Ba.

Boreal Sea

Untended Lands

Black Mtn.

Grey Mtns.

Fjordland

Morkfjord

Kath

Dragon's Roost

Great Maelstrom

Seabane Is.

Steppes of Jord

Kaagor Pass

Naad

Grimwall Mtns.

Wolfwood

Xian

Khal

Aralan

Rigga Mtns.

Gron

City of Dendor

Aven

Gorìa

Shoe

Landover Road

City of Dael

Mineholt North

Riamon

Alban

Darda Galion

City of Rondor

Hèl's Crucible

Ganar

Valon

R. Argon

Jago

Pellar

The Islands of Stone

Voran Is.

Hurn

Scale

0   200   400

Miles

Arbalin Is.

Thell Cove

Caer Pendwyr

Avagon Sea

Sarain

Aban

בוכבהשׂד

Gjeen Is.

Thayra

Chabba

Sabra

The Karoo

Khem

Nizari

City of Dendor

Aven

Go

City of Dael

Mineholt North

Riamon

Darda Galion

City of Rondor

Hèl's Crucible

Valon

INTO THE
FIRE

Novels by Dennis L. McKiernan:

HÈL'S CRUCIBLE:
Book 1: *Into the Forge*
Book 2: *Into the Fire*

The Dragonstone
Caverns of Socrates
Voyage of the Fox Rider
The Eye of the Hunter
Dragondoom

THE SILVER CALL DUOLOGY:
Book 1: *Trek to Kraggen-cor*
Book 2: *The Brega Path*

THE IRON TOWER TRILOGY:
Book 1: *The Dark Tide*
Book 2: *Shadows of Doom*
Book 3: *The Darkest Day*

The Vulgmaster (the graphic novel)
Tales of Mithgar (a story collection)

INTO THE FIRE

HÈL'S CRUCIBLE BOOK 2

Dennis L. McKiernan

A ROC BOOK

ROC
Published by the Penguin Group
Penguin Putnam Inc., 375 Hudson Street,
New York, New York 10014, U.S.A.
Penguin Books Ltd, 27 Wrights Lane,
London W85TZ, England
Penguin Books Australia Ltd, Ringwood,
Victoria, Australia
Penguin Books Canada Ltd, 10 Alcorn Avenue,
Toronto, Ontario, Canada M4V 3B2
Penguin Books (N.Z.) Ltd, 182–190 Wairau Road,
Auckland 10, New Zealand

Penguin Books Ltd, Registered Offices:
Harmondsworth, Middlesex, England

First published by Roc, an imprint of Dutton NAL,
a member of Penguin Putnam Inc.

First Printing, September, 1998
10 9 8 7 6 5 4 3 2 1

 REGISTERED TRADEMARK—MARCA REGISTRADA

LIBRARY OF CONGRESS CATALOGING-IN-PUBLICATION DATA:

McKiernan, Dennis L., 1932–
   Into the fire / Dennis L. McKiernan.
     p.   cm. —(Hel's crucible ; bk. 2)
   ISBN 0-451-45701-3 (acid-free paper)
     1. Fantastic fiction, American.   I. Title.   II. Series:
McKiernan, Dennis L., 1932–   Hel's crucible ; bk. 2.
PS3563.C376I56   1998
813.'54—dc21

                                                    98-5247
                                                    CIP

Printed in the United States of America
Set in Trump Mediaeval
Designed by Leonard Telesca

To the Tanque Wordies
and
other writers' groups
whose sole aim is to raise the quality
of that which others will read

FOREWORD

*T*hroughout my lifetime various tales I've read are about people with special <powers> or abilities, or about people who believe they are ordinary, yet they are really sons or daughters of royalty or wizards or other such and are hidden away in some obscure place where the powers of evil will not think to look. In these tales, suddenly they are thrust into the thick of things where their <powers> or uncommon abilities or heritage will prove the linchpin to all.

These are not tales about common people thrust into uncommon situations and struggling to meet the challenge; instead they are about uncommon people with <powers> and heritages and abilities, and you know darn well they *will* meet the challenge and crush it.

Rather than such a tale, I wanted to write about ordinary people who find themselves caught up in events they neither control nor have any special heritage or <power> or extraordinary abilities to resolve. In other words, I wanted to write about common "soldiers" who must struggle with things as they happen, "common" people in uncommon situations who may or may not have the ability to rise to the challenge.

This tale is about Tipperton Thistledown and Beau Darby, two "common" Warrows caught up in events not of their doing. They are not hidden royalty, not mages, not folk with extraordinary abilities, extraordinary powers, extraordinary brains and wit; instead they are mere common soldiers, assuming of course there is such a thing . . . common people caught up in uncommon events struggling to soldier through.

Oh, perhaps they do have an extraordinary thing going for them . . . and that is uncommon heart.

If there is such a thing as a common soldier's tale, then this is it. Yet is there such a thing as a common soldier?

You decide.

May you enjoy what you find herein.

—Dennis L. McKiernan
July 1997

AUTHOR'S NOTES

*I*nto the Fire is the second book of the duology of HÈL'S CRU-
CIBLE. Along with the first book, *Into the Forge*, it tells the tale
of the Great War of the Ban, as seen through the eyes of two
Warrows, Tipperton Thistledown and Beau Darby.

It is a story which begins in the year 2195 of the Second Era
of Mithgar, a time when the *Rûpt* are free to roam about in daylight as well as night, although it is told that they prefer to do
their deeds in darkness rather than under the sun.

The story of the Ban War was reconstructed from several
sources, not the least of which were the Thistledown Lays.
I have in several places filled in the gaps with assumptions
of my own, but in the main the tale is true to its source
material.

As occurs in other of my Mithgarian works, there are many
instances where in the press of the moment, the Humans,
Mages, Elves, and others spoke in their native tongues; yet to
avoid burdensome translations, where necessary I have rendered their words in Pellarion, the Common Tongue of Mithgar. However, in several cases I have left the language
unchanged, to demonstrate the fact that many tongues were
found throughout Mithgar. Additionally, some words and
phrases do not lend themselves to translation, and these I've
either left unchanged or, in special cases, I have enclosed in
angle brackets a substitute term which gives the "flavor" of
the word (i.e., <see>, <fire>, and the like). Additionally, sundry
words may look to be in error, but indeed are correct—e.g.,
DelfLord is but a single word though a capital L nestles among
its letters.

The Elven language of Sylva is rather archaic and formal. To capture this flavor, I have properly used thee and thou, hast, dost, and the like; however, in the interest of readability, I have tried to do so in a minimal fashion, eliminating some of the more archaic terms.

For the curious, the *w* in Rwn takes on the sound of *uu* (w *is* after all a double-u), which in turn can be said to sound like *oo* (as in spoon). Hence, Rwn is *not* pronounced Renn, but instead *is* pronounced Roon, or Rune.

SYNOPSIS

*T*his is the second part of HÈL'S CRUCIBLE.

In the first part, *Into the Forge,* on a winter's night Tipperton Thistledown, a Warrow miller, was awakened from a sound sleep by a skirmish on his very doorstone. In the battle a lone man managed to kill all nine of the Foul Folk foe, but he himself was terribly wounded. Tip dragged the man into the mill, bandaged him as well as he could, and, during the process, the man gave Tip a small, drab, pewter coin on a thong and told him, "Go east . . . warn all . . . take this to Agron." Tip didn't know who or what Agron was, but didn't question the man, and instead ran to get a healer, another Warrow, Beau Darby. When they got back to the mill, the man's throat had been cut by Spawn who had come while Tip was away, Foul Folk whose tracks then headed on westward into the Dellin Downs.

As Tip and Beau built a pyre on which to cremate all of the slain, a balefire burned afar on Beacontor, calling for muster.

Men from the nearby town of Twoforks, seeing the smoke of the funeral pyre, came to investigate and, together with the Warrows, they discovered that the dead man's slain horse bore the brand of the High King.

Believing a Kingsman's mission more important than a wee Warrow joining the muster at Beacontor, Tip decided to take the coin east to Agron, whoever or whatever it might be.

Beau chose to join Tip on the journey, and they set out eastward and within the week entered Drearwood, a dismal and forbidding place. On the very first night in that dreadful forest they saw a great Horde of Foul Folk marching to the west.

On the second day, as darkness fell, a freezing rain began, and it lasted all night; when daylight came, Drearwood was sheathed in ice. Slipping and sliding, they pushed on, making little progress on the thick glaze. In the night there was an attack on their camp by a huge monster only half-seen in the dark: the ponies were killed, but Tip and Beau managed to escape.

Afoot, they attempted to sneak through the rest of Drearwood, and more than once they barely escaped discovery by searching bands of Foul Folk.

Weary and hungry beyond measure, as they reached the far fringes of Drearwood they were ambushed and captured, but it was by a band of Lian Guardians, Elven warriors, led by Vanidor.

Vanidor told them that Agron was the king of Aven, a realm beyond the Grimwall Mountains. Vanidor assigned an Elf named Loric to take them to the Lian strongholt of Arden Vale, where they could tell Lord Talarin of the things they'd seen.

Upon reaching Arden Vale, Talarin and other Elves told the Warrows that Modru, a powerful Black Mage in Gron, had been gathering Foul Folk: they were pouring across the "in-between," coming into Mithgar on the Middle Plane from Neddra on the Lower. It was also rumored that Modru wooed Dragons to his cause.

Talarin assigned Loric and a female Lian, Phais, to accompany the Warrows to Dendor, the capital city of Aven. But it was yet winter, and so they waited for the spring thaw to clear the way through the Grimwall Mountains.

On Springday, Eloran, a Dylvana Elf, arrived from Adonar to report that Adon had sundered the in-between way from Neddra to Mithgar. Eloran also confirmed that Modru of Gron had indeed started a wide war, and that High King Blaine was calling for an alliance of men, Elves, Dwarves, and Mages to fight this great threat.

The Elves blamed the evil god Gyphon for this war, saying that Modru was but His servant, and if Modru conquered Mithgar, then Gyphon would displace Adon as the master of all creation.

During these discussions, Talarin's consort, Rael, a seeress, in a trance spoke a rede: "Seek the aid of those not men to quench the fires of war . . ." No one knew just who "those not men" were, or who the rede was meant for.

The spring thaw finally came, but before Tip and Beau and Phais and Loric could embark on their mission, a scout brought word that Crestan Pass was held by the Spawn. And so the four set out for Aven along one of their alternate routes, one that would add miles and months to their journey.

South through Rell they went, aiming for the pass at Stormhelm, one of the four mountains of the Quadran under which the Dwarvenholt of Drimmen-deeve was carved. Yet when they arrived they came upon a battle between the Dwarves of Drimmen-deeve and the Foul Folk. During the battle, Skail of the Barrens, a renegade Drake, came swooping down spouting fire and drove the Dwarves back into Drimmen-deeve.

With all ways cut off over the Quadran and under as well, the foursome rode on south, along yet another alternate way, one that was even longer.

In Gûnar they encountered a squad of Dwarves and were told that Gûnarring Gap was occupied by a Horde, hence that route was blocked to them.

To keep the foursome from needing to go on an even longer route, the Dwarves revealed a secret path across the Gûnarring: the Walkover, so named because of a low tunnel along the way, where only people afoot and small ponies could pass through.

Giving up their horses, the four crossed on foot, and when they came down into the realm of Valon, there too was war, for smoke from a burning town rose into the sky.

Battling storms and avoiding detection, they made their way northeastward, heading across the Plains of Valon for the Elven strongholt of Darda Galion, some several hundred miles away, but as they drew near their goal they were discovered.

They were yet some forty-five miles from safety, and they made a run for it. The foursome was saved at the last moment by a squad of Lian Elves who saw the pursuit from their encampment atop the Great Escarpment and came in rescue.

Several days later the foursome reached Wood's-heart, the Elven stronghold central to Darda Galion. There they found the Lian preparing to go to the aid of the besieged Drimmen-deeve folk.

Although they would have liked to aid in this mission, the four felt it necessary to proceed on to Aven and deliver the coin.

Once again ahorse, the four headed for Caer Lindor, a fortress on the River Rissanin, garrisoned by Lian and Dylvana Elves and by Greatwood Baeron.

In Caer Lindor they found a company of Warrow archers whose village of Springwater had been destroyed by the Foul Folk. Among these Warrows, Tip met Rynna Fenrush, leader of the band, but even though he fell desperately in love with her, and she with him, he had a mission to fulfill and so did she.

A Horde was still roaming along the eastern boundaries of Darda Erynian, and to avoid this Swarm, Tip, Beau, Phais, and Loric decided to push on for Aven by going north through Darda Erynian. On the day the four prepared to set out, a group of Rivermen came to the fortress and asked for sanctuary. Neither Tip nor Rynna liked the look of these men, for something just didn't seem right. But Tip had to go on his mission to deliver the coin, and Rynna had to stay behind to captain the Warrows, and so the lovers parted.

Tip, Beau, Loric, and Phais eventually came to Bircehyll, the Dylvana strongholt in Darda Erynian. While they rested, word came via the Groaning Stones and the fox-riding Pysks that Caer Lindor had fallen and all Warrows had been killed in the fight. This news devastated Tip.

To gain revenge and slay Foul Folk, Tip and Beau pledged themselves to Coron Ruar, leader of the Dylvana: they would go with Ruar's army to help lift the siege of Mineholt North, a Dwarvenholt in the Rimmen Mountains in Riamon.

With Tip roving as a scout, and Beau riding as a healer, they traveled with a thousand Dylvana Elves up through Darda Erynian, where they rendezvoused with a force of Baeron.

At Rimmen Gape the Allies defeated a segment of Spawn and then continued on their mission to lift the Foul Folk's siege of the Dwarvenholt.

As they neared Mineholt North, they were challenged by a force of men from the town of Dael. Among this band was Bekki, a Dwarf of Mineholt North. Led by Prince Loden, this company was also bent on lifting the siege of the mineholt.

Coron Ruar called a strategy meeting, and many plans were proposed, but all were met with objections. Finally, based on a skirmish with a squad of Rûpt, Tipperton devised a plan they all accepted.

Bekki chose Tip as the emissary to go with him, and they entered the mineholt through the secret entrance and proceeded through corridors and passages and crossed above deeps to reach distant Dwarven chambers, where they found DelfLord Borl, Bekki's father, in his throne room.

Tip explained his plan.

Two days later the Dylvana, Baeron, and Daelsmen rode to the vale of the mineholt and arrayed themselves before the Horde. The Horde jeered, for they outnumbered the Allies five to one.

That night Tip and a battalion of Dwarves, camouflaged in

grey to match the stone, slipped through the side postern and took places against the flank of the mountain at the rear of the Horde.

As dawn stood barely below the lip of the world, the Allies in front drew the Horde forward to face them, and from the rear the camouflaged Dwarves slipped down and hurled clay vessels of a flammable liquid to crash into and upon the Horde's supply wagons, with vessels of smoldering firecoke following, and the wagons were set afire. Elements of the Horde, including all six monstrous Trolls, turned against the Dwarves. Dwarves cast flammable liquid upon three of the Trolls, but managed to set only one afire. The Allies to the fore attacked to divert the Horde from the Dwarves.

With fighting to the front and rear, confusion reigned among the Horde.

From a burning wagon, Tip lit one of his signal arrows and launched it into two of the liquid-drenched Trolls, setting them aflame, though Tip himself was nearly slain by a Ghûl in the process. The remaining Trolls fled, afraid of the "magic fire." When the Trolls ran away, the Rûcks panicked and ran as well, and the siege was broken.

Many of the Allies were slain in this battle—Daelsmen, Baeron, Dwarves, Dylvana—and many were wounded as well, including Phais, terribly pierced by a poisoned arrow.

After the funerals, the Allies set off in pursuit of the remnants of the Horde, but Tip, Loric, and Beau remained behind in Mineholt North with wounded Phais.

Bekki, too, remained behind, for he had pledged himself to go with Tip to deliver the coin.

Using a gift given him in Arden Vale, the mint gwynthyme, an antidote to poison, Beau struggled desperately to save Phais's life and barely managed to do so.

After two and a half months, Phais was fit enough to ride. And so, on the fifteenth of December, Tip, Beau, Phais, and Loric set out once more to deliver the coin, Bekki now among them. . . .

. . . And as *Into the Fire* begins, we join the five as they ride away from Mineholt North.

Freedom is not free. . . .

INTO THE
FIRE

1

*D*own from the now-free gates of Mineholt North rode the five—Tipperton, Beau, Phais, Loric, and Bekki—three on ponies, two on horses, and drawing two pack animals behind. Down from the portal and along the road on the eastern side of the mountain vale they fared—two Warrows, two Elves, and a Dwarf—riding southward, soon to turn east and follow the tradeway to the city of Dael. Of the mighty battle which had raged before the gates a mere ten weeks past, the battle which had shattered the Foul Folk siege of the Dwarvenholt, the battle which had sent one of Modru's Hordes fleeing in panic, of that battle there remained little sign, for all was covered with unmarked December snow, and not even the great scorching of the funeral pyres from the aftermath showed through, though rounded hummocks under the whiteness betokened where lay the Daelsmen's burial knolls.

Past this field of blood rode the five, alongside a mountain flank, slitted eyewear protecting their sight from the blinding glare of the white pristine 'scape, the bright winter sun shedding little warmth down upon them all.

"I say," queried Beau, peering at Tip, "just how far is it to Dael?"

"Thirty, thirty-five leagues by road," replied Tipperton, "shorter could we fly."

At these words, Beau looked long at the sky. No birds were in sight, though the forward edge of feather-thin clouds eked southward high above. "Huah. Even if I were a bird, I'd think it too cold to fly. No, Tip, I'll stick to my pony even though it'll take us five or six days in all."

"Five or six days, Beau, that's just to Dael. We'll be forty, forty-five days on the road to Dendor, and that's if we don't run into trouble."

"Forty-five da—?"

"It's two hundred sixty, two hundred seventy leagues away, bucco."

"Oh my, eight hundred miles or so?"

"So Bekki says, Beau."

Bekki grunted and said, "It is two hundred sixty-six leagues and two miles and some paces by the route we will go if all steps out as planned."

Beau nodded, then began counting on the fingers of one gloved hand. After a while he said, "You are right, Tip: at six or seven leagues a day, that *will* take some forty or forty-five days." Beau shook his head. "A long time of eating field rations."

"Oh, Beau, take heart," said Tip, "there are towns along the way."

Beau shook his head. "We can't count on that, Tip, with Foul Folk all about. I mean, look at how far we had to go after leaving Arden Vale before we had a good hot meal. All the way down and through the Grimwall and over the Gûnarring and back up to Darda Galion."

Tip shook his head. "You're forgetting the marmot and rabbit we cooked on the Plains of Valon."

"All right, all right, so that's, what, one hot meal in a thousand miles? Not exactly what I'd call eating well."

Tip turned up his hands, then said, "We ate quite well in Darda Galion, and then again in Caer"—Tip's face fell, yet he managed to say—"Lindor."

Beau looked across at his sad-eyed friend, then jerked his thumb over his shoulder and added, "In Mineholt North, too."

Tip glanced at Beau and smiled through his tears. "Yes, we did." Then he sighed and wiped his cheeks with the heels of his gloved hands. "I'm sorry, Beau, but whenever I think of Caer Lindor, it brings it all back."

"I know, bucco," said Beau. "I know. And it's all right."

They rode along in morose silence for another mile or so, and a chill wind kicked up at their backs and they drew their cloaks tightly 'round.

Finally they came to the mouth of the vale, and the road swung easterly. Along this way they turned, making new tracks in the unmarked snow as thickening clouds slid overhead.

Phais looked at the sky and removed her eyewear. "I think we're in for a blow."

"Oh my," said Beau. "Should we turn back? I mean, we're not too far from the shelter of the mineholt."

Phais glanced at Loric, and he shook his head and said, " 'Tis the winter season, Beau, and no matter when we set out snow will fly . . . lest thou wouldst have us wait until spring is upon us."

"Oh no," said Beau, pushing out a hand in negation. "We've been on this mission too long as it is to dawdle about waiting for fair weather. Besides, whatever message or meaning or charm or hex the coin bears, we need to get it to the one it is meant for."

At this mention of potential magic, Tip's brow furrowed, and he nervously touched his eiderdown jacket high on his chest. "Beau, I wish you'd leave this talk of spellcraft behind. I mean it's enough that we bear the coin without having to talk about enchantments or magic or whatever."

"All right, bucco," replied Beau. "I'll be quiet. I know it makes you uncomfortable and all to think that something actually touching your skin might be charmed in some way. I mean, if a Mage cast a spell upon the coin, or if a Sorceress laid a hex, or a Wizard incanted a—"

"Beau, enough!"

Beau's eyes flew wide, and then he frowned in puzzlement. Finally he grinned sheepishly and said, "Oh, right."

Loric looked at Phais and she at him, and although they tried to remain solemn, they failed, and laughter rang out across the snow to be slapped back by the towering mountains to their left, and soon Beau was laughing, and finally stern Bekki joined in.

Tipperton scowled at them all, but at last even he grinned.

And the south-flowing clouds above thickened.

"Oh my," said Beau, pointing ahead and left, air hissing in through clenched teeth. "Modru's sigil."

A standard pole with a tattered flag jutted up out from the snow, the symbol a ring of fire on black.

"Abandoned by the fleeing Horde, I ween," said Phais.

"There's something under the snow," said Loric, spurring his horse to the flag and dismounting.

"Take care," called Beau.

Loric knelt and with a gloved hand brushed away the blanket of white.

"What is it?" asked Tip.

"A dead Ruch," replied Loric, looking down at the swart face revealed. He brushed away more snow, uncovering a long gash in the quilted armor along the Rûck's torso. Loric looked up at the others. "He took a cut from a blade. Probably in the battle. Got this far before he bled to death."

Tip blew out a breath, frosty white in the cold air. "I would rather die quickly in combat than a slow painful death such as that."

"Oh my, yes," said Beau. "But better still, what say we die of old age instead?"

As Loric remounted, Tip laughed and said, "Indeed, and after a long and fruitful life, eh?"

As Beau nodded in agreement, Bekki said, "I would have a long and fruitful life—three or four centuries—then die in glorious battle. If not battle, then old age must serve."

Once again they started easterly. Of a sudden Beau frowned and looked at Phais.

"We do not die of old age, Beau," said Phais, "if that is what thou art mulling. Instead 'tis by violence or accident, or by poison as nearly did I."

"Oh my," said Beau, his eyes filling with distress. "Nothing peaceful whatsoever?"

Phais shook her head.

Beau glanced at his medical kit. "Illnesses?"

Phais spread her hands. "There are but few which affect Elvenkind, and those most virulent."

"Oh my," said Beau. "Oh my."

And easterly they rode, while the wind blew chill and brooding clouds darkened the skies above.

"This way," called Bekki above the howling wind, and Tip, next in line, could but barely hear him. Still Tipperton turned and shouted behind, "This way! This way!" and whether Beau heard him and shouted the word on, Tipperton could not say.

Blindly they followed Bekki through the hurling white, barely able to see the horse or pony ahead as they tramped in file, each drawing an animal or two behind.

Finally they reached a vertical flank of mountain stone, and Bekki turned rightward to the east, while the frigid blast shrieked down from the heights above, carrying stinging ice and hurtling snow on its furious wings.

"I say," called Tip toward Bekki, but his words were shredded on the squalling wind and carried to shrieking oblivion. *I say, wouldn't it be better if we were roped together?* But no one could hear him or read his thoughts, and so, unattached, he followed Bekki, and Beau followed him, with Phais coming after and then Loric. To the right loomed shapes—trees?—he did not know. He was just about to try yelling to Bekki again when of a sudden the fury abated, and he came into a cavernous vault, with stone overhanging above and rubble underfoot, and in the dimness he could see Bekki and his pony trudging on ahead, back into recesses of the great hollow.

Tip led his pony on inward and turned to see Beau and his mount coming after, and then Phais drawing her animal behind with a packhorse in tow as well, and finally Loric with two steeds after.

Bekki nodded at the fire. "Before we leave, we shall gather wood to replace that which we burn."

Beau gazed around at the vaulted chamber, a semidome of sorts, sides curving 'round to the back, ceiling arcing down to the back as well, the rubble-strewn floor more or less level. They sat at the rear of the hollow in relative comfort, snow flying and wind howling a hundred feet away at the bowed mouth of the wide cavity.

Beau turned to Bekki. "Oh my, Bekki, how did you ever find this place?"

"It is a Châkka wayfarers' shelter. I have been here before."

Beau looked at the cords of wood stacked against the back of the chamber. "Yes, but with all the snow, I mean, how could you see?"

"I could not, but as I said, I have been here before."

Beau threw up his hands in a gesture of puzzlement.

Bekki glanced at Tip, then said, "Châkka cannot lose their footsteps. Once we have been to a place, the way is always within us. It is a gift from Elwydd."

Beau looked out into the shrieking snow. "Oh my, quite a marvelous gift, I should say." He turned to Tip. "I wonder if we have a gift . . . Warrows, that is."

Tip sighed and tapped his chest at the point of the coin. "Perseverance, I shouldn't wonder."

Phais shook her head and looked at the Warrows, then said, "Nay, Tipperton, 'tis heart."

They spent that night and all the next day in the cavernous shelter, the wind screaming past. It was during Bekki's watch on the second night that the storm began to abate, and by the next morning there was nought of it left but a few gentle flakes drifting down. The five scoured for deadwood among the broad stand of trees ranging before the hollow to replace the wood they had used. And then they set out once again to the east, the ponies and horses at times broaching deep drifts, at other times faring across ground scoured clean by the blow.

Slowly the skies cleared, and by midafternoon the comrades rode beneath a glacial sky, the sun remote and chill, the air numbingly cold, their breath streaming white, the vapor freezing on crusted scarves wrapped 'round faces, and Bekki's beard was clotted with the ice of his exhalations.

Through the slits of his eyewear, Beau looked at Tip, the other buccan with his cloak wrapped 'round. "Lor', Tip, but I don't think I'll ever be warm again. I mean, this is even worse than when we were in Drearwood."

"Let's walk awhile, Beau," said Tip, swinging a leg over the saddle forecantle and hopping down. "It'll warm us."

"I'm all for that," replied Beau, dismounting as well. "I mean, I'd walk all the way to Dendor if it'd keep me warm."

"There'll be a warm inn in Dael," said Tip, "with good hot food and something steaming to drink."

"Oh my, hot wine mulled with spices," groaned Beau. "I can taste it now."

Walking behind and leading two animals, Phais said, "A warm bath would serve better."

"Oh yes," agreed Beau. "A hot bath with hot wine to sip even as we soak."

Tip's mind flashed back to their first bath in Arden Vale, its warmth driving away the chill in their bones. And then he blushed, remembering dark-haired, blue-eyed Lady Elissan walking in on him as he stood naked in the bath washing his hair, his eyes closed against the soap running down, and he recalled her words at their last parting: *When next thou doth take a bath, keep thine eyes open, else thou mayest once again have thy splendor revealed.*

Tipperton laughed, his breath puffing white in the brumal air. Beau looked at him. "What?"

Tip shook his head. "Oh, nothing."

And on they trudged, now and again coming across the bodies of Foul Folk who had died of wounds sustained in the battle before the gates of Mineholt North, wounds which ultimately proved fatal during the retreat as the Horde had fled. Yet they could not say how many other dead Rûpt they had unknowingly passed hidden beneath the snow.

Early on the nineteenth of December the road they followed entered Daelwood, a wide forest in Riamon. Frost covered the stark limbs of the wintering trees, the boughs barren and hard.

"Oh my," said Beau, as they wended through the desolate

wood, "but with the branches scraping at the sky, well, it reminds me somewhat of Drearwood."

"Nay, my friend," said Phais. "Dhruousdarda is an evil tangle; *Arindarda* is not."

Beau frowned. "Arindarda? —Oh, you mean Daelwood."

"Aye."

Tipperton nodded. "I agree. There was an evil air to Drearwood, whereas here there is none." Then he turned to Phais. "I say: Arindarda: doesn't that mean, um, Ringwood?"

"Aye, it does. Once nearly all of the land within the ring of the Rimmen Mountains was covered with this forest, but men have hewn it down until but a remnant remains."

"Goodness," said Tip, shaking his head as he remembered the rolling plains he had scouted with Vail, "what a loss."

On they fared within the forest, and late in the day they crossed an ice-covered stone bridge above a frozen tributary of the Ironwater River. On the far side, the road swung southeastward, following along the stream.

"We'll camp here at the turn," said Bekki, glancing through bleak limbs at the cheerless sun.

"How much farther to Dael?" asked Beau, dismounting.

"Ten leagues and one mile minus some paces will bring us to the city walls," replied Bekki, loosening the cinch strap on his shag-haired pony.

"Barn rats," groaned Beau. "I was hoping we'd get to an inn tomorrow, but it looks more like two days, eh?"

Bekki turned and shook his head. "Not quite. Even with this snow and ice, a day and a half should see us there."

Beau hauled the saddle from his pony. "A day and a half, Tip, and then it's hot mulled wine and a bath for me."

Late the next day they came across a frozen man. With his cloak wrapped 'round and his back to a tree, he sat next to the road. Snow covered his feet and legs, and a white frost clung to him from the waist up. His icy face was chalky, and his eyes were frozen shut.

"Is it one of the Horde?" asked Tip.

Bekki shook his head. "Nay, I think not. By his garb it looks more to be a Daelsman. Caught in the storm, I deem."

"Aye," said Phais. "Though late in the storm, I would think. There is little snow clinging unto him."

"It could have been blown away," said Tip.

Loric cocked an eyebrow. "Mayhap, though I ween the words of Dara Phais more like to be true."

Beau finished his examination and turned to the others.

"Well, he's frozen through and through; there's nothing we can do for him now." He looked at Bekki. "Maybe a pyre, for we won't be able to bury him in this rock-hard winter ground."

Bekki shook his head. "Instead we'll report him to the town militia. They will come with a wagon and bear him back to Dael. His kith need to identify him and mourn him properly."

"What about Wolves or such," asked Tip, "won't they be likely to, um—?"

"Nay, Tipperton," said Loric. "He is frozen solid and bears little scent, and though the storm was four days past, nought has yet defiled his remains. I deem he will stay untouched until the militia comes, unless there is a warming."

"I'll see if there's anything on him to say just who he was," said Beau, squatting down and prying open frozen pockets.

Tip frowned at this necessary yet rather grim business, but said nought.

Beau moved to the other side and in moments stood and shook his head.

Another mile down the road they found a frozen horse, one leg broken.

"Hmm," mused Loric. "A mystery this."

"How so?" asked Tip.

"If this is the frozen man's horse, then he went onward instead of turning back toward Dael."

"He might have been confused," said Beau. "Lost in the storm. Or so chill that he had no wits."

"Mayhap," growled Bekki, "yet I think instead he was fleeing."

Tip's eyes widened. "Fleeing? Fleeing what?"

Bekki gestured at the animal. "See the frozen hair? Lather turned to ice, I think. The horse mayhap was running when he broke a leg. And who would run a horse on ice but a fleeing man? Too, its throat is not cut, and so I ask, who would leave behind a broken-legged horse alive and in pain? Someone fleeing, that's who. Someone running in panic."

"Yes, but still you haven't answered Tip's question," said Beau. "What was the man fleeing from?"

Bekki shrugged and looked southeasterly along the road and then muttered, "Mayhap he was fleeing the city of Dael."

The next day they came upon another frozen man, and then another, and then three together, all of them covered with snow and ice and frost. And as the five rode onward, more and more frozen corpses were encountered, the road littered with the cold dead—men, women, children—some clearly had been travelling afoot while others had been riding, and still more were found frozen in carts and wains, horses lying blizzard-slain and rock-hard as well. And all were heading northwest-erly along the road, a road which led to Mineholt North and nowhere else.

As the five now rode onward, Loric turned to Phais. "Refugees?"

She nodded grimly. "Bekki I deem grasped the truth of it when he saw the very first man; he was fleeing the city of Dael, as I ween were these others."

"But what's in Dael?" asked Beau, looking about in trepida-tion. "I mean, why would they run?"

Loric turned up his gloved hands. "We cannot answer that question until we arrive, Beau."

"Perhaps we ought to skirt the city altogether," said Tip. "I mean, if something perilous is there—a Gargon or such—"

"Oh my," gasped Phais, looking at Loric, "mayhap indeed it *is* a Draedan."

"Gargon, Draedan, Ghath," growled Bekki, "we should draw near enough to know." He gestured southward. "Somewhere my sire and the rest of the Allies hie after Squam, and we need to warn all if a Ghath strides Dael."

Reluctantly Loric nodded. "Bekki is right. We need to see for ourselves what may lie therein. And if needs be, warn Coron and DelfLord and Chieftain and Prince alike."

Tip pulled his bow from its saddle scabbard and took an arrow in hand. "Fetch out your sling and bullets, Beau; we're riding into Dael."

They sat atop the hill and looked eastward down the fall of land toward where the city of Dael should have been. Yet they saw nought of what they expected—a riverport town sur-rounded by high stone walls—but a mass of snow-covered rub-ble instead. Not a whole structure stood, though here and there a damaged wall or stark chimney reared up where a building had been. Broken battlements surrounded the wrack, the high stone bulwark breached, ruptured, smashed in a hundred places, cleft with great wide gaps. And a chill wind swirled through the gapes and among the ruins beyond.

"Lor'," breathed Beau, surveying the destruction, "what could have caused this? The Horde?"

Phais shook her head. "Nay. They were in flight, our allies after. They had not the time to do such."

"A Gargon?" asked Tip, his heart thudding.

Again Phais shook her head. "They are a terrible foe, but not even they could cause such ruin."

"Too," said Loric, "I feel not the dread of one."

Tip's mind flashed back to the time at Gûnarring Gap when his heart had hammered with twisting apprehension from even a distant Gargon. No such anxiety writhed through his veins here.

"I see no movement," growled Bekki, looking at the others.

"Nor I," said Phais.

"What'll we do?" asked Beau. "Pass it by?"

Loric shook his head. "Nay. We must see what has befallen; others will want to know." Loric kicked his heels to the flanks of his mount, drawing his sword as he moved downslope.

And so did they all follow: Bekki with his hammer in hand, Phais with her blade, Beau with his bullet-laden sling, and Tip with an arrow strung.

They rode across the remains of crashed-down gates and into the rubble beyond, and hard-frozen bodies lay everywhere, yet some were burned as well. Too, not only were buildings smashed, but charred timbers and ash attested to raging fire.

And Phais and Loric looked at one another and nodded in unspoken agreement.

"What?" asked Beau.

"Drake," replied Phais.

The swirling air muttered among the wrack like whispering wraiths on the wind, as through the devastation and toward the palace they rode, now following Bekki, threading their way among snow and ice and burned wreckage and the dead. But when they reached the site of the mansion they found nought but blackened corpses amid shattered, charred ruins.

Beau looked about, shaking his head in disbelief, his eyes wide and filled with distress.

"I wonder—" began Tip—

—but Phais threw up a hand. "*Hist!*"

While the chill wind spun through splinter and burn and stone, Phais cocked her head this way and that, and then she looked at Loric and gestured toward the river.

He nodded, and softly said, "I agree."

Bekki frowned. "I do not hear—"

"But they do," said Beau, canting his head toward the Elves.

"What is it?" breathed Tip.

"Laughter. Weeping," murmured Loric.

"Mounted or afoot?" asked Phais, gripping her sword.

"Mounted, I think," replied Loric, easing his horse ahead.

Now Beau frowned in puzzlement. "The weeping, the laughing, is mounted?"

"No," whispered Tip. "It's we who will go mounted rather than on foot down to the river's edge."

"Oh," breathed Beau in understanding.

"Spread wide," said Phais, "a street or so. 'Twould not do for us all to ride into the same ambush."

Beau looked at Tip and silently mouthed [Ambush?]

Tip shrugged and *chrk*ed his pony rightward to start away.

Taking a deep breath, Beau went leftward.

Widely spread, down through the snow- and ice-laden wrack they rode in a ragged line abreast, down toward the frozen Ironwater, Bekki in the center, with Phais a cobbled street to the right and Loric a street to the left. Beyond Phais rode Tip, with Beau to Loric's left.

And now Tip could hear an intermittent hissing and babbling, spates of unrecognizable words interspersed by giggling and weeping . . . and silence. Onward he rode, now able to see the frozen surface of the waterway ahead, bone-white under the grey overcast above. At last he came to a long stone wharf bordering the Ironwater River itself, with a great number of boat slips and barge landings along its considerable length, all empty in the winter cold. His bow at the ready, Tip waited for the others to reach the long, long pier, and as he held position, again he heard distant hissed words, as if someone were revealing secrets to a confidant, though what was said Tip did not know, for it was in a tongue he spoke not.

To the left, bucco, and near. But wait for the others.

Now Beau appeared on the stone pier a distance away, and in quick succession Bekki and Phais and Loric rode onto the windswept stone.

Phais turned rightward and held out a shushing hand to Tipperton. Quietly she dismounted.

Tip did likewise, carefully and silently swinging a leg over and down.

Moving toward the Dara, Tip listened and looked and tried to hear and see everything all at once. And as he passed a wide ramp pull-way leading up from the river to the pier and across to the collapsed ruins of a dockside warehouse, from within the wreckage a giggling babble and weep sissed forth.

Tip turned toward the warehouse ruin and signalled to Phais it was here. And he waited for her to arrive.

Together they crept in among the shatter and char, and found whence the hissings came: from 'neath an overturned barge.

And as Bekki and Loric and Beau came in among the rubble, Phais and Tip knelt and peered under.

And in the shadows they saw—

"Lord Tain!" gasped Tipperton.

The white-haired man was holding the frozen corpse of a burnt woman and muttering into her ear.

As weeping and babbling and hissed secrets came sissing from under the barge, Bekki stood up and growled. "I say we kill him now."

"What?" blurted Tip.

"He fled from the field of battle and deserves nothing more than a coward's death."

Loric put a hand on Bekki's shoulder. "Aye, my friend, he did flee from the Rûpt at Mineholt North, yet he was advisor to Prince Loden, hence justice is King Enrik's to do and not ours."

"King Loden, you mean," said Bekki.

Tip frowned up at Bekki. "Prince Loden?"

Bekki shook his head. "Nay, Tipperton, Loden is now king. Enrik is dead."

"How do you know this?"

Bekki gestured at the upturned barge. "Craven Tain says so."

"You understand the tongue he babbles?"

Bekki nodded. "It is Riamonian."

"What is he saying?"

Of a sudden Bekki's eyes softened, and he sighed sadly.

"What is it, Bekki?" asked Tip.

"He just now said her name."

"Whose name?"

"The corpse he holds: it is Lady Jolet, his daughter."

In that moment Beau came back into the rubble, his satchel of medicks in hand. "Is he still under there? I need him here to treat him."

Bekki shook his head. "He is too fear-stricken and won't come out."

"Then I'll go in," said Beau.

"Nay, Beau," said Loric. "Thou dost not know what he may do, for his wits are gone."

Beau looked at Phais.

"Hast thou aught to set madness aside?" she asked.

Beau shook his head.

"Then thou canst do no good, whereas in his state he may do great ill to thee."

"Nevertheless . . ." said Beau.

Bekki ground his teeth and said, "Wait, I will try to call him forth."

Bekki squatted and peered under the edge of the barge. "*Radca Tain, wychodzic.*"

Lord Tain held the corpse and rocked and whispered on.

"*Radca Tain, proze wychodzic.*"

Still there was no response from Tain.

Bekki turned to Beau. "He does not know we are here."

"Then I'm going in," said Beau, and before anyone could stop him he scrambled under the edge.

"Tipperton," snapped Bekki. "Set arrow to bow and hold against Tain. If he makes an ill move, kill him."

"But I might hit Beau," protested Tip.

"Not so," said Phais, "for thine aim is true. And Bekki is right. 'Tis better to slay a madman than to lose a friend."

Hastily Tip nocked an arrow and knelt and made ready should Lord Tain try to do ill to Beau.

Bekki squatted at Tip's side.

Still Tain muttered on.

"What is he saying?"

Bekki took a deep breath. "Among his babblings he now speaks of a Dragon, Sleeth, wreaking havoc."

"One of the renegades," whispered Phais.

"Now he tells that King Enrik is dead," continued Bekki, "killed by Dragonfire."

Beau opened his medick bag and took out a small jar: a salve. He applied it to the burn on Tain's forehead. The man did not note the buccan's ministrations.

Still Bekki translated, sifting information from babble: "Again he says Enrik is dead, but adds that Lady Jolet now bears Enrik's child in her womb, a child who will be the one true heir."

Phais gasped, "Oh Adon, she was with child." Phais reached out and took Loric's hand as tears brimmed her eyes.

Bekki looked up. "He believes that all the princes of Riamon are now slain: some by Dragon, some by cold, and he deems Loden and Brandt could not escape death at the hands of the overwhelming Horde in the battle at Mineholt North." Bekki shook his head. "He does not know Lady Jolet is dead, and he speaks of the child, the prince, the king to come from her loins."

Under the barge Beau spoke softly as he wound a bandage about Tain's head, yet the counsellor babbled on.

"Again he tells of Sleeth and the ravaging of Dael and speaks ill of those who fled from the city, calling them cowards all. Pah! As if Tain himself were not a runaway coward."

Beau closed his satchel, and Tipperton gasped and pulled the arrow to the full, for Beau tugged on Tain's sleeve, trying to draw him forth from under the barge. "Watch out, Beau," called Tip, "he's likely to do you harm."

Beau looked at Tip and then back at Counsellor Tain and tugged again, saying, "My Lord Tain, we must leave now, the kingdom has need of you."

But Tain did not note the Warrow's presence and sat and rocked and keened.

Finally, shaking his head, Beau took up his satchel and came out from under.

Tip exhaled a sigh of relief and relaxed his draw.

Southeasterly along the Sea Road they fared and away from the ruins of Dael, for none would stay in that city of death, none but the dead and the mad. And all along the tradeway they passed among the frozen blizzard-slain.

Ere they had departed, Bekki had led them to a market square, and there they had managed to find in the rubble a frozen slab of bacon, a whole side of venison, a number of grain-sacks of oats and two kegs of pickled herring, along with several sacks of beans. Some of this they packed on their horses, but most they bore back to Counsellor Tain's shelter and set it there for him to have. Too, they left him with a found oil lantern along with flint and steel. As for firewood, there were many unburned splintered timbers he could use, though none of the comrades thought he would. As Bekki said, and they all agreed, "He is mad and in his madness knows only what he mutters."

And they had ridden throughout the ruins and searched for other survivors, calling out for any who might yet be alive . . . but nothing stirred and no one answered and so they had ridden away, having done all they reasonably could.

And now they fared down the Sea Road among the frozen dead.

Loric gestured about. "This is why the Horde marched past Dael and set siege to Mineholt North instead."

"I don't understand," said Beau.

"Modru knew Sleeth would attack here and so did not cast his Horde against the walled city."

"But that was months back," said Tip, "and Lord Tain babbled of Sleeth attacking just ere the blizzard came."

"Modru is master of the cold," said Bekki. "He waited for his season ere loosing Sleeth to set fire to Dael, to crush its walls and batter down its dwellings, and he sent the blizzard flying on the Dragon's tail, for without shelter any survivors would die in the grasp of its frigid blast."

"I say," chimed in Beau, "d' y' think that's why he set siege to Mineholt North, to cut off that place of refuge should any make it through?"

Bekki shrugged. "Who knows the mind of Modru? Not I, Beau. Not I."

They set camp alongside the road, in a stretch where no frozen dead lay. And as they huddled about their nightly fire and sipped hot tea, Tip said, "It's my understanding that Drakes are vain, selfish, arrogant, and very powerful. How could Modru command such a creature to destroy Dael?"

"Perhaps he bribed him with a treasure," said Bekki.

"A treasure, eh?" said Beau. "What do you suppose it was? Or for that matter, what did he offer Skail of the Barrens to attack the Dwarves at Drimmen-deeve?"

Bekki shrugged, but Tip said, "Delon the Bard offered Raudhrskal a mate." Suddenly Tip's eyes widened. "Oh my, but I just thought of something."

Phais looked at Tip, an eyebrow raised.

"What if Modru has offered the renegade Drakes the Dragonstone?"

Phais shook her head. " 'Twas lost with the destruction of Rwn."

"But what if he's found it? I mean, that's why they became renegades in the first place, isn't it? They didn't want to give up the Dragonstone."

"Mayhap," replied Phais, "though Dara Arin herself said 'twas more likely they became renegades because in their arrogance they did not wish to be bound by the strictures of a pledge to *anyone*, much less the one devised by the Mages of Black Mountain."

"Now wait a moment," said Beau, throwing up a hand. "Look, didn't you just say Dragons were selfish and arrogant and powerful?" At Tipperton's nod, Beau plunged on: "Well if that's so, then which one of them would hold this Dragonstone? I mean they couldn't all have possession of this precious thing. So how could Modru promise the renegades the Dragonstone?"

"Perhaps," growled Bekki, "he secretly told each one that he would give over the stone to him and him alone—Skail, Sleeth, and any other Drake he would bribe—separately promising each one the same."

Loric nodded. "A Black Mage would do such."

Tip shook his head. "But wouldn't the Dragons take retribution against Modru for doing such an underhanded thing?"

Now it was Phais who shook her head. "Not with Gyphon as Modru's protector."

Beau yawned and stretched. "Well, I must say it's all quite beyond me. It's enough that we'll be done with it when we've delivered the coin."

"Oh, Beau, we won't be done with it until the entire war itself is done," said Tip, sipping the last of his tea and sliding his cup into a saddlebag. "It's all connected, you know."

Beau's eyes widened, and he nodded, pondering, then said, "You're right, Tip, but listen: nothing will ever be over, even after this war is done, for indeed all is connected, all is linked, past, present, and future, at hand and near and far, from all that has ever gone before to all that is yet to come."

As Tip took up his bow to stand the first turn at watch he said, "Well, Beau, you may be right about that, but if we can just get to the end of this war and win, for me that will be enough."

Beau did not reply as Tip stepped away from the fire and into the cold dark beyond.

*S*outh-southeasterly they fared, passing by the frozen corpses of those who had fled from the city of Dael, had fled from the raging Dragonfire, had fled from the whelmings of Sleeth, had fled into the countryside only to be blizzard-slain. Men, women, children, babies, horses, dogs: Modru's storm had spared none. And they lay scattered along the road as testament to his cruel power.

"Oh Adon," said Beau, his tilted amber eyes wide with distress, "why didn't some survive?"

"They had no chance to prepare when they ran from Sleeth's ravagement," growled Bekki.

"But they should have made fires, found shelter, anything but this."

"Oh, Beau," said Tip, "don't you remember the shrieking wind? The blinding snow? I mean, if it hadn't been for Bekki, we would have been hard-pressed to survive ourselves, and we're well prepared for the cold."

"Aye," said Phais, smiling at Bekki, " 'twas Fortune Herself who favored us with the company of this Drimm."

Bekki shot the Dara a quick glance, then looked at the road ahead, the Dwarf somehow disconcerted by her regard.

Beau sighed, then said, "Ah, me, and wellaway, but it is so tragic for so many to come to this grievous end."

"It's just one more thing that Gyphon and all his get will have to answer for," said Tip.

Loric looked at Tipperton. "Art thou still consumed by the need for revenge, wee one?"

Tip shook his head. "No, Loric. I but speak the truth."

Loric nodded and said no more as on down the Sea Road they fared, riding now in silence.

The next day, the shortest of the year, they passed beyond the reach of the frozen dead, and that night, as a waning gibbous moon rose in a clear sky, Phais, Loric, Tip, and Beau all took places to step through the Elven Winterday rite, the Dara facing north, the Alor and Waerlinga facing south. And as they looked upon one another, Phais began to sing, to chant, for it was something of each. Then Loric took up the chant, the song, and surprisingly he was joined by Tipperton, the Waerling in harmony. And Loric and Phais both smiled down at the buccan, while Beau looked at him in astonishment.

And in the argent light of the silvery moon shining down on white snow, Phais and Loric and Tip and Beau began stepping out the turning of the seasons.

Singing, chanting, and pacing slowly slowly pacing, they followed an ancient ritual reaching back to the dawn of Elvenkind. And enveloped by moonlight and melody and harmony and descant and counterpoint and feet soft in the moonlit snow, they trod solemnly, gravely . . . but with filling hearts.

Step . . . pause . . . shift . . . pause . . . turn . . . pause . . . step.

Slowly, slowly, move and pause. One voice rising; two voices falling. Liquid notes from the dawn of time. Harmony. Euphony. Step . . . pause . . . step. Phais turning. Loric turning, Waerlinga in his wake. Dara passing. Alor pausing. Buccen pausing as well. Counterpoint. Descant. Step . . . pause . . . step. . . .

And all were lost in the ritual . . . step . . . pause . . . step.

When the rite at last came to an end—voices dwindling, song diminishing, movement slowing, till all was silent and still— Lian and Waerlinga once again stood in their beginning places: female facing north, males facing south. And when they were finished it seemed as if the weight of the last few days had been lifted from them, and they were gladdened.

"I say," exclaimed Beau, breathlessly, "we almost know how it's done, eh?"

Loric grinned, but Tip shook his head. "Oh no. If it wasn't for Loric, we'd've floundered about in the snow."

Beau grinned back at Loric. "Even so, we're beginning to get the hang of it, neh?"

"Aye," said Loric. "Ye are at that, though e'en if ye practiced each day, still 'twould take long ere ye would be masters of the rite."

"I say, if we were Dwarves, we could master it at one pass, couldn't we?" asked Beau.

"The steps, aye, but the chant, the song, and its relation to the steps, that would take awhile."

"Speaking of Dwarves," said Tip, looking about the sparsely wooded clearing, "where has Bekki gotten to?"

Phais pointed. Atop a nearby hill stood Bekki, his arms stretched wide to the sky above. And they could hear his voice chanting words.

"What's he doing?" asked Beau.

" 'Tis the Drimmen rite of Winternight, a calling out to Elwydd," said Loric.

"Elwydd, eh?" said Tip.

"Aye, for She is their patron."

"What's he saying?" asked Beau.

"Words nearly as ancient as the Drimma themselves," replied Loric. "I was taught the rite by Kelek, when we were ship-wrecked in the Bright Sea. To do it properly, the DelfLord acts as cantor, the Drimma of the Dwarvenholt act as chorale, in alternating litany."

"Can you chant it to us?" asked Tip. "In Common, please."

Loric glanced upslope, then shook his head and said, "Even though thou and I art Châk-Sol, Tipperton, Bekki will have to do so, for it is their most solemn rite, a thing of the Drimma and not of the Lian."

"Oh," said Tip, looking up at Bekki on the moonlit hill, the snow asparkle in the silvery light, "I understand."

After a moment, Beau looked at Tip and said, "You know, we don't have solemn rites."

Tip frowned. "Who, Beau? Who doesn't have solemn rites?"

"Warrows, Tip. Warrows of the Boskydells, that is. I mean, although we note Summerday, Winterday, Springday, and Autumnday, they're all happy affairs, the best being Summerday."

"Oh?"

Beau nodded enthusiastically. "Oh my, yes. Look, Tip, you weren't raised in the Bosky, but on Summerday, Year's Long Day, Mid-Year's Day, there's a fair in Rood, and parades, and contests. And that's the day, Year's Long Day, when we hold a birthday celebration for anyone who's had a birthday in the past year, which of course includes everyone. —Oh my, I just thought of something."

Tip raised an eyebrow.

"We didn't celebrate our birthdays on Year's Long Day," said Beau.

"Hmph," grunted Tip. "It seems to me that on Year's Long Day we were hiking across Valon in the night with Hyrinians and Chabbains all about trying to do us in, Beau."

"Pah," said Beau, frowning, "be that as it may, still we should have celebrated. In fact, we should celebrate our birthdays right now."

"But, Beau, it isn't Year's Long Day, but Year's Short Day instead," protested Tip. "We'll be six months late or six months early, depending on how you want to look at it."

"Well, late or early, Tip, what better day for Warrows to celebrate? A short day for a short folk, eh?" Beau turned to Phais, who was grinning behind her hand. "I say, Phais, have we any of that venison? —And tea? Yes, tea. We must have a birthday tea, with mian if we yet have some, or crue if not. And, Tip, you must play your lute: 'The Merry Man of Boskledee' will do just fine. It's a good birthday song."

"Let's wait for Bekki," said Tipperton, glancing up at the crest of the hill. But Bekki wasn't there. Instead the Dwarf came flying downslope. "What th—? Bekki!"

Loric looked up and sprang to his feet. "Quench the fire," he hissed, his hand on the grip of his sword. "Be ready to fly."

As Beau kicked the campfire into the snow, Loric and Phais stepped to the horses and began casting on saddle blankets, Tipperton doing likewise to the ponies.

"A band," huffed Bekki, as he came into the site.

"Band?" asked Beau, catching up his saddle and stepping to his pony.

"Aye. To the south along the road. Tramping this way. Squam, I think."

"How many?" asked Phais, cinching a saddle tight.

"Too many," gritted Bekki, lifting his own saddle into place. "A hundred or so."

"Does it have to be Rûcks and such?" asked Beau, reaching under his pony for the belly strap dangling down opposite. "I mean, couldn't it be Daelsmen?"

"Mayhap," replied Bekki. "Though were it Loden's men, I would expect them to be riding and not on foot."

"We are well off the road," said Tip, threading cinch strap through binding rings.

"Even so . . ." said Phais, now turning toward one of the pack-horses.

Quickly all was ready for flight, and Bekki growled, "I would keep them in sight."

Phais nodded. "Let us ride to the far side of the knoll, and then go afoot to the top."

"Aye," said Loric, " 'tis Rûpt."

In the distance, in the moonlight, Tip could see the company of Foul Folk tramping northerly along the road.

"Oh my," said Beau, "they're marching to Dael. Shouldn't we ride back and warn—?"

"There is nought back there but ruins and the dead," growled Bekki.

"What about Lord Tain?" said Beau. "He's not dead."

Bekki looked at the buccan. "He might as well be."

"Nevertheless," said Beau, turning to Phais, "shouldn't he be warned?"

Phais sighed. "Thou must harden thy heart, Beau, for many will be the time the needs of the mission outweigh the needs of one."

"Barn rats, but I don't think I like that one bit."

"Still, 'tis the way of war, Beau."

"Oh, I understand the need, Phais. Even so, I don't have to like it, do I?"

"Nay, thou dost not."

"Why would they be going to Dael?" asked Tip.

"To loot," gritted Bekki. "It lies in ruins ripe for plunder."

"But how would they know it's been destroyed? I mean, if this is part of the runaway Horde, how would they know? They would think it a well-fortified city."

"Mayhap they go there at the behest of Modru," said Loric.

"But we killed his surrogate," said Tip, his mind returning to that desperate dawn in the tent. "Bekki did, that is. And since we killed Modru's eyes and ears and voice, how would they know?"

"He has more than one surrogate," said Phais.

"Perhaps they're simply deserters from the Horde," said Beau. "Running away from the fighting. Heading for the mountains."

"Well, deserters or not, fleeing or not, even if they are going to Dael," said Tip, turning to Beau, "still they might not find Lord Tain; he is well hidden, and all he needs do is remain silent."

Beau shook his head. "Not likely in his madness."

"If they do find Coward Tain," growled Bekki, "mayhap the Grg will save Loden the task of dispensing the king's justice."

Beau sighed but said nought in reply.

Long they lay atop the hill and watched the maggot-folk

march up the road and past and away while the waning gibbous moon sailed overhead and down, and Beau fell asleep with the waiting. And when finally the Spawn were gone from sight, Phais awakened the buccan and down the slope they all went, back to the horses and ponies, Beau grumbling that Year's Short Day was now also gone and they hadn't gotten to have their birthday party.

"Bekki says there's a town some miles ahead," said Tip, thumbing among his map sketches, finding the one he sought and showing it to Beau. "It's here at the fork where the Ironwater meets this tributary. Perhaps we can have a good hot meal and a bath and a mug of ale."

"Oh, Tip, don't say that."

"Wha—?" Tip looked at his friend. "Why not?"

"Well, every time we've counted on getting a good hot meal and a warm bath and a good bed and such in the next town, we arrive only to find it destroyed—Stede, Annory, that town in Valon, Braeton, Dael."

"See what I mean?" hissed Beau.

They stood in the woods and peered across the frozen Ironwater River at the small town on the far bank, where a company of swart maggot-folk looted and burned.

Tip sighed. "There are too many to fight."

Phais nodded. "We must ride on. To do otherwise is to risk the mission."

Bekki growled. "I like not this leaving of foe at our backs, yet I agree."

As they trudged among the trees toward the horses and ponies, Tip said, "There was a time, Bekki, when all I wanted was to kill Spawn. But no more. The death of Alor Lerren and others at Braeton was the first time I realized that people I knew would actually be killed while I sought my revenge. And then there were the terrible losses at Mineholt North . . . the price we pay is too high."

Loric looked down at the buccan. "The price paid for vengeance indeed is oft too great, wee one, yet no price is too high to pay for liberty, for it is precious beyond reckoning."

Bekki grunted. "Loric, I would argue with you concerning the worth of vengeance, yet not on the value of liberty."

They came to the place where the animals were tethered and mounted up and rode slowly through the woods, out of sight of the plundering Rûpt, passing the town by, each of the comrades feeling somewhat guilty at leaving living enemy behind.

*   *   *

Days passed and days more, and still they followed the road through the woods bordering the Ironwater River, and ten days after leaving the ruins of Dael, they neared the town of Bridgeton, there where a gap forty miles wide broached the ring of the Rimmen Mountains. And through this gap the waterway flowed southerly, the Sea Road following along as both wended down to the far Avagon Sea. And faring across, stretching east and west, through the breach ran the Landover Road, the Grimwall Mountains at one end, far Xian at the other.

And as the five comrades neared the gap, through the river-border trees they could see trails of smoke blearing the sky.

"Oh no," groaned Beau.

None else said aught as they rode onward.

Yet at last they emerged from the woods, and Beau broke into tears, for in the gap ahead they saw a town yet whole, smoke from chimneys rising into the air.

3

*I*t was Year's End Day, the last day of December, the last day of the two thousand one hundred ninety-fifth year of the Second Era of Mithgar, when Tip and Beau and Phais and Loric and Bekki rode toward the shut and warded town gates of Bridgeton. It was, as well, the very last day of the very first year of a great and terrible war.

And as the five approached, horns were sounded and flinty-eyed watchmen with crossbows in hand stood atop the western walls and looked upon these nearing strangers hooded against the cold. And when the horses and ponies were drawn up before the gates—

"*Uw zaak!*" demanded one of the guards.

Bekki glanced up at the blue-and-white tabarded watchman above the gate and at the flag of Riamon higher still and then called back, "*Wij zoeken schutting.*" Bekki cast back his hood and motioned for the others to do as well, which drew a murmur from the guards. Elves and Dwarves they recognized for what they were, but as to Tip and Beau—

"My lord and lady," called down the chief warder, now speaking Common, "to travel with your children in these troubled times—"

"We are Warrows!" interrupted Beau—

Volksklein? The guards looked down in wonder, for seldom had Small Folk been seen in Bridgeton, though it was said some Waldans lived on the banks of the River Rissanin just beyond the Rimmen Mountains on the western borders of Riamon.

—"And if you please," continued Beau, "would you open the gates? We need hot baths and mulled wine and warm meals and good beds to sleep in."

The warder laughed and turned and called down to someone within, then turned back to the five. "Meals and baths and mulled wine are within, but as to the beds, we've a scarcity of such, for Prince Loden and the Allies occupy many a cot."

"Loden?" blurted Tip, his companions surprised as well.

"Aye," replied the warder, as within the gate there ground a rumble of gears.

"What of my sire Borl?" called Bekki above the grinding sound. "DelfLord of Mineholt North."

The chief warder's eyes widened. "The DelfLord can be found at the Red Goose. Straight ahead and on the right. You can't miss it."

"And Coron Ruar?" called Loric.

"Coron, DelfLord, Chieftain, Prince: you will find them all at the Red Goose."

Now a side postern opened, and a man beckoned. Dismounting, inward strode the five, drawing the animals after. Through a wrenching corridor under the wall they went, much like the twisting passageway at Caer Lindor, with portcullises and barred gates at each end and murder holes overhead.

And then they came in among the streets of Bridgeton, the city abustle, for it was Year's End Day, and the citizenry would celebrate in spite of Modru's war.

"And it was Sleeth you say?"

"Aye, King Loden," replied Bekki, sitting across the table from the stunned young man.

Prince Brandt stood at the fireplace, tears running down his face. "We've got to kill him."

"Kill who?" asked Beau, sitting at the edge of the hearth.

"Sleeth."

Bekki cocked an eyebrow and shook his head, and beside him, DelfLord Borl said, "It cannot be done, for none has ever slain a Drake and likely none ever will."

"What about Gurd? He slew Kram," declared Brandt.

Phais glanced at Tip, then turned to Brandt. " 'Tis but a fanciful song the Bards sing."

Loden nodded grimly. "Brother of mine, Lord Borl and Lady Phais are right: should we go after Sleeth then we would merely be casting our lives away."

"But he slew our father, our brothers . . . Lady Pietja."
Brandt's face twisted in grief.

"I know," replied Loden, his eyes desolate. "I know."

"It's Modru who is responsible for the destruction of Dael and
the deaths of so many," said Tipperton, "for not only did Renegade Sleeth whelm the city, but the blizzard Modru sent was
perhaps even more deadly."

"Aye," said Coron Ruar, the Dylvana Elf staring into his mug
of tea. He looked up at Tip. "It nearly proved our undoing as
well."

"Oh?"

"Aye. Yet Fortune smiled upon us, for we were near Bridgeton
when the blizzard struck."

"What of the foe, the Horde?" asked Tip.

"Fully half of them perished," said Chieftain Gara, "slain by
the breath of Waroo, or so we thought."

"Waroo?"

"A hearthtale, Sir Tipperton: he is the Great White Bear from
the north who claws over the tops of the mountains and blasts
his chill breath down on all, bringing hard winters onto the
land, or so our legends say."

A silence fell upon those gathered 'round the table, and only
the crackle of the fire on the hearth filled the void. Finally Borl
said, "Regardless of the Baeron fables, we thought this blizzard
was at Fortune's behest, but now we find it was Modru
instead."

"Modru, aye," said Loric, "yet beyond stands Gyphon, the
root of all ill."

Another silence fell, and a knot popped in the fireplace, star-
tling Beau. He looked about sheepishly, then said, "What'll you
do about the company of Foul Folk we saw marching toward the
ruins of Dael?"

Loden shook his head. "Rather than pursue a small band of
deserters into a dead city, there are some two thousand Foul
Folk—the remnants of the Horde—yet east of here. Those we
must deal with first."

"But what about Lord Tain?" asked Beau. "He's in Dael and
yet lives."

"Coward Tain," growled Bekki.

"Mad Tain," replied Beau. A bleak look drew over the buccan's face. "He whispers to the corpse of his daughter."

"Mad he may be," said Bekki, then he looked at Loden, "yet
a proven coward he is, and deserves nought but the king's justice."

Loden shook his head. "From what you say, my friend, Lord

Tain's punishment was greater than any king's justice I might have decreed."

Bekki frowned but remained silent.

"Speaking of justice," said Borl, "it is fitting half of what remained of Modru's Horde were slain by his own hand."

"Devastated they may be," said Gara, "yet gone they are not. I say we go forward as planned and set forth on the morrow to renew our harassment of them."

"But there are only two thousand of them left," said Brandt, "and the scouts say they run for the Skarpal Mountains. Why not let them fly, while we go back to Dael instead. In spite of what we've been told, perhaps Lady Pietja survived; others too."

Bekki shook his head. "I tell you, Prince Brandt, we found none in the city alive but Coward Tain."

"She may have been hidden," cried Brandt.

Bekki growled but did not reply.

Loden looked at his brother. "Brandt, I, too, would like to go back and seek those who may have escaped, and give those we love a fitting funeral. Yet we cannot allow even two segments of a Horde to remain in the kingdom. Nay, Chieftain Gara is right: now is the time to pursue the Wrg, to slay them or drive them entirely out. Our warriors are well rested, the steeds, too, and the remainder of the Horde is now weary and weak." King Loden looked about the table for affirmation and received nods from Chieftain Gara, DelfLord Borl, and Coron Ruar. "Good. It is settled then. On the morrow we ride."

Ruar turned to Tipperton and raised an eyebrow. "No, Coron Ruar," said Tip, glancing at Beau and Bekki and Loric and Phais. "Our business lies elsewhere—in Dendor, in Aven, with King Agron—for we have a coin to deliver."

"Two thousand?" asked Tip.

"Aye," replied Vail. "Of the full Horde, two thousand were slain outright before the gates of Mineholt North. Another thousand of their fallen perished on the field at the hands of the mercy bringers. Another two thousand or so perished from their battle wounds along the way of the retreat. We slew another thousand in raids along their route. And finally the blizzard slew half of those who remained."

Beau was counting on his fingers. "Huah! That leaves two thousand, right enough, of the ten thousand they started with."

"What about our own casualties?" asked Tip.

Vail shook her head, sudden tears springing into her eyes. "We came away not unscathed. Fully two hundred fifty or so of our own will ne'er answer the bugle again."

"Two hundred fifty Dylvana?" blurted Beau. "But that's fully—"

Vail pushed out a hand. "Nay, not Dylvana only, but Drimma and Baeron and Daelsmen as well."

"Still, it is a lot to lose," said Tip.

"Aye," replied Vail, tears streaming. "And one was Andal . . . his death rede . . . it came to me. I did not even know he loved—" Vail choked back a sob.

Tipperton reached out and took her hand, almost as small as his own.

They sat in silence for a while as Vail regained her composure, and finally Beau looked about the common room of the Red Goose and said, "Tip, why don't you play and sing a song."

Tip looked at Vail—her features drawn, her eyes glistering. She smiled wanly. "Something gay, if thou wouldst."

The next morning dawned to a grey overcast, the skies threatening snow, while below, in the streets of Bridgeton, riders assembled in the morn. Prancing they came, and plodding as well, mounted warriors with eyes deadly grim: Dylvana and Daelsmen on swift horses, Baeron on massive steeds, Dwarves on ponies.

Throughout the night rumors had flown that Prince Brandt and his guard had ridden away in the dark, heading for the ruins of Dael, yet Brandt came riding in among his kinsmen, putting the lie to such.

Tip and Beau, Loric and Phais and Bekki, they all stood on the stoop of the Red Goose and watched as the Allies assembled, and Vail rode to the porch and said good-bye to them all, dismounting long enough to embrace Tipperton and wish him well.

Melor, too, came to the stoop, especially to bid Beau goodbye. Yet even as he did so, bugles blew, and the column, like a ponderous multilegged beast of great length, surged into motion and slowly drew away, heading for the eastern gate of Bridgeton. And Tipperton could see at the back of the train the heavy wains of the Baeron coming last, with Wagonleader Bwen standing on the seat of her wain and bellowing some command in her native tongue at the drivers of the wagons behind. She turned about and plopped down in time to wave a cheery farewell to the Warrows and Lian and Bekki the Dwarf, and then she, too, was past and away.

"Come," said Beau. And he led Tip running along the column and to the gate and up a ramp to the top of the beringing city wall, Phais and Loric and Bekki following after. And they all watched as the column and train emerged from the east gate to clop and rumble across the bridge spanning the Ironwater River, each of the five feeling somewhat guilty for not riding with the Allies to war. Yet Tipperton had his own mission to follow, the others to ride with him as well. And so they watched as Dylvana and Daelsmen and Dwarves and Baeron rode out from the city and into the land beyond.

Long they stood in the chill winter air as the column drew away. And finally, when the last wain rumbled 'round a far turn, Beau said, "Well, that's that." Even so they remained where they were, watching and watching still. And as they did a flutter of flakes began drifting down in the day. It was Year's Start Day, the first day of January, the first day of the two thousand one hundred ninety-sixth year of the Second Era of Mithgar as Tip and Beau and Phais and Loric and Bekki stood on the Bridgeton walls. It was, as well, the very first day of the second year of a great and terrible war.

4

*T*he rest of that day and all the next, Tip and Beau, Phais and Loric, and Bekki took advantage of the services of the Red Goose Inn, enjoying hot baths and hot meals and cool ale and rich red wine . . . and sleeping on soft feather beds. And they sang sad and sweet and rousing songs in the common room of the inn, to the delight of the townsfolk and guests alike, for although a force of Dylvana had been ensconced in Bridgeton for several days and had sung in the taverns and inns, still the townsfolk never got enough of Elves and their singing, for they were the best bards of all . . . or so it was said. Yet here not only were the Lian singing, but one of the Volksklein as well— ". . . Him with his silver stringed lute and his high, sweet voice, and the other wee Volksklein dancing a jig now and then. And would you believe it, one of the *Dwergvolk* sometimes bursts forth with one of those *Dwergish* chants, his own voice sounding much like a load of gravel sliding from a wheelbarrow, I'd say. And you can't understand a word he utters—pah! that language of theirs. Even so, I must admit it truly stirs the blood. And at times when the *Dwerg* sings, that little Waldan, the one who dances, he marches about with his chest stuck out and mug of ale in hand, and sometimes the crowd follows after. And occasionally that Lian Guardian, Elven lord that he is, he joins right in, and don't you wonder how an Elven voice can wrap itself around that tongue? But best of all is when the Elven lady sings and the lute-playing Waldan sings harmony and the Elven lord sings counterpoint."

Needless to say the common room was packed to overflowing when the news spread that "A Waldan and a Dwarf and two Lian were singing in the Red Goose, and another Waldan danced to their tunes."

And for two days, two Waldans, two Elves, and a Dwerg sang and chanted simple songs, tragic songs, glad songs, and songs of derring-do, of ships on the sea and Dragons in the air, of lost loves and loves found, of storms and rainbows and treasures vast, of hewing stone and harvesting grain, and of Silverlarks and Draega—the great Silver Wolves of Adonar, large as ponies and deadly foe of the Vulgs—and other such creatures of legend. And more, much more, did they sing and chant and march and dance, and all the peoples of Bridgeton, it seems, came to the Red Goose Inn.

Over those same two days as well, the comrades tended and cared for their animals, feeding them good grain and sweet water and giving them rest. The five also replenished their diminished supplies, Beau especially making certain that there was enough tea to last all the way to Dendor. "It's going to be cold, bucco," he said to Tip, "and hot drink will come in handy, right enough, morning and evening both. —Nighttime, too."

"Assuming we can build fires," replied Tip.

"Oh, Tip, do you think the whole of the way will be rife with Rûcks and such?"

Tip threw an arm over his friend's shoulders. "Surely not, yet regardless, we'll take all the tea with us."

And so, for two days the companions relaxed and sang and danced and drank and ate . . . and made ready to resume their quest, a journey ahead of them still, for on a thong about a small neck there rested a plain pewter coin, a coin that one of them had promised to deliver and fulfill the wish of a long-dead man.

On the third morning after the Allies had gone from Bridgeton, Tip, Beau, Phais, Loric, and Bekki rode forth as well, faring eastward across the stone bridge above the Ironwater River, frozen in winter's cold. They followed the Landover Road, and intended to stay on this route until they reached the gap where Riamon ended and Garia began; then they would turn almost due north and after some days cross the Crystal River to come at last into Aven. Even then, it was some leagues more they would have to travel through that land to reach King

Agron's court. Altogether it would be a journey of some five hundred twenty-five miles from the walls of Bridgeton in Riamon to the walls of Dendor in Aven.

Beau moaned when he heard of the distance they yet had to go, but gestured behind and said to Tipperton, "Well, bucco, at least we got our hot bath and mulled wine, and, oh, but wasn't the singing fun?"

"Don't forget the hot meals and soft beds, Beau, for I imagine we'll not see the likes again for many a day . . . perhaps not until we reach Dendor itself."

"How many days till then, do you think?"

"Twenty-five or thirty, if nothing goes wrong."

Beau groaned. "Oh no, a full month."

"Belike," growled Bekki riding alongside. "But there are towns along the way, and if they are yet standing—"

"Oh, Bekki," interjected Beau, thrusting out a gloved hand, "don't talk about towns along the way. I mean, no sooner said than something awful is likely to happen to them."

Riding in the fore, Loric turned and asked, "Dost thou think that merely speaking of them can bring ill fortune?"

"You never know," replied Beau. "Everything's all connected somehow, and I wouldn't want to tempt fate."

Bekki snorted, but said nought.

Sighing, Tip looked at Beau and said, "Sometimes, Beau, I wish I hadn't told you about events and stones and ripples in ponds."

Out front, Phais laughed, but Beau's jaw shot forward and he said, "Well it is, you know . . . all connected, I mean."

And Phais called back, "Good and bad alike, Beau, good and bad alike."

Beau frowned and looked at Tip and turned up his hands, and Tip said, "I believe what she means is that you are thinking only of the bad things bringing bad. But good things bring good as well."

Beau's eyes narrowed. "Hoy, now, if good brings good, and bad brings bad, does that mean good can sometimes bring bad? —Huah! Of course it does. Just as bad can bring good."

"Take care, my friend," called Phais, "for thou art now on a slippery slant, where thou mayst conclude that a good end justifies even the most foul of means."

"Oh no, I wouldn't do that," protested Beau.

Bekki glanced over at him. "Honor wouldn't permit."

"Indeed," replied Beau. "Indeed."

And down the Landover they fared.

*   *   *

Eastward they rode, ever eastward, an arc of the Rimmen Mountains in the distance to their left, the miles passing cold beneath the shod hooves. They rode by day and stayed in crofters' haylofts and open-air camps by night, the wayside inns along the way burnt to the ground or yet standing but abandoned, and these they stayed in as well and left a few coins upon counters when they rode away the next day.

In the late afternoon on the sixth day out they passed a wide swath in the snow where a well-churned track swung away from the road and beat east-southeasterly. Tip rode down and looked long at the trail and then remounted his pony. He gestured at the ground and called out, "These are the marks of shod hooves and the ruts of wagon wheels. It's where the Allies left the road."

"Pursuing the Rûpt," said Loric.

Bekki shaded his eyes, peering southeastward. "There," he pointed. "There lies the Skarpal Range."

Standing low on the horizon, snowy crests just visible across the rolling land, loomed the jagged peaks of a mountain range.

"That's where the Squam are heading," added Bekki.

"May Loden drive them all the way to their haunts," said Phais.

"May all the Grg be dead before any arrive," growled Bekki in response.

Tip spurred his pony up the slight slope and back onto the road, then he, too, turned and looked at the range afar. "They won't follow any surviving maggot-folk into the mountains, will they?"

Phais shook her head. "Not likely. To battle on one's home grounds is one thing; to battle on the foe's is quite another. Nay, I would think they pursue and fell the foe at opportunity—ambushes, swift strikes, and such. But when they reach yon slopes, I think the Allies will disengage, for the ground is not well suited to battle."

"Is any ground ever such?" asked Beau.

Phais looked at the buccan and made a negating gesture. "Nay, Beau, neither plains nor mountains nor fields nor fens: no ground is ever meant to be blooded, yet there are times when nought else will serve. And if one must do battle, then one must choose wisely, for on occasion the ground determines all."

Tip sighed. "I suppose if any foe reach the mountains, it's better just to let them go, eh?"

Loric shrugged. "Some may follow."

Bekki grunted, then said, "As to fighting among the peaks and crags, none are better than the Châkka. If any pursue the Grg, it will be my sire and kindred."

"Well," said Tip, "pursue or not, kindred or not, as concerns our mission, 'tis moot. I say we push on, for the sun is low, and this is not a place to stay."

As twilight deepened they came to a stand of oaks sheltering a wayside inn, the hostel seemingly abandoned, for no lights shone through the darkened windows, and all was silent and still. Yet when they tried to enter, they found the door to be barred within. Bekki drew the hand axe from his belt, and Loric and Phais drew blades.

"Maybe they left by the back way," said Beau, puzzled.

"Hush," hissed Bekki. "If the door is barred, mayhap there are Grg inside."

"Oh my," murmured Beau, backing away and plucking his sling from his belt, lading it with a lead shot.

Down from the porch they crept, where Tip took his bow from its saddle scabbard and nocked an arrow. Bekki slid his axe back into his belt and took up his war hammer.

"Ye three wait here," said Loric to Phais, "while Bekki and I go 'round back."

Phais nodded, and then as Loric and Bekki slipped through the shadows, she and Tip and Beau drew the animals after and took shelter behind broad trunks of oak. "Should any come running out," said Phais, "loose thy missiles at will. Yet should they draw nigh, take refuge behind me. And if there are too many, then leap astride thy ponies and flee."

"And leave you alone?" protested Tip.

"I will draw the horses behind and ride 'round for Loric and Bekki."

"You forget, Phais: Bekki won't ride a horse," said Tip. "I'll take his pony to him."

"And I'll ride alongside Tip," said Beau, "just in case a sling is needed."

Phais looked long at the buccen, then nodded.

Moments passed and the only thing Tip heard was the pounding of his own heart. But of a sudden—

"Yahh!" came Bekki's bellow, and the sound of splintering wood.

Gasping, Tip drew his arrow to the head, and Beau whirled his sling 'round and 'round.

Screams came from within, and the front door flew open, and Tip aimed—

"Hold!" shrieked Phais. " 'Tis women!"

Down the steps they fled, two women, as behind and backing out came a man with a bung hammer in hand.

Tip relaxed his draw and stepped out before the fleeing women, Beau stepping out as well.

"Rutcha!" shrilled one of the women, veering sharply leftward in spite of her bulk, the other following after, the pair only to run straight at Phais, who had stepped out as well.

"Drôkh!" shrieked the woman, turning again and running at the horses, then screaming, "Hèlsteeds!" and spinning in her tracks to dart back toward the inn, the second one running on the heels of the first all the time, hardly a handspan between them.

Beau fell down laughing.

"We thought ye the foe," said the innkeeper, a beefy man, as he poured another ale.

"As did we think of you," growled Bekki. "Finding a locked inn is cause for suspicion. It could have been full of Grg."

The innkeeper nodded. "The ways were barred, for the times, they are troubled."

"Aye," said Bekki as he threw a handful of copper on the table. "This should pay for your back door."

In the flickering light of but a single candle the 'keep looked at the coins a moment and then scooped them into his apron pocket, saying, "It will at that."

"I'm sorry I laughed at your wife and daughter," said Beau. "They must have truly been frightened."

"Aye," said the man, "as were we all. But it's them you should apologize to and not me."

Just then from the kitchen came the two women, bearing trenchers and bowls and spoons and knives and a cold joint of beef and two loaves of bread and an onion and a tureen of soup. "I'm sorry, but it's all cold now," said the wife. "The fire, you see, we don't burn one at night. It might be seen, even though the drapes are drawn."

"But it's winter," said Tip. "Surely you need a fire."

"Only in the daytime, sir," said the daughter.

"And then but a small one to keep the smoke down," said the innkeeper, "and we huddle close 'round warming ourselves for the night. 'Tis no way to live."

"We're thinking of leaving, you know," said the wife, a large red-faced woman with ginger hair. "The others nearabout along this road, they're gone, and winter travel, though usually slow, has completely disappeared. You are the first we've seen in weeks and weeks."

"Where will you go?" asked Tip, tearing off a hunk of bread.

"We have relatives in Dael who will put us up until all this blows over."

"Oh my," said Beau. "Oh my."

Phais sighed. "Then we bear ill news for ye, I'm afraid."

"Ill news?" said the daughter, a slender image of her mother, glancing at her dam and sire. "For us?"

"Aye," said Phais, "and there's no soft way to tell ye."

"Then just tell us," said the innkeeper, reaching out and grasping his wife's hand.

"Dael is destroyed," said Phais, "by Dragon and fire and blizzard storm."

"My sister," breathed the wife, her eyes pleading.

"There were no survivors," said Phais.

Bekki growled but said nought . . .

. . . as softly fell the tears.

On the twelfth day after leaving Bridgeton they rode up a long slope toward a low set of hills, and late on the following day they crossed over a running ridge connecting the Rimmen Mountains in the north to the Skarpals in the south. It was the fifteenth day of January when they came into Garia and rode down the far slope and onto the broad plains of that land. At last they had gotten past all the mountains that stood between them and their goal. And so due north they turned, smiles on every face, for from here it was but two hundred eighty straight miles over gentle rolling hills to Dendor in Aven, where they hoped to deliver a coin.

*A*nd you said this was going to be the easy part," hissed Beau as he lay bellydown in the snow, sling in hand.

"Beau, I only said that the land would be gentle, with rolling hills and such," replied Tip, peering at the campsite below, arrow ready, "and nothing about maggot-folk at all."

On the far side of the Crystal River—the border 'tween Garia and Aven—a small company of Foul Folk stirred. In the still air the smoke from their fire rose straight into the sky. It was this plume which had alerted the comrades as they had ridden northward in the morning, the sixth after coming into Garia.

Tip turned to Bekki. "Why do you think they're guarding the ford? I mean, it's winter and the river frozen. We can cross anywhere."

"Who knows the minds of Grg?" replied Bekki, his knuckles white on his war hammer.

"Gyphon," said Beau. "Modru."

Bekki scowled at Beau but said nothing.

"Mayhap they were sent by Modru to wait for the turning of spring," said Phais, "for then this will be the singular crossing in the region."

"They could be deserters," said Beau, "like those we saw in Riamon."

"Deserters or no, warders or no, still we must pass them by," said Loric, "for they are too many to engage."

Bekki hissed in exasperation but said, "Aye. Still, I do not like running from Grg."

"We'll not be running," said Tip.

"Nevertheless," growled Bekki.

Phais pointed leftward. "Yon, toward the slopes of the Rimmen Ring, there on the far flank of the second hill west, there where the river curves 'round, we should be able to cross over unseen."

Carefully they backed away from the crest and fared downslope to the animals.

Steel-shod hooves knelled on the ice.

"Can they hear the river ringing?" hissed Beau. "—The Rûpt, I mean."

"Mayhap," said Loric, spurring his horse. "Swift now!"

Across the frozen river they dashed, two horses and three ponies, their riders astride, drawing two pack animals behind. Up the far bank and into the hill country beyond they galloped, and if there was any pursuit, the comrades saw it not, for the Spawn were afoot and could not catch the running steeds even if they ran after.

"Foul Folk in Aven," said Tipperton as the snow drifted gently down. "It does not bode well."

"I think in this war they'll be everywhere," replied Beau. "I mean, way back when we first saw the fire on Beacontor, Tip, you said it could signal wide war, and now we find it is true. Indeed, wide war does burn on Mithgar; we can certainly testify to that."

Bekki reached across the small sheltered fire for the pot of tea. "Aye. War burns, yet we skulk past the foe."

"We should do nought to jeopardize the mission," said Phais, "or delay it."

"Indeed," replied Bekki, setting the pot back on the fire, snowflakes sissing in the flames. "Even so, as I have said before, it galls me to leave living foe behind; there is no honor in that."

"Nor at need is there any disgrace," said Phais.

Bekki looked at her and raised an eyebrow. "Mayhap not, yet the sooner we deliver the coin, the sooner we can engage."

"Wisely, I hope, and not rashly," said Tip.

"Ha!" barked Bekki. "This from the one who said 'Rescue me from behind' and leapt up in the face of the Grg."

Tip turned to Loric and appealed, "Did you think that was rash?"

Loric sighed. "Let us merely say 'twas precipitous."

Tip turned to Bekki to smile in triumph, only to find the Dwarf grinning.

"Wull," said Beau, "let's just hope that we don't find any more Foul Folk lurking between here and Dendor. I mean, Tip promised me a gentle trip across Aven, and a gentle trip I would have."

"The village is ablaze," said Phais. "We'll have to swing 'round."

"But what if they need help?" asked Beau, peering at the smudge in the sky.

"Just as we did in Valon," said Tip, "we'll have to pass burning towns by."

Beau looked at Bekki. "I'm beginning to agree with you, Bekki: the sooner we get rid of that blasted coin, the sooner we can help. In that, we are much alike."

Bekki glanced at the healer's satchel behind Beau's saddle and shook his head. "Alike? I think not. For you would engage to save lives, my friend, whereas I mean to quench them instead."

Wide of the conflagration they rode, slipping past the foe. And the next day they did likewise, for another hamlet was in flames, this one filled with Foul Folk running amok.

Beau sighed. "Oh, Tip, it is as you feared: Rûcks and such are indeed in Aven, slaying, looting, destroying all."

Tipperton shook his head grimly. "I wonder, Beau, given the foe are here, just what does it portend for Dendor beyond?"

Instead of ten days from the Crystal River to Dendor it took two weeks for the five to cross the two hundred miles between, for Spaunen patrols swept the land. Often the companions had to wait for night to avoid being spied on the plains. And on one of these days they were seen by a lone Rûck running westerly, going where for what reason none knew. And Loric ahorse rode him down from behind and slew him ere any alarm could be raised.

Yet north and north they went through weather foul and fair, avoiding discovery, swinging wide of their intended route, lying low for candlemarks on end, but coming ever back to the course.

And no longer did they build campfires, much to Beau's dismay. "Tea," he said. "I need my tea, and the Foul Folk are keeping me from it. If for no other reason, Bekki, you can kill them for depriving me of such."

Closer they came and closer still until at last they rode up through the hills which would bring them to the ridge above Dendor, and Tip's heart lay uneasy within his breast. And the closer they came the more he dreaded looking down upon the plain.

And Loric glanced at Phais, her lips drawn grim. "Dost thou hear, chier?"

She nodded.

"What?" asked Beau. "What do you hear?"

"Drums," replied Phais, "bugles, shouting, and the clash of arms."

"Drums?" asked Tip. "Like those that pounded before the gates of Mineholt North?"

"Aye," replied Loric. "Spaunen drums."

"Lor'," said Tip. "I can't hear them, nor the shouts nor clash of arms, but my heart is pounding so."

"As is mine," said Phais.

"And mine," said Beau.

Bekki only nodded.

"I fear what it betokens," said Loric.

"Look!" cried Tip, and he pointed to a trail of dark smoke blowing high across the sky.

"Oh my," said Beau.

"Vash!" gritted Loric, and he spurred forward, the other four following after.

On they rode up through the hills, and now all could hear the drums and bugles and shouts and the clash of arms . . . and still smoke plumed in air filled with the odor of char . . .

. . . and still the dread grew . . .

. . . and Tip looked at Beau to see another buccan blanched nearly white, a face reflecting his own.

At last they topped the final hill to look down on the plain below, and there stood the walled city of Dendor, some of it ablaze, though most not, and bucket brigades battled the flames. Yet the fires were not what drew the eye, for the city itself was beringed by battle, armies washing to and fro—Rûpt and men in chaotic struggle, red slaughter on the land.

To Tip's eye, all seemed a howling madness, as riders on horses charged the enemy, running regiments alongside on foot, only to be met by Ghûls on Hèlsteeds, with Hlôks and Rûcks in escort. Lance, barbed spear, saber, tulwar, bilaxe, glaive, hammer, club, mace, scimitar, falchion, flail, whip, mattock, . . . : they clove, bludgeoned, pierced, slashed, crushed, gutted, punctured, hammered, ripped, and broke men and Rûpt alike. And arrows flew in swarms of hissing doom, black shafts to be answered by white fletchings, deadly in their flight. Horses fell flailing, men screamed, hewn down, and Rûcks and Hlôks shrieked in death.

And behind the Rûptish foe, giant trebuchets and towers and great rams stood ready, should there be a need. Yet these were not advanced to the fore, there where fury reigned.

"Oh Adon," moaned Tip, his heart hammering in dread, "but I hoped to never witness such again."

"Do you see it?" asked Loric.

Beau, his face pale and drawn, looked at the grim-lipped Alor. "Do I see what?"

But Loric's gaze was fixed on the field, and he did not reply.

"Aye," groaned Phais, "there it is," and she pointed a trembling hand.

Tipperton's sight followed the line of her outstretched arm to see—

On the west side of the city, men quailed back from the foe, most to turn and run toward the gates of Dendor behind.

And alone midst the advancing Spawn strode a monster, grey in the midday light, and it walked upright on two legs, like an Ogru but no Ogru this . . .

. . . and then Tip knew why his heart hammered so, for it could be nought but a Gargon, a fear caster, and before it the men broke and ran, though some simply fell to their knees in terror, unable even to flee.

Even this far away Tip could tell it was massive, for the creature stood half again as tall as a man, and Tip thought he could detect the glint of scales on its flesh, though at this distance he could not be sure. And it ponderously stalked forward in a circle of emptiness, for not even the Foul Folk could stand to be near, so great was its terrible power.

And it seemed invincible, spreading terror as it went.

Yet of a sudden the fleeing men slowed and turned, and gripped their weapons, those they had not cast aside. And the men who had fallen to their knees scrambled up and ran back to join the ranks.

"See, chier, atop the walls," cried Phais.

"Aye," replied Loric.

"What is it?" demanded Tip, discerning nought but a milling throng along the banquette, though he did see men wheeling a ballista toward the point of attack, the giant bow laded with a spear. "Is it a trick? Do they lure the Gargon within range?"

"Nay, wee one," replied Loric, " 'tis a Mage on the wall instead. —Or mayhap more than one."

"What do they do?" cried Beau, scanning the ramparts, unable to single out anyone who might be a Mage.

"Quench the power of the Draedan," said Phais.

"But my heart yet pounds," said Tipperton.

"As does mine," said Bekki. "As does mine."

"For their protection to reach up here would drain them

beyond their means," said Loric. "They but shield the men below, those on the point of attack, lessening their fear."

A Rûptish horn blatted, the advancing Spawn stopped, and the Gargon roared in thwarted fury, echoes of rage ringing from the nearby hills.

The horn blatted again, and the advancing foe withdrew.

Yet elsewhere about the city, battle seethed and the slaughter grew, shouting men and yawling Rûpt slaying one another.

Time passed, measured in death, but at last the outnumbered men were driven back and back and back again, until they fled across the stone bridges above a dry moat and through the gates and into the streets beyond, portals slamming to behind, great bars clanging down.

And now the city of Dendor was under siege, none to pass either in or out through the clutching grip of cold iron.

In spite of a heart pounding in dread—*"Dahet malum scaths!"*—Tipperton cursed in the ancient Warrow tongue of Twyll, his rage cresting above fear, for this day was precisely one year to the day after a deadly skirmish at his small mill in the Wilderland, one year to the day from when he had accepted a small pewter coin to deliver, one year to the day after making a vow to honor a dying man's wish—one year to the day precisely—and on this day he had finally reached the threshold of completing his hard quest . . . only to find that he and his comrades were now completely shut out.

Oh my," said Beau, as he and the others stood atop the ridge and looked down at the Swarm beringing Dendor, "to come so close only to be thwarted."

"I should have ridden down during the battle and gone in through the gates with the men," said Tipperton.

"But then we would have been trapped," said Beau.

Tip sighed. "No, Beau, I wouldn't have had you and the others risk it. I should have ridden down alone. At least I would have delivered the coin."

Beau glowered at Tipperton. "Look, bucco, d'y' think I'd've let you go it alone after coming with you all this way? Besides, I want to know what this coin's all about."

"I just want to be rid of it," replied Tip.

" 'Tis a heavy burden to bear, no matter its weight," said Phais.

"Yet honor permits no less," said Bekki. "Even so, with Modru's Squam besieging the city, it will be difficult to keep your pledge, Tipperton."

Tip nodded glumly. "Let us wait and see, there may be another battle. And look, no matter what Beau says, there's no need for all of us to be trapped in Dendor should the men fail to break the siege. No one else need go."

Beau cleared his throat and shook his head. "Didn't you hear what I said, Tip? I'll not let you go it alone. I mean to stick to you like a burr. But as to Phais and Loric and Bekki, now—"

Bekki growled, "I am pledged by my DelfLord to ward you on this mission, Tipperton, and ward you I will."

"Most likely if ye go without us," said Loric, "ye three will be taken for Rucha by the men and slain out of hand or by cast. But accompanied by Guardians, such as Dara Phais and I, ye and we will likely survive."

"Oh my," said Beau. "He's right, Tip. Remember what happened back at the inn. We *were* taken for Rûcks."

"Yes, Beau, but that was at night and by frightened women. Remember, they took Phais for a Hlôk, and the horses for Hèl-steeds. Probably in the dark they took Loric for a Hlôk as well. As for Bekki, I don't know what he might have been mistaken for, mayhap a tiny Ogru."

"Kruk!" growled Bekki, but grinned.

"Even so, Tipperton," said Phais, "the vision of Humankind is poor in darkness, and if we attempt to join with the men in the night, whether afield or on the walls, they are most likely to take us for Foul Folk."

"Then we need go in the daytime," said Beau.

"Ah, but then, my friend," said Loric, "the Rûpt are like to discover us for what we are."

"Barn rats," growled Beau.

"Tipperton has the right of it," said Bekki. "If the men mount another assault, it is then we slip through in the confusion."

They spent the night camped back in the hills, but sleep was a long time coming, for still the pulse of Gargon dread beat within their veins.

The following day once again they made their way to the ridge, but on this day no attack came . . . nor the day after . . . nor the one after that.

But on the fifth day there sounded a great *thwack*! followed by cheering shouts and the beating of the Rûptish drums. And a wave of dread flowed and ebbed. And then another *thwack*! and more shouting and blatting of bugles and the deep booming of drums, and another wave of dread.

The comrades reached the crest of the ridge just in time to see the arm of one of the trebuchets swing up and over and—*thwack*!—hurl a scatter of tumbling objects to rain down within the city.

"Oh, Loric," said Phais, turning away in abhorrence.

Even as a wave of dread flowed over the five, "What is it?" asked Beau. "What are they throw—"

But then Beau saw, and he gasped in horror, as did Tip at his side.

Corpses had been dragged through the snow to the trebuchets, and the bodies hacked and severed and wrenched asunder. Heads, arms, legs, torsos: all were randomly laded into the
trebuchet slings, and then—*thwack!*—cast in high arcs, body
parts spinning, gyring, tumbling, to rain down onto the roofs
and into the streets of Dendor city beyond.

And horns blatted and drums thundered and waves of dread
rolled on.

"Oh lor', how ghastly," said Beau, tears streaming down his
cheeks.

thwack!

"We've got to do something," said Tip. "I mean, to just stand
and watch and wait for the Dendorians to break the siege isn't
enough."

"But, Tip," protested Beau, "we are just five. It isn't as if we
have an army here as we did at Mineholt North—one to attack
from the front while another strikes from the rear."

"That's it, Beau," said Tip, "you've hit upon it. What we need
is another army, and a coordinated attack—one head-on from
the city and one rear-on from, from—"

"That's just it, Tip: where are we going to get that second
army?"

thwack!

"Kachar," said Bekki. "We shall ride to Kachar."

Tip turned to Bekki. "Kachar?"

"The Châkkaholt nigh Kaagor Pass," said Bekki. "It is closest."

"Closer than the Allies?"

"Aye. Kachar is but a hundred sixty miles north, whereas the
Allies are twice as far or farther still, should they yet be pursuing the Horde in among the Skarpals."

thwack!

"But what if Kachar itself is under siege?" asked Beau. "I
mean, it's a Dwarvenholt after all, and Modru seems to have a
special grudge against your folk."

"If it is under siege," said Loric, "then we can appeal to the
Jordians, can we hie through Kaagor Pass."

"Dost thou think the pass to be held by Foul Folk?" asked
Phais.

Loric shrugged.

"Regardless," said Tip, "we've got to try. I mean, if we're ever
to stop those monsters down there, if I'm *ever* to deliver this
coin, then we've got to break this siege. And to do that, we need
fetch an army here and now."

" 'Seek the aid of those not men to quench the fires of war. . . .' " quoted Beau, hearking back to the mysterious rede they'd heard uttered by Dara Rael in council months past, but for whom the rede had been meant, none knew.

thwack!

Beau turned to Tip. "Let's go get Bekki's Dwarves."

They backed down from the ridge, then mounted and rode to their campsite, where they gathered up their goods and laded them on the packhorses, then rode straightaway to the west. When they had gone three leagues or so, they rode back through the hills above the plains and then waited until darkness fell, and that night beneath a gibbous waxing moon they crossed the flat treeless grassland covered with winter snow, reaching the other side some twenty miles away just after cold dawn.

They rested all that day and the following night, and then started out early next morn.

On the sixth day they came to the banks of the great Argon River, here curving in from the east and running away westerly; its frozen surface stretched wide before them. Along the bank stood the remains of a burnt dock, its charred pilings frozen in the river ice. The ashen remnants of a small shack stood on the bank above.

Bekki gritted his teeth and said, "Grg have been here."

"What is this place?" asked Beau.

"The southern landing of the Kaagor Ferry," replied Loric.

"We were going to take a ferry?"

Loric canted his head. "Aye, were the river running free and had the Spaunen not destroyed all. But even were the ferry yet whole, it runs not when the river is frozen, and all must wait . . . or chance the ice."

Still growling, Bekki dismounted and took his axe in hand. "I will see if the ice will bear us."

"Hold," said Loric, "this is not like the other streams we've crossed, but flows wide and deep instead. I will ready a rope."

Beau turned to Tip and whispered, "Hoy, when we crossed the Crystal River we didn't test the ice."

"With the maggot-folk downstream we couldn't test it," answered Tip. "Remember how the ice knelled under hoof? Besides, some rivers may run warmer. I mean, there were places below my mill on the Wilder that never seemed to fully ice over."

Bekki tied the line about his waist and gingerly stepped out on the ice. Then he stamped his foot. "It seems solid enough."

Walking out a ways and kneeling, he began chopping. Shards flew, and after a while Bekki looked up and said, "I am over two handspans deep and have still to break through. This will support an army. Even so, walk the animals onto the ice, while I go onward and test again. . . ."

. . . It took nearly three candlemarks to cross the Argon, yet cross it they did, the ice in the cold, cold winter thick enough to bear all.

"We are yet some fifty-two miles from Kachar," said Bekki, as they mounted again. "Two days and some should see us there."

"Let us just hope that when we arrive Kachar is not under siege," said Tipperton.

Through the Silverwood they rode, so named because of the trees of silver birch within its bounds, though trembling aspen and splendid high pine were sheltered as well in the cupping mountain bowl. And when they approached the far side, Bekki slowed them all, saying, "The vale of Kachar lies just beyond, yet if there are besiegers, I hear them not."

He looked at Loric and then Phais, and both Lian shook their heads, *No*.

Dismounting, they walked the last several strides among the trees to the very fringe of the wood, and they looked out to see in the midmorn light . . .

. . . nought but a snow-covered dale rising to meet the dark stone of the mountains beyond.

"There," said Bekki, pointing at a dull gleam of iron embedded in a wall of stone. "There be the gates of Kachar."

"They tried to hold Kaagor Pass," said Valk, "but we drove them down and slew them all." The redheaded DelfLord slammed the butt of his clenched fist to the stone table. "Yet now you say Dendor is beleaguered. Elwydd, but when will it end?"

"When Modru is defeated or slain," said Loric.

Valk grunted, then said, "But as you say, with Dragons at his beck, and Ghaths, it will not be easy."

"As to the Draedan," said Loric, "there is a Mage at Dendor who seems to be able to combat the dread. But the renegade Drakes, anow, they are a different matter altogether. Still, in a year we have seen but one—Skail—though Lord Tain in Dael babbled 'twas Sleeth destroyed the city. Mayhap Drake forays are rare, for I deem Modru need promise them something they cherish ere they act. What this might be, I nor my companions can say, though we have speculated long."

"Perhaps Tip's got the answer," said Beau, and when Tip looked at him blankly, Beau added, "they might want the Dragonstone."

"It is lost," growled Valk, "or so I have heard."

Phais nodded. "Lost with Rwn." She glanced at Tipperton. "Even so, the renegade Drakes mayhap would do Modru a service for the promise of such a token."

"Still," said Bekki, "that is neither here nor there. The problem before us is to rescue Dendor."

Valk nodded. "Aye. They are a valuable trading partner to this Châkkaholt, and we have a treaty with King Agron to come to his aid at need."

"Well, they certainly need you now," blurted Beau.

Valk looked at Beau and growled, "Fear not, Waeran, we Châkka honor our pacts"—he gestured across the chamber at the flag of the Dwarvenholt: crossed silver axes on a field of black—"especially the Châkka of Kachar."

"Oh my," said Beau, flustered, "I wasn't, I didn't—"

"He knows, Sir Beau," said Phais. "He knows."

Valk grunted and reached for a pullcord. "It is time to call in my captains, for we have a battle to plan."

As Valk and his captains met for the second day, with Tip, Beau, Phais, Loric, and Bekki in attendance, there remained one obstacle to completing the plan.

Bekki peered down at the map, with its movable symbols denoting segments of the Swarm surrounding the walls of Dendor. Shown also were the Dwarven routes of attack, as well as the likely paths the men would take in response upon issuing from the city. Bekki grunted and looked across at Valk. "There is left but this, DelfLord: how will the men know we have come, and how will they know the plan? Unlike Mineholt North, there is no secret entrance to Dendor, none I know of, that is." He looked across at Valk.

Valk shook his head. "There may be a tunnel, but Agron has never spoken to me of it, if so."

Silence fell as all considered the map. Finally Valk said, "All here know our chances for victory run high can we coordinate the attacks, and defeat will come knocking can we not. This then is the crux of the matter: how to let King Agron know."

The DelfLord's gaze swept about the table in challenge. "Let us delve how this may be done."

Long they spoke, considering plans and counterplans, finding strengths and weaknesses in each:

Some advocated the use of message arrows, could they get

one or more archers in range, or perhaps long-range ballistas instead. But then others asked, would the messages be found? And would King Agron believe such missives aught but a ruse? Still others noted that even if he did believe, what if a message fell into the Foul Folk hands? Through a miscast arrow or a captured archer, if a message fell into the wrong hands, then all plans would be revealed, for there was no secret code between DelfLord Valk and King Agron.

They also noted that signals flashed from the ridge above could be intercepted as well.

Other plans were examined and rejected . . . such as searching for a secret tunnel which may or may not be there. "Huah," said Bekki. "If there were a tunnel, do you not think that Agron would have sent someone to ask for aid?"

"Worse yet," said Loric, "if there were a secret tunnel and if found by the Rûpt, they would use it to invade."

Seated next to Tipperton, one of the captains, a black-haired Dwarf named Kaldi, said, "Could we not march and array ourselves along the southern ridge to let King Agron see we've come? Then mayhap when we attack from without he will sally forth from within."

Valk shook his head. "It is a worthy plan, Kaldi, and one we may come to in the end, but then there is this: with a surrogate in the Swarm, Modru would be alerted by our array and then mayhap a Drake will come. Nay, if we can, we should take them by surprise."

"Barn rats!" said Beau. "With a Swarm about the walls, it's not as if we can just walk up to the gates and knock for admittance."

Silence fell, and Dwarves about the table shook their heads and gritted their teeth in frustration. But then Tip glanced at the flag of Kachar and of a sudden said, "Wait a moment, Beau, I think you've hit upon it."

"Wha—?" began Beau, but Tip cut him off.

"Have you still got that flag of Modru's?"

Beau frowned but said, "It's still in my saddleba—"

"Good!" said Tip, smiling. "Here's what we can do: I'll take the flag and walk through the Swarm till I reach the—"

"Good grief, Tip, that's madness! They'll kill you dead!"

"No-no," said Tip. "Hear me out. You said it yourself, Beau: in the dark, Warrows can be taken for Rûcks, just as we were taken for them by the folks at the inn. And since I'll be carrying a flag of the Spawn, who among them would look at me twice?"

"Sir Tipperton," said Phais, "if it means walking through a Swarm, Sir Beau is right. 'Tis a mad plan fraught with risk."

Beau nodded his total agreement, but Bekki looked at Tip in admiration and clenched a fist of support.

Tip held up a hand. "Oh, Phais, as I said to Beau, hear me out."

Phais sighed, but nodded.

Tip took a deep breath and said, "When I get through the ring of Swarm, I'll cross the open land between them and the city—"

"You will be seen," said one of the captains.

Bekki shook his head and said, "He is a Waeran," as if that explained all.

"Even so," said Valk, "I would hear the whole, for he is not yet done." He gestured for Tip to continue.

Tip nodded and said, "I'll cross the land between and—"

"And what?" cried Beau. "Knock on the gate?"

Tipperton nodded. "Exactly so, Beau. Knock on the gate."

"But they'll quill you with crossbow bolts," declared Beau. "I mean, you said it yourself, you'll be taken for a Rûck."

"No, Beau, by that time I will have shed Modru's flag and will instead show the flag of Kachar." He gestured at the black flag with its crossed silver axes. "Surely they will know it, eh?" He turned to Valk.

Grudgingly the DelfLord nodded. "Even so, Waeran, you are not Châkka. They will not admit you, thinking it a trick of Modru."

"No," said Tip, "I am not 'Châkka,' but then I've got this." With these words Tip reached down the collar of his shirt and drew out the coin on a thong.

"Ha!" snorted Kaldi, next to Tip, the Dwarf leaning over the better to see. "Do you think they will accept an all but worthless toll?"

Tip looked at Kaldi and said, "If we are right, Captain Kaldi, Agron will certainly accept this coin."

Valk looked at Tipperton. "I do not understand."

Tip sighed. "DelfLord, let me tell you about a night in the Wilderland, when I was awakened in my mill by a battle to the death on my doorstone. . . ."

Finally the coin came back 'round the table to Tip. As he slipped the thong over his head, an elderly Dwarf across the table said, "It is a Gjeenian penny—an alloy of *zin* and *chod*—mayhap the most worthless coin in all of Mithgar."

"Gjeenian?" said Tip, looking across at the Dwarf.

"From Gjeen, an island in the Avagon Sea off the coast of the Karoo. How it bears on your mission, I cannot say."

Tip frowned and peered at the coin and mumbled, "Knowing where it comes from doesn't enlighten me one whit."

He looked at Loric, who turned up his hands and shrugged.

"All of this talk about where a coin comes from and its worth doesn't matter a hill of beans," said Beau. "What matters is this harebrained scheme of Tip's—I mean, him marching through a Swarm of maggot-folk who will kill him dead . . . and then sneaking across the land in between warring armies to the walls, where the men above will kill him dead . . . and then knocking politely as if you please on the doors of Dendor, where the guards on the gate will kill him dead."

Silence fell, and after a moment Tip asked, "Have you a better plan, Beau? If so, I'm sure we'd all like to hear it."

"Oh, Tip, of course I don't have a better plan. It's just that I'm worried sick that, Foul Folk or men, one or the other will kill you dead."

The circle of captains discussed the merits of Tipperton's "harebrained scheme," until finally Valk called for quiet. He glanced 'round the table, his gaze settling on Tipperton last. Valk smiled. "Once long past when faced with a perilous choice Breakdeath Durek said, 'The gamble is great, the stakes are high, yet he who dares, wins.' Sir Tipperton, I accept this mad plan of yours."

Tipperton exhaled pent breath.

"And a Waeran must do this thing," Valk continued, "for none else might pass as a Rûck, albeit a small one, and none will be better at stealing across land between, and with a flag of Kachar to keep him from getting slain out of hand and the coin as a means of admittance, well then, who better than Sir Tipperton?"

"What about me?" asked Beau.

"Oh no, Beau," objected Tip. "It's my mad plan and I should bear the risk."

Beau looked at Bekki. "It is his right," said the Dwarf.

"Wull then, I'll just go with him," replied Beau.

Phais shook her head. "Nay, Sir Beau. Fortune favors one alone, but not two."

"But I went through Drearwood with Tip, and it was just as dangerous."

"Aye, perhaps just as dangerous, yet 'twas not the same. There in Dhruousdarda ye twain needed pass through nought but trees while avoiding scattered Rûpt and lone dire creatures of that wood. But in this Tip must walk through the heart of a Swarm and cross from its fringe to the walls of Dendor and then seek admittance. One alone has a better chance than two together of getting through the Swarm, and two together represent more of a threat to the men on the gate than a single one alone."

Tears came to Beau's eyes, but he nodded bitterly.

"It is decided, then," said DelfLord Valk. He turned to Tipperton. "Hear me now: two things can occur with your mission: it may fail; it may succeed.

"Should it fail, then when we arrive we will array ourselves on the ridge south of the city for a day and attack the next, and that should give Agron enough time to see us and set his forces to attack when we do, though it will also give Modru enough time through his surrogate to see us as well and to act, all surprise being lost.

"Ah, but should your mission succeed . . . You have seen and know our plan and you must convey it to Agron. Tell him I come with three thousand Châkka no more than a week after you. Have him each night and dawn loose fire arrows from above the four gates, signifying that all is ready. Just ere the dawn the day of attack, we will loose one fire arrow in return and then in the darkness ride down to war and attack with the coming of the sun. Let Agron's men come forth at that time, and together we shall win." As Tipperton nodded, Valk raised his axe. "Châkka shok! Châkka cor!" his voice rang.

Châkka shok! Châkka cor! responded the captains all 'round.

The DelfLord then looked at Tip and said, "Sir Tipperton Thistledown, may the smiling face of Fortune be turned your way, and may Elwydd watch over you." Valk grasped the helve of his axe nigh the head and held it before him and slapped a hand to the blade and called out, "*Shok Châkka amonu!*" and so did all the captains as well.

Tip glanced up at Loric, and the Alor said, "The axes of the Dwarves are with you."

Eleven days later, in the early March evening as the sun sank low in the west, once again the comrades stood among the trees atop the ridge overlooking Dendor. Still the Swarm ringed 'round the city below.

"It looks thinnest near the south gate," said Loric, pointing straight ahead.

"Then that's where I'll go," said Tipperton, his heart hammering, for not only was he about to set out on a mission dire, somewhere below a fear-casting Gargon stalked among the Swarm.

Phais gestured at the remains of remote winter sun sliding

below the horizon, all but its upper limb now gone, the thin arc of a crescent moon sinking down just above. "When the sun disappears and the moon sets, then thou must go, for dark night will be full upon the land."

Tip nodded and looked at Beau, and that buccan's face was drawn. "Cheer up, bucco," said Tip, as he folded the flag of Kachar and stuffed it under his jacket. "We'll see each other after."

"Oh, Tip, it seems you are always going off into danger, while I but do hang back."

The last of the sun disappeared, and the fingernail moon edged down.

"Huah!" barked Tip. "Who walked with me through Drearwood, eh? Was it you or some stranger instead? Some stranger who saved me from that strangling Hlôk, hit him in the head with a rock? And who came rushing to my aid at Annory? A stranger still? And who—?"

"Look, bucco, I know we are both in it up to our necks, but this time it seems more, more—"

"Harebrained?"

Beau laughed in spite of himself. "Well, perhaps not harebrained, but dangerous nonetheless."

"I know, Beau, and that's why I'll be all the more careful."

As the moon itself slid into the land Bekki glanced through the twilight at Tip. "There may come a time when boldness will better serve."

Tip nodded, but Beau said, "If it comes to needing to being bold, Tip, remember what I once told you."

Tip raised an eyebrow, and Beau grinned, and said, "If you're going to be bold, then do it timidly."

Tip smiled, remembering, and while the moon sank below the horizon, he said, "With that Gargon down there, I'll be way beyond timidity and into stark terror instead."

A look of distress crossed Beau's face. "Oh, don't say that, Tip. I mean this mission is bad enough without throwing in a Gargon, too."

"Well, we can't very well throw him out, now can we?"

Now the moon was gone altogether, the night lit by remote frigid stars in a cold crystal sky above.

Phais knelt and embraced Tip. "Fare well, my friend." She kissed him on the cheek.

Loric, too, embraced the buccan, as did Bekki, much to Tip's surprise.

Last of all, Beau gave him a hug, tears running down. "Hear me, Tipperton, you take care," he managed to choke out.

"You, too, Beau. You too," replied Tip, his own voice trembling.

Loric handed the buccan a pole, Modru's standard atop, and, with his heart thudding in dread, Tip took a deep breath and said, "Well, I'm off."

Bearing a ring of fire on black, and bearing their hopes as well, the wee Warrow set off afoot down through the winter snow.

Ahead lay the gates of Dendor.

Ahead lay a deadly Swarm.

7

*H*is heart hammering, Tip lay in the snow for long candle-marks, watching the outer-perimeter guards passing to and fro, the maggot-folk silhouetted by the fires of the Swarm, the buc-can trying to gauge when best to attempt to slip across the space and step in among the teeming Spawn.

As planned, Tip had aimed for the south gate, yet the closer he had come toward the Swarm, the harder he had found it to breathe—

Fool, you fool, you'll never pull this off.

—and the more his guts had churned with dread.

But even so he had worked his way through the shadows until at last he had come to the very perimeter itself, and now he hid behind a snowy outcropping and watched the Rûcks and such tromp past, some patrols marching deasil and others widder-shins; and they frequently passed where he lay.

Still he had seen enough to know there were good gaps, and so he made ready for the attempt . . . his pulse thudding in his ears.

The patrol passed before him, and as they trod away into the night, Tip glanced leftward toward the squad following—

—A long way off.

Still he waited for the right moment, his heart racing, his breathing shallow and quick.

Leftward in the distance came the patrol.

Tip reached out and gripped the flagstaff lying beside him and gathered his feet under and glanced rightward at the retreating squad . . . and groaned—

—Oh no. Another band just beyond . . . coming this way.

Tip slumped back into the snow and watched.

As the two groups rightward met, the Hlôks in the lead stopped to confer, their squads jostling to stumbling halts behind.

Hoy! Now, bucco, now!

His heart thudding, blood hurtling through his veins, Tip scuttled low into the wide space of the perimeter, expecting shouts of alarm even as he scrambled across. . . .

Oh Adon Adon Adon . . .

. . . but none came.

And then he was in among the maggot-folk.

And his breath came even faster.

With his hood cast over his head, his features in shadow, and his heart hammering against his ribs like a wild caged bird against bars, Tip unfurled Modru's standard, and with the pole over one shoulder he headed inward, threading his way amid the campfires of Rûcks and Hlôks and Ghûls, while fear rose up through his stomach and threatened to spew outward in vomit.

On he went and on, past maggot-folk, Foul Folk, Spawn, his heart beating even more wildly with each and every step . . . and then he came to a wide place where no fires whatsoever burned . . .

. . . and the stench of vipers swept over him . . .

. . . and billowing terror engulfed him, his heart, his being, his very soul drowning in overwhelming fear, and he shrieked in uncontrollable dread and whirled about and plunged away, running heedlessly, running back the way he had come, running back past maggot-folk, Foul Folk, Spawn, screaming and running back and away from a large, round black tent sitting alone in the snow . . .

. . . and Ghûls laughed at the small, shrilling, flag-bearing figure fleeing headlong among the campfires. . . .

Running in blind terror, Tipperton slammed into the wheel of a wagon and fell backwards into churned-up snow. Stunned and disoriented, he floundered to his feet, and would have fallen again, but he managed to grab on to a spoke and steady himself, his heart yet racing in terror.

He looked hindward the way he had come and gasped when he saw the solitary tent, his mind flashing back to Gûnarring Gap, where a tent just like this one had blocked the way.

There in the Gap it was the tent of a Gargon.

Here it could be no less.

Oh, bucco, bucco, bucco, no wonder your heart is trying to fly away—it's the dread of the Gargon you feel.

Tip drew in a deep shuddering breath and stooped to pick up the flag.

No wonder as well the tent sits alone: none can deal with the fear. And no wonder the path to the south gate seems thinned of surrounding Foul Folk: a Gargon stands in the way.

Gasping and trembling and leaning on the flagpole as if it were a staff, Tipperton looked through the Swarm and past the tent and toward the distant gate beyond.

Well, bucco, the south gate's out and that's for certain. I mean, you can't get past that dreadful thing.

He looked left and then right. Foul Folk teemed both ways.

Which gate, bucco, which gate?

Trying hard to steady himself, at last Tipperton chose:

The west gate . . . that's where the Mage was. Besides, from the Wilderland to here, I've travelled east far enough.

With his pulse hammering and on trembling legs, once again Tip started moving among the wavering shadows cast by the fires of the Swarm, arcing westward within the ring of Foul Folk, praying to Adon that none would see through his too easily revealed masquerade.

"Where do you think he is now?" asked Beau, looking up at the wheeling stars and trying to gauge the time.

"In these candlemarks ere mid of night," said Phais, "if all has gone well, he should be nigh Dendor's south gate."

"If all has gone well? Oh, don't say that, Dara. I mean, there's no cause to bring down misfortune on his head. Surely all has gone well."

Tipperton continued winding his way among elements of the Swarm, turning aside when maggot-folk seemed to be stepping toward him, turning aside as well when it seemed someone was following after.

And still dread pulsed through his veins and still his heart hammered, and still his breath came in gasps, but less so than before, for the black tent was nearly an eighth of a circle behind. Even so, Terror paced alongside the buccan, keeping him company on his perilous path.

"He is probably lying in hiding nigh the south gate and waiting for dawn," said Bekki, "the flag of Kachar in hand."

"Oh, do you think so?" said Beau, glancing again at the starry sky.

Bekki, too, looked upward, just in time to see a streak of fire race overhead.

"Oh look!" cried Beau. "A falling star. Make a wish, make a wish."

The Warrow turned to Bekki, only to find the Dwarf with his hood cast over his head and staring at the snowy ground.

"What is it, Bekki? What's wrong?"

But Bekki refused to say, and he turned his back to the city.

Tipperton worked his way toward the fringe of the Swarm, peering ahead to see where he might slip out from the ring and toward the west gate.

And he gasped, for another tent stood in his path. Yet no dread washed over him, and no reek of vipers filled the air. Instead this shelter was warded . . . by Ghûls, no less.

I wonder—⁈ Oh my, perhaps it's another of Modru's surrogates. Yes, bucco, I believe you are right: it has to be the tent of a surrogate. If Bekki were here he'd say, "Kill him now and take away Modru's eyes and ears and voice." Yes, that's what he'd say. But me, I've other things to do.

Seeking to find a way 'round, Tip was shunted aside by a tramping squad of Rûcks.

Stepping leftward, Tip passed nigh the rear of the tent. And from inside he could hear a whispering and hissing in a tongue he did not know.

Modru in council⁈

Again Tip turned aside as a Ghûl came walking near.

"It means, Beau, that someone he knows has died."

Beau looked up at Loric in alarm. "Oh no. Do you think it could be Tip?" Beau stared down at Dendor, as if willing his sight to fly overland to wherever Tip might be. Yet though false dawn glimmered in the sky, only shadow 'round the city met his gaze, darkness relieved but slightly by the brittle stars high above and the campfires of the Foul Folk below.

Loric turned up his hands. "All Drimma believe that falling stars foretell of fallen friends."

"Wull, let's just hope it's nothing but wild superstition," said Beau, the buccan pacing back and forth while peering down at the city. "Oh, Loric, I told Tip it was a harebrained scheme, and now we have falling stars. And you tell me the Dwarves—oh, surely it can't be true. I mean, stars fall all the time." Beau turned to Loric for confirmation, but Loric was looking at Bekki sitting beneath a tree some distance away, the Dwarf with his hood cast over his head in mourning.

* * *

At last Tipperton reached the inner fringe of the Swarm. Ahead some quarter mile or so stood the west gate of Dendor. His heart yet pulsing with the distant dread of the Gargon, Tip looked for a way across. Yet this perimeter was more heavily patrolled, maggot-folk marching the verge. Too, sentries stood watch along this periphery.

Oh lor', but I'll never get out unseen.

Tip glanced at the sky above. False dawn glimmered.

Elwydd, show me the way.

And then to the left, a figure, a Rûck, walked past a sentry and out and down into a shallow gully, while another came trudging back, fastening his breeks as he came from the meager draw. The picket paid little heed.

Tip moved closer and the reek of feces and urine wafted on the air.

Sucking in a deep breath and making certain that his hood was well about his face, Tip hefted the standard and with his stomach squinching he walked past the warder and into the draw, past a Hlôk voiding his bladder, past a Rûck defecating, past them all and to the distant end of the gully—

—where he squatted behind an outcropping of rock and waited, trying with little success to ignore the reeking fumes.

In the last of the darkness before dawn, Beau sat on the ridge with his back to a tree, the dread of the Gargon pulsing in his veins, his stomach roiling with anxiety. He cast his eyes to the night sky above, winter-bright stars coldly glittering.

Oh, Adon, Elwydd, Garlon, Fyrra, and anyone else who cares, watch over Tip. Keep him safe. He's my best friend, you know.

Staying low and taking advantage of every fragment, every fraction, every scrap of cover—dips in the ground, scatters of rock, ditches alongside the road—Tip crawled through the snow toward the west gate, still hundreds of yards away. Pausing by a winter-dead bush, Tip caught his breath and looked back toward the Swarm. He found he was more or less halfway between death at the hands of the Rûcks who would kill him for a Warrow and death at the hands of the men who would kill him for a Rûck.

Gritting his teeth, Tip crawled on, the sky in the east turning pale.

"Watch the south gate with your eagle eyes, Phais," said Beau, the buccan's own eyes bloodshot and red-rimmed, his face haggard. "Surely you'll see if—no! surely you'll see *when* Tip goes in."

"I will," replied the Dara.

"As will I," said Loric.

And the four of them stood atop the ridge and peered down at the south gate, as dawn came to the sky.

Moments passed and moments more, and the gate remained shut.

"Oh no," groaned Beau. "He's been captured, he's been captured . . . or something worse."

Phais knelt and placed an arm about the buccan's shoulders and drew him to her. "Take heart, wee one."

"Huah!" grunted Bekki. "Look left. Something stirs."

" 'Tis Ghûls on Hèlsteeds," said Loric, staring. Then his eyes widened. "Ai, look now, but they do race through the shadows aslant and toward the west gate of Dendor."

Dng! Dng! Tip, his hood cast back, hammered the butt of the flagpole against the iron of the enshadowed west gate deep-set in the stone walls of Dendor.

"I'm not a Rûck! I'm not a Rûck!" he shouted in Common over and again as—*Dng! Dng!*—he pounded on the metal door, flakes of hoarfrost scaling down.

Iron scraped on stone left and right and above, and dimly Tip saw the steel points of crossbow quarrels aimed at him from unshuttered dark arrow slits to each side, and murder holes overhead now yawned wide in the gloom above.

"I am not a Rûck! I am not a Rûck!" cried Tip, waving the standard back and forth—a black flag bearing crossed silver axes—the emblem of Kachar.

A slot in the iron gate slid aside. Eyes peered out to see the fluttering banner sweeping back and forth.

"*Vad är det här!*" growled a voice, and then the eyes shifted down. "*Jo, jo! Är det a Rutch!*"

"I am not a Rûck!" shouted Tip in the dawn shadows, turning his head left and right so that the warder might see his features. "I'm not a Rûck , I'm not a Rûck , and I bear a token for King Agron."

The eyes left the small portal, and a voice shouted, "*Kapten, jag behöva dig!*"

"King Agron, King Agron, I need to see King Agron." Tip jerked the coin out from under his jerkin. "I bear a token for King Agron."

Atop the wall a horn sounded.

Tip stepped back a dozen or so paces out from under the wall and to the stone bridge, and still waving the flag he peered upward.

But the men above were not staring down at the buccan but instead were looking out toward the Swarm.

Tip turned to see two Ghûls on Hèlsteeds hammering through the slanting dawn shadows and toward the gate where he stood, snow flying from cloven hooves.

Tip spun back toward the shut portal and ran to the frost-laden steel doors. "Let me in, let me in!"

"*Nej! Det är skoj!*"

The iron panel slammed shut and crossbows in arrow-slits were raised and pointed at Tipperton, while Hèlsteeds thundered toward the gate and cruel barbed spears glimmered in the dawn.

Tipperton whirled and dropped the standard and whipped off his cloak, revealing the Elven bow fastened crosswise over chest and back. Quickly he looped it free and snatched an arrow from the quiver at his thigh.

But even as he did so, a hail of arrows hissed out from the wall above, most to miss, though some struck the Ghûls, piercing arms and legs and necks . . . and they howled in glee and thundered on.

And trapped outside the gate, Tip aimed and loosed his arrow to strike the lead Hèlsteed square in the chest, the beast to grunt in pain and run another handful of strides ere tumbling down dead and hurling the Ghûl over its head as it crashed into the snow.

Yet as the following Hèlsteed hammered by, the downed Ghûl gained his feet and came running on, his deadly barbed spear in hand.

Now a second flight of arrows hissed out from the wall above to strike at the remaining Ghûl and Hèlsteed; quilled, the cloven-hoofed beast reared up squealing, while the rider cursed in Slûk and cruelly sawed on the reins, fighting for control.

"Let me in! Let me in!" shouted Tipperton, even as he strung a second arrow.

And down through the murder holes—"Open the side postern, you fools!" snapped a voice. "Can you not see he's a Warrow! *Öppna den små port! Skynda dig!*"

Even as the Ghûl afoot ran forward, arrows hissing all 'round, to Tipperton's left a side postern clanged open. Tipperton risked a sideways glance and saw an armored man frantically gesturing him inward and shouting, "*Skynda på! Skynda på!*" while three warriors stood farther back, their crossbows leveled at the Warrow.

Tip turned and loosed his arrow at the onrushing Ghûl now running onto the stone of the bridge, the shaft to slam into the creature's stomach, yet it did not slow him one step and across the span he came. Then Tip snatched up his cloak and the flag and bolted in through the gate—*Clang!*—the men slamming it to after, an iron bar sliding home.

Outside the Ghûl howled in frustrated rage as arrows and arrows rained down.

Tip found himself in a twisting corridor, more murder holes overhead, more shuttered arrow-slits along the sides, and escorted by four suspicious Avenian warriors along the cobbled way he went . . . to emerge in the city beyond.

It was only when he came out from the shadows of the tunnel and into the slanting light of the morning sun that the men looked on in wonder and relaxed their guard, for here was one of the *Litenfolk* of legend, seldom if ever seen.

Down a ramp and toward Tipperton strode a stern-faced warrior of Dendor. He was dressed much like the ones who had escorted the buccan under the wall: fleece jacket over a chain mail shirt, with quilted brown breeks and fleece-lined boots. A broadsword was girted about his waist, and a metal helm rode on his head. Yet this warrior was not the one who caught Tip's eye, for walking alongside came another. Tipperton frowned, for this "other," was he an Elf or a man? The Warrow could not say. Different from Human, he was, and different from Elf as well, yet in his features he held something of each, or so it seemed to the buccan. Man height he was, six foot or so, and in this was taller than most Lian, and his eyes held the hint of a tilt, though less than one might expect of an Elf. And his ears were tipped, though not as sharply as those of either Lian or Dylvana. His hair was dark and held streaks of grey, and his features sharp, like those of a fox, though no fox this. Dressed in black, he was: heavy woolen coat, and pants, boots, and gloves all ebony. And he bore no weapon whatsoever, or so it seemed. And when he came to where Tip awaited, the guards shuffled back a bit, as if in respect or awe, though they did salute the warrior accompanying him, mumbling, "*Kapten.*"

But it was the Elf, the man, the one with dark eyes nearly black beneath black eyebrows, who looked down at the wee buccan and said, "Now what would a Warrow be doing at the gates of a city surrounded by Modru's Swarm? And carrying a Dwarven flag at that, eh?"

"Sir," said Tipperton, his own gemlike eyes of blue staring up into eyes of jet, "I stand in for a Kingsman slain and bear a token for King Agron." Tip pulled the coin up and showed it to the pair.

The captain held out a hand. "I would have it."

Tipperton frowned and shook his head. "Nay, it is for King Agron alone. I have pledged to see it delivered."

"Pah! As I thought: this is trickery."

The man, the Elf, the one in black turned toward the captain. "Trickery, Captain Brud? I see no trickery here."

"Mage Alvaron, it must be trickery, for he came to the gate from the Swarm."

"I came *through* the Swarm," snapped Tip angrily, "and let me—" Of a sudden his words jerked to a halt and his jaw dropped open as he gaped at the one in black. *Mage? Mage? This is a Mage, a Wizard?* Tip stared at the man, the Elf . . . the Mage.

"Through the Swarm?" sneered Captain Brud. "Nothing could get past that—"

"He is a Warrow," interrupted Alvaron as if that explained all, the Wizard smiling down at Tip. "And your name, my lad?"

"I am Sir Tipperton Thistledown, a miller from the Wilderland."

Alvaron's brow furrowed. "From across the Grimwall?" At Tip's nod, Alvaron added, "Then you've come a long way, Sir Tipperton."

"Longer than ever I dreamed," replied Tip.

"Huah," grunted Brud. "A miller giving himself airs, if miller he even is, calling himself 'Sir,' is he now?"

"A title given me by the Elves of Arden Vale," retorted Tip as Alvaron glared at the captain, "though I lay little claim to it myself . . . except at need."

"Well," said Alvaron, smiling, "I see you need no defending by me." He turned to Brud. "We must take him to King Agron."

"But, sir," said one of the escort yet standing nigh, his face turning pale. "What of the Gargon? I mean, if you leave us unprotected here, then—"

"Imongar is on the south gate. Tell her I've gone to see the king; she will see to the Dread."

As that man sped away, Captain Brud scowled and said, "Very well, Mage Alvaron, we'll go to the king . . . if to do nought else but expose this spy. Yet he'll not go armed into my liege lord's presence."

Brud held out his hand, and Tipperton gave over his Elven bow and quiver of arrows, saying, "I'd like them back, if you please."

Brud paused momentarily and frowned down at the weapons, surprised to see such splendid crafting in the hands of an agent of Modru. But then he shook his head and said, "The flagpole, too."

"Oh," said Tip, handing over the standard of Kachar, seeing for the first time that the staff itself could be used as a weapon as well.

"Search him," said Brud to one of the nearby soldiers.

As the captain rolled the pole horizontally to furl the flag, the soldier ran his hands over Tipperton, confiscating a small dagger, and then—"*Jo, vad är det?*" He reached into the buccan's jacket and pulled forth the other flag. Turning—"*Kapten*"—he displayed the ring of fire on black.

"Ha!" barked Captain Brud. "I knew it! A Wrgish spy."

"No, no," protested Tip. "That's how I got through the Horde! Bearing that flag. They thought I was a Rûck!"

"And Rutch you might be," shot back Brud.

"Nonsense, Captain," said Alvaron. "He is plainly a Warrow, and has a token for the king, a token of perhaps some importance. I say we go to Agron now!"

"But what if he is an assassin?"

Tip's mouth dropped open, yet ere he could say aught, Alvaron said, "Pah! He is without weapons. And with you along and me at your side and perhaps one of your men, what can he do?"

Reluctantly, Captain Brud stepped back and called to the ramparts above, "*Löjtnant, föra över en stund.*"

In spite of the fact that Mage Alvaron and Captain Brud and a soldier waited outside the Dendorian war room with, of all things, one of the Litenfolk, still it was long moments ere the four were received by the king, a young castle page announcing them. And when they entered, they found in the chamber a tall, slender, dark-haired man, perhaps in his early fifties judging by the silver at his temples; he stood at a map-scattered table, frowning down at a chart. And as they entered, the king looked up, his pale blue gaze to widen. "Ah, so they told me true, it *is* one of the Wee Folk, or do my eyes deceive?"

Alvaron smiled and said, "I assure you, King Agron, Sir Tipperton is no apparition."

"My lord," said Captain Brud, one hand on Tipperton's shoulder, his grip firm, "no apparition, perhaps, but a phantom instead, for he claims to have come through the Swarm disguised with nought but this." Brud nodded to the soldier, who displayed the ring of fire on black.

The king smiled and looked at Tip. "Very clever, I must say. And why did you take such risk?"

"He claims to bear a message," said Brud.

"A token," corrected Tipperton.

"A token," amended Brud.

The king peered at Tip. "This token, Sir Tipperton, may I see?"

Tipperton reached down and pulled the coin and thong over his head. He started to step forward, but Brud held him fast.

The king looked up at the captain. "Release him."

Brud sighed. "Aye, my lord." And his hand fell away from Tip, yet went to the sword at his side.

Tip stepped to the king and of a sudden found himself reluctant to hand over the coin. After all, he had borne it a full year, and it seemed a part of him. Even so, with a trembling hand, he gave over the token to the king.

As Agron took the coin, just as suddenly Tip felt a sense of relief mingled with a sense of loss, as if he had laid down a weighty burden while at the same time had been cast adrift. The mission was done. The task accomplished. The coin passed on. His promise to a dying warrior kept. But now what? What would he do? Where would he go? Back to Twoforks? Back to his mill? With a war raging on?

Agron sighed and softly said, "I hoped to never see this."

The king stepped to a chair and seated himself, his face haggard. He looked at Tip, the Warrow yet waiting. "'Tis from High King Blaine. A summons."

"A summons?" asked Tip.

"Aye, a summons; a call for aid."

"But it is we who need aid," blurted Captain Brud.

"Aye," agreed King Agron.

"I have brought aid," said Tipperton, and he gestured at the flagstaff in Brud's hand.

Brud looked at the furled standard he yet held and then stood the staff upright, the flag uncurling to loosely drape down, silver axes on black showing.

"Kachar," breathed King Agron, and with hope in his eyes he looked at Tip.

"Aye, Kachar. DelfLord Valk will be here with three thousand Dwarven warriors within the week, and well do I know his plan."

That night from each of Dendor's four gates, fire arrows sailed up in the air.

The beringing Swarm jeered and japed at this paltry show of arms.

But high on a ridge south of the city, four people shed glad tears, for at last they knew that Tipperton Thistledown, friend and companion, was not captured or dead, but had gone into Dendor instead.

As they took a late private supper, Tipperton glanced at the coin lying on the table near the king's right hand and said, "Lord Agron, I have borne that penny for a full year trying to reach you, and now you tell me it is a summons. Yet surely there's more to the tale than that. I mean, because of the token my friends and I, well, our lives have been changed in ways none could have imagined a year back, and little of it for the better. Too, Kingsmen have died bearing that coin. Oh, not that the token is at the root of the ills besetting Mithgar—Modru and Gyphon bear the blame for that. Still, it is the penny and a promise which set me and my friend Beau Darby on our way to find you, and much has happened since then, and I would hear the full story behind the coin, if you please."

Agron nodded. "You deserve that and much more, Sir Tipperton."

"Tip," replied the buccan.

"Eh?"

"Please, lord, call me Tip, or Tipperton. 'Sir Tipperton' sounds so very formal."

The king smiled and said, "Would that I could do the same, Tip. —Simply to be called Agron, I mean."

Tipperton grinned and then suddenly and without volition yawned, then looked apologetically at Agron. "Your pardon, my lord, I assure you it's not the company, but the truth is I've not slept for nigh two days—lurking the night among Spawn and then crawling 'cross the land between as it were. Even so, I would hear of the coin."

Agron turned up a hand and said, "It is a simple tale, Tip, one begun some forty years past. You see, Blaine and I first met in the Greatwood when we were but lads. As is the custom, our sires had sent each of us there in the spring of our tenth year to live in the care of the Baeron throughout the summer, to learn how to listen to the land and to hearken unto its voice, to learn its ways and foster its well-being. And it was there in the Greatwood where we became fast friends, Blaine and I . . . blood brothers, more or less. But the summer, as all summers do, finally came to an end, and with the onset of autumn we were to part: he to Caer Pendwyr, I to Dendor. It so happened I had with me two Gjeenian pennies, the cheapest coin of any realm, and as the day of our parting drew nigh, I strung the coins on leather straps and gave one to Blaine and kept one myself. And we pledged that should one of us need the full help of the other, the penny is what we would send." Agron lifted a thong about his own neck, and on it dangled another of the plain pewter coins, holed in the middle. Then he took up the like token Tipperton had given him and gripped the leather cord tightly, his knuckles showing white. "As I said, 'tis a summons, this Gjeenian penny, a call for aid, a call to muster all forces and ride to war. And this cheapest of coins, this base pittance, this Gjeenian penny would pay for all."

"Oh my," said Tip. "Oh my. So *that's* what it's all about. Would that the Kingsman had been able to tell me, but he died by Spaunen hand ere I got back with aid." Tip shook his head in regret.

"Good men die in war," said Agron, then amended, "good people, that is." The king sighed and looked at Tip. "Still he gave the coin, the mission, over to you, and in that he chose well. —I wonder, did he have a name?"

"None he gave me, sire, but whoever he was, he saved my life. Would that I could have saved his."

They sat in silence for a while, and then Tip added, "Young he was, twenty-five or so I would guess, though when it comes to Humans, I am not the best judge of age. Still, he was young . . . slender . . . like you, my lord, and about your height, though once again I have trouble judging, you Humans being nearly double height to me. He had dark hair, nearly black and short-cropped, and pale blue eyes, pale as ice, so pale as to seem nearly—"

"White?" blurted Agron, bolting upright.

"Why, yes, my lord," said Tipperton in surprise. "Eyes so pale as to seem nearly white, a bit like yours, though more so."

"Marks, any marks?"

"Marks?"

"Distinguishing marks."

Tip frowned in concentration, trying to remember a year past. "N-no . . . —Oh wait! Yes, a scar above one eye, the left, I believe."

Agron's face drained of blood, and he gestured over his own left eyebrow, his finger jagging down, then up. "V-shaped?"

"How did you know?"

Anguish flooded Agron's face. "He took it in practice. I gave it to him." The king's voice fell to a whisper. "An accident."

"You know this man?"

"He was my son, Dular my son, my one and only heir."

Agron shoved back from the table and fled the room . . .

. . . leaving Tip alone shedding tears.

A time later a page came, and he led Tip to a bedchamber within the castle, where, in spite of the pulse of the Gargon running through his veins, the buccan fell asleep while undressing and slept the whole night through, his right boot lying on the floor, the left one yet on his foot.

After a hot bath, a page brought Tip clean clothes to wear, clothes outgrown by a child of the castle staff. Too, the page tied a black band about the buccan's left wrist. As Tip looked on in puzzlement, the youth somberly pointed to the band he himself wore, saying, "It is a mourning band, sir, worn on the left wrist, closest to the heart. The king, his son Prince Dular . . . word has come he was killed by the Foul Folk." The page sighed and stepped back and looked at the buccan. Apparently finding Tipperton passable, he then led the Warrow down to a great hall to break fast with the king and members of the court.

Tip came into a large chamber filled with people taking breakfast, and black wristbands of mourning were worn by each person there. At the high table sat Agron, his face haggard, as if he had not slept at all. And the air of the chamber was doleful. As the buccan stood looking, Mage Alvaron waved Tip to a vacant seat at hand.

"Here, lad, sit next to me and tell us of your ventures dire, for surely you had many a trial in coming here, and we need a bit of distraction."

Tip climbed onto the bench beside Alvaron and knelt on his knees to be at a height to eat comfortably.

Across the table sat a flaxen-haired lady of indeterminate age, though had Tip to guess he would have put her just beyond her young-maiden years. And although she spoke to Alvaron, her somewhat tilted blue eyes were upon Tipperton. "Hush, Alvaron; let him be, at least until he gets some provender within." She smiled at the buccan, her face lighting up.

Alvaron grinned and said, "Sir Tipperton Thistledown may I present Mage Imongar."

"Oh my, another Mage," said Tip, unaware that he'd spoken aloud.

"Indeed," said Imongar, "and there are four more besides."

Tip flushed, but then added, "Six Mages in Dendor?"

"Aye." Imongar pointed. "Veran and Ridich are over there, breaking fast. Delander and Letha are on the walls keeping ward over the Dread. Night and day we set watch in turn, for all are needed to contain the Gargon's fear."

"Well then I am most glad to meet you, lady, and glad as well that there are six of you altogether, for the Dread is terrible."

As Alvaron waved a servingman over and gestured at the Warrow's empty cup, Imongar looked closely at the buccan, as if gauging. "You speak from experience." Her words were not a question but a statement instead.

"Aye." While the man poured Tip a mug of tea and Imongar passed him the basket of toast along with some peach preserves, Tip said, "I nearly stepped into its tent out there in the Swarm south of the south gate."

"Into its tent?" Alvaron turned his piercing black eyes the buccan's way.

"Well, not exactly into its tent, but upon the bare ground surrounding."

"Even so, 'tis closer than I could have come," said Imongar, looking at the buccan in speculation.

Tip slathered preserves on a slice of toast. "Oh, I'll tell you I bolted, I did. Blindly, too. If I hadn't slammed into a wagon wheel, well, I'd be running still—knocked me flat on my back, it did."

Alvaron raised his cup. "Here's to wagon wheels which jump in the way, else we would not now be breaking fast with a true herald of glad tidings."

"True herald?"

"You, my boy. You. Though you brought sad news of the death of a prince, you brought good news as well, for salvation comes riding on your shoulder, or so we hope."

Imongar frowned. " 'Twill not be easy, Alvaron, and it will take all six of us working together as well as a company of men to lay the Gargon by the heels."

Tip looked up in surprise, for although he had known it was up to the Dendorians to deal with the Dread, still he had not known just how they would succeed. Oh, he knew that a Wizard was critical to accomplishing this objective, but now he discovered there were six Wizards involved and not just the one he first met.

"I say," said Tip, "if six Mages and a group of Dendorian warriors can combine to slay the Gargon, then why hasn't he already been? —Been killed, that is."

Alvaron sighed, but Imongar said, "We tried, but we could not win through—the Dread was too well protected by the Swarm."

Imongar looked at Alvaron, and he said, "But with the Dwarves attacking elsewhere and drawing their forces away, well then . . . perhaps this time we will succeed."

Tip frowned at the two Mages. "You sound in doubt, yet I would have thought magic powerful enough to deal with any threat."

Imongar shook her head. "What you call 'magic,' Sir Tipperton, has its limitations. Astral <fire> can be warped to do many things, some most powerful indeed, but at a cost none can bear for long."

Alvaron nodded and plucked at a lock of hair. "This was black when the Spaunen first came, and now it is shot through with grey."

Tip raised an eyebrow, and at his puzzled cast of face, Imongar said, "To manipulate <fire>, one must spend one's own <power> at the cost of youth, and the greater the cast, the greater the cost."

"Adon," said Tip, his eyes widening. "You mean magic ages you? Each spell makes you grow older?"

Imongar nodded. "Aye, our astral <fire> dwindles with each cast, and the more powerful the spell, the greater the drain."

"Still," said Alvaron, "we can recover that <fire> by resting a special way, though now that Rwn is gone, we cannot return to Vadaria, and the cost to recover in Mithgarian years is staggering."

"Goodness, and here all along I thought magic was, um, free."

As Tip was served from a platter of eggs, rashers of bacon on the side, Alvaron shook his head. "Oh no, my lad, in spite of what some innkeepers claim, a lunch is never free, nor breakfasts for that matter. We all must pay as we go, more or less, and that includes Mages as well."

Tip frowned in thought and looked at his meal and then across the room at King Agron at the high table. The king, he had paid a high price: his only son and heir was dead. And what had Tipperton paid? A vision of Rynna filled Tipperton's mind, and his eyes brimmed, and in that moment a sense of shared sorrow swept over the buccan.

Without speaking and with tears sliding down, Tip clambered from the bench and stepped across the chamber to where the king sat, the buccan to kneel beside Agron. With a puzzled look the king turned toward the Warrow, and Tip said, "My lord, the mission to deliver the coin is finished, yet I am a scout well trained. I ask that you take me in your service until this war is done."

"You would pledge to me?"

"Aye, my lord, as a scout."

King Agron's face fell grim, and his hand strayed to the black band at his left wrist. "For what I have in mind, Sir Tipperton, scouts will be in high peril."

"Nevertheless, my lord."

"Then rise, Sir Tipperton, scout of Aven, until this war is done."

After breakfast, his sense of purpose renewed, Tip strode with Imongar toward the south gate. "So, then, it was you, Tipperton, who bore the king the woeful news as well as the good you did bring."

Tip sighed. "Yes, though I didn't know at the time that it was the king's son Dular who had died at my mill. Why it was he bearing the coin, I do not know."

"He was in service to High King Blaine," said Imongar, "and would have been the obvious choice for Blaine to send to Dendor . . . not only to fetch aid but to remove Dular from harm's way."

"Remove him from harm's way?"

"Aye. Did you not tell the war council that Challerain Keep had fallen?"

Tip nodded.

"Well then, I think Blaine sent Dular away ere that battle began . . . as I said, to take him out of harm's way."

Tip frowned and said, "In my experience, Lady Mage Imongar, all of Mithgar stands before harm."

Imongar canted her head. "Aye, Sir Tipperton, it does at that."

At last they arrived at the gate and made their way up to the ramparts above. There Imongar relieved Delander, another tall

Mage like Alvaron, though Delander's hair was a rich golden brown, a shade nearly matching his eyes. After greeting Imongar and meeting Tipperton, Delander went down to take a meal and then to rest, for his was the first shift, midnight to morn, and standing watch on a Gargon was a task most fatiguing and dire, especially here where the pulse of the Dread was strongest.

Climbing to the weapons shelf, Tip stood and looked south. Teeming maggot-folk yet beringed the city, but the buccan had expected no less. Somewhere a deep drum thudded relentlessly, out among the Swarm. In their midst the Gargon's tent stood alone, Foul Folk all 'round but no nearer it seemed than a hundred long paces nigh. As to the Draedan itself, no creature was in evidence; but it was not gone from the city, nay, for the racking dread yet pulsed, a thudding in the gut keeping pace with the beat of the drum.

Tip tried to ignore all these things as he stood and looked long at the distant ridge south, trying to see . . . trying to see . . .

"Beau and the others are up there somewhere," he said. "I wonder how they fare?"

"How did they fare when you left, Tipperton?"

"Unh . . . on cold rations and camping in snow," replied Tip, sighing, "but otherwise they were hale."

"Then I suspect that they fare that way still."

Tip drew in a deep breath and let it out. "It's no way to live, you know—on the ground with no fire and nought but cold food to eat."

Imongar nodded. "Much like an animal, neh?"

They stood and looked a moment longer, then Tip said, "Did they launch the fire arrows?"

"Aye, as planned," replied Imongar, "last night and this dawn as well."

"Good," said Tip. "By that sign alone they will know I am safe."

"Ha!" barked Imongar, "I would not call being surrounded by a Swarm to be safe by any means." Imongar looked about, and seeing that none were near, she added in a low voice, "Too, here in Dendor a dreadful sickness has come, cast over the walls by the Spaunen."

Tip looked at her wide-eyed. "Dreadful sickness? Cast over the walls?"

"Aye, a dark ill. Some twenty-four days agone the—"

Tip shuddered and said, "They cut up the dead and flung the parts over the walls, using those, those—"

"Trebuchets," supplied Imongar.

"Yes, those trebuchets." Tip looked out. The great catapults were yet there, along with other siege engines: tall towers on ponderous wheels and dry-moat spans and scaling ladders and the massive rams. "We saw what they did, Imongar, my comrades and I. From the ridge. From up there it was appalling, but down here it must have been horrible beyond all words. That was the day we left for Kachar to fetch the army of Dwarves."

"Well, Tipperton, that was but the first day of their vile casting. For three more days they flung the dismembered dead into the city—Rucha, Loka, Gulka, men—it mattered not to the Rûpt, their own dead or ours, all were cloven asunder and the parts hurled over the walls.

"The king ordered all and sundry to gather up the remains and bear them to the plaza to be thrown on a great flaming pyre." Imongar now shuddered. "Ai, the smell of burning flesh, 'twas whelming throughout all of Dendor."

"But what has this to do with the illness?" asked Tipperton. "I mean, how came such a sickness to be?"

"Ah, Tipperton, you ask a question which has puzzled healers down through the ages. Some say it is a curse, some a spell, some say divine retribution . . . yet this we know: the first to fall victim were a handful of those who had borne remains to the fires, but others have been stricken since. Buboes pustulant and black, boils seeping, raging fever, a terrible stench: those are the symptoms. Few survive, despite what the healers do, and those who die are burnt, just as were the dismembered battle dead, though in the prison yard instead of the city plaza."

"Prison yard?"

"Aye, that's where they burn those slain by the scourge."

Tip frowned but did not pursue the story behind that strange custom. "Is it widespread?"

"Not yet, but with pestilence, none can ever say."

Tip looked south. "If this dark illness is what Beau has told me of, then he has a cure, or thinks he might."

"Beau?"

Tip pointed at the far ridge. "One of my companions."

"And this cure . . . ?"

Tip frowned in concentration. "Silverroot and gwynthyme, if I remember correctly."

"Silverroot I've heard of, but gwynthyme?"

"I seem to recall that both have other names: what these may be I have no idea, but Beau can tell us when the siege is broken. All I know is that gwynthyme is a golden mint and proof against poison. It saved Lady Phais from death by envenomed Rûck arrow. Vulg poison they said."

"Vulg poison? Ai, this golden mint must be potent."

Tip nodded. "So I would say."

"Well then, Tipperton, you must go to the healers and tell them what you know."

"Well, I don't exactly *know* much more than what I just said. It's Beau who knows the cure, if a cure it is."

"Still . . ."

"Look, we don't even know if this is the same disease Beau told me about," said Tip, hopping down to the banquette. "Regardless, where do I go?"

"To the prison—that's where they quarantine the ill—but you will need a pass. Captain Brud on the west gate can give you one."

"Oh, Brud," said Tip, sighing. "He and I didn't exactly hit it off when first we met."

"Nevertheless, he can give you a pass to the healers. And don't discount him, Tipperton, he is a good warrior, though stern."

"And suspicious," said Tip, then barked a laugh. "I mean, who else would believe one of the so-called Litenfolk to be a Rûptish spy?" Again Tip laughed, and Imongar smiled. Then Tip looked west and north along the banquette toward the distant west gate. "But all right, it's the dark ill we are speaking of and if I can help . . . —I'll go see him now."

As Tip walked away, Imongar turned and faced south, faced the Swarm, faced into the pulse of the Dread and stood ready to spend years of her youth should the need arise.

"A cure for the scourge, and you would see the healers?" asked Captain Brud, his voice low.

Tip nodded.

The man pulled a drawer open in the table and took out a parchment. As he dipped the nib of the quill into the inkwell, he said, "Take care to whom you speak of this illness, Sir Tipperton, for even the knowledge that pestilence is within Dendor will drive some men to rash acts."

At hand, Alvaron grunted. "Perhaps so, Captain Brud, but if indeed it is the dark plague, then it will not remain a secret long."

Brud nodded grimly and then stood and pointed out a back window of the upper gatehouse and said to Tip, "That grey building, squarish, made of stone, next to the tower, see you it?"

"The one with the wall all 'round?"

"Aye," said Brud. "It is the prison."

"Gaol," said Alvaron.

"Oh my, a jail that big?"

Brud shrugged. "Not all of it is a prison . . . just the upper floor. The rest is where the town wardens live, or used to."

"Used to?"

"Aye. Instead of warding those walls, now all are warding these."

"As are the former inmates," said Alvaron. "Pardoned by the king if they would but wage war."

Brud grimaced as if at something repugnant, but then said, "Regardless, that's where you'll find the healers."

Tip shook his head and cocked an eyebrow. "Who would have thought it: healers in jail. I wonder what Beau will say when I tell him."

"It is the safest place to take those who have fallen to the"— Brud paused.

"The pestilence," said Alvaron. "Modru's gift to Dendor, I would say."

"Oh."

Brud folded the paper and held it up for Tip to see. "This pass will admit you through the wall gate and to the door, but not inside, for I would not lose you to this dark ill."

Tip looked up at Brud in surprise, and Brud said, "Sir Tipperton, I was wrong about you. Even so, I do not apologize, for you came from the Swarm and asked to see my liege lord, and I beg no pardon for thinking of him first. And now you are one of his scouts, and for that I am glad: anyone who can slip undetected through an entire Swarm is welcome to serve my lord, and I am pleased we now stand together."

Brud smiled and stuck out his hand, and Tip grinned and took it, his own small grip lost in the man's.

"And now, your pass." Brud handed the Warrow the signed parchment.

"Gwynthyme, eh, the rare golden mint. Yes, I know of it, though we call it *bladguld*—goldleaf. Even so, we have none. But *rotensilver*—the root of silver—that we have in plenty, though it saves precious few of those stricken."

Tip's face fell. "Oh my, and Beau used the remainder of his gwynthyme to cure Lady Phais, five doses in all."

"Well I'm afraid that it'll take more than five doses, my lad," said the healer through the bars on the door, "for within these walls there are many who have fallen victim to the scourge and many more yet to—" Of a sudden the healer's words jerked to a halt and he looked past the buccan. Tip turned about, and there behind him and through the warded gate of the prison wall came a white wagon driven by a man in white, white scarf about his face.

"Stand well off," hissed the healer, covering his own face with a white scarf.

As Tip backed aside and away, the wagon circled 'round to come alongside the barred door. And as it turned, in the bed of the wagon Tip could see three people: a man and a woman and a child, all flush with fever and moaning, their lips cracked but not bleeding. And Tip saw dark, pus-running boils on the arms and face of the child.

That evening, Tip stood on the walls and watched as flaming signal arrows were lofted from each and every gate. He momentarily thought of sending his last red-fletched arrow up from the one in the south, yet did not, for it was the last thing of Rynna's he had, but for memories bittersweet. And so he watched as arrows were sent skyward, and he listened to the jeers of the Spawn all 'round.

The next morning, just ere dawn, a wedge of men mustered within the walls and waited, King Agron at its head, and with their ballista all stood ready while those above watched for a flaming arrow to fly from the south ridge afar. And Tipperton, his Elven bow in hand, stood with them, for he would not be left behind.

There as well were the six Mages, ready to smother the Gargon's fear, and these were among the foremost at the south gate, as was Tipperton.

"Would that Farrin were here," said Ridich. "Of us all, he is the most powerful."

"Farrin?" asked Tip, looking up at the Mage.

"Aye. A year past he was with us in Black Mountain, part of our Circle of Seven. It was there one night he dreamt of the oncoming war. He told Sage Oran of this dream, and the Sage, after long consideration, asked us to come to Dendor for perhaps Farrin had Truedreamed. Farrin himself set out on a quest of his own: to find the Utruni and entreat them to join the Free Folk against Modru and his master Gyphon. We have not seen him since."

"He is not likely to find the Utruni," said Letha, "deep in the rock as they are."

"Even if he does find them," said Ridich, "they are not likely to join, for even though they are said to ward the Kammerling,

Utruni are above the affairs of the world, or in their case, far below."

Letha sighed. "Would that he could persuade them, for with the <power> they hold over stone, mayhap 'tis true a single Utrun alone can fell an entire mountain."

Tip's eyes flew wide. "Can fell an entire mountain? —I say, these Utruni—Dara Aleen mentioned them once, as did Bekki—just what are they?"

"Stone Giants," replied Imongar.

"Stone Giants? But they're just myths. Giants with gemstones for eyes? Giants that move through the rock deep underfoot?"

"Oh no, wee one," said Alvaron, "they are no more myths than, say, the Hidden Ones."

"Or the Litenfolk," added Veran, sotto voce.

Imongar laughed. "Just ask a Dwarf, Tipperton, they'll tell you it's so. Long past, First Durek was saved by a Stone Giant, or so they do say."

"That's what Bekki said: Durek was saved by the hand of the Utruni." Tip shook his head and shrugged. "At the time I didn't know what he meant, but it didn't seem important. —I say, this First Durek, was he also called Breakdeath Durek?"

"Aye," replied Imongar, "though not until much later, after he was dead and reborn."

Tip frowned at this seeming paradox but said, "Bekki once quoted this Breakdeath Durek: 'He who dares, wins.' I thought it quite apt, for at the time I was planning to sneak through the Swarm and knock on the door to Dendor."

"A foolish scheme," said Veran.

"Harebrained," agreed Tip.

"As is our plan to slay the Gargon," said Alvaron.

Dawn came, and fire arrows were loosed into the sky, Tipperton climbing up to the south gate and taking one of the flaming man-sized shafts and loosing it along with the others, his to sail in an arc even higher than those of the men. And they looked on in wonder at this wee Litenfolk with his magic Elven bow, or so they believed it was. Yet there was no return signal from the south ridge, so the muster stood down, though the ward atop the wall did not.

The next day was much the same, with the men and Mages and the buccan mustering at the south gate in the predawn marks, but still no signal came from the south ridge, and so once again the muster stood down.

Tip counted on his fingers: *Five days, bucco, it's been five days. Five days since we sighted Dendor after coming back from Kachar; four since I made it inside. Has something happened to the Dwarves? Oh surely not. Besides, Valk said he'd come within a week, and the week's not up yet.*

Tip found he could not relax—*If I only had my lute, but no, it's back in the camp with Beau*—and he spent most of the day pacing the walls of Dendor, dread hammering at his heart as he walked all 'round the city high on the ramparts above.

On the sixth day, again there was no signal and Tip fretted and paced anew, and he tramped along the walls and down in the city streets. Yet his pacing stood him in no good stead, for he felt as if a doom were poised, ready to be unleashed, but whether this was a true premonition or instead the Gargon's incessant pulse of fear, he could not say.

Yet while walking down one of the Dendorian streets, he saw three white wagons, three drivers in white, the wains rumbling along the cobbles, people crying out as they passed, and the wagons drove toward the grey walls around a grey stone building, where a column of smoke rose into the grey sky behind. And Tip wondered how many more white wagons had rolled through the streets that day.

The seventh dawn came without a signal, and once more the muster stood down. And after breaking his fast, again Tip took to the ramparts above, fuming and fretting and wondering: *Where in all of Mithgar are Valk and his army of Dwarves?*

But on this day in midmorn, of a sudden all the drums of the Swarm began to pound and Rûptish horns began to blat and waves of dread poured over the walls.

"Something is afoot," said Imongar grimly, her eyes seeking sign of assault.

Tip jumped to the weapons shelf and peered out through a crenel. "Oh, surely you don't think they've, they've . . ."

Imongar looked at him. "They've what, Tipperton?"

"Oh, I don't know. I don't know! Perhaps discovered the Dwarves on the march, captured my friends, captured Beau, I just don't know." Tip looked at her in appeal as the Gargon spread fear over all.

Imongar shrugged and turned her gaze back to the Swarm, and of a sudden called out, "Bugler, sound the summons. The Gargon is on the move."

Tip looked and gasped in dismay, for out from the tent strode the hideous monster: grey and stonelike it was, and scaled like a serpent but walking upright on two legs—a huge and reptilian malevolent parody of a man, and waves of fear rolled outward.

Snow bursting upward about its heavy tread, the ponderous Mandrak advanced: eight feet tall, taloned hands and feet, glittering rows of fangs in a lizard-snouted face. And the Draedan, the Ghath, the Horror, the Dread stalked forward in a circle of emptiness as the Foul Folk gave back, some shrieking and bolting away, for not even they could stand to be near, so great was its terrible power.

The earth beneath its feet seemed to shake with each and every step, and Tip shuddered as well.

"Stand ready," called Imongar, her face white, drained of blood.

But as this hideous creature reached the inner rim of the Swarm, leftward it turned, leftward, and toward the western periphery.

And as it stalked away, the bugler, trembling, managed to raise the clarion to his lips and to sound the call on his second attempt.

"Come," said Imongar, walking west along the wall, matching her stride to that of the monster without.

Tip, his air coming in gasps, trotted along the weapons shelf a pace or two behind the Mage, for he didn't want to block her view. And as he and Imongar went west, armed and armored men poured through the streets and to the walls, most gathering about the four gates.

And the king came riding, a cavalry at his back.

Circling, west went Tip and Imongar, to finally come to the west gate. And opposite stopped the Gargon, standing in a circle alone.

And to the west gate came the other four Mages, Alvaron already there.

More Rûptish horns blared, and drums pounded.

And King Agron and his cavalry rode to the west gate and stood below waiting.

But then Captain Brud called down, "Sire, they wave the grey flag of truce!"

"What?" called the king.

"They would parley," shouted Alvaron.

"'Tis likely a trick," called Brud.

"Nevertheless, captain," called up Agron, riding to the ramp and dismounting, "raise the flag of truce."

Without another word, Captain Brud signalled to a soldier, and in moments the grey flag was located and raised above the gate.

And the drums and horns of the Swarm fell silent.

As the king came onto the rampart, he said, "Bugler, sound the call to stand ready to repel an attack. If this is a trick, I want all gates, all walls, all warriors on alert."

The command was sounded, and the air fell silent again, as if each side held its breath, though the waves of fear yet rolled.

Then there came a horn blat from the Swarm straight ahead to the west, and out from the tent midst the Rûpt, a man was led by a Ghûl toward a waiting Hèlsteed. The man bore a burden under one arm, and was boosted onto the 'steed, encumbrance and all. When mounted, the man shifted the burden to his lap and held it close.

"A surrogate," hissed Tip.

"You know of them?" asked Imongar.

"There was one at Mineholt North."

Now a mounted Ghûl took up the reins of the surrogate's Hèlsteed and rode toward the Dendorian west gate, towing the surrogate behind.

Just to the right of the oncoming pair trotted a Rûck bearing the grey flag of truce, and on the left trotted another, the flag on his pole waving black.

And as they came on, Tip frowned in puzzlement, for there was something about the man . . . but Tip couldn't quite put his finger on—

"Oh my lord!" exclaimed Tipperton.

"What is it?" asked Imongar.

"The surrogate, if that's what he is," said Tip in dismay, "it's Lord Tain."

"Lord Tain?"

"A Daelsman. The only one who survived the destruction of that city, as far as we knew. All else were killed by Sleeth . . . or died in the blizzard thereafter. His daughter was slain. It drove him mad."

Onward came the Ghûl and Rûcks and Hèlsteeds and man, Lord Tain's white beard long and unkempt, his white hair stringing down, and the burden he bore—

"Oh Adon," groaned Tip.

—was the desiccated corpse of Jolet.

And Tain whispered and hissed into her ear, and gestured at the city before him.

And they came to the foot of the bridge and stopped and the Rûcks planted the flagstaffs in the snow, grey flag on one side, the black with its crimson ring of fire on the other. As if this were a signal, the pulsating dread completely ceased.

And a sigh of deliverance rose up from the city, Tip staggering in sudden relief.

The Ghûl backed his Hèlsteed alongside Lord Tain's, the man yet babbling and hissing and whispering into desiccated Jolet's ear.

"*Gluktu!*" sounded the Ghûl, as from a voice of the dead.

And Lord Tain's babbling and hissing ceased, the madness in his gaze replaced by a malignant glare. No longer did a madman look through these eyes, but a vile presence instead. And it turned Tain's head and looked at the cadaver . . . and laughed in vile exultation, and one-handedly thrust the desiccated corpse into the air, her arms and legs and head flopping loosely, stringy dark hair and tattered silken garments dangling down, one foot bare, the other yet encased in a slipper.

Tip turned aside in revulsion, and tears stood in his eyes.

"My Lord Agron," called the foul entity, "*this*"—he thrust up again the corpse, its dangling arms and legs flopping, head joggling—"*this* is the fate of all who resist me."

King Agron did not reply.

But Alvaron called, "Begone, Modru, you have no business here."

The surrogate's gaze shifted to the Mage. "Quiet, fool, I speak with your better."

Now the glare swung back to the king, but suddenly changed to malicious glee. "I meant to inquire, my lord, how does your citizenry fare? All in good health? None ill?" Wild laughter burst forth from the surrogate, and he stroked the matted hair of dead Jolet.

Agron stood atop the wall and remained silent, his arms folded, his lips clamped tight.

The surrogate's laughter chopped shut and a malevolent gloat filled his gaze, and he gestured toward the Swarm and the massive siege engines beyond. "As you can see, you are completely at my mercy, but do not despair, for I am a merciful lord and these are my merciful terms: if you surrender, then you will become my allies, whereas if you do not, then I will slay you all, all warriors, women, children, oldsters, babes, animals . . . all, and you will end such as this." And he turned his gaze to the corpse and kissed it on the lips, then grinned malevolently and called out, "I give you a day to decide."

The surrogate flung up a hand and suddenly the glare was gone, replaced by madness—

And in that same moment a blast of terror slammed into them all, some men shrieking and fleeing, others falling to their knees, Tip shrilling in unendurable dread. . . .

Below, the Rûcks fell to the snow and screamed in horror, and even the Ghûl scrunched down in his saddle as if to grow small, and his Hèlsteed seemed frozen in place.

Only Lord Tain appeared unaffected as he clutched Jolet's corpse to his bosom and whispered and hissed deep secrets into a shriveled ear.

And then the blast of horror ceased, to be replaced by pulsing fear.

10

*T*he days and nights eked slowly by for Beau and Bekki, Phais and Loric, south along the ridge, the comrades set on edge by the distant thread of fear pulsing through their veins. Turn by turn they stood watch on the besieged city below, but only the fire arrows streaking up at dusk and dawn from the four Dendorian gates broke their weary ward. And back in the camp when he wasn't standing watch, Beau seesawed between pacing and fretting and sitting and fretting—mostly pacing—until finally Bekki exploded: "Argh! Sit down, Beau, else you will dither me to death."

Beau plopped down in the snow. "Oh, Bekki, it's just that, well, you know."

Bekki looked up from the face of the war hammer he was buffing for perhaps the hundredth time. "Aye, Beau, I do know. Pace at need; I will try to hold my tongue."

"It's all this wanting and waiting, Bekki: wanting hot meals and hot baths and hot drink; wanting to be before a good roaring fire; wanting a soft bed to sleep in; wanting to see Tip again—"

"Waiting for Valk and the army to arrive so that we can get on with this war," interjected Bekki, inspecting the bindings 'round the haft.

"Oh, more than that, Bekki, more than that. What I'd really like is for this war to be over and done and Modru and Gyphon to be, to be—"

"Dead!" growled Bekki.

"All right, all right, dead . . . though I was simply wishing them somehow to be gone."

"Dead is better."

Silence fell between the two, and Beau looked upslope through the pines to where Phais and Loric stood ward in the midmorn, peering at the city beyond the ridge from the camp.

Beau sighed and gestured at Tip's lute safely enwrapped in its velvet and leather casings and lying atop Tip's other gear. "If I knew how to play, I would entertain us . . . if only I knew how to play."

Bekki barked a laugh. "And if I had the voice of a Fjordlander *engel*, then would I soar into song with you."

"Engel?"

Bekki smiled. "One who lives beyond the sky, or so say the Fjordlanders. Lovely in face and form are the engels, and they sing sweeter than larks"

"Oh."

"But you cannot play, and I cannot sing, and so we sit and wait."

"I dunno, Bekki, those songs you sang back in Bridgeton seemed quite good."

Bekki shook his head. "Songs? Nay, not songs; I did not sing; instead they were cants I chanted: of war and death and blood and fire, things to stir a warrior's heart. Nay, we Châkka do not sing songs; instead true singing is left to the, left to the . . ." Bekki's voice fell to nought, and his eyes took on a distant gaze, as if he were looking through Beau.

"Left to the Châkia," completed Beau. "I know, for I heard them in Mineholt North. In fact, Tip played a song to which they sang, sweeter than larks I might say."

Of a sudden Bekki wiped a sleeve across his abruptly full eyes and cleared his throat. "Indeed, we heard it: it filled the entire mineholt."

Again silence fell between the two. After a while, Beau sighed. "I didn't hear any in Kachar, Châkia singing that is. —And say"—Beau leapt to his feet—"just how long has it been since we were there? Or more to the point, how long has it been since we returned?" Beau began toting on his fingers.

"This is the seventh day since coming back," said Bekki.

Beau held up five fingers on one hand and two on the other. "That's what I come up with, too. —Oh, Bekki, where are Valk and the army? Shouldn't they be here by now? He said they would come within a sevenday, and—"

Bekki threw up a hand for silence. "Hush, Beau, and listen! Something is afoot."

From beyond the crest sounded drums and horns.

Hammer in hand, Bekki jumped to his feet, and together he and Beau ran for the ridge above.

"The Draedan is on the move," said Phais, as the two came panting nigh.

Down below, drums hammered and horns blatted as the Draedan stalked deasil along the inner edge of the ring of Spaunen encamped 'round the walls of Dendor. Toward the western extent he bore, an empty space all about as Rûcks and Hlôks and Ghûls alike gave way before his dreadful power.

Atop the city walls, armed and armored men rushed to take up station.

"What do you think is going on?" asked Beau.

"A parley," said Loric, pointing.

To the west flew a grey flag before a tent the comrades believed to be the surrogate's, given that it was warded by Ghûls, their Hèlsteeds close at hand.

At last the Gargon came to a place out from the western gate, and there it halted.

Time passed, and still the horns sounded and the drums beat, and then—

"Look!" said Bekki. "Above the western gate. Another grey flag is raised. Are they mad? To parley with Modru is to parley with Lord Treachery himself."

"Even so," said Phais, "they may gain information from such a meeting."

Bekki growled but did not reply.

Of a sudden the drums and horns of the Swarm fell silent, though a clarion call from within the walls of Dendor sounded. What it signified, none on the ridge could say.

And still the Gargon's fear pulsed within each heart.

A Rûptish horn blatted, and out from the surrogate's tent a man was led by a Ghûl toward a waiting Hèlsteed. The man bore a bundle of some sort under one arm, and he was boosted onto the 'steed by the Ghûl.

"Modru's eyes and ears," growled Bekki.

"Modru's voice," added Loric.

"An abomination," said Phais.

"When we ride to battle," said Bekki, "he is the one we should seek and slay."

Beau shuddered but said nought.

Among the Spawn a second Ghûl, this one mounted, reached down and grasped the reins of the surrogate's 'steed and rode out and away from the Swarm and toward the Dendorian west gate, the man trailing after.

On the near side of the surrogate's Hèlsteed loped a Rûck bearing the grey flag of truce, and on the far side trotted another, the flag on his pole waving black.

The man himself held his bundle close and gestured toward the city ahead.

They came to the foot of the bridge above the moat and stopped. As the Rûcks planted the flagstaffs in the snow, of a sudden the Gargon's fear completely ceased.

Beau took in a deep breath of relief, and Phais reached out for Loric's hand. Bekki merely grunted.

The Ghûl backed his Hèlsteed alongside the surrogate's, and turned toward the man, and of a sudden the man thrust the bundle into the air, parts of it dangling down.

"Elwydd," breathed Phais.

"What is it?" asked Beau.

"A corpse," gritted Loric. "It is a corpse he holds on high."

"Oh my. But why would Modru display a corpse?"

"Terror," growled Bekki. "He seeks to drive terror into the hearts of those he faces."

Beau frowned. "I would think the Gargon enough to do that."

Loric glanced down at the buccan. "He uses the corpse as an example should Agron not bend to his will."

Beau's mouth formed a silent O.

And down below in the distance, still did the mounted surrogate sit before the wall, now gesturing up toward the men above the western gate, now gesturing out and away.

"What do they say?" asked Beau.

"No doubt he demands their surrender," gritted Bekki, his knuckles white on his war hammer.

Now the surrogate flung up a hand, and atop the walls men collapsed to their knees while others ran, and before the gate the flag-bearing Rûcks fell to the snow and groveled, and though distant were they all, shrieks of terror could be heard even up on the ridge. "The Horror throws all his dread at them," said Phais.

Suddenly the pulse of fear returned to the comrades, as in the distance the surrogate was led away from the gate and toward his tent along the western periphery.

"Oh my," gasped Beau, "how awful; it's back. I wonder if I'll ever get used to being afraid."

That evening during the last of Beau's watch, even as fire arrows sailed up into the gathering night from each of Dendor's four gates, Phais came running silently up the slope.

With Rûcken drums thudding afar and Gargon dread threading through his very soul, "What is it?" called Beau, even more alarmed.

"Hsst, take cover," said Phais, grabbing him by the arm.

"Cover?" Beau clutched his sling all the tighter.

As the Dara hauled him in among the trees, she hissed, "Aye, someone or something comes through the vale behind."

In Beau's mind flashed the ill-formed image of a half-seen monster in Drearwood, a monster that had come crunching 'cross the ice toward Tip and him to nearly kill them both.

11

*O*ne *day left, one day, and where are the Dwarves?*
Tip paced atop the ramparts, unable to sleep. Oh, he had tried, but slumber would not come, and so in the candlemarks before mid of night he arose from his bed and dressed and took up his bow and quiver of arrows and walked from the castle to the walls.

And now he paced along them, fretting, worrying, his heart thudding with Gargon fear, or perhaps with the dread of what the morrow would bring.

Now and again he clambered up to the weapons shelf and by the light of the half-moon sinking low in the west he peered out at the Swarm and the massive siege engines beyond and wondered how such a great force with their mighty tools of war could be thwarted.

And all the while a deep Rûcken drum boomed incessantly.

In the southeast quadrant as Tip paced he came upon Brud, the Dendorian warrior leaning on his hands in the crenel between flanking merlons and peering outward.

"Captain," said Tip, as he drew near.

Brud turned. "Sir Tipperton, I did not hear you come."

"Argh, but who could hear aught above that Squamish beat?" said Tip.

Brud shook his head. "I think, Sir Tipperton, e'en were it dead silent, I would not likely have heard, for 'tis said the Litenfolk move so quiet that whispers sound as shouts by compare."

Tip grinned. "Well, captain, I don't know about that, but we Warrows do step softly."

The buccan climbed up to the shelf and looked out through the adjacent crenel. Then he sighed and said, "There are so many of the foe, it seems they would have attacked weeks past, what with those mighty towers and such, rams too."

Brud made a negating gesture. "Nay, Sir Tipperton. Had they attacked weeks past, we would have given them a battle dire, and though we might have lost, still we would have devastated them. Instead they seek to grind our spirits down and make the victory all the easier."

"Grind down?"

"Aye. The drums, the horns, the casting of fire, the hurling of hacked-apart corpses into the city, the dark illness . . . but most of all, the relentless Gargon fear. These things, they sap the will, the spirit, the strength of even the most resolute."

"But what about them?" asked Tipperton, motioning toward the Swarm. "I mean, they also seem to fear the Gargon. Won't it sap their will as well?"

"Aye, but that monster directs the force of his regard toward Dendor, and 'tis we who suffer the most."

"Oh, I see."

Tip sighed, and the two of them stood together for long moments more, while the fires of the Swarm died down. After a while, Brud said, "You spoke a word: Squamish."

Tip grinned. "It comes from Squam, a Dwarven word. My friend Bekki oft says it when he refers to the Spawn."

Brud nodded. "I like that word Squam; it seems to speak volumes."

They stood awhile longer. The half-moon set. Mid of night had come. And still drum thudded and dread flowed.

Brud turned to Tipperton. "The morrow will be hard enough without being worn from lack of rest. I'm for bed, and you should be, too."

"I think I'll remain awhile," said Tip, the buccan still too keyed-up to rest.

"As you will, my friend," said Brud, "and I bid you good night." The captain then stepped away, leaving Tip alone . . . but for the men of the night watch ringing the ramparts all 'round.

And after long moments more, Tip resumed his pacing and fretting, and ever did his eye turn to the south where stood the ridge—*Where are Valk and his army? Have they fallen to ill fortune?*—but a signal, if any, would come in the deeps ere dawn, awhile from now.

Candlemarks fled, false dawn came and went, and then the

fires of the Swarm disappeared completely, as if they had all been . . . snuffed out.

And about the city, the great Rûcken drums began to beat.

What . . . ?

More candlemarks eked by, and then Tip heard—

What is it?

—under the thud of drums—

I can almost make out . . .

—a squeak and rumble, as of axles turned by ponderous wheels.

And peering by starlight he could see . . . shadow on shadow . . . motion . . . something dark in the dark moving . . . something huge.

Oh lor', the siege engines!

In that moment a bugle sounded within the walls, a bugle answered by another, and another still.

It was a call to arms.

A call to muster.

A call to defend the walls.

And these clarions were answered by the blats of maggot-folk horns and the howls of the Swarm raised in a wordless collective yawl.

thwack!

From the darkness a fireball rose up and, whooshing and sputtering, hurtled overhead to crash down in the city, other fireballs from other quadrants raining down as well.

"Modru, you skut, you liar!" shouted Tipperton out through the castellated ramparts just west of the southern gate. "You said we would have a day to decide!"

"He is a deceiver," said a voice beside him, and Tip turned to see Mage Delander at hand.

thwack!

Another fireball rose up, and Tip groaned to see by its sputtering light hundreds of Rûcks haling on ropes and wheeling the lofty siege towers toward the walls, while other Foul Folk drew a mighty ram across the snow and toward the gate below.

thwack!

Men poured through the streets of the city and up the ramps to the walls, while others rushed to and fro below, some to battle the fires, others on errands unknown.

Tip heard the sound of a liquid thickly gurgling, as of a heavy stream runnelling, and odor rose up—reeking of oil—from the walls below.

At Tip's frown, Delander said, "They fill the dry moat with what oil they have to ring the city with fire; as long as it burns it should keep the Rûpt from using their scaling ladders, though I'm afraid it will not stop the towers."

thwack!

"What about the rams?"

"Flaming oil will be poured down through the murder holes," replied the Mage. "Even so it will stop them but awhile, for the supply is limited."

"How long will it burn, the moat I mean?"

"Wood, brush, whatever will kindle will be cast into the moat to make the fires endure, but even so, as a great flaming barrier to bar the Rûpt, it will not last overlong."

thwack!

Drums thudding, horns blaring, onward came the howling Swarm, and rumbling in their midst, axles squealing in protest, the great towers trundled forward . . . and so, too, did the rams. And still the trebuchets cast fiery missiles over the walls and into the city beyond.

"My Lord Mage, look!" cried a voice.

And Tip turned to see a soldier pointing out beyond the walls, beyond the Swarm, where in the darkness to the south an arrow aflame streaked up in the night from the ridge afar.

12

As the burning arrow arced scarlet high through the dark of the predawn sky, "Swift now," called Mage Delander to the captain of the ward, "send a courier to King Agron. Tell him the Dwarves have come."

Within but heartbeats a runner raced down the ramp and leapt astride a waiting horse, as—*thwack!*—another fireball sputtered overhead, hurled by a Spaunen catapult, the blazing mass to burst apart upon striking a roof in the city, flaming rivulets of fire splattering outward.

And still the mighty siege engines rolled forward amid the yowling Swarm, the tall towers and massive rams alike, and still the waves of numbing fear beat outward from the Gargon, pulsing to the boom of the drums.

"Hurry with that ballista!" shouted Agron, now among the gathering muster at the south gate.

As the mighty spear-caster was wheeled forward, a distant clarion rang out, and then another. And someone atop the wall shouted down, "My Lord King, they swarm through the moat with scaling ladders, and the ram now crosses the bridge."

As black-shafted arrows whispering of death hissed over the walls to be answered in kind by crossbows, King Agron called back, "Quarrels only at the ram, and sound the call to fire the moat at will."

As the signal rang out, Veran and Ridich came pressing

through the back of the muster and toward their fellow Mages.

There sounded a clacking as wood slammed up against the outer stone of the walls, and men above shouted *Ladders!*

Braving the darts of the Rûpt, crossbowmen loosed deadly bolts down into the darkness below, and crews of burly men took up long, forked poles to shove the ladders back and away. Still other men lighted torches to sling over the wall at command.

"Cast fire!" shouted the captain above, and men flung torches through the crenels.

phoom! Flames leapt upward from the moat, lighting the sky lurid red, and Tipperton, in the midst of the muster at the gate, heard shrieking coming from the far side, the men on the wall above howling in glee.

"Where are the Dwarves?" panted Ridich as he and Veran came in among the Mages.

Letha shook her head. "The arrow flew not a candlemark past. They've not yet arrived."

"Stand ready," called King Agron.

"But we did not plan our attack to occur when the Rûpt were attacking as well," protested Ridich.

Tip barked a laugh. "As my da used to say, 'Life is what happens while you're making plans.' Well, we made our plans, and good plans they were, but it seems Life is running all over us, or perhaps in this case it is Death."

"Sir Tipperton, be it Life or Death," said Agron, "we must make do with what the Fates have cast our way. And e'en though the Rûpt assail our walls, our immediate objective is to slay the Gargon, and by Adon, slay him we will!"

"Where is the Gargon?" Alvaron called up to Delander, the Mage peering into the night.

"Yet at the fore of his tent," came the shouted reply.

dng!

"What th—?" muttered Tip, then, "Oh, the ram."

Above and from within the embracing walls crossbows twanged, hurling quarrels at the batterers before the outer gate.

dng!

"Ready at the bar," Agron commanded the inner gate warders.

"King Agron, do we not wait for the Dwarves?" asked Alvaron.

dng!

Agron shook his head. "What better time to attack than in the midst of all. Their forces are spread along the moat. The

Gargon stands behind them alone, and can we break through the ring of Rûpt we will take him undefended."

Alvaron shook his head. "A Gargon is never undefended, my lord, for the casting of dread shields him from harm."

"Nevertheless," said Agron, and he signed for the gate to be opened.

dng!

The great drawbar was pulled away and, squealing, the portcullis was raised.

Delander came rushing down from above and joined his fellow Mages, the six bracing themselves for what was to come.

The inner gate swung open—

Dng!

—and wheeling the ballista amid them, afoot they entered the twisting way under the wall—King Agron and his handpicked company of men. And among the armed and armored Dendorians strode six Mages, only two of which even bore staffs. And among the Mages walked one wee Warrow, his Elven bow at the ready.

Dng!

When they were all within the dark, twisting confines of the tunnel, with a clang the gates behind were shut, and the portcullis squealed down.

Passing below the murder holes and alongside the arrow-slits in the tunnel walls, in moments they reached the last turn, and the outer gate stood before them.

DNG!

In the fore, Agron stepped to the side postern and cautiously drew aside a small viewing panel and looked outward, and a ruddy flicker from without dimly lighted up the passage. In the wavering reddish light, Tip looked up at Imongar and said, "I am minded of what DelfLord Borl once told me."

DNG!

Imongar raised an eyebrow.

Tip smiled grimly. "He said, the moment the battle begins is the moment all goes wrong."

DNG!

"Well then, Tipperton, let us hope in this case it is DelfLord Borl who is wrong and everything here goes according to plan."

Agron closed the viewing port. "Stand ready," he commanded. "The battering ram and its crew of Drôkha are in the way. Pavises shield the Wrg from the crossbows above and to the sides. We'll have to charge in among them and hurl them back and then shove the ram away to get the ballista out through the main gate and past."

Dng!

"Signal the men aside and above to cease the attack on the ram," said Agron.

As word was swiftly passed through the flanking arrow-slits to the crossbowmen in the passages behind the tunnel walls and to the crew at the murder holes above, two men began to remove the bar from the side postern.

"Wait, my lord," called Veran, pressing forward through the ranks. "Mayhap I can serve here."

King Agron turned.

"A ruse," said Veran. "Let me at the viewing port."

Dng!

"What's he doing?" hissed Tipperton, the wee buccan down among the men and trying to peer past. "I can't see."

"He readies a casting," replied Imongar.

"Oh, goodness."

"Here," muttered Alvaron, bending over and lifting Tipperton up.

Tip held his breath and squinted his eyes and turned his head slightly aside in trepidation, for *magic* was about to be loosed.

Dng!

And Veran at the port muttered, "*Casus incendio!*"

Yaaaaah! Shrieks and wrauls came from without, and King Agron bellowed, "By damn, I said no fire from above! It will only delay us."

Without turning, Veran said, " 'Tis not true fire, my lord, but instead a mere glamour of fire cascading down which serves to rout the Spaunen." Veran paused, then added, "I believe we can go now. Fear not the fire, for it does not burn."

The side postern was flung open, and crying *For king and Dular!* Agron and half his captains and men charged outward, swords and axes ready to rive, maces and morning stars to bash, but the foe was gone, abandoning the ram and pavises and fleeing back across the stone bridge and into an angry sheeting of crossbow bolts sissing down from the walls above.

Of a sudden the inner portcullis began to squeal upward, and the drawbar of the main gate slid aside and men sprang forward to open the portal. As Alvaron lowered Tipperton back to the cobbles, the iron panels swung wide, and lurid scarlet light flooded into the passage, turning it a ghastly bloody red.

For king and Dular! shouted the men in the tunnel, surging forward, Tipperton surging forward as well, only to stop dead in his tracks, for the soldiers in the lead strode into burning flames, or so it seemed. And midst the conflagration, fire bellowed up and whirled about the crew who shoved against a huge battering ram, pushing it back and away, back over the bridge to unblock the span, a span now guarded by Agron and others, while in the distance Hlôks fled. Other men hurled aside the pavises, abandoned by the fleeing Rûpt. And beyond the ram, yet other men cast dead Foul Folk off the bridge and into the flaming moat, the Spaunen brought down by crossbow quarrels as they had run away.

Out from the tunnel surged the men, and into the flames wheeled the ballista, the weapon they hoped would slay the dreadful Gargon.

Now following, Tip drew back as he came to the fire, and Imongar, standing within the blaze, turned and beckoned to the Warrow and held out her hand to him.

His heart thudding—whether from fear of fire or from the Gargon's cast or from fear of magic, Tip did not know—the buccan screwed his courage to the sticking point and stepped within.

The world all around him roared with raging blaze, yet it touched him not. Even so he rushed forward, running ahead, passing the wheeled ballista, the buccan trying not to scream.

And then he was beyond the illusory flames and onto the stone span, and still ruddy fire roared up and about, yet this was from the burning moat and real, and scorching heat hammered at the Warrow.

Even so, even though true fire was but an arm's span away, even though scathing incandescence blasted against his exposed skin trying to incinerate this fool, it could not reach him on the stone bridge, and now only the dread cast by the Gargon made his hammering heart race.

Waves of black smoke from the flaming moat billowed over the bridge and, coughing and hacking, his nostrils filled with the thick smell of burning oil, Tipperton pressed forward, to come to the foot of the bridge.

He turned to see where the ballista was and gasped, for behind stood the high stone walls of Dendor, the raging fire in the moat casting its ruddy light over all for as far as the eye could see.

It seemed a city aflame.

And eastward, yowling Rûcks and Hlôks and Ghûls swarmed toward a massive siege tower and upward, toward the ramp above which spanned from tower to top of wall, a ramp bridging high above the flames of the burning oil.

And up on the wall, men quailed back, some to flee screaming.

The Gargon! Tip turned and looked southerly to see where the dreadful creature was, yet all he saw by the wavering light was but an abandoned dark tent.

No, you fool! Look straight out from the tower! Tip looked east to the place at the wall where the men had fled and Foul Folk were now pouring over the battlement, and then he swung his gaze outward . . . and his heart leapt to his throat—

Adon! There it is!

But not alone!

—for a company of Foul Folk marched well before and another company trailed a distance after. And the Ghath, the Gargon, the Draedan, the Horror, ponderously strode eastward, its dreadful stare locked on the wall above, casting frightful terror upward to drive the men screaming away, leaving great sections of the parapet undefended.

And beyond that tower stood another, Foul Folk gathered at the base and waiting.

Oh Elwydd, that's the plan! To swarm into the city a tower at a time, the Gargon opening the way.

"One side, Waldan!" came a shout, and Tip looked to see the ballista rolling out from the illusory flames, men pushing.

Tipperton ran onward and past the great ram now being shoved to one side.

And then Tip realized, *The scaling ladders, the rams at the gates, they are but a ruse; the real invasion pours over the wall at the towers.*

"King Agron," called Tip as he came to the King and his men guarding the way, "the Gargon moves yon."

Agron glanced at the Warrow. "Aye, we see him and his escort."

Now the men pushed the ballista onto the snowy plain, turning east at the king's command.

"Hurry," called Tipperton, "the Gargon, he's already at the next tower."

And on the wall at that second tower, men shrieked and fled along the parapet and away, while Ghûls led the yowling Foul Folk across the now-bridging ramp.

And still at the first tower, howling Rûpt clambered up to pour over the wall, shouting men now returning to fight valiantly, attempting to hurl back those already on the banquette. Yet the baying Spaunen pressed forward, for Ghûls in the fore took terrible wounds which affected them not, while the wounds to the men were deadly.

Down on the plain eastward at a run pressed the king and men and Mages and one lone Warrow, the ballista trundling among them. But the massive Gargon, unaware of pursuit, now came to the third tower.

And once again the men above fled screaming, while howling

Rûpt clambered up the framework, the ramp to thud down upon the merlons, bridging from tower to wall. Led by the Ghûls, across swarmed the Foul Folk, while down below the Gargon with its fore and aft convoy moved onward, striding widdershins about the city, the massive creature stalking through rolling black smoke and crimson light cast by burning oil.

"Oh hurry, hurry," panted Tipperton, his breath blowing white in the winter air, the buccan running down among the men and alongside the ballista, fear pulsing in his veins, the wee Warrow unable to see past the tall Dendorians, but for a glimpse now and then. And so he did not know how near or far was the foe, until of a sudden the wedge of men crashed into the rear escort.

"For Dular!" shouted Agron, his sword riving.

For king and Dular! shouted the Dendorian warriors, swords and axes, maces and morning stars bashing aside dhals and sipars and tulwars and scimitars and cudgels, the Foul Folk taken by surprise from behind, but turning to meet the attack even as the men smashed through.

His heart hammering with fear, Tipperton leapt onto the ballista platform to gain height, hoping to catch sight of the Gargon and let fly a shaft from his Elven bow, yet as small as he was, he could not see over the battle raging all 'round, as yelling men and shrieking Rûpt now crashed to and fro, bashing, cleaving, crushing, steel rending, steel bludgeoning into flesh, bone, brain, muscle, and gut.

From somewhere blatted a Squamish horn, and in the fore the Gargon slowed and paused and began to turn.

"Now!" shouted Alvaron. "Loose now!"

"But my Lord Mage," protested a ballista-man, "the range."

"By damn, I said now!" bellowed Alvaron.

The man leapt onto the platform and took up the stock, while "Out of the way, Waldan!" shouted another, shoving Tipperton aside, the buccan barely able to keep his feet as he pitched to the ground.

"Wait!" called Imongar, trying to reach the spear-caster, but then—

—Thuun!—

—right above Tipperton the great ballista loosed, the spear to hurtle away in the oil-fired crimson dark, and the man who had shoved Tip aside began frantically turning a crank handle, a ratchet clattering as the ballista bow was drawn once again to reload.

Down on the ground, battle but an arm's span or two away, Tipperton dodged this way and that, dancing back while trying

to see the flight of the great bolt, to no avail, for clashing men
and Foul Folk raged back and forth and blocked the view.

"Missed!" shouted Alvaron. "Loose another. Mages, stand
ready, the *Draedan* turns."

And just as a second shaft was dropped into the waiting
groove—

—unendurable terror whelmed into Tipperton, and he
dropped his bow and fell to his knees in the churned up snow
and covered his face in his hands and shrilled in dread, while all
about men and Rûpt alike shrieked and howled and collapsed to
the snow as well.

And the Mages, the clustered Mages, they stood as if frozen,
for the Gargon had captured every last one in his dreadful glare,
and waves of paralyzing fear washed over them all.

Alvaron, his features stark, all the blood now fled from his
face, Alvaron alone managed to grit out, "*Averto formido; abigo
timeo.*"

But solely he could not stave off the dreadful force of the
mighty Gargon, and Alvaron's manipulation of astral <power>
faded to nought ere he could bring any to bear.

And now the hideous Mandrak began to move—

thdd!

thdd!

—stalking forward, toward the frozen Mages, toward the
downed Warrow, toward the squalling king and his screaming
men and the screeching Foul Folk, its mighty claws set to rend,
to tear, to shred these groveling fools who had dared to seek its
life.

thdd!

thdd!

On ponderous feet like stone it came, the monster scaled and
grey, the frozen ground shaking under its massive tread.

Thdd!

Thdd!

Men screaming, Foul Folk shrieking at its nearing approach,
still it came on.

THDD!

THDD!

Through the smoke and smell of burning oil and the shiver of
crimson light the Fearcaster came. Now it passed into the
fringes of the shrilling flock, none able to flee, to run away, for
its dread was too strong. And as it stalked forward, it shredded
all those within its immediate reach—men, Rûcks, Hlôks,
Ghûls—it mattered not whether it was friend or foe, all that
mattered was the rending. Heads, limbs, faces: through the air

they flew, trailing blood both red and black, riven from shrieking victims as the hideous creature waded past downed prey.

But as it stalked forward riving, a distant bugle rang, a clarion call from the darkness, from the south.

And a faint tremor quivered through the ground, and still the bugle sounded—

—*ta-rah . . . ta-rah . . . ta-ra, ta-ra, ta-ra . . .*

Louder it blew, and louder still, and the earth shivered with the beat of hooves.

And now the Gargon slowed.

Ta-rah . . . ta-rah . . . ta-ra, ta- ra, ta-ra . . .

To the distant west and east and even from the far north rang answering bugles belling in the predawn.

Ta-rah . . . ta-rah . . . ta-ra, ta- ra, ta-ra . . .

And now the earth boomed with the hammer of hooves.

The Gargon, eyes glaring, claws dripping blood, turned its fang-filled, lizard-snouted face southerly.

And ponies driving, bugles blowing, out from the darkness and into the crimson light thundered five hundred warriors, axes and hammers in hand.

The Dwarves had come at last.

And the Ghath, the Dread, the Gargon, the Horror, roared in rage and turned his terror upon them.

Ponies reared up and back, and Dwarves shrieked and fell away. And Foul Folk at the next tower turned to see the foe, and they took up their tulwars and scimitars and cudgels and pikes and ran to aid the Dread, for he was their key to victory.

With the Gargon gaze averted, Tipperton, still screaming, found he could move, and he snatched up his bow and turned to flee. But then his eye fell upon Imongar and Alvaron and the others, yet frozen where they stood.

Shrilling in fear, Tip sprang to the platform of the ballista, only to find—

Shrieking in dread, he jerked out an arrow from the quiver at his thigh and jumped to the ground and stabbed Imongar in the leg and squealed, "It's too high, too high!"

Imongar reeled back, her own voice now screaming in terror, and she turned to run, but Tip kicked her behind the knee, and she fell to the ground.

"The ballista!" shrieked Tipperton, snatching a fistful of her hair and jerking her about in the snow.

Imongar batted his hand aside and struggled to her feet, and whining in horror she stumbled to the spear-caster, while all about, men and Foul Folk and Dwarves screamed, and Mages stood frozen in dread.

Imongar struggled to the platform, and wrenched up the rail of the ballista, and aimed, and the Dread turned her way—

—*Thunn!*—

—the spear was loosed—

—*"Verutum ferio cor!"* shrilled Imongar, stabbing a finger toward the Gargon—

—the javelin to shift course slightly and slam into and through the hideous beast's chest.

YAAAAWWWW! bellowed the monster, and great waves of unendurable dread blasted outward, and Tip was hurled backwards onto the ground shrieking, his hammering heart all but bursting asunder. And everywhere about the city, this side and that, ponies squealed and bolted, while wailing Dwarves fell from the steeds and groveled in the snow in dread, their axes and hammers forgotten. Men, too, dropped howling in terror, many to pitch from the battlements to the cobbles below, breaking their bones, crushing their skulls, dying even as they screamed.

Foul Folk as well tumbled from the towers and ramparts, some to burn in the fire of the moat, while others crashed to the stone streets. Elsewhere on the walls and the ground outside the city, Rûcks and Hlôks and Ghûls crumpled down and yawled in terror, while Hèlsteeds fled across the icy cold plains.

And somewhere nigh the western perimeter, a second wee buccan along with two Elves and a fierce Dwarf groveled in the snow in fear.

And just as suddenly as it began, the hideous dread ceased altogether.

Alvaron collapsed to the snow.

Her leg bleeding from a deep arrow stab, Imongar hobbled to the other Mages, while all about men and Dwarves and Foul Folk began to stir, though some without visible wounds lay utterly still.

As Tipperton floundered to his feet, behind him a Hlôk staggered upright as well, the Spawn with a tulwar in hand.

"*Waeran!*" came a cry.

Tip spun about to see the Hlôk, tulwar upraised to strike, the Spawn plunging down at him—"*Waugh!*"—to fall dead at the buccan's feet, a crossbow bolt embedded in the Hlôk's back.

And beyond the dead Grg sat a Dwarf in the snow, spent crossbow in hand.

Tipperton grinned and saluted, receiving a like grin in return, but on all sides the Foul Folk snatched up weapons and scrambled to their feet, only to meet Dwarves with weapons in hand scrambling up as well, the men yet floundering.

Tip whirled and caught up his bow from the ground and,

dodging and ducking, sprang to the bed of the slack ballista. And he loosed arrow after arrow into the Spawn, bringing down any who came nigh the Wizards at hand. But then the Dwarves cleared the way, driving the Squam back, though more Foul Folk came rushing toward the fray.

Among the Mages, Imongar shook Delander and Letha, and then Ridich and Veran. "Quick, now," she called, "gather your energies. We are outnumbered, and all our power will be needed."

As the four Mages shook off the dregs of the dread, Imongar bent down to waken Alvaron, only to fall to her knees weeping.

With an arrow nocked, Tipperton leapt down from the platform to step to her side. "What is it?"

"He's dead," sobbed Imongar. "Alvaron is dead."

"Dead?"

"Slain by the Draedan's death throes. Oh Adon, he died in terror."

Tipperton looked from Alvaron toward the Gargon and then to Imongar, and grief welled up in his eyes. He glanced at the arrow-nocked bow in his hands and said, "Lady Mage, I will ward you and him from harm until the battle is ended."

Imongar shook her head, tears yet streaming. "Nay, Tipperton, he would not want it that way. Instead we must carry the fight."

And with that she stood and gathered herself, blood running down her leg, and as Letha knelt by her side and laid a palm over the wound, Imongar said, "Veran, I would have a thousand warriors charge at the Foul Folk nigh."

Veran ran a shaky hand across his brow. "Aye, Imongar."

Now Letha took her hand away from Imongar's leg, the wound no longer bleeding. "Take care, Imongar, and move not in too much haste, else the wound will reopen."

Imongar nodded distractedly as she stared toward the city. Then she turned toward Delander and Ridich. "Can you two turn that fire in the moat against the towers?"

Delander nodded and said, "Aye, but we must get closer."

"You'll need an escort, then. Letha, hearten the Dwarves."

Letha stood and shook her head and pointed at the Dwarves, most of whom had gained their feet and weaponry and now fought savagely. "Nay, Imongar, they need it not. 'Tis the king and his men who would be braced."

Tip's eyes widened. *The king! I had forgotten.* And he turned about, trying to find Agron, but gasped when he saw massive warriors, armored in glittering plate and bearing two-handed swords, running out from the darkness toward the battle raging 'round.

"Baeron!" shouted Tipperton. *But wait, Baeron in bright plate armor? And whence came they?*

Tipperton was not the only one who saw the oncoming throng, for the Foul Folk at hand saw them, too. And with wails of dismay, they turned to flee, some to be cut down by the Dwarves and King Agron and some of his men, most of the Spawn to escape howling.

And as the plated warriors reached the battlefield—

—they simply and utterly vanished.

"Good cast, Veran," said Imongar, peering 'round. "And now, let's destroy those towers."

"Inside or out?" asked Ridich.

"Wha—?" Tipperton frowned.

"Inside, I think," replied Imongar. "From the walls above." She turned to Tip. "Run, fetch the king. We need an escort to get Delander and Ridich back through the gate."

But as Tip turned to go, King Agron and a handful of warriors came striding to the Mages. A look of regret flashed over Agron's face when he saw Alvaron lying dead. But it quickly passed in this moment of exigency.

"My Lord Agron," said Imongar, "we need escort for these two back inside. They will use the fire of the moat to burn the towers."

"Aye," replied Agron, and he turned to one of the men. "Kapten Harn, find a *Dvärgkapten* and tell him that I go to the city to gather the men to carry out as much of the original plan as I can. Have him spread the word among the rest of the *Dvärgfolk*, those here as well the rest of Valk's divided legion nigh the other three gates: the cavalry and foot soldiers and I will issue into the field within two candlemarks.

"And, Harn, when that is done fetch some of those Dvärgfolk and cut the head from the Gargon. I will meet you at the south gate with a horse and a pike. You will spit the Fearcaster's head on the lance and bear it into battle at my side."

As Captain Harn turned toward the Dwarves, Agron motioned to Delander and Ridich. "Come and set your fires," he said, and with an escort of armed and armored men, the king and the two Mages set off at a trot for the south gate.

Watching them go, Imongar said to Letha, "The Dwarf herald will need a pony. Can you fetch one?"

Letha nodded and closed her eyes, muttering, *"Manni, convenire hic!"*

Now Imongar turned to Tip and the others. "Come, let us also find the captain of these Dwarves and see what we can do to salvage their part of the plan."

"What about the wounded?" asked Tipperton. "Shouldn't some stay and ward them?"

Imongar looked at Veran. He sighed and nodded. "I will ring them about with a phantom force, though I will not stay."

Tip frowned in concern.

" 'Tis the best we can do," said Imongar, as a pony came galloping in, and then another, and twenty more, followed by another hundred or so, all to gather about Letha.

"I asked for one," said Imongar, smiling, ponies stirring and pressing all 'round.

"I summoned them all, two thousand, I believe, if all Dwarves nigh and far were unhorsed. —Unponied, I mean," replied Letha, grinning back as the ground thundered with more little steeds galloping in. "We must needs get them back to Valk's army."

"Not all," said Imongar, "for I'll need one. I've been stabbed in the leg, you know."

"Oh, Imongar," appealed Tip, "it was the only way I could think of to bring you out from—"

"I know, wee one, I know," said Imongar, frowning and rubbing her head. "And I forgive you as well for pulling my hair out by the roots."

The battle was hard-fought and long, dawn coming and then the morn, yet by the noontide, the Foul Folk were routed, their towers burned, their Hèlsteeds gone, half of the Swarm lying slain. And the king and his cavalry and foot soldiers were deadly, as were the savage Dwarves; and with massive warriors appearing out of nowhere to rush across the field at them, many of the Squam had panicked and fled.

And sometime in midmorn and on a pony circling far out on the plains and well away from the fight, Tip saw Beau, the other buccan mounted as well, for Letha had led the little steeds wide 'round the walls, remounting the forces of Kachar.

"Beau! Beau! Hiyo, Beau!" shouted Tipperton, kicking his pony into a dead run as he espied his friend galloping out from the field and leaving the battle behind.

And Beau veered his mount and came racing, shouting, "Oh, Tip, we thought you— I thought you— Oh, Tip, it's so good to see you alive."

And they rode together and haled up side to side facing one another and reached across and clasped hands and grinned great grins, simply glad to be reunited.

"Loric, Phais, Bekki—?"

"They're all right, Tip. Loric and Phais are in the thick of it,

Bekki, too, though he's bashing aside all comers while looking for Modru's surrogate."

"Oh, Beau, the surrogate: it's Lord Tain."

"Tain?"

"Yes." Tip shuddered. "And he bears the corpse of his daughter, Lady Jolet, and yet whispers his mad dreams to her."

"Oh my."

"He's completely unhinged, Beau, unlike that other surrogate at Mineholt North, who seemed nought but witless."

Beau frowned. "Mayhap by being mad or without wit, mayhap that's what allows Modru to exert his hideous control."

Tip sighed and canted his head and said, "Perhaps you're right, Beau; who knows? Not I, and that's for certain. But that's neither here nor there, and I'm just glad we're together again. And, I say, just where were you going so Hèlbent?"

Beau held up his sling. "I'm all out. There's a stream nearby, and I was riding to gather up more stones."

Tip held up his bow. "Me too. —All out of arrows, I mean, all but for the red-fletched one Rynna gave me, and I'll not use that. Instead, when I can find them I've been plucking shafts from dead Rûpt and using them to kill others still. —Say, you wouldn't happen to have a spare sling, now, would you?"

"No, but we could make one, can we find some leather."

"I know just the place," said Tipperton, "a leather tent nearby. It once housed a Gargon."

Holding tight to the ponies' reins to keep them from bolting away, Beau's face wrinkled in disgust. "Lor', it smells like a snake's den."

Pulling on the slice of leather, Tip made the final cut through the tent with his knife. The strip came free. "There." He held up the strap. "Crude, but perhaps I can make do after a bit of trimming."

He glanced at Beau's twisted visage and burst out laughing. "I say, Beau, you look as if you just swallowed a stinkbug."

Beau grinned. "I think I'd rather that than this." He gestured at the tent.

Tip canted his head. "Aye. But the Gargon himself smells worse. Like a monstrous viper—putrid rot and diseased blood and a hideous coppery tang you can't seem to clear from your tongue. Would you like to see him?"

Beau blanched. "Oh, Tip."

"He's dead, you know, his head on a pike, at Agron's side in the battle," said Tipperton, now squatting on the hard-frozen ground and slicing away on the strap.

"Is *that* what that terrible thing was?" asked Beau. "I didn't know, though wherever it was borne it seemed to take the heart out of the foe when they saw it coming."

"Yet they still fight," said Tip.

"Aye, but much less savagely." Beau watched as Tip trimmed the leather. "Say, how was it killed? —The Gargon I mean."

"Spitted by a spear. Imongar killed him."

Beau frowned. "This Imongar, a mighty champion, eh?"

"Well, I wouldn't exactly call her a—"

"Her? The Gargon was killed by a *her*?"

"Indeed," said Tip. "Shot the Gargon with a ballis—"

"Is she one of these Jordian warrior maidens I've heard about? Or did one of those great strapping Baeron women come here? Bwen perhaps?"

Tip shook his head. "No, Beau; Imongar is a Mage."

"A Mage? Did she kill him with magic?"

"I don't think so, though she did shriek something and the spear hit the Gargon dead center."

"Magic," said Beau, nodding sagely. Then—"Oh, speaking of magic, what about the coin? Was it an amulet or some such?"

"No, Beau, it was merely a summons: from Blaine to Agron. They were boyhood chums. I'll tell you about it later."

"Huah," said Beau, his face falling in disappointment, "I was hoping it was somehow charmed."

"It wasn't," said Tip, "and for that I'm glad." Then he glanced at his black wristband. "One thing, though, the man who gave me the coin, the one who was slain at my mill, he was Dular, King Agron's own son."

"Oh my," breathed Beau, his features now falling to sadness.

Silence fell between them as Tip made a final cut, and only the distant clang of battle disturbed the quiet.

Finally Beau said, "Where is this headless Gargon?"

"Yon," replied Tipperton, pointing with the knife, "east a ways."

"I say," said Beau, peering, "who are those big warriors standing in a ring? They look formidable. And why aren't they in the fight? Better that than guarding the headless corpse of a Gargon, I would say."

Tip laughed. "Magic, Beau, guarding some of the wounded, it's magic come to light. And come to think of it"—Tip held up the strap and frowned at it and then nodded—"I'd rather we go for slingstones and rejoin the battle than to walk through those magical phantoms just to see a dead Gargon with no head, as wondrous as that may be." Tip stood and slipped his knife back into its sheath.

"All right," said Beau, handing Tip's reins over to him and then mounting up. "Follow me to the rocks, and then we'll join up with Loric and Phais and Bekki."

And so, off to the creek galloped the two buccen to gather up slingstones, and then back to the fight, where their bullets hurtled into the Foul Folk, one of the wee slingsters significantly more deadly than the other.

Time and again they returned to the creek, breaking through the ice to fish through new pockets of pebbles, and their fingers suffered the worse for it.

And the sun rose up in the sky, and as the noontide came, away fled the last of the Swarm, scattering in all directions. None of the Allies, as weary as they were, gave more than a token chase; not even the Dwarves of Kachar long pursued their enemies of old fleeing across the plains.

13

On appropriated mounts they rode through a field of carnage: past the dead and dying, past healers tending wounded men and Dwarves, past Dwarven mercy squads striding among the downed Foul Folk and relieving them of all suffering forever. At last they came to the ring of phantasmal warriors, did Tip and Beau, Phais and Loric, and Bekki, a strong malodor hanging o'er all. Tip took a deep breath and plunged through the conjuration, while Beau paused to admire the glamour, Veran's illusion yet standing.

"Come on, Beau, there's wounded here," called Tip, leaping down from his pony, the animal skitting and shying, Tip holding tight to the reins to keep the steed from bolting. *And also a dead Gargon.*

Beau kicked his heels to his pony's flanks and rode within the circle. "Phew!" Beau's face screwed into a look of disgust. "The Gargon, a pit of a thousand vipers could smell no worse."

"Here," said Loric, "hand the reins over to me. I will tend the steeds in this rank place."

Dismounting, Beau gave over the pony to Loric and took up his medical satchel. "Tip, Phais, Bekki—walk among the downed and make certain of life."

Bekki growled, "There are Grg here as well, and for those I will make certain of death."

Slowly they moved among the men and Dwarves and Foul Folk, Bekki now and again slitting a throat.

As they worked, Letha came into the ring of phantom warriors, and where she moved she laid on hands and whispered, "*Concrescere!*" and stopped the leak of blood.

Beau looked at her amazed. "Oh my goodness, what a wonderful gift you have."

She smiled and moved on, as did the others.

"Huah!" grunted Bekki, a frown on his face, "some of these dead have no wounds at all."

"They were slain by terror, I think," said Tipperton. He gestured at the headless Gargon, the haft of the ballista-hurled spear jutting out from its chest, the gore-smeared blade protruding from its back. "When he was felled a great blast of fear whelmed all who were nigh."

"We felt it, too, and we were far," said Bekki, prodding a disemboweled Hrôk as if to make certain it was truly dead and not somehow lying midst its own entrails and feigning.

Tip looked at where Alvaron yet lay. "It was terrible, that outpouring of dread, and killed Alvaron and these others. For a moment I thought my own heart would burst."

Bekki frowned. "Alvaron?"

"A Mage . . . there," replied Tipperton, gesturing and then wiping away tears. "One of six."

Bekki shook his head. "Six Mages, and they could not stop the Ghath?"

Tip shrugged, but nearby Letha said, "We had just run far and had come into combat and had no time to marshal our <fire>."

"Time?" asked Tip.

Letha nodded without looking up from the wound she was treating. "It takes time to summon <power>: only an instant for the lesser things; long moments for the greater. Fending a Draedan is of the greater."

"Oh."

"I say, Tip," called Beau. "Ride to the city and fetch some help to move the wounded to shelter. We can't leave them lying about in the cold like this, you know. They've been here long enough as it is."

A day passed, and then another, and though King Agron had the battlefield thoroughly searched, of Lord Tain and his dreadful burden there was no sign. It was as if Modru's surrogate had vanished into the icy air. When Beau asked why it was so important to find Mad Tain, Bekki replied, "As long as Coward Tain is alive, Modru has a tool to rally the runaway Grg."

On this day as well, the head of the Gargon was mounted atop a spire at the west gate to face distant Gron, Modru's realm afar, as a grim warning to any and all who would set their hand against this city and against this land. At this raising of the dread monster's head, Agron's captains, fresh from war council, seemed more dour than the ceremony would warrant.

Nine more days passed and rumors flew, for every day the captains came muttering from the war room, and rumor had it that the king had been driven mad by the death of his son Dular.

During these same nine days, the battlefield was cleared of bodies, and funeral pyres were set aflame, for the earth was yet frozen even though the last of these days was the twenty-first of March: spring had come unto the land though snow yet covered all.

And out on the snowy plains under a waning gibbous moon, on Springday night Tip, Beau, Phais, and Loric paced the Elven rite of the turning of the seasons, while in the distance nigh the city walls the last of the funeral pyres burned scarlet as women and children wept and Dwarves and men tore at their beards and beat their chests and swore vengeance dire.

On the third day following the last of the battlefield funerals, most of the Dwarven army rode away, wagons bearing their wounded among them, for they hoped to cross the Argon ere that river thawed . . . or to cross on the Kaagor Ferry if its rebuilding were done, for Valk had left behind crafters to do so in anticipation of the army's return. Only DelfLord Valk and a few of his warriors remained in Dendor, for there was to be a ceremony held in the throne room, and the honored DelfLord would attend. Too, Tip and Beau were invited, along with Phais and Loric and Bekki, as well as a host of others.

That evening, the Warrows were dressed in their finest, though it was but a spare set of clean clothes, their goods having been fetched by Bekki from their abandoned camp on the south ridge. When Bekki had returned with their belongings, the first thing Tip had examined had been his marvelous Elven lute, finding it no worse for the wear, and yet in tune even though cold to the touch. But now he set the instrument aside and made his way with the others unto the great throne room.

The chamber was thronged with people and filled with a babble of sound—men, women, Dwarves, others, milling about and in noisy converse while waiting for the king.

"Adon, but I can hardly hear myself think," Beau called above the gabble when they came in among the clamorous press.

Pushing through the crowd, Tip and Beau eventually found themselves among the Mages, splendid in flowing robes.

Beau looked up at Letha. "I say," he called, nearly shouting to be heard, "could you teach me that trick of yours? —Stopping bleeding, I mean. It would be most handy for me to know, being a healer and all."

Letha gazed with brown eyes down at the tiny buccan and called back, "I am afraid not only would you need long training to master such, but a touch of wild magic as well."

"Wild magic?"

Letha brushed a stray lock of her brown hair away from her eyes, then leaned down and spoke into his ear. "Aye, unless you can see <fire>, that is."

"Oh no," groaned Beau. "<Fire>. I've heard of it before. From Delgar."

"Delgar?"

Beau nodded. "A Mage."

"Oh, I know who Delgar is. I was just wondering where you came across him."

"In the Bosky. —The Boskydells, that is. He was passing through when I was but a stripling. I must have been about twelve; that would make it some eleven years back, or so. He gave me a book about herbs and simples and philters and physicks and medicks and got me apprenticed to a healer in Willowdell, he did. —And say, you know him?"

"Indeed," replied Letha. "He is my sire."

"Oh my," said Beau—

—but in that moment a staff knelled thrice upon the marble floor, and a voice rang out above the babble, "My lords and ladies and honored guests, all kneel before King Agron, son of Morgon and sire of slain Dular."

Silence fell, and the crowd pushed back from the central aisle, a multitude closing about the buccen. And all in the assembly but Phais and Loric and DelfLord Valk fell to their knees, ladies included.

Dressed in red, a black band on his left wrist, King Agron paced through the lane opened and toward his throne, while down on one knee beside Tip and amid the throng, Beau leaned this way and that, trying to peer past the men and women and Dwarves. "I can't see a thing down here," he muttered to Tip. "—Can you?"

"Not at all," whispered Tip. "Much like when we were running after the Gargon. I couldn't see a thing there either, down among the Big Folk as it were."

"Well, they ought to put us up front, or let us stand, or something that would put our eyes on level with the others," grumbled Beau.

Tip merely shrugged.

From the direction of the throne, King Agron called out, "My lords, ladies, and honored guests, please rise."

As they all stood, Beau whispered, "Come on, let's move to

where we can see." And he and Tip looked all 'round for a way through the press.

"We are gathered here to celebrate our victory over the forces of darkness," began Agron . . .

Hemmed about on all sides by Big Folk, Beau finally dropped to hands and knees and with Tip following began to crawl among polished boots and around the flowing hems of full skirts belled out with petticoats and hoops, people looking down in consternation and drawing aside as the two Warrows came crawling by.

". . . without the help of DelfLord Valk and his legion it would have been nigh impossible . . ." continued Agron, as the buccen crawled on, now nearing the central aisle, only to find it occupied, lords and ladies and warriors and guests having moved therein. Beau turned rightward, now crawling toward the throne.

". . . and it was Lady Mage Imongar who loosed the spear that slew the Gargon . . ."

A cheer rang out above Agron's words, and still the buccen crawled forward.

". . . and I name her a Heroine of the Realm . . ."

Again a cheer rang out, and the crowd parted to make way for Imongar to come to the throne, only to reveal two Warrows down on hands and knees crawling forward.

"Unh, Beau," hissed Tipperton, slowly clambering to his feet, his face flushed red with embarrassment.

Beau crawled on.

"Beau," hissed Tip again, louder.

"What? What? We're almost there," replied Beau.

Led by the king, the crowd burst out in laughter.

Beau looked up . . . and then tried to sink through the floor.

'Mid the hoots and howls and giggles and titters, Imongar limped to the prostrate buccan and reached down to help him rise.

Many were praised that night:

DelfLord Valk of Kachar was singled out, the flag of that Dwarvenholt to henceforth hang in a place of honor in the throne room of Aven.

The Mages of Black Mountain were lauded: Delander and Ridich for their burning destruction of the siege towers; Veran for the phantasmal warriors rushing at the Swarm to make the Rûpt bolt; Letha for rounding up the ponies and for her healing hand; Imongar for the slaying of the Gargon and her leadership thereafter, though she told all that Tipperton Thistledown, stabbing her in the leg as he had done and yanking her about by the hair, he was the one who truly deserved the credit for the Gargon's demise; and lastly, Mage Alvaron, for ere he was slain he had been their leader, and more than once in the days before had protected the Dendorian warriors from the Gargon's dread.

Others were honored as well—captains, warriors, healers, advisors—but none so praised as the five who had come bearing a coin: two Litenfolk, two Alfs, and a Dvärg. For without them the Dvägfolk of Kachar would not have come. Without them Dendor would have fallen. And without especially Sir Tipperton Thistledown, all would now be dead.

Tip was summoned to the throne dais, and when he stood beside the king, calls of *Speech!* and *Hålla et tal!* rang out.

Tipperton frowned and looked out at the crowd and raised his hands. When silence fell, he said, "No single person alone is responsible for a victory or even for a defeat. If you would praise anyone, then I say, praise each and every single one who stands against Modru and his ilk. Together we will cast him down."

His words were met by a resounding cheer.

And finally King Agron called for quiet. In the stillness which followed, he looked down at the buccan and then out at his captains and warriors, his lords and ladies, his healers . . . his subjects. "Sir Tipperton's words are prophetic: together we *can* defeat Modru. To that end I plan to carry the fight unto the vile one himself, the killer of my son Dular. When the army is rested, wounds healed, strength recovered, supplies laid in, wagons assembled, then we will bear the fight to Modru, into his own realm, for I plan to march my armies into Gron and assail his foul minions there."

But for a collective intake of breath, a stunned silence met these dire words.

14

*I*nvading *Gron?* some in the taverns muttered over their mugs of ale, while others whispered across back fences: *Modru's realm? Modru, the Black Mage? Is the king mad?* Still others looked wisely at one another and proclaimed, *He has a plan which will end the war swiftly, does the king . . . after all, didn't he kill the Gargon?* Yet some avowed in hushed tones to any and all who would listen, *'Tis Dular's ghost roaming the ramparts and demanding vengeance which drives the king to do such.* Regardless as to what the rumors alleged, riders bearing the king's gold and blue colors spread out across the land and bore the message that King Agron called for all able-bodied men to take up their arms and armor and leave their steads by the October moon to muster in the river town of Älvstad in the west of Aven by mid-November; as far as the king's subjects were concerned, *That settled that.*

Even so, in advisory conference with the king, the DelfLord of Kachar counseled against such a rash move, Valk calling it self-slaughter, with Imongar, representing the Mages of Black Mountain, siding with him.

"What say you, Lian Guardians?" asked Agron.

Loric looked to Phais, and she said, "I would suggest, my lord, that thou shouldst instead march thine armies to the aid of High King Blaine."

"My lady, what I plan will aid Blaine even though I will not be at his side."

"Aye," agreed Phais, "it will, though still I advise thee to find the High King instead."

"Where is Blaine?" asked DelfLord Valk.

"West of the Grimwall when last we knew," said Loric, "retreating from the fall of Challerain Keep and fighting a running battle."

Imongar frowned. "If he was at Challerain Keep, then he may have difficulty in reaching Pellar, for did you not say that all routes across the Grimwalls were blocked?"

Loric nodded. "Crestan Pass, Quadran Pass, Gûnarring Gap: all are held by the Rûpt."

"Pardon, my lord," said Agron, "but Arden Vale lies beyond those cols. If all are blocked, how did you come from that side to this?"

"That, my lord, I am not at liberty to tell, for we are pledged to hold secret the way we came. Yet I will say this: the route is insufficient for your armies to use. We ourselves came afoot—did the Waerlinga and Dara Phais and I—leaving our horses behind, the way too narrow for them, though a pony could cross."

At these words, DelfLord Valk raised an eyebrow and nodded slightly toward the Elves.

"Does any fight to open the ways?" asked Imongar.

"Aye," said Phais. "The Lian of Arden Vale and the Baeron of Darda Erynian battle to open Crestan Pass, and the Dwarves of the Red Hills seek to quash the Horde at Gûnarring Gap, though a Draedan helps bar that slot. As to Quadran Pass, mayhap the siege of Drimmen-deeve is broken and the Dwarves of that holt and the Lian of Darda Galion have command of that way. Yet we do not know if any of these passes are open, for our knowledge is seasons old."

Agron frowned but said, "Well then, if they are yet closed, where do you hope to find Blaine?"

"Pellar is where I would seek him," said Loric. "If he is not now at Caer Pendwyr, then there he will come soon or late."

Valk nodded. "I plan on taking my warriors to Pellar to be at the High King's side. Even so, for the long campaign it promises to be, we will not set forth until after the harvest of this year's crops in our mountain vales, for an army cannot live long off the country alone."

Agron turned to Imongar. "And what will Magekind do?"

Imongar sighed. "We, too, shall set out for Pellar, for the High King will need all the aid he can muster, Magekind most of all, for Modru has at his beck not only Foul Folk but <power> and Gargons and Dragons and other fell beasts which only we can ward against."

Phais's eyes widened. "Ye can fend Dragons?"

A grim look came over Imongar's face. "Mayhap in a great conjoinment of Mages, can we find a sorcerer to be the focus and wielder of the bonded <fire>, though the casting needed is like to slay all thus merged."

Phais shook her head and opened her mouth to speak, but Agron declared, "Then I march into Gron alone." His defiant gaze swept from DelfLord to Guardian to Mage.

Loric, too, looked 'round at the others and then said, "Regretfully so, my lord; thou and thine army wilt go alone and without our aid, for we deem victory will come at the High King's side, wherever he may be, and not in the colds of Gron."

Agron drew in a deep breath and then let it out. "It may be as you say, Lord Loric, yet hear me. By marching into Gron I will give Modru pause and perhaps buy Blaine some time, time to forge the alliance needed to throw down the vile one. In the very least, I will cause Modru to hold back several Hordes merely to meet my threat, Hordes which will not be cast against Blaine." Agron took up a thong from the table, a thong laced through a pewter coin. "That you will find him, I do not doubt, and so I ask but this: take back to him this token and say to him when you meet, the coin he sent by my son Dular, whom Modru most foully slew, the coin borne to me by others, that coin will be well spent."

Loric accepted the token and, glancing at Phais, said, "My lord, though we disagree on this mission to Gron thou dost undertake, Dara Phais and I will seek out the High King wherever he may be and deliver the coin and thy message. This we do so pledge."

And so it was: of DelfLord and Wizard and Lian Guardian, none could dissuade King Agron from his chosen course, Dwarf and Mage and Elves to go a separate way, leaving Agron and his men to march into Modru's realm. And yet it was not only men who would be marching into Gron, but a wee Warrow was pledged to scout for the king on his perilous course, and wherever that wee Warrow scout would go, a wee healer would go as well.

"I say, Beau, we've been cooped up indoors for days on end; what say we go outside and you teach me some of those slingster tricks of yours, eh? I mean, any arrows I take into battle are like to be entirely spent ere the fighting is done, whereas rocks always seem to be at hand. And if I am to carry on the fight when my quiver is empty, then a sling seems the best choice, and I could use a trick or two."

Beau looked at Tip. "Ho, me teach you tricks? This from the one who saw me try to lob rocks at a tree and nearly brain my own self?"

Tip laughed, remembering. "Ah, but Beau, that was back more than a year past, and you've improved a wee bit since then."

Beau grinned. "Well then, we'll have to get Phais to make you a sling, for she is the one who made mine."

"Hoy, what's wrong with the one I cut from the Gargon's tent?"

Beau shook his head and said, "Wait'll you use mine, bucco; then you'll see."

They trudged out to an ornamental garden behind the mansion and gathered up chill pebbles amid the melting snow, then walked to an open space along the city wall.

"All right, bucco, here's what Phais taught me: first you've got to adjust the loop 'round your thumb: too tight, you cut off the blood; too loose, and you'll hurl the sling away with the bullet. And speaking of bullets, the best are not perfectly round, but elongated instead: they fit the sling pocket better for a better throw and seem more deadly when they strike. And another thing . . ."

Thus did Beau begin teaching Tip all he knew about slings and bullets and deadly casting, underhand and overhand and sidearm and backhand, for one never knew just where one might be when it came time to throw—on a cliff or hanging onto a tree trunk or peering over a wall or standing still or running or riding a pony or horse—at targets left and right, near and far, high and low, at stationary targets and moving ones, big and little both, speaking of the best places to strike the foe to bring him down or kill him outright. Although Tip was a quick learner, there was much more to slinging than he had ever suspected.

The following day, Valk and his remaining warriors prepared to set out for Kachar, and the Mages of Black Mountain for distant Pellar. As to Phais and Loric, they would not leave for a time to come, yet hoping to turn King Agron away from his mission to Gron and toward Pellar instead. Bekki though was of a mind to remain at Tipperton's side, for although his pledge to see the Waeran safely to Dendor had been fulfilled, still he felt an obligation to the wee Châk-Sol; besides, what better place to find Grg to kill than in the wastes of Gron.

Long were the farewells, Tip, Beau, Phais, Loric, and Bekki saying good-bye to Valk and the Mages. Imongar came limping to Tipperton and embraced the buccan and whispered her thanks to him in spite of his having stabbed her in the leg with one of his very sharp arrows.

And as they rode away, the Dwarves to the north, the Mages to the south, clarions called from the walls of Dendor, announcing to one and all that on this day heroes now rode across the plains of Aven.

It was on the third day of sling practice, when Beau frowned at something afar. "I say, Tip, what's that? It's the fourth one I've seen today."

Tip turned and looked. A white wagon, its driver in white, made its way down the cobbled side street. "Oh, it's a wagon for the sick, Beau, heading for the prison."

"Prison?"

"Aye. There's a dark disease in the city. Modru caused. When he had the corpses cast over the city walls—"

"Dark disease?"

Tip nodded, his face grim. "Awful. Pus-running boils. Dark rin—"

"Black nodules under the armpits, the groin?" broke in Beau. "Fever?"

"Well I don't know about nodules, but fever, yes, and dark rings about sunken eyes."

"Oh my," said Beau. "It sounds like the plague."

"Plague? But I thought a plague was something widespread, whereas this is not extensive. Just those who bore the corpses to the fires seem—"

"Perhaps it's not widespread yet," declared Beau, gathering up his jacket and cloak, "but if it's what I think it is, it'll bring down the entire city if it's not stopped."

"Where are you going?"

"To this prison, wherever it is. I've got to see for myself. Besides, they can use my help."

Tip began donning his own jacket. "I'll take you there, but as far as helping them, I dunno, Beau. The healer I talked to acted as if not many would survive."

"Oh my, but I was hoping I would never see this day," said Beau, the look on his face grim.

"Then it is the plague?" asked Tip.

Beau nodded. "Even though I've never seen it before, it fits all the descriptions I've ever read, particularly the one in my red healer's book."

Phais glanced at Loric. "Our help will be needed, chier."

Loric nodded in silent reply.

Beau sighed. "They've silverroot aplenty but none of the golden mint."

Bekki looked up from his plate of food. "Golden mint?"

"Yes. Gwynthyme. I've thought a tisane of golden mint mixed with silverroot might aid in curing the plague, yet I have no gwynthyme left. Do you know where there is some?"

Bekki shrugged. "Mayhap. Once when I was prospecting in the Grimwall above Nordlake I saw quite a lot of a golden mint growing in cracks and crevices along the face of the steeps. But whether this is what you are seeking, I cannot say."

"Quite a lot? Oh my, just what we need, if gwynthyme it is." Beau jumped down from the bench at the table. "Hold on, I'll show you a picture of it."

Moments later the buccan was back, his thin, faded-red-leather healer's book in hand. Riffling through the pages, quickly Beau found the one he sought. "Here it is." He showed the drawing to Bekki.

The Dwarf grunted and looked up from the picture. "Perhaps it is what I saw." He glanced again at the page and then frowned in puzzlement. "These words, I cannot read them."

"The book, it's written in a simple code," said Beau. "Here, I'll read it for you." Beau took the book back and, his brow furrowing in concentration, read, " 'Gwynthyme: a trefoil with serrated trifoliate aromatic leaves and nearly regular pale yellow flowers.' " Beau looked up to see Bekki yet frowning.

"The yellow flowers I understand," grumbled Bekki. "But the rest of it . . ." Bekki shrugged.

"Delgar writes like that, Bekki: jaw-breaking words and all. It took me awhile to learn what they meant."

Bekki raised an eyebrow. "Delgar?"

Beau nodded and tapped the red book. "The Mage who gave me this."

"Ah. Mage talk. I see," growled Bekki. "What is he really trying to say about gwynthyme?"

Beau gestured at the sketch. "Think of it as an ordinary mint, Bekki, but with three jagged-edged leaves at each stem, golden in color with a minty odor. Is that what you saw?"

Bekki looked again at the picture and then nodded. "Aye, as near as I can remember."

"Oh my. Oh my," said Beau. "Then that's just what we need, I think. This place where you saw the mint, can you find it again?"

Bekki scowled at the Warrow. "Did I not tell you I am Châkka, wee one, and cannot lose my feet?"

"Oh, right."

"Look," said Tip, "Agron's muster isn't until November, nearly eight months from now, so I should be able to go along. What do we harvest, the flowers or the leaves?"

"The leaves, Tip. The flowers are gone by the time the mint turns golden."

"And when is this? Now? In the springtime? Oh, Beau, what I'm really trying to ask is when do we harvest it? When do we have to be at Nordlake?"

Beau glanced at his red book, and then his face fell and he groaned. "Oh, barn rats, I had forgotten."

"Forgotten what?" asked Tip.

"One of the reasons gwynthyme is rare is that it only flourishes between the moons of August and September, and by then the plague may have a death grip on this city."

"Even so"—Tip looked at Bekki—"that's well before Agron's muster in November. We should go after the mint, can we get there and back ere then. When are these moons?"

"The moon of August occurs on the tenth," said Loric. "The one in September shines full on the ninth."

"Well," said Beau, looking at his book, "according to this, the mint turns golden on the full moon of September following the August full moon, and it must be harvested before the following dark of the moon occurs."

"The dark following the September full moon?" asked Tip, shaking his head, slightly confused.

Beau nodded.

Tip turned to Loric, the Alor answering his question ere it was asked, saying, "The dark of the moon falls on the twenty-fourth."

Tip looked to Beau. "So we've got between the ninth of September and the twenty-fourth to harvest it?"

Beau looked up from his book. "Right, for on the dark of the moon it turns brown and becomes deadly poison."

"Elwydd," exclaimed Bekki, "ruin and rescue in one?"

Beau nodded and said, "Aye, and it's vital you get there in time to harvest the rescue and not the ruin." Beau closed his book and asked Bekki, "Where is this Nordlake, and how long will it take to get there and back?"

"Just a moment," said Tip, "I'll get my maps and then we'll see."

"Here is a ford," said Bekki, jabbing a forefinger down to the sketch.

"Wait a moment," said Beau. "What about using the Kaagor Ferry? Wouldn't that way be shorter?"

"It is burnt," said Phais.

"But Valk left behind crafters to rebuild it ere he brought his army here. That was a month or so past. Surely it is done by now, or will be when it is time to go for the mint."

Loric nodded. "Even so, it may fall prey again unto the Spaunen, whereas the ford may not."

Tip stroked his chin, remembering. "Beau may have a point: the maggot-folk could have wards set up at the ford, just like they did at the Hâth River in Rell."

"And the Crystal River into Aven," added Beau.

Bekki shook his head and pointed once again at the ford. "Unlike the ferry, there is nothing vital nigh these shallows: no cities, towns, holts, passes . . . nothing—not even Squam strongholts, I ween. It is not likely the Grg will think it worthy to spend their forces there. Nay, I deem they will not ward it, though they could use it to cross over to do ill in distant parts."

Tip frowned and pointed at a spur of the Grimwalls. " 'Tis moot, I think, for here the mountains must be rounded; hence, by ferry or ford, I gauge the ways nigh equal."

Beau peered at the map. "Oh well, never mind."

"All right," said Tip, "ford it is." Then measuring with his thumb—"Um, that's some two hundred seventy, two hundred eighty miles to the ford, and"— he measured again—"another hundred twenty or so to Nordlake." He looked up at Bekki.

"A day or two to get to the face of the mountain where I saw the mint," said the Dwarf.

Tip nodded. "By pony, then, I make it some two weeks to the ford, another week to the lake, and a couple of days to the mint: twenty-three, twenty-four days altogether."

"Add leeway for unexpected delay," said Bekki. "Squam may yet roam between here and there, with Squam in the mountains as well."

"Perhaps more than just you four ought to go," said Beau.

"You're not going?" asked Tip, surprised.

"I've got to stay here, Tip, and help out. This dark scourge will get much worse before it gets better. But Phais and Loric can go with you and Bekki."

A frown crossed Loric's face. "Nay, we cannot."

Tip looked up at the Alor.

"Elvenkind does not fall ill to this scourge," said Loric. "And if it is as Beau says, then we will be needed here in the days to come. Yet King Agron could lend whatever aid is needed to harvest the mint."

Bekki shook his head. "It is better that just two of us go than a large band, for as I said, Grg may lie between here and there, and two alone have a better chance of slipping past their wards than would an entire company."

"Look," said Tip, "we can cross that bridge when we come to it. But for now we will plan on going alone, just you and me, Bekki . . . in, what, mid-July?"—Tip counted on his fingers—"Say, fifteen weeks from now?"

Again Beau groaned at the length of time.

"According to your book, Beau, it can't be helped," said Tip. "I mean, if the mint doesn't come to fruition until the September moon, then I can't see setting out from here before mid-July. That will give us four weeks or so to get to Nordlake in time for the August moon. And then we'll have another four weeks to find *all* the places where the mint grows, and be entirely ready to harvest it. And lastly, two weeks or so to gather it in. Then three weeks from Nordlake to Dendor"—again Tip counted on his fingers—"that'd make it around mid-October when we return. That's plenty of time for me to get to the muster in Älvstad by mid-November. —Oh, I say, Beau, we'll need a drawing of what the mint looks like before it turns golden . . . and tell me, just how much of this mint do you need?"

"As much as you can bring, Tip, but according to the book you also have to leave enough behind so that more will grow in subsequent years."

Tip frowned, and Bekki growled, "A gardener I am not, nor an herbalist. How much should we leave behind? Does anyone know how to judge?"

Beau smiled and tapped the faded cover of the book. "Delgar does. He wrote it all down, and I'll tell you what he said."

And so, from his Mage-written manual, Beau began educating Tip and Bekki in the ways of the golden mint, though he himself had no experience with the growing of it.

During this same time, in King Agron's war room long into the night, obstacles to the king's war plan were raised and solutions conceived:

"The army is sapped, my lord, many of our best are wounded."

"That is why we wait for autumn, captain, to give many the time to heal."

"The crops, sire, what of them? We cannot leave a hungry nation behind."

"Much will be harvested ere we set forth."

"Ah, but Älvstad is far to the west, my lord, and it will take many a day for those in the east to reach the muster on the Argon River."

"Let them ride instead to the Crystal and Green Rivers on the east, for they are Argon tributaries. Let those in the north ride to the Argon as well. By raft and boat they can journey to Älvstad, for river legs never tire and it will make the passage swift."

"Even so, my lord, still there are late crops to gather in and next spring's tilling and planting as well."

"In those cases, where oldsters and women and children are not enough, by lottery leave behind sufficient of the able-bodied to bring in their own and their neighbors' crops and plant for the following year."

A captain on the far side of the map table cleared his throat and said, "My lord, was it wise to announce to the public your plans to invade Gron? What of spies bearing word to Modru himself?"

Agron's icy gaze swept 'round the table, and he clenched a fist. "I want him to know we are coming. I want to give him pause. Yet heed, he will not know by what route we will advance, and must needs hold back his forces instead of spending them to carry the fight to others."

"My lord, how will we enter Gron?" The captain gestured at the map. "It lies on the far side of the Grimwall, and I have heard that all passes are warded. Do we march north from Älvstad through Jord and take to the Boreal Sea and around?"

Agron shook his head. "Nay, we do not, though mayhap Modru will think so. Instead we enter by an unexpected way." The king looked up from the map. "This knowledge will not leave this room." After receiving nods from his captains, Agron traced a route across the chart. "We ford the river here at Älvstad, then march through Jallor Pass and into this corner of Jord. Here we turn to the west and enter the Gronfangs, for at this point there is a narrow twisting pass through that dire range, all but forgotten, blocked by a slide, and who would clear a slide for passage into the cold wastes of Gron, eh?"

At the captains' astonished gazes, Agron added, "I have seen it myself, for when I was but twenty, Prince Halfar of Jord and I rode in on a lark—a test of bravery then; but in hindsight nought but a foolish risk.

"Regardless, far within there is a slide, but one which an army can clear, providing a way to come upon Gron unawares."

An elder statesman leaned forward. "Sire, we will be marching across Jord, or a part thereof."

The king raised an eyebrow.

"What I mean, my lord, is that we should send an emissary to Jordkeep and apprise King Ranor."

Agron nodded and said, "Prepare a missive, Lord Vengar. I will set my seal to it." The elder statesman nodded.

Across the table a captain said, "My lord, what of this dark ill which strikes down the healthy?"

"The healers are doing their best, captain. Yet this I say: I have chosen for the muster to take place in Älvstad instead of Dendor for more than one reason, among them is this: my healers tell me that by waiting for the ill to run its course, we isolate the muster from the scourge. Although Modru's disease is in Dendor, we will keep it from spreading."

"Do you mean to quarantine the city, my lord?"

Agron nodded. "Aye. Not only that, but round up any who handled the Modru-flung corpses and set them off in separate quarters away from the general populace until this scourge is gone. Have the healers attend to them, and set apart those who seem healthy from those who seem not. Too, burn the houses of any who fall ill."

"But my lord, much of the city is already in ashes from the Wrgish fireballs."

Agron sighed. "I know, captain, yet drastic times call for drastic measures. We would not have these ill vapors spread to others, and fire purifies all."

To Agron's left, a captain cleared his throat.

"My lord, we will be marching into Gron in the dead of winter."

Agron nodded, then said, "We will not be ready until then, captain. And yes, winter campaigns are hard. Yet what better time to invade but when least expected?"

"But what I meant, my lord, is . . . the pass may be blocked by snow."

"The pass is low through the mountains, captain, and when Halfar and I rode in, it was nearly Yule, yet, but for a dusting of snow, the way was clear. Prince Halfar said it was due to the Gwasp, warm air flowing up from that vast mire keeping the way open."

"Sire," said another captain, glancing about, "*I* will say what none else has: it will be a winter campaign, and it is said that Modru is master of the cold."

Agron looked about the table, ice in his pale blue eyes. "Then we will prepare for the cold, captain, and let Modru waste his power."

Agron's cold gaze swept from captain to captain, and each and every one nodded in assent, though some but reluctantly. "It will be a long campaign," he said, "requiring much in the way of food and other supplies. Let us now reckon the total, based on six months, one year, and two. Then we can gauge how many horses and wains we'll need, and what supplies that will add to the whole."

And so the planning went.

The following day the gates of Dendor were shut, not to keep a foe without, but to keep the people within, all but those farmers and their families who the healers could declare to be plague-free; they were allowed to return to their steads to rebuild their homes and to grow needed crops and round up any animals that had survived. Too, the king's messengers were allowed like passage, for they were critical to the coming campaign. All else needed the king's exception to pass through the gates, for Agron was determined to keep the plague from spreading beyond Dendor's walls.

April came and went, winter loosing its grasp. Fields were tilled and crops planted, while buds broke forth on the trees. Yet even as the warmth of returning spring greened the land, within the quarantined city a darkness grew, for every day more stricken were brought to the healers. The prison was filled to overflowing with the ill and the dying, where they were treated with potions of silverroot. Yet this brew proved wanting, for, just as Beau's red journal had stated, in spite of the medick, six of seven died in agony. Even so, without the brew, only one or two in a hundred would live.

Just as he had in the aftermath of the Battle of Mineholt North, Tip took up his lute and visited the wards of those who had been wounded in this battle as well. He sang and played for them and lifted their hearts. Yet when he suggested to Beau that he do the same for those afflicted by the dark ill, Beau would not let him, saying that nought but healers were allowed within the prison wards.

May came, and with it the flowers and warmth and more tilling, and the leaves broke forth, and preparations for the muster continued. Some of those wounded in the Battle of Dendor healed, while others so wounded died . . . and Tip grieved for those lost, yet he continued to play and sing.

And still the dark ill spread, houses burning in its black wake, and there was great unease in the city, for people were frightened. Some tried to leave, but were turned back, and the quarantine held firm.

In the prison and the now-sequestrated buildings ringing

'round, as the numbers of stricken grew, there was little that Beau and Phais and Loric and the healers could do but comfort the ill and dying, though one in seven survived. And it was in this month that some of the healers themselves fell ill.

"Oh, Beau, are you in danger?"

"This dark illness, Tip, it can strike anyone. —Elves excepted."

"How can this be? I thought it struck only those who handled the hacked-up corpses Modru had flung over the walls."

"No, Tip. Even people who touched no part of a corpse have fallen ill, whereas others who bore remains to the fires have stayed hale. Look, Tip, I am certain that this is the same plague that killed my parents. And they and the others who died that year certainly didn't deal with any dead bodies flung by anyone."

"Then where does it come from?"

"I dunno, Tip. Some say it's bad vapors. Others say that it's a curse. Some say it's foul creatures slipping into the bedroom at night and inflicting the unwary with an unfelt bite, while others lay it on the doorstone of Modru and all his ilk. Whatever it is, it's a scourge, all right, and one which needs to be rooted out and entirely and utterly destroyed."

"Well, Beau, whatever it is, you take care to see that it doesn't get a hold of you, eh?"

Beau turned up a hand. "Perhaps in some manner I am like the Elves, Tip. I mean, it killed my parents but completely passed me by, even though I lived in the same house with them, while distant Warrows miles away came down with it and died."

"Hoy, is *this* why you wouldn't let me play and sing for those so stricken? You thought I might come down with it?"

Beau merely shrugged.

Tip frowned. "Wull look, bucco, by your own words, it doesn't seem to matter whether a person is near or far, so I think I'll go with you when—"

"No, Tip. You can't come. I think you are safer out here than in there, and I won't have you risk it. I'll just tell the guards to throw you out."

Seeing how serious Beau was, Tipperton said no more, though late in the night a sweet voice sang outside the prison walls.

June arrived, and with it the Dendorian herald returned from Jordkeep. And word raced through the city, for riding alongside came a female, a Jordian warrior maiden no less, the emissary of King Ranor. Tall she was and coppery haired, and she wore a chain mail shirt and a helm sporting a long horsehair gaud. A sword was at her side, and a spear in her hand, and snapping in the breeze high on the haft fluttered a pennon of Jord—white horse rampant on a field of green.

"Open the gate," called the captain above as they approached, for he had his orders. And into the stricken city she fared alongside the herald, her horse spirited and prancing, and people ran out to see as she rode down the streets to the castle walls and within.

"Even as we speak, my lord, Modru's Swarms march into Jord, debarking from ships along our western shore, there at the end of the Gronfangs. Yet the balefires atop the warcairns are lit and the red flag has been borne unto all corners of our nation, and we make ready to hurl the foe back into the sea."

Agron nodded. "Lady Ryla, mayhap he does so for he believes I plan on striking Gron by marching my armies across Jord and then taking to the sea to come at his northern shore."

"Mayhap, my lord, yet I deem he would have assaulted Jord regardless. Even so, King Ranor welcomes your invasion of Modru's realm, for perhaps that will cause him to withdraw some of his Hordes back to the Iron Tower. When and if that happens, or when we defeat those who now step within our borders, King Ranor will send aid to you.

"Yet my king also says to tell you as soon as he can he plans to send warriors to Pellar to fight at the side of the High King."

"Lady Ryla, that Modru assails Jord is ill indeed, though as you say, not unexpected. And Ranor's pledge of aid is most welcome. Yet bear this word to your king and his plan to join with the High King: none knows where Blaine is. Yes, he may now be in Caer Pendwyr, and if so, he will welcome the aid. But then again he may not be in Pellar at all, for when last we knew— more than a year agone, now—he was retreating from Challerain Keep, a small garrison which fell before one of Modru's Hordes. And the ways to Caer Pendwyr from Challerain Keep are held by the Foul Folk."

The warrior maiden turned up a hand. "Even so, my lord, surely by the time we push Modru back into the sea and come unto Pellar there will be word of the High King's whereabouts. But even if there is not, sooner or later Modru will make a stab at Caer Pendwyr. And when he does, Jord will be there."

Within two days Ryla rode forth from the afflicted city of Dendor, for Agron would not have her risk the dark ill stalking those within. And she bore with her a missive: King Agron's words of thanks to King Ranor and his wishes for a successful campaign. And as the emissary rode away, trailing a packhorse after, two Warrows stood atop the north gate of Dendor and watched, their jewel-like eyes glittering at the sight of this warrior maiden of Jord.

The twentieth of June was Year's Long Day, and Beau insisted that he and Tip and Phais and Loric and Bekki hold their own private party for anyone who'd celebrated a birthday within the past year, which of course included everyone. But Tip had insisted they leave out Modru and all of his blackhearted ilk.

"Oh my," said Beau, "I never thought of that. I never thought of Modru as ever having a birthday, of being born, being a child, growing up. I wonder if his parents are proud of him."

Bekki just growled and spat.

"In fact, Beau," said Tip, "let's rule out anyone allied with Gyphon: the Hyrinians, Chabbains, Kistanians, and whoever else sides with that monster, especially the Foul Folk."

"Foul Folk? Foul Folk? Celebrate for them? Of course not, Tip. Besides, I don't think they're born, but hatched instead . . . and from rotten eggs."

Phais grinned and glanced at Loric, the Alor smiling as well.

Bekki, though, snorted and shook his head.

And so, with these disqualifications, they celebrated the birthdays of everyone who was left, which of course included Phais and Loric and Bekki and naturally their very own selves.

Later that evening, they stepped through the Elven ritual of the turn of the seasons, and this time Bekki joined the stately dance, while Tipperton joined in the singing.

Yet when the rite came to an end they were not as exhilarated as in times past, for a scourge pressed down on the city all 'round.

In the heat of early July, wagons began moving west across the land of Aven, laded with goods for the muster in Älvstad, passing quarantined Dendor by. And people stood atop the walls and called down messages to be given to their kindred afar, and the wain riders promised they would try to see their words delivered. Yet in shadowy corners of taverns within the city itself, dark mutterings whispered from mouth to ear, driven so by grim forebodings and sullen unease.

And as July commenced, farmers began bringing cheese and eggs and meat and produce to market. Yet they were stopped just without the city walls, for the gates yet remained closed, and only the king's buyers were allowed outside to purchase the city's needs and to send the crofters home again. When the farmers were gone, soldiers drove wagons out to bear the goods into the city for distribution within.

Too, in July messengers came riding from afar, carrying news of the war, but of High King Blaine's whereabouts there was as of yet no word.

In the early days of this month as well, Tip and Bekki prepared for their journey to Nordlake. Six ponies in all they decided to take: two for riding and four for carrying supplies—food for the most part and grain for the ponies. They would take as well two sets of climbing gear, for Bekki said that the golden mint grew in the cracks on cliffs of sheer stone. Tipperton paled when he heard of this, yet he had climbed sheer faces before, when Phais had trained Beau and him to scale the bluffs of Arden Vale. They added to their cargo the tools to harvest the mint, and twine and cloth for ripping into swathes to bundle it in—eleven sprigs to a bundle as per Delgar's written instructions in Beau's leather-bound book—and ten large sacks to pack the bundles within and lade them on the ponies, should there be that much golden mint to harvest, though Bekki doubted it would be so.

"Oh lor'," breathed Beau. "If you fill but one of these sacks, I think I could treat the entire city to a cup of gwynthyme and silverroot tea, should absolutely everyone fall ill."

"The entire city?" asked Tip, his eyes wide.

"Aye, Tip. A little goes a long way."

They prepared to set out on the twelfth of the month, the day of the July moon, for as Tip had said, "It seems only fitting, since our entire mission for the golden mint seems governed by the phases of Elwydd's light."

Bright dawn of the twelfth came to a cloudless sky and, after a hearty breakfast, Tip and Bekki carried to the stables the goods for their journey, making repeated trips to do so. By midmorn the riding ponies were saddled and the pack animals laded and at last all was ready. Beau and Phais and Loric came from comforting the ill to say farewell.

"Now you take care, bucco," said Beau, "for as Bekki here says, there's Foul Folk yet afoot in Aven, to say nothing of those in the Grimwall."

"Wull, Beau, it's not me and Bekki I'm worried about but you instead . . . here as you are in a plague-ridden city."

"Oh, we'll be just fine, Tip," said Beau, turning to Phais, "won't we, now?"

Yet in that very moment the Dara's face blenched, and with a moan she fell to her knees, Loric collapsing beside her, the Alor covering his face in his hands and crying out in distress.

Phais reached out blindly, shock and agony and grief whelming her features, tears flooding her eyes, and with a cry of despair she fell back in a swoon.

"What is it? What is it?" cried Beau, springing forward, but Bekki was first to the Dara's side, indecision and anguish on his face. The Dwarf looked to Beau for aid and called out to the Warrow, yet what he said could not be heard above Loric's howl of torment.

And Tip on his knees in front of the Alor reached up and gently pulled Loric's hands away from his face . . . to reveal an aspect of bleak desolation as great choking sobs tore from Loric's very soul. And the Elf reached out and clasped the buccan to him and wept as if he were nought but a child.

And Dara Phais, though consciousness had fled her, wept tears of anguish as well.

Shaken, Loric and Phais gripped one another's hands, their lips yet drawn thin by distress.

"It was like . . . a death rede, oh, but different, so different," said Phais.

"A deathcry," said Loric, his features twisting once again into anguish with but the memory of it. "A deathcry of hundreds and hundreds."

"Pardon, Lord Loric," said Bekki. "Hundreds and hundreds of . . . ?"

"Lian, Lord Bekki. Lian," said Loric, choking on his own words. "A wailing deathcry of hundreds upon hundreds of Lian, blowing like an icy wind through our very souls."

"What does it mean?" asked Beau. "What does such a dreadful thing mean?"

Phais looked at Loric, her eyes flooding once again with tears, and she said, "That a great disaster has occurred somewhere and countless of our kindred have perished."

Tip and Bekki decided to stay in Dendor that day to comfort their bereaved companions, though Phais and Loric asked not. Yet it was plain to see that their solace was needed, for both Lian would shed tears at erratic times, and a touch or a word or an embrace acted to ease the pain. Even Bekki gave comfort, though when he embraced Dara Phais, his own expression was one of distress, either that or entirely unreadable.

And none knew what had happed, yet when Beau speculated that it was Modru's doing, Phais shook her head and said, "Nay, my friend, something of this enormity can only be the work of Gyphon Himself."

In the midafternoon of that clear July day a thunderous boom rolled over the land below and across the sky above, echoing from building and wall, rattling dish and window and roof alike, jarring the city entire. Then it was gone, the air still once again. And all looked at one another in startlement and fear, yet none knew whence it came or its cause.

The following morning, pressed by their mission, Tip and Bekki again saddled two ponies and laded four others with goods. And saying farewell for a second time, they set out at last for Nordlake afar.

They rode out through the west gate, King Agron's pass letting them through, Captain Brud personally escorting them to the bridge, the wound on his face all but healed, leaving a long scar behind. And as they rode away, Tip turned and waved at Beau and Phais and Loric standing on the wall above, the Elves yet wan, yet pale.

"Take care, Tip," called Beau. "You, too, Bekki."

"You as well," shouted Tipperton back, "and we'll bring you some golden mint."

And then he turned and faced west, he and Bekki riding away, trailing four ponies after. West they rode and west, across the summer land, leaving behind three close friends in a quarantined city rife with a dark affliction.

Just past the noontide there came a rolling boom, knelling as would a diminished echo of the sound of the day before.

Tip looked at Bekki. "Did you hear that?"

"Aye, I did."

"Oh, Bekki, you don't suppose another disaster has occurred, do you?"

Bekki frowned and shook his head. "That I cannot say, Tipperton, for I am not an Elf."

And in the silent deeps of the night, as Tipperton stood midwatch, there came to his ears another faint boom, this one diminished even further. He fretted and wondered if he should waken Bekki, but in the end decided not, for neither could do aught regardless.

15

*A*t first I thought they were falling victim to the plague," said Tipperton, urging his pony around a tangle of brush, two pack ponies following. "Even though both Loric and Phais had said Elves don't fall ill to the dark scourge."

Bekki nodded but otherwise did not reply.

"It must be awful, this 'gift' of theirs—more like a curse if you ask me—to know when someone dies."

"This was not a `Death Rede' sent from one Elf to another," said Bekki, "but a thing much worse: not a single 'someone' calling out in death, but hundreds and hundreds crying out instead."

Tipperton shivered, as if struck by a sudden chill. "Still, I would think it somehow connected to their gift. . . . How horrible it must have been: like a ghastly wind blowing cold through the souls of all Elvenkind."

Bekki grunted, then said, "I cannot but think the thunderous sounds we heard—the first one and then the one after—are in some manner connected to the deaths of so many."

"Oh, Bekki, did I tell you I heard another just like it only fainter in the depths of the night?"

Bekki looked at Tip.

"Three or four candlemarks past mid of night, I would say," added Tip.

"Hmm, three rolling thunders in all." Brow furrowed, Bekki fell into thought, then said, "Mayhap as loud as was the first, mayhap the sound came to the walls of the world and was echoed back. . . . Yes, that must be it, Tipperton, for it would account for each echo being less than the one before."

Tip shrugged, saying, "Or if the Elves are right and the world is truly a ball, a sphere, perhaps the noise circles all the way 'round and passes by again."

Bekki snorted in disbelief as on they rode, angling slightly north of west.

"Oh, Bekki, whether an echo from the walls of the world or the sound passing 'round the world, if we are right, it means there's not another disaster, or two or three, but the sound of the first knelling over and again."

They rode another mile, and then Bekki said, "Aye, Tipperton, yet think: if the sound reaches all the way to the walls of the world to echo again and again, then what a terrible blast it must have been."

As Tip stood the midwatch, just ere mid of night, another faint thunder grumbled. *Another echo from the walls of the world? That or the sound ringing 'round.*

Onward they rode, and in late morn of the third day from Dendor, Tip thought he heard a very dim echo of the boom again, yet he couldn't be sure.

"I say, Bekki, did you hear that?"

"Hear what?"

"The sound, so weak as to be all but silent."

Bekki shook his head.

They rode a bit farther, then Tip said, "A final echo from the walls of the world, do you think?"

"That, or distant thunder," replied Bekki, then he looked at the clear July day and shook his head and the two of them rode onward.

On the fourth day out from Dendor, Tip looked up at the sky and said, "Ho, Bekki. Does it seem to you that the day isn't as bright as it ought to be?"

Bekki nodded. "Aye, though I see no mist, no fog, no clouds."

But as they fared west, the light diminished, as if the sun itself somehow weakened.

That evening, a layer of clouds began to form high above.

"There is our answer," said Bekki.

"Answer?"

"Aye. It is preparing to rain."

"And . . . ?"

"And the light grew dimmer and dimmer today as the rain started gathering above," declared Bekki.

"Perhaps," said Tip, uncertain.

They rode awhile in silence, then Bekki said, "There is a thicket ahead where we can camp."

But Tip was staring beyond the thicket at the cloud-filled sky made bloodred by the setting sun, and a shiver went down his spine.

It began to rain in the night, and when Tip was awakened for the midwatch, Bekki said, "There is something strange about this rain, Tipperton."

"Oh?"

"Aye. The drops are cloudy."

"Cloudy?"

In the lanternlight Bekki held out a tin cup filled with rainwater.

Tip looked. "Lor', Bekki, it's cloudy all right, positively dusty looking. What do you think it means?"

Bekki shook his head. "That, my friend, I do not know."

It rained throughout the night, and continued the next morning, and by the noontide the drops falling on the ponies and cloaks left long smears behind.

"Adon, Bekki, but it's raining mud."

"More like rain through rock dust," replied Bekki.

"Rain through rock dust?"

"Aye. In the quarries, when it rains, it leaves long grey smears like these."

"But how would rock dust get up in the sky? I mean, are there quarries nearby?"

Bekki shook his head. "None I know of. —Even if there were, by this time all the rock dust would have been washed from the air, yet this is still coming down."

On they rode through a rain falling stone-grey.

The next day dawned to a breathtaking sunrise, the entire vault shifting in stages from indigo to violet to lavender to a bloodred to peach, and then the sun rose in a pale grey-blue sky. Still the morning seemed wan, in spite of the striking dawn.

The day itself grew darker as westerly they rode, as of a grey curtain being drawn up from the west and riding over the sky above.

"Adon, Bekki, but do you think it more dust? Rock dust?"

"Aye, riding on the high winds, it is."

"Gray on grey it is," said Tipperton, turning about. "Running over the sky, behind as well as ahead."

All morning the grey deepened, and by midafternoon it was as if dusk had come, and the sun was dim in the sky.

And then rock dust began to drift down like snow on a July day, coating all things with a layer of pale grey.

"We need cover our mouths with cloth," said Bekki, "and cloth over the noses of the ponies, too."

"I'll do it," said Tip, dismounting. And pulling some of the linen from the sacks, he ripped seven wide strips, gaining the swathes needed to cover the noses of the ponies and Bekki and himself. "Lor', Bekki, lor', what can be the cause?"

"I have never seen such ere now, Tipperton, though I have heard that firemountains at times belch out such dust, or so say the old tales."

"Firemountains, eh?" said Tipperton, glancing into the darkening sky. "I've heard of them but have never seen one. Is there a firemountain nearby?"

"The nearest I know of is Dragonslair in the Grimwall Mountains," replied Bekki, "though I do not think it the cause of this."

"Why not? I mean, if it is a firemountain—"

"The winds are wrong," said Bekki. "This rock dust comes from the west, whereas Dragonslair is far to the east of Kachar, east of Dendor, a thousand miles or more. Too, I am told the fire of that mountain does not burn, though wisps of steam are said to flow into the sky now and again."

"Oh," said Tip, now tying a cloth over his own mouth and nose. "By the bye, just why is it called Dragonslair?"

"It is said that Black Kalgalath holes up in that mountain," said Bekki.

"Black Kalgalath? Isn't he the greatest Dragon of all?"

"Mayhap it's Daagor instead," replied Bekki, now binding a cloth across his face.

"Daagor the renegade?"

Bekki grunted, tying a knot behind.

"I suppose that's neither here nor there," said Tip, his voice a bit muffled by the covering. "Instead, if this is caused by a firemountain somewhere downwind, just which firemountain could it be? Are there such in Gron? Rian? Or farther still in distant Dalara or even beyond in Thol?"

Bekki shook his head. "The only one west I have heard of is Karak on the Isle of Atala, but that is somewhere in the Weston Ocean and far, far removed from here—four thousand miles in the least. Too far I would think to be the cause of this."

Mouths and noses covered, Bekki and Tip donned their all-weather cloaks and mounted the ponies and began riding west through the drifting down dust, and after a while, Tip said, "Tell me, Bekki, what causes firemountains to spew?"

Bekki shrugged. "I know not, though some have said the earth shudders when firemountains roar, yet whether the shudder causes the roaring or the roaring causes the shudder, I cannot say."

They rode another mile before Bekki said, "I suppose the Stone Giants would know."

"Know what?"

"What causes firemountains to spew," replied Bekki.

"Oh," said Tip, brushing rock dust from his shoulders and thighs, a losing effort at best. "You know, until the Mages talked about them in Dendor, I always thought Stone Giants a myth."

"Not so, Tipperton. Not so," said Bekki. "Did I not say that First Durek was saved by the Utruni, the Stone Giants?"

Tip turned up his hands. "I thought it but a tale grown tall in the telling and becoming legend o'er time."

Bekki barked a laugh. "If that were so, then Kraggen-cor would not have been discovered."

"Oh?"

"Aye. First Durek—"

"First Durek? This is Breakdeath Durek, right?"

Bekki nodded. "Aye, we call him that. Deathbreaker Durek, too."

"Why do you call him 'Deathbreaker'?"

"Recall, Tipperton, we Châkka believe that after death, spirits are reborn to walk the earth again, some more often than others. The spirit of First Durek is one which breaks the bonds of Death often."

"Oh, I see. Well then, go on with the tale of the Stone Giants and Durek and Kraggen-cor."

Bekki cleared his throat. "First Durek was exploring in the Grimwalls when he was assaulted by a band of Grg. Howling in glee, from a high stone ledge they flung him into the *Vorvor* and—"

"Oh wait, Bekki, just what is this, um, Vorvor?"

Bekki growled and held up a hand. "Tipperton, I will never get through this tale if you keep interrupting."

Tip's fingers flew to the dust-laden cloth over his mouth as if to seal his lips, yet he still managed to say, "But, Bekki, you keep using terms I don't know. It's not as if you and I had the same schooling."

Bekki sighed. "Perhaps you are right, Tipperton. Perhaps I need tell it as do the Châkka Loremasters."

"Oh please, Bekki, and I promise not to interrupt again."

Behind the cloth over mouth and nose, Bekki smiled. Then, casting his thoughts back to his tutelage in Mineholt North, Bekki said, "On the northeast quadrant of the Quadran stands a mountain of blue stone— oh, not that it is truly blue, but it bears a tinge of that color. The mountain itself is known as *Ghatan*, or in the common tongue, Loftcrag.

"In a great fold of stone on Ghatan's southern flank stands the Vorvor, a whirling churning gurge deeply entwined in Châkka legend: there a secret river bursts forth from the understone of Ghatan to rage around a great rock basin and plunge down into the dark again; this is the Vorvor, a great gaping whirlpool raving endlessly, sucking at the sky and funneling deep into the black depths below.

"When the world was young and First Durek trod its margins, he came unto this place. And vile Ükhs, shouting in glee, captured him and from a high stone ledge they flung him into the spin, and the sucking maw drew him down. None else had ever survived that fate; yet First Durek did, though how, it is not said. To the very edge of the Realm of Death, and perhaps beyond, he was taken, yet Life at last found him on a rocky shore within a vast, undelved, undermountain realm; and First Durek strode where none else had gone before—treading through that Kingdom which was to become Kraggen-cor. But at last he came again unto the light of day, and it is said that *Daün* Gate stands upon the very spot where he walked out through the mountainside.

"Many have wondered how he managed to live for days, weeks, even months in what to them is nought but a cold stone realm, and to them it remains an enigma. But the Châkka know that he was aided by the Utruni—the Stone Giants—for Utruni admire the work the Châkkakyth do in the undermountain realm, unlike that of the Grg, who destroy the living stone rather than enhance it.

"And so, aided by the Stone Giants, Durek survived to found the great holt of Kraggen-cor, the mightiest Châkkaholt of the five Châkkakyth and one of the few places on Mithgar where starsilver is found.

"Long have the Ükhs rued the day they cast Durek from that high stone ledge, for on that day the enmity with Squam began, more deadly by far than the ravening whirl of the roaring Vorvor."

With eyes wide, Tipperton looked at Bekki. "But Kraggen-cor has been a holt for millennia."

Bekki nodded. "Indeed."

Tip shrugged. "Are you telling me that something which happened thousands of years past still drives you and your kindred to kill Foul Folk?"

Bekki clenched a fist and gritted, "He who seeks the enmity of the Châkka finds it, forever!"

Tipperton shook his head in incomprehension. "I always thought old grudges must die last in the endless days of time."

"Strange will be the day a Châk forgives and forgets."

They rode in silence for a while, the grey stone dust drifting down and down. Finally Tipperton said, "Tell me if you can, how did Durek survive? How did he see in the darkness below? Do you know?"

Bekki shrugged. "As to how he did see, there is a glowing lichen which grows on some rocks nigh understone rivers. Too, there is a phosphorescent moss in some of the caverns. Kraggencor in places has both of these. We use a preparation, a leaching, of the lichen and moss to make the Châkka lanterns, wherein no fire need be kindled, nor fuel consumed.

"As to what he did eat: blind fish and water weed, the glowing moss, mushrooms—"

"Mushrooms?"

"Aye, they grow at times in the very same caverns where the moss is found."

"Oh. I see. —But wait. The fish. Did he eat them raw?"

"Aye," replied Bekki, "that and other living things, for he could kindle no fire."

"Other living things?"

"Blind beetles, spiders, wor—"

"Enough, Bekki," cried Tip, shuddering.

Bekki barked a laugh . . .

. . . and on they rode through drifting down stone dust under the darkling sky.

They came to the village of *Grönkulle*, nought but a hamlet on a rounded hill, all the buildings now covered with the stone dust, the town overall a pale grey. But both Tip and Bekki were glad of the village, for as they rode through the powder-covered streets and past dust-laden, canvas-topped wagons, they found it had an inn.

Dismounting, they tied up the ponies at the railing, and through the door and into the common room they trod, shaking dust from cloak and clothing and removing the cloth from their faces. Men sitting at several of the tables—men in armor and bearing weapons—drew in their breaths at the sight of the two.

Moving on inward, Tip and Bekki halted before a man in an apron stooping over and whisking a pile of grey dirt into a dustpan.

"*Det är en mork dag vilken bringa du—*" Straightening up, the innkeeper's words jerked to a halt when he saw who these new patrons were.

"Sorry, but we don't speak Avenian," said Tipperton, stamping dust from his boots.

"Um, I was saying, it is a dark day which brings you to my inn," replied the 'keep, setting aside the pan and whisk broom. "What will it be?"

"Be?" growled Bekki.

"I mean, what will you have? Rooms? Food? Drink? We've not but a couple of rooms left"—he nodded toward the men at the tables—"what with the drivers and guards heading for the muster, as it were."

"All three, and a bath, too," said Tipperton, briskly rubbing his head, stone dust flying, the innkeeper frowning as it drifted to the floor.

"Have you someone to see to our ponies?" asked Bekki.

"Jarl!" shouted the innkeeper. "*Ponnis er ute gata.*"

A young lad came scrambling down the stairs, his eyes flying wide when he saw the guests, but then he bolted out the door, Tipperton calling after: "Bring in our gear!" Yet whether the lad heard or understood, he did not know.

"A Dwarf and a Waldan: we don't get your like too often 'round here," said the innkeeper, bustling behind the bar. At Bekki's scowl, the man blurted, "Oh, not that there's aught wrong with it—"

"How many other Warrows have you put up?" asked Tip, grinning. "Or for that matter, how many other Dwarves?"

"Well, now that I think of it, you two are the first."

"Hah!" barked Bekki.

The 'keep stooped down and looked under the bar. "Um, will you be wanting one room or two? And will that be a bath before or after a meal and a mug?"

"One room is fine," said Bekki.

"The bath before," added Tip. "I've got to get free of this dust."

The innkeeper straightened up, latchkey in hand. "Top of the stairs, third room on the right. The bathing room is out back. Jarl will see to the water."

As the two made their way up the stairs, from a nearby table one of the patrons stood and hurried from the room.

Quickly the news spread throughout the village:

One of the Litenfolk—

—Travelling with a Dvärg, no less—

—From Kachar? Them what saved Dendor?—
—The little one, can he be the one?—
—The one what the kingsherald told us about?—
—Him what snuck through the whole of the Horde?—
And as the news spread, folks came through the still-falling dust and into *Den Grönkulle Vädrshus*—The Greenknoll Inn—though now it and the hill it stood on was anything but green.

"Aye, some came past, months agone, but they steered wide," said one of the men.

"Running for the Grimwall, we think," added the woman at his side.

"Running for the ford, I shouldn't wonder," opined another, lifting her mug.

Tip shoved away his empty wooden bowl, the stew having gone down well. As he took up a chunk of bread, Bekki said, "The ford?"

"Aye, over the Argon, west and north a deal."

"More west than north," amended another.

Bekki glanced at Tip, then said, "The ford a bit west of Nordlake?"

"Aye," came the response.

"If that's where you are headed," added the innkeeper, "then I'd advise not. But if you are bound to go regardless, then watch your necks."

A murmur of agreement muttered 'round the room.

"And if it's to Nordlake you be bound, watch out for the *Vattenvidunder*," cautioned another.

This brought derisive laughter from some and wide-eyed agreement from others.

Tip frowned. "What is this, um, Vatten—?"

"Vattenvidunder," said the innkeeper, refreshing Tip's mug of ale, then Bekki's. The 'keep cocked an eyebrow at several in the crowd, and added, "A water monster which some believe lives in Nordlake."

"He does! He does!" averred the one who had first spoken the name. "He comes up the Argon from the sea now and again and into Nordlake. Why? For what? Who knows?"

"Oh, Norge," pooh-poohed someone in the crowd, "and just how does he get past the shallows of the fords?"

"He comes and goes in flood times," huffed Norge.

Tip shook his head. "Beg pardon, Goodmaster Norge, but flood or no, a creature coming up the Argon from the sea would have to swim over Bellon Falls, and that's a thousand-foot-high cataract. I know, for I have seen it."

"Wull, then he swims around it."

Again Tip shook his head. "I'm sorry, but there are no rivers 'round."

This brought a laugh from several in the crowd, and someone called out, "See!"

Norge frowned and jutted out his jaw. "Wull, whether or no he comes from the sea, still there's a Vattenvidunder in Nord-lake, for my da, ere he died, bless his spirit, saw it."

"Or so he said," called out someone, laughing as he did so.

Norge leapt to his feet, fists clenched, but Tip called out, "A song. I'll play a song." And he reached for his silver-stringed lute as a cheer greeted his words.

A glare in his eyes, Norge sat back down, and thus was a fight averted.

The next morning, stone dust yet drifted down from the grey sky above. The wagon drivers and guards decided to wait another day or so, but Bekki and Tip rode onward, for the moon did not tarry in its path, nor would golden mint pause in its growth, though what this falling grey might do to the gwyn-thyme, neither Tip nor Bekki could say.

"Rûpt and water monsters and falling rock dust," said Tip as they left the bounds of Grönkulle. "I wonder what else lies in our path."

"Dust, yes; Squam, perhaps; but Vattenvidunder? I think not," said Bekki.

"Oh? And why not the Vatten—, uh, Vatten—"

"Vidunder," completed Bekki. "I think not because I have been to Nordlake, and no monster did I see."

"Oh. —Well I've never seen a Stone Giant, yet you tell me they are real."

"Ah, but, Tipperton, you have never spent most of your life under the living stone, as have I."

"And, Bekki, you have never spent most of your life along the shores of Nordlake."

"True," admitted Bekki.

"Well then?"

Beneath his face covering, Bekki frowned but held his tongue.

They rode awhile in silence, but then Tip said, "Have you seen a Stone Giant?"

Bekki shook his head, dust drifting off his cloak hood. "Nay."

"Oh," said Tip, disappointed. "I was just wondering what they did. I mean, I've heard some of the legends—how they can move through stone, how they have real gemstones for eyes—but I've never heard of their purpose. I mean, why are there Stone Giants?"

Bekki laughed. "Ah, my friend, let me ask you this: why are there Waerans?"

Now Tip laughed under his protective covering. "Unh, I see what you mean."

They rode a bit farther and came to a stream, the water silted grey. Under an oak, Bekki found a pool, and with swipes of his hands he cleared the surface. As they watched the ponies drink, Tip said, "Back in Dendor the Mages told me that a Wizard named Farrin is seeking the Stone Giants and if he finds them he will try to enlist them to aid the Allies in this war against Modru."

Bekki grunted, then said, "Against Gyphon you mean."

"Oh, right."

Bekki stepped to one side and relieved himself. Then he said, "Mage Farrin is not likely to succeed in his mission, for even though the Utruni aided First Durek, and even though they are said to ward the Kammerling, they remain aloof from the affairs of Mithgar."

"That's what Ridich said—I mean, about them being above the concerns of Mithgar, or, as he put it, in this case far below."

Now Tip stepped away to relieve himself. As he came back to the pool he said, "You said something about a Kammerling?"

Bekki nodded.

"Well then, Bekki. What's that all about? Look, tell me everything you know about the Utruni."

Bekki barked a laugh. "Ha! What I know of the Utruni would not fill a thimble."

"Even so, Bekki, surely it is more than I know."

Bekki sighed. "All right, my friend, this is what I've been told:

"Indeed they do have gemstones for eyes, and they dwell in the living stone; in that, you are correct. Yet there is this, too: it is said they can somehow move through solid rock itself, and they work along the faces of the deep stone, where rock slides past rock, and they ease the tension that builds up. By doing so it is said that great earthquakes are avoided, though just how, I cannot imagine. On the other hand, I am told the Utruni believe that deep within the rock, perhaps at the very heart of Mithgar itself, a great Stone Giant slumbers, and it is when he turns over in his sleep the land quakes. Just how that jibes with the easing of tension along the deep rock faces is anyone's guess.

"There is not much more I can tell you of the Stone Giants, other than it is said the Utruni ward the Rage Hammer, the Kammerling itself. It is believed Adon gave them this token of power to watch over until the time comes for its wielding. Just who is to wield it, I cannot say, but its purpose is well-known among my folk."

"What is it? I mean the Kammerling. And what is its purpose?"

"It is a great silveron war hammer, said to be forged of star-silver by Adon Himself. And it is intended to be used against the greatest Dragon of all."

"Oh, that's, um, Black Kalgalath, right?"

"Or mayhap Daagor," replied Bekki.

"Oh my. Even with the Kammerling, one would have to be mad to go up against either of them. I mean, who can oppose a Dragon? Fire and all. Power and all. Monsters that they are."

All ponies watered, again they set out for the distant ford.

"We saw one, you know," said Tipperton.

"One what?"

"Dragon. Skail of the Barrens, or so did Phais and Loric say. Huge. Devastating. Alone, it drove the entire Dwarven army of Drimmen-deeve back into their Dwarvenholt."

Bekki growled in suppressed rage.

"No sir, I don't want to ever have to face a Dragon," said Tip, and on through the sifting fall they rode.

For four days the stone dust fell from the sky, covering all in a thin layer of silt, the amount of fall diminishing with each day. And during these same days, the land grew chill, for the sun was wan above, and July summer was fled away though July itself yet lay on the land.

On the fifth day it began to rain, the drops yet clouded grey. For three more days it drizzled and stormed and misted and pelted, washing the world with water, the silt being carried by tumbling streams northerly toward the Argon.

And on the next day in a chill morning fog, leading their ponies, Tip and Bekki crept to the banks of that river, yet no warding Spawn did they find. But the river, the river itself, it was flooded, the water boiling past, a racing tumult under a thick and cold blanket of enshrouding grey vapor.

"Kruk!" snarled Bekki. "We can't cross in that."

"Any other fords nearby?" asked Tipperton.

Bekki shook his head. "The one at Älvstad is far to the west—sixteen or seventeen days—and it is no doubt flooded, too."

"What about the ferry at Kaagor? Isn't it closer than Älvstad? Someone said that Jordian warrior maiden told it had been rebuilt."

"Aye, Captain Brud said the ferry once more crosses the Argon. Too, he told me it is warded by two companies of

Agron's best. And you are right: it is closer than the ford at Älvstad. Twelve or thirteen days from here. Indeed we could use it, have the Squam not burned it again . . . unlikely with Agron's soldiers on guard. But heed, even if we set out today, by the time we got there and back, surely we would have long past crossed through this ford, and it would have been a lengthy trip for nought, nigh another month altogether."

"A month? Oh my. Well then, there's nothing for it," said Tip, "we'll just have to wait."

Bekki sighed. "It may be many a day ere we can cross, Tipperton. Pray to Garlon He sends no more rain."

Even as Bekki said it, the sky began to drizzle, chill water falling through the clasping fog.

16

*B*eau and Phais and Loric stood a long while, watching as Tip and Bekki rode away from the walls of Dendor. But at last Beau glanced at the sun and said, "Well, I've rounds to make and more silverroot to brew, though little good it does."

Phais looked at Loric, then said to Beau, "For the next while, thou must do without our aid, for Agron has granted us permission to go to the solitude of the hills to mourn."

"The hills?"

"Aye, our old campsite on the south ridge. If thou dost need us, thou wilt find us in the stand of evergreen."

"How long will you be gone?"

"Two days, mayhap three, no more, for the want here is great. Even so, we need the time alone to come to terms with our grief." Phais looked to the west, where Tip and Bekki could yet be seen, though she did not note them, her mind looking elsewhere. "So many souls crying out," she murmured. "So very many souls."

"Well then," said Beau, "you two take all the time you need. I'm certain the other healers and I can manage."

Loric nodded and took Phais by the hand. "Come, chier."

With one last look at Tip and Bekki—"Oh, I *do* hope they find some gwynthyme"—Beau set off for the prison, while the Alor and Dara made their way toward the stables.

The fresh scent of pine about them mingled with the smell of a small cedar fire ablaze in a circle of stones, and with birds flitting through the July air, some singing on the wing, Phais and Loric sat in deep meditation, he on one side of the ring, she opposite. The sun had passed the zenith, and all was calm, there in the dappled shade.

Yet of a sudden there came a surging boom, as if distant thunder rumbled across the clear blue sky.

Phais's eyes flew open. "Didst thou hear, chier?"

Over the small flame, Loric looked at her. "Aye." He frowned in concentration. "It seemed an echo of the rolling blast of yester's Day of Anguish."

Phais nodded and said, "Yet this time I felt no . . . no deathcry beforehand. Oh, Loric, was it an echo, or dost thou think another disaster has occurred? One not involving the death of our kind?"

Loric lowered his head into his hands. "That I cannot say."

Phais moved about the circle and embraced Loric, saying, "What has happened, chier? Tell me, what has happened."

Loric did not reply.

Freshly cut pine boughs lay in a circle where once burned a fire, and a nearly full moon sailed through the stars above, the glittering spangle wheeling slowly across a sky made indigo by the bright waning moon. Once again Phais and Loric knelt in meditation, having sung an Elven Deathsong for those who had passed beyond, and now only the sound of calling crickets filled the air of the light-washed night.

Yet another rolling boom surged past, diminished from the one before.

Phais looked at Loric, but he did not move, his eyes remaining closed. She, too, closed her eyes, and silently asked Elwydd to calm her heart.

In late midmorn of the second day of meditation and fasting, once more the sky rumbled, well diminished from that of the night before.

"Again," said Loric.

"And again I felt no deathcry," said Phais.

"E'en so, 'tis the same sound, though greatly quelled."

"Aye," agreed Phais.

Late that night came the sound again, even more attenuated.

Another day they fasted, the third of their retreat, and on this day there came but a single faint boom, this one in late midmorn.

*   *   *

The next day Phais and Loric broke camp to return to Dendor. Yet as they rode back toward the city, Loric said, "Look, chier, the sky: it faintly darkens."

Phais nodded. "As of a caul being drawn over the vault above, west to east it flows."

"Mayhap there is a distant fire," said Loric.

"Mayhap," replied Phais, and on to Dendor they rode.

Yet ere they reached the city, again there came a boom.

That evening, Loric saddled a steed and rode away from the city, his pass permitting egress. And when he was well clear of the sounds of Dendor, he waited 'neath a darkening sky. And as twilight drew on the land, and night swept across the caul-laden vault, there came a faint rolling boom, this one even more quelled.

Later that night rain began falling, borne on a western wind, and in the rain, the rain itself, the water was clouded grey.

All the next day, the grey water fell. Even so, nigh the unseen sunset, Loric rode to the plains, and though the rain fell steadily, once again he heard the sound.

Sometime in the night the grey rain stopped.

And in the darkness just ere the next dawn, Loric awakened Phais and said, "Ride with me, chier."

Away from the city, away from the sounds of man they fared, out under the open sky.

And in that dawn, again came the sound, though even to Elven ears it was so faint as to be nigh gone.

"Oh, Loric, nine times has come the sound, each time diminished from the time before. Dost thou think nine calamities in all have occurred?"

"Nay, chier, 'tis this I think: nine times in all we have heard the sound, each time as that of the first, though weakened and weakened more with each passing. I deem it is but the sound of the very first blast we hear over and again, a blast so loud it circles 'round both sides of the world, the far girth and the near, and comes to our ears anew, though diminished each time."

Of a sudden the Dara's face fell and twisted into anguish. "But, oh, my love, what a terrible blast it must have been to have sounded 'round the world nine times."

Loric reached out and embraced her, saying, "I ween it still echoes, chier, but now too faintly to hear."

*   *   *

As the pair rode back to the city in the light of a spectacular sunrise, Phais shifted her gaze from the east and peered west. "Loric, does it seem to thee that the sky darkens yon?"

Loric looked. "Aye, it does at that. Strange, I would say, for the rain should have washed the sky clean of the caul, yet this may be another coming."

In through the southern gate they rode and onward to the stable. After grooming the steeds and eating breakfast with Beau, to the prison they fared, bracing themselves for another day of agony and dying.

The day itself grew darker as the sun rose up in the sky, as of a shadowy curtain being drawn up from the west and riding over the vault above and on toward the east. Throughout the morning the darkness deepened and grew deeper still as the noontide came and went, and by midafternoon it was as if a gloom had come over the world, for the sun was dim in the sky. And lanterns and candles were lighted, though it was a July day.

In that same July midafternoon, into the prison wards a healer came rushing. "Adon, but if I didn't know better, I would say the sky is falling."

Beau looked at Phais and said, "Let us find Loric and go out and see just what this calamity is."

When they reached the prison yard, they found pale grey dust drifting down from the sky above, coating all things with a powdery layer.

"Huah," exclaimed Beau, running his finger through. "Like the stuff that came down with the rain, though this is dry whereas that was wet." The buccan looked at the Lian. "Just what do you think it is?"

Loric, too, ran his finger through the dust. "I have seen this once, or its like, on the island of Ryodo, nigh Jinga far to the east. There it was the spew of a blasting firemountain blowing into the sky."

Beau ran his finger through the dust again and rubbed it against his thumb. "I say, do you think this is the blast of a firemountain, too? If so, which one."

Loric looked at Phais. "The only one to the west I know of is—"

"Karak on Atala," said Phais, her eyes wide in horror. "Oh Adon, Adon." She clutched Loric to her.

"What?" cried Beau. "What is it?"

Loric embraced Phais and with tears in his eyes said, "The firemountain of Karak is on the isle of Atala in the reach of the Weston Ocean. This rock dust falling from the sky, the blast we heard, oh, the mighty blast, and the deathcry of a thousand or more Elves, these could only have come from Atala. Karak itself must have exploded, for nought else explains all. Karak exploded, destroying not only itself but all life at hand: the Elves of the city of Duellin; the Elves of Darda Immer, the Brightwood of Atala; Humans and Dwarves and Wee Folk and Hidden Ones as well. Karak must have exploded, and if it did so, then not only people and plants and animals perished, but with a blast so mighty the island itself must be gone." .

"Oh my," said Beau, peering at the falling dust, "if an entire island exploded and vanished, what did it do to the ocean all 'round?"

Still the grey descended down and down, while Loric clutched Phais and they wept.

17

The rain fell down through the morning vapor, and Tip and Bekki led their ponies easterly into the woods, well off the trace leading to the ford. Finding a suitable site, they began setting up camp. As he constructed a lean-to, Bekki said, "A week or so, and then if the river doesn't fall, we will hie for the Kaagor Ferry . . . that or build a raft." Bekki lashed another pine bough in place. "One way or another, we will get across."

Tip paused a moment in his care of the ponies. "I don't know much about making rafts, Bekki, but if that's what it takes, I'm willing. But I say, couldn't we swim it? I'm fairly good in the water. And the ponies, well—"

"Swim?" blurted Bekki, blanching. "Nay, Tipperton. Swimming is not common among Châkka."

"You can't, uh, er, that is . . ."

Bekki shook his head.

Tip turned back to the pony at hand. "Oh well, then, if it comes to building a raft, I'm willing."

Bekki grunted and frowned. "With five ponies, it will take a large one . . . either that or several trips."

"Not really, Bekki," said Tipperton. "Just one."

"One?"

"Certainly. The raft will serve to keep you and me and our goods dry as we paddle across. But the ponies, now, well that's an altogether different thing: as I started to say, they can swim, so all we need do is tether them behind as we float from this side to that."

"Um," said Bekki, nodding. "Still, I would rather ride a pony across the ford than ride a raft over. Too many things can go

wrong otherwise: a pony could panic; some might resist swimming and tug the opposite way; one of us could fall in. . . . Nay,
if it comes to rafting, let us build one and haul the ponies
across."

Tip shrugged and turned up his hands. "As you wish, Bekki.
As you wish. But say, if it takes several trips, that will be a lot
of paddling."

"Nay, Tipperton, instead we will tie ropes to trees on each
side and swing across on the current. Paddle across once; haul
and swing thereafter."

"It's a wide river," said Tip. "Have we enough rope?"

"We will find a narrower place, should it come to rafting,"
replied Bekki.

Tip frowned. "Even so . . ."

The drizzle ended by midday, yet a grey pall hung over all;
whether it was from a rain-gloomed sky or from grey dust aloft,
neither Tip nor Bekki could say. Under this dismal cast, Bekki
and Tip rode upstream along the banks of the Argon looking for
a narrow enough site to cross on a rope-swung raft. Yet the river
was wide, and nowhere did they find a place where all the rope
they had with them would reach even once from bank to bank,
much less there and back.

"I'm afraid it's paddling we must do," said Tip, sighing.

"On the morrow we will ride the opposite direction, downstream then," said Bekki. "Mayhap there we will find a narrow
enough place to span. If not, let us hope the waters wane, for I
would rather ride the ford than ride a raft."

But when they returned to the camp and then walked to the
ford, they discovered the river had risen even more, and the
crossing was wider than ever.

"It has not crested as yet," growled Bekki.

"Maybe it never will," replied Tip, looking at the glum sky
above.

Although it did not rain the following day, still the waters rose
even farther, encroaching up the bank and toward the campsite.
And in their ride downstream they found no narrow place.

"If this keeps up," said Tip, "we'll never get to the gwynthyme."

"Tomorrow it is a raft we begin crafting," said Bekki.

"Have you ever made one?" asked Tip.

Bekki shook his head and said, "Nay, I have not. Even so, how
hard can it be?"

*   *   *

Using nought but Bekki's small handaxe, it took all day to fell three trees nigh the riverbank and trim away the branches.

"At this rate, Bekki, we'll be a week or so just building a float."

Glumly, Bekki nodded.

Tip sighed. "Mayhap instead of waiting a week we ought to set out for the Kaagor Ferry on the morrow. Oh my, that will add nigh another month of travel just to get to the gwynthyme. It's a good thing we included time for unexpected delay, for delay this certainly is. Even so, with another wait, we could miss the golden days of the mint altogether." He got to his feet and took up his bow and quiver and said, "I think I'll go check on the ford again."

Bekki caught up his war hammer and shield. "I will go with you."

As they approached the flooded crossing, Tip frowned. "I say, Bekki, has the water receded? I seem to recall it was past that boulder, but now it doesn't quite reach it."

Bekki stepped down to the water's edge and peered at the distant far side. Then, casting about, he took up a rock the size of his fist and set it down at the brink of the water. "There. In the morning we shall know."

"Unless someone moved the rock in the night, the river is receding," said Tip, smiling.

In the wan morning light the river flowed past, the water a good two yards down the shallow bank from the stone.

Bekki nodded. "Aye. The Argon has waxed and now wanes."

"How soon do you gauge we can cross?" asked Tipperton.

Bekki shrugged. "Let us lay another stone down and see where it stands tomorrow, and then we can judge."

As Bekki carried another rock to the river's edge, Tip looked up the shoreline toward where the logs lay. "Are we going to continue on the raft?"

Bekki's hand strayed to the small axe at his belt. "Let us wait and see."

Tip grinned but remained silent.

On the eighth morning after arriving at the unnamed ford, Tip and Bekki crossed over, the slow-moving water belly high on the ponies. Yet no steed was swept from its feet, much to Bekki's relief.

As they rode away from the northern bank, Tip looked back across the river. "Making a raft, how hard can it be? Mighty hard, if you want my opinion."

"Especially with nought but a handaxe," growled Bekki.

Up and out from the river valley they rode, up through the river border forest and toward the Grimwalls glimpsed now and then through the woodland, the mighty range towering in the distance, their peaks snowcapped.

And still the days were glum and chill, the sun weak, as if autumn had come, even though it was but early August.

"Do you think there's dust yet in the sky, Bekki, shielding us from Adon's warmth?"

"The air is always sharp nigh the Grimwall, Tipperton, though it seems more so these days."

Onward they rode, and toward evening it began to rain down in the foothills where they were, though high in the mountains snow fell instead.

A sevenday after crossing the ford they came to a large lake embraced in the arms of the mountains. Its waters were cloudy blue and wide; its distant shore fetched up against a steep rise in the land some thirty miles afar.

"Nordlake," grunted Bekki, his breath blowing white in the chill air.

"Home of the Vattenvidunder, eh?" said Tip, peering at the broad expanse.

Bekki merely snorted.

"All right," said Tip, "where is this set of cliffs holding the gwynthyme?"

Bekki pointed. Past the far side of the lake and up the slope of land, a stone massif on a mountain flank rose sheer. Vertical it was, and tall, and topped by a broad ledge, or so Bekki had said. Beyond the ledge the mountain rose again "Two or three days yon, if indeed it is gwynthyme growing in the crevices."

"Lor', Bekki, we're not going to have to climb up that, are we?"

Bekki laughed. "Nay, Tipperton. The face of that great bluff is more than a mile high, a mile or so up to the shelf above, where we will set camp among the wide stretch of aspens. A trail leads upward the ponies can manage, and that is how we will get there. Nay, we will not climb up that sheer face, but dangle downward instead, hanging on ropes and rock-nails."

A mile! A mile high! Even from this distance Tip could tell that the face they would be on was straight up and down. His stomach squinched and his heart thudded deep in his chest, and he wondered if he could force himself to dangle on nought but a spindly rope down that vertical stone.

Onward they rode, and that night they camped beside the waters of Nordlake.

*   *   *

Under a glum sky the next morning, when filling the water-skins Bekki said, "Huah, the lake was clearer some years back when last I saw it, but cloudy now."

"Perhaps the dust fell here, too," said Tip.

"Aye, that must be it."

On they rode and on, following the shoreline of the great lake, the mountains ahead seeming to draw no closer. Once again they spent a night along the shore.

The next day they rode in among the foothills north of the lake, the vertical massif in the distance ahead seeming to grow taller, its stone grey and brown, the grey matching the grey of the sky above.

As they topped a hill, Tip halted his pony and peered long and finally called to Bekki, "I say, isn't that something pale yellow way high? Or is it tan stone instead?"

Bekki stopped his steed and shaded his eyes and finally said, "Yellow, I ween."

"Flowers, do you think? Gwynthyme blossoms?"

Bekki shrugged.

"Oh, I do hope so," said Tip, "for if it is, then there's a great crop up there."

Bekki grunted and replied, "Pray to Elwydd it is gwynthyme and not yellow oxeye daisies."

That evening they camped at the foot of the trail leading toward the top of the mile-high cliff. The length of the perpendicular bluff itself ran to the east for perhaps ten miles and towered into the sky; sheer it was, with long vertical ripples running down the drop of the stone face, now glowing bloodred in the setting sun.

Tip peered at the vast expanse and shuddered, but whether from fear of what was to come or from the chill air, he could not say.

It was raining the next morning as they twisted and turned up the narrow trail, Bekki riding in the lead, two pack ponies trailing, then Tipperton came after on his steed with two pack ponies following him as well. At times they dismounted and took to foot to give the ponies a breather, and at other times they stopped altogether, giving all a rest. But soon they would continue onward, climbing the steep, winding trail; and the higher they gained, the sheerer the drop to the right, and the closer to the left fared Tip, his heart racing at the thought of the fall but a pace or so away.

Yet at last nigh the noontide, the rain stopped just as they came to the top of the bluff and into an aspen woodland, the green leaves trembling and dripping water in the drift of cold air sliding down from the white mountain slopes far above, where more snow had fallen instead of rain.

"Let us ride onward," said Bekki, "five miles or so, to the midpoint atop the massif, to my campsite of old. Then we will look for the golden flowers."

"All right," said Tip, his breath coming easy now that he was surrounded by trees on all sides.

Tip forced himself to the lip of the stone and peered downward, only to quickly draw back. "There's nothing there but a long fall."

Bekki, standing on the very brim, leaned over and looked down as well. "It has an overhang, Tipperton. You have to look inward. And, ah, there are flowers. Leftward."

Tip stepped toward the edge and flopped down on his belly and pulled himself forward to peer beyond the lip. *You can do this, bucco. Just remember, a thirty-foot fall will kill you just as dead as a fall of a mile or so, and you've been well beyond thirty feet before. The only difference being, at this height you'll get to scream much longer on the way down.*

His heart hammering, Tip looked leftward. There in the near distance he could see pale yellow blossoms nodding in the chill air. Farther beyond he could see another patch, and several even farther. Tip looked to the right, and yellow flowers nodded there, too. "Oh my, Bekki, what a wondrous trove you have found."

"Growing in the cracks like I said," muttered Bekki. Then he looked at Tip, his eyes widening in surprise to see the buccan lying at the lip on his stomach as if he were afraid of heights. Shaking his head, Bekki grunted, then said, "Come, Tipperton, let us climb down and see if these are gwynthyme blossoms or are oxeye daisies instead."

"They're not oxeye daisies," said Tipperton above the long drop, his voice tight with tension. "Daisies have yellow centers, but their petals are white, and these petals are yellow."

"Well, some other all-yellow flower then," said Bekki. "Marigolds or some such."

Tip slid back from the lip and stood. "Marigolds grow in swamps, or so I've heard, and not in stone cracks along mountain faces."

"Regardless!" snapped Bekki, striding off to the left.

"Look, Bekki," said Tip, running after, "you just happened to pick the only two flowers I know anything about. Oh, and roses. It's not as if I'm an expert. Oh, clover, too. —And bluebells, and yellow-eyed violets and . . ."

Bekki stopped along the brim and looked down and inward. "Here they are," he growled, then turned to Tip. "Have you the sketch?"

Tip patted his jacket pocket.

"Good," said Bekki, surveying the stone. "I'll fetch one, and then we'll see."

"I'll get the ropes and rock-nails and such," said Tip, turning to go back to the camp.

"They won't be needed," said Bekki, and he clambered over the brim to begin free-climbing down.

"But the stone is wet," called Tip.

"Not here under the overhang," drifted up Bekki's reply.

Tip flopped down and slid to the edge and held his breath more than once, closing his eyes at times, as Bekki edged downward to the blossoms.

"It's gwynthyme, all right," exclaimed Tip, grinning, comparing the sketch Beau had drawn to the sprig in Bekki's hand.

Bekki grinned fiercely, too, and growled, "Serrated trifoliate aromatic leaves and all," then burst out laughing.

Giggling, Tip folded the vellum and slipped it back into his pocket. As they made their way toward camp, Tip said, "Tomorrow we will begin marking all the places where the gwynthyme grows, and when comes the full moon of September—um, twenty-six days from now—then we begin the harvest."

Now that he had a task to do, Tipperton was much less timorous at the lip of the massif. Rain or shine, he and Bekki spent the next eleven days roaming along the verge of the precipice and stacking small piles of stones at each place along the rim where they could see the pale yellow blossoms of gwynthyme growing in cracks and crevices below.

But on the twelfth day, when they came again to the lip, Tip looked over the rim to see blossoms and petals falling away in the wind, spiralling downward in a pale golden shower, as the gwynthyme shed its flowers.

"Oh my, but this will make it harder to spot the mint below."

Bekki nodded but then said, "Harder for us but nevertheless a good sign, for the gwynthyme is coming to fruition."

"I wonder why it picks now to do so?" asked Tip. "I mean, cast off its flowers."

Bekki frowned, then his visage brightened. "You said it your-self, Tipperton, months past."

Tip looked at Bekki in puzzlement. "I did?"

"Aye. This mission, the gwynthyme, all is governed by Elwydd's light, and this day, this night, is the dark of the moon altogether."

"Ah, so it is, Bekki. So it is."

Later that day, it began to rain along the massif and to snow in the mountains above. Tipperton sighed and said, "I say, Bekki, does it seem to you it's been raining more lately?"

Bekki looked up into the drizzle. "Aye, it does."

Tip shook his head, then said, "What do you suppose causes it? Could it have something to do with the dust high in the sky, blowing about on the wind? I mean, even on the best of days, still the sky is a bit grey and the sun seems pale and there is a chill in the air. And add to that the frequent rain. So what do you think, eh?"

Bekki shrugged. "Who knows how Garlon makes the rain?"

Tip frowned. "Garlon?"

Bekki looked at Tip in surprise. "He is master of water. How else do you think it rains?"

Tip turned up his hands. "I dunno. The wind. Water. Perhaps the wind blows across the water and lifts some up to come down elsewhere as rain."

Bekki snorted. "Then how would you explain the Karoo?"

"The Karoo?"

"Aye. The great desert beyond the Avagon Sea. It has wind. It has the ocean at hand. Yet it seldom rains in that place of dunes, full of sand as it were. And even when it does rain there, the water is pure and not salt from the sea. —Windblown water? Nay, Tipperton. I'll take Garlon instead."

Tip shook his head but remained silent, and he and Bekki continued along the rim.

That night under the gloom above, Bekki awakened Tipper-ton, a finger to the buccan's lips.

"What is it?" whispered Tip.

"Someone comes along the rim," gritted Bekki, a shield on his arm, his war hammer in hand.

Tipperton listened, and to the east he could hear the thud of jogging feet. "More than one someone," hissed the Warrow, reaching for his bow and quiver.

"The ponies," growled Bekki. "We must keep them quiet."

And he and Tipperton slipped among the trees to the rope pen where the steeds dozed.

Long moments later in the distance the thud of shod feet passed by to finally fade away westerly.

"Who was it?" breathed Tipperton. "A squad of Squam?"

"Who else?" growled Bekki.

"Oh my, but this does complicate things. I mean, if there's a maggot-folk holt nearby, we may have trouble harvesting the mint."

In that moment came a prolonged low calling, as of a mournful horn winded afar.

Tip's eyes flew wide. "Goodness, what was that? A Spaunen signal, do you think?"

Bekki shook his head. "It's not like any Squam horn I've ever heard, nor any owl for that matter. But horn or no, owl or no, I deem we need move our camp farther back among the trees, farther back from the rim."

"Now? Tonight?"

"Aye."

The next day, in the rain-dampened soil along the rim they found boot tracks heading westerly.

"Hobnails," said Tipperton. "Rûpt, all right, twenty or so, I gauge. It's good we had no fire in the rain, else they would have spotted us. From now on any fire we set will have to be in the day and smokeless."

"If it were not for the gathering of the mint," growled Bekki, "we would track them down and kill them all."

Tip looked southward, where in the distance Nordlake lay like a dull iron sheet in the wan morning sun. "The gwynthyme takes precedence o'er all, Bekki, including getting it back to Beau. And speaking of gwynthyme"—Tip looked over his shoulder—"I think our searching for more patches of mint is over, at least in the daytime. I mean, they may see us walking out on the rim. They may, in fact, be watching us even now."

Bekki sighed. "Aye. Let us get back among the trees."

As they slipped into the woodland again, Bekki said, "I will pull down our old lean-to and move it to our new camp."

In the next several days, it rained off and on and, even though they heard no more Squam pass by, neither Tip nor Bekki ventured forth in the light of the day from the woodland where they camped. During these same days the moon grew toward fullness, advancing from a fingernail-thin crescent to a half-moon and then onward.

And when it grew on toward fullness, in the nights Tip and

Bekki slipped through the woodland and to the rim and searched through the argent light spilling down the precipice for more gwynthyme below.

And still no Rûpt passed by.

"Perhaps it was a one-time occurrence," said Tipperton. "Mayhap there is no maggot-folk holt at hand."

Bekki shrugged. "Mayhap you are right, Tipperton, but then again mayhap not."

Tip sighed. "I know. I know. It's better we don't gamble."

At last the September moon came full, and the mint turned golden overnight, and down the massif on spindly ropes dangled a Dwarf and a Warrow, Tip having forced himself over the lip and down. Each wore a sack on a strap 'round his shoulder, and in the moonlight each cut the aromatic mint, leaving one sprig behind for every one they took. Bekki with great climbing skill harvested twice over what Tip could take, the Dwarf on his rope walking sideways across the face of the massif to gather in more sprigs.

During the morning light of the day ere taking turns at sleeping, they sat in camp and bundled the sprigs together, rolled and bound in strips of cloth, eleven to the bunch.

And as he rolled another packet, Tip said, "I say, Bekki, I believe I once told you that Phais taught Beau and me to climb, but you put us to shame. I mean, you are a splendid climber. Where did you ever learn?"

"Nine, ten, eleven," said Bekki, counting out sprigs of golden mint onto a swathe of cloth. Then he looked up from the array. "Nearly all Châkka have climbing skills, for the inside of the mountain needs more climbing than the outside ever did. As for me, my sire spent time teaching me, and his skills put mine to shame."

"Oh," said Tip, "then what a wonder it must be to see him climb if he's better than you."

Bekki nodded and then rolled the gwynthyme into the cloth binding. "Aye, he is among the very best, though there are better still."

"Oh my," said Tipperton, reaching for another handful of sprigs.

In the moonshadows of the fourth night of harvesting— "Ssst!"—hissed Tipperton, gaining Bekki's attention. "Someone comes."

Together they dangled on their spidery ropes, unmoving against the moonlit stone. Above on the lip of the precipice, a tramping could be heard, nearing. And on this night there was harsh talking, voices in Slûk, the Foul Folk tongue.

Clinging to the massif, Tip looked down a mile of sheer stone, his heart hammering wildly—*Oh lor', if they find our anchors, they'll cut us free and we'll*—and he thought he might scream out in terror, but bit his lip and managed to hold his fear in.

Above tramped the feet, and a voice called out—

Tipperton clutched his rope. *They've found us!*

—but the maggot-folk ignored the call and marched on.

Directly above, a voice muttered.

One has stopped! Why?

Then a stream of urine arched outward and down, falling toward the shadows below.

And there sounded a far-off hooting, like a forlorn horn cry. From the south it came, and distant.

"Waugh!" blurted the voice above, and the urine cut off in midstream, and Tipperton heard fleeing footsteps thudding away, running after the others.

As the steps faded, Tip loosed pent breath he was unaware he'd been holding and looked toward Bekki, to find the Dwarf once again in the moonlight harvesting golden mint.

Eight more nights they harvested, the moon waning with each nighttide, the silver orb growing thinner and rising later each eve as it approached the dark of the moon.

Ere they set out on the ninth night, Tip said, "It's the eve of the equinox, Bekki, and back in Dendor, Beau and Phais and Loric are stepping out the turning of the seasons. Would that I could, but I don't know the steps, for I always followed Loric."

Bekki looked at Tip. "If you accept me as a poor substitute, Tipperton, I will pace you through them."

Tip's mouth fell open. "You know the steps?"

"Did I not join you on the summer solstice?"

"Yes, but how do you—? Oh, right! You are a Dwarf."

And so, in the aspen woodland, with Bekki infallibly leading and Tip singing softly, they paced through the Elven rite. And when they were done, Tip looked at Bekki, and said, "Thank you, my friend. That was splendid. Now let's go harvest gwyn-thyme."

Bekki nodded, and as they gathered their climbing gear and harvesting tools, he said, "Mayhap the Elves have it right by celebrating each turn of the seasons. The greatest of the Châkka celebrations occurs on one of these nights—Year's Long Night."

"I remember," said Tip. "It was Year's Long Night, the same

night we saw the Squam marching north along the Ironwater,
that you were speaking some rite atop a hill."

"I was praying to Elwydd as we Châkka do at that turn of the
seasons."

"Elwydd?"

"Aye, Châk-Sol; we believe she made the Châkka and set
them on Mithgar. Each year in acknowledgement of Her deed,
we pray that we may touch the stars."

"Touch the stars? What do you mean by that?"

"The stars are Elwydd's, and we with our crafting attempt to
make something nigh as perfect as are they."

"Oh, I see. And you pray for guidance in this task?"

Bekki stood and cast wide his arms and chanted as if cantor
and chorale:

> *Elwydd—*
> *—Daughter of Adon,*
> *We thank Thee—*
> *—For Thy gentle hand.*
> *That gave to us—*
> *—The Breath of Life.*
> *May this be—*
> *—The golden year*
> *The Châkka—*
> *—Touch the stars.*

Two more nights altogether they harvested, alert for the
tramp of maggot-folk. But no more came these two nights, nor
in the past ten nights altogether.

In the early light of the new day in a thin drizzle they bundled the last of the harvest, and with that they were done, for
although there was one more night ere the dark of the moon,
they had found no more sites of the mint. They decided to set
out on the morrow, for the climbing had been hard and they
needed a full day and a full night of rest before starting back.
As to the gwynthyme itself, altogether over the fourteen nights
of collecting, they had managed to reap three full sacks of the
golden mint. "Enough to treat Dendor three times over if
Beau's guess is right," said Tip. "It's a rather good harvest
we've done."

Bekki nodded, glum in the icy rain, and gestured at the sky.
"Now our task is to get it back to the city."

"Let us hope the ford is low," said Tip.

"With Garlon's rain, who knows?" replied Bekki.

*   *   *

The next morning ere they set out, Tip and Bekki rode to the nearest set of markers and dismounted and looked down the precipice one last time. A billowing mist lay below the lip, as if it were a fog trying to gain the rim. But it was not this mist they sought, but the patch of gwynthyme instead. "Right on schedule," Tip said, pointing down at the mint below. "It's as brown as an old leather shoe, just as Beau said it would be."

"Rescue to ruin," said Bekki, then looked at one of the sacks on a pack pony. "Rescue and ruin in one."

Mounting up and turning west, Tip and Bekki made their way toward the narrow, tortuous path leading to the foothills below. Along this way they twisted and turned, riding down into the mist. And in the greyness Tip was glad that he couldn't see the sheer fall beyond the drop-off on the left, though he knew it was there.

Down they rode and down, to finally come unto the rolling hills. Without a glance behind, southward they turned, aiming for the ford.

The fog gripped the world for three days, and on the third of these days as they rode along the shores of Nordlake, a mournful hooting, loud in the quiet, sounded out upon the water.

"Oh my," exclaimed Tip, startled, peering through the fog, seeing nought but grey mist. "That's what we heard in the night on the cliff. It's not a horn, not a horn at all."

Bekki scowled and tried to peer through the fog, having no more luck than Tip. "Mayhap it is a bird," he said, his voice not at all confident. "A loon or cob or some such."

"Oh no, Bekki, oh no. It's the Vattenvidunder, I ween."

Tip raised his hands and cupped them to his mouth and shouted out onto the lake. "Thank you, O water monster. You mayhap saved our lives with your cry."

There came no response but a huge splash, as if something large had dived down.

The next morning Tip awakened to a heavy frost. Bekki on watch said, "It crept here in the night."

"But it's still September, Bekki. Too early for a frost."

"The weather these days is strange, Tipperton: rain, a wan sun, cold nights."

"And now an early frost," said Tip. "I wonder the cause of it all."

"Mayhap it is as you said, Tipperton. Mayhap it is the dust on the wind above, shielding us from Adon's warmth."

Breaking camp, on they rode, the ford long miles ahead.

*   *   *

Through frosted mornings and chill days, they rode alto- gether another week ere coming to the shallows over the Argon. The water was low and they crossed with ease.

East they turned, now riding in Aven, and still the weather was fickle, rain or a dusting of snow falling now and again. Even so, on the days the air seemed clear, sunrises and sunsets were spectacular.

But late in the day of the seventeenth of October they espied the walls of Dendor, and smoke from within rose up in the twi- light, as if part of the city burned. And on they pushed, night drawing over them as they rode for the battlements yon.

"Open the gate," bellowed Bekki to the ward above.

A lantern swung over the parapet, and a soldier looked down. Bekki threw back his hood to reveal his features. "Nay, Dvärg, the city is closed."

"But we've returned from Nordlake," shouted Tipperton, casting back his own hood. "We have a pass from King Agron himself."

The soldier turned and spoke to someone, and then Captain Brud came to the wall. "Is that you, Sir Tipperton, Lord Bekki?"

"It is," growled Bekki.

"Aye," called Tipperton, gesturing at the pack ponies behind, "and we've brought gwynthyme."

"A moment," called Brud, and disappeared from view.

After a while, the side postern opened, and Brud stepped out, a soldier at his side holding a lantern to light the way. "I have your escort."

Tipperton frowned. "Escort?"

"Aye, Sir Tipperton. You and Lord Bekki will need escort and protection. The city is under curfew. The citizens have rioted twice."

As Tip and Bekki dismounted to walk their ponies through the gate, Tip said, "Rioted? Why?"

"The plague. It runs wild. Fully a quarter of the citizens have died."

"Then take us to the prison," growled Bekki, "to Sir Beau Darby. We have what he needs."

Brud's face fell, and Tip's heart flopped over.

"But he's dead, Lord Bekki," blurted the soldier at Brud's side. "Beau Darby is dead of the plague."

18

The air went out of Tip's lungs. Blenching, he turned to Bekki, tears flooding the buccan's eyes, and he fell to his knees.

Captain Brud leapt forward to aid Tipperton, but Bekki was there before him. With a flinty gaze, Bekki looked up at the soldier who had blurted out the woeful news and then back to the captain. "Dead? Beau is dead?"

Brud cast his aide a withering glance, then turned to Bekki and Tip. "We are told he died this morning."

Tip struggled to his feet. "Oh, let us hie to the prison. I would see him one more time ere they burn him with the others."

Through the twisting way under the walls they hurried, and beyond the inner gate a mounted escort waited. Captain Brud sprang to the back of a horse and said, "Come. I will lead the way."

Now astride their ponies, Tip and Bekki rode into the city, mounted soldiers fore and aft. Along the narrow streets they ran, hooves aclatter on the cobbles. Past shattered doors and broken windows they went, and buildings burnt to nought but charred shells. Through soldier-warded barricades they passed, Captain Brud's orders opening the way. Soldiers afoot and on patrol watched as they cantered by, as did citizens from windows above, citizens pale with fear and shouting imprecations. It was clear that dread ruled the city, as in the days of the Gargon, though no Gargon this; for a Gargon could be slain, but what, by Adon, would slay a plague?

None of this ruin and fear did Tipperton note, for his chest was hollow, his heart numb, his mind filled with grief.

Oh, if only we'd come earlier. . . . If only . . .

At last they drew up before the gates of the prison. Bekki sprang down and helped Tipperton to dismount. "Bring those three large sacks," he snapped at Captain Brud, then at Tipperton's side stepped to the prison gate.

A soldier on duty stood across their path. "You cannot go in."

"Out of the way," growled Bekki, his knuckles white on the haft of his war hammer.

Confusion filled the soldier's eyes, and he turned to Captain Brud. "Let them pass," called the captain, but Bekki had already shoved by, Tipperton in hand.

Toward the prison doors they strode, Brud and two others following, these latter three each bearing a sack of gwynthyme.

As they entered the prison, a man at an entryway table looked up and protested, "Here now—"

"Sir Beau Darby, where does he lie?" snapped Bekki.

The man looked to Captain Brud, who nodded.

"Third floor"—the man pointed at a flight of stairs—"that way. The Alfs are—"

But Bekki did not stop to listen to what the man said, and instead with Tipperton headed up the steps.

Up they went and up, cries of delirium and pain echoing through the halls and along the walls of the stairwell. On the way up they passed two white-clothed men coming downward, bearing a litter on which a small corpse lay.

Tip drew in his breath. "Is it—?" No, it was instead a child: nought but skin and bones and black boils.

On up went Bekki and Tip, Brud following, the captain yet bearing a sack. Of the other two soldiers, there was no sign.

They reached the third floor and stepped through an iron-barred gate standing open. Down a central hallway they went, open-gated cells left and right, cells filled with the beds of the sick and dying, stricken people moaning in pain, fevered, covered with pus-running boils and writhing in agony, some not stirring at all. White-clothed people moved among the victims, soothing brows with cloths of cold water, feeding them sips of a liquid, closing the eyes of the dead and drawing sheets over their bodies.

They came at last to the cell where Phais and Loric sat vigil. And at hand in one of the cots was a small form. It was Beau. Gaunt, wasted, boils oozing, darkness in his armpits and groin, Beau lay unmoving. Tip gasped, a trembling hand flying to his mouth upon seeing Beau's emaciated frame.

Weeping, Tip stepped to the bedside. "Oh, Beau, Beau, why

did you have to catch this awful scourge. Why did you have to go and di—"

A shallow breath rattled through Beau's cracked lips and into his lungs.

"He's not dead!" cried Tipperton. "Bekki, Phais, Loric, he's not dead!" Tip fell on his knees beside the bed and grasped one of Beau's limp hands. "Oh, Beau, you're not dead."

Phais knelt beside the buccan and circled an arm about him. "Not yet, Tipperton, but soon. Soon."

"Not if we can help it," snarled Bekki. "We've brought gwynthyme." Bekki turned and snatched the sack from Captain Brud.

Phais's eyes widened and she looked back at Bekki. "Gwynthyme? Ye twain were successful?"

He dropped the bag beside her. "Aye. That we were."

Phais's eyes widened. "So much?"

"There's two more bags like it," said Bekki, turning to Brud.

"Downstairs at the entry," said the captain.

"Oh my," said Phais.

"A tisane of gwynthyme and silverroot," said Bekki. "That is what Beau said."

Loric's fingers flew as he untied the sack. "Aye, he did, but what proportions the ingredients?"

Anguished, Bekki shook his head.

Loric snatched out a cloth-wrapped bundle of sprigs and turned to Tip. "Tipperton, dost thou remember the proportions?"

"Proportions?"

"How much gwynthyme to silverroot."

Tip frowned, trying to remember. "I think he said in equal measure. Yes, half and half, that's what I recall."

"Swift, chier," urged Phais as Loric darted away, "there is not much time."

Another shallow breath rattled in and out of Beau.

And then another.

And another. . . .

Within a candlemark Loric returned, a steaming cup in hand. "Whether or no this is in equal measure only Adon can say."

"Pray to Elwydd it is so," said Bekki.

Loric spooned small amounts of the brew into Beau's lips, while Tip held the buccan's hand and Phais held Tip to her. Bekki paced back and forth, and Captain Brud squatted in the cell door.

As Bekki came past the captain for perhaps the hundredth

time, Brud said, "Lord Bekki, I just recall: a Dvärg emissary in King Agron's halls awaits your return."

Bekki stopped his pacing. "An emissary?"

"Aye. From Mineholt North, he said. Rode to our gates in August. Insisted on waiting for you. Wouldn't take no for an answer. King Agron himself came and talked to him, and then allowed the emissary in, though he did send the Dvärg escort away. I think they are quartered in a farmhouse nigh."

"Do you know why they have come?"

Brud shook his head.

"There," said Loric, setting aside the empty cup and spoon, "it is done. Now all we can do is wait."

In the early candlemarks of the morning, Beau's breathing eased. Phais laid a hand on the buccan's brow, then said, "His fever has diminished."

Tip burst out in tears.

Loric took up the bag of gwynthyme. "I will instruct the healers in the way of its preparation."

Brud stood. "Lord Bekki, I will escort you to the palace." Brud turned to Tipperton. "You, too, wee one. You need the rest."

Tip rubbed a sleeve across his eyes and shook his head. "No thank you, captain; I'll sleep on the floor right here."

Phais reached out to the buccan. "Nay, Tipperton, for the risk is high that thou wilt come down with the scourge should thee stay."

As Tip started to stubbornly shake his head, Brud said, "The muster, my friend, we must soon answer. And better a healthy scout than a sick one."

Tip's shoulders slumped. "The muster. I had forgotten." He turned to Beau and squeezed the unconscious buccan's hand. "I'll be back on the morrow, bucco, you can count on that. You get better, you hear me?"

Beau did not respond in any manner whatsoever.

As they entered the palace, a footman leapt to his feet. "My Lord Bekki, you are back."

Bekki cocked an eyebrow at the footman.

"My lord, I have been instructed to have you wait in the anteroom while I fetch Emissary Dalk."

"Dalk is here?"

"Aye."

Bekki looked at Tip, and at the buccan's frown, Bekki said, "From Mineholt North. He has a yellow beard."

"Oh yes. Now I remember. One of the council of captains."

As Tip and Bekki stepped into an anteroom, the servant hurried away.

Within a candlemark, yet buttoning a shirt, Dalk hurried into the chamber and knelt.

Bekki's face blanched to see such a move.

Dalk glanced at Tipperton.

"He is Châk-Sol," said Bekki, his voice but a whisper, his fists clenched as if for a blow.

"I bear ill tidings, DelfLord Bekki, your sire, DelfLord Borl, is dead."

"Oh no," said Tipperton, dismayed.

Bekki's knuckles went white on his clenched fists. "How?"

"A Squam arrow in the Skarpal Mountains."

Bekki slammed the butt of a fist to a table, the wood splitting with the force of the blow, Tipperton jumping in startlement.

"We wreaked great vengeance," said Dalk.

Slowly, Bekki released his clenched hands and cast his hood over his head in the Châkka gesture of mourning. A silence fell upon the room for long moments. Finally Bekki asked, "The mineholt?"

"It is in Lord Berk's capable hands. Even so, DelfLord, your holtwarder grandsire calls you back, for war burns upon the land and the mineholt needs your rule."

Yet covered with dark pus-running boils and black buboes in armpits and groin, Beau did not waken the following day. Even so, his fever continued to abate and his breathing to ease, and he took water and kept it down.

The day after as Tip sat vigil beside the bed, just as Phais stopped by to see to the buccan, Beau opened his eyes and smiled wanly at Tip.

"Oh, Beau, Beau, I thought we had lost you. Captain Brud said you were dead."

Beau weakly lifted a finger and beckoned, and when Tip leaned down to hear, Beau whispered, "The report of my death was quite premature."

Tipperton laughed, and Beau faintly smiled, but Phais shook her head. "By less than a candlemark, I ween."

Beau's hand dropped back to the cover, and he closed his eyes. Tip waited, but it soon became apparent that Beau's exhausted body demanded sleep.

"Come, Tipperton, we do not want to overtire him," said Phais.

As they walked out from the makeshift infirmary, Tip asked, "What of the other patients?"

"All but a handful are responding to the infusion."

"Getting better, you mean?"

"Aye. It seems that Beau has struck upon a thing sought after for untold ages: a sweeping cure for the plague."

The news flashed throughout the city, yet the quarantine was held in place, for before lifting it the king would be certain that all was as it seemed. Nevertheless, the citizens celebrated, for Litenfolk and Elves and Dvärgs could not be wrong, now could they? And in the palace, Agron breathed a sigh of relief, for a fear-driven revolt was averted, though but barely. He sent criers throughout the city, proclaiming the quarantine would be set aside as soon as all was deemed well. The criers also proclaimed the king's amnesty for any crimes short of murder committed during the panic of the past month. And the citizens themselves, casting about for any excuse, laid the guilt for such acts on the doorstone of Modru.

Within the week it was clear that the combination of gwynthyme and silverroot was effective, and instead of six out of seven falling to the scourge, only one in a hundred died . . . and these perhaps from complications rather than from the plague itself. And so the king declared the city open. The gates were cast wide, but only a few people seized the opportunity to flee Dendor, for wonder of wonders, something had been found which would entirely slay the plague.

Yet none had the heart to tell the citizenry that silverroot, plentiful in Dendor, only grew in certain places, and gwynthyme, golden gwynthyme, was extremely rare in spite of the surplus the healers now enjoyed.

During this same sevenday, the king readied for his journey west to the muster at Älvstad. And Tipperton, too, prepared for the day of leaving. Even so, he spent many a candlemark at Beau's bedside, chatting with his ill friend and playing his lute and singing to all of the stricken.

As for Beau, within a day of his regaining consciousness he began taking broth for sustenance; and the next day he ate soup and bread sopped with the liquid; and finally he ate a bit of solid food on the day after. "This grub will put some meat back on those bones of yours," said Tip as he carried a full tray into the cell on that third day.

Slowly the pustulant boils began to recede and the black buboes to wane. Nevertheless, Beau looked a mess, or so he did say the day he caught his reflection in the small mirror from his medical bag, a glass he used to check for breath and breathing.

"Captain Brud, he said I was dead, eh?"

"Not Brud, Beau, but an aide instead, though it was just a repeated rumor," replied Tip. "He has since apologized."

Beau took one last look in the mirror. "Well I can't say I blame the one who started the rumor for thinking so; I'm quite ghastly, you know."

"Beau, if you think you look bad now, you should have seen yourself three days past. I mean, you looked—" Of a sudden Tip's eyes flooded. "Oh, Beau, I thought you were dead."

Beau's own eyes filled with tears. "So did I, Tip. So did I." And he reached out and squeezed Tip's hand.

Tip smiled and then looked at the buccan. "But you didn't die, Beau, and that's all that counts . . . that and finding a cure for the plague."

Beau's eyes widened. "Oh my, I did, didn't I? Even so, I wish it had been twenty-five or thirty or more years ago and by someone other than me."

Tip raised an eyebrow. "How so?"

"Well, if any had known of it back then, perhaps my parents would still be alive."

"Oh. I see."

The buccen fell to silence, each wrapped in memories and thoughts, but after a while Tip said, "Bekki's leaving in a day or so; he's DelfLord of Mineholt North, you know."

"Yes, and I am terribly sorry that his da was killed. I told him so yesternight."

Tip looked out the barred slit of a window. "I'll be leaving too. Riding in the king's cavalcade. The muster in Älvstad is but three or so weeks hence. Agron says we'll be using remounts, for time is short but the journey long."

"Oh, right." Beau sighed, then said, "I'll follow when I'm better."

"Oh, Beau, I'd rather you'd not. It will be perilous in Gron, and—"

Beau thrust out a negating palm. "All the more reason I need to be there, Tip. I mean, who's going to take care of you when and if you require healing."

Tip smiled wanly. "I don't plan on needing any stitching or other such, bucco. Besides, your healing is wanted here."

"Not so. The plague is as good as gone, what with the gwynthyme you and Bekki brought back, and the locals can deal with whatever else needs doing. No, bucco, as soon as I can, I'm coming after you. I'm certain that it will take the two of us Litenfolk to throw Modru down."

Tip grinned and shrugged, and Beau smiled in return. Yet of a sudden Beau's face took on a serious cast. "See here, Tip, we don't really know what the future will bring . . . but the fact that we are separating must mean something. Look, everything that happens has some bearing on events as yet untold. It's all connected, you know."

Tip laughed aloud and then said, "Let us just hope that by me leaving now and you coming later, well, that it is for the best."

Again a silence fell between them. Tip took up his lute and strummed a few soft chords. But then Beau said, "Oh, did I tell you that Phais and Loric believe that a firemountain on Atala blew up, and mayhap the entire island has sunk?"

Tip set aside his lute. "Because of the blast we heard ringing 'round the world?"

"That and the dust which fell here. Did any fall on you and Bekki?"

Tip nodded. "Yes. From the west it came, flowing over the sky and then falling down. Bekki said it was rock dust, perhaps from a firemountain, and the only firemountain he knew of west of here was Karak on Atala."

Beau drew in a deep breath and slowly let it out. "Karak, yes. Phais said that many Elves and others lived nigh the slopes, and when it exploded, well, it killed them all, all in one terrible blast, and that was the awful doom she and Loric felt that dreadful day. She said others lived on that isle—Humans, Dwarves, Hidden Ones, even some Warrows—but it was the deaths of so many Elves all at once that blew through them like an ill wind."

"Oh my," said Tip. "Oh my."

Three days later in early morn, Tip came to Beau's bedside. Bekki came as well, along with Phais and Loric. Even King Agron came to see Beau, for this was the day of parting: Bekki was going with his Dwarven escort back to Mineholt North. And now that the plague was well in hand, Phais and Loric would ride southerly with Bekki and the Dwarves until they came to the Landover Road, the Dwarves to turn west and the Lian to continue south, for the Elves were sworn to deliver Agron's message to High King Blaine along with a small pewter coin. As for Agron and Tip, they were heading to Älvstad. And for the moment, wan and weak, Beau would go nowhere, confined to his bed as he was.

But on this morning, King Agron stood at the side of the frail buccan's bed. "Sir Beau, not only did you save Dendor, but the whole of Mithgar owes you a debt it can never repay, for ever has the plague beset all folk, and you have found the cure. Others have been named Hero of the Realm, but I name you Hero of the Entire World."

"Hear, hear!" said Tip.

Under the remaining dark pustules, Beau blushed. "Oh, I'm not a hero at all, not like everyone here—"

"Nonsense," snapped Bekki. "King Agron is right, and I here and now proclaim you Châk-Sol of Mineholt North, Beau Darby, Master of the Plague. So I have said; so shall it be."

"Oh my," said Beau, as Tip grinned.

Agron now turned to Tipperton. "Sir Tipperton, I know you are pledged to ride scout for me. Yet this I say: instead of joining my winter campaign in Gron, mayhap you and Beau should go with the Lian Guardians and represent the interests of the Litenfolk to High King Blaine, wherever he may be."

Tip glanced at Phais and Loric, friends he had come to love. It would be so easy to go with them and search for the High King rather than ride into the cold wastes of Gron. He gazed down at the floor, remembering the courageous young man who had saved his life at his mill. Tip looked back up at Agron. "Nay, my lord, I am pledged to you to avenge the death of Dular. A scout I am, and a scout I will be."

Agron then looked at Beau, that buccan to shake his head. "Nay, my lord, wherever Tip goes, so will I go. We started this war together, and together we will be when it ends. That we are separated is temporary, or so I do believe. Besides, you will need healers in this winter campaign, after all, and you can use my hands. I'm a hero, you know; you said so yourself."

And so it was decided: the comrades would go their separate ways—three south, one west, and one to remain behind until he was well enough to follow.

Agron glanced at the light beyond the prison window; outside, snow had begun drifting down. " 'Tis time we were going, Sir Tipperton, on this winter morn." One by one, Agron looked at the others. "Fare ye well, Sir Beau. Fare ye well DelfLord Bekki, Dara Phais, Alor Loric. May Adon watch over ye all." Agron turned on his heel and strode down the passageway.

Bekki growled, "Would that I were going into Gron with you, Tip, to lay Grg by the heels." Bekki then smiled at Beau. "Hear me, Châk-Sol: when you are well enough to follow Tipperton, take plenty of bullets for your sling, for surely you will need them."

Beau nodded, then said, "Oh, Bekki, that reminds me. Take a goodly amount of the gwynthyme and silverroot back to your mineholt; the Châkia will need it there. And, you, Phais and Loric, take some silverroot and gwynthyme, too. You as well, Tip, you as well; you never know when it will come in handy."

Phais nodded and then leaned down and kissed Beau on the cheek in spite of his pustules. "Take care, wee one. We shall meet again."

Loric also kissed Beau, and laid a hand on the buccan's thin shoulder. "I, too, think we shall meet again, little one."

"Oh, Phais, Loric, Bekki, Tip, it is as if I am losing everyone I love."

"Nonsense," said Tip, embracing his friend, "we shall meet again soon. After all, you said it yourself: everything is connected."

"Connected, yes, but that doesn't mean we will all meet again."

Bekki shrugged. "In this war, who can say?"

A horn cry drifted in through the window slit.

"Oh my, Beau, I've got to go now," said Tip, catching up his lute. "Get well, and soon."

"I will, bucco, and you can wager on it."

Bekki, Phais, Loric, and Tip: they all stepped from the prison cell. "Remember," cried Beau, his voice tight with emotion, "stop by the healer station and get gwynthyme and silverroot to take with you."

Beau heard Tipperton call back, "We will," and there came a chord on the lute, and Tipperton's voice lifted in song:

> *Oh—fiddle-dee hi, fiddle-dee ho,*
> *Fiddle-dee hay ha hee.*
> *Wiggle-dee die, wiggle-dee doe,*
> *Wiggle-dee pig die dee.*
>
> *Once there was a very merry man*
> *Who came to Boskledee . . .*

Tipperton's voice faded away as he went down the hall and into the stairwell. And Beau sat propped in his bed, tears running down his face, humming along with Tip's song, Beau's favorite: "The Merry Man of Boskledee."

Long moments later Beau heard a second horn cry, followed by the shouting of voices and the clack of hooves on the cobbles below, the ching of arms and armor and the clatter of the cavalcade to fade into the distance. . . .

. . . And then he could hear nothing more but the silence of the prison.

19

*I*n the last seven days of October and the first nine of November, Agron's cavalcade pressed on toward the muster at Älvstad. And during these sixteen days of travel, snow fell five of them altogether, unusual in Aven this time of year. Some claimed 'twas Modru's doing, while others claimed 'twas not. Regardless, in spite of the early snowfall and the cold, Agron's company finally arrived at their goal on November the ninth.

Älvstad itself was a stockaded city nigh the banks of the River Argon, yet with the muster at this place it was more tents and wagons ringed all 'round than buildings of wood within. Down through this gathering fared the cavalcade, down through snow churned to mud. And when the blue and gold of the king passed by, followed by the king himself, men stood along the route and cheered their monarch, slayer of the Gargon and conqueror of Modru's Swarm. Coming after the king and astraddle a horse towed behind a mounted soldier rode a legend alive: one of the Litenfolk.

Through cheering men and into the town proper fared Agron King, Tipperton and others following in his wake. At last they stopped before an inn, the king to dismount and signal a handful of others to follow, Tip among these latter. The remaining soldiers gathered up the horses and rode on toward the town stables, where they would quarter until time to leave.

As Tipperton stepped into the inn, he was glad this part of the journey was over, for he did not enjoy being on a tall horse tethered behind one of Agron's kingsmen, nor did he enjoy sleeping on the hard ground. Yet it seemed as if he had done nothing but such for absolutely ever so long, and for this night and the next several, he would sit adoze before a hearth and wallow in a soft, soft bed.

As a wide-eyed serving maid brought him a sweet-smelling cup of hot mulled wine, Tip shed his cloak and jacket and plopped down in comfort dear. A week from now they would be leaving for the wastes of Gron—but that was a week from now . . . practically forever.

In Älvstad as Agron had promised, there were several stables where ponies were available, and the very next day Tip spent long candlemarks looking over the stock before finally selecting two for his own use: a small brown pony from the hills nigh the Rimmens, and a black from the Steppes of Jord.

"If I were you, I'd ride the black," advised the stablehand.

"I fully intended to, but why did you say?" asked Tipperton.

"Why, lad, it's from Jord," replied the hand, as if that were explanation enough.

Tip shook his head and grinned, then outfitted the black with a small enough saddle and shortened the stirrups to length. The hand threw in a blanket and bridle for the good king's coin he received. Saddlebags and a currycomb were added to the goods, along with a stock blanket and lade-rack for the brown, as well as nosebags and other such. Tip arranged for the keep of the ponies until it was time to march, but when the stablemaster found that the buccan was a kingsscout, he would accept no pay for such. "Doin' my part for the war," said the man. "Doin' my part for the war."

Over the next five days more wagons and men and soldiers on horses drifted in, but on the sixth, the bugles blew and Agron's army set forth—wagons rolling, men marching, horses prancing—the army thirty thousand strong, all led by a wee buccan riding far-point along with another scout, that one a grizzled man.

Across the Argon River they passed, crossing at the wide ford, breaking through a thin layer of ice all the way to the opposite bank. Behind Tip and his companion, as each ridden horse and each drawn wagon came to the ford, they paused to wait for the marching men, each rider taking on a walking soldier, each wagon taking several men. And thus they crossed the Argon, horses bearing double, wagons hauling more, as through the shallows they fared.

In all it took until late midmorn for the entire army to cross, for many were the men and wagons and horses, and the whole stretched for miles altogether.

Up through snow toward Jallor Pass they fared, the route through the Grimwall Mountains standing against the distant sky some thirty miles and three days away, for an army is a slow beast when faring across open land. And although Jallor Pass was a principal trade route between western Jord and Aven, still there was no maintained road between . . . but for a rough track the merchants' wagons and horses had made.

Ten miles a day and only ten would the army try to achieve, for as King Agron had said, " 'Tis a long march and better to arrive with ready soldiers than with an army worn by haste."

And miles out front rode Tipperton and Auly, the two far-point scouts.

Two days, three days, they fared up the land, Tip and Auly now deep in the grip of the pass, the army just then reaching the southern gape. And again snow fell, a chill descending down.

"Oh my, but I hope this weather doesn't bode ill," said Tip, drawing his cloak tight around.

"Here in the col it could be a bane," said Auly, a veteran of battles past, "but down in the flats, it's more likely a blessing."

"How so?"

Auly scratched his greying beard and gestured about. "Unlike the flats below, up here the snow is like to get deep, hindering horse and wain and marching men all. But down in the flats, if it doesn't snow a deal, the cold will actually aid us. It'll freeze the ground, you see, and the harder the ground, the less likely a wagon will mire."

"Ah, yes," said Tipperton, nodding in understanding.

They fared onward through the slot, scanning the slopes and the col ahead for any sign of foe. But the way seemed clear, and the two rode mostly without speaking. Yet at last, Auly said, "What I'm truly worried about is that Modru is master of the cold, or so I hear, and I don't want him casting his power against us."

"I am not certain he will, Auly. When I was in Dendor, six Mages were there as well. They said some castings take an enormous amount of, um, <fire>. I would think that raising a blizzard is one of these . . . though Modru might have done so after the city of Dael was destroyed by Sleeth."

"The Dragon?"

"Yes. He whelmed the city with fire and might until no shelter was left, and then the blizzard came. Whether or no Modru sent it, I cannot say, though others tell it was so."

"And you saw this?"

"Only the aftermath. We waited out the storm in a shelter of sorts many miles and several days away and only came to Dael after the dark deed was done."

"Well I just hope Black Modru doesn't send a storm down on us, though when you think about it, what better target than an enemy army marching on the land?"

Tipperton shivered and did not reply, and the snow came down and down.

On the ninth day after leaving Älvstad the army marched out of the col and down into the Jordian town of Jallorby at the northern reach of the pass. Two more days they rested in this far corner of Jord, there on the flank of the Grimwall Mountains. But on the third day they set out once again, their short respite over.

Moving westerly, they aimed for a distant mountain range and the slide-blocked pass within, Tip and Auly riding far-point, some ten or so miles in advance of the army. And always to their left the Grimwall loomed, reaching for the Gronfangs ahead.

On the fifth day out, as Tip and Auly topped a rise in the land, straight before them and low on the horizon the snow-laden caps of mountains came into view, the range marching off northerly. Tip drew in a breath, the air seeming extra cold.

"There they are, the Gronfangs," said Auly. "As evil a stretch as can be."

"Evil?"

"Aye, filled with Rutcha and Drôkha and Guula and such."

Tip looked at the far reach. "Perhaps less so, now that Modru's Hordes are spread across the lands."

Auly grunted but otherwise did not reply, and urged his horse forward and down the slope ahead, Tip following.

"Look, leftward by the big rock," said Auly.

Lying on his belly atop the hill, Tip peered through the midday light at the ridge nigh the mouth of the pass. Movement stirred among the snow-laden stone on high. "I see."

It was the twelfth day after leaving Jallorby, and the two far-point scouts had come nigh the entrance of the pass through the Gronfangs, no more than a quarter mile ahead. The army itself was a day or so behind.

"Spawn, do you think?" asked Tip.

"Who else?" replied Auly.

"So the pass is not unguarded." Tip's words were a statement and not a question.

Auly shook his head.

"Well then," said Tip, "we need ride back to King Agron."

"Not yet, Tipperton. First let us see what else we can."

And so they waited and watched as the sun edged down the sky.

"A company, we think," said Auly.

"In the gape of the pass?"

"Aye, my lord."

King Agron looked to Tipperton, and the buccan nodded. "Thirty or forty, we saw, Lord Agron. If there are others, they are well back in the slot. Even so, given five we did not see for each one we counted, then a company in all stand ward. Yet that is but a guess; there could be many more within."

Agron sighed. "Then a brigade, or segment, or even a full Horde could bar the way."

"My lord, if it is a segment or Horde," said Captain Brud, standing at hand, "the pass is strait, and it will be difficult winning through."

"Aye, captain, yet we cannot expect to reach Modru without a skirmish or two." Agron paused, then said, "Call my council of captains. We have a battle to plan."

Dressed in white and stealing through the moonlight, across the snow came Agron's vanguard afoot, nigh invisible in the alabaster night. Behind a mile or so, the cavalry awaited the signal, and more soldiers afoot stood ready.

Far to the left and ahead of those advancing moved Tipperton and Auly, guiding a small force of raiders. Their assignment was to negate the lookouts atop the southern ridge.

Across the snow the raiders glided, quiet in their approach, and they came at last to the stone flank of the mountain. Then north they turned and up a slope they advanced, Tipperton in the lead, his bow at the ready, the Warrow silent upon the land.

At last they reached the crest of the ridge, and in the moonlight Tipperton could see, down among the boulders, dark forms lying upon the ground. Holding a hand out to stop those following, Tip took a deep breath to calm himself and slowly let it out, then surveyed the scene below.

A squad of maggot-folk. Asleep. But wait!

He espied one of the Rûpt on ward, peering southerly.

Silently, Tip signalled the men behind to advance, but quietly. Auly came up alongside the buccan. When it seemed the raiders were in place, Tip's whispered command was relayed down the line, and carefully he raised his bow, arrow nocked to the string.

Inhale full; exhale half; draw and aim and loose.

The Rûck was completely unaware.

Even though reluctant to slay an unsuspecting foe, Tipperton's mind flashed back to a similar time at Rimmen Gape, recalling Dara Lyra's words: *Think of all who have been slain by his ilk.*

thun! The arrow whispered through the moonlight to take the Rûck in the neck, and gargling inarticulately he fell sideways to the snow. Yet in that same moment a second Rûck stepped from behind a boulder. And ere Tip could load and loose another arrow, *"Waugh!"* cried the Rûck and raised a horn to his lips.

Even as the signal blew, Auly's shaft took the sentry under the arm, slamming the Rûck aside to fall unmoving to the snow; but the alarm had sounded, and more Rûpt sprang to their feet as arrows sleeted down from above.

With cries of dismay and fear, maggot-folk dodged behind boulders, and again a Rûptish horn blatted, to be answered in kind by a blare from the narrow pass below.

And yet out on the plain another bugle blew, and with a cry of *For king and Dular,* men rose up from the snow and came rushing into the gape, their weapons slashing. And a mile or so away, clarions sounded amid the hammer of hooves.

Still Tipperton and Auly and the men above nocked shafts and let fly, and the Spaunen squad below was devastated, shrieking Rûcks running, only to be brought down as they fled.

"Quick, now, let us see if we can help the king," cried Auly, and the raiders scrambled down the slope and to the ground formerly held by the sentries.

They came to the drop into the gap, and below, men and Rûpt fought savagely. Tipperton could not loose an arrow down into the battle for fear of hitting his own, yet Spawn at the back pressed forward, and there did Tip and the men above wing their shafts.

And still the bugles out on the plains blew, and the thunder of hooves hammered across the hard-frozen land, and farther back came men running, a wordless howl on their lips.

And just as the riders arrived, down in the gape the king and his men parted left- and rightward, to let the horses thunder through, the cavalry to smash into and over the Rûpt here in the mouth of the gap.

Screaming in fear, the Foul Folk turned to flee toward the strait, yet many were felled as they ran, though some did scramble up the slopes to escape the warriors on horses, only to be pursued by men on foot.

And then the main army arrived, men running and shouting, to find the battle nigh ended, for it was but a small company warding the way.

"I'm sorry, my lord, but I did not see the Rûpt behind the boulder, and so the signal was sounded."

King Agron pushed out a negating hand. "Hush, Sir Tipperton, the fault lies not with you. Besides, you said it yourself some months back as we set forth to slay the Gargon: the moment the battle begins is the moment all goes wrong."

"Aye, my lord, but in this case—"

"Nonsense. Our casualties were light, and the Spawn yet caught in the dregs of sleep even though a horn did cry."

"Would that all our victories come at such a cheap price," said Captain Brud. "But I fear we will not escape so lightly in the days to come."

King Agron frowned at Brud. "You and I know that, captain, but for now say nought and let the men celebrate."

"Aye, my lord."

Eyeing the snow-laden steeps above, Tip and Auly rode along the slot of the pass between confining walls, the defile twisting this way and that, jinking in the near distance ahead, angling in the distance behind. No more than a quarter mile aft came the vanguard, yet often Tip and Auly lost sight of any followers as the two point-scouts twined beyond turns in the zigzags of the channel. Farther back and lagging, came the bulk of the army along with the wagons and much of the cavalry, for Agron and the vanguard would ride ahead and clear the foe before them, striving to win completely through and ward the far end until the slower wagons and men afoot could arrive. And so, through the pass rode scouts in the lead, the vanguard and others following. And at the fore of this twisting strait fared Tipperton and Auly on point.

At times the walls were sheer, rising four or five hundred feet or more; at other times but a bit less vertical, sloping upward at steep angles to either side. Yet always the walls were close, no more than a hundred feet apart, narrowing down to twenty-five feet or a bit less for long stretches at a time.

"Lor', Auly, I feel like we're in a vise."

"We are, my lad, we are," said Auly. "And should we meet an army within, it will be quite dreadful."

Snow lay in the slot, in places three or four feet deep, though in other places the rock was bare. In the white-laden stretches,

Auly would lead the way, his horse broaching a path for Tip on his pony to follow.

And always there were maggot-folk tracks in the snow. "Fleeing, I ween," said Tipperton, kneeling and examining the trace, "running somewhere ahead of us." Tipperton stood and mounted the black again.

Occasionally they came to rubble and scree ramped against the walls and running out across the slot. Here they would pick their way carefully and then ride onward, the vanguard in their wake, all outstripping the remainder of the cavalry and the wagons and the men afoot. Yet often a horn signal came drifting along the passage from behind, noting to those who understood its code that the supply train was temporarily stopped, waiting for a path to be cleared of drifts or loose rock so that the wagons could roll on.

The sun rode beyond gathering clouds in a glum winter sky, its rays but rarely reaching the floor of the twisting slot here and there, and a chill drift of air flowed up the passage. As they rode toward a turn in the channel, Tip said, "Huah, but I thought Agron said that warm air from the Gwasp in Gron kept this passage clear, but you know what? It seems to me—"

Tip's speech broke off. Ahead the walls pinched inward, and across the way stood a high barricade made of logs, Foul Folk on the far side.

The second skirmish was hard-fought, stone raining down from above. Black-shafted arrows hissed through the air, slamming into the pavises borne by the men.

Unable to o'ertop the barricade, finally Agron sent a group of archers—Tip among them—back down the pass to scale the walls and come forward again to fly shafts at the missileers and rock throwers on the rampart ahead and send them scurrying. And the archers rained arrows down into the Foul Folk defenders below, receiving deadly dark shafts in return.

And as the fighting raged, the wagons and marching men came 'round the turn, the foot soldiers to join in, though only a company or so at a time could be brought to bear on the Rûptish fortification.

The strife lasted nigh half the glum daylight in all, even though the Rûpt were outnumbered at least a hundred to one. Yet in the end Agron's army prevailed, though the casualties sustained were considerable.

"As I said," muttered Auly to Tip, the two of them watching men tear down the barricade, "we're in a vise . . . a place where a handful can oppose many, as a handful of Spawn did here."

That night and still at the place of the barricade, as the army tarried to rest awhile and to take a meal, Captain Brud came forward to join Tip and Auly at the fire they shared. As they sat and chatted, riding on the wind and echoing up the slot from the darkness ahead there came from afar a shuddering howl to be answered by howls even farther.

"Oh my," said Tip, pausing in his trimming of long arrow shafts to fit the length of his draw, "is that what I believe it is?"

"If it's Vulgs you are thinking of," said Brud around a mouthful of bread, "well then you are right. It's Modru's curs. *Fordervelig Värgs!*"

By the firelight Auly sighted down one of his arrow shafts, saying, "Have you ever seen any?"

Tip swallowed, remembering the beasts in Drearwood. He nodded. "Black and Wolflike, they are, but as large as a pony, or near. Beau and I escaped from one once, though many sought our track. I'm told they have a poison bite."

As Auly looked at Tip and nodded, Brud said, "Vulg's black bite slays at night."

A shiver trembled down Tipperton's spine at Captain Brud's ominous words. "I've heard that," said the buccan. "And a bad poison it is; a Châkia healer once claimed it was a Vulg-poisoned arrow that nearly slew Phais. We almost lost her."

Auly shook his head and looked westward into the dark of the pass. "Laddie, let us hope we don't run into any Vulgs out on point as we are."

Just as Tip nodded in agreement, another howl juddered the swirling air.

Under a dark churning sky, Tip and Auly came riding in haste back to the vanguard. "There's a large slide ahead blocking the way," said Auly. "Mayhap the one you spoke of to the captains, King Agron, back when you first planned this campaign. It's quite a pile and will take a heap of clearing to get the wagons through. But the trouble is, Spawn are using it as a rampart. We're going to have to fight them again."

"Ah me," said Agron, "but I was hoping the way was abandoned. It seems as if Modru has set a watch on this pass, even though I had hoped he would think we would march to the Boreal and take to Fjordlander Dragonships and invade along his north shore. We must hurry now that he knows we are here."

"My lord," said Captain Jorgen of the council, "how would he know we are in this pass? The Iron Tower is days north."

Agron sighed. "Did you not hear the *Värgs* last night? They are Modru's scouts, and I have no doubt they've carried the word to him. Even now a Horde may be on the march to block the far end. We must hurl the Rûpt down from the rampart of rubble and clear it away, and quickly, for I would not have a Horde come upon us while we are yet confined herein, where our cavalry is more of a hindrance than an asset. Out in the open we have the advantage, but herein the leverage is theirs."

Once again the battle was fierce, the footing up the ice-clad, snow-laden scree treacherous, the Rûpt holding the narrow way to the last. Yet finally the king and his men prevailed, for Agron sent men climbing up and across the ravine walls on each side and through a hail of deadly black arrows to come at the Spawn from the rear, the foe to break and run, Agron's forces winning the way. Even so, the wounding of men was disproportionate: the Spawn had slain at least three for each casualty of their own.

Now did the vanguard wait for the bulk of the army and the wagons to arrive, for the slide was formidable, and it would take many men long, long candlemarks to clear the way.

In early morn as a dark day came churning on the land, the king called Tip and Auly unto him. Above the rising wind Agron said, "With all thirty thousand of us laboring together, we should clear the bulk of the blockage in a day or so, at least well enough to get the wagons through. Ere then I would have ye both ride along the remainder of the pass, to see if any Spawn yet lurk. As soon as we can, the vanguard and I will follow after ye. Meanwhile, take care, for there may be a full Horde lying in wait, and I would not have ye fall into a Spawnish trap."

Tip gestured at the slide. "Lord King, you bid us to ride ahead, yet we cannot ride over that."

Agron nodded. "Nay, ye cannot. Yet I ween my men can get your two steeds across. It will take many hands, but get them across we will."

And so, in the swirling wind, angling up and across the slide and angling down again, horse and pony scrambled and skidded and lunged and stiff-leggedly balked, as slowly they scrabbled up and over the slide and down again, men all 'round the steeds to shore with strong arms and hands and to coax and wheedle and haul with ropes, and to support and prop and brace, to lift and tow, other men atop the rubble anchoring ropes on both the ascent and descent, an occasional man slipping and falling and rising again to aid those yet afoot. But at last the steeds came down the far side of the pile and to the floor of the pass beyond, Tip and Auly fretting and fuming every struggling step of the way.

"Lor'," said Auly, inspecting his bay, finding her none the worse for the ordeal though her eyes were yet wide and rolling, "but it's a wonder a leg wasn't broken—on horse, pony, or man."

"I think my black had an easier time of it," replied Tip, the little pony standing calmly as the buccan checked the cinch strap and made certain his bedroll and saddlebags and lute were lashed firmly to the rear cantle, and his bow and extra quiver lashed firmly to the one in front. And he settled a sack holding three days half-rations of grain across the steed's withers. Though Tip's pony and Auly's horse would be on half-rations for the next few days, they would let the black and bay eat their fill when they came to the army again.

"Ready?" asked Auly, glancing at the dark roiling sky above.

"Ready," replied Tip, turning and waving at Agron atop the heap and receiving a salute in return.

As they mounted up and started down the grim slot ahead, Auly said, "I don't like the looks of what might be riding on the whirling wings of this wind. Methinks for the past two days there's been a storm brewing, mayhap one conjured by Modru, Master of the Cold."

"If so," said Tip, pulling his flapping cloak about his shoulders, "then perhaps he's wasting his power."

"Oh?"

"Aye, for should he hurl blizzard at us, then down here in this narrow slot we should be well out of the worst of it."

The blizzard came screaming in late afternoon, trapping Tip and Auly in a howling white Hèl, the pass acting as a giant funnel to channel the shrieking wind and hurtling ice and snow up the slot to the deep-laden steeps above. The world was now a darkling white, and Tip could but barely see Auly's dim form straight ahead, though he was but a handful of paces away.

Seeking shelter, they rode along the north slope of the slot, for there the wind seemed a bit less strong. Even so, it pummelled and battered at them and at their steeds, seeking to hammer them into oblivion, or to freeze them where they stood. And so Tip and Auly sought refuge from the wind, needing to find it quickly ere darkness fell, ere the blast could wrench away life. They were some twelve miles west of the army and nigh the outlet of the pass, and in those twelve miles they had seen no sign of the enemy, but for a scramble of tracks running away. Yet neither friend nor foe were on their minds, but finding safe haven instead.

Of a sudden Auly in the lead veered leftward, angling across the pass, Tip following, and in among high boulders they rode. How Auly had seen them through the hurling white, had seen them through the oncoming night, Tip could not say, yet he was relieved that they had found a shelter of sorts. Still the wind shrieked among the stones, less fierce than out in the open. Auly dismounted and called something back to Tip, but the howling air shredded Auly's words and flung them away on the wind. Yet Tip guessed at what Auly had perhaps called and dismounted as well—

—just as a huge black form hurtled through the shrieking white and over Tip's head and crashed into the pony, slamming the steed sideways and to the ground.

"*Waugh!*" shrilled Tip, only to hear Auly's scream and a horrid yowl. Tip's floundering pony squealed in terror, a terror chopped off in mid scream as the black creature atop tore out the little steed's throat. Tip jerked an arrow from his quiver as, slavering blood, the dark creature whirled toward the buccan and leaped. The Warrow only had time to shove the arrow out before himself as the beast smashed into Tipperton and knocked him backwards, Tip's upflung arm to be caught in the creature's jaws, as together they crashed to the ground, the monster slamming down atop the buccan, knocking the wind from his lungs. Stunned, unable to breathe, Tip feebly pushed at the beast, but it crushed down on him, its fangs locked on Tip's limb.

Oh lor', what a way to—

Ghuuhhh!

Tip managed to inhale.

In the shrieking white, the creature atop him did not move, its crushing weight pinning the buccan.

Ripping his forearm free of the fang-filled jaws, blood flowing unchecked through the shredded cloth of his jacket sleeve, desperately Tip kicked and shoved at the beast, finally struggling out from under the dark creature.

Floundering to his feet, Tip looked down to see—*Vulg! It's a Vulg!*—the buccan's arrow driven deeply into the beast's chest. But Tip did not pause to wonder at this turn of fortune. Instead—

Auly!

Now Tip snatched his bow from the scabbard on his dead pony and set an arrow to string and whirled toward where Auly had been, though there was little he could see. With the wind screaming and whiteness hurtling all 'round, Tip pressed through the blizzard to find—

Oh, Auly.

Where the scout's throat had been there was nought but a gaping ruin, spewn red blood staining crimson the snow. Auly's dead eyes stared wide with fright, locked on the hurtling ice and snow of the blizzard shrieking above. Lying next to him was a dead Vulg, a dagger embedded to the hilt in its baleful left eye. Of Auly's horse there was no sign.

Tip fell to his knees in the snow beside the grizzled man and gently closed his eyes.

Auly, Auly, with force of arms you slew your murderer, whereas mine was slain by chance.

Overlaid on the yowling wind came a howl of a different sort.

Tip leapt to his feet—*Vulgs! More Vulgs!*—his bow at the ready. *Oh lor', the blood, the scent of the blood, it will bring them running. But wait, the wind, they might not— Never mind, bucco, you've got to get out of here, out of the pass altogether.*

Darting back to his dead pony, Tip unlashed his bedroll and saddlebags and lute from the rear cantle and shouldered all. He turned toward Auly's body. *Oh, Auly, I cannot leave you here for the Vulgs to—*

Another howl cut through the wind, this one louder.

Faced with little or no choice, Tipperton turned in the yowling blizzard and the falling dark and began scrambling through pummelling wind and shrieking white and up the canted slope, the snow cascading down the slant behind.

Higher he climbed and higher, air and ice screaming all 'round, the wind stealing his heat even as he sought safe haven. He came to the face of a bluff, a bluff he hadn't the strength to climb even were there no blizzard plucking his life away. Leftward he turned, away from the hammering blast and back toward the army miles hence, though it was not the army he sought but shelter instead—boulders, a cave, a fold in the stone—anything out of the wind.

Pushed by the yawling blast at his back, across the slope and alongside the bluff he struggled, the deep snow grasping at his trembling shanks, the buccan growing weaker with every stride, a fever seeming to rage through his veins. Ahead through the racing whiteness, he saw what appeared to be a darkness on the stone of the bluff. *A shadow, but wait, night is at hand, so how—?*

Slammed from behind by the blizzard, Tip was smashed to his knees, but when he tried to stand again, he had not the strength. Crawling, floundering, creeping through snow, Tipperton made for the dark place ahead . . . to come to a low opening in the stone, a hollow out of the wind.

Scrabbling, struggling, back among the rubble he crept, as far from the blizzard as he could get, ten or twelve feet at most. Panting, he dropped his saddlebags and lute—his bedroll had been lost or abandoned somewhere along the way—and he hitched about and faced the opening, sweat runnelling down his forehead and cheeks in spite of the cold.

And he was burning up.

Blearily, Tip felt along his ripped sleeve to find his arm bleeding beneath. *Oh lor', I've been bitten by a Vulg.*

Captain Brud's ominous words echoed in Tip's mind: *"Vulg's black bite slays at night . . . slays at night . . . at night . . . night."*

As darkness clasped the land, searing with fever Tip leaned back against the fissured, crack-raddled rock, Vulg poison raging in his veins, while outside on the shrieking wind there yawled a juddering howl.

20

In the Dendorian prison, Beau languished abed, too weak, too enervated to rise. Even though his pustulant boils and dark buboes continued to recede, he recovered but slowly, his fever-wasted flesh stubbornly refusing to fill out on his bones no matter how much he ate, though to say fair, his appetite seemed to languish as well. That he had been ill was patently clear, for to the edge of death he had been borne by the plague, to the edge and nearly beyond. Yet the blending of silverroot and gwyn-thyme in a single tisane had drawn him back, had rescued him, along with some five hundred others, though it had come too late for nearly three thousand more.

People came to the prison to see the wee healer, for surely he was Adon-blessed—how else could you explain the miracle he had brought to the city? But the wee one was entirely too weak to accept public accolades, and so many who sought audience were turned away at the prison gates.

Even so, over the next weeks, Beau had a number of visitors, particularly healers who came to praise him, and those who came to worship: patients yet in the prison who had been saved by the remarkable grace of his cure. And in the early days of these visits, he would tire quickly, and often a caller who came to see him would find the wee buccan asleep. Many left him small gifts; many simply knelt and kissed his hand, and if Beau was awake at the time, he was deeply embarrassed by such adulation.

Lor', but this must be how Tip felt, the Hero of Dendor and all; the Hero of Mineholt North, too, though there the Dwarves were a deal more level-headed than the Humans here seem to be.

Ten days after Tip and Bekki and Phais and Loric and even King Agron had said farewell, Beau was allowed to rise. And though his legs quivered and it seemed as if he would faint, still he vowed never again would he lie a prisoner abed, even if he had to crawl to the privy, never again. With help he tottered to the toilet at the end of the hall, and when he returned to collapse on his cot exhausted, he first set his bedpan outside the cell and muttered, "Never again," again.

Another three weeks passed, Beau now gaining flesh, and every day he grew stronger.

Anxious to follow Tipperton, Beau marched into the chief healer's office nigh the prison door. Sitting at the desk within was Halga, leader of the healers ever since Bragan had died of the plague. She looked up from her work as Beau came purposefully in. "I'm fit to travel," he pronounced.

"No you are not," declared Halga.

"I am, too."

"Nay, wee one. Shall I demonstrate?"

Beau groaned. "Look, Lady Halga, just because I need to sit down and rest when I get to the top of the stairs, that doesn't mean—"

"Oh, but it does, Sir Beau. Tell me: what would you advise a like patient who happened to be in your care?"

"Why, I'd tell him to go and do whatever he—"

Halga squatted and looked into Beau's eyes.

"—um, er, that is—" Beau couldn't meet her gaze, and finally he said, "All right. You win. But just as soon as I can top those stairs without stopping to rest, then I'm going, permission or not."

"Beau, even now you need no one's permission to get up and go. Yet heed: if you do go now, then there is every chance you will become a liability along the way and never reach the end."

Beau sighed and nodded, and Halga said, "Another week or so, and then we'll see."

During the week, Beau helped the other healers tend a handful of patients much in the same shape as he, the few who had been drawn back from death's door. All other living victims of the plague had recovered wholly, had been discharged, and the sequestrated surrounding buildings had been given back over to their original purposes.

Those patients left had been moved to the lower quarters of the prison. And the prison itself had once again become a jail, though the inmates were few, most having marched off to war; now in the cells were new-caught felons waiting for the king's steward to pass judgement on them.

In any event, Beau tended a few patients, and every day practiced walking the stairs, getting stronger with each pass up and down.

On the sixth day after confronting Halga, there came a bustle at the front gate, and a guard was assigned to escort a tall person into the lower halls.

Beau was summoned.

As he stepped into the chamber, Beau saw a man, an Elf, nay, a Mage. Tall he was with brown eyes and auburn hair and dressed in a brown robe. He seemed to be youthful, though with Mages one could never tell.

The Mage scowled at the buccan. "So you are Sir Beau Darby, the Litenfolk who found the cure for the plague?"

At Beau's nod, the Mage smiled and sat down and gestured toward a second chair. "I am Farrin, late of Black Mountain."

"I've heard of you, Mage Farrin," said Beau, climbing into the seat.

At Farrin's raised eyebrows, Beau added, "From Mage Imongar and the others. You were part of their circle of seven, or so Tip did say, though you were off looking for Stone Giants to get them to side with us. Did you find them and will they join in the battle against Modru and his ilk?"

A brooding look came over Farrin's features. "Aye, find them I did. But as for siding with us, the chances of that are slim."

"You must tell me all about it, for Tip will want to know."

"The other Waerling? The one who went off with the king?"

Beau nodded. "Yes, and I hope to catch up with him soon and join with— Oh my." A look of dismay crossed Beau's features.

"What is it?" asked Farrin, glancing 'round. Finding nothing to note alarm, he turned back to the Warrow.

Beau looked up at the Mage. "Dara Rael's rede."

"Rede?"

"Aye. 'Seek the aid of those not men to quench the fires of war.' That's what she said, there in Arden Vale, when she looked in the crystal, though at the time she said it, she spoke in the Elven tongue; Dara Faeon rendered it into Common."

Farrin canted his head. "For whom was the rede intended?"

"That's just it," said Beau. "We don't know. A number of Elves were in the room at the time, along with two ragtag Warrows— Tip and me—and Rael said it could be meant for any one of us."

Farrin nodded, then said, "And what does this have to do with your dismay?"

"Well, you see, if the rede is indeed meant for either Tip or me—though I don't think it likely—then Tip has gone off with King Agron, you see, and his entire army, and I am soon to follow."

Farrin turned up a hand. "And . . . ?"

"And they're all men," replied Beau.

"Ah," said Farrin, nodding. "And the rede says to seek the aid of those not men. I see your concern. Of course, that assumes the rede was not meant for the Elves but for you or him or both."

Beau sighed, and he faintly smiled up at the Mage. "Not likely, eh?"

Farrin turned up both hands. "With wild magic, one can never say."

Silence fell between them, but finally Beau asked, "Do you think he is in any danger?"

"Who?"

"Tip."

"Why would you say that?"

"Well if he's with men instead of not-men . . ." Beau looked at Farrin and shrugged.

"He was with men at the battle of Dendor, wasn't he?"

Beau nodded, then said, "Yes, but with Mages, too. And aren't you not-men? Uh, er, I mean, well, that is— Oh, barn rats, you know what I mean."

Farrin laughed. "Yes, Sir Beau, we Mages indeed are not men but another race altogether. Yet, hear me: I would think Sir Tipperton is in no more danger than anyone else marching with an army into the wastes of Gron, even though there are no not-men from whom he can seek aid."

Before Beau could answer, a gong sounded. At Farrin's raised eyebrow, Beau said, "Dinner. Would you join me? You can tell me all about the Stone Giants."

As they stood and stepped from the room and strolled down the hall, Farrin said, "Well, there's not that much to tell. I found them under the Grimwall north of the Skög—"

"The most ancient forest?"

"Aye, though how did you— Oh, the Elves?"

Beau nodded. "Phais and Loric spoke of it. But what about the Stone Giants?"

"They spoke in a tongue most peculiar, like rocks sliding over one another. I managed to teach three or four of the younger ones an old form of Common. When I explained to them why I had come, and they in turn told the elders, well, the elders replied that they wanted no part of a war among surface dwellers."

"Surface dwellers?"

"Aye, that's what they call those of us who live on the land and not within it."

"What about the Dwarves? They are in this fight, and although they live on the land, they live in it as well."

Farrin smiled. "The very point I made to them, Beau. Yet though they admire the work of the Dwarves and revile that of the Rûpt, still the elders refused. On the other hand, a few of the younger ones seemed somewhat reluctant to say yea or nay."

"Did you tell 'em about Gyphon and what it might mean should he be victorious?"

"I did. Even so, they were not swayed."

"Hmm," mused Beau, and he turned from the hallway and entered a common room, Farrin coming after. Taking up trenchers and knives and spoons from a side stand and taking up earthenware mugs as well, they filled their plates from an array of food on a central table and filled their cups with tea. As they moved to a bench and settled in to eat, Beau asked, "What do they look like? —The Stone Giants, I mean."

"Tall. Some even taller than Trolls. Fourteen, fifteen, sixteen feet and more they stand. And they have gemstones for eyes."

"Real gemstones?" asked Beau, tearing off a hunk of bread.

"So it appears," said Farrin, nodding and sipping his tea, then adding, "Glittering eyes, much like those of your folk."

"How do they dress?" Beau managed to say around a mouthful.

"They don't. Clothes would turn to tatters where they dwell, where they work, down along the grinding seams of the living stone itself."

"Oh my, no clothes; weren't you embarrassed?"

Farrin exploded in laughter.

They ate in silence for a while, and finally Farrin said, "When do you plan on starting out for Gron?"

"Tomorrow should see me declared fit to travel," replied Beau. "Though I am not quite up to my old self, still I can climb several times to the top of the stairs before becoming too winded to continue."

Farrin smiled. "The stairs are your measure?"

"Not mine. Halga's." Beau nodded toward where Halga sat a table away.

"It is a rough gauge of fitness," said Halga. "Yesterweek he couldn't make it from bottom to top without stopping at least twice. Still, he would have left had I not stopped him."

As Farrin looked askance at Beau, the buccan said, "She was right, even though it cost me a sevenday delay. In the long run I think I'll reach Agron's army sooner by leaving later than later had I left sooner."

Farrin laughed aloud, then said, "I know how you feel, Beau, wanting to rejoin your comrade. I, too, go to join my companions; I may have failed with the Utruni, but when I find my colleagues the circle of seven will be whole again."

"Oh my," said Beau, his face falling, "didn't anyone tell you?"

Farrin canted his head, puzzled, faintly smiling, a spoonful of beans lifted partway to his mouth. "Tell me what?"

Beau reached out to touch Farrin's free hand. "One of your circle—Alvaron by name—the Gargon slew him in its death throes."

The wind went out of Farrin's lungs and he dropped his spoon with a clatter. "Alvaron?"

Beau nodded.

"Dead?"

Again Beau nodded.

Farrin pushed his trencher away and stood. "I need to be alone."

Beau watched as the Mage stepped through the doorway and was gone. Sighing, the buccan, too, pushed his own trencher away. Turning to Halga, he said, "I think I'm going for a walk, Halga. Out to the city walls, if I might."

She looked at him long and finally nodded, saying, "Dress warmly, Beau."

Beau trudged to his room and took up his quilted jacket and gloves and cloak, and moments later stepped out through the front gate. A light snow drifted down through stillness to settle on the town, and Beau pulled his collar 'round and looked up through the drifting flakes at the grey sky overhead. As he took a deep breath of chill air, he suddenly realized that this was the first time in over two months he had been free of the prison behind. Yet even though he should have felt joy at his deliverance he did not, for his wee buccan heart was heavily weighed with an old grief again made new.

The next day, as Beau returned from an early-morning walk, a grim Farrin came riding toward the prison, a pack animal in tow behind. Beau stopped at the gate and waited, and Farrin rode to him and drew up. Without dismounting, the Mage looked down at the Warrow. "I'm going now to seek the remainder of my circle. In Pellar, I am told, they might be found, and find them I will. I hope you find your own friend, wherever he may be. Yet, heed, Beau Darby, and heed me well, for I came to tell you this: where you intend to go is a place of a most ill nature, for Gron is Modru's realm, and the land follows his lead. To go alone toward that dire place is certainly risk enough, but to enter alone is madness. You must seek aid to find your friend, and another comes who may help."

Beau's eyes widened. "Another?"

Farrin nodded. "Aye. I met him as I rode from the Skög. When I told him I was bound for Dendor, he said therein was a Waerling who had found a cure for the plague. How he knew this I did not ask, yet hear me: he said he would come to Dendor just to look at you. I would ask him for his aid, were I in your place. None better can you find to help you find your friend."

"Who is he?"

Farrin's somber cast was broken slightly by a faint smile. "You will know him when he comes."

Impatiently, Beau shook his head. "Look, Mage Farrin, Halga declared me fit to travel, and travel I will. Within the week. If he's not here before I go, he will just have to find me along the way."

Farrin cocked an eyebrow and slightly shook his head. "Ah, me, but this is rash and ill-advised, yet I know you are driven, just as am I. Still I would ask of you this: wait out the week, the full sevenday, ere you set forth on your own, for he may come within that allotted time. But if not, leave word that you travel alone for Gron, and also leave word as to the route you intend to take so that he may follow if he is of a mind to do so."

With that, Farrin reined his horse about, then again glanced down at Beau and said, "Look to the east, for he will come thence, and soon I would say, for he is curious to see just who it was broke Modru's plague."

Without another word Farrin rode away, the packhorse drawn on a tether after.

Nettled, puzzled, Beau watched as the Mage fared down the cobbled street, snow lying white on the stone. At last the buccan called out, "Good fortune. May you find what you seek."

Without looking back or slowing, Farrin momentarily raised a hand in reply and kept riding southerly, heading for the distant south gate and the way to Pellar beyond.

His breath blowing white on the cold air, Beau watched until Farrin turned beyond a corner building, then the buccan trudged into the prison.

Over that day and the one after, Beau began assembling the

things he would need on his journey, especially taking care to select a good variety of medicks. Too, he went to the king's stables to see to his pony, and found the little steed in good stead, having been well cared for by the stableboy.

Remembering Bekki's words, Beau went to the armory and chose several pouches of lead sling bullets, then on second thought, exchanged them for bullets of steel.

"That's a fair choice," said the armorer, a beefy man. "Steel is less heavy, and you never know when you'll need to run or climb or such, and the lighter the load, the easier the task. But these here"—he turned and took up a handful of elongated bullets, shiny earthen-brown in color—"are lighter still, and almost as deadly. Clay, they are, fired in our own kilns; the glaze makes them extra hard. Would you care to try some?"

Beau took a double handful and stepped out back. When he returned he had a smile on his face. "Splendid," he said. "Fired clay it is."

And so, for two days, Beau made his preparations, but Farrin's words ever echoed in his mind: *"Gron is Modru's realm . . . to enter alone is madness . . . you must seek aid . . . another comes who may help."*

Each dawn and noon and evening, Beau strode the walls of Dendor—*"Look to the east, for he will come thence"*—but no one did Beau see.

Although he was ready to travel by the second day, Beau delayed for a third, and he paced the ramparts along the eastern merge. *Come what may, I'm leaving tomorrow, and that's certain.* But again Farrin's words came to mind: *"Wait out the week, the full sevenday . . ."*

The sun was verging on the western rim of the world, when out on the eastern plain a glimmer of movement caught Beau's eye. A shimmer of white on white it seemed . . .

Lor' but what is it?

. . . silvery-white shapes running toward Dendor across the glittering snow.

"Hoy," Beau called to the guard and pointed. "Look. To the east."

Onward they came, drawing ever closer.

What is it I am seeing?

Beside Beau a clanging sounded as the guard hammered an iron bar 'round and 'round within a hanging iron triangle.

One, two, three—Beau counted—*four altogether. —No, six . . . seven.*

He waited as on they came, and he counted again.

Seven, definitely seven.

And still the running silver shapes defied his eye to resolve into something he could recognize.

And the sun fell halfway into the lip of the world, red rays west running to violet in the eastern sky. And against fading sunlight glancing on snow, seven shapes raced across the plains, running silver on pale crimson white.

Soldiers with crossbows scrambled up the ramps to come to the banquette, and the captain of the guard came to the bastion and peered east as well. "Stand ready," ordered the captain.

Of a sudden in a flash of recognition, Beau knew what he was seeing though he'd never seen them before and in fact had only heard of them as sung in an Elven song, and amazement filled his gaze. "Wait, captain, loose no quarrels!" he called. "These are not the foe!"

The captain turned to the buccan. "Then, by Adon, what is it that comes?"

"Draega, captain, Draega. Draega from Adonar. They can't be anything else."

"Draega?"

"Oh my, oh my," exclaimed Beau, not answering, racing back and forth along the weapons shelf, stopping long enough to look again, and then run to another crenel.

Exasperated, the captain turned to his men. "Stand ready, but do as the Litenfolk says: loose no quarrels."

And they watched as seven silver shapes came running, until all could see what they were: seven Silver Wolves from legend, plunging o'er the snow, seven Silver Wolves, seven in all, racing toward Dendor and Beau.

*S*omething important. Something im—

Again a Vulg howl sounded on the screaming wind.

—*portant.*

But what it was, Tip could not remember, his mind ahaze with poison raging in his veins, while just beyond the mouth of the sheltering hollow a blizzard shrieked past in the darkness, hurtling ice and snow onto steep mountain slopes above and along the gorge below.

Tip leaned his head back against the cracked stone and closed his eyes, and just as he was losing consciousness—

Tip jerked upright and called out, "What? What did you say, Beau?" His voice was lost under the yowl of the wind outside.

I'm certain I heard him call out.

Again Tip spoke aloud into the darkness. "Oh, Beau, are you in trouble?"

There was no answer.

His breath coming harsh, Tip sat in blackness, his bow grasped loosely in his hands, the arrow fallen away.

What did you say, Beau?

Fevered and muttering aloud—" 'You're in a terrible fix, bucco.' That's what you would tell me, as if I didn't know. Well, my friend, it's not like you were in any better shape, the last time I saw you." Unable to hold himself upright, Tip slowly fell over sideways. He lay on his left side, his cheek against cold rubble, and looked down at Beau in his prison cot, pustulant boils all over the buccan's face. "But Bekki and I, we saved your neck, bringing back th— Oh lor', that's it!"

Hissing and muttering, Tip struggled, trying to upright himself, but he could not. His wounded left arm trapped beneath his own body, Tip floundered about with his free hand in the ground-up barley, making certain the great rumbling buhrstones didn't crush his fingers or arm as he searched through the flour for his saddlebags. "That's what you were trying to tell me, Beau. That's what you were trying to—" His hand fell upon leather and, straining, cursing, he dragged the thing to him. "Oh no. It's my lute."

Feebly pushing aside the dead pony, not wondering how it had gotten here, Tip again fumbled across the rubble and found—"Is it my blanket ro—? No, no. This is leather."

He managed to drag the pouches to him and after a long, one-handed struggle succeeded in unbuckling one side. "I hope this is the bag I put it in, for I haven't the strength to—" With the fire burning atop Beacontor in the distance, Tip's hand fell across a cloth bundle, and he pulled it free of the pouch. Gripping the bundle and using his teeth, he loosened the twine and rolled open the cloth to free the sprigs inside.

Yet lying on the cold rocks, Tip called out, "But I can't make gwynthyme tea, Beau; what'll I do?"

Only the howl of the blizzard answered the buccan, beautiful, exotic, unveiled Châkia singing in the wind.

Answering his own question—"Well, there's nothing for it, bucco, you'll just have to make do with what you have"—Tip began chewing on one of the sprigs, his bare bit of saliva mixing with the juice of the golden mint as Hyrinian riders galloped across the Plains of Valon.

"Should I swallow it, Beau? Should I swallow? It's not tea, but it's the best I can do." Tip laughed in fevered hysteria and looked up to see DelfLord Borl. "Hoy, Lord Borl, I'm eating precious gwynthyme; will you have some? Your son and I crawled all over that mountain to get this yellow weed, and surely you— I say, Loric, here we have a most rare treat, and I do mean rare."

Tipperton took up another sprig and began to chew, and the heartening fragrance of mint filled his mouth and nostrils. As Borl and Loric faded, Tip managed to shove himself upright, looking about the Dwarvenholt to see where they went. But Phais lay abed before him, pale in countenance. Tip began weeping. "Oh, Phais, you are sorely wounded by a poisoned black shaft. Don't die as my Rynna did. Here, we need to put a gwynthyme poultice on your arrow wound." But Phais vanished even as he reached for her.

Struggling, giggling, weeping, raging, Tip managed to free his wounded arm from the left sleeve of his jacket. And he unbuttoned and slid the sleeve of his jerkin up to his elbow, exposing the jagged wound. "No tea, Beau, no tea," he shouted above the roar of Bellon Falls.

Tip took up another sprig and shoved the whole of it into his mouth. And he chewed and spat upon the ripped flesh of his forearm time and again, until juice and saliva and blood slathered over all. And while sitting on the ramparts of Caer Lindor he wept and watched the bordering woods for Rynna to appear, and he placed the chewed pulp over the gashes, but it did not cover all. Tip took up another sprig and chewed and spat and swallowed some of the juice and chewed more and spat more and finally added the pulp of this sprig to that of the other. He fumbled about on the floor of his mill, shoving aside coins with holes in them until he found the cloth the gwynthyme had been wrapped in and used it to bind his wound and hold the poultice against the deep slashes.

And still the moon howled over the twisted trees of Drearwood—or was it a Vulg howling on the wind?—as Tipperton fell screaming down the sheer stone above Nordlake and into waters below, while a forlorn hooting sounded within the fog.

"What is it?" asked Tip.

Rynna smiled and gestured at a basket. "Come and see."

Tip stepped to the damman, and there asleep in a rumple of blanket was a—

"Oh!" Tip startled awake.

It was dark, and still a blizzard howled outside the mouth of the cavity. Tip was shuddering with cold. He managed to struggle his bandaged left arm back into the sleeve of his jacket and wrap his cloak around ere swooning again.

The next time he awakened, night had gone, but the blizzard had not, for the wind yet howled and ice yet hurtled across the low opening of the cavity, a drift covering fully half of the breach.

Terribly thirsty, Tip fished under his jacket to his right hip and pulled out his waterskin, looped on a thong over his head and across his chest. Drinking, drinking, it seemed as if his parched throat would never be satisfied. Finally he stopped, his thirst yet burning, but he was too exhausted to hold the container aloft. And then he retched and retched again, vomit spewing out, the buccan barely turning aside in time to keep from soiling himself. He slumped back against the stone, and even as he swiped his sleeve across his mouth, he lost consciousness.

Tipperton's own screaming wrenched him awake. "The Gargon! The Gargon! Eeee . . . !" Confused, he thrashed about. "Where . . . where am . . . ?"

Outside in darkness the savage blizzard howled.

Oh, the cave. I'm still in the cave. I, I wonder what day . . . ? I wonder what . . . ? Tip's muddled mind could not complete the thought.

Thirsty.

"But I threw up," he said aloud. He fumbled among the stones alongside. "Gwynthyme. Mint. Settle my stomach."

Locating a sprig, Tip began to chew, the juice of the golden plant eking forth a bit of saliva.

"I could eat snow," he told the dark shapes hidden in the blackness. Their answers were lost in the howl of the wind.

"Eat snow . . . but wait, Beau said not. 'It'll just steal our heat, and we've no food to replenish it,' he said." Tip looked about, still chewing. "Didn't you say that in Drearwood, Beau?" But Tip couldn't find his friend, and so he spoke 'round his mouthful of gwynthyme to the surrounding dark, while outside the yawling blizzard raged. "That's what he said. But I have some crue in my saddlebag. And more gwynthyme. I could eat crue and gwynthyme and maybe even silverroot."

The juice of the mint now gone, Tip managed to swallow the pulp. After a moment he took up the waterskin and drained it dry. This time he kept the water down.

In the stillness he heard a *tink* and then another. *What th—?*

tink

Water?

tink

Tip opened his eyes. In the snow-laden mouth of the tiny cave light shone through the small gap between the top of the drift and the stone above it.

tink

But wait. I hear a drip and not a howl. How can . . . ? Oh. The blizzard. It's blown itself out.

Struggling, Tip tried to lean forward to crawl to the opening. He managed to catch himself before he fell on his face. Pushing back, Tip leaned against the wall once more. *Too weak. I've got to eat.*

tink

Tip dragged the saddlebags to him and fumbled with the

buckles of the yet unopened side, finally managing to free the straps. Exhausted, he rested awhile before extracting a biscuit of crue.

tink

To his right along the back wall, in one of the small crevices water dripped. Tip fished into his saddlebags and found his tin cup. It just barely managed to fit in the cranny under the drip.

Tip fell asleep while waiting.

A thundering rumble awakened the buccan, and he opened his eyes to see whiteness roaring past the entry.

What th—!

Snow boiled inward, toward the buccan—

Avalanche!

—and blackness fell within the tiny cave as dense snow blocked all light, but the thunder rumbled on . . . and on . . . and finally fell to silence.

plip

In total darkness, drips fell into a cup of water.

Tip found the crevice and the cup and drank all the water within, then slid the cup back under the drip and took a bite of crue.

I'll dig out when I've the strength.

Tip could not tell how long he had been asleep or whether it was night or day outside. After drinking another cup of water and setting the tin back under the drip, in the darkness he carefully unwrapped his wounded arm. The flesh was terribly hot, the arm sore to the touch. Wincing, he cleaned the remains of the poultice away and took up the last two sprigs from the opened bundle of gwynthyme, and once again he chewed and spat the juice onto the damaged flesh. And he made a poultice out of the resulting pulp.

Of the two bundles of gwynthyme you took, bucco, you've only one bundle left. Oh, and the silverroot, too.

Calling out in the dark, he said, "Beau, should I ration the gwynthyme or should instead I use it at need?"

Only the *plip* of water dripping into the cup answered his query.

Muttering aloud—"I had three days of crue and jerky with me in my saddlebags."—*Oh Adon, Auly is dead*—"If I ration my food carefully, I might be able to make it stretch for days. But if I do that, then how will I gain the strength to dig my way clear of the slide. Oh, I wish I had taken my pony's sack of grain . . . but then, weak as I was, I would never have made it to this place. Lor', lor', it was a choice between being slain by Vulgs or getting in here and being trapped by a slide."

Wait just a moment, bucco, you can't blame yourself for being trapped by a slide.

Tip drank the water in the cup and slid the little container back into the crevice.

tink

"Hoy, Beau, where do you suggest we pee?" Tip called out and laughed, remembering. "No cliff here to dribble over." He patted the stone behind. "No way back into the woods, either. And for that matter, after eating, where do you suggest I—"

From somewhere outside and muffled by the snow there sounded a prolonged howl.

Tip's heart skipped a beat. *Damned Vulgs. They killed Auly, and now they search for me.*

Tip had no way to know the passage of time. *If I were an Elf . . . but I'm not.*

"Hey, Beau. How many days have passed?"

Sitting in the dark for long, long candlemarks, Tip had thought of an elaborate scheme to gauge the passage of time. First he would count heartbeats while the more or less regular drips of water slowly filled the cup. Then he would cipher out how many candlemarks that might be. Next, he would set his waterskin under the drip and wait until it was full, and then measure it in cupfuls, and that would give him a gauge as to how long it took the skin to fill. And then he could use that from then on to measure time: it would be a waterclock of sorts. But when he tried to put the plan into effect, he found he could fit the mouth of his waterskin into the crevice such that the drips went in, but the bulk of the skin was upslope, hence it would never fill. And without a large container collecting drips even as he slept, the scheme wouldn't work at all.

In trying to determine how long he had been in the cave, he seemed to recall that the blizzard had lasted two or three days . . . but because he had drifted in and out of delirium, of this he wasn't certain at all. And then the slide, the avalanche, came, and that was on the third day, perhaps, or mayhap it was the fourth. And his food had lasted the following three days, assuming he ate more or less on schedule, though again that may or may not have been true. He had eaten all of his food trying to regain the strength to dig his way free, but had not recovered sufficiently to do so. And his food had run out two days past, and now he was on the verge of fainting.

His mind drifted, wandered, roamed the darkness, spinning

the same thoughts over and again, though occasionally ranging into new territory.

Lor, I've been trapped, what? Six days, eight days?

His left arm had swollen and seemed filled with fire, and neither gwynthyme nor silverroot had sufficed, though all of that was now gone as well.

And still there came Vulgs' howls, some seeming nearer than others. *Do they search for me?* Though Tip had long since become accustomed to the smell of his own vomit and urine and feces permeating the tiny cave, he prayed to Adon none would leak out for the Vulgs to catch the scent.

Tip drank another cup of water, a cup replenished just fast enough to barely keep his thirst at bay.

I wonder where the army is. Perhaps even now they're somewhere below digging through snow. Oh, if I could only hear a bugle, a bugle, a bugle, I'd yell and hope someone would hear me.

As he set the tin back under the drip, his hand brushed across his lute. *Lor, but I do miss my music. But I can't play a thing with this hot bloated limb; my fingers don't even work.*

I wonder what day it is? Has Year's Long Night come, or is it yet to be?

A tear ran down Tip's cheek. *Come on, bucco, is this any way to act? Here, now, put some iron in that spine of yours. And think, even if it is Winterday, Year's Long Night, you don't need that arm of yours to have music. You still have your voice.*

Softly Tip began to sing the Elven rite of the changing of the seasons, smiling in remembrance of Bekki pacing him through the ritual on the eve of Autumnday, weeping in remembrance of stepping the Springday rite among the Elves of Arden Vale.

Lost in the ritual it was awhile before Tip heard the sounds of digging. And he chopped his voice to silence and listened.

Still the digging went on.

Rescue!

"I'm in here, I'm in here," yelled Tip in the ebon dark.

His shout was answered by a growl.

Oh Adon, it's Vulgs. They've found me!

Now the digging came faster, as if more than one creature clawed to get through the snow and at the buccan.

Tip felt about and found his bow, but he could but barely grip it with his left hand; and e'en should he switch hands, his fiery swollen arm certainly would not withstand the draw.

My sling!

Searching through the saddlebags, Tip fumbled for the sling, but before he could find it, light began filtering in.

Too close! They're too close!

Snatching up an arrow, Tip squinted against the light, pain lacing through his unaccustomed eyes, for he had been in total darkness for days on end.

Weak, his head swimming with dizziness, his left arm useless, his eyes nearly blinded, arrow in hand like a dagger, Tip struggled to his knees, too weak to rise fully, and snarled, "All right you Vulg bastards, Modru's curs, you've found me, but to Hèl with you and your Gyphon."

And then a dark, fanged muzzle broke through the snow and lunged into the cave, just as blackness overtook Tipperton and he fell forward on his face.

22

*S*even Silver Wolves, seven Draega, came trotting across the eastern stone bridge above the dry moat and into the embrasure below the eastern parapet. And then out from under the wall and into the open stepped a man, an Elf, nay, a Mage. How he had come to the gate itself, Beau could not say. Yet it was plain to see that the Mage was there at the bridge below, and huge Silver Wolves, large as ponies, milled about him.

"My friends and I ask permission to enter your city," called up the Mage.

"And who are you and what is your business, Lord Mage?" asked the captain of the east ward.

"I am Dalavar of Darda Vrka, though some know me by the name Wolfmage, and I have come to see the Waerling who put down Modru's plague."

"Oh lor'," blurted Beau, "he's come to see me." The buccan turned to the captain. "He's come to see me. Farrin said someone would come to me from the east, and perhaps Mage Dalavar is the one. Oh, do let him in, captain. Do let him in."

As Beau ran down the ramp and toward the inner portal, the captain of the eastern gate hesitated and glanced down at the Mage with his waiting 'Wolves, but finally nodded to the men at the portcullis winch, and called a command down to the soldiers in the passage below.

Beau jittered from one foot to another as the iron inner grille squealed upward, and then men unbarred the inner side-postern and opened it. One after another, through the gate came the huge Silver Wolves, trotting out on their long legs, their eyes shifting this way and that, their silver muzzles in the air as if to sense friend or foe. Warders gave back before them in awe, for they were beasts of legend, yet Beau stood his ground, transfixed in wonder, and two came straight at the buccan and loomed over him, red tongues lolling over white fangs.

"Oh my," breathed Beau, reaching tentatively out to touch one of the great beasts.

"I would not look them straight in the eye if I were you, Waerling. They do not take kindly to such boldness." Beau looked up to see the Mage, to see Dalavar, standing at hand.

Man height he was, six foot or so, and as with all Magekind his eyes held the hint of a tilt and his ears were pointed, though less so than those of Elves . . . or Waerlings for that matter. His hair was long and silvery-white, and it hung down beyond his shoulders, its sheen much the same as Silver Wolf fur, though somehow darker. In spite of his whitish hair, he looked to be no more than thirty. He was dressed in soft grey leathers, black belt with silver buckle clasped at his waist. His feet were shod in black boots, supple and soft on the land. His eyes were as piercing as those of a falcon, their color perhaps a pale grey. At his throat was a glimmer of silver, mayhap an amulet upon leather thong. He bore no visible weapons and did not bear a staff.

"I say," said Beau, the beast at hand tolerating his touch, "they really *are* the size of ponies."

Dalavar laughed. "Indeed."

"What's his name?" asked Beau, running his hand along the silvery-white flank of the creature, a thick layer of soft white fur beneath.

"*Her* name, if you must have one . . ."—Dalavar frowned, then said—". . . is Shimmer of Moonlight on the Water as the Gentle Breeze Brings Scents from Near and Far . . . or that's as close as I can say it in Common."

"Oh my, what a mouthful," said Beau, unable to keep his hands from the magnificent creature.

"Not in Draega," replied Dalavar. "You may call her Shimmer."

"Shimmer," said Beau, trying to hug the pony-sized Draega, his cheek lying alongside her chest as he inhaled her clean scent. Shimmer looked up at the Wolfmage as if seeking advice, but endured the wee one's embrace.

"And your name . . . ?" asked Dalavar.

Beau stepped back from Shimmer. "My name? Oh, I'm Beau Darby. I think I'm the one you've come to see."

* * *

"... and so you see, with what I had learned from Delgar's book and from Elby Roh in Willowdell and from my own studies, well then, it just seemed natural to try a tisane of silverroot and gwynthyme."

Dalavar nodded as Beau took a swig of ale, the Mage himself not touching the small glass of brandy before him.

The buccan and the Mage sat in the common room of the Leaping Stag, a tavern near the prison. Silver Wolves lolled outside, and few people had the courage to step past them and into the alehouse itself. Hence, but for the 'keep and a patron or two, Beau and Dalavar had the place nearly unto themselves.

Beau looked up at the Wolfmage. "Surely I am not the first to have thought of doing so."

"Perhaps not, Beau, yet you are the first to have thought of mixing the two *and* to have had the ingredients on hand when plague raged on the land."

"Oh, but I didn't have all the ingredients, just the silverroot. It was Tip and Bekki who got the gwynthyme."

"Tip? Bekki?"

"Bekki is a Dwarf . . . now DelfLord of Mineholt North. His da, you see, was killed in the Skarpal Mountains fighting Foul Folk. But Bekki was here at the Battle of Dendor, and he knew where a patch of gwynthyme grew. And Tip, well, he is Tipperton Thistledown, another Warrow like me; he now is a scout with King Agron's army in Gron."

Dalavar slowly shook his head. "So Agron has foolishly marched into Gron in the wintertime."

Beau's heart lurched. "Is that bad?"

"It is Modru's season, Beau."

"Oh my, that's what the others said. But no one—not Phais, Loric, Imongar, or any of the others—could talk Agron out of his winter campaign. Some said that it was Prince Dular's death that drove Agron to such an act."

"When did he set forth?"

Beau frowned. "Well, the muster was to take place in Älvstad in mid-November . . . the fifteenth, I think. That's when he was to start the march toward Gron."

"And do you know how he was to enter that grim land?"

"Tip said they were going through a narrow pass in the Gronfangs somewhere west of Jallorby."

Dalavar took in a deep breath and let it out. "I know of it. A grim slot, that."

Beau turned up a hand. "Well, grim or not, that's where I'm headed."

"You?"

"Yes, Mage Dalavar. I plan on going into Gron."

Dalavar frowned. "Why?"

"Well, I'm going after Agron's army. As I said, Tip is a scout for the king, and Tip and I have been through a lot together. We started out this war together and, by the grace of Elwydd, we plan on finishing it together."

For long moments the Wolfmage looked at Beau. Finally he said, "Friendship, loyalty, they are precious things."

Beau took another swig from his mug. "Mage Dalavar, Farrin said you might aid me in reaching my friend, at least I think he was referring to you. He said he met someone as he rode from the Skög, someone who would come from the east to see me. And since you are the only one who has come from the east lately, and to see me, well . . ."

"Yes, I did meet Farrin nigh the Skög. And he said I might aid you, eh?"

Beau nodded.

The Wolfmage gazed into his brandy as if to find something within. At last he took up the glass and held it toward the window and peered through the amber liquid at the light and said, "Well then, we can't let Farrin down, eh?"

Beau's eyes flew wide. "You mean you'll help me?"

Dalavar drank the brandy all in one gulp, and said, "Indeed. Mayhap I can overtake Agron ere he marches too far into Modru's realm, ere he makes the mistake of his life. When can you be ready to leave?"

"Right now," said Beau. "I mean, I've already gathered the goods I intend to take. But look, there is no way my pony can reach Tip and Agron and the others before they are well into Gron."

The Wolfmage smiled and got to his feet. "You will need no pony, my friend. And dawn will be soon enough. Pack your goods in saddlebags."

Beau scrambled down from the bench. "Unh, if you don't mind, I'll keep my red healer's book and a few other things in a bindle across my back."

Though Dalavar had no money whatsoever, the innkeeper would take no coin from Beau, saying that the buccan had already paid for all: "It was you what cured my laddie of Modru's malice, and bless you, sir."

As they stepped to the porch and the street beyond, Beau looked about. "I say, Dalavar, one of your 'Wolves has gone missing. There are but six Draega here." Beau looked up and down the street. "I don't see him anywhere."

Dalavar smiled. "First let me say, these are not *my* 'Wolves,

wee one, but my friends instead. And as to one of them missing, fear not; he may be nearer than you think."

As dawn came, Beau said good-bye to Halga, the only healer
other than himself left at the prison caring for the three remaining victims of the plague. Beau also said goodbye to the trio of
patients and to the prison staff, for he had come to know all of
them well during his recovery.

Looping the strap of·his bindle over his head and across his
chest, and bearing two pairs of saddlebags, he passed through
the prison door and trudged through the snow to the iron gate,
where the guard swung the grille wide.

Outside stood Dalavar and six Silver Wolves and behind them a
large crowd of Dendorians who cheered when Beau stepped forth.
The Draega seemed somewhat uncomfortable with the press of
people, even though all in the throng gave the 'Wolves wide berth.

Stepping forward came Jaegar, Steward of Aven now that
Agron was gone. And for all peoples everywhere, Jaegar bade the
young buccan farewell and praised him for what he had done.
Embarrassed, Beau shuffled his feet, and when the crowd called
for him to speak, Beau said, "Look, I just happened to be in the
right place at the right time, or perhaps the wrong place at the
wrong time. Regardless, my friend Tipperton once said that no
one person is responsible for victory. The same can be said
about winning the fight against the plague in Dendor: it took
many hands to deal with this scourge. So praise all those who
worked tirelessly, for their battle to defeat Modru's pestilence
was no less courageous, no less deadly, than that fought on the
walls and in the field against Modru's Horde. Seek out the healers, the caregivers, and all else who risked their lives in the battle against the scourge, and tell them how you feel. But as for
me, my friends, I thank you for your thoughts and for your well
wishes, but I must go; there is work yet to be done."

As Beau stepped back and toward Dalavar and the Silver
Wolves, the crowd erupted in a prolonged cheer, and many
called out blessings on the wee buccan, and those who would
seek to touch him were held at bay by the sight of the Draega
he walked among.

"Here," said the Wolfmage, taking Beau's saddlebags from
him and draping a pair across one Silver Wolf and the second
pair across another, "we will bear these burdens."

Beau looked about. "But how will we go, Dalavar? Are you
going to cast a spell? Are we to fly?"

Dalavar laughed. "Nay, wee one. Instead, you will ride."

"Ride?"

"Aye." The Wolfmage gestured at a nearby Draega. "I have asked Shimmer, and she has said she will bear you."

"Oh, Shimmer." Again Beau embraced the Silver Wolf, and again she tolerated it.

Beau looked up at Dalavar. "Will I need a saddle?"

Dalavar laughed. "Nay. She will not let you fall."

Dalavar boosted Beau onto the great 'Wolf's back, saying, "Twine your fingers in her fur. She will not mind."

Hitching his bindle 'round to his back and then lacing his fingers into the soft fur, Beau looked about, and said, "But how will you come, Dalavar? Will you ride? And I say, where is that seventh 'Wolf? He seems to be missing again."

"Fear not, Beau. He will be at the western gate."

Dalavar spoke a strange word unto the Draega and then stepped away and into the crowd, and though Beau was watching, of a sudden he lost sight of the Mage; it was as if Dalavar had simply vanished.

Following the largest of the Silver Wolves, Shimmer moved smoothly into a trot, the other Draega forming a cordon 'round. Hastily, the crowd parted, giving back before the buccan and his extraordinary escort, though they cheered him on his way. And when the Silver Wolves passed beyond the throng, they broke into a lope, a steady, easy gait.

Westerly they fared through the streets of the city, now and then veering down a side street only to turn west again, and people afoot and those mounted or in horse-drawn vehicles moved aside to let them by, though they shouted out benedictions and acclaim as the Draega ran past.

To the western gate they came, the passage standing open below the parapet, and under wall and out across the stone bridge they loped, where another Silver Wolf awaited, this one somehow darker than the rest. And this 'Wolf matched his gait to that of the leader, and out onto the snow-covered plains the pack ran, while behind, soldiers atop the wall cheered them on.

Of Dalavar there was no sign.

Across the wide reaches of Aven they loped, miles vanishing behind their long strides, Shimmer and the other Silver Wolves running easily. And Beau watched the land flow by, seeing it with new eyes, for wonder of wonders he was riding a Draega.

Miles fled and miles more, and yet the Silver Wolves didn't seem to tire. Even so, as if by some silent signal, they stopped now and again, most of the time nigh thickets, where they allowed Beau to dismount and stretch his legs and relieve himself. The 'Wolves, too, went about the thicket, marking the trees, but whether they were claiming the territory or simply leaving the message that they had been here, Beau did not know. Yet soon they would signal the Warrow that it was time to be on their way again, Shimmer standing steadily as Beau vaulted astride.

As the sun reached the noontide, the 'Wolves veered from their course and stopped at a small stand of trees. And there the Draega bearing the saddlebags came to Beau and with a shiver, dropped the pouches at his feet.

"Ho, what is it?" And then Beau's eyes widened in revelation. "Oh, I see. You've stopped for me to have a wee spot of lunch, eh?"

Three Silver Wolves took station about the stand and stood ward, while the remaining four plopped down in the snow and waited.

Beau fished a biscuit of crue from one of the saddlebags, and he sat in the snow with his back to a tree and slowly ate the waybread. "Oh, I say, where are my manners?" Beau fished out another biscuit and extended it to Shimmer, but she turned her head away from the offering. "I don't blame you, Shimmer. Rather tasteless, this. But here, I've some jerky." Shimmer turned this down as well.

Beau finished his biscuit and drank some water and then relieved himself. Two of the Draega came and stood beside the saddlebags, and Beau settled the pouches across their backs. Shimmer once again came to the buccan and stood without moving as he sprang to her back. When he twined his fingers through her fur, she and the others set out westerly, the large one and the dark one yet taking the lead.

And across the rolling plains they tirelessly ran.

Nigh sunset, again the pack stopped, and once more Beau took a meal. But soon they were on their way again, and across the snow and through the dusk fared the Silver Wolves, Beau yet mounted on Shimmer. And under her long loping stride, Beau on her back with his stomach full, laid his head down and in moments fell sound asleep, though his fingers remained entwined.

The moon rose, gibbous but waning, and across glittering snow and through argent light sped the silver-white 'Wolves, nearly invisible in the winter night, a buccan asleep in their midst.

Beau wakened as Dalavar took him from Shimmer and bore him among trees to the side of a fallen log. "Sleep, Beau, we will watch." Muzzy and but half awake, Beau undid his bindle and spread his blanket and lay down, sleep overtaking him again. He wasn't aware when two Draega came and lay next to him, their soft fur to keep him warm.

"I say, how far have we come?"

Dalavar squinted to the east at the morning light. "Thirty-three leagues, more or less."

"Oh my, a hundred miles? Goodness. A hundred miles in a day."

" 'Tis no more than a pack of ordinary Wolves could do."

"You mean Wolves other than Draega can run a hundred miles a day?"

Dalavar nodded. "Aye, Beau." Then he gestured about. "But this pack can run twice that at need."

"Well then, why don't—?" Suddenly Beau's face fell. "Oh, it's because of me, isn't it? I mean, having to deal with me slows you down. You ought to leave me, you know. In a town where I can get a pony."

Dalavar shook his head. "Nay, Beau. Although we could run two hundred miles in a day, still we could not keep it up day after day. Even Draega need to rest and eat. Too, in Farrin's name I promised to help you, and so I will."

Beau took a drink from his waterskin, then looked at it puzzled. "I say, it was nigh empty last night."

"I replenished it," said the Mage.

"Oh." Beau looked about but did not see a stream or pool.

Watching the buccan, Dalavar smiled and then added, "It will be full every morn, whether or no there is a nearby stream."

Beau's eyes widened and he looked at his waterskin. "I say, is this going to be one of those magic bags? I mean like those of the hearthtales? Oh, that would be splendid."

Dalavar laughed and shook his head. "Oh no, Beau, it is but an ordinary waterskin."

They sat in silence for a while, Beau finishing the last of his breakfast jerky. A gleam at Dalavar's throat caught the buccan's eye, where dangled a small silvery nugget on a thong.

"That's what got us into this mess, Tip and me."

Dalavar raised an eyebrow.

"Only in our case it was a coin on a thong and not a small chunk of silver. As it turned out, the coin was a summons, a call for aid, and that's why Agron is marching into Gron."

"Someone summoned Agron to Gron?"

"No. Actually it was a call from High King Blaine to summon Agron and his army to Blaine's side, but since no one knows where Blaine is, Agron decided to invade Gron instead."

Dalavar shook his head.

After a while, Beau said, "The coin was a Gjeenian penny, practically worthless in and of itself. Yet now an army marches into Gron because of it."

Dalavar sighed and fingered the silver nugget. "Many tokens of power are that way: rather plain in and of themselves, but mighty in what they bring."

Beau watched Dalavar absently worry the silver piece. "And what might that be about your neck?"

Dalavar took his hand away from the nugget. "It is silveron, Beau, starsilver, an amulet of sorts, and I but hold it temporarily."

"Temporarily?"

"Yes. It is meant for two who are yet to come: One to hide; One to guide. Ask me no more, for I am pledged."

"But—?"

Dalavar abruptly stood. From their places nearby, Draega stood as well. "Let us be on our way."

Beau rolled his bindle and packed the saddlebags, and when he looked up, Dalavar was nowhere to be seen.

Sighing, Beau climbed atop the fallen log and draped the pouches over the two Silver Wolves who came for them. Shimmer stood beside the log, and Beau stepped astraddle, and as the pack trotted from the woods they were joined once more by the dark Silver Wolf who awaited them at the marge.

The second day out of Dendor, the sky overhead began to turn grey, and on the third day, dark clouds gathered above. As far as Beau was concerned, though, each of these days was much the same, Dalavar disappearing a bit after dayrise and reappearing on the nighttide, the Draega ever bearing westerly, miles vanishing under their long strides. And still they paused to let Beau stretch his legs and relieve himself and eat a midday meal. Too, they paused at streams not yet frozen for him to take on water, the Draega lapping water as well.

During his nighttime conversations with Dalavar, Beau learned all the 'Wolves' names, or at least a short, common-tongue equivalent he could use: The largest of the Draega was Greylight, who seemed to lead the pack. Then there were Shimmer and Beam, the two females, much alike in carriage and manner, though Beam seemed always to defer to Shimmer. Seeker and Trace and Longshank were three of the males, but when Beau asked about the dark 'Wolf, Dalavar laughed and said, "I think you can call him . . . Shifter . . . yes, Shifter will do."

*   *   *

Just after dawn on the fourth day of running, a harsh wind rose, hurtling snow riding on its wings, filling the day with blinding whiteness. Although the Silver Wolves seemed to relish running into the teeth of the storm, Beau pulled his hood 'round tightly and buried his face in Shimmer's fur and away from the wind-driven snow. That evening in the shelter of the thicket, as the wind and white howled overhead, Dalavar said, "This blizzard comes from afar, Beau, from the Gronfangs in the least."

"Oh my, do you think it's Modru's doings?"

For long moments Dalavar looked into the hurtling snow, as if seeking . . . seeking . . . what? Beau did not know. Again he asked, "Do you think it's Modru's doings?"

The Mage turned to the buccan. "That, wee one, I cannot yet say, though it does have a taint of <dark power>."

The wind and snow continued racing by on the fifth day out from Dendor, and once again Beau kept tight to Shimmer's fur. And just after nightfall, through the swirling whiteness gone black in the dark, they espied the lanterns of Älvstad, where the muster had taken place. In all, the pack had travelled some five hundred and forty miles in but five days, yet they seemed none the worse for the wear.

As the 'Wolves stood in the storm on the downslope of the hill surveying what could be seen of the town below, Dalavar came striding over the crest behind. "We will stop here for a day, Beau," he called above the wind.

"Stop? But shouldn't we be moving on? I mean, it's plain to see the army is gone, else there'd be tents and such surrounding the town."

"You may think them invincible, my friend, but even Draega need to hunt, to eat, to rest. They will run tonight and bring down a stag or two. They will rest after filling their bellies. You and I will stay in the town below tonight and tomorrow and tomorrow night as well. But the morning after you will meet the pack at the ford, yon, and then press on."

"How can they hunt in this blizzard, Dalavar?"

"The storm will end ere morrow's dawn, wee one. They will hunt then."

As Dalavar took up the saddlebags from Longshank and Trace, Beau stepped through the wind to Shimmer. "I'm sorry, sweet Shimmer, but I didn't think. Do go. Hunt. Eat. Rest if you can in this blizzard. I will see you at the ford."

Shimmer's great tongue lapped Beau's cheek, then she looked to Dalavar.

The Wolfmage turned to Greylight and spoke—neither a word nor a growl, but something in between—and then started off downslope through the storm. Beau gave Shimmer a final pat and then hastened after the Mage, the wee Warrow following in Dalavar's track through the deep snow. Partway downhill, Beau turned 'round to look back upslope, but the Silver Wolves were gone. Sighing, the buccan faced into the wind again and followed Dalavar down to the town.

Following the gate warden's instructions, they stepped out of the blow and into the *Kunghus,* as the hostel had been renamed following Agron's stay at the time of the muster even though the sign out front yet bore the image of the head of a red boar. After arranging for beds and a hot bath, Dalavar and Beau took places at a table in the sparsely populated common room and called for a good hot meal.

Dalavar ate as if he had gone without food for days on end, the Wolfmage signalling several times for the serving girl to bring more fare. And though he ate as if starved, to Beau's eye Dalavar seemed no thinner than usual, nor fatter after consuming what seemed to the buccan to be more than anyone could possibly eat.

Long after Beau had been sated, the Wolfmage finally pushed back from the table and joined the buccan in front of the fire, where together they called for hot mugs of spiced mulled wine.

" 'Tis not often I enjoy such luxuries," said Dalavar, as he took his mug from the maid.

Beau sighed. "Me neither. I think the last time I had mulled wine was back in Bridgeton."

The serving girl looked at Beau. "That's what the other Litenfolk said."

Beau looked up at her. "The other Litenfolk?"

"Sir Tipperton, he was, and a scout," she replied. "He stayed here with King Agron."

"How did he look? Was he all right?"

"Oh yes sir."

Across the room another patron signalled the maid, and as she took up her tray she said, "He rode off with the king and the army, um, a month back it was."

As the girl stepped away, Beau looked at Dalavar. "At least we're on his trail."

They sat without speaking for a while, the moan of the blizzard groaning down the chimney, the wind hammering on the clapboards of the inn. Finally, Dalavar said, "This storm, Beau, it indeed carries traces of Modru's <dark fire>."

"<Dark fire>?"

"<Fire> wrenched from others, stolen from victims through torture, through fear and pain and agony and death."

"Oh my," said Beau, a sudden shiver running along his spine.

Dalavar's features grew grim. "Like all Black Mages, Modru cares not what happens to others; only his own gratification is paramount. Hence, rather than use his own, he wrenches <fire> from victims and uses it to <power> his castings . . . in this case, he has used <dark fire> to raise a storm in the cold reaches of the Boreal Sea, or in the Barrens, and has guided it to fall on those he would crush."

The wind whistled 'round the *Kunghus* and moaned in the chimney, stirring the flames in the hearth.

Beau looked into his cup and said, "Well, in spite of Modru, I would think in their snug winter gear Tip and the army are safe. I mean, we are no worse for the wear having come through the very same storm."

Dalavar sighed. "Beau, we cannot judge by that which blows without, for it may be considerably more brutal where they are."

As Beau frowned up at the Mage, Dalavar gestured toward the window, where illuminated by lanternlight white snow hurtled past. "Ere the storm reached us it had lost much of its strength, for two great barriers stand across the way—the Gronfangs and the Grimwall—where much of the blow has been lost, dashed against mountain stone."

"Oh my," said Beau. "Oh my."

And the wind without rattled the walls of the inn.

The next morning dawned to stillness, the blizzard completely gone, having blown itself out sometime in the night; not even a faint breeze remained. All that day Beau and Dalavar rested, though "rested" might be the wrong term, for, except for acquiring some crue and jerky to replace that which he had consumed, Beau paced agitatedly, anxious to be on the way. As to Dalavar, he downed meal after meal, as if stoking up for some great effort, or as if recovering from one. Again it seemed as if he would never get filled, though at last he did stop.

The day wore on, and finally night fell, and from the nearby hills there came a prolonged howl, and of a sudden the night was alive with yips and yammers and whines and more howls. Below in the town, doors slammed, doors opened, some shutting, others being flung wide, and lanterns were held on high, casting their light across snow. Finally, silence fell, and doors in the thorp slammed to again, latches clicking, bolts throwing home, bars banging down into brackets; the stockaded town entire closed up tight.

The next morning when Beau awakened, Dalavar was gone. Dressing quickly, Beau took up his bindle and saddlebags and his replenished waterskin and hurried downstairs. When he tried to pay the innkeeper, someone had more than settled the bill with a fresh-killed stag. "Brought down by dogs, I think," said the 'keep, "for there's nary an arrow mark on it, but a throat torn out by teeth."

As the innkeeper stepped into the kitchen and snatched up a biscuit and some rashers of bacon for the wee Litenfolk, Beau slung on his jacket and cloak and fitted his bindle-strap over all. He looked about, seeking Dalavar, but did not see the Mage, yet was not surprised by such, what with Dalavar's "magical" comings and goings. Carrying his saddlebags and munching the food, Beau stepped from the inn and strode out the north gate and down toward the river and the ford, where he found the pack waiting, all seven of the 'Wolves.

Across the Argon they fared, and toward the mountain pass through the Grimwalls ahead, their travel slowed by blizzard fall. Through Jallor Pass, Shimmer with Beau came last, running in the path through the snow broken by the others. Night had fallen ere they came down from the mountains and into Jallorby, and there they stopped and rested another day, for it had been a difficult passage. Yet in spite of the deep snow, still the pack had run some seventy-five miles in all.

Leaving Jallorby, west they fared, toward the Gronfangs afar, and here in this corner of Jord the snow lay deep on the land. Even so, even though stopping more often and resting longer each time, the pack covered seventy miles altogether, and when they stopped for the night, the Gronfangs were visible in the distance ahead.

In early morn of the next day, they came to the narrow pass, and snow ramped high within, rising up some two hundred feet or so here at the entrance.

Beau's heart lurched, and he involuntarily clutched Shimmer's fur. "Oh, Shimmer," breathed the buccan into the great 'Wolf's ear, "the way is blocked."

The pack paused and looked toward Greylight, but he in turn looked at Shifter. And that dark 'Wolf took the lead and scrambled up the snow along the southern flank.

All day they struggled along the slopes above the south rim of the slot, now climbing across mountain flanks, now faring along high ledges, now breasting through chest-deep snow. And the farther into the pass they went, the deeper was the snow down in the gorge, as if the way entire had been buried by an avalanche. Seldom did they fare in the snow-filled pass itself, for there they would sink deep and struggle hard simply to go a few yards. But now and again the stone flanks of the Gronfangs would be bare, for clearly all snow and rocks that should be lying on them had slid down into the gulch below. Across these barren places the pack loped easily, though all too soon they would come unto snow-laden steeps again. And often they stopped to rest, Silver Wolves lying on their sides and panting, their great tongues lolling, dripping, even in the frigid air.

By late afternoon they had covered but some twenty miles in all along the jinking, twisting, snow-choked pass, when Greylight paused, his nose held high in the air. So, too, did the other 'Wolves stop, their noses up, their lungs taking in deep breaths, scenting and then snorting and then scenting again. Shimmer whined, and her tail drooped, as did those of the other Draega, all but Shifter, who peered down at the snow in the blocked pass below and growled.

"What is it, girl?" asked Beau, but Shimmer whined, as did Beam, and Longshank raised his muzzle and howled.

Greylight swung about and stared fixedly at Longshank, and the 'Wolf howl chopped shut. And then Shifter turned away from the snow below and took up the trek again, the rest of the pack following.

At last the sun sank, night rushing on, and Shifter found a more or less level place on a mountainside, and there the pack stopped. Shifter went on alone, passing from sight beyond a turn in the stone.

Beau took the saddlebags from Longshank and Trace, and cast them down to the snow, and then unlooped his bindle-strap and dropped the roll as well. Kneeling, Beau dug into a saddlebag, and as he did so, Dalavar said, "I bear ill news, Beau."

Beau, now used to the Wolfmage's abrupt comings and goings, looked up, a biscuit of crue in hand. "Ill news? Does this have anything to do with the pack's strange behavior a few miles back?"

"I'm afraid so. You see, w— the pack, that is, caught a faint scent of men and horses and other such back there."

Beau frowned. "And . . . ?"

"It lasted for nearly two miles altogether."

Beau turned up a hand. "How is this ill news?"

"Beau, I believe that Agron's army is buried back there, under the snow, under an avalanche."

The air went out from Beau's lungs, and he felt as if he had been struck a blow. Gasping, he slumped back into the snow. "The army? The whole army?" He gestured toward the snow-filled pass, glimmering grey in the light of remote, icy stars. "Under all of that?"

"I cannot think of aught else to account for the spoor," said Dalavar. "A slain soldier or slain horse or even a hundred would not be scented were they under all of that snow, two or three hundred feet deep in the least, perhaps five hundred in places. Yet even five hundred feet of snow is not enough to conceal from Draega the scent of an entire army."

Tears filled Beau's eyes. "Oh, oh . . ."

Dalavar knelt beside him.

Not seeing, Beau looked at the Wolfmage. "Tip. What about Tip? Is he . . . is he . . . ?"

"Ah, wee one, I cannot say. He could be there or not."

Shimmer came and lay beside the buccan.

Beau reached out and twined his fingers in her fur. "I don't want him to be there. I don't want— Look, we've got to go on. Tip was, Tip is a scout. He may be ahead somewhere. He may be ahead."

"Perhaps," said Dalavar, standing and peering west. "Perhaps."

The Wolfmage glanced down at the buccan. "On the morrow we will look."

Dalavar walked away and squatted by Greylight, leaving Beau in his misery behind. And the buccan buried his face in Shimmer's fur and wept, and the she-'Wolf laid her head down and did not move from his side.

Beau awakened just ere dawn, a fingernail-thin crescent moon leading the sun into the sky. Remembering back to when they had been in Jallorby, Beau counted on his fingers. It was Winterday, the shortest day of the year, and tonight would be Year's Long Night. Just one year past on the solstice, he and Tip had stepped out the Elven rite of the change of the seasons, and Bekki had been on the hill above praying to Elwydd.

Perhaps this is an omen for good.

But then Beau remembered that Foul Folk had come through the dark and had spoiled the night for them.

Perhaps it is an omen for ill.

Beau managed to choke down a biscuit of crue and drink a bit of water from his full waterskin.

The sun rose in the cold dawn sky turning indigo through red to icy blue. About Beau the 'Wolves stood and shook snow from their fur and with tails low and fawning they gathered 'round Greylight, just as they did every morn. From beyond the turn appeared dark Shifter, trotting into view, and as if that were a signal, Longshank and Trace came to Beau for the saddlebags and Shimmer came for the buccan himself.

Westerly they fared along slopes above the pass, following its twists and turns, the snow yet deep and hindering. They had travelled but twenty-four miles the previous day, an extraordinary distance, given the conditions, and yet for Beau, used by now to going a hundred or more miles a day, it had seemed a crawl, and this day seemed no better. And worry gnawed at Beau's stomach, his gut a knot of anxiety.

Oh, Tip, Tip, you've just got to be alive somewhere in the miles ahead.

And onward across the laden slopes they struggled, the frigid morning growing colder with each and every step.

As the pack came closer and closer to the far eastern end of the pass, the snow within began to diminish as the gape widened. Even so, even though the rim and walls could now be seen, given that this end of the pass was much like that at the beginning, the snow yet stood a hundred feet deep or more, or so Beau judged.

Still they had seen no sign of life, yet they forged ahead, the remote sun shedding no warmth as it neared the midday mark.

In the lead, Shifter pressed on, but Greylight suddenly stopped, the pack behind stopping as well, and Greylight cocked his head this way and that, as if listening, as if catching an elusive sound.

"Whuff," called Greylight, and Shifter turned and trotted back. But Greylight bounded down the high-ramped snow and into the slot of the pass itself, clouds of white flying in his wake, and though the great Silver Wolf was half-buried, he turned toward the nearside wall of the pass and began frantically digging.

Shifter, too, sprang down the steep snow slope to come alongside Greylight, the dark 'Wolf to dig as well.

Shimmer came to the rim above and stopped, and Beau dismounted, looking down.

And then Beau heard a muffled cry of sorts, and it didn't sound as would a 'Wolf.

Greylight looked toward the rim and growled, and Beam and Seeker slithered down through the snow to aid in the digging.

And then there came a shrill shout, but what was said, Beau did not know, yet he cried out and leaped down the ramped snow, tumbling through the deep white.

And as he struggled to his feet, he saw Shifter, the dark 'Wolf, plunge into the wall of snow and disappear from sight, while Greylight backed away, whuffing and snorting and trying to clear his nostrils as if something inside the hole stank.

And as Beau floundered forward, Dalavar emerged from the hole, and in his arms he carried an unconscious buccan—Tipperton Thistledown.

*H*is face is flush, as if—" On his knees in the snow beside Tipperton's still form, Beau bent over and placed his cheek against the unconscious buccan's forehead. As Beau did so, he looked across at Dalavar. "He's fevered, all right." Beau straightened up. "What do you imagine— Oh lor'. Look. His sleeve. It's torn. I think he's been wounded. Help me get him out of his jacket. Just that arm. I don't want him to freeze out here."

Swiftly, Dalavar and Beau pulled Tip's arm from the jacket sleeve, Tip moaning but not wakening. Greylight, Seeker, and Beam gathered 'round, the great Silver Wolves providing a windbreak, while on the rim above, Trace, Longshank, and Shimmer stood ward.

"He's treated it," said Beau, carefully unwrapping the cloth bandaged about the limb, "and with gwynthyme. See the pulp? Oh Adon, but his arm, it's all inflamed and swollen. What could he have—? Oh my, deep gouges, festered."

" 'Tis a Vulg bite," said Dalavar.

"Vulg bite?" Beau drew in a deep breath. "Vulg venom." He glanced up at the Draega on the rim above. "I'll need my kit. It's in the saddlebags."

Dalavar raised his face and spoke something akin to a growl. Trace and Longshank came bounding down the ramp of snow, whiteness churning in their wake.

As Beau dragged his saddlebags from the backs of the 'Wolves he said. "From the looks of Tip's wounds, he was bitten some days back." Beau rummaged through the pouches and hauled out his kit and a bundle of sprigs. "Even so, it's Vulg venom, and Dara Phais took long to recover from her poisoned wound, and so may Tip. I must dose him with more golden mint . . . tea, preferably, and for that we'll need a fire and a place to work out of the snow." Beau glanced up at Dalavar.

The Wolfmage gestured toward the small cave. "Yon is the only place free of snow. I will bear Tipperton back within." Dalavar stooped and took up Tip's limp form. As he stood, he looked at Greylight and spoke another growling word, and the great Silver Wolf turned and bounded away, Seeker following.

Catching up his saddlebags, Beau headed for the entrance to the cave, the wee buccan breasting through the snow. Following him and bearing Tipperton, Dalavar said, "Vulg bites are not only poison, they are foul as well. This wound may be clear of venom, but festered with the taint of the Vulg's mouth. A wound such as this needs cleansing in addition to gwynthyme."

"We'll want hot water," said Beau, finally reaching the entrance. "Oh my," he said as he stepped inside, his face wrinkling in disgust, "but this place smells like an outhouse."

"Tipperton was trapped here long," said Dalavar, stooping and following Beau in, "days at least. Regardless of the odor, 'tis out of the snow."

Gently, the Wolfmage lay the buccan down, and then moved to the entrance of the small cave and stepped outside and began knocking down snow hanging overhead and clearing it away. "As soon as Greylight and Seeker return we'll build the fire here," he called in to Beau.

Beau nodded but did not reply as he unrolled clean cloth and laid out gwynthyme and bandages and a cup. And he set his waterskin at hand as well. Then he turned and looked about; and he gathered up Tip's belongings—saddlebags, lute, bow, quiver of arrows—and arranged them nearby. Too, he espied Tip's cup sitting in a small crevice, the container nearly full, a drop forming on the stone above.

Well, at least you had water, bucco, though precious little from the looks of it.

The droplet fell:

tink

Sighing, Beau turned just as Beam entered the small cave and lay down next to Tipperton.

"Doesn't the odor bother you, girl?" asked Beau.

Beam did not reply.

Beau shook his head and looked out at Dalavar, the Wolfmage still clearing snow from the entrance. "I say, Dalavar," called

Beau, "just how did Greylight find this place? How did he find Tip? The smell of the Warrow? The rank smell of this cave? What?"

Dalavar shook his head, then said, "None of those, Beau. Instead, Greylight said he heard him singing."

"Singing?"

Dalavar nodded.

Beau cocked his head. "And he told you this?"

Dalavar nodded again.

"And Greylight said it was 'singing' he heard?"

Yet again, Dalavar nodded.

Beau frowned. "How would Greylight even know what singing was?"

Dalavar stooped and looked inside, looked at Beau in surprise. "Why, all Wolves sing, my friend . . . and laugh as well. Have you not heard them at night? Have you not seen them grin?"

"Oh my, but I never thought of it that w—"

Beam's ears flicked forward and her head came up from between her paws. A shadow darkened the entrance to the cave, and Greylight, a long pine bough in his mouth, stood before the opening, Seeker standing just behind, that Draega with a leafless limb of some sort long twisted by the wind. At a signal from Dalavar they dropped the branches and bounded away.

Dalavar shook the snow from the bough and the limb and stooped inside and began breaking off stems. "This will get us started," said the Wolfmage. "Greylight, Seeker, Longshank, and Trace have gone for more."

"Here," said Beau, turning toward his saddlebags, "I'll get out my flint and steel and tinder, and then we'll have us a—"

But at that moment a ruddy flicker lighted the hollow. Beau turned back to see Dalavar feeding barren twigs into a small flame. How the Wolfmage had started the blaze, Beau could not say. Even so, he took up Tip's tin cup and added a bit of water to it and said, "Here, set this to boil."

Dalavar arranged three rocks about the tiny fire and set the cup atop, the flames licking the tin bottom.

After soaking the wounds and cleaning away the yellowish skims of forming scabs and draining the pus as best he could, Beau said, "Oh Adon, Tip may lose his arm." Tears welled up in Beau's eyes and he turned to the Wolfmage. "Oh, Dalavar, I-I've never cut off a limb before, though I've seen it done on the battlefield. It was awful, the knives, the saws . . . the screaming. And now I may have to do the same, though I don't even have . . .

I don't even have . . ." Beau's words choked to a halt, and he could not bring himself to say what it was he didn't have.

Beau turned to see Beam licking Tip's wounds. "Here, now, Beam," protested Beau, starting to rise, but Dalavar reached out a hand and stopped the buccan.

"Let her treat him, Beau. You've done all the cleansing you can. Now let her do her best. When she is finished, lay on your poultice and bandage him. On the morrow, we shall see."

Sometime nigh mid of night, Tipperton opened his eyes and in the flicker of firelight looked up to see Beau smiling down.

"Oh, hullo, Beau," he rasped, his voice but a whisper. "I was having the most horrible drea—" Tipperton glanced about, his eyes flying wide in panic at the sight of the great 'Wolf lying at his side, and he scrabbled feebly at the rubble, trying but failing to get away, moaning.

"Tip, Tip, it's not a Vulg," said Beau, embracing Tipperton to keep him from flailing. "Not a Vulg. It's a Draega, a Silver Wolf instead. Her name is Beam. She's a friend."

Yet thrashing, Tip looked wildly at Beau. "Shh, shh, Tip," soothed Beau. "She's not a Vulg, not a Vulg, but a friend instead; a Silver Wolf. Remember the song Phais sang in Bridgeton; Draega are deadly foe of the Vulgs."

Allayed by Beau, his panic subsiding, Tip timorously looked at the 'Wolf, and Beam cocked her head side to side and looked back.

Beau reached down and turned Tip's face toward him. "Dalavar says not to look them directly in the eye; they don't take kindly to such boldness."

Now Tip glanced at the stone overhead and rasped, "Oh my, I'm still in the cave. It wasn't a dream after all."

"No, bucco. It wasn't a dream."

Tip strained to reach . . . to reach . . . but fell back. "My cup, Beau. It's in a crack somewhere."

Beau snatched up his waterskin and filled one of the tin cups, then supported Tip and aided him to drink. After that cup and two more, Tip looked up at Beau cradling him. "Oh, Beau, it's so good to see you. How did you get here? Did you come across Agron's army? Are they all right? The blizzard . . . the slide . . ."

Tears filled Beau's eyes. "Oh, bucco, I bring ill news. King Agron, his army, we think they're all dead. The avalanche . . ."

Tip fell asleep weeping.

Beau came awake in time to add another branch to the dying embers, rekindling the small fire. As he turned he found Tip struggling to sit upright, sucking air through his teeth from the pain.

"Here, bucco, let me help," said Beau, scrabbling over rubble and past Beam in order to get to Tip, where he helped Tip to sit up and slide hindward to place his back against the side wall of the cave for support, the wounded buccan groaning a bit from the pain of movement.

Tip smiled weakly. "You wouldn't happen to have something to eat, now would you? I'm rather famished. Thirsty, too."

Beau snatched up his waterskin and a saddlebag and, as he filled a cup with water, said, "I've some crue and jerky."

"Crue please. I don't have the strength for jerky."

Tip took the cup and drank it all down, then Beau handed him a biscuit. As Tip took a bite, he laughed softly.

Beau looked across at him. "What?"

Tip chewed long moments and then swallowed. "I was just remembering what you said at a morning meal just before we entered Drearwood, Beau." As Beau frowned in puzzlement, Tip said, "You asked, 'Is anything else as tasteless as a crue biscuit?' and then added, 'And jerky is called jerky 'cause it's so accursed tough that it'll jerk your teeth out by the roots just trying to gnaw off a simple bite.' That's what you said, bucco. But let me tell you, right now this crue biscuit tastes quite scrumptious." Tip took another bite.

Beau smiled and watched as Tip chewed, a cup at hand in the event Tip asked for more water.

Tip glanced at Beam and then turned to Beau. "Where did she come from? I mean, when last I saw you, you were lying abed in a prison, just back from Death's door. And the plague, what of the plague? And by the bye, I ate all of the gwynthyme and silverroot, or most of it, that is: two bundles, five roots. Oh, some of the gwynthyme I put on the Vulg bite."

"It probably saved your life, Tip. —The gwynthyme, I mean. Just as it saved mine." Of a sudden Beau's eyes widened and he said, "Oh my."

Tip looked left and right, then asked around a mouthful of crue. "What?"

"Well, it just struck me, Tip: Modru's plague. . . ."

Tip waited, and then gestured with the remainder of the biscuit.

"Oh," said Beau, as if returning from wherever his thoughts had taken him. "Modru's plague, it needed gwynthyme and silverroot to allay it. Silverroot I had, but no gwynthyme. Bekki knew where there was some. You and Bekki harvested it. The plague was put down. You had some gwynthyme with you when you were Vulg bitten and it kept you from dying. Dalavar and the Draega came because Dalavar wanted to see the one who had found the cure for the plague. He helped me to come after you. And it was the Silver Wolves who found you, buried behind snow in this cave."

Beau fell silent, and Tip cocked an eyebrow.

"Oh, Tip, don't you see? Everything *is* connected. Because of Modru's Plague, Greylight found you."

"Greylight?"

"Another of the Draega."

Tip glanced at Beam, and then said, "Beau, it was a long chain of events that put me here, and a long chain that brought you to this same place. As to cause and effect, there is no direct link between Modru's plague and our being together at this place at this time. No, this chain was forged link by link, and it easily could have gone a different direction."

"But don't you see, it didn't, Tip. It didn't. All the links led to this place and no other."

Tip sighed and took the last bite of the biscuit, but managed to say, "Just where is this Dalavar you've mentioned several times?"

Beau looked at the opening of the cave. "Oh, he took my rope and knife and went off with several of the Draega. Said he would be back before daylight."

Beau filled the cup with water and handed it to Tip, then crawled forward to place another branch on the fire. As he did so there came a clink of tin on stone, and Beau turned to find Tip asleep, the empty tin cup by his side. Beau crawled back and eased the sleeping buccan away from the wall to lie down next to Beam.

Dalavar returned just ere dawn. He said something to Beam, and that great 'Wolf went out from the small cave, and Trace came inward to take her place.

"I have made a travois, Beau, and as soon as Tipperton is strong enough to travel, we will head for Jallorby."

"D' y' think we can drag him back across the Gronfangs? I mean, some of that passage was right hard."

Dalavar smiled. "I have asked my friends if they would be willing to harness up and haul him. Each of them said yes."

Beau looked at Tip. "He ate something and I think his fever is down, though he is still quite flush. And with that arm . . . well, it could be awhile. We could run out of food."

Dalavar barked a laugh. "With six Draega hunting? Not likely, my friend."

Beau smiled then frowned. "I'm a bit worried about the fire, what with Vulgs about and Foul Folk. I mean, won't they see the smoke?"

Dalavar's brow furrowed and he shook his head. "As to the fire, the breeze blows what little smoke there is back the way we came, and I think with the avalanche now blocking this way into Gron, this passage is now abandoned by Modru's lackeys both within and without, for we scented no spoor of Spawn when we went to make the travois."

In that moment, Greylight appeared at the mouth of the cave and dropped a hare to the snow. "Ah," said Dalavar, "your breakfast meal is here."

In late midmorn Tip awakened to the smell of coney sizzling on a spit above the fire, Beau squatting and turning it now and again.

"I have to pee, Beau, and I'd rather not foul this nest anymore."

"Oh, Tip, but you are too—"

"Look, bucco, I'm going to go out there if I have to crawl."

"No need for that," said Dalavar, stepping into view and entering the hollow, the Mage stooping and moving inward. He took up the buccan and bore him outward, saying, "I'm Dalavar of Darda Vrka, though some know me as the Wolfmage."

". . . and so, in the howl of the blizzard the Vulgs jumped us. I killed one with an arrow, though he bit me, and Auly killed the other one, though he was slain in doing so." Tip paused and leaned back against the stone wall, gathering the remnants of his strength to continue. Beau gave him a drink of gwynthyme tea. Tipperton took a sip and then whispered on. "My pony was dead, and Auly's horse was gone. More Vulgs were coming, and so I grabbed what I could and fled. I thought they would search for me down in the pass, so I climbed the slope and by pure happenstance found this cave and crawled inside." Again Tip paused and took another sip of tea. After a while, and in spite of Beau's protestations, Tip took up the tale once more, his voice trembling with the effort. "A bit later I realized that I was bitten, a Vulg bite, a poison bite, and, Beau, I swear, I heard you trying to remind me of the gwynthyme. I could make no tea such as this, but I ate some mint and I chewed some and spit the juice onto the wound and made a poultice, and . . . and . . . Oh well, you know the rest." Tip paused, his breathing thready.

"Fortune turned Her smiling face your way, Waerling," said Dalavar, "for without Her favor you would not have found this cave and would now be buried out yon."

Tip's eyes brimmed and he whispered, "Like thirty thousand others, Dalavar. Thirty thousand."

A grim look came over Dalavar's features. "Modru has much to answer for."

"If I could get my hands on him, I'd kill him dead," growled Beau.

Dalavar looked at both Warrows. "Leave vengeance for these deaths to me, my wee friends. Modru and I have crossed paths before, to his regret . . . though in that case as in yours, Tipperton, Fortune smiled down on me."

Tip sighed and murmured, "Fortune may have turned Her smile toward me in the end, but She was glaring ere then."

"Be glad that Her hidden face remained turned away, else death under snow would have been sweet by compare."

Beau shuddered. "Oh, enough of this talk of Fortune's three faces and of dooms dire. Instead, let us have a look at that wound."

Frowning slightly as Trace licked the gashes, Tip whispered, "Won't it hurt him if some of the Vulg poison yet lies in the bite?"

Dalavar shook his head. "Nay. Draega are not harmed by Vulg venom. Too, if some trace of the poison remained, then you would now be dead."

With exhausted eyes, Tip glanced at Beau, and Beau said, "Besides, Tip, the swelling has gone down a bit, I think due to the ministrations of Beam—she cleaned the wound yester. So let Trace do what he will and on the morrow we shall see again."

Tip fell asleep watching.

"How many of the 'Wolves are there?" asked Tip, taking a bite of rabbit left over from the day before.

"Seven," said Beau, "though I haven't seen Shifter in a while. He's like the others, only a bit darker of fur."

Longshank lay at the feet of the wounded buccan, watching with interest as Tip nibbled the cold meat.

They sat in silence for a while. Finally Tip finished off the bit of leg and looked at Beau. "Do you think a rabbit bone will hurt this 'Wolf?"

Beau shrugged. "Longshank? I don't see why it should. I mean, Wolves, regular Wolves, that is, they eat coneys raw, bones and all. And surely a Silver Wolf can outdo one of them."

Tip held out the bone toward Longshank, and very gently the great beast took it from him, and then with a snap and a crunch it was gone.

"Well, that was short work, Longshank," said Tip.

"Water?" asked Beau, filling a cup.

Tip nodded, and Beau handed the cup to him and then filled another for himself.

As Tipperton took a small sip, he looked across the cup at the exit from the cave. "I say, Beau, when will we be leaving?"

Beau frowned, then said, "As soon as you can walk out from here and pee on your own."

"Oh," said Tip, disappointed. Then—"Now that you mention it, Beau . . ."

On the sixth day after being freed by the Draega, Tip managed to totter from the cave without any aid. When he returned on shaking legs he smiled and declared, "Time to go."

Dalavar took one look at the buccan standing and sweating and trembling, then the Wolfmage turned to Beau. "We have a travois."

Beau shrugged. "On the morrow?"

Dalavar nodded. "On the morrow."

With a grunt, Tipperton sat down, unable to stand any longer.

The following dawn, Dalavar scrambled up to the rim above and, using Tipperton's rope, hauled up all the gear. Beau's bindle blanket was then used to complete the bed of the travois. Then Dalavar hauled up the buccen: Tipperton first, then Beau.

Longshank came to be harnessed to the travois, and Tip and his bow and lute were roped in. As Dalavar stepped out somewhere ahead, Beau settled all saddlebags across Draega backs—Beam, Trace, and Seeker each carrying pouches. And when that was done, Beau leapt astraddle Shimmer.

Greylight looked at Beau, and then turned and trotted away, the other Draega following . . . and 'round a bend they caught up to Shifter, the dark 'Wolf waiting there.

And across the snow-covered slopes they went: Shifter and Greylight in the lead, followed by Seeker then Longshank haling the travois, with Shimmer and Beam after, and Trace bringing up the rear.

"Where's Dalavar?" called Tip back to Beau coming after.

Beau shrugged. "He comes and goes—rather abruptly at times—but will show up tonight. At least he always has."

It took nearly three days altogether for the pack just to reach the eastern end of the pass, some eleven or twelve leagues of travel, for in many places the going was slow, the travois a hindrance over the precipitous ways. And both Beau and Tipperton were glad to see the long, rolling stretches of Jord lying before them when they came down from the steeps. Even so, even though they had reached the relative flats, still the going was slow, for Longshank would not jounce the wee buccan he was drawing behind.

And so another two days, nearly three altogether, they fared ere the lights of Jallorby came into view, for they had pressed on into the night. And just after mid of night came, six great Silver Wolves trotted to the marge of that town, where they found Dalavar waiting.

He led them all to the White Horse Inn; and there he unladed the travois and set Tip on the edge of the porch as Beau retrieved the saddlebags.

"Well, let's go in," said Beau, "and have some hot mulled wine."

Dalavar shook his head. "Nay, my wee comrades, go on alone; my friends and I, we have many missions to attend to and we must be on our way. Yet I deem ere this war is ended, we shall meet again."

"You're leaving?" asked Beau, his face chapfallen.

"Aye."

Beau stepped to Shimmer and hugged her. "Farewell, sweet Shimmer, and take care."

She lapped him with her tongue.

One by one the great 'Wolves came to each of the buccen and suffered their touch, all but Greylight, that is, the pack leader standing aloof.

And Tipperton hugged each of them, and Longshank, last in line, gave a single tentative lick to the buccan's cheek. "Take care, my friend," whispered Tipperton. "Perhaps one day we'll share another rabbit."

Beau stepped up to the porch and helped Tip to stand and then said, "Farewell, Dalavar, and we thank you for all you have done. And I say, but where has Shifter gotten to? I would tell him good-bye."

Dalavar smiled and then said, "Ah, but you already have." And a gloom gathered about Dalavar, enveloping him, his shape changing, growing large, silvery-grey, with black claws and glistening fangs, the shifting form dropping to all fours, and where Dalavar had been now grinned a Draega, though one somehow darker than the others. And a silveron nugget dangled on a thong around Shifter's neck.

"Oh my!" exclaimed Beau, as Tip gasped in wonder.

Yipping and yammering, the great Silver Wolves milled about, and of a sudden and almost as one they turned and sped from the town.

And in the wee candlemarks of Year's Start Day, the first day of January, the first day of the two thousand one hundred ninety seventh year of the Second Era of Mithgar, the very first day of the third year of a great and terrible war, Tip stood with Beau's support on the porch of the White Horse Inn, the buccen watching as seven Silver Wolves loped away to the west under a sky of cold, crystalline stars.

When they were gone from sight, Beau looked at Tip and said, "Well, bucco, let's go get that mulled wine."

24

*S*eek the aid of those not men,' " intoned Beau, staring into the flames and quoting Dara Rael of Arden, "and we did, for surely Dalavar and the Silver Wolves were not men—"

"Oh, Beau, you are assuming her rede was meant for us," replied Tip, "and there were too many persons of renown in that chamber for it to have been aimed at two insignificant Warrows. Besides, the rede goes on to say, 'to quench the fires of war,' and we certainly didn't do that."

The buccen sat before the hearth at the White Horse Inn and sipped on flagons of ale. They had been in Jallorby for a month altogether, with Tip growing stronger every day. The swelling in his arm had finally subsided, much to Beau's relief, for he had dreaded the thought of having to sever the limb to save Tipperton's life. Even so, even though Tip seemed well on the way to full recovery, still Beau gauged it would take weeks more ere they would be ready to travel.

"Oh, Tip, I know we didn't quench any fires of war," protested Beau. "The point I was trying to make was something I told Farrin on the very first day I met him."

Tip's eyes widened. "You met Farrin? Farrin the Mage?"

"Oh yes, didn't I tell you?"

Tip shook his head.

"Well, he came to Dendor about a week before I left. I told him about the rede and that none of us knew who it was meant for. I went on to say that you had gone off with an army of men, and it worried me. He understood my concern and said that especially with 'wild magic' none can ever tell what a rede might mean or who it's intended for. Regardless, there you were, off to Gron, marching with only men and no not-men . . . and you nearly lost your life because of it."

Tip growled. "Beau, yes, I nearly lost my life, but it was not because I was surrounded by men; instead it was because of a not-man."

Beau looked quizzically across the rim of his mug, and Tip added, "A not-man Vulg, in fact."

"Yes, Tip, but contrary to Dara Rael's rede, you most certainly were not seeking that not-man's aid."

Tip grinned ruefully. "Ah, bucco, you're right about that."

A knot of wood popped in the fireplace, and Tip said, "Rede or no rede, tell me more of Farrin. Did he find the Utruni? Will they help?"

Beau let out a long, low sigh and said, "Yes, he found them, and, no, they'll not help . . . at least not the elder Utruni. They consider this war an affair of the surface dwellers—that's us— and not the business of those who dwell within the living stone."

"What about the Dwarves?" asked Tip. "They live in the stone; they fight in this war."

"Exactly what I asked," said Beau, "and exactly what Farrin himself asked the Stone Giants. But still they declined . . . even though the Dwarves are caught up in this war, the Utruni elders refused to join an alliance, although some of the youngers seemed undecided."

"Oh," said Tip, dejected. "I was hoping they would help, for Mage Letha once said that with their <power> over stone mayhap a single Utrun alone could fell an entire mountain."

"Adon," said Beau. "What powerful allies they would be."

Tip nodded and sighed. After a while he took a swig of his ale and rolled it around in his mouth and then swallowed. At length, he said, "Tell me more of Farrin."

Beau shrugged. "Well, there's not that much more to tell. He was looking forward to finding his friends and completing the circle of seven again. When I told him that Alvaron had been killed, it struck him like a thunderbolt—it seems no one at the castle had said a word. He left the very next day to find the remaining five. But before he did he came to me and told me to wait for Dalavar. —Er, that is, he didn't single out Dalavar by name, but said that someone would come from the east who might help me. Sure enough, it was Dalavar and the Draega . . . a pack of not-men, you see."

Tip threw up a hand in surrender. "All right, Beau. I give up. From now on we'll try to make certain that at least a few not-men are among those we join or aid or ask for aid."

Beau grinned. "Even if the not-men are Foul Folk? Rûcks and such and Vulgs?"

"No, no," said Tip, smiling back at his friend, "those not-men I'd rather thwart."

Beau looked long at the fire, then turned to Tipperton. "I say, Tip, just where will we go when you are back up to full strength? I mean, look, for a year or more we had a mission: we carried a coin, trying to deliver it. And so we did. And when that was done, well, there was the plague to deal with, and so you went after gwynthyme while I tended the ill. Then you took on the mission of scouting for King Agron and I came as soon as I could. But now, Tip, with the coin delivered, the plague put down, and King Agron's army no more, well, I feel like a buccan without a purpose, like I'm on the fringes instead of where I should be. I mean, here we are in Jallorby sipping ale, while across the face of Mithgar a terrible war rages. It just doesn't seem right that we're not helping out."

"You're right, Beau: we shouldn't be sitting on the margins, what with a war to be fought, an evil to be stopped. And we can't just sit in Jallorby and wait till all's done."

Beau took a pull on his mug. Then wiping the foam from his mouth he said, "Right, then. So I ask again, what shall we do, where shall we go, when you are up to full strength?"

Tip sighed and flexed his fingers, yet somewhat stiff from long disuse. "When do you think that'll be, Beau?"

Beau frowned. "By the spring thaw, I would gauge. Certainly by the time Jallor Pass is clear, if we go south, that is. But that begs the question I asked: where next? To Caer Pendwyr in Pellar? That's where Phais and Loric headed. Like them, should we try to find the High King, wherever he may be? Or how about we go to Darda Galion? I mean, if Drimmen-deeve is still under siege, well we could help out there. Then there's always the Wilderland where we started, though that's a long trip. On the other hand, I suppose we could go to Jordkeep and help out the Jordians . . . I mean, we *are* already in Jord. So what say, bucco? Where next? —I mean as soon as you are fit."

Tip shrugged, then said, "How about we go to Darda Erynian?"

Beau sucked in air between his teeth. "Blackwood? But why?"

Tip paused and took a sip from his mug. Then he glanced at Beau and said. "Look, Beau, but for the Wilderland and Jord, the other places you named—Caer Pendwyr, Pellar, Darda Galion, Drimmen-deeve—lie south of here, as does Darda Erynian, the Great Greenhall."

Beau turned up a hand. "Yes, but—"

"No 'yes-buts' at all, my friend," said Tip, "that broad forest is along the way, and somewhere in Darda Erynian live the Springwater Warrows—Rynna's people. I've never been among many Warrows, you know, except for that brief time at Caer Lindor, and right now for some reason I feel the need to be with our kind, if only for a week or so."

"Warrows in Blackwood, yes, Tip, but also in Blackwood live the Hidden Ones—"

"As do the Dylvana," interjected Tip. "The Baeron too."

Beau sighed. "Well, except for the Baeron—and I'm not certain just what they are, being so big and all, and rumors saying that some Baeron can take on the shapes of Bears and Wolves—the others you've named are certainly not-men all, even the Hidden Ones. —But, say, just how will this help in the war? I mean, what is there to do in Darda Erynian?"

"Well, last we knew there was a Horde somewhere along the eastern marge of the Great Greenhall. Perhaps we can use our skills to do something about them. —Oh, Beau, we won't know until we get to Darda Erynian whether there is a task we can fulfill in that woodland or whether we should press on. Surely someone there—Dylvana, Baeron, Warrow, or someone else altogether—can help us decide where we could do the most good. But task or not, advice or not, I would like to see others of our kind ere pressing on. Besides, I made a promise, you know, that when the coin was delivered, I would come back to Darda Erynian."

"A pledge to Rynna?"

Tip swallowed and nodded, then said, "For some reason I feel a strong need to keep that promise now."

Beau sighed. "Wull, bucco, promise or not, you know how I feel about the Blackwood—haunted and all as it is—but I'd like to see some Warrows, too. And even if we stay but a short while, still . . ."

And so it was decided: as soon as they could fare through Jallor Pass, south they would go, to Darda Erynian, to the Great Greenhall, to Blackwood, could they but find the means to do so, for no ponies were to be had in all of Jallorby.

The following day Tipperton took up his lute once more and, in spite of the stiff fingers of his left hand, still he managed the simpler of his tunes. When the people of Jallorby heard that one of the wee folk was playing and singing at the White Horse, they came to listen and to lift a mug or two.

And when they found out Beau was a healer, his skills were in heavy demand; after all, there seemed to be something special about one of the wee folk prescribing various teas and herbs and poultices and other medicks to citizens with ails.

And so with the extra patronage the innkeeper struck a bargain with the wee buccen: should Tip continue to play and sing, and should Beau continue to set up shop in the White Horse Inn, then free room and board would be theirs for the taking as well as any coin the citizens bestowed their way.

Hence, every night the inn was filled with those who came for a drink and a song and a dance, while every day people came with coughs and aches and pains and other complaints, folk who would take a dram or two of brandy on their way in or out. And as the townsfolk came and went, so too did the rumors, but it was clear to Tip and Beau that whatever was happening in the conduct of the war, none here knew the truth of it, for too often did the rumors contradict one another, and too often did they say what the Warrows knew to be false.

Days grew longer and nights shorter until Springday arrived with its balance of light and dark, but icy winter yet gripped the land, for a thick blanket of white yet lay across the plains, and the pass into Aven remained blocked by snow. It was as if Modru's cold hand clutched the world . . . that or the hand of Gyphon. Some said the lack of spring had to do with the fall of stone dust from out of the sky above, while others claimed it was clearly a magical curse. Still others said that they had seen winters in their childhood which were certainly as cold and had lasted as long. But just as it was with the rumors concerning the war, none in Jallorby knew fact from fiction, none knew the cause.

And Springday came with no relief. Even so, on that night after the thin crescent moon had long set, under the crystalline stars two Warrows attempted to pace out the Elven ritual of the turning of the seasons, but they became hopelessly entangled in their own steps, for Bekki the Dwarf was not there to guide them nor were any of the Elves . . . though Tip's song did remain true to the rite.

The days edged toward April, and still cruel winter gripped the land and still Tipperton continued to play and sing to the folks at the White Horse, and still did Beau treat those with ills. But daily they also spent time behind the inn: Beau casting bullets at silhouettes; Tip regaining his eye with bow and arrow, loosing shafts at pinned-leaf targets on shocks of hay, his left arm now well enough and strong enough to handle the draw of the bow. Yet Tip came away from each of these sessions in a doleful mood, for the last time he had practiced such, it was with Rynna Fenrush at Caer Lindor, the fortress betrayed by Rivermen, and among those slain were all the Warrows within, and only a few Elves and a handful of men had managed to escape. And so, casting arrows at pinned-leaf hearts only brought back bittersweet memories of Rynna his dammia, Rynna his truelove, she and her pennywhistle, she and her red-brown hair and amber eyes and quick smile and quick temper and gentle gaze and fiery glance. When the buccen came in from practice, Tip would sit quietly by the fire and strum softly on his Elven lute, which seemed to give him a measure of solace, though whether his heart would ever mend . . . Beau, who would sit quietly nearby and listen, could not say.

Just after the dawn a week beyond Springday the buccen were wakened by black-oxen horns blowing in alarm. Oldsters and youngsters and women caught up axes and bows and swords and rakes and brooms and cudgels and shovels and whatever else came to hand, and they rushed to the streets to defend the town. Tip and Beau scrambled out of bed and into their clothes and snatched up their own weapons, and when they came running outward, they looked where the townsfolk were staring and pointing. Riding across the snow-laden plains came a large mounted force, long shadows cast by the Grimwalls obscuring just who they might be. On they came and on, as citizens took up a defensive stance, and Tip nocked an arrow, while Beau laded his sling. And from the approaching riders a horn sounded, deep and ringing, and mutters of hope ran among Jallorby defenders, for it was the call of a black-oxen horn. In that moment through the low-hanging overcast a shaft of eastern sunlight burst along a vale in the mountains to banish the gloom on the plains below and illuminate the oncoming riders. Someone among the townsfolk began to cheer, followed by the glad shouts of others, for now all could see the green-and-white banner flying from a lance in the fore of the force and the wheeled chariots within, and the horses were prancing proud steeds.

"Who is it?" called Tip to one of the citizens, an oldster who frequented the inn, a billet of firewood in hand.

"Jordian warriors, lad, Jordian warriors," said the man, looking at the wooden weapon he held, then casting it to the porch of the inn. "Looks to be a regiment all told. Mayhap it's our sons and daughters come back from the war."

Across the plains they came riding and into the streets of Jallorby, tall men on tall horses, women too, fiery warrior maidens of Jord. Vanadurin all, they looked proud and hard, riding as they did, their weapons at the ready, their visages resolute and framed by coppery hair, their clear eyes flinty as if seeking foe of the realm.

The townsfolk cheered and shouted *Harlingar!* and *Vanadurin!* and rushed to and fro and called out for any news of their kindred, and the warriors broke into great smiles and called back answers, though for the most part they knew nought of the sons and daughters of Jallorby.

Beau tugged at Tip's sleeve and pointed. Rumbling toward them came one of the two-wheeled chariots: drawn by four horses abreast, the war wagon carried two warrior maidens—one driving, one bearing a spear and buckler. The wagon itself seemed made of wood and covered with a hide—armor of sorts. The wheels were large, the iron rims wide, the better to run over rough ground, and wicked blades turned on the hubs, glittering and slashing and deadly. A cluster of spears—perhaps ten or twelve in all—stood to the right side and rear, and the buccen could see a readied bow racked on the right-side handrail.

As the chariot neared, Tip turned his attention away from the wagon itself and to the warrior maidens within. Tall and fair they were, with coppery hair curling down. Steel helms they wore, dark and glintless, one sporting a long, trailing gaud of white horsehair, the other bearing raven's wings flaring. Fleece vests covered chain-link shirts, and long cloaks draped from their shoulders to ward away the icy chill of the wintry late-March air.

"Lor'," breathed Beau, "but don't they look formidable?"

Tip frowned. "Formidable?"

"Aye, what with that red hair blazing," replied Beau, "and fire in their eyes."

"But they're smiling, Beau."

"Yar. Now. But I was imagining what they'd look like thundering across the plains and bearing down on some hapless foe, the blades on the wheels flashing deadly. Lethal, wouldn't you say?"

Tip shrugged. "Um, I suppose so. But for now they just look happy to me."

As the chariot rumbled past, the spear wielder's eyes widened and she elbowed the driver in the ribs and pointed at Tip and Beau and both warrior maidens smiled at the Warrows and waved, the buccen making low sweeping bows in return.

*   *   *

"Dediana," she said above the babble of the crowd jammed inside the White Horse.

"Wull, I'm Beau Darby, and this is Tipperton Thistledown," shouted Beau.

Dediana smiled and gestured toward her companion, who was at that moment quaffing a hot cup of spiced wine. "Linde."

"What?"

Dediana leaned across the table. "Her name is Linde."

"Oh," said Beau.

Tip bobbed his head. "We are most pleased to meet you, Dediana, Linde, but pray tell, how goes the war?"

A dark look swept over Dediana's face. "Not well. The *fördömlig maskfolk* drove all the way to Jordkeep ere we got them turned. They left a trail of ruination behind: slaughter, pillage, burnings—"

"Horses slain for meat," interjected Linde, slamming her empty cup to the table.

Dediana nodded fiercely and clenched a fist. "Just as we thought the keep fallen, the Fjordlanders attacked from the rear. Now the *Svärm* has been driven north and east, toward Kath and Naud. Those two nations have been reluctant to join in the fight, but now they will have no choice."

"North and east?" Tip frowned. "Hmm. Rumors in Dendor had it that Lady Ryla said you would push the Foul Folk back into the Boreal Sea, and that would be west, now, wouldn't it?"

"Would that we could push them west, Sir Tipperton, for should they return to the ocean they will discover that the Fjordlanders burnt all their ships, and into the sea we would drive them to perish in those cold waters. But that does not seem fated to be, for they fight a running battle in a different direction altogether."

Beau canted his head sideways. "Running battle? Say, wouldn't that favor Jord, being on horses, that is?"

"Aye," said Dediana, "though they have Guula on Hèlsteeds. Still, we strike and withdraw, strike and withdraw, hitting them at their weakest as they flee across our realm to escape."

Dediana paused to quaff from her cup, and Linde said, "Of course, the Naudrons and Kathians will blame Jord for turning the Svärm north and east and driving them toward those lands. It will serve to fuel old hatreds which burn between Jord and those two *förbannad* realms . . . all started by many dark deeds done by them long past." She smacked a fist into open palm, fire burning in her eyes.

"Pardon, my lady," said Tip, "but if the fight yet rages in the north and east, then I ask what is your regiment doing here in

Jallorby, south and west and yet in Jord but as far from the battle as one can get?"

"Argh," growled Linde and shook her head, but Dediana said, "We were among the wounded, all of us in this regiment. King Ranor came unto us and said that as soon as enough were healed, we were to form a regiment and to head for Caer Pendwyr. King Ranor felt the need to send some aid to High King Blaine, and this is that contingent, a token force to show support and to fight by the High King's side until the rest of Jord can come."

"But as far as I know," said Tip, "King Blaine's whereabouts are uncertain. Didn't Lady Ryla convey that message?"

Dediana nodded. "King Ranor said King Blaine might not be in Pellar, but surely he will come there soon or late."

"*Fördömlig taggspjut!*" Linde peeled up her mail shirt and the padding 'neath and the silken undershirt beyond and looked at a long, pink scar running across her stomach. "If it weren't for that blasted Guul, I'd be with the Vanadurin right now."

Dediana frowned and gestured about. "Linde, you *are* with the Vanadurin."

Linde dropped her shirt. "You know what I mean, Dediana. If I hadn't taken the wound, I'd be fighting up north."

"Hoy, now," protested Beau. "It's no disgrace to take a wound. I've seen plenty of them, and on the toughest of fighters, too: Dwarves, Baeron, Elves, Humans, Warrows—well, one Warrow, Tipperton here who took a Vulg bite. Show 'em your scars, Tip. Stitched up plenty of them, too. I'm a healer, you know."

"You took a Värg bite and lived?" Dediana asked Tip.

"Of course he did," said Beau. "Show 'em your scars, Tip, show 'em your scars."

Reluctantly, Tip slid up his left sleeve, exposing the furrows made by fangs.

"What of the Värg?" asked Linde, peering at the wound.

"He's dead," said Beau. "Tip stabbed him with an arrow."

Dediana looked at Tip. "Slew a Värg with nought but a handheld arrow?"

"Actually," said Tip, "I had the arrow in my right hand when the Vulg leaped at me. I fell backwards, my left arm in his mouth; the nock of the arrow jammed against the ground and the Vulg managed to impale himself as he came down atop me."

Dediana shook her head. "Fortune certainly smiled down upon you, Tipperton Thistledown, for had She not then the arrow would not have been straight on dead center and would have simply snapped and you would have been his meal."

"What of the *gift*?" asked Linde.

"Gift?"

"Um . . ." Linde searched for the word in the common tongue. Then she turned to Dediana. *"Um, vad är gift på den gemensam tunga?"*

"Venom," supplied Dediana. "Poison."

Linde looked at Tip and raised her eyebrows.

"Oh well, I happened to have some gwynthyme with me. It did the work of countering the poison, but Vulg mouths are befouled and an infection set in and . . . well, Beau came along and healed me."

Again Linde turned to Dediana. *"Vad är gwynthyme?"*

Dediana shrugged, then looked at the buccen. "What is gwynthyme?"

Beau reached into his pocket and pulled out the small silver case given to him by Aris back in Arden Vale. He snapped it open, saying, "I've more in my medical bag." Once again the small metal container held sprigs of mint.

"Ah," said Dediana. *"Guldgul mynta."*

Linde nodded and said to Tipperton, "Again Lady Fortune smiled your way."

Tip ruefully shook his head. "Would that She had smiled down just a bit earlier such that no Vulgs whatsoever were in that pass."

Linde shrugged and said, "It sounds as if there is a tale here for the telling, and since you know why we are here in Jallorby I think it's time we found out just how you two *mygga* ended up here."

Beau looked at Linde. "Mygga?"

Linde laughed. "Gnats."

Beau grinned. "Oh, so we are gnats, now, eh? Wull, I think you'll be a bit surprised by what these 'gnats' have been through. Tell 'em, Tip. Tell 'em."

Tip's mouth fell open—"Unh!"—and he looked at Beau wide-eyed.

"Go on, Tip, tell 'em," urged Beau, turning to Linde. "It's quite a long tale, you know."

Dediana reached out and hooked a passing serving wench by the arm. "Bring us a full pitcher and four full flagons. We've a long story to hear."

"Oooh, my head," groaned Beau, shielding his eyes from the early-morning sunlight backlighting the oiled-hide window.

Tip sat up and peered about, squeezing his eyes shut repeatedly and smacking his tongue against the roof of his mouth as if tasting something unpleasant. Then he looked at Beau and barked a laugh and immediately winced from the sound.

"Wha'r' you laughing about, bucco?" whispered Beau.

"Your eyes, Beau. Your eyes. They look like two yellow holes in the snow."

"You're one to talk, my friend, you who are about to bleed to death through those ruddy orbs of yours."

Tip groaned and started to crawl from the bed only to draw back in haste. "Beau," he hissed, "we've guests."

Beau looked over the edge of the berth. "Um, that'd be, uh, Dediana, Linde, and the twins, Irana and Ilea."

Tip frowned. "What are they—?"

"Don't you remember, Tip? You invited them to stay in our room rather than bunk in the stables."

"I did?"

"You did."

Tipperton pressed the heels of his hands against his forehead as he surveyed the four warrior maidens lying on blankets on the floor, and Beau said, "Look, Tip, they've offered to take us with them as they head south for Caer Pendwyr. I mean, they should go right past the Blackwood, and travel'll be a lot safer, what with us surrounded by an entire brigade of Jordians, a thousand warriors altogether, or thereabout. Besides, don't you see, the ones we'll actually be going with, well, they're all warrior maidens."

Tip nodded, then groaned from waggling his head and held it in two hands. "Oh, now I remember. And, Beau, you'll get no argument from me. I agree; we should go with them." Then Tip looked across at Beau and frowned. "But what does their being warrior maidens have to do with anything?"

"Well, bucco, the way I see it, warrior maidens are not-men."

As Beau intoned " 'Seek the aid of those not men' " Tip threw up his hands and sighed.

That same day a warm wind began blowing through the pass from the south, and some said it was an omen of good, while others claimed it was the usual spring wind. Still others said 'twas Modru's eye turned elsewhere. Yet omen or not, usual or not, or a lapse of the Evil One's gaze, winter reluctantly began to loosen its grasp on the plains below Jallorby, the land slowly clearing of snow to reveal thick yellow grass waiting to green. In the warm-driven air and in spite of the mud, laughing children romped through the streets, and everywhere faces held smiles. And every day, Vanadurin scouts rode up into the col, only to come back and report that it was yet blocked by snow though there was considerable melt. A week passed, and still the wind blew, and another five days all told, and on the very next day, the tenth day of April, the wind stopped altogether.

Nevertheless, the scouts returned to say the way south, though yet hampered by snow, perhaps was now passable.

And so, on the eleventh day of April, with Beau Darby riding in the war chariot driven by Dediana, spear-caster Linde at her side, and with Tipperton Thistledown riding in the chariot driven by Ilea, her twin Irana at the lances, beneath glowering skies, the brigade of Vanadurin left Jallorby behind, the townsfolk standing along the way and largely cheering, though some wept as well.

As the chariots rumbled up the rough trace and into the pass, Irana said, "Here, Tipperton, there's no need to remain standing all the way south." She pivoted up two padded boards hinged to the interior chariot walls, the attached sliding braces clacking into place, providing a seat on each side of the wain.

"But where will Ilea sit?" protested Tip, glancing up at the dark-haired driver.

Ilea turned and looked with blue eyes at the buccan and smiled. "Fear not, wee one, we will all three take turns, for legs get tired of standing, while bottoms tire of sitting, especially over rough ground."

As Irana sat down, Tip clambered up onto the other seat and grasped a rail to steady himself against the jounce of the war wagon rumbling up the uneven way. He twisted about and looked at Dediana's chariot following directly behind and saw that Beau was now seated, too, his face showing just above the rail. Beau grinned and waved, and Tip waved back then turned about once more, and up into the pass they rode, a long line of Vanadurin warriors stretching out fore and aft.

As they trundled upward, Ilea said over her shoulder, "We are now in the Grimwalls, Tipperton, where the fördömlig maskfolk dwell. Should it come to combat, I will slow long enough for you to leap from the chariot, for Irana and I cannot fight effectively with you underfoot. Get to a place of safety. We will come for you when the battle is done."

"You'll need take that with you, as well," said Irana, pointing at Tip's bundle of goods: lute and pack and bedroll lashed together, bow and quiver lying atop.

Tip nodded but did not reply as up through the slot in the mountains they fared.

The higher they climbed, the colder became the chill air, and banks of unmelted snow lay to either side in the shadows of crags and cracks where the sun shone not and the warm wind of the past several days had failed to reach. Soon their breaths were blowing white, and Tip gathered his cloak around, as still they pressed onward, the chariot wheels now and again running in a layer of white or skidding over ice.

Often Tip stood and held on to the rail, and either Ilea or Irana would take his place, one or the other of the twins command-ing the reins even though seated, for the horses simply followed the ones ahead, needing little or no guidance. Now and again they would stop to rest the horses, either that or they would walk alongside the steeds. Both Tip and Beau found these strolls a welcome relief from the jolting of the wain, and together they would trudge through the snow and slip across ice. Occasion-ally they would come to wide drifts attempting to block the way, yet, with a quarter of the train before them, the horses and wains passing through ahead, by the time the buccen arrived, snow barriers were tramped down well enough that the struggle was brief if at all.

Shortly after the noontide they topped the crest of the col and started on the long descent, for as Dediana had said, glancing at the leaden sky, "In spite of yesterweek's warm wind, in spite of Dame Fortune's goodwill, we'll not remain in the pass through the night, for cold yet grasps the land, especially at these heights, where wintry storms may come of a sudden and trap us entirely."

"Oh my, Dediana, don't say that," hissed Beau. "I mean, don't ask for trouble when there is none."

And so down they went and down, and in the chill midafter-noon, as if Dediana's words were prophetic, an icy wind began to blow at their backs, and dark clouds roiled above. Within but a few candlemarks, a howling blizzard came screaming across the range.

Night had long fallen by the time they had battled their way to the foothills below, the supply wagons and their escort com-ing through the hurling white last of all. Into a woodland they struggled, seeking the shelter of the trees, though the wall of mountains behind afforded some protection from the worst of the blow. And even though they could not see more than a few yards through the fling, *Hrosmarshal* Hannor set a picket about as the remainder of the warriors made camp.

The next day, though snow yet fell, on southward and down they pressed, the wagons and wains and horses struggling through high drifts. Yet the farther they went, the less the fall, the less that covered the ground. For here the warm wind of the past days had scoured the land clean, and the new-fallen snow lay shallow.

* * *

"We now come to the river, Tipperton," said Ilea, the sun low to the horizon. "Recall, if battle comes upon us, I will slow long enough for you to leap from the chariot. Irana and I will return when all is done."

Tip nodded, his lute and pack and bedroll now strapped to his back, his bow in hand, his quiver at his thigh, for the Vanadurin scouts had come riding in with the news that Älvstad was destroyed. And though the scouts had seen no Foul Folk and reported the ruins looked to be weeks old, still Hrosmarshal Hannor had ordered the Vanadurin to be battle ready.

Through the light of the afternoon sun, Tip looked back up the slope at the chariot behind and saw that Beau was poised as well, and down the embankment and across the shallows they fared, Älvstad ahead, the palisade shattered, charred timbers beyond, black burn jutting up through windblown layers of white.

"Retribution, I would say," said Tip, averting his gaze from the remains of those who had been slain, remains for the most part now covered by snow, "for here was held the muster of Agron's army."

"Just plain evil, if you ask me," said Beau, his breath frosty on the air.

Tip gestured toward the charred stables. "Well, Beau, the ponies we were counting on are all gone—"

"Probably eaten by the maggot-folk," gritted Beau, slamming a fist into palm.

Tip nodded, then said, "I've seen enough. Let us get back to the camp."

Up the snowy hill they trudged and over the crest and through the ring of pickets beyond.

South fared the Vanadurin and south, crossing a ford on the North Rimm River that day and the South Rimm River the one after, the ring of Rimmen Mountains running out of the east and curving south. Through the foothills they wended, the days growing longer, the nights shorter. Late in the third day after leaving Älvstad, they sighted a forest before them; it was the northern reach of Darda Erynian, and even the Vanadurin looked upon the yet-barren woodland with chary eyes, for no matter what its name—Darda Erynian, the Great Greenhall, Blackwood—the repute of the forest was ill, though Tipperton said otherwise. Even so, when Dediana and Linde looked to Beau, that buccan shook his head and said, "There's dark things in there, even though we travelled its length."

East they turned for a day, skirting 'round the marge, then south the following day, riding between the Rimmens on their left and the woodland on their right, a quarter of the Vanadurin before them, three-quarters coming after. And now only occasionally did snow lie on the land, for in spite of all, spring seemed to march on its inexorable path: grass underfoot and -hoof was turning green; new buds could be seen on the Blackwood trees, and returning birds flew among the branches and sang their territorial songs of mating; and the air had the smell of melt and of earth and of water running. Even so, the nights were yet quite chill, though the recent days had been warmer.

That night, Tip and Beau asked permission to see Hrosmarshal Hannor, and they were led by Dediana to his fire. There they found a tall slender man, dark-haired with greying temples. With hawklike eyes he looked at the *Waldfolc* as Dediana said, "Hrosmarshal Hannor, this is Sir Tipperton Thistledown and Sir Beau Darby, those I've been telling you of."

Without glancing at Dediana, he said, "So these are the passengers you bear south."

"In my wain and one other, hrosmarshal, that of the twins."

Hannor grinned, then said, "Which of you is the healer?"

"U-uh, that'd be me, sir," said Beau, stepping forward.

Hannor sat down on a nearby rock and in the firelight held out a hand, forefinger extended. "I have this splinter. . . ."

Beau frowned. "Have you a pin? A needle will do."

"Arald!" called the hrosmarshal. "A pin or needle."

Moments later, a Harlingar youth stepped from the shadows, a needle in hand.

Beau took up a burning brand and as he gingerly passed the needle back and forth through the flame, Tipperton said, "Sir, there is a Horde somewhere along this eastern marge of Blackwood, or at least there was when last we were here."

Beau frowned and took Hannor's finger in hand and began picking at the splinter. "Half a Horde, Tip. Remember?"

Tip nodded. "Aye, we heard from Dara Cein that half had been destroyed by the Hidden Ones as they fled from the ruins of Caer Lindor."

Hannor cocked an eyebrow. "Five segments, eh? And somewhere along this merge?"

"Yes sir. Down along the River Rissanin."

"How recent is this news?"

"Um"—Tip thought back—"some twenty months, now."

Beau nodded.

Hannor shook his head. "A bit more than a year and a half, eh? Well then, it's not likely they yet roam this bound, for what would be their mission with Caer Lindor now gone as you say?"

Tip turned up a hand and said, "Perhaps they are holding Eryn Ford."

"Perhaps they are along this marge to keep the Hidden Ones from marching south to Caer Pendwyr," said Beau. Then, "Ah, got it." He held up the needle, a small splint of wood impaled on the point. He showed it to the hrosmarshal and said, "I'd stick that finger of yours in some brandy if I were you, sir."

"Hmph, a waste of good brandy, Sir Beau."

"Nevertheless," said Beau, handing the needle to Arald.

Hannor glanced up at the youth. "A tot of brandy, my lad."

Arald stepped into the shadows once again, and Hannor said, "Not likely that the Hidden Ones would emerge for any reason. Still, on the off chance that a Horde or a part yet wards the marge or holds the ford, I will make certain the scouts are apprised."

As Arald returned with the brandy, Hannor stuck his finger into the cup and swirled it about and then removed his finger and sucked the liquor off, then slugged the remaining brandy down. As he wiped his mouth he turned to Tip. "Tell me, Sir Tipperton, is your lute nearby? If so, do you feel like a song?"

Three days later they came unto the Landover Road a few miles west of Braeton, the town just inside the Rimmen Gape that had been razed by the Rûpt.

"Lor'," said Beau that night, "but we've come in a big circle. What was it, September two years back when we were here ago?"

"You were here?" asked Ilea.

Tip nodded. "Aye. And it was at Braeton we destroyed a segment of Foul Folk."

Irana cocked a blue eye. "Single-handed?"

"Not quite," said Beau, smiling. "We had a wee bit of help: a thousand Dylvana and five hundred Baeron, to be exact." Beau looked about and then added, "The Baeron on giant horses smashed them down and the Dylvana on lighter steeds a bit like yours came after, with Tip and me on ponies riding alongside."

"Hai!" called Irana, snatching up a lance and leaping to her feet and flashing the spear toward the sky. "Sir Beau and Sir Tipperton: *Krigares av den Hros!*"

The other three warrior maidens called out *Hai!*

Beau frowned, and asked Ilea, "What did your sister say?"

Ilea smiled. "She named you two as warriors of the horse."

"Um, Lady Irana . . ." said Beau, looking up at the twin.

Irana looked down at the buccan and frowned.

"Not that I would contradict you," said Beau, "but if warriors we must be, then you should call us warriors of the pony, instead."

Irana burst out in laughter and raised her spear to the sky and managed to proclaim through her guffaws, "*Krigares av den Ponny!*"

Dediana, Linde, and Ilea all whooped in jubilance.

"What?" appealed Beau. "What did she say?"

"W-war-warriors," gasped Linde, "o-of—"

"Of the pony?" asked Beau. At Linde's nod, Beau demanded, "What's so funny about that?"

This only brought on more whoops, but finally Dediana, tears running down her face, managed to say, "Although at times we raise ponies to sell to others, even as children we Harlingar, we Vanadurin, we do not ride them, and to hear that someone is a warrior, no less, of the p-po-pony—" Dediana's voice rose in a squeal of laughter, shared by warrior maidens all 'round.

Beau looked at Tipperton, and Tip shrugged and turned up his hands and said, "It must be a Harlingar thing."

Instead of following the marge of Blackwood, Hrosmarshal Hannor struck south-southwest, aiming directly for distant Eryn Ford, leading the column out onto the open wold. And as the Harlingar moved southerly, the eaves of Darda Erynian receded to the west until the forest could no longer be seen, much to the relief of the Jordians, much to the relief of Beau as well, for they would be quit of even the sight of that wood of dire repute. All day long they followed this course, and when they came to camp that night, the edge of Blackwood lay eight or ten leagues to the west.

"I say, Tip, just where will we leave the Jordians?" Beau looked across the fire at Dediana, Linde, Ilea, and Irana and said, "Oh, not that you aren't good company, but now that we've come this far, Tip and I could strike overland to reach the Blackwood, and, well, though I'd rather we were going elsewhere, the 'wood is where we are bound."

All four warrior maidens looked beyond the buccen in the direction where lay unseen the far-off eaves of shadowy Blackwood and frowned, but none said aught.

"Well, Beau, I'm of a mind to ride all the way to Eryn Ford. Then we can make our way down the Rissanin River to Caer Lindor, for I would see for myself the ruins where . . . where . . ."—Tip's eyes teared and his voice fell to a whisper—"where Rynna died." The buccan wiped his fingers across his cheeks and then with strength in his voice said, "From there we'll make our way north to Bircehyll and the Dylvana. Someone there should know where the Springwater Warrows live."

A stricken look came over Beau's face. "Oh my."

Tipperton frowned in puzzlement. "What is it?"

"Oh, Tip, from Caer Lindor Phais and Loric guided us to Bircehyll, but this time we'll be on our own."

"And . . . ?"

"And, well, who will guide us past the forbidden places?"

"Forbidden places?" asked Irana.

Beau nodded. "Places forbidden to outsiders, Lady Irana. Places where one shouldn't go."

Again all four warrior maidens glanced toward the west where lay the woods, and Linde said, "From what I hear, the entire forest is forbidden."

Dediana nodded. "Even in Jord the name Blackwood alone is enough to quell the spirit."

"Well," said Tip, "the Dylvana don't think so . . . nor do the Baeron. And now there are Warrows within, and I would think they do not quail at the name."

Ilea cocked an eye at Tipperton. "If they are yet alive in that dark place, then perhaps they do not quail."

Beau gasped, "Oh, don't say that, Ilea. Don't even think it, if you please."

Tip sighed. "Beau, you know it isn't all that bad. I mean, we spent a goodly while in there and nought ill came of it."

Beau reluctantly nodded.

Dediana again glanced west across the wold in the light of the thin crescent moon chasing after the long-set sun. "What did you see in there?"

Tip shrugged and turned up a hand. "Trees. Elves—"

"Shadows that follow along," interjected Beau. "Hills that move. Things in the woods where foxes bark. Things that groan in the ground." Beau shuddered, a shiver echoed by the warrior maidens. "That's what I've seen and heard in those haunted woods. Hidden things and Hidden Ones: that's what's in there."

"Oh, Beau," said Tip, "I don't believe the woods are haunted . . . and besides, even if they are, why be afraid of shadows, of phantoms, of specters?"

Beau pointed a finger at Tip. "You should talk, bucco. I mean"—Beau reached into the pack at his side and pulled out his red-bound book and thrust it toward Tipperton—"why be afraid of magic?"

Tip gasped and leaned away from the book, but said, "But magic is real, Beau."

"And so I believe are ghosts," shot back Beau, jamming the book into his pack once again.

Southerly across the open wold they fared, did the Jordian brigade, aiming for Eryn Ford across the River Rissanin. And nigh sunset of the twenty-third of April they came to a bend in that river, where the waterway had swung northerly to turn northeastward again. Here they made camp among the trees of the river-border forest. Both Tip and Beau were comforted by the rush of the river and the shush of a breeze through the trees. Yet their ease was short-lived, for in the night a rumor circulated among the fires that the scouts had not yet returned.

The next morning, when the brigade broke camp, the rumor persisted; it seems no scouts had reported in all night. And as they readied to ride forth, the command came down from the hrosmarshal to be in a state of high alert, for the rumor was no rumor, but truth instead.

Again Ilea and Dediana warned Tip and Beau that should it come to combat, they would slow enough for the Waldans to jump out and would fetch them after the battle was done. And so Tip and Beau lashed their goods to their backs and kept their weapons in hand.

And away to the south they rode.

Down they went and down, angling away from the bend in the river and faring across the wold, aiming now directly for Eryn Ford, the crossing but some eight leagues south-southwest of their riverside encampment. And still no scouts reported back, though new ones had been dispatched.

The sun marched up and across the sky and down again as the column fared southerly, and relay riders came alongside and spoke orders in Valur, the Battle-tongue of the Vanadurin.

And now to the west they could see Darda Erynian once more, the forest nearing as the brigade neared the ford.

As dusk approached, the column of Harlingar passed through a set of low hills, and a mile or so before them they could again see the river-border forest, and beyond the trees water lay gleaming like cold grey iron in the dying rays of the sun.

Tip found his breath coming harshly, and he said, "Even though Hrosmarshal Hannor thinks the Foul Folk gone, if there's an ambush waiting, 'tis likely at the ford. At least that's where one awaited us at Hâth Ford on the far side of the Grimwalls."

"Mayhap I should let you off here," said Ilea.

"No," said Tip. "If there's fighting to be done, then my arrows and Beau's bullets will be needed."

Ilea glanced at her twin, and Irana said, "I've come to trust the worth of these *Waldfolc* warriors. They can leap out if a battle begins. Till then let them ride."

Ilea nodded and called back to Dediana, who nodded her agreement as well.

On they trundled, Tip's unease growing, and he looked back to see Beau, that buccan's features grim as well.

A relay rider came galloping by, calling out in Valur. As Ilea swung rightward, Tip looked up at Irana, and she said, "Hrosmarshal Hannor agrees with you, Tip. And we are warned that an ambuscade may lie in wait at the ford."

Dediana pulled forward and swung wide to the left, and Tip looked to see that all the chariots had paired up two by two . . . and then four by four as two others swung wide alongside, wheelblades turning wickedly.

A line to hit the foe hard, if foe there is.

Weapons ready, spears and sabers in hand, Tipperton's arrow nocked, Beau's sling laden with a bullet, toward the river forest they went.

And still anxiety gnawed in Tipperton's gut, growing greater with each turn of wain wheel south.

A furlong ahead rode the vanguard, the riders now in battle array, the chariots coming after, warrior maidens with lances at the ready and bucklers on their left arms.

Tipperton's heart hammered hard in his chest, his breathing coming in gasps, and the closer they came to the crossing, the more dread coursed in his veins.

Lor', what's the matter with me? True, I've been out of battle awhile, yet . . . —Oh, Adon, can it be—?

"Lady Irana, sound your horn, call for retreat, there's a Gar—"

—The blast of fear slammed into them, horses rearing and bolting, warriors shrieking in horror, chariots thundering beyond control, the drivers whelmed with dread.

Shrilling in terror, Tipperton pitched from the wain, the sudden jerk of bolting horses causing him to tumble and fall to the ground amid hammering hooves and thundering wheels as horses and chariots ran amok.

And then the terror lessened, and yawling wordless howls, Rûcks and Hlôks and Ghûls on Hèlsteeds rose up from surrounding hills to charge downslope, scimitars and tulwars and cudgels and whips and barbed spears set to slay, to kill.

And stalking out from the trees came the massive Gargon and

toward the fore of unhorsed Harlingar, their steeds panicked and run away, the men afoot frozen in paralyzing dread, caught in the creature's terrible glare, the monster's horrid claws set to rend, to tear.

25

Scrambling to his feet, Tipperton ducked and dodged among the squealing, stampeding horses, and leapt away from the paths of careening chariots with their wicked, spinning blades. Above the thunder of wheels and pounding of hooves and screams of horses and the cries of Jordians, and above the howls of the onrushing Spaunen—"*Tip! Tip!*"—Tipperton heard someone cry out his name. He turned to see Beau darting among the bolting steeds, the buccan attempting to reach Tip's side.

And on came the yawling Spawn, as the Vanadurin fought to gain control of their steeds. And just as some Harlingar managed to master their mounts, the first of the Ghûls smashed in among the Jordians, the stench of the Hèlsteeds causing many of the horses to bolt again. And cruel barbed spears took their toll as the corpse-foe swept through the disarray.

Still dodging and darting down among the horses and Hèlsteeds and runaway chariots, Tip and Beau managed to reach one another.

In that moment the dread of the Fearcaster abated further, and Tip, still dodging, looked to see the horrid, eight-foot-tall creature ponderously striding among terror-frozen men and slaughtering with its terrible claws, its deadly power now focused on them.

"They've got a Gargon!" cried Tip. "We've no Mages, no ballistas, nothing to fight him with."

"How about a chariot?" shouted Beau, loosing a bullet to fell one of the Spawn as they came rushing among the Harlingar. As Tip aimed and loosed an arrow to impale a Hlôk, Beau cried, "If we could get a chariot we could cut the Gargon down with those wheelblades."

Even as Beau suggested it, one of the chariots raced toward the monster, wheelblades spinning, but the creature, its claws slathered with blood, turned its gaze upon the oncoming threat, and the horses squealed and veered, one to lose its footing and fall, and the wain tumbled and cartwheeled, flinging the driver and spear maiden out, a white horsehair gaud on one of the helmets spinning in the setting sun.

"Dediana, Linde!" cried Tipperton, as he nocked another arrow. "Oh Adon."

But then the battle washed over the buccen and now they fought for their lives, dodging and darting and loosing and running as the dying sun washed the sky bloodred to match the crimson of the blood-soaked soil.

To the rear they could hear howling Rûpt on their trail, the Spawn yawling in glee. And from the fore a horn blat sounded.

"L-lor', they've cut us off," panted Beau, skewing rightward, running alongside Tipperton among the craggy hills lying between them and the Blackwood.

"We've got to get to a place of safety," huffed Tip.

Beau pointed rightward where stood a tall crag, and both buccen veered that way.

Gasping, blowing, the pair clambered up the steep of the uplift, a nearly half-moon angling westward lighting the climb in the night.

"Have you any bullets left?" wheezed Tip.

"One or two," heaved Beau. "How about you?"

"All I've left is the red signal arrow. But if there're any rocks up here, I've got my sling."

"Well, bucco, rocks or not, I say we hide," gasped Beau.

Behind they could hear Foul Folk yelling in Slûk, yet what they shouted, the buccen knew not. And somewhere in the distance farther back, a terrible dread pulsed.

Tip and then Beau clambered over the last of the acclivity and onto the confined, stony flat above. They slipped their goods from their backs, for even though pursued, they had found no time to abandon them.

From below there came a shout, and Tip moved to the west brim of the steep-sided crag and groaned, "Oh no. Here comes another band."

Panting, Beau stepped beside Tip to look. In the moonlight a second squad of Foul Folk ran toward the uplift. Beau turned back the way they had come. Maggot-folk loped toward the crag. "The ones behind must have spotted us, signalled the others," said Beau. "Both groups know we're here." He began searching the ground for rocks suitable to sling.

"Look, bucco," said Tip, helping him find apt stones, "you're better with the strap than I'll ever be, so when they get here, you sling stone bullets at them while I heave some bigger rocks down."

"I never thought I'd ever say that I'd've liked to run among those trees, Tip, but if we could have only gotten to Blackwood, well, I don't think they would have followed us in."

Tip glanced up from seeking slingstones to look westerly toward the forest, no more than two or three furlongs away. Then he resumed searching for proper rocks, saying, "Had we gotten to Blackwood, Beau, whether or not they followed, I think we would have given them the slip."

A black-shafted arrow hissed overhead.

"Oh my, we'll have to be careful," said Beau, flinching down, "else they'll spit us for certain."

Now there came a clamor at the base of the crag. Tip peeked over the edge. "Here they come," he gritted, turning about to take up a large rock even as another black shaft hissed up and past from the shadows below and into the moonlight above.

"Here, too," called Beau from the opposite side, and he spun his sling and loosed. "Barn rats!" he cursed, lading his sling again.

Tip glanced over the edge and stepped leftward and cast the jagged slab down the face of the steep, where it smashed into one of the climbers, the Rûck to silently plummet back to the sward, dead even as he fell, the rock to bound from an output and graze another climber, who shrieked in pain and tumbled down.

Someone below Beau screamed, as Tip took up another large stone.

"Move about!" cried Beau. "They're climbing up all 'round." And he hurled another bullet downward, followed by a Rûckish scream.

As a black arrow arced up and past, Tip hove the stone down the side of the crag, then moved to the left to drop another, both to crash into climbing maggot-folk, breaking bones in one and killing the other outright.

Shouting in fear, Rûpt fled downward, scrambling, leaping, running back and away from the crag.

"We've got 'em on the run," shouted Beau jubilantly.

But Tip shook his head. "No cause for celebration, bucco, for they've still got us trapped."

In moonshadow below, Foul Folk huddled, and then one went trotting away.

"What do you think they're planning?" hissed Beau.

As Tip moved stones to the perimeter of the flat, he watched the jog-trotting Rûck pass beyond the shoulder of an adjacent hill south and west of the crag. "I'm afraid that's the Squam who's been loosing arrows at us. And if he gains the top of that hill, he'll have us in his aim."

Beau, searching among the pebbles, looked up to see where Tip pointed, then he went back to his hunt.

Moments later, in the near distance to the north and east there sounded a resonant horn cry. "Ho," exclaimed Tip, "that's a black-oxen horn. Some of the Vanadurin yet live."

"Would that they were here, bucco," said Beau. "We could use their help right now."

Tip glanced at the quiver at his hip. A lone red arrow rested within, his last vestige of Rynna. Taking a deep breath he stepped to his pack and drew out a small lantern with striker. "Mayhap we can summon some help." Raising the hood, he lit the lantern, a lambent glow to add to the slanting moonlight and suffuse the air atop the crag.

"Oh lor', but what fine targets we are," groaned Beau, as he loaded his sling with his last good fired-clay bullet.

Taking up his Elven bow, Tip set the red shaft to string, and then he jabbed the point of the arrow into the flame of the lantern, as from the nearby hill came an exultant shout.

Whrrr . . . sounded the spin of Beau's sling as the arrow caught fire, and Tipperton hauled back and aimed the shaft skyward, and loosed, and Beau loosed, and a streak of red soared upward, leaving a long train of fire behind, as a streak of black flew from hill to crag and a spinning bullet flew in reverse.

Sssssss . . . hissing black death whispered past Tipperton's ear—

Thock! The bullet crashed into the eye of the bow-bearing Rûck, the maggot-folk to pitch backwards down the far slope of the hill, dead as he tumbled slack.

And as Tip watched the scarlet burn fly, Beau stepped to the lantern and blew it out and slammed down the hood. "No need to help them any more than we have to, bucco."

And still the incandescent arrow arced upward, leaving a phosphorescent red streak behind, a glowing trail of sparkling crimson fading in the night.

"Well, Beau, there it goes, shouting that we are here. Let's just hope it's friends who answer and not foe." Tip then looked at his comrade and added, "Though what worries me most, bucco, is that it might be the Gargon who is drawn to this crag instead."

"Here they come again," hissed Beau, cocking an ear to the furtive scrabbling from below.

"You take that half, I'll take this," said Tipperton, gesturing, then springing to his feet.

As Beau started to rise, he cried, "Tip! Look out!" and jerked Tipperton back down just as a black-shafted arrow hissed past in the moonlight. "They've got another archer on the hill."

Tip looked round the shoulder of the boulder they had been leaning against and at the crest of the adjacent hill. "Where?"

"By that tree."

"I don't see— Oh, there he is." Tip turned to Beau. "Can you—?"

Beau shook his head. "Not likely, Tip. My last good bullet was used on the other one, and these stones we've got, well, they stray a lot, especially at long range."

Still the buccen could hear stealthy movement below. "Well then, bucco," said Tip, looking about for the nearest jagged stone, "we'll just have to make ourselves be difficult targets— duck and dodge and dart—else those Foul Folk climbing are like to reach this flat, and rocks and fists are no match for scimitar and cudgel and whatever other weapons they bring."

In the silvery light of the argent half-moon Beau nodded and curled to a crouch, as did Tipperton.

"Ready?" asked Tip.

"Ready," said Beau, lading his sling.

"Then . . . now!" barked Tip.

And the Warrows darted out from the protection of the boulder, Tip to scoop up a large rock, Beau to run, sling spinning.

A yell came from the adjacent hill, and something *sissed* past Beau.

Tipperton darted to the edge, the large stone held in two hands, and he peered over the brim of the crag—"*Waugh!*"— straight into the face of a Hlôk but a foot or so below, the Spawn to yell and throw up an arm as the buccan bashed the rock down on him, the Hlôk to plummet screaming into the shadows below, the rock crashing down after.

Dodging and darting and running zigzag, Tip scooped up another stone, for two Rûcks climbed just to the left of where the Hlôk fell, the pair now clambering up over the edge.

"Beau!" cried Tip, rock in hand, the buccan leaping forward

just as a black-shafted arrow sissed through the air where he had been. Tip rushed toward one of the Rûcks, as the other shrieked and fell back, Beau's slingstone crashing into his chest, pitching him from the crag.

Rock first, Tip smashed into the second Rûck, knocking him hindward, and as he teetered on the edge, Tip slammed him again, and over the brim the Rûck toppled, screeching as he plunged down the steep, crashing into stone and toppling onward.

With the rock yet in hand, Tip darted along the perimeter, and still more climbers swarmed upward.

Sooner or later a black arrow will get us, either me or Beau, but till then . . .

He hurled his rock down at a climber, but the plummeting stone missed.

Glancing about, he scooped up another rock, and this time he didn't miss, yet other Spawn kept swarming upward, determined to gain the top and slaughter these two.

Slingstone after slingstone Beau hurled down at the oncoming Foul Folk, some to hit, others to miss. Yet still upward came the foe.

And as Beau laded his sling again, he glanced toward the nearby hill, for no more black shafts came their way. "He's run out of arrows, I think!" Beau shouted, but then in the moonshadows he saw— "Oh lor', Tip, there's more coming."

Down the hill slope and across the sward came small forms running, and shadows in moonshadow as well.

But Tip couldn't look to see, for Rûcks and Hlôks clawed upward, some reaching the brim, and with his large rock he smashed fingers and hands and wrists and arms groping over the edge, bones shattering, Foul Folk screaming as they tumbled back down.

And then from the shadows below, arrows flew to pierce Rûck backs and maggot-folk fell away shrieking. And yet some tumbled down for no visible reason that either Tip or Beau could see.

And of a sudden the attack was done, all Foul Folk lying dead.

And Tip sat down with a thump, his breath heaving harsh in his throat. And yet he managed to flounder to his feet and stagger toward Beau.

"Is anyone up there still alive?" called a female voice.

"A couple of buccen," cried Beau, standing back from the edge, as yet unwilling to expose himself to whoever it was below. "Who is it down there who's saved us?"

"A couple of buccen? Oh my. I'm a Warrow, too: Rynna Fenrush of Springwater."

"Rynna!" shouted Beau, stepping to the brim. "How can it be? You died at the fall of, of . . ."

Below in the moonlight stood Rynna, lowering her bow, relaxing the draw, a second Warrow nearby, along with a handful of small shadows shifting about in the moonlight.

"Oh, Rynna, it's me, Beau Darby, and Tipperton, too!"

Beau turned toward Tipperton to find that buccan collapsed to his knees, his face covered in his hands.

And then he looked back down to see Rynna come running forward to scramble up the side.

And somewhere nearby a black-oxen horn sounded, to be answered by Rûptish blats.

And sweeping over all came growing dread as a terrible horror stalked forward.

*E*ven as Rynna ran forward, another Rûptish horn blatted, this one nearer, and Beau called to her, "No, wait, Rynna, the Rûcks and such are too close! We'll climb down."

Beau turned and stepped to Tipperton. "Come on, bucco, we've got to go."

Tears running down his face, Tip looked up. "They said she was dead."

"Well, she's not," said Beau, taking up his goods and then holding Tip's out to him. "Time to go. Unless you'd rather wait for the Foul Folk to get here."

Tip scrambled to his feet and shouldered his pack and lute. With Beau he stepped to the edge of the crag, his heart to swell near to bursting as he looked down in the moonlight to see his Rynna standing below. And Rynna's hand flew to her mouth, and she wept at the sight of her buccaran.

Yet in that same moment a third Warrow and a cluster of shadows came trotting 'round the flank of the crag, and the buccan called, "Ryn, Ryn, we've got to go! Maggot-folk are on the way!"

Rynna looked toward him. "How many?"

"Too many."

Tip turned to see a mass of Foul Folk in the near distance loping toward the uplift. Horns blatted and were answered by other horns farther away. Shucking his goods, Tip said, "Get out your rope, Beau, we'll have to rappel, else they'll trap us again. We'll tie to that big rock."

Beau dropped his own pack to the flat and fetched his line, and cinched the two ropes together, while Tip tied their goods to the far end. And as Beau anchored the lines to the boulder, Tip lowered the packs and lute to those waiting below. Then, looping the doubled line across his back and under one thigh and diagonally up and over the opposite shoulder and down his back again, Tip turned about and said, "Ready?" At Beau's nod, Tip stepped backward off the rim and dropped down the face of the crag, his left hand high and guiding while the right was down and behind and braced and braking, the buccan fending and footing as Phais had taught him and Beau back in Arden Vale.

Quickly he reached the base of the uplift and called, "All clear. Come on, Beau."

As Beau stepped backwards over the lip above, Tip turned about and Rynna flew into his arms. And he gathered her in and held her tightly and kissed her ever so gently then whispered, "Rynna, my Rynna." It mattered not that a vanguard of Foul Folk approached, nor that somewhere a dreadful Gargon stalked. Nay, all that mattered at this moment was that once again he held his Rynna in his arms. And with tears running down his cheeks, he said, "Oh, my dammia, they said you were slain, that all Warrows were slain at the fall of Caer Lindor, but here I find you alive."

Rynna kissed Tip again and fiercely clung to him. She looked into his face as if she couldn't get enough of the sight of him. And then she gestured to the other two Warrows and said, "Farly and Nix and I were with Aravan and Arnu and Velera at Olorin Isle and then Darda Galion beyond, seeing to the truth of the Rivermen's story. We found it to be a lie, but ere we could return, the strongholt had been betrayed by those same Rivermen—"

"I knew it!" spat Tipperton. "We never should have let them—"

But Rynna silenced him with another kiss and then said, "Oh my buccaran, you thought I was dead, and as for me, I didn't know where you were or even if you lived. Yet when I saw the red flare of the arrow, I did not dare to hope, though hope I did. And when we came, you were here." With tears in her eyes, once again Rynna kissed Tip, and in that moment Beau came to the base of the crag.

"Time for reunions later," puffed Beau, unlooping the line from 'round his body, "the maggot-folk are—"

Abruptly, Beau's words jerked to a halt as he looked directly at one of the small shifting shadows nigh. "Oh lor', but do I see there in that gathering of darkness a Fox Rider? What Phais called a Pysk?"

Before anyone could answer, a horn blatted on the far side of the crag.

"We must run to the sanctuary of Darda Erynian," said Rynna.

"My pack," barked Beau.

"My lute," added Tip.

"Farly and Nix have them," said Rynna, and Tip and Beau turned to see the two buccen, the rescued goods on their backs.

In that moment past the shoulder of the crag a small shadow came racing, and a voice cried out, "*Adreem! Adreem! A va Naxdow! Va Sleg ra an slait!*"

"Run!" cried Rynna, and pulling at Tip, westerly she darted toward the Blackwood, two or three furlongs away, Tip, Beau, Farly, and Nix, and a cluster of small shadows all flying for the safety of the woods.

And from the rear they heard Rûptish voices howling and horns blowing as Spawn sighted the fleeing Wee Folk.

Black-shafted arrows hissed through the air to stab into the ground, some falling short, others flying long, some coming perilously close.

"*Adreem!*" shouted Rynna to the shadow-wrapped Pysks, "*Adreem! Ne ata!*" But even though they were riding swift foxes, the Fey Folk coursed fore and aft and aflank the running Warrows, and they did not obey Rynna's command to fly on ahead and escape.

Howling, yawling, on came the Foul Folk, their longer strides overhauling the Warrows, and unlike a time in the past when Tip had fled before Rûpt, only those who would slay him pursued, with no one running after to rescue him or his companions from behind. Yet the eaves of the Blackwood were nigh; if they could just reach the safety of that forest . . .

Tipperton cast a look back. "We're not going to make it," he cried. But even as he did so, a resonant black-oxen horn sounded nearby, and thundering through the moonlight 'round the shoulder of a hill came Jordian horses and Jordian riders, Harlingar spears lowered and charging.

And upon the back of one of the steeds rode a warrior maiden, the white horsehair gaud on her helm flying out behind.

"Linde!" cried Tipperton nigh the eaves of the forest, the buccan pausing in his flight, Rynna and three of the enshadowed Fey Folk stopping as well, while the remainder of the wee force scuttled across the remaining space and into the woods beyond.

And as Rynna tugged Tipperton toward the forest, Tip shouted, "Linde, to me! To me!"

But she paid no heed as into the fore of the dismayed Foul Folk crashed the Vanadurin, Rûpt crying out in fear and turning to flee, Harlingar spears impaling them even as they ran, Jordian horses bashing down Spawn and trampling them underhoof.

Now at the brim of the woods, "Linde! Linde!" cried Tipperton, as the Harlingar thundered through the Foul Folk ranks and circled 'round to come at the Spawn again.

This time the warrior maiden heard the buccan's shout and she came riding nigh, her horse panting and snorting, eyes rolling wide, the scent of spilled blood in its nostrils shouting that battle was at hand.

"Tipperton, I thought you slain!" cried out Linde, her own eyes wide and flaring. And she looked to see Rynna at Tip's side, as well as three clustered shadows with nought whatsoever to cast them.

"Linde, Linde, there are too many Spawn to fight! Come with us. We run to the safety of Blackwood, for it's not likely the Foul Folk will follow us in."

"You are asking that we flee?" demanded Linde.

"Yes, to battle another day!"

Linde's knuckles turned white.

"Please, Linde. Not even the Vanadurin can fight a Gargon."

Of a sudden Linde's shoulders sagged and the wildness left her eyes, and she glanced in the direction of the battle yet raging.

"Come with us to the Blackwood," pled Tipperton, and he swept a hand toward the forest and the dark galleries within.

Rynna stepped forward and looked up at Linde. "Can you swear an oath to which all your comrades will hew?"

Linde nodded. "Though baseborn, I am cousin to King Ranor, and with Hrosmarshal Hannor dead, I captain this remnant."

Rynna gestured toward Darda Erynian. "Then if you will warrant those you command as well as yourself to secrecy, the Hidden Ones will yield sanctuary." Rynna turned to the shadows surrounding Tip. "And so that you may know our trust . . ." Rynna signed to the clusters of darkness, and the shadows vanished and three black-footed red foxes appeared, each bearing a small rider astride, none more than a foot or so tall, each with a tiny bow, tiny arrows nocked, and they motioned toward the shadowed forest at hand.

Linde's eyes flew wide in startlement, for beings of legend—Fox Riders—stood before her. She glanced toward the forest and then to the battle and then back to the wee folk afoot with the Hidden Ones at their side, Hidden Ones no longer hidden.

"Please, Linde," Tipperton beseeched, gesturing at the strife. "They are but the vanguard of the Foul Folk. More are yet on the way, and with them comes the Gargon."

Reluctantly Linde nodded and then her look became resolute and she said, "By Adon and Elwydd I do so pledge the Hidden Ones our secrecy, I and the Vanadurin all." Then she lifted her black-oxen horn to her lips and blew a call, the resonant cry cleaving through the clash of combat.

And as the Harlingar responded to Linde's signal to form up on her, from the distance there answered the collective blats of a score or more brazen trumps, Foul Folk responding in challenge.

And a wash of dread flowed over all.

A Gargon was yet unsatisfied with the horrific extent of the slaughter so far.

As the unremitting fear grew ever stronger, into the darkness of Blackwood went the Vanadurin, the Jordians now afoot and leading their steeds and following Nix, that Warrow bearing a small lantern, its distant light bobbing among the trees like a will-o'-the-wisp leading the Harlingar within.

And while the warriors and horses passed into the woods, with Linde standing at the eaves of the forest and urging them on, Tip and Rynna and Beau and Farly remained nearby and watched the Spawn in the moonlight aslant, the Foul Folk having drawn back from Darda Erynian to shift and stir among themselves and call out with horns to the oncoming Spawn, those signals growing ever closer . . .

. . . as did the pounding fear.

Beau had recovered his pack from Nix, and Tip his own goods from Farly, and as they slung them onto their backs, Tip took a deep breath, his heart racing. "If for some reason they come within, I'll need arrows; I'm all out."

"And I'll need bullets," said Beau, his lips drawn thin with dread, "though I do yet have a few rocks from the crag."

"Farly, how many arrows have you left?" asked Rynna.

"Um, three, five, six altogether, Ryn," he answered.

"And I've four," said Rynna. "I'm afraid we're all of us just about out, Tip. And as for sling bullets, Beau, we have none, though not far ahead there's a stream where we might find suitable pebbles." She turned to Farly. "Give Tip three of your arrows, and I'll give him one of mine."

"Now wait, Rynna," protested Tip. "I can't strip—"

"Nonsense," said the damman. "Better that three of us be winging shafts than just two."

The last of the Harlingar passed by, and Linde said, "That's it. Ninety-seven Vanadurin in all."

"Ninety-seven?" groaned Tip. "Then that means—"

"Nine hundred warriors have fallen to the Foul Folk," gritted Linde, "forty-five score. And they will pay, this I vow." She looked with hatred at the Foul Folk beyond, and then gasped in dismay—

—for 'round the shoulder of the hill trod the dreadful Gargon.

A seething mass of Rûcks and Hlôks came after the appalling terror, and those who had been waiting gave way before its hideous power, none able to withstand even its muted fear. Surrounded by allies, still it stalked alone, empty space all around, none of the Spawn able to come nigh; not even the seemingly fearless Ghûls could endure its horrid might.

The Foul Folk who had been waiting called out and pointed toward the Blackwood, and the Gargon turned its terrible gaze upon that mighty forest, and dread poured forth in a torrent, whelming all, nearly felling Linde and the Warrows. But then the fear abated.

"Run!" hissed Tip. "It can't see us, though it knows we are here."

Into the shadows of Darda Erynian they fled.

"Oh Elwydd," hissed Rynna, scrambling backwards and down the slope, Tip and one of the enshadowed Pysks scrambling down after, "it's coming into the forest and bringing the Foul Folk with it. Tipperton, we can't stand against a Gargon. Instead we've got to fetch Lark and the others and flee."

"Lark?"

"Yes. She is—"

Dreadful terror swept over them and past, and both Warrows gasped in fear as it raked by, their hearts hammering in horror. And the small shadow cried out, *"Af slait! Adreem!"*

Rynna grabbed Tip's arm and pulled him after. "We must follow the Fox Rider."

On into the forest they ran, the darkness-cloaked Pysk on her black-footed fox darting ahead, then pausing to let them catch up, then darting ahead again.

And somewhere behind came terror, four thousand Spawn at its back.

Gasping and wheezing, at last the two Warrows caught up with the retreating column, and onward they strode, following the others deeper into the woods.

"Well?" said Beau, dropping back to walk alongside, his face drawn tight with fear.

"It's coming into the woods," said Tip.

"Bringing what's left of the Horde with it," added Rynna.

"I thought as much," Beau groaned.

And again dread swept past them, as if the Terror used its hideous <power> to search the forest for sign of the fleeing foe.

"Look, Ryn," said Tip, "we can't lead the Gargon to the Springwater Warrows or to the dwellings of the Hidden Ones. We can't expose them to such horror."

"The Pysks have a plan," said Farly.

"A plan?"

Farly nodded. "It seems that one of their own managed to slay a Gargon way back near the end of the First Era, or so says Phero."

"And . . . ?" demanded Rynna.

"Phero now rides to the Eio Wa Suk to ask them to send a message far north and find out how it was done. In the meanwhile we are to keep beyond the dread Gargon's stare."

"You mean run, don't you? Just as we are doing?"

"Yes," replied Farly, "until Phero finds out how 'twas done."

At the tail of the column of fleeing allies, on they pressed through the moonshadowed forest, a bobbing lantern far ahead as Nix continued to lead the way; and tiny lights now winked alongside the file, yet whence came these blinking glows, neither Tip nor Beau could say. And still a dread raked across them now and again as the Gargon's terror swept back and forth, the monster seeking prey.

"Look," said Tip, catching his breath after one of these sweeps, "although we can't lead the Foul Folk to the Springwater Warrows, perhaps there is a place we can lure them to; if we can get far enough ahead, mayhap we can make a trap, a spiked pit or some such to slay the Gargon ourselves." As he strode, Tip looked at Rynna in the shadows cast by the half-moon sliding down the indigo vault of the western sky.

Rynna frowned and shook her head. "I can't think of a place where we could be certain that the Gargon would step into—" Of a sudden, her eyes widened, and she glanced at Farly and then back to Tip, saying. "Oh, Tip, there may be another way: if we can cause his escort of Foul Folk to flee, perhaps the Gargon itself will quit this place."

"How would we do that?" asked Tip. "How would we make the Spawn abandon the Gargon, run away altogether?"

"You said it yourself, my love: we lead them, but in this case we lead the Gargon and Foul Folk into a place the Foul Folk fear."

Farly looked at Rynna in puzzlement. "What have you in mind, commander?"

"Eio Wa Suk," answered Rynna.

"Yes!" cried Farly, hope gleaming.

Upon hearing the name again that night, Tip frowned in concentration, trying to recollect. Then his eyes widened. "Eio Wa Suk; Groaning Stones?"

"Yes, Tipperton, Groaning Stones. There is an aggregate nearby. That's where Phero has gone."

"These are those who make the ground grumble?" asked Beau, his eyes filled with trepidation.

"Yes," replied Rynna.

"Oh my," said Beau. "I am not certain at all I want to walk among things that groan in the ground. It gives me the willies just thinking of it."

"That's what I'm counting on, Beau. —Oh, not you shrinking from walking among the stones, but that the Foul Folk dread them even more."

"Ha!" barked Farly. "They have run from the Stones in the past."

"Do not get your hopes too high," warned Rynna. "With the Gargon among them, it may not work at all."

"Speaking of the Dread," said Tipperton, "will the Gargon's fear not hurt the Stones?"

Rynna frowned and called one of the moving shadows to her side, and they spoke for long moments in the Fey Folk tongue. And even as they did so, a sweep of fear passed over all.

Finally, Rynna turned to Tipperton. "Rali does not think so, my love. She says the Eio Wa Suk are but partially awake and fear no thing except perhaps a great shaking of the land."

"Nevertheless . . ." said Tipperton, "it *is* a Gargon after all."

Rynna spoke again with the Fox Rider, and off darted the shadow toward the head of the column. The damman turned to the others. "Rali has gone ahead to tell Nix to strike for the aggregate and through. Then she will ride onward and speak with the Stones themselves, and if necessary we will change our plan. But for now, it's through the aggregate we will go and hope the Foul Folk will not."

Beau shivered and said, "If we must."

Ryn looked at Farly. "Farly, you go forward and warn Lady Linde what we are to do, for she and the Vanadurin must keep their horses in check should the Stones rumble as we pass among them. And tell her to relay the word for all to step softly, else the Stones *will* grumble."

Even as Farly darted forward, the dread of the Gargon swept over them once more, the monster leading the howling Spawn toward slaughter anew.

*   *   *

Among the shadows of lithic giants wended the column of horses, the half-moon low and nearly set, casting long darkness easterly. Here was an aggregate of Eio Wa Suk, a wide vale of enormous Stones, ranging from tall, standing monoliths soaring skyward, some towering upward fifty feet or more, to great boulders half-buried in the ground, squat and rotund in comparison. Huge and rough were they all, the lofty ones looming up in the pale yellow light cast by the sinking moon, the smaller ones—no less imposing—lurking in shadows below. Some of the Stones were barren and dark, others barren and light, and still others were covered with moss or vines or were splotched with dottles of lichen splayed in long runs of greenish white.

And as the column moved among these great rocks, Tip could hear the howls of the oncoming Foul Folk behind, for the entire file of Jordians and Warrows and fox-riding Pysks had slowed to let the Spawn draw nigh. And the dread of the Gargon was now locked onto the hammering hearts of those it would slay, terror coursing through the veins of horses and foxes and Harlingar and Wee Folk and Hidden Ones all, as amid massive Stones they fled.

Twisting and winding and moving apace, among lofty rocks they hastened, the Stones rumbling low at the tread of horses jarring the ground. But the Vanadurin held tightly to the reins near the bits as they trotted before their steeds, pulling the beasts after.

Down this vale of Groaning Stones fled the Free Folk, and up a long ridge out of the dell, where they came to the last of the great rough rocks.

"Go on," cried Rynna to Linde, the hindmost Jordian in line. "We will see if the plan has worked and then come running after."

And as the last of the moon fell away, Linde saluted and over the crest and downslope she went, following after the others, leaving Tip, Beau, Rynna, and two of the Fox Riders on the ridge behind.

"Lor', but I wish we had the vision of Elves," said Beau, tasting fear and peering into the darkened valley, looking back the way they had come. "Then we could see by starlight alone."

"Fear not, Beau," said Rynna, gesturing into the shadows at hand, "we have at our sides the eyes of the Pysks."

His palms sweating, his heart hammering, Tipperton reached out and took Rynna's hand as howls echoed along the vale. "They come," he said, and then amended, "No, what I mean is *it* comes."

Rynna's breath fluttered in short, rapid puffs. "In moments we will see."

No sooner were the words out of her mouth than there began a groaning rumble.

One of the Fox Riders spoke: *"Va Dreeth ar en va dep un visin den Eio Wa Suk."*

"The Gargon is in the valley," translated Rynna, "moving among the Stones."

Louder and louder came the groaning, and the howls of the Foul Folk juddered to a halt.

"Mayhap it is working," said Tip, squeezing Rynna's hand.

Rynna nodded, saying, "Aye, mayhap," though doubt dwelled deep in her voice.

Louder and louder groaned the Stones, the rumbling ground itself beginning to shiver, and Beau looked about in dread as if seeking a place of solidity.

And still the Draedan came onward, its terror growing with every massive stride.

"Oh, love, I just remembered," called Tip above the collective moan filling the air, the buccan's voice shaking with dread, "the Gargon, his tread is ponderous, as if moving on massive feet of stone."

Her breath jerking in and out of her lungs, Rynna managed to say, "Good . . . that will . . . anger . . . the Eio Wa Suk."

Now the whole vale shook with a collective deep grinding, a vast unending stentorian groan, the very earth thrumming in response, as if the whole world howled.

Beau clapped his hands over his ears and squeezed his eyes tightly shut.

And from his place on the ridge, Tip could see down in the starlight and among the Stones, where—

—He screamed in unending terror and fell to his knees and shrieked and shrieked and shrieked.

And beside him Rynna and Beau stood frozen in horror and shrilled, as did the Fox Riders, the Pysks and foxes suddenly bereft of shadow. . . .

Through a gap between monoliths, the Gargon had them trapped in its glare.

Yet as the creature stalked toward the gaze-stricken victims, it passed behind a Stone, and suddenly all were free, though pounding dread yet coursed through their veins.

"Run!" cried Tip, but even as they started to turn, Tip's eyes flew wide for he beheld—

—one of the huge monoliths tilting, tilting, falling, falling, falling—

—down—

—down—

WHUUUMP!

—the entire vale quaked with the shock of the thunderous crash—

—and great waves of unendurable dread blasted outward, and Tip, Rynna, Beau, foxes and Pysks, all were hurled to the ground shrieking, their blood hurtling along their veins, their hammering hearts ready to explode. And screaming in boundless terror they groveled on the ground beyond all reasoning, beyond all control.

And then it was gone.

Completely.

His breath coming in gasps, Tip managed to say, "The Gargon is dead."

And an angry roar rose up from the Groaning Stones, a sound so loud that it rattled the very bones, and the earth itself quaked and trembled under the thunderous blast. Stumbling and falling and rising and running across the shivering land, Rûcks and Hlôks and Ghûls on Hèlsteeds fled away in mortal fear, though many did not live beyond a mere few paces, their very beings bursting apart in the bellowing rage below.

27

The angry roaring thundered out across the land, the enraged fury of lithic giants hammering throughout Darda Erynian and under the Rissanin River and into the Greatwood beyond, the earth juddering for miles uncounted—loam, soil, detritus, muck, glades, hills, vales, fens, streams, pools, meres, swards, bushes, trees, all shuddering in response. And on the very edge of the aggregate, Tip, Beau, Rynna, Pysks, and foxes, all were knocked from their feet in the jolting, bellowing blast of wrath. Warrows and Pysks slapped hands over their ears, while foxes turned their own back and down, yet the roaring thundered through flesh and bones to deafen them regardless. And just over the crest of the vale and down in the woods below—horses and Harlingar, foxes and Pysks, and Warrows afoot—all reeled under the onslaught, and animals tried to flee, those who had not run away during the death throes of the Gargon.

Exactly how long the rage lasted, none on the ridge or beyond could say, yet of a sudden the bellowing ceased altogether, to be replaced by a low, anguished groaning. And in distant places throughout the forest and elsewhere in Mithgar, other aggregates of Eio Wa Suk took up the mournful cry.

On the valeside, as Pysks stroked foxes and soothed them, the animals wide-eyed and jittery, Tip struggled to his feet and helped Rynna to stand as well. He then called out to Beau, but Beau sat on the ground and looked down into the vale and paid him no heed, for with their hearing aggrieved neither Tip nor

Beau nor Rynna could comprehend a word said. Tip stepped to the buccan and held out a hand, yet Beau waved any aid away and simply remained sitting, though he did say something that neither Tip nor Rynna understood.

And so, Tip and Rynna took places beside him, and all peered down into the aggregate below, seeking any sign of movement, Tip with his arm about his dammia as they waited for their hearing to return.

Moments later, up the back of the ridge came three Pysks riding, shadow gathered 'round. Coming after was Farly the Warrow as well as Linde and another Harlingar, the Vanadurin astride horses.

The gathered darkness about one of the Pysks vanished as she stopped before Rynna and said something, but Rynna touched her ear and shook her head.

The Pysk nodded in understanding, and called out to the others, and Farly turned and spoke to the Vanadurin and then sat down beside Beau, Jordians and Pysks dismounting to wait as well.

As April stars wheeled through the dark velvet sky above, they sat and gazed into the valley where Groaning Stones mourned. How long they waited, none could strike a mark, yet after a lengthy while, again the Pysk stepped before Rynna and said, "Ya e a va dep a vis elt ve crued a Eio Wa Suk."

Although the Fox Rider's voice seemed muted, Tip realized he could now discern the words.

Rynna turned to Tip. "The Fox Riders are going down into the aggregate to see what has befallen the Groaning Stones."

"Then we should also go," said Tip. "You never know what might be lurking therein."

"You need not worry about the Pysks, love," replied Rynna. "Those tiny arrows of theirs are quite lethal."

"Should they face danger," said Linde, "Sten and I ride with them." She gestured toward the male Vanadurin who had ridden back with her.

"Nevertheless . . ." said Tip, rising to his feet and helping Rynna up. Then he turned to Beau. "We're going back down into the vale, bucco."

An unwilling look swept over Beau's features, but he stood, though reluctantly, and laded his sling with a nearby pebble and said, "If we must."

The Pysk spoke again to Rynna, and she in turn said to Linde, "Leave your horses behind. Their heavy tread might anger the Stones. And walk softly, please."

Linde nodded, then said, "It is dark down there and unlike Waldana and Pyska, Sten and I will need light to see by."

Beau took a small hooded lantern from his pack and lit it, raising the shield a crack. "Here," he said, and held it out to Linde. But Sten stepped forward and took the light.

Then Tip, Rynna, and Farly all nocked arrows, and Linde and Sten each took a saber in hand.

And so, stepping lightly, down into the aggregate they went—six shadows, four Warrows, and two Jordians—while all about them arose a dolorous collective groan.

"Oh my," said Rynna, disheartened, as she looked through the starlight at the huge, vine-covered Stone, the great long monolith broken in twain where it had fallen to the ground. Lying on its side, some eight feet up and eight feet across it was, and nearly sixty feet in length altogether, including the ten feet or so that had ripped out of the valeside when it had pitched forward and down. And now it lay sundered—like a toppled broken obelisk from an ancient age unknown.

And the vale was filled with a low moaning, grievous in tone and timbre.

No longer enshadowed, Pysks had dismounted to step to the Stone and touch it and lay their cheeks against it, and tears coursed down their faces. One looked at Rynna and spoke awhile and then turned back to the monolith. Rynna then stepped to Tip and Beau, and above the doleful groaning she said, "Tynvyr tells me that this was one of the greater Stones. She named it the Grandsire of the Vale, saying it always seemed to be the patriarch of this aggregate, standing as protectorate over all. She tells me that many a warning did this Stone relay, many a summons too—musters, rallyes, conclaves, assemblies, forgatherings. It will be sorely missed by all the Hidden Ones and by those it sheltered so well."

"Sheltered?" asked Beau.

"In its covering of vines," replied Rynna, gesturing at a half-formed nest a pair of springtime birds had begun.

"Oh," said Beau.

" 'Round here!" called Farly above the lamenting of Stones, the buccan and Harlingar on the opposite side of the broken monolith.

To the near end and around went Tip, Rynna, Beau, and the Fox Riders, to find Farly and Linde and Sten staring by lantern-light at the remains of the Gargon, the monster crushed by the fallen Stone, only its head and shoulders and one arm out from under. And the smell of vipers rose up all 'round, foxes snorting as if to rid themselves of the foul odor.

"Lor' but it's ugly," said Farly, peering down at the dead creature.

"Huah!" exclaimed Beau. "It looks just like the one Tip and Imongar slew back at Dendor."

Farly looked at Tip in wonder. "You slew a Gargon?"

Tip shook his head. "Imongar did. Shot it with a great ballista. Put a spear through its heart."

"She couldn't have done it without Tip, though," said Beau.

"And it looked like this one, you say?" asked Farly, peering back at the creature.

"Yes," said Tip, "ugly thing that it is."

"King Agron put its head on a pike and carried it into battle," added Beau. "It seemed to dishearten the Foul Folk to see such a powerful one of their own be reduced to nought but a pate on a pole."

Linde glanced at Rynna. "Would you like to do such?"

"Oh no," replied Rynna, looking at Tip and Beau and Farly, the buccen all shaking their heads, *No*.

"Well then, if you have no use of it . . ." said Linde.

"Please . . ." responded Rynna, stepping aside and sweeping a hand at the remains not crushed.

Linde waved them back and with Sten holding the lantern nigh, she took her saber to the monster, with little effect. She looked at her blade and then back at the creature. "Hmm, this is like hacking a log."

"It took a Dwarven battle-axe to lop through the other one's neck," said Tip.

Linde turned to Sten and took the lantern and said, "Ride and tell the others what we have seen, that the Gargon is slain by this Stone. Tell them as well the Spawn have fled, though some did not live to escape this vale. When that is done, fetch Thurl. He yet has an axe. Though not Dwarven, mayhap 'twill do."

Sten nodded and turned to make his way up and out from the vale, the man stepping softly as deep lamentation rose up all 'round.

"Over here," hissed Rynna.

Tip stepped to her side and looked where she pointed.

"I think this one is a Human," said Rynna, no longer flinching from the sight of those slain by the rage of the Stones.

Bones and organs shattered, blood oozing over ruptured flesh, a man lay dead among several Ghûls, the Foul Folk slain as well. Limp they lay, somewhat formless, like split bags of mush-filled skin. As to the man, he had been pale white with long white hair, and like all the other dead, he reeked of blood and feces and urine and vomit.

"A surrogate, I think," said Tip.

"Surrogate?"

"Someone whom Modru can possess. I think they are all without wit, and this gives Foul Modru a way to see and hear and speak. He commands his far-flung armies through the use of such empty men."

"Oh my," said Rynna, her hand flying to her mouth. "How dreadful."

On they went, continuing their count of those felled by the wrath of the Stones.

After a while Rynna said, "Madness."

"Madness?"

"Modru. Instead of such a hideous means, I would think he would choose those wise in the ways of war to lead his armies."

Tip shook his head. "I think he does not trust command to anyone but himself."

Rynna frowned, then said, "Either that, or he believes but for him all others to be fools."

Tip nodded and said, "Madness indeed."

"With your count and ours," said Tip, "if I've toted it right, some seven hundred Spawn did not escape this vale."

"Oh my," said Beau, looking back down into the valley from the ridge where they all now stood. "No wonder the Foul Folk fear the Groaning Stones."

Rynna spoke with Tynvyr, then turned to the others. "She tells me that never have so many been slaughtered by Eio Wa Suk, yet never before has a Stone died to kill a Spawn."

"How did he do it?" asked Beau. "—Grandsire, I mean. How did he manage to move at all? It isn't as if rocks or such can stir about under their own power."

Tears came into Rynna's eyes. "As to how he managed to move, that I cannot say, yet Eio Wa Suk are not ordinary rocks as you well can see."

"As I can see and hear," said Beau, the sad groaning rising up from the vale.

"Aye, and hear," agreed Rynna. "As to Grandsire, I believe he forfeited his own life to save those of the Pysks we were with; had we been alone, Beau, you and Tip and I, then perhaps he would yet be . . . alive. See here, I am not certain at all the Groaning Stones sense aught but Fox Riders and other Stones and the trembling of the land. Mayhap he knew of the Gargon by means other than its heavy tread, but I do believe he sensed the fear of the Pysks and thought them trapped, not knowing even as he pitched over, that we had broken free and were turning to run. Yet no matter the which of it, he is dead, the Gargon is dead, and the remaining Foul Folk are gone."

Tynvyr spoke to Farly, and he in turn said, "The Fox Riders will hold a funeral within a day or so."

"Not for the Foul Folk, I would hope," replied a Vanadurin man, striding up the slope toward them, a bloody axe in hand. Following came Sten, the Gargon's head on a spear.

"Nay, Thurl," said Linde. "They mourn the broken Stone, as we will mourn our own slain, though how we will bury them properly . . ." Linde's words trailed off, and she rubbed her fingers across her eyes, wiping away tears.

They stood without speaking for a moment, the sound of woe filling the air. Finally, Tip said, "What about the Spawn that got away? Shouldn't we gather the Dylvana and Baeron and lay them by the heels?"

Rynna shook her head. "The Dylvana and Baeron, most are not in Darda Erynian or Darda Stor: those of the Blackwood are struggling to free Crestan Pass, while Baeron of the Greatwood are at Drimmen-deeve, fighting to break the siege of that Dwarvenholt."

"The Lian from Darda Galion, then," said Tip, "can they not come?"

Rynna shook her head. "They struggle in the Grimwall and along the wold between there and the Argon River, as well as protect the borders of the Larkenwald. In the main, though, they strive to rid Drimmen-deeve of the besetting Swarm, but Modru's forces are formidable."

Beau blurted, "Both Crestan Pass and Drimmen-deeve are yet beset by the Rûpt? Oh my, that was so more than a year agone . . . almost two, by now."

Tip looked about. "With the Dylvana elsewhere, who protects Darda Erynian?"

Rynna turned up her hands. "Why, we do."

"We?"

"The Hidden Ones and a handful of Warrows, along with the Dylvana and Baeron who were assigned to remain behind. But spread throughout this forest and the Greatwood as we are, a sparse few protect any given region. Even so, Spawn give us wide berth."

"The Gargon didn't," said Thurl, looking up at the head on the pike.

"Aye," agreed Rynna, "it did not."

"Why didn't it attack before?" asked Beau. "I mean, it seemed to have no fear of the Blackwood, so what kept it at bay?"

Rynna shook her head. "The Gargon, it was not here even a sevenday past."

Linde cocked an eyebrow, but remained silent.

"We make occasional scouting trips to see to the where-abouts of the Spawn," explained Rynna, "as we were doing this night." She reached out and took Tip's hand. "When last we went they were holding Eryn Ford, with no Gargon in sight."

Linde sighed. "Would that you had warned us of the numbers holding the ford. We would have crossed elsewhere: upriver most likely."

Farly shook his head. "We did not even know you were nigh. Oh, word came that a force of Vanadurin was circling 'round the north of Darda Erynian and down the eastern flank, but when you came to the Landover Road we lost track of your brigade. We thought you had turned easterly, through Riamon Gape."

Linde shook her head. "We struck southerly, taking the short-est way to the ford. Besides, tales of Blackwood are dire, and we were eager to ride well away from its eaves."

"Your mistake," said Farly.

Linde nodded morosely. "Aye, and nine hundred paid with their lives." Again she wiped her eyes, then said, " 'Neath green turves they need be honored, yet there are nine hundred slain and but ninety-seven of us, and Foul Folk yon stand across the way."

Rynna looked up at the warrior maiden. "In mounds would you bury them?"

As Linde canted her head in assent, Tip's thoughts returned to Mineholt North, to the Daelsmen's rites, for they too buried their dead in mounds.

Rynna spoke with Tynvyr some moments, and then said to Linde, "Fear not, for the Pysks will arrange all."

Linde frowned. "But how—?"

Rynna pushed forth a hand, palm out. "I did not question, yet I believe it will be done."

The faint light of the oncoming dawn began to illume the eastern sky. Rynna looked at the pale glow and said, "Come. We must get to a sheltered place, where wounds can be treated and all can rest and recover. 'Tis a new day, and much is yet to be done."

And so as the sky slowly brightened, they passed across the ridge and down into the forest beyond, while in the vale behind, huge Stones groaned a doleful dirge.

"Are we going to where the Springwater Warrows live?" asked Tip.

"In time," said Rynna, smiling. "But first we will stop at our bowers. There's someone I want you to meet."

"Bowers?" asked Beau, striding alongside.

"Aye, shelters at a place where we camp when on patrol. This night—or rather this morn—you will stay with Farly or Nix, while Tip"—Rynna reached out and took his hand—"will stay with me."

"Oh, right," said Beau, looking sidewise at Tip and grinning.

"This someone you want me to meet," said Tip, "is it family? An uncle or aunt or some such?"

"Some such," said Rynna.

"Well, for that I am glad," replied Tip. "Would that I could find relatives, too, what with my own dam and sire now being gone, just as are yours, my dammia. Kith and kin and kind and friends: all are important, or so I have come to believe."

And on they went as the sun rose and morning light filled the sky.

As the Vanadurin made camp in the small grassy dell, and Beau went off with Farly, Rynna led Tipperton up the western slope of the hollow and to the edge of the woods, where a modest shelter woven of saplings stood hidden back among the trees.

Rynna, smiling a secretive smile, stepped inside, Tipperton following. As Tip set his bow against one wall and removed his quiver and lute and pack and set them to the earthen floor beside it, he looked about at the sparse furnishings—a straw-filled pallet, some cooking gear, a few supplies, and such. Quietly, Rynna set her own bow and quiver aside and then stepped silently across sunlight shining through the doorway and moved into the dimness beyond, where sat a large open oblong woven basket of withes. And she looked down and her face softened and she whispered. "Come, Tipperton, I want you to see."

"What is it?" asked Tip. Suddenly a fleeting memory flitted across his mind but vanished ere he could capture it, leaving behind the uncanny sensation that this had happened before, yet just where . . .

Rynna smiled and gestured at the basket. "Come and see."

Tip stepped to the damman, and there asleep in a rumple of blanket—

—it was a wee Warrow child, nought but a tot—

"This is Lark."

—who opened her eyes, her glorious green eyes—

"Lark?"

—and smiled, oh how she smiled—

"Your dammsel, Tipperton. Your daughter."

"My . . . my . . ."

"Your dammsel," repeated Rynna, taking her up, "or rather I should say ours."

"Ours?" breathed Tipperton, wide-eyed, and he tentatively reached out to touch the wee youngling, but drew back and looked at Rynna.

"Well, go on," said Rynna, laughing. "It isn't as if she'll break."

Tip stroked the back of a finger across the child's cheek, the tot looking askance at him in response. "She's so soft."

"Here," said Rynna, holding out the moppet.

"Oh my, but I don't—"

"Nonsense."

Tentatively, Tipperton took the child, and he grinned down at her. Lark looked up at him and frowned, as though to ask just who this stranger was, but then smiled as if finding him worthy of her aspect.

And Tip looked up at Rynna. "She's grinning."

"Oh, Tipperton, she is grinning because her da is here."

Upon hearing a familiar word—"Da. Da. Da-da. Da-da-da-da . . ." chirped Lark, the words finally running together into a trill.

Tipperton looked up at Rynna in wonderment, and Rynna said, "She's been saying that for a week now, almost as if she knew you were coming."

"She can talk?"

"She's beginning to say words, love."

"Lark, my Lark," breathed Tipperton. Then he looked at Rynna. "When?"

"She was born a year ago tomorrow, and I could not have asked for a finer birthday gift than her sire coming home."

"Home?" Tip looked about at the bower, then smiled back down at the wee child.

"Anywhere we three are, Tipperton," replied Rynna.

Lark squealed and reached up a tiny hand, striving to clutch Tip's nose, and then she struggled and fussed, and Tip shifted her to a more upright position against his chest. Lark then seized a button on Tip's jacket, thoroughly fascinated by its roundness.

Tip grinned, but then frowned. "Say, love, she hasn't been here all alone, has she?"

"Of course not, Tip," said Rynna, glancing 'round, "though just where Prym or Melli have gotten to . . . Well, no doubt one or the other is—"

A shadow darkened the doorway, and an eld damman bearing

an armful of clean white cloths hurried into the bower. Her face gladdened upon seeing Rynna returned, and she one-arm embraced the young damman, saying, "Rynna, Rynna, you are back and safe. And oh my, but these Big Men on horses, well, did they ever give me a start, coming into the glade as they did. But I saw the Fox Riders were with them and Nix, too, and so I ran down to greet him, this armful of nappies and all." She turned to Tipperton. "He's my bucco, you know. —Nix I mean."

Rynna grinned. "Aunt Melli, this is my buccaran, Tipperton."

"Lark's da? Him that went off to foreign lands? Oh, how wonderful." Melli stepped forward and would have embraced Tip, but for the tot in his arms, and so she settled for a kiss on his cheek.

"Now you two rest, for Nix told me of the Gargon and all— as if I didn't see that horrible thing's head bobbing about on a pike—and I'll make a bit of breakfast." She turned to Tip. "Will hot tea and a rasher or two along with some eggs do? —And a crust of bread, of course."

"Oh, Melli, the crust alone would do," said Tip, "but tea and eggs and a couple of rashers, I cannot think of aught better."

Lark held her arms out to be taken by Melli and gurgled her approval as well.

As darkness fell, Beau arose from his pallet in Farly's hut and stepped out into the woods to relieve himself. As he came back, he could see movement across the glade. His eyes flew wide, and he rubbed them in disbelief, for the far end of the canted field was now covered entirely with mounds, each some eight or ten feet high and twice as wide at the base, each hillock veiled with a strawlike yellowish grass, or what seemed to be grass . . . *and they were moving*, these mounds, moving westerly, small creatures and Fox Riders faring alongside, heading in the direction where stood the aggregate of Stones, and farther off the eaves of the forest and the open wold beyond.

With his heart thudding, Beau watched in wonder and recalled when last he'd seen mounds like these: it was when he and Tip and Loric and Phais had ridden north through the Blackwood nearly two years ago. *I told Tip then I saw one of them move, and now here they march across Blackwood like an army off to battle.* Beau wondered whether he should go waken Tip . . . or Rynna . . . or Nix or Farly, but in the end decided not. Long he watched as the Living Mounds crossed the distant sward, and when the last of the massive column passed in among the trees to disappear from view, Beau went back into the hut and lay down on his pallet.

Sleep was a long time coming.

In the middle of the night with moonlight glowing down through the doorway, as Tip and Rynna slept soundly, Lark, using the edge of her withy-woven bassinet, pulled up and stood and jiggled. Just outside, a tall creature—seeming nought but entangled twigs and tendrils and greenery—turned and stooped and entered the bower, and paused to look down on the two lovers dreaming in one another's arms, and then it took up the restless wee youngling and crooned it to sleep as well.

And Tynvyr passed by the bower woven of saplings and paused to listen to Prym's singing, the voice of the Vred Tre rustling like leaves in the wind.

28

*T*he Fox Riders report that the Foul Folk have fled from Eryn Ford," said Nix.

Sitting on the ground, Rynna paused in her fletching of arrows and squinted up at Nix. "Fled?"

"Aye. She says they ran away when they saw the Liv Vols coming across the wold."

Tip shifted Lark to his other knee. "Liv Vols?"

"Uh, Living Mounds," replied Nix.

"See!" exclaimed Beau, turning to Tip. "I told you."

"Are the Spawn gone for good?" asked Melli.

Nix shrugged and looked toward Rynna.

"I don't think so, Melli," replied Rynna, returning to her fletching. "Although they fled the field, still they seem to be here for a purpose, though just what that could be . . ."

"We thought it might be to keep the Hidden Ones from joining the Free Folk," said Tip, "keep them trapped in the woods, so to speak."

Rynna shook her head and set the arrow aside and took up another shaft. "I don't think so, Tip. Although the Hidden Ones are deadly, nearly invincible, within their dardas, out in the open they are quite vulnerable, almost ineffective, and that's why they will not join any alliance outside of their own domain."

"But didn't the Rûcks and such run from them just now?" asked Beau. "—Or rather, last night? And that was out in the open."

"Aye, but the maggot-folk had just suffered a calamity among Eio Wa Suk, and mayhap they thought another disaster was upon them."

Lark, losing her fascination with Tip, wriggled free and, stepping on unsteady feet over the uneven ground, she toddled to Rynna's side and plopped down and took up a feather to taste. As Tip scooted over and slipped it from Lark's fingers and used it to tickle the dammsel's nose, he asked, "Did you not say the Gargon had recently come to their ranks?"

Rynna nodded. "Within the sevenday."

Tipperton grinned at Lark, but his words to the others held an ominous note. "Then it seems to me as if Modru is expecting something rather momentous along this flank and wanted the Gargon to stop it."

Beau looked at Linde. "Perhaps that monster was brought here to stop the Jordians."

Linde glanced at Sten and then back at Beau and slowly shook her head. "I think not, for we are, or were, just a brigade. Why spend a Gargon to deal with such a small force?"

Beau shrugged, a pensive look on his face. "I dunno, yet I do think Tip is right: something is brewing, else I'll eat my hat."

Tip laughed.

"What?" said Beau.

"You don't have a hat, bucco."

Lark squealed as if she agreed, and that set them all to laughing.

In that moment, Tynvyr came striding up the slope, her black-footed red fox following. She and Rynna spoke for long moments, then Tynvyr leapt astraddle the fox and rode down and away.

Rynna turned to Linde. "Tynvyr says that with the ford abandoned, now is the time for the Vanadurin to go if you yet aim for Pellar, though you are welcome to stay within the woodland. She believes it will be a few days ere the Spawn regain their courage to come once more to the eaves of Darda Erynian or those of Darda Stor."

Linde raised an eyebrow. "Darda Stor?"

"The Greatwood to the south."

"Oh."

"What about our slain?" asked Sten. "Are we to leave them lying afield?"

An unspoken question on her lips, Linde looked at Rynna.

"Tynvyr says the Fey have kept their word," answered Rynna.

In the mead north of the ford, ninety-seven Vanadurin ahorse and five Warrows on ponies rode past destroyed war chariots and wrecked supply wagons and in among raised mounds of grassy turves, for here were buried the Harlingar: Hrosmarshal Hannor, Warrior Maidens Dediana and Ilea and Irana, and nine hundred other Jordians.

How they had been buried and by whom, none could say, though Beau declared it had to have been done by the Living Mounds.

Of the slain Spawn there was no sign, neither here nor by the marge of Darda Erynian . . . nor was there any sign of the maggot-folk, those who had been slaughtered among the Groaning Stones. And in this, too, Beau claimed it to be the work of the Living Mounds. "I mean, who else could have done it?"

And now as evening drew down on the land, Warrows and weeping Harlingar—many of the Jordians bearing battle wounds now bound—made their way to the midmost mound among the many barrows. And there Linde called for a halt and all dismounted. She raised her black-oxen horn to her lips and blew a ringing note and cried out so all could hear:

> Ride forth, Harlingar, ride forth,
> Along the Shadowed Way,
> Where only Heroes gallop
> And Steeds never tire.
>
> Hál, Warriors of the Spear and Saber!
> Hál, Warriors of the Knife and Arrow!
> Hál, Warriors of the Horn and Horse!
> Ride forth, my comrades, ride forth!

And Linde blew her black-oxen horn again, as did all the Vanadurin, and the spirited horses of the Harlingar raised their heads and belled out challenges and pawed at the earth, for the horn call was for war.

Then Linde stepped to the Warrows and embraced and kissed each and every one, and when she came to Rynna, she whispered, "Thank you for saving us. And tell Tynvyr this: what little we know of the secrets of Blackwood are locked in word-bond forever."

Rynna returned her embrace, and said, "I will tell her."

As Linde stood, "Have you adequate supplies to carry on?" asked Farly.

Linde nodded and gestured at the many packhorses among the Vanadurin. These were the surviving horses of those who had been slain in the battle, horses that had scattered before the Gargon. Yet trained as they were, they had come to the sound of a horn call, and now they were laded with goods. "Aye. Some of the supply wagons were left undamaged—unplundered as well—and we gathered in enough food and grain to last us unto Caer Pendwyr."

"Use that food with caution," said Nix. "The maggot-folk may have tainted it with poison and left it apurpose."

Linde nodded.

"I will miss riding with you," said Beau.

"And I will miss your company, too," replied Linde—she turned to Tipperton—"and your playing and singing, my wee friend." She hesitated a moment, but then stepped to her saddlebag and drew out a black-oxen horn and handed it to Tipperton. "Here, wee one, this was Dediana's. Use it at dire need."

Tip's eyes flew wide. "Oh, but I couldn't—"

Linde looped the strap over his head. "You are a scout, my friend, and this may came in handy one day."

Tip nodded, acceding to her wishes.

Linde mounted, and looked down. "We shall meet again, my comrades, of that I do not doubt."

"Fare you well, Warrior Maiden," said Tip, "so do we all you bid."

Linde raised her horn to her lips and blew another call, and all the Jordians mounted. Sten rode forward to Linde's side, the butt of his spear couched in his stirrup cup, the Gargon's head on the blade. And when all had formed up in a rank behind, a thicket of upright spears stirring, Linde cried out an elder benediction of the Vanadurin:

> *Arise, Harlingar, to Arms!*
> *Fortune's three faces now turn our way:*
> *One smiling, one grim, one secret;*
> *May the never-seen face remain always hidden.*
>
> *Hál, Warriors of the Spear and Saber!*
> *Hál, Warriors of the Knife and Arrow!*
> *Hál, Warriors of the Horn and Horse!*
> *Ride forth, Harlingar, ride forth!*

And in the gathering darkness, again she blew her horn and, drawing packhorses behind, out from the mounds and across the ford ninety-seven fierce warriors rode, aiming for Caer Pendwyr to serve as a pledge from King Ranor to High King Blaine that the nation of Jord as soon as it could would ride to his side as well.

Tip, Rynna, Beau, Nix, and Farly all watched till the Vanadurin were across and away, and then they turned their ponies back to Darda Erynian, and when twilight faded into night they were safely within the grasp of that mysterious, shadowed wood.

The next day, waving farewell to Nix and Farly and Tynvyr and several Pysks at Tynvyr's side, Tip, Rynna, Beau, and Melli with Lark, all rode out from the ward camp and west, aiming for the holding of the Springwater Warrows, the site some thirty miles away. And as they rode, a warm breeze blew from the south, bearing with it the promise of spring, though chill nights yet grasped the land, and frost seemed but a nip away. Nevertheless, buds swelled, and here and there crocuses bloomed along with yellow winter aconite, and bees stirred among these sparse blossoms. The land smelled of wetness, though it hadn't rained within the week, yet bournes flowed sprightly and clear. Birds flitted among the branches above, readying for the season yet to come, much to Lark's delight, the wee youngling standing and joggling in her bassinet, the basket hanging from the forecantle of Melli's saddle.

And as the Warrows slowly wended among the trees and through the galleries of Darda Erynian, they spoke of many things:

"Aye," said Rynna, "Silverleaf and Aravan did indeed escape, both wounded, Silverleaf near fatally. Others managed to win free, managed to fight their way to the west gate and out."

"But none of the Warrows?" asked Tip.

Rynna shook her head and her voice choked. "None of the Warrows at the fort survived. And had not Nix and Farly and I been at Olorin Isle and in Darda Galion beyond, then we, too, would have fallen, that I do not doubt. But we were with Aravan and Arnu and Velera and finding the Rivermen's tale to be a lie."

"Arnu? Velera?" asked Beau.

"Arnu is a Baeran; Lady Velera a Lian."

"What of the Horde?" asked Tipperton.

"They destroyed Caer Lindor. It is now nought but ruins. But by the Spawn taking the days to bring down the walls, the Hidden Ones had time to muster and subsequently attack. The Foul Folk fled, but fully half did not live to escape Darda Erynian and Darda Stor. Those that did learned to fear them both. And I believe had not the Gargon been with them this last time, I think they would not have entered Blackwood again."

"Not even if Modru's surrogate demanded it?"

Rynna turned up a hand. "This I do know: the maggot-folk survivors of Caer Lindor, they fled the woods but did not keep running. Instead, they reassembled, perhaps at the command of the surrogate, and they continued to patrol up and down the eastern eaves as if they yet had a mission to fulfill. They are the ones who attacked the Jordians, though I do not believe that was their purpose for being here. Instead I think they have a different task, though what it may be, who knows? Yet if it calls for them to enter Blackwood or the Greatwood again, then I think they shall, for Modru will demand such of them. Yet they will not find us unprepared, for Tynvyr and the others even now make ready for such an event. Never again will they catch us unaware."

They paused at a stream to let the ponies take on water, and Tip said, "What of Silverleaf and Aravan? Where are they now?"

"Silverleaf, I believe, captains a band of raiders somewhere along the Grimwall. Aravan now serves Coron Eiron of Darda Galion; I think he rides with Galarun."

"Oh, we met Galarun," said Beau, then barked a laugh. "He saved our bacon, and the next day we savored his."

Rynna wrinkled her nose and looked at Tipperton. "A small jest," said Tip.

"A very small jest," she replied, as they took up the journey again.

Tip, Rynna, and Beau rode without speaking for a while, lost together in thought, though Lark, hanging onto the side of her basket, jiggled about and babbled and pointed at birds and scurrying voles and other woodland creatures disturbed by the passage of the ponies, while Melli called out their names.

Finally Tip said, "I'd like to see Caer Lindor for myself."

"Though its battlements and halls are nought but rubble, I will take you there," said Rynna, and onward they fared.

"Oh my," said Beau, his eyes glittering in the light of the campfire as he peered through the darkness and into the forest beyond and fumbled for his sling.

"What is it?" asked Tip, setting aside his lute and taking up his bow and standing and turning to face the direction where Beau stared.

"Something out there. Moving. I swear it looked like nothing more than a bundle of twigs and vines. And don't you say I didn't see such, Tip. You pooh-poohed it when I first saw a mound that moved, and now it's withy and leaves stirring about out there."

Melli looked where Beau pointed. "Oh," she said, "it's just Prym."

"Prym?" said Tip, turning to Rynna. "Say, isn't that who you named as being one of Lark's wards?"

"Yes," replied Rynna. "She usually watches over her at night."

"What is she?" asked Tip, stepping forward for a better view. But Prym backed away in the darkness. "Oh, I frightened her," added Tip, disappointed.

Rynna laughed. "Frightened? Oh no, my love. She's one of the Vred Tres, shy as are they all. Too, she does not trust fire. But frightened of us she is not."

"Twigs and vines and leaves?" asked Beau, his eyes wide.

"Um, yes, that's what they seem. Some would call her a Woodwer, and savage is she and all her kind when someone endeavors to clear away any part of the woodland in which they dwell, clear it away without their specific permission, that is." Rynna took up her pennywhistle again and said, "Come, Tip, Lark needs another song."

Reluctantly turning away from the perimeter, Tip stepped to his log and set aside his bow. He resumed his seat and picked up his lute, and soon a lively tune rang through the woodland along with Lark's laughter. And among the trees, Prym moved forward again, the better to see and hear.

Nigh the noontide of the next day, they rode through a ring of warders—striplings and maidens and eld buccen for the most part, bearing bows and slings, though a few seemed to have no weapons at all—and into the holding of the Springwater Warrows.

"I think you'll like it here, Beau," said Melli, smiling, as she watched him swiveling about to look back at the maidens.

Rynna grinned, too, and then looked at Tip and growled, "You, my bucco, are taken."

Tip's mouth dropped open. "But I wouldn't—I mean—I—"

Rynna laughed gaily and rode on ahead. And the four ponies and their passengers trotted past pigpens and coops and fields tilled for planting, past a rope pen where ponies were held. And they fared in among sapling-woven bowers, where a handful of younglings came running alongside, calling out for any news, while other Warrows stepped through their doorways and watched and listened and called out as well.

"This evening," said Rynna, fending off the queries, "when we hold a town meeting. No need to tell it twice."

Town meeting? Tip looked about and estimated altogether there were some thirty or thirty-five huts. *More like a hamlet, I would say.*

Rynna dismounted before one of the bowers, and said, "Here is our place, Tip. Beau, you can take one of the empty—"

"Nonsense," declared Melli. "Beau, you will stay with—"

"Mum," cried a feminine voice, "you're back."

Beau turned to see an amber-eyed brown-haired maiden, verging on her young damman years, come rushing to Melli, and they embraced one another.

Then Melli turned to Beau. "As I was saying, you can stay with Linnet and me. Linnet, this is Beau Darby. Beau, my dammsel Linnet, sister of Nix and cousin of Rynna."

"Oh my," breathed Beau, entirely unaware he was speaking aloud, "but you are beautiful."

And as Linnet blushed and lowered her eyes, Melli turned aside and smiled unto herself.

". . . killed a Gargon, you say?"

"Yes, Will," replied Rynna. "Crushed it."

A mutter of voices rose up. "Good riddance," called out someone amid the babble.

"And good riddance for the Foul Folk slain by the Vanadurin," said someone else.

"And those killed by the Stones," added another.

And someone cheered, others to take it up, for all slain Spawn were from the Horde that had devastated the village of Springwater.

Rynna held up her hands and raised her voice and called for quiet. As the gathering of Warrows settled down, Rynna said, "The ill news is that many of the Foul Folk managed to escape and they yet range along the eastern eaves of the wood."

A collective sigh rose up from the Warrows, but Rynna spoke on: "Yet there is much good news as well."

"Like what?"

"Well, for one"—she gestured at Beau—"this buccan has found a cure for the plague—"

A cure? For the plague? Can it be? Oh my!

"—and saved the city of Dendor entire."

Again a babble rose up, but Rynna called out, "And together with their allies"—quietness fell and Rynna repeated—"and together with their allies—the Dwarves of Kachar and the Men of Dendor—Tip and Beau broke Modru's siege of the city. But here, I'll let those two buccen tell the tale for themselves." She turned to the twain and gestured for them to take places on the slope beside her, saying, "Tip, Beau, if you will."

Reluctantly the two stepped upslope and turned to face the gathering. And Beau shoved Tip to the fore. All through the telling, Beau shuffled uncomfortably, for ten or so dammen looked upon him adoringly, especially the maiden Linnet.

* * *

The very next day, Tip, Beau, Rynna, and an older buccan named Delby prepared to set out for Caer Lindor. Melli stood by with Lark in her arms, for she and Prym would care for the child while the two were gone, though the Woodwer had not been seen since the night they had camped in the forest. Even so, Melli assured them that Prym was nigh at hand. Too, Melli slipped a smoke-cured slab of bacon into Beau's saddlebag among his other provisions, saying, "It'll be tasty on the trail."

As they mounted up to ride away, Linnet, who had been hanging back, stepped forward and hesitantly asked, "Beau, um, would you carry my favor for luck?"

Mutely, Beau nodded, and she unwove a pale brown ribbon from her dark brown hair. Beau leaned over as she tied it 'round his upper arm. And as he was bent down, she quickly kissed him and fled away in the direction of her bower.

Beau looked after her in amazement, and with Melli smiling and wee Lark squealing in joy, away spurred Rynna and Tip and Delby, Tip calling out, "Come on, Beau, the sun waits for no one."

Jerking to his senses, Beau heeled the flanks of his pony and followed after, though his thoughts ran elsewhere.

And when he caught up with them, Rynna said, "I hope you realize, Beau, just what a precious gift you have been given."

Beau looked down at the ribbon.

"Not the ribbon, Beau," said Rynna, "though that is precious as well."

"The ribbon?" asked Tip.

"Aye. For when we all fled Springwater, there was little time to take away the things we valued. Most was lost to the pillaging Spawn. And Linnet, well, one of the few things she rescued was that cherished ribbon she has just given away."

"Oh my," said Beau. "I'll ride back and return it now."

"No you don't, bucco," growled Tip. "Even I, as dense as I am, even I know better than that."

And on through the Blackwood they fared, Beau ever glancing down at the dear ribbon now tied 'round his arm.

Southwesterly they rode through Darda Erynian all that day and the next, and on the second day they came to the Rissanin River, to follow along its banks. And late in the afternoon of the third day, they sighted the wreckage of Caer Lindor, the island fortress nought but rubble, only the thickest part of the walls yet standing, no more than ten or twelve feet high in places, less in others. Of its towers and turrets and the great hall, nothing but broken stone remained.

"Goodness," groaned Beau.

"Goodness had nought to do with it," growled Delby.

Tip sighed and said, "I would like to ride in, but I suppose they destroyed the bridges as well."

"They were going to," said Delby, "but the Hidden Ones attacked just then. A good thing, too."

"Good thing?"

"Aye. It allowed the Hidden Ones to cross over and harry and hound the Spawn from the Greatwood as well as Darda Erynian, and many more of the maggot-folk were slain. Too, this is a major crossing over the Rissanin, and the Baeron and Elves would not have it otherwise. The Hidden Ones ward it now."

"Ah, I see," said Tip, looking 'round, seeing no one at all.

And so, as twilight crept upon the land, over the western pontoon bridge they rode and into the shadowed rubble beyond, the mighty portcullises and ironclad gates nought but twisted metal.

"Lor', what wrack," said Beau, gazing about at shattered stone. "And Trolls did this?"

"Yes," replied Rynna.

"What of the slain?" asked Tip.

Rynna pointed to a clear space on the courtyard pave, where a great blackened scorch marked the stone. "We recovered as many as we could . . . and set a pyre. The Baeron, though, took their own dead into the Greatwood. But there are those we never found, and we think they were thrown into the Rissanin and were borne down to the sea."

Beau shuddered and glanced at Tip, and Tip shook his head slightly, both buccen perhaps recalling the corpses they had seen partly consumed, yet neither said aught to Rynna.

"Well," said Delby, "if you've seen enough, it's time we were making camp."

"But not in this place of death and ruin," said Beau, shivering, "not in this place of loss."

"Look," hissed Beau, pointing.

Among the trees along the western bank of the Rissanin there burned several small fires.

"Someone is camped," said Rynna.

"Someones, you mean," said Delby.

"A small force?" asked Tip.

"Who could it be?" asked Beau. "Foul Folk?"

"Perhaps, though not likely. They fear this place," said Rynna.

"Rivermen?"

Rynna took up her bow and said, "There's but one way to find out. Leave the ponies tied."

Moving as only Warrows can move, silent in their steps, among the trees the four crept, ever nearing the fires. And then Rynna reached out and stopped Tip at her side. She pointed, and among the shadowed wood and away from the light there stood a sentry.

Tip looked to see where Beau and Delby had gotten to, but they were nowhere in sight. And so, silently hand signalling Rynna to proceed and receiving a nod in return, arrows nocked, creeping low, toward the warder slipped the two, the damman angling away to Tipperton's right, ten paces from his flank.

Tip was no more than twenty feet from the sentry when the warder turned his face toward the firelight, and Tip smiled and stood up and softly said, "Hadron, 'tis I, Tipperton Thistledown, and I no longer have the soap."

Hadron started and looked Tip's way, and then he laughed.

As Hadron escorted them to the fires, Rynna asked, "What's all this about soap?"

"Hadron was with Galarun's company, the Lian who rescued us from the Hyrinians on the Plains of Valon. In any event, he gave Beau and me a bar of scented soap as a parting gift when we went on. Like wildflowers it smelled."

"I remember," said Rynna. "The scent, that is. It was on you when first we met . . . and the night before we parted."

In that moment they walked in among the campfires, and a company of Lian looked up as they came striding by.

"Oh, Hadron," said Tip, "Beau and another Warrow are out there somewhere, perhaps we ought to whistle them i—"

"We're not out there," said Beau, he and Delby stepping from behind an enshadowed tree.

"Ha!" barked Hadron. "So much for Elven warders where the Wee Folk are concerned."

"Rynna," called a voice. Rynna looked across the fires. It was Aravan, and beside him stood another Elf.

"Alor Galarun," exclaimed Beau, "hál and well met again, and would you happen to have any bacon?"

Night had deepened and the fires had fallen to embers when Aravan looked at Galarun. "Somehow, I think Modru knows of what we seek, and the Gargon was placed at Eryn Ford to thwart this mission. 'Twas only happenstance the Vanadurin sprang their trap."

Beau's eyes widened. "Oh lor', it's all connected."

"Gyphon," spat Galarun. He turned to the Waerlinga. "And ye say the Spawn are yet nigh the ford?"

Rynna nodded.

"Then we need change our route."

"Where are you bound?" asked Tipperton.

Galarun glanced at Aravan and then said, "To Black Mountain."

"In Xian?" blurted Beau, then immediately said, "Of course, you ninnyhammer, Black Mountain is in Xian."

"Why would you be going to the Wizardholt?" asked Tip. "—If I may ask, that is."

"Great events are under way," said Galarun, "and we are sent for a mighty token of power: a silver sword."

"Silver? Not steel?"

"So I was told. Yet whether it is silver plain or starsilver, or dark silveron, I know not."

Rynna cast a small twig into the fire. "You spoke of great events under way . . . ?"

Galarun took a deep breath. "Know ye that Atala is destroyed?"

Tip looked at Beau then back at Galarun. "We suspected as much, but now you confirm it?"

Galarun nodded. "Aye. A survivor, Talar, rode unto Darda Galion, looking for his *jaian* Riatha."

"Jaian?" asked Delby.

"Sister," said Tipperton. "Jaian is Sylva for sister."

"Oh."

Tip turned back to Galarun. "Then this Talar, he is an Elf."

"Aye. A Lian."

"Go on with the tale," said Beau.

Galarun smiled. "Talar's jaian Riatha, she is among those warding the wold north of Darda Galion, though I understand she and her band cross over into Darda Erynian now and again. Regardless, ere Talar went onward, he told us Karak had exploded, and great tidal waves rolled outward and engulfed many coastal lands, destroying cities, and slaying thousands. Hardest hit were the isles of Gelen, though the coasts of Thol, Gothon, Basq, and Vancha were inundated as well. For a calamity so great, only Gyphon could do such."

"But why?" asked Delby.

"We think it was to destroy the city of Duellin, for weapons of great might are forged therein, or were forged, I should say . . . swords in the main. And these Gyphon would keep from the hands of those who would oppose Him."

Galarun fell silent, but Aravan said, "Many Lian lived on that isle as well—in Darda Immer, the Brightwood of Atala—and would have been a formidable force to bring to bear."

"We knew of the Brightwood," said Tipperton, "and of the Lian, but not of the blades of Duellin."

"This silver sword," said Rynna, "what will it do, and why is it needed now?"

Aravan looked at Galarun, and at a slight nod, turned to the Waerlinga and said, "We know not its intended purpose, though some say it will slay the High Vûlk Himself."

"High Vûlk?"

"Gyphon."

"Oh my," said Beau. "No wonder they sent a Gargon to stop you."

Rynna frowned. "But why now? Why fetch it now? —The silver sword, I mean. And once fetched, who will wield it?"

Aravan clenched a fist. "Gyphon and a large force of Rûpt have invaded from the Low to the High Plane, and a great battle rages thereupon."

"Oh no," cried Tip. "If He wins Adonar—"

"Then He will control all," blurted Beau.

"Can Gyphon win?" asked Delby.

Aravan turned up his hands. "Until He was thwarted, He seemed to be striking for an in-between to Mithgar."

"To Mithgar?"

"Aye, for with the ways sundered between Neddra and Mithgar, Gyphon's direct invasion of the Middle Plane is stopped."

"You say He was thwarted?" said Rynna.

Aravan nodded. "Aye. Many Elves and others crossed to the High Plane to help stop Gyphon, for it seems His strategy was to breach the High Plane and come to Mithgar, at which point he will have won. But Adon has now sundered all ways between the Planes except the ways of the blood."

"Ways of the blood: what are they?"

Aravan steepled his fingers. "For those who know how, who know the in-between rites, they can go home, but nowhere else. They will not be able to cross over to a Plane not of their blood. Hence, Elves away from the High Plane can return to Adonar but will not be able to cross to any other Plane. Foul Folk away from the Low Plane can go to Neddra, but nowhere else. Those of Mithgar can come here but cannot go to Adonar or Neddra. Of course, horses and animals can go as well, as long as there is someone to chant the way. Already Darda Galion is poorer for the Sundering, for the Silverlarks have disappeared. These are the blood ways, Tipperton, the ways that will allow one to return home, the ways that bar all else."

"Oh, I see. But what of the battle on the High Plane. Where does it stand?"

Aravan turned up his hands. "With the Sundering, Gyphon's plan to invade Mithgar by marching across Adonar is thwarted, yet we can only assume that the battle for control of the High Plane rages on, for not only must Modru be defeated on Mithgar, Gyphon must be defeated upon Adonar as well, for if Gyphon wins on the High Plane, or if Modru wins on the Middle Plane then, as ye say, Gyphon rules all."

"What about Neddra?" asked Beau.

Aravan sighed. "We believe that before the Sundering a regiment of Free Folk had invaded the Low Plane, and fighting goes on there as well, but with only a regiment they cannot succeed but only can harass."

"All right, then," said Rynna, "we understand. Now answer my last question: who is to wield the silver sword?"

Aravan shrugged, but Galarun said, "This and no more do we know: my company and I are to fetch it from Black Mountain and bear it to Darda Galion. My sire, Coron Eiron, will then decide who is to ride the blood way and take it to the High Plane. That it is to go there makes me believe it is meant for the hand of Adon, Himself."

"Well then," said Rynna, "if Modru knows of your mission, then he will do all to stop you."

Both Aravan and Galarun nodded, and Rynna went on to say, "And to prevent Modru from stopping you at the marge of Darda Erynian, what I would advise is for you to let us guide you through the Greatwood and to the plains of Riamon south of where the Spaunen lie in wait. That way you can skirt entirely 'round them, and a spur of the Rimmens will stand across their way and thwart them from pursuit."

Galarun grinned at Rynna and exclaimed, "Done and done!"

In the morn at break of fast, Galarun said, "Sorry, Beau, but of bacon we have none. Mian, yes, for we travel light."

"Wull, then," said Beau, "as for travelling light, on this trip the Warrows do not, even though we were expecting to go just to Caer Lindor and then back again. And so, I'll share out what bacon we have with you and yours as far as it will go, returning your favor of months past, if you please."

As he cut slices off the slab Melli had put in his saddlebag, Beau asked, "How goes the war at Drimmen-deeve?"

" 'Tis done. The siege broken not a month past. And although they took grievous losses, the Drimma now harry the Rûpt, fighting in the Grimwall—in this they are aided by Baeron and Lian. As soon as the rage of the Drimma is spent, they will be ready to aid the High King."

"If I know anything of Dwarves," said Tip, "it is this: long will it be ere a Dwarven rage is satisfied."

Galarun laughed. "Ah, Waerling, thou dost know them well."

"Speaking of the High King," said Beau, "does anyone know of his whereabouts?"

Galarun shook his head. "Talar said—"

"Talar—that's the one who survived the destruction of Atala?" asked Beau.

"Aye. He was saved by passing ship and borne to a Gothon port. In that port there are rumors the High King fights to the west of the Grimwall—in Rian and Wellen and Dalara and Trellinath—though how any came by this news, neither Talar nor his sources could say. But the Gothonians had been constructing ships to join with a mighty fleet, for the Straits of Kistan are blockaded, and it will take such a fleet to break through. But the great waves from the destruction of Atala destroyed the ships and much of the sheltered port as well. Yet the Gothonians have started anew and are laying keels again, the ships huge and many decked, to carry both men and horses. With all the ways across the Grimwalls held by the Rûpt, we believe the High King plans to sail with that fleet to come unto Pellar."

"But all the ways are not blocked," said Tip. "You told us yourself that Drimmen-deeve is free."

"Aye, but the High King may know it not, though Coron Eiron has now sent messengers across Quadran Pass to find King Blaine and tell him that way is now unfettered."

As they rode among the trees of the Greatwood—"Aye, Tipperton, a Pysk did slay a Draedan," said Aravan. "I was there when 'twas done."

"How did this come about?" asked Tip. "And how can a tiny Pysk slay a mighty Gargon?"

"Jinnarin, a Pysk, and Alamar, a Mage, came asking for my help to find her mate Farrix. Across the world we voyaged, and when we found him at last, 'twas then she slew the Mandrak, though not in a corporeal state."

"Not in a what?" asked Tip.

"Corporeal state," answered Beau. "Not in a physical form." Then Beau frowned and looked at Aravan. "Not in a physical form?"

Aravan nodded. "It was as she dreamwalked, and she slew the Draedan's spirit therein but not its body, though its body did die as well."

"When was this and where?" asked Tip.

A look of pain flared deep in Aravan's eyes. "It was on a small

isle in the Sindhu Sea in the time of the destruction of
Rwn. . . ."

On the sixth day of May Galarun looked out on the open
plain, empty for as far as the eye could see, though a hawk circled in the distant sky. To the left a spur of the Rimmen Mountains guarded the north. Galarun turned to the Waerlinga. "I
thank ye all for the warning and for guiding us here. That we
would have fallen into a Rûptish trap is mayhap certain. Yet
now ye have steered us 'round their flank, and 'tis on to Xian we
ride. Long will it take to reach there, and long will be the journey back.

"Yet heed, as ye have guided us, I would have ye keep track
of the whereabouts of the Spaunen and lead other folk safely
past them as well."

"But we were thinking of going to Pellar and aiding the High
King," said Tip.

Rynna looked startled.

Tip turned to Rynna. "It is war, love, and as well we know, in
war loves and lovers are parted, though I would dwell with you
awhile."

Rynna nodded in anguish but said, "I understand."

"I say, though," exclaimed Beau, "in the meantime, if we can
get the Drimmen-deeve Dwarves to come to Darda Erynian,
then we can destroy the remnants of the Foul Folk who wait at
Eryn Ford, and then we won't have to worry about them at all."

Aravan shook his head. "Nay, Beau, 'tis better those Spaunen
be left alone, for where they are they do little good in Modru's
cause, and little harm in ours."

"But they slew nearly all the Vanadurin," protested Beau,
"and if that's little harm, then I don't know what harm is."

"Aye, that was indeed harm. Yet heed, as Galarun says, we
would have ye Waerlinga keep track of the Rûpt and guide others past them as ye have guided us. And in that way they will
be ineffective, a waste of Modru's power."

Galarun nodded. "The Horde is best set along a margin where
they are doing no good whatsoever, though Modru knows it not.
Mayhap it will lead him to believe we have not set out at all,
and are yet to fall into his trap. If so, then mayhap our mission
to Black Mountain will go forth unmolested. Hence, leave them
be, and this I promise, when we return we will lay the Rûpt by
the heels. And when the time to go to Pellar comes, we will
proudly ride with ye.

"But now our mission is not to aid the High King, but to fetch a
sword instead, and I would have Modru think we are yet to come."

Rynna nodded, as did Tip, though his assent came reluctantly.

Galarun smiled and then said, "Fare ye well, my friends, and may Adon ward each and every one of ye."

And Galarun signed to his company, and with Aravan at his side, out into the plains they all rode, packhorses and remounts trailing, the Lian on an enigmatic mission to receive a silver sword from Mages and bear it back to war.

"Farewell," cried Rynna. "May Elwydd keep you all."

As they watched the Elven company ride away, Tipperton sighed and said, "I suppose they're right, though leaving two segments of Foul Folk on our very doorstone sits askew with me. Nevertheless, if keeping track of the Spawn and guiding others past will serve the needs of all best, well then, I suppose it'll have to do."

Rynna nodded, then said, "We have done well these six days, steering Galarun and his company 'round a danger lying in wait. Let us go back to Darda Erynian and see how to best carry out the mission he has charged us with."

The four Warrows set out for Caer Lindor, where they would cross back over into the Blackwood once more. And as they rode, Beau said, "Well, Tip, with Warrows and Pysks and Groaning Stones, with Living Mounds and Woodwers, there's not a man among them. We couldn't find a better group of not-men."

"Not-men they are, that I agree, but I ask you this: are we using their aid to quench the fires of war or simply to avoid strife?"

Beau frowned and did not answer Tipperton's question as into the Greatwood they rode.

29

Summer came at last, though it seemed more chill than summers before. "I wouldn't doubt that it's all the fault of Gyphon," said Beau, his back to a boulder as he watched the slope behind.

"Gyphon?" asked Linnet, keeping vigil the opposite way, Linnet now a young damman, her twentieth birthday having come just a week past on Summerday—Year's Long Day itself.

"Wull, Tip thinks it's due to Karak blowing up and sending stone dust into the sky, and Phais and Loric seemed to think that as well. If they're right, then this chill summer is due to the hand of Gyphon. It's all connected, you know."

"You keep saying that, Beau, about all things being connected."

"Well, they are. Let me tell you how events falling upon the world are like stones being cast into ponds, the consequences like waves, mixing and mingling and affecting one another—"

"*Hsst!*" shushed Linnet. "Ogru."

Beau and Linnet crouched low against the ridge and peered through the boulders and down. Below, a massive Troll plodded through the moonlight and across the wold. Linnet took up an arrow and set it to bowstring.

"Might as well put that aside, Linnet," said Beau. "It'd be nothing more than a pesky gallinipper to him."

"Gallinipper?'

Beau grinned. "A biting fly, Linnet. It's an old Bosky term."

Long they watched from the overlook, viewing the wold east of Eryn Ford, the ridge part of the spur of the Rimmen Mountains extending down to the Greatwood. Finally the Ogru trod 'round a flank of stone to disappear from view.

"Should we follow?" asked Linnet.

Beau shook his head and resumed his watch on the slope behind. "I think he's heading up to his Troll hole again."

For the past seven weeks, Warrows and Fox Riders had been keeping watch on the Spawn, and they knew much of their movements by now. This particular Ogru had a lair in the spur of the mountains a bit north of where Linnet and Beau now sat vigil.

As to the remainder of the Spawn, they yet sent patrols along the margins of Darda Erynian and Darda Stor, though they kept a goodly distance away from the eaves themselves.

In the early days of the vigil, acting on Galarun's request, Tynvyr had ridden to the Dylvana and asked them to join in the watch on the Spaunen, and to guide travellers past. In the meantime, Tipperton and Rynna had ridden into the Greatwood to find the Baeron and ask them to do the same.

It was as they were riding northwesterly away from The Clearing—a vast open space in the Greatwood, on the verge of which they had met with the Baeron—that Rynna and Tip had come across a vine-covered dell filled with huge broken stones—shattered, cracked, toppled and burst asunder—none were whole but one, and this a tall monolith, tilted askew, leaning against the steep valeside. . . .

"This looks like an aggregate of Groaning Stones," said Tip.

Rynna nodded and peered into the vale, tears springing into her eyes. "Oh, Tip, so many Eio Wa Suk slain. What ever could have happened here?"

"I don't know," replied Tip, "but whatever it was, it was horribly ruinous."

Rynna sighed and tugged on the reins of her pony, the steed's head coming up from cropping grass. "Let us go away from this place, Tip. I will have one of the Fox Riders come and discover what happened here and when."

"Do only Fox Riders know how to speak with the Stones?"

"Aye, Tip. Except for other Eio Wa Suk, the Stones will listen to none but a Pysk."

And on toward the Blackwood rode the two, leaving the dell behind, their mission to the Baeron successful.

*   *   *

And so it was that Fox Riders and Warrows, Dylvana and Baeron, all sat watch on the eaves of the woods and escorted the few who would fare through the region safely past the Spawn.

On the ridge Beau glanced up at the waxing, gibbous moon and said, "Our relief should come soon."

Linnet nodded, but did not take her gaze from the wold below. "You were saying about stones and ponds . . ."

"Oh well, it's just this: events are like stones cast into water, some large, some small, some tiny. And the consequences of the events ripple outward, like waves on the water to mingle and mix with other waves, at times adding, at other times cancelling, and sometimes having no effect at all. But all the waves from all the events—from enormous to tiny—sooner or later cross one another, hence all things are connected."

Linnet glanced across at Beau, then returned her gaze to the wold below. "It's rather like my mum says."

"Your mum?"

"Aye, she speaks of the great web of life, and how if you pluck a strand here, it causes movement there, some strands more important than others, for if you pluck one of those, it causes the whole web to shake violently . . . and if you break a strand, a part of the web will collapse, and the more important the strand, the greater the ruin it causes. And so, like your stones and ripples, perhaps events are like plucking the strands, causing the web to shudder."

"Huah!" exclaimed Beau. "Stones in water or shaking the web—they aren't all that much different."

They sat without speaking for a while, and then Beau added, "Y' know, Linnet, I think Modru hopes to sit in the center of the web like some great bloated spider and control all."

"Modru on Mithgar," said Linnet, "but Gyphon over all."

The moon fell near to setting, and a cluster of shadow came scrambling up the slope.

"Our relief is here," said Beau, and moments later a Pysk and fox came unto their side.

Speaking the few words of Fey they had been taught by Rynna—[Ogru go. Many Spawn no move.]—Beau and Linnet left the Fox Rider and fox on ward, and made their way down the slant to where the ponies were tethered.

A month passed and then another, and during this time Rynna taught the Fey language to the Warrows. When all became well enough versed in the tongue of Pysks, the Fox Riders themselves began to add words to the Warrows' store.

*   *   *

Summer came and went, and as autumn drew nigh, Tip and Rynna and Melli with Lark, along with Beau and Linnet, rode north to Bircehyll to be with the Dylvana on Autumnday, for Tip and Beau would step out the Elven rite again.

They found Bircehyll sparsely inhabited, for most of the Dylvana were off to war—up in the Crestan Pass and within the peaks of the Grimwall nigh. Even among those yet in Darda Erynian—now with the harvest in—many had rejoined the others patrolling the woodland eaves. Hence there were but twenty or so Dylvana at the Elvenholt proper, along with two Lian: a golden-haired Dara named Riatha, and her golden-haired brother Talar, both with eyes so pale grey as to seem a shade of silver—Talar the Elf who had survived the destruction of Atala; yet none spoke of that calamity but celebrated Autumnday instead.

All throughout the day and eve Dylvana came to hold wee Lark, she hardly bigger than a Pysk, yet no Pysk was this but a Warrowchild dammsel instead, and totally beguiling.

After the feasting, singing in procession, Elves and Warrows wound through the woods to come to a bowl-shaped vale the Dylvana called *Sur Kolaré*—Whisper Hollow—a grassy slope facing a high stone concave wall. It was a natural amphitheater, and all sat on the sward facing toward the wall, where the performers stood on a stagelike mound cupped by the stone. There was music and singing and sagas told and odes spoken, and Tip and Rynna marvelled at the wall and noted the shape of its curve, for even the slightest whisper could be heard . . . especially when the performer faced completely away and spoke to the stone itself. Here Tip played his silver-stringed lute and Rynna her pennywhistle, and turn by turn they sang, to the delight of all.

Finally that eve and again singing in procession, all wound through the woods and to the crest of the hill above the Elven dwellings, where the clusters of silver birch trees thereon were sparse and widely spaced. And the Dylvana asked the two Lian—Riatha and Talar, *jaian* and *jarin*, sister and brother—to take the place of honor and lead the Elven rite of Autumnday.

And there 'neath the swelling half-moon, singing, chanting, and pacing slowly pacing, they began a ritual timeless by mortal gauge. And enveloped by moonlight and melody and harmony and descant and counterpoint, with feet soft on the sward, the Elves trod solemnly, gravely . . . yet their hearts were full of joy.

Step . . . pause . . . shift . . . pause . . . turn . . . pause . . . step.

Slowly, slowly, move and pause. Voices rising. Voices falling. Gliding notes from the dawn of the world itself. Harmony. Euphony. Step . . . pause . . . step. Riatha turning. Talar turning, Dylvana turning in unison. Darai passing. Alori pausing. Counterpoint. Descant. Step . . . pause . . . step. . . .

And down among the shifting Dylvana and treading at Talar's side, Tip and Beau were lost in the ritual, Tip singing, Beau pacing—step . . . pause . . . step—just as Rynna and Linnet and Melli paced alongside golden Riatha, she of the argent eyes.

And out on the fringes and among the silver birch stood a tall figure of leaves and twigs and vines, Lark asleep in its arms, Prym singing along with the rite, a rustle of leaves in the wind.

In early October two Pysks—Nia and Kell—came riding their foxes through the autumnal forest, leaves golden and red and russet and brown. The cool summer past, frost had come early, and chill was in the air. Into the vale they rode, into the ward camp, where they sought out and spoke with Tynvyr for a time. Finally, Tynvyr came to Rynna and Tipperton and said, [The Stone you found in Darda Stor among the shattered Eio Wa Suk in the broken dell, it is ancient beyond counting, and sorely does it grieve from an ancient hurt as well.]

[What happened?] asked Tip, speaking Fey.

Tynvyr shook her head. [Though yet alive it is damaged and no longer knows what befell the aggregate, and only the sorrow remains.]

[Damaged?]

[Aye. As you have seen, it had nearly been uprooted.]

Rynna looked at Tipperton. [It *was* tilted.] She turned to Tynvyr. [Would that do it? Tilting I mean? Damage but not slay?]

Tynvyr's eyes filled with tears. [This I do know: when one falls or is moved a distance from its source, it no longer speaks.]

Rynna turned to Tip again. [When this war is done, Tipperton, we will ask the Baeron and others to set it upright again. Mayhap that will restore it to its source and repair the damage done.]

Tipperton sighed and nodded and gazed out on the autumn woods. [Can it speak with other Stones?]

[Nia and Kell say not. It was all they could do to reach past its grief and find the Stone within. Its voice is given to soft mourning, and not to speaking afar. Mayhap, afflicted as it is, it can no longer do such.]

October faded, the leaves turning brown, yet nought else nigh Eryn Ford seemed to change—Warrows and Fox Riders keeping station, watching the maggot-folk, guiding a traveller or two past the Spawn now and again. But in the first days of November—

[The Rûpt are on the move!] came the cry. Both Tynvyr and Rynna looked up to see Picyn come racing into the camp. Tynvyr stood and jammed two fingers into her mouth and blew, and although Rynna couldn't hear it, she knew a shrill whistle pierced the air. Picyn called out to his fox and it turned for the damman's hut, where Rynna and Tynvyr had been conferring. Up the slope raced Picyn, his fox to skid to a halt before the bower. Breathlessly he leapt down and repeated, [The Rûpt are on the move!]

[How many and which way?] snapped Tynvyr.

[All, and north, and they have a dark-haired, pale-skinned man with them: a Human.]

[A surrogate,] hissed Rynna.

[And some Ghûls on Hèlsteeds have ridden ahead,] added Picyn, [or mayhap *raced ahead* is a better way to put it.]

Rynna frowned. [For those two segments to be marching north and with a surrogate, and for Ghûls to be riding ahead and swiftly, something momentous is likely afoot.] She turned to Tynvyr. [Fetch as many as you can, and send word by Eio Wa Suk for others to foregather in the woodland along their route.]

At Tynvyr's nod, Picyn leapt astride his fox and started to turn, but Rynna cried, [Wait!] Picyn turned back. [Tipperton, what does he do?]

[He trails north, Lady Rynna, wide on their eastern flank, Nix too.]

Rynna's hand flew to her mouth. [Oh my!] But then she looked at the Fox Rider. [Thank you, Picyn. Now go, go, time is of the essence.]

Rynna once again turned to Tynvyr and said, [Raise the camp. We must hie.]

Tynvyr called her fox and mounted and rode swiftly away, rousing those in their huts 'round the perimeter of the dell.

"Aunt Melli!" cried Rynna, dashing into the bower.

At the small table the eld damman looked up from her work, Lark standing on a stool at her side looking up as well, the child's face and arms streaked with flour. "Bread, bread, bread," said Lark, holding out her white-powdered hands to show to her dam.

"What is it?" asked Melli, trying to keep her voice calm in front of the child, but her words quavered regardless.

"Bread," said Lark, looking at Melli.

Rynna snatched up her arrows. "The Spawn are on the move," she said as she fastened the quiver to her hip. "Heading north. Tipperton is on their east flank." She strung her bow and looped it over her shoulder. "With Nix." Now she took up her saddlebags and blanket roll.

"Nix? Going north and on the east flank? Riding the open wold between the maggot-folk and the mountains?"

"Yes," gritted Rynna.

"Oh my," groaned Melli, "but that means they're trapped."

Lark looked back and forth between Melli and Rynna, anxiety coming over her tiny face.

"No, not trapped. Not trapped. Not precisely," averred Rynna, as if to assure not only Melli but herself as well. "Yet if the Foul Folk turn . . ."

Lark began to cry.

Rynna set down the saddlebags and bedroll and scooped her up and said, "There, there," but Lark only cried all the harder.

Despairing, Rynna turned to the eld damman. "Melli, I must go."

Melli stepped forward and took the child from Rynna and embraced her and in spite of her own tears muttered a soothing word or two, the tot inconsolable. But then Melli asked, "Do you want me to go back to the Springwater holding?"

"Perhaps it's best," said Rynna, taking up her bedroll and saddlebags again. She stepped to the door. "I'll be there as soon as I'm able."

And then she was gone.

And Lark looked up at the empty doorway and said, "Byebye," and she rested her head on Melli's shoulder and sobbed, Melli weeping as well.

"Why are they marching north, and in such a hurry?" asked Nix, urging his pony 'round an outcrop of rock.

Riding in the lead, Tipperton glanced back. "I don't know, Nix, but with a surrogate, and what with the Ghûls racing ahead, I think it must be urgent."

"Well, should we double back and cross at the ford? The Rissanin is somewhere ahead, you know."

"I don't think so, Nix. I mean, I don't think we should double back. I don't know where they are going but, wherever it is, we've got to keep up."

"How will we cross the river?"

"Swim, bucco, swim."

"Argh," groaned Nix. "I suspected as much."

"Oh my," exclaimed Beau. "On the wold on the eastern flank? That's not good being out in the open like that."

Linnet, riding on Rynna's left, said, "Can't they always double back and cross at Eryn Ford? I mean if it is abandoned . . ."

"It may not be," said Rynna. "They may have left a contingent behind. But fear not, Tip and Nix know what they are doing."

"I hope," said Beau. "I hope. —Oh, *I* should have been with him, not Nix."

Rynna shook her head. "Not so, Beau, for who better to take Linnet under wing than you? —as fond of her as you are."

Linnet gasped, and Rynna reached out to her cousin. "Linnet, 'tis nought but the plain and simple truth. You needed someone skilled in the ways of war to apprentice under, and since Beau cherishes you, I knew he would—" Rynna's words came to a halt, for they had reached the eaves of the darda.

"Here they come," said Farly.

In the distance out on the plain the massed Foul Folk boiled northerly.

After a while Beau said, "Lor', but look at them go."

" 'Tis a forced march," said Rynna. "They are in a hurry."

"I'd not like to be in their way," said Farly.

"And somewhere ahead ride Ghûls," said Linnet.

Both Rynna and Beau nodded but remained silent.

They watched moments more, and then Rynna spurred forward and out onto the wold, the others following, the four Warrows heading northerly on a course parallel to that of the distant march.

And in the dimness of Darda Erynian, enshadowed Fox Riders coursed a like route within, though Tynvyr and Picyn rode out on the wold with the Warrows.

"I do hope that you are right about Tip and Nix," said Beau.

Her eyebrow cocked, Rynna looked at him.

"That they know what they are doing," explained Beau.

"L-lor', l-lor', b-but this w-water is c-cold," said Nix, his teeth chattering, the two buccen hanging on to pony saddles and urging the little steeds through the water, the horselings drifting downstream in the current as they valiantly struggled across. "W-we should have k-kept on our c-clothes and b-boots."

"N-no," chattered Tip. "We'll n-need them w-when we get to the s-side opposite."

"If we d-don't f-freeze first," said Nix.

At last, numb and shuddering uncontrollably, they reached the far bank, both buccen staggering up out of the water and into the woods beyond.

"S-s-swift, now," said Tip, "unbundle everything, d-dry on the, the blanket, and, and g-get dressed."

But Nix needed no instruction, for even as Tip spoke, in spite of his numb fingers Nix untied the tightly wrapped all-weather cloak from 'round his blanket roll, which in itself was wrapped around his garments and weaponry and a few supplies. Quickly he dried on the blanket, and then donned his clothes, and looked up to see that Tip had done the same.

Both Tip and Nix wiped down their ponies, using the blankets here too, the labor serving to warm the two buccen. Wringing out as much water as they could, they rerolled their blankets 'round their meager supplies and lashed them to the saddles.

Fastening his quiver to his thigh and his bow scabbard to the saddle, Tip said, "Quick now, we've got to get ahead of the Foul Folk and track them from the fore. That way they can't trap us against the mountains. Too, by the tracks of the Hèlsteeds we can see whether or no the Spawn follow wherever the Ghûls have gone."

"Speaking of Ghûls, what'll we do about them?" asked Nix.

Tip shook his head. "I don't think our ponies can keep up with Hèlsteeds, but surely we can outpace maggot-folk afoot."

Mounting his steed, Nix said, "No, Tip, what I meant was: with Ghûls ahead, are we likely to run into a trap?"

Swinging up and astride his own pony, Tip said, "Well, bucco, we'll just have to keep a sharp eye out." With that he heeled his pony in the flanks, Nix following, and off they rode, wide to the right of the march.

"Lor'," said Beau, "are they never going to stop?"

"I think not," said Rynna. "At such a pace they think it urgent to get to wherever it is they are going."

"*Hsst!*" sissed Linnet. "Something or someone comes 'cross the wold."

In the twilight to the fore and left they could see a mounted force riding from the direction of Darda Erynian, the eaves of the forest now some fifteen miles to the west.

"Hai," said Beau, kicking heels into pony flanks, "come on. It's Dylvana."

Weary, eyes rimmed red, Tip looked hindward through the dawn light, a waning half-moon overhead. "They're still marching."

"If they keep this up," said Nix, "—no, what I really mean is: if *we* keep this up, we'll kill the ponies."

"They're tougher than you think, bucco," replied Tip, gazing to the fore. "I don't see any Ghûls, so what say we again ride far enough ahead so to dismount and walk awhile?"

"All right." Nix urged his pony into a slow canter. "But let me ask you this: where are the maggot-folk bound?"

Pony jogging, Tip reached into his saddlebag and pulled out his map sketches and unbound them from their waterproof wrappings. "I don't know their final goal, but they haven't changed direction for the last twenty miles. North-northeast they fare."

"What's to the north-northeast?"

Flipping through his sketches, Tip said, "Well, the first place of any note they'll come to is Rimmen Gape. That's where Braeton lies."

Nix canted his head and pursed his lips, then said, "Perhaps they intend to sack the town."

"No, that's not it. The town was taken by the Spawn two years ago. There is nought left to plunder."

"Two years—?"

"Aye. We came upon them in the ruins of Braeton, did the Dylvana and Baeron and Beau and I. They had murdered the citizens and pillaged the town, and we slaughtered them—Foul Folk all—and avenged the folks they had killed. As far as I know, it's an empty town."

"Oh no, Tip, not empty, but filled with ghosts instead."

"But," protested Beau, looking up at Dara Cein, "there's nothing whatsoever at Braeton. And so I ask you: why would Modru send his forces haring off that way?"

Linnet, Beau, Rynna, Farly, and Cein rode side by side in the second rank of a small cavalcade of Dylvana faring north-northeasterly across the open wold, paralleling but a mile or so west of the course set by the hard-marching maggot-folk. Except for short rests, they had not stopped since the march began yestereve, Modru's Spawn yet tramping an undeviating line.

Tynvyr and Picyn had long since ridden back unto Darda Erynian, saying that they would gather their forces along the eastern marge of the forest and lie in wait at three principal places: at the Landover Road; at Eryn Ford; and halfway between those two points. No better strategy could any devise, and so the Fox Riders had turned away from the open wold to seek the advantage of the woods.

Cein pondered awhile and then said to Beau, "As to why Modru would hie his forces northeasterly, along his march lies Rimmen Gape, a choke point where the Landover Road drives through the Rimmen Mountains. Mayhap he wants to set blockade upon that passage."

"Why would he block it now?" asked Beau. "I mean, it's been

lying open for two years and more—ever since we destroyed all the Foul Folk that had ravaged Braeton."

Cein shook her head. "I do not say he intends to do so, wee one, for blockading the Rimmen Gape is but one of sundry possibilities; there are many places beyond where this force may be bound."

Farly scowled and looked at Cein. "But Beau did ask a good question: why would Modru send his forces running to Rimmen Gape? —Assuming, of course, that's their goal."

Cein turned up a hand. "I know not the mind of Modru, nor such would I desire."

"Well, whatever his reason, wherever they are bound," said Rynna, peering at the distant march, "it must be important for him to drive his forces so."

Beau frowned in puzzlement, for with Rynna's dire words an ephemeral thought had flickered through his mind, but ere he could capture it, it was gone.

Walking, riding, and at times resting, Tip and Nix maintained a good distance between the maggot-folk and themselves. Weary were Warrows and ponies alike, their steps lagging, for they had been on the move for a day and a night and another full day and part of the second night as well, and only starlight illumed the land. Even so, in the distance ahead, the two buccen could see the notch of Rimmen Gape silhouetted against the indigo sky.

"We've got to be careful now," said Tip, stepping 'round a grassy hummock, "for if the Ghûls are nearabout, it'll be in the pass where they've stopped, or so I would think. It's a choke point, you know. Anyone coming or going along Landover Road has to pass through there."

Plodding at Tip's side, Nix looked across at him. "Who might that be? —I mean, who or what is so important that Modru would send his Ghûls ahead to lay a trap along the Landover, and his maggot-folk to follow after?"

Tip shook his head, and on they walked in the starlit shadows, leading the ponies after.

"They're still faring for Rimmen Gape," said Dara Cein, looking at the stars above. "At the pace they set, they'll come to it by dawn at the latest."

"Good," said Beau, his voice weary.

Linnet looked at the buccan. "Good?"

Beau nodded. "The Blackwood curves around and nearly reaches the slot, and if Tynvyr and Picyn have succeeded, there'll be a force of Hidden Ones nigh."

"Dylvana and Baeron, too," said Rynna, awake from her doze in the saddle.

They rode without speaking for long moments more, but finally Rynna once again asked, "What could be driving them so?"

"There," whispered Tip. "Just behind the hillocks on either side. See?"

Nix peered down where Tip pointed. "Hèlsteeds."

"And look just above on this side of the crests," breathed Tipperton, "Ghûls waiting and watching."

From the slopes above Braeton, the two buccen looked through the predawn light and down at the ambush set along the Landover Road.

"Some thirty or so, I tally," said Nix.

"Aye," said Tip. "The whole of the Ghûls from Eryn Ford I would imagine, but for the few escorting the surrogate."

Dawn pinked the sky.

Tip peered southerly. "Here come the maggot-folk."

Out on the wold some two or three miles distant and boiling northeasterly came the Spawn.

"Tip, look! On the road east."

Tip swung his gaze toward where Nix pointed. "Oh Adon," groaned Tip, "*this* is why they set ambush."

East of Braeton and riding toward Rimmen Gape came a band of Elven riders, travel-worn, drooping, wounded.

"I should have known! I should have known!" cried Tip in despair. He leaped to his feet and headed for his pony, no longer trying to remain hidden.

"What? What is it?" appealed Nix, jumping up and following.

"It's Galarun and Aravan and the company, or what's left of it," gritted Tip. "We've got to do something."

As the buccen swung up onto the ponies, Nix turned to Tip. "Why would Modru pull his Spawn from Eryn Ford and set an ambush for these few Elves?"

"If they've succeeded in their mission, they are bearing a great token of power, a silver sword, one that'll slay Gyphon Himself, if the rumors are true. Modru hopes to stop them."

"All right, then, what'll we do?"

Air hissed in and out through Tip's clenched teeth, and then he said, "Stampede the Hèlsteeds before the Ghûls can reach them and mount up to waylay Galarun."

Nix nodded. "If the ponies don't flee from the stench."

Kicking his heels into his weary steed's flanks—"You take

this side; I'll take that"—Tip galloped down the slope, Nix riding after.

Down the slant they ran, toward the Hèlsteeds tethered on either side of the road, and even as the Ghûls started down the slope toward the scaled creatures, Tip flew past the first group, while Nix rode among them crying "Yah, yah!" And Hèlsteeds began to kick and bite at the darting pony and at one another, and jerk loose from their tetherings to squeal and mill and clash.

And Tip galloped across the road and in among the other 'Steeds, and as he did so, he raised to his lips the black-oxen horn—Dediana's horn given to him by Linde—and blew blast after blast as he charged through the cloven-hoofed rout. And the sound of the Harlingar horn panicked the beasts, both on this side and that of the road, and squealing and grunting in alarm, they scattered.

And on the road, Lian Elves raised weary heads, and unsheathed swords and took lances in hand in the dawn.

"*Krystallopýr!*" whispered Aravan, gripping his spear and true-naming it, making ready for combat. Even as the horn sounded, the small, blue stone amulet at his throat grew chill with peril . . . as it had done so many times on the journey to Black Mountain and back. And now it and the black-oxen horn called out danger, and neither would be denied.

"Ready!" barked Galarun, sword in hand, another sword—one of silver—strapped across his back. And he motioned to Larana, and she raised an argent clarion to her lips and blew an answer to the oxen horn, the silvery notes belling clear.

The sound of a Harlingar horn rang over the wold, and Spawn hearing it hesitated. Yet the Ghûls surrounding the surrogate cried out in their foul tongue, and whips lashed about and the maggot-folk began to run through the daybreak shadows and toward the gap ahead. And then a silver note rang, but the Spawn stopped not in their race.

"That's Tip's horn!" cried Beau. "He's in trouble!" And he leaped astride his pony and spurred forward, galloping after Rynna flying across the wold, Linnet and Farly and all the Dylvana racing after. And then an Elven horn sounded in the distance ahead.

As the Hèlsteeds scattered before the buccen, Ghûls sprang up from their ambuscade and yawled in fury and with cruelly barbed spears in hand they ran toward the two Warrows on ponies, the corpse-folk ready to slay.

"Ride! Ride!" called Tip, and he and Nix wrenched their over-tired ponies 'round to flee down the Landover Road, only to see a vanguard of Spawn scrambling across the way, two thousand others shrieking war cries and racing after.

And behind the buccen came savage Ghûls, the corpse-foe overtaking the two ponies, the little steeds stumbling in exhaustion.

Tip raised the black-oxen horn once again to his lips and blew a second time, and Rûpt quailed back from the sound, and the Ghûls slowed a step or two in their pursuit—

—and Lian slammed into them from the rear, lances piercing, swords riving, Aravan's truenamed spear *burning* wherever it struck flesh, Ghûls howling even as they died upon the dark crystallic blade. Yet Elves died too, impaled by barbed spear. But the corpse-foe could not withstand Aravan's deadly lance nor the beheading strikes of swords, and they yielded back from the Lian, no longer disputing the way.

And toward Tipperton and Nix did Galarun and company ride and toward Darda Erynian beyond.

And yet two thousand Spawn stood across the way.

A third time did Tipperton blow Dediana's horn, and lo! the call was answered from the nearby woodland as a horse-borne company of Dylvana and Baeron came charging out from the trees, while at the same time a small band of Dylvana came racing across the wold, four Warrows on ponies running alongside, arrows flying and sling bullets hurtling to slam into the Spawn.

Even as Galarun and Aravan and other Lian surrounded Tip and Nix, the Rûpt reeled hindward from the charge of the Baeron and Dylvana.

"Quickly!" called Galarun. " 'Round to the right and into Darda Erynian."

None argued with his command, for all the Allies together were yet outnumbered ten to one.

Rightward they fled, running for the trees, spent ponies and weary horses faltering even as they ran, giving their all to the riders.

And Larana blew a horn cry—a signal to withdraw—and now the company of Dylvana and Baeron and the small force of Dylvana and four Warrows turned their own steeds and fled for the forest as well.

With howling Rûpt on their heels, into the Blackwood they ran, past gathered shadows slipping twixt the trees, and huge yellowish mounds standing still, and tall bundles of twigs and vines and tendrils looming in the darkness and rustling as leaves in the wind. Among these and other such things they passed, the forest enshadowed a grim grey though the sun shone aslant through the brown-leafed November trees.

"Shouldn't we stop and help?" called Tip, urging his exhausted pony across a streamlet and up.

"Nay, love," replied Rynna. "As Tynvyr has often told me, we would just be in the way."

30

*S*heltered by Darda Erynian, the Elves, Baeron, and Warrows rode another five miles westerly ere making camp within a small glade just north of the Landover Road. And while the Baeron and Dylvana stood ward, exhausted Warrows and Lian and the Elves who had ridden with Dara Cein slept the sleep of the dead. After taking water and a hearty ration of oats, spent ponies and horses dozed as well, some standing, but most lying on the sward. Through the remainder of that day and the full of the night and into the next morning did they sleep, though Elves and Warrows awakened long enough to relieve themselves as necessary and to take a meal in the evening.

In midmorn, riding into camp came a Pysk. Dressed in varying shades of grey, she was, and her hair was mouse brown and her eyes cobalt blue, and a tiny bow and an empty quiver were slung across her back.

"I would speak with the commander here," she said to the Elven sentry, her words in the common tongue.

"Lady Pysk, we have several commanders here," replied the guard, peering down at her twelve-inch height. "Dara Cein, Alor Galarun, Alor Perin, Rark of the Baeron, Lady Rynna of the Waerlinga—"

"Who is nearest?" interjected the Pysk.

The sentry gestured at one of the small campfires. "Dara Cein and Lady Rynna sit yon with Alor Aravan."

"Aravan!" exclaimed the Pysk, her gaze seeking him out. "Oh my. Thank you." She urged her fox forward.

As she arrived at the fire, Aravan, Cein, and Rynna turned to look at her. Dismounting, she spoke a word to the fox, and it stepped some paces away and turned about in circles to finally lie down nose to tail.

Now the Pysk faced Aravan. "Alor Aravan, I am Aylissa, *iníon*—daughter—of Farrix and Jinnarin."

"Daughter of—?"

"Yes." Aylissa smiled. "They named me after . . ."

Loss befell Aravan's features, and Aylissa's words stumbled to a halt. But then Aravan smiled—the hurt retreating deep within his eyes once again—and softly he said, "Well met, Lady Aylissa, and how fare thy sire and dam?"

"They are well, Alor, and ward the northwestern marge of the Great Greenhall. Had they known you would be here, they would have come in place of others to face the foe."

Aravan held out a negating hand. "Would that I had seen them, yet some must remain behind to guard."

Rynna cleared her throat, and Aravan said, "Lady Aylissa, may I present Lady Rynna and Dara Cein."

Rynna and Cein smiled, and Aylissa canted her head in acknowledgement.

"I note your quiver is empty," said Rynna.

"All spent driving the Spaunen from Darda Erynian," said Aylissa.

"Then they are gone?" asked Cein.

"Aye. They have fled, though fully half did not live to escape."

"What of the surrogate?" asked Tipperton, yawning widely, the buccan just then joining the others at the fire.

Aravan looked across the flames and said, "Lady Aylissa, Sir Tipperton Thistledown."

"Hullo," said Tip, yawning again, and then taking a place on the ground beside Rynna. "Your pardon, Lady Aylissa, but sleep seems not yet done with me."

Aylissa smiled. "You must be one of those who rode from Eryn Ford."

"I was."

" 'Twas he who blew the Harlingar horn to scatter the Hèl-steeds and alert us to the Ghûlka lying in ambush," said Aravan.

"We heard it as we approached," said Aylissa. "Another trump as well."

"That was Larana's horn."

Tip yawned once more and repeated, "What of the surrogate? Did he escape?"

Aylissa frowned. "Surrogate?"

"Modru's eyes and ears and voice," replied Tip. "A Human. Pale skin, dark hair. The only one among the Spaunen, I think."

"Ah," said Aylissa. "Such a Human was felled." She gestured at her bow. "By a Pysk arrow, I believe."

"Then he is slain," said Tip with certainty, for the tiny arrows were deadly, their points coated with a fatal bane, lethal in but a heartbeat or two.

Rynna looked at Tipperton. "Even so, love, that yet leaves some thousand Foul Folk loose on the wold."

"Ah, yes, but now they are without Modru's guidance."

Rynna grinned ruefully. "That may make them all the more deadly."

Tipperton sighed and turned up a hand.

Aylissa then said to Aravan, "My sire and dam oft speak of you and the *Eroean*. They will be eager for news of you and will want to know what has befallen since last they saw your face centuries agone."

Aravan nodded, then said, "I spent a time dwelling in solitude in Darda Erynian along the banks of the Argon. Finally I was ready to be with others, and so I went unto Caer Lindor. There did I stay for uncounted seasons, working at sundry craft—blacksmith, stable hand, scout, cook, horse master, sentry, mason, chandler, weapons master, and many another trade—until came this war and the fortress was betrayed and the walls themselves were cast down.

"Then did I go unto Darda Galion to join with my kindred. We fought before Drimmen-deeve and in the mountains above, and there I became comrade to Galarun. When his sire, Coron Eiron, sent Galarun unto the forges of the Mages, there below Black Mountain in Xian, he asked me if I would go with his son, but I would have gone regardless."

Aravan's hand strayed to the blue stone at his throat and his eyes glanced at the black-hafted crystal-bladed spear at his side. "Fraught with danger was our journey, for we were opposed by many. It was as if the foe knew of our mission and sought to bar the way. Yet unto Black Mountain we came at last, fully a quarter of our company slain along the way. Nevertheless, into the black stone of that Wizardholt the Mages asked Galarun to come, but they bade the rest of us to wait, and we know not what transpired within.

"When Galarun emerged, he had the silver sword—named the Dawn Sword—in his grasp. Grim was his face, yet he mounted up and we rode away in silence.

"Westerly we fared, through Xian and Aralan, across Khal to Garia and into Riamon, at times fighting, at times fleeing, for Spaunen lay in wait at every turn, and slowly our ranks dwindled as comrades fell unto the foe.

"I can but hope this battle at Rimmen Gape is the last Modru casts in our way, yet there are many leagues 'tween here and Darda Galion, and I fear there are more battles to come."

As Aravan fell to silence, Tip glanced afar to where Galarun, the silver sword rigged across his back, stood conferring with one of the Dylvana. "I say, Aravan, does he use the sword in battle?"

Aravan shook his head. "Nay, Tipperton. It is meant for another foe altogether."

"Why is it called the Dawn Sword?" asked Rynna.

"That is what Galarun named it when he bore it forth from the Wizardholt. Yet he does not say why."

"Hmm," mused Tip. "A mystery, that."

"Even more so," replied Aravan.

"Oh? What else is there?"

"Galarun does not let any other bear it, nor touch it whatsoever. And he blanched when I said I would carry it should he fall in battle. Yet he disputes me not, for such is mine to do should the need arise, for he has named me second-in-command."

Rynna nodded and looked at Tipperton, but neither spoke. Finally, Aylissa asked, "What next, Alor Aravan? Where do you go from here?"

"We are bound for Darda Galion and time flows swiftly, and so we hie for Landover Ford and the wide wold beyond, where we will turn south and ride in haste over the rolling land."

"But Aravan," protested Cein, "there are safer ways to go: through Darda Erynian, for one."

Aravan nodded. "Aye, safer ways, but none swifter that that which we plan to take."

"Why the hurry?" asked Tipperton, though he suspected the answer.

Aravan poked the fire with a stick. "Nigh four months it took to reach Black Mountain, and nigh that will it be to return, and much can happen and has no doubt happened upon Adonar in the while between. And if this silver sword—this Dawn Sword—is the key to victory, then we must get it there as swiftly as we can, and riding the open wold is that way."

Silence fell among those at the fire, but finally Aravan turned to Aylissa and said, "Say this unto thy sire and dam, Aylissa of Darda Erynian: should we meet after the war, long will we talk of things that were, of things that are, and of things yet to be.

Say this to them as well: I am pleased that thou art named Aylissa."

Without another word, Aravan rose and walked away, and all watched him go, Aylissa with tears in her eyes.

Only that day did Galarun and company rest in the safety of Darda Erynian, and the very next morning they prepared to set forth on fresh horses borrowed from the Dylvana. Galarun mounted up, the silver sword scabbarded across his back, and he called out to all: "We were sent to fetch a sword to be borne unto Adonar, where last we knew war raged. Modru has striven mightily to thwart us from doing so, yet thanks to ye all and the Hidden Ones he has failed once again. Would that we could bide awhile, yet we cannot, for our mission is most urgent. Fare ye well, my friends, and now we must go."

At a signal from Galarun, Larana sounded her silver trump and, as the argent notes faded into the shadowed galleries of the Great Greenhall, forth spurred Galarun, Aravan at his side, a column of Lian following.

And so, amid shouted farewells and good-byes, Waerlinga, Pyska, Baeron, and Dylvana watched the Silver Sword Company ride westward, angling for the Landover Road. They would follow that route to the ford across the Argon and the wide wold beyond, the river and rolling plain some fifty-five leagues hence, where they would turn for Darda Galion, another eighty leagues south, the only appreciable barrier the Dalgor Fens halfway between.

And as they went from sight, Rynna turned to Tipperton and said, "Oh, I do hope they have taken the best way." And then she shuddered, as if the icy breath of the Dark One himself had whispered in her ear.

31

A full sevenday after Galarun and Aravan and the remainder of Galarun's company had ridden westerly, the Warrows prepared to depart the campsite and head down along the wold. The Warrows were the last to go, for the Dylvana, Baeron, and Pysks had left days before, the Elves of northern Darda Erynian taking all weary horses with them, for their journey was but a short one. Hence, only Tip, Rynna, Beau, Linnet, Farly, and Nix were left in the camp, and they had waited until the ponies were ready to travel before they set out, for the little steeds had been utterly spent, having trod one hundred forty miles in but two days. The Warrows, too, had been wearied, yet they had recovered first.

But now all were well rested, Warrows and ponies alike, and so south they fared, crossing the Landover Road and passing down through the eastern fringe of Darda Galion, aiming for their camp within the wood nigh Eryn Ford, some hundred fifty miles in all by the route they would take, following along the arc of the forest eave. They set out in a cold winter drizzle, for although it was but mid-November, the chill season itself was upon them more than a month early. And the woods were drear and silent but for the rain falling through brown leaves, carrying them down from the limbs to the ground to add to the humus below. Not voles nor hares nor limb runners nor beasts of any kind did scurry among the trees, nor did birds flit among the branches, for they had long past sensed the onset of winter and had flown away to warmer climes, taking their bright songs with them.

Through the edge of this dismal and stark wood did the Warrows ride, speaking little among themselves, their spirits dampened as well.

Five chill days they rode southerly, the nights frigid in camp, and although they kept watch on the eastern wold as they fared down its west flank, no sign did they see of the Foul Folk, those who had survived.

Late in the eve of the eighteenth of November and through a falling snow, the Warrows came unto the glade where the Eryn Ford watchers encamped. As they dismounted before their bowers, Tynvyr came riding her fox, and she stopped and sprang to the ground and looked up at them.

[Know you what passed nigh Rimmen Gape?] asked Rynna.

[Aye, the Eio Wa Suk carried the news,] replied Tynvyr.

[The Foul Folk, we have not seen them since. Are they back at Eryn Ford?] asked Tipperton.

Tynvyr shook her head.

"Barn rats!" exclaimed Beau, and then speaking Fey, added, [Where have they gotten to, I wonder?]

"No matter where," said Linnet in Common, "they can be up to no good"

"No matter where," agreed Farly, the look on his face glum.

[I would think that if they've not returned to the ford,] said Tip, in the Fey tongue, [then it is most likely they are somewhere in the Rimmens licking their wounds.]

[That, or waiting for another surrogate,] said Beau.

Rynna sighed. [Well, there's nought we can do for the moment, and I am tired and cold and hungry. Tip, you and the others see to the ponies, and I will see to a good fire and a meal.]

[I will help,] said Linnet, handing the reins of her pony to Beau.

Rynna looked at Linnet in some surprise, for as far as Rynna knew, her cousin would rather care for a pony than to help prepare a meal.

As the buccen and Tynvyr returned from the makeshift stables westerly in the woods, Rynna looked at Beau and grinned, while Linnet turned away in some haste and busied herself at things already done, color high in her cheeks.

That night Linnet drew Beau into her bower, her mother Melli away at the Springwater holding and the last thing on the young damman's mind.

*   *   *

"Oh, Tip," said Beau. "I've loved her ever since the first moment I saw her, but I am so plain and she is so beautiful, and yet she feels the same. Isn't that marvelous?"

"Indeed, Beau, indeed. But I knew it all along, what with you mooning about and watching her every move and her casting sly eyes at you."

"Rather like you and Rynna, eh?"

Tip laughed and slapped a hand over his heart. "Argh, bucco, sling bullets are not all you throw."

Beau grinned, then turned serious. "I say, Tip, what say we get married?"

"Married?"

"Aye. Not to each other, of course, but you to Rynna and me to Linnet."

"But Beau, there's a war on."

"In spite of the war, Tip, life goes on," declared Beau. "What better time to plight troth?"

Tipperton frowned and looked eastward, where stood the eaves of Darda Erynian some five miles away through the forest.

"Look," said Beau, "I think we'll have a bit of respite while the Foul Folk are off licking their wounds, and so we ought to take the time to have a wedding or two. Besides, Linnet is my heartmate."

"Have you asked her?"

"Well, not exactly, but I will. And you should think on asking Rynna, too, what with Lark and all. A child needs a father, you know."

"But Beau, she *has* a father. Me! Or did you think Lark fell out of a nest on one of those branches above?"

"Of course not, Tip. But I just think you ought to get married, and we can make it a double."

"Oh, Beau, don't you think Rynna and I want to be married? We've talked about it often, but there's no mayor or Adonite cleric or Elwyddian priestess about."

"What about up in Bircehyll, or over in Darda Galion for that matter? In Wood's-heart. Surely there's a cleric or priestess in one of the two."

"Married by the Elves?"

Beau nodded.

Tip smiled. "When?"

"How about Winterday?"

"Year's Long Night?"

Again Beau nodded.

"All right, Beau. Let's get the Pysks to ask the Groaning Stones to see if a cleric or priestess is available."

[Is something amiss?] asked Tynvyr, sitting before a wee fire outside her tiny bower.

[Oh no,] replied Tipperton, [we've come on another matter altogether.]

[Would you like a small cup of tea,] said Tynvyr, laughing as she held up an acorn-sized mug. As both buccen declined, Tynvyr canted her head and said, [Well then, what is this—how did you put it? Oh yes—this another matter altogether?]

Tip glanced at Beau and then said to Tynvyr, [Would you ask the Eio Wa Suk to send a message to Bircehyll and to Wood's-heart to see if a priestess or cleric is among the Elves? If so, we'd ask that they come to the holding of the Springwater Warrows to perform a wedding ceremony, and if they cannot, then we'd travel to wherever they might be.]

Tynvyr smiled. [Wedding ceremony?]

[Yes,] said Beau, grinning. [Linnet and me, and Tip and Rynna. We need a cleric or priestess to do it since we haven't any mayors on hand.]

Tynvyr pursed her lips and then said, [There are no Eio Wa Suk in Darda Galion, and so we cannot send messages there by that means. Too, I can say now there are no clerics or priestesses among the Elves, unless one haps to be passing through.]

[Oh my,] said Tip, and he turned to Beau. [If none is available, how will we get it done?]

Beau frowned and shook his head, but then his eyes lighted and he turned to Tynvyr and exclaimed, [I say, who performs the ceremony for Pysks and Vred Tres and Living Mounds and other such among the Hidden Ones?]

Tynvyr turned up a hand. [No one. We simply declare ourselves bonded, and that's that.]

Beau looked at Tip. [Hmm. Much like you and Rynna did.]

Tip nodded. [But we always knew one day we'd take formal vows.]

[Would you instead accept a coron?] asked Tynvyr.

Tip raised an eyebrow. [A coron?]

[Rather than priestesses or clerics, corons perform the ceremonies for the Elves.]

[Ruar or Eiron?] asked Tip.

Tynvyr nodded. [Ruar, Eiron, or, for that matter, Silverleaf, for he was coron apast.]

Tip looked at Beau and grinned, and together they nodded.

Tynvyr smiled and called her fox and rode away toward the aggregate.

"With Ruar gone, we will have to chance that Eiron is in Darda Galion," said Tip.

"Chance?" Rynna frowned.

"There are no Hidden Ones," said Tip, "no Eio Wa Suk, in the Larkenwald, love, and so we do not know if the coron is even there."

"Ah," said Linnet, grinning at Beau. "Well, I say we trust to Fortune he *is* there."

"I dunno," said Beau. "Dame Fortune has looked askance at us before."

"But She's also smiled, Beau," said Tipperton, "else you and I would be long dead."

Rynna gasped. "Oh, Tip, don't ever say that. —About being dead, I mean."

Tip pulled her close and kissed her, then said, "To travel to Darda Galion means we need cross the Argon. When last we heard, the Baeron were plying the ferry. Yet things change, and what if they've been called away? We'll still need to cross the Argon."

Rynna and Linnet nodded, and Rynna said, "And . . . ?"

"And, well, how will we do so?" added Tip. "I mean, I don't trust the Rivermen."

"The Rivermen are gone," said Rynna.

"Gone? From Olorin Isle?"

Rynna nodded. "Aye. None were there when we went to see to the truth of their story. Even so, and even if the ferry is abandoned, when last Farly and Nix and I crossed with Aravan and Velera and Arnu, we used Elven boats, and I know where they are cached."

Tip turned to Beau. "Do you know how to row?"

Beau shook his head.

"Neither do I," said Tip. "And I don't want to be swept miles downriver and over Bellon Falls." He turned to Rynna. "Elven boats are out, love."

Rynna glared at both Tip and Beau. "And just what makes you think that Linnet and I don't know how to ply an oar?"

"W-well—" stammered Tip—

—but Rynna cut him short and gritted, "Buccen."

Beau turned to Linnet. "You know how to row?"

"The term is paddle, my love. And yes, I know how to ply an oar. After all, I lived all my life along the Rissanin, and the river was our playground."

"Huah," said Tip. "I lived all my life along the Bog and the Wilder, and I never learned one whit about boats."

"Well then, it is time you did," said Rynna.

"Uh, how do we get the ponies across?" asked Beau.

"We don't," said Rynna, "if all we have are the Elven boats. But I would think someone yet plies the ferry; after all, it *is* a vital link, you know."

Beau frowned. "But if not . . . ?"

Rynna shook her head and turned up her hands.

"Perhaps the march-ward will lend us spare horses and someone to haul us along behind," said Tip, looking at Beau. "Just as when we fared southward from Arden Vale."

Linnet touched Rynna's arm. "Why don't we ask my brother to ride ahead and arrange for the ferry to meet us."

Rynna clapped her hands. "Good. Nix will be glad to go. After all, he should be there for the wedding."

"My dam and Lark, too," added Linnet.

"Um," said Tip, "but what about the watch on the wold? The way I see it, it'll take us ten or so days to get to Wood's-heart, and ten or so to return, and that's a deal of time to be away from the eastern marge."

They looked at one another for moments without speaking, but then Rynna said, "If the maggot-folk return, then we will postpone our journey. But if they remain among the missing, mayhap we can go with a clear mind. I will speak with Tynvyr on this, and get her advice."

"Ah, love," said Tipperton, "what she will say is that should the Foul Folk return, we would just be in the way."

"If necessary," said Linnet, "we can ask the Baeron of the Greatwood or the Dylvana of the Blackwood to stand in our stead."

"Oh, I don't think that'll be necessary," said Beau, "I have already spoken with Farly, and he says that when it comes to it he and some others in the Springwater holding can guide the occasional traveller past any Spawn."

Linnet glowered at Beau. "Are you telling me that everyone else knew about us getting married *before* you even came and asked me?"

Beau's eyes flew wide. "W-wull, not everyone. Just Tipperton and Tynvyr and—"

Linnet looked at Rynna.

"—and Farly—"

"Can you believe this, Rynna?"

"—and of course the Eio Wa Suk and the Fox Riders—" Rynna shook her head.

"—and the Elves in Bircehyll and probably some Baeron, that's all."

Rynna glared at Tipperton. "I said it before and I say it again: buccen!"

Tipperton's gaze darted about the bower, as if seeking a means of escape, and Beau peered at the earthen floor as if he would be better off some ten feet under the dirt.

But then Rynna burst out laughing, Linnet, too, and they embraced their buccarans, and both Beau and Tipperton breathed a sigh of relief.

On the ninth of December they set out from the campsite to journey to Wood's-heart some two hundred miles and ten days away. In the Springwater holding they took up Melli and Lark, and amid cries of well-wishers they rode on. Nix and the ferry were waiting for them to cross the mighty Argon, and now did they see that Dwarves plied the ferry at Olorin Isle, Dwarves from Kraggen-cor, the Châkkaholt no longer besieged. One set of the grim warriors plied between the east bank and the isle, another set plied the west.

"We trade off with the Baeron and the Elves," replied one of the crew to Beau's question, "moon by moon by moon."

"Well, that's good," replied Beau, grinning, "else we'd have a deal of trouble getting to Wood's-heart." He gestured at Linnet and Tipperton and Rynna, his grin growing all the wider. "We're off to be married, you know."

The Dwarf nodded and looked at the Waerans and wee laughing Lark and smiled and tugged on his forked beard and said, "May Elwydd keep you all."

But then the ferry reached the west bank of the Argon, and the Warrows debarked and rode onward.

Over the Rothro they fared and the next day the Quadrill, and they rode through the towering eld trees, silent now, the Silverlarks absent, what with all but the bloodways sundered. Still Linnet and Melli and even wee Lark gaped upward at the towering giants, their leaves yet gathering twilight to suffuse down through the air to the snow-covered floor below. And Nix and Rynna and Tip and Beau gaped as well, for although they had been in Darda Galion before, still it was a wonder.

On the nineteenth of December they arrived in Wood's-heart, where they heard the terrible news.

"Dead? Galarun's dead?" Tipperton's eyes filled with tears.

"Aye," said Aravan, his own gaze brimming. "Slain by a man with yellow eyes, the silver sword lost."

"This man—?" said Beau.

"What hap—?" asked Rynna.

"Where—?" asked Linnet.

Aravan held forth a hand, palm out. He wiped the tears from his cheeks and said, "As ye know, a day we spent resting in Darda Erynian . . ."

A day they spent resting, but no more, for their mission was urgent, and they rode away the following morn, did Galarun and his company. West they fared, crossing the mighty River Argon to come into the wide wold 'tween river and mountain, where they turned south for Darda Galion, the Grimwalls on their right, the Argon to their left.

Three days they rode down the wold, coming unto the Dalgor Marches, where they were joined by a company of Lian warriors patrolling the fens. Here it was that Aravan first met Riatha and Talar, riding among that company.

The next dawn, into the fens they rode, horses splashing through reeds and water, mire sucking at hooves, the way slow and shallow, arduous but fordable, unlike the swift deep waters of the Dalgor River upstream flowing down from the high Grimwalls to the west. Deep into the watery lowland they fared, at times dismounting and wading, giving the horses respite.

It was near the noontide, that November day, when Aravan warned Galarun that the blue stone on the thong grew chill, and so the warning went out to all that peril was nigh. On they rode and a pale sun shone overhead, and one of the outriders called unto the main body. At a nod from Galarun, Aravan rode out to see what was amiss. He came unto the rider, Eryndar, and the Elf pointed eastward. From the direction of the Argon, rolling through the fen like a grey wall rushing came fog, flowing over them in a thick wave, obscuring all in its wake, for Aravan and Eryndar could but barely see one another less than an arm's span away. And from behind there sounded the clash and clangor and shout of combat.

"To me! To me!" came Galarun's call, muffled and distant in the fog there in the Dalgor Fens, confusing to mind and ear.

Though Aravan could not see more than two strides ahead, he spurred his horse to come to his comrades' aid, riding to the sounds of steel on steel, though they too were muted and remote and seemed to echo where no echoes should have been. He charged into a deep slough, the horse foundering, Aravan nearly losing his seat. And up from out of the water rose an enormous dark shape, and a webbed hand struck at him, claws raking past his face as the horse screamed and reared, the Elf ducking aside from the deadly blow. *"Krystallopýr,"* whispered Aravan, truenaming the spear, thrusting the weapon into the half-seen *thing* looming above him; and a hideous yawl split the air as the blade burned and sizzled in cold flesh. With a huge splash the creature was gone, back into the mire.

Still, somewhere in the murk a battle raged—clang and clangor and shouts. Again Aravan rode toward the sound, trusting to his horse in the treacherous footing. Shapes rose up from the reeds and attacked—Rûpt, they were, Rucha and Loka alike— but the crystal spear pierced them and burned them, and they fell dead or fled screaming.

Of a sudden the battle ended, the foe fading back into the cloaking fog, vanishing in the grey murk. And it seemed as if the strange echoing disappeared as well, the muffling gone. And the blue stone at Aravan's neck grew warm.

"Galarun!" called Aravan. *"Galarun . . . !"* Other voices, too, took up the cry.

Slowly they came together, did the scattered survivors, riding to one another's calls, and Galarun was not among them.

The wan sun gradually burned away the fog, and the company searched for their captain. They found him at last, pierced by crossbow quarrel and cruel barbed spear, lying in the water among the reeds, he and his horse slain—the silver sword gone.

Three days they searched for that token of power, there in the Dalgor Fen. Yet in the end they found nought but an abandoned Ruchen campsite, a campsite used less than a full day. ". . . Perhaps they went back to Neddra," suggested Eryndar, as cold rain fell down and down.

At last, hearts filled with rage and grief, they took up slain Galarun and the five others who had fallen, and they rode for Darda Galion across the wide wold. Two days passed and part of another ere they forded the River Rothro on the edge of the Eldwood forest, snow lying on the ground. Travelling among the massive boles of the great trees, the following day they forded the Quadrill and later the River Cellener to come at last unto Wood's-heart, the Elvenholt central to the great forest of Darda Galion.

Aravan bore Galarun's blanket-wrapped body into the coronhall, where were gathered Lian waiting, mourning. Through a corridor of Elvenkind strode Aravan, toward the Elvenking, and nought but silence greeted him. Eiron stepped down from the throne at this homecoming of his son, moving forward and holding out his arms to receive the body. Tears stood in Aravan's eyes as he gave over the lifeless Elf. Eiron tenderly cradled

Galarun unto himself and turned and slowly walked the last few steps unto the dais, where he laid his slain child down.

Aravan's voice was choked with emotion. "I failed him, my coron, for I was not at Galarun's side when he most needed me. I have failed thee and Adon as well, for thy son is dead and the silver sword lost."

Coron Eiron looked up from the blanket-wrapped corpse, his eyes brimming, his voice a whisper. "Take no blame unto thyself, Aravan, for the death of Galarun was foretold—"

"Foretold!" exclaimed Aravan.

"—by the Mages of Black Mountain."

"If thou didst know this, then why didst thou send thy son?"

"I did not know."

"Then how—?"

"Galarun's Death Rede," explained Eiron. "The Mages told Galarun that he who first bore the weapon would die within the year."

Aravan remembered the grim look on Galarun's face when he had emerged from the Wizardholt of Black Mountain.

Kneeling, slowly the coron undid the bindings on the blankets, folding back the edge, revealing Galarun's visage, the features pale and bloodless. From behind, Aravan's voice came softly. "He let none else touch the sword, and now I know why."

Coron Eiron stood, motioning to attendants, and they came and took up Galarun's body, bearing it out from the coron-hall.

When they had gone, Aravan turned once again unto Eiron. "His Death Rede: was there . . . more?"

The coron sat on the edge of the dais. "Aye: a vision of the one responsible. It was a pale white one who slew my Galarun; like a Human he looked, but no mortal was he. Mayhap a Mage instead. Mayhap a Demon. Pallid he was and tall, with black hair and hands long and slender . . . and wild, yellow eyes. His face was long and narrow, his nose straight and thin, his white cheeks unbearded. More I cannot say."

"And the sword. Did Galarun—?"

Aravan's words were cut short by a negative shake of Eiron's head. "The blade was yet with my son when he died."

Frustration and anger colored Aravan's voice. "But now it is missing, is the Dawn Sword. Long we searched, finding nought."

After a moment Eiron spoke: "If not lost in the fen, then it is stolen. And if any has the Dawn Sword, it is he, the pallid one with yellow eyes. Find him and thou mayest find the blade."

Aravan stepped back and unslung his spear from its shoulder harness; he planted the butt of the weapon to the wooden floor and knelt on one knee. "My coron, I will search for the killer and for the sword. If he or it is to be found—"

Aravan never finished, for the coron began to weep. And so Aravan put aside the crystal blade and sat next to his liege, and with tears in his own eyes, spoke to him of the last days of his valiant son.

"After the funeral, I rode back unto the fen, and long did I search, aided by Dara Riatha's company, but to no avail, for no blade did I find. At last I gave up the hunt, for war yet burns across Mithgar, and my spear is needed." Aravan fell silent.

After a moment, Tipperton said, "But with no silver sword to take to Adon . . ."

Aravan sighed, then said, "We can only trust that the Lian and others who are upon Adonar can carry the day."

"Carry the day?" asked Linnet.

"Win the war upon the High Plane," clarified Aravan.

"As we must win the war here," said Rynna, her voice resolute, her face grim.

'Twas grievous news, the loss of Galarun and the silver sword, and though it had happened some five weeks past, still it was new to the Warrows, and they wept for slain Galarun and those who had died with him.

Nevertheless, as Beau had remarked, in spite of war, life goes on. And so, two days after arriving, Rynna and Tipperton, Beau and Linnet, they took their vows on Winterday eve, Year's Long Night, First Yule, Coron Eiron presiding. And Nix and Melli and Lark and Alor Aravan and other Alori and Darai attended the wedding as well, though most Lian were yet warding the marges of Darda Galion, or were fighting alongside the Châkka of Kraggen-cor and rooting out pockets of Rûpt left over from the siege of that Dwarvenholt.

And so they gathered in the coron-hall, Elves and Warrows alike, with Nix standing at Melli's side, Lark in Melli's arms, Darai casting delighted glances at the wee tot, now some twenty months old. And Coron Eiron stood before them all, Tip and Rynna, Beau and Linnet, facing the Elven lord, Aravan and Velera and Riatha and Talar standing to the sides and behind. And all fell quiet as Coron Eiron raised his hands, but for Lark, and she giggled at a wink from an admiring Dara.

Yet ere the coron uttered the formal vows, he spoke long on the sharing not only of love but on the sharing of work as well. Too, he spoke of the common ground they needs must nourish to keep their love alive, and among his words were these:

"'Till death do us part' is not a phrase used in Elven vows, for Death was ever meant to be a stranger unto Elvenkind. Yet heed, our vows are worthy, regardless of mortality or not."

"Worthy," said Lark. "Worthy, worthy, worthy." Melli whispered in Lark's ear, and the child fell silent.

Coron Eiron smiled and then said, "As does this babe grow and learn and change, so, too, do all things change with the passing of seasons, for change is a fact of life. Some changes are imperceptible, whereas others are swift; some bode well for life; others are harbingers of death."

"Life," said Lark, and then "*Saol.*" Nix looked at her in surprise, for she had spoken Fey, the word "saol" meaning "life." But then Nix turned back to the ceremony as Coron Eiron spoke on:

"Individuals, too, change with the passing of seasons, and vows made should not bind one in a relationship in which common ground no longer exists, no matter the oath, be it for mating, fealty, vengeance, or aught else. For just as death may part one from a vow, so too does the loss of critical common ground.

"Hence, to keep thine own relationships strong ye must share equally in the cultivation of the common ground and in nurturing the vows between; and ye must sort among all duties and participate willingly and fully in all which can be shared."

Lark made a *shssh*ing noise, as of wind among the leaves, and again Melli whispered in her ear and once more she fell silent.

Eiron stepped to Beau and Linnet and softly asked, "Do ye understand the meaning of that which I say?"

"I do," said Beau, looking at Linnet, and with tears in her eyes, Linnet said, "I do."

Eiron stepped to Tipperton and Rynna and asked, "Do ye understand the meaning of that which I say?"

And Tipperton took Rynna by the hand and said, "I do."

"I do," said Rynna, squeezing Tipperton's hand.

Eiron then stepped back and raised his voice. "Then I ask ye to speak true: dost thou vow to thy trothmate to tend the common ground and to nurture the pledges given and received?"

I do vow, they said in unison.

"Then speak true: will ye plight thy troth to one another, forsaking all who would come between?"

I do vow.

Eiron then placed Linnet's hand in Beau's and clasped their joined hands in his. "Then Beau Darby and Linnet Fenrush, each having spoken true, go forth from here together and share thy joys and thy burdens in equal measure until thine individual destinies determine otherwise."

Eiron then stepped to Rynna and Tipperton and clasped their joined hands in his. "Then Tipperton Thistledown and Rynna Fenrush, each having spoken true, go forth from here together and share thy joys and thy burdens in equal measure until thine individual destinies determine otherwise."

Eiron then stepped back from the two couples and called out in a clear voice unto the assembled Lian, "*Alori e Darai, va da Waerlinga, Linnet Fenrush e Beau Darby, e va da Waerlinga, Rynna Fenrush e Tipperton Thistledown, avan taeya e evon a plith!*" And a great shout went up from all, with Lark laughing gaily and Melli weeping tears of joy and Nix hugging the dammen and slapping both Beau and Tip on the back.

Escorted by Riatha and Talar, and by Aravan and Velera, Beau and Linnet and Tipperton and Rynna were led through the gathering, lutes and flutes and harps and pipes and timbrels playing a merry tune, and Elven voices were raised in song.

Out through the doors they were led, the gathered Elves following, and to a snow-covered glade, where paper lanterns were hung—yellow and red and blue and green and many hues in between—and there they took their places among the Elves and stepped and chanted and paced and sang and celebrated not only their weddings but the turn of the seasons as well.

And held by Melli, Lark looked over Melli's shoulder and into the shadow-wrapped galleries of the Eldwood, and again the tot made the sound of the *shssh*ing of leaves in the wind and held out her hands toward the gloom. And in the dimness just beyond the fringes of light cast by the colorful lanterns, there stood a tall creature of limbs and leaves and vines and tendrils. How Prym had gotten to Darda Galion is not told, yet in Darda Galion she was, swaying in time to the Elven rite and keeping watch on her wee Warrow charge.

It was snowing the next day, the second of Yule, and the Warrows spent much of their time before warm fires in the guest-house, talking with Aravan and gleaning what meager news there was of the war, though now and again Beau and Linnet or Tip and Rynna would slip off to be alone. But the following day, the third of Yule, feeling the need to get back to their duties, they said their good-byes and bundled well against the cold, Lark in particular, they set out for Blackwood again.

Among the great eld trees they went, riding by day, camping by night, heading for the ferry at Olorin Isle. And on the eve of the third day, they reached the west bank of the Argon, where this time it was Baeron crews who rowed them across, the full moon having come the eve before.

*　　*　　*

It was twelfth Yule, Year's Start Day, the first day of January, the first day of the two thousand one hundred ninety-eighth year of the Second Era of Mithgar when the wedding party rode through the snow to come in among the withy-woven bowers of the holding of the Springwater Warrows, where they were greeted by the grim news that the Spawn had returned to the eastern wold.

It was, as well, the very first day of the fourth year of a great and terrible war.

*N*ot only have they returned," said Farly, "but there's something afoot on the wold and in the Rimmens."

"Something afoot?" Rynna glanced at Tip and then back to Farly. "What?"

"Well, they've increased their patrols along the eaves two- or threefold above what they were before they went haring off for Rimmen Gape. —Not bigger patrols, mind you, but just more of them. The same is true of their watch posts along the Rimmen Spur: they've increased the number and have shifted their old ones to new places. In addition to that, they've begun scouring the heights trying to locate ours."

"Oh my," exclaimed Beau, taking Linnet's hand. "Have any been hurt? —Any of our watchers, that is."

"Not so far," replied Farly, "though there's been one or two close calls."

Nix frowned and looked at Rynna. "I wonder what it all means?"

Rynna paused in thought and then said, "Perhaps they do not want a repeat of what happened at Rimmen Gape, their trap being sprung and all."

Slowly, Tip shook his head. "It seems to me that something greater may be afoot, but what it might be I cannot say."

"Who knows the mind of Modru?" muttered Beau.

"All we can do," said Rynna, "is keep a wary watch."

* * *

Three days later, Rynna stood at the map table in the ward camp, Warrows gathered 'round. A handful of Pysks stood on the table itself and looked at the map Tip had sketched on a broad sheet of vellum. Rynna looked across at Tynvyr and said, [The news is grim.] Picyn and Tynvyr glanced at one another, their features giving way to dismay.

[Tell us,] said Tynvyr.

Rynna sighed and spoke on: [When the siege of Drimmendeeve was lifted, Coron Eiron sent heralds across Quadran Pass to find High King Blaine. Though there were many foe along the way, some of the couriers managed to get through—and back as well. This is what they learned:

[In the opening days of the war, Modru's forces swept out from Gron and 'round the northern end of the Rigga Mountains. Down through Rian they came, and assaulted Challerain Keep. It fell in a pitched battle, but not before the balefires were lit. The High King and some of his forces managed to escape, and they fought a series of running skirmishes as they fled south and west.]

Beau stabbed a finger to the map. [Here near Stonehill there were several battles in a set of downs, and it was here Blaine and his forces smashed the foe, for here the High King won. But more Foul Folk marched down through Rian, and still more came from the east, and so the King and survivors went west, past the Bosky and into Wellen beyond.] Beau grinned. [Eiron said the Boskydells themselves are yet safe, for the maggot-folk can't breach the Thornwall ringing it all 'round.]

Rynna's finger traced a route on the map: [The maggot-folk who came at the King from the east had marched through Grûwen Pass and into Drearwood and then west, for Modru hoped to catch the King between this force and the Spawn to the north.]

[These were the ones we saw when we came through Drearwood,] said Beau, looking at Tip.

Tip nodded but did not reply as Rynna continued:

[Still in the north, the maggot-folk took Crestan Pass, and Quadran Pass, and set siege upon Drimmen-deeve.

[Too, they blocked the Gûnarring Gap.]

[As we found out,] muttered Beau, looking at the map.

[Is there no end to Modru's vile greed?] asked Phero, stepping across the map to view it from the other side.

[You've not heard the half of it,] said Linnet, gesturing for Rynna to go on.

Rynna jabbed a finger to the map at several points: [Here they set siege upon Mineholt North, and here they occupied

Rimmen Gape. And here they set siege on Dendor in Aven, and as Tip and Beau have reported]—her hand swept across the Boreal—[from the sea the Spawn invaded the Steppes of Jord.]

Rynna looked up from the map. [Of course, the sieges of Rimmen Gape and Mineholt North and Drimmen-deeve and the city of Dendor have all been broken, and it seems that the Jordians have the maggot-folk on the run, though that news is old and may have taken a turn for the worse.]

[Yes,] said Tynvyr, [but what of the High King, and what of the Hyrinians and Kistanians and Chabbains?]

Rynna's hand swept south and west. [Eiron's own forces have reported that in the south the Lakh of Hyree were ferried across the Straits of Kistan by the Rovers, and up through Vancha and Tugal they came, ravaging as they went.

[The Kistanians themselves, after burning the ships in the harbors of Arbalin, landed a force in Hoven, though for the most, their ships block the Straits of Kistan.

[And also to the south, across the Avagon Sea came the Chabbains, and they invaded Jugo and Pellar.

[Meanwhile, the Fists of Rakka have revealed themselves once more, and they swept out from Sarain to take Hurn and Alban.]

Phero looked up from the map. [Fists of Rakka?]

[A religious sect,] said Rynna. [Put down long past when a woman from Ryodo rallied the oppressed.]

[And this Rakka . . . ?]

[Another name for Gyphon,] replied Tip, [or so the Lian say.]

[Ah,] said Tynvyr. Then she looked back at the map as Rynna continued:

[Together, these four nations—Hyree, Kistan, Chabba, and Sarain—control the Karoo, Khem, Thyra, Hurn, Alban, Vancha, Tugal, and parts of Hoven, Jugo, Valon, and Pellar.] As she named them off, Rynna's hand swept 'round the whole of the Avagon Sea.

[Oh my,] said Picyn, [can things be worse?]

[Things *are* worse,] said Tipperton. [Atala has been destroyed, and the silver sword is lost.]

[That's right,] said Beau. [And Gyphon has invaded the High Plane, and the ways between are sundered—all but the bloodways—yet that seems neither here nor there to Warrows]—he turned to Tynvyr—[although it might to Pysks.]

Tynvyr shook her head. [We fled from our home to Mithgar and will never go back to our own Plane.]

[Oh?] said Linnet.

All five Pysks nodded grimly, but none added more.

Tynvyr turned to Rynna. [Can you answer my other question? What of the High King?]

[He is hard-pressed in the west. Still, the men of Wellen and Dalara and Thol, of Jute and Gothon and Gelen, and the warriors of Fjordland—who've sailed across the Boreal Sea and 'round to the Ryngar Arm to join Blaine in the fight—they all stand fast, in spite of bad blood between nations.]

[Old adversaries unite against a common foe,] said Farly.

[Enemy of my enemy, enemy of mine,] affirmed Nix.

Rynna frowned at this statement but shrugged and then said, [And the High King prepares a great fleet in the harbors of the shipbuilders along the Weston Ocean—]

[A great fleet? What for?] asked Nia, looking at her mate, Kell. He, in turn, looked at Rynna.

Rynna turned up a hand. [I think he plans on breaking the Rovers' blockade of the Kistanian Straits and invading the occupied lands from the south.]

[If and when he does,] said Nix, [that's the time we Warrows need to rally to his banner and take the fight to these Hyrinians and Kistanians and other men.]

[As well as to the Rûcks and Hlôks,] added Farly.

Her voice aquaver, Linnet said, [And Ghûls on Hèlsteeds—and Trolls.]

[And Gargons,] Rynna added, memory drawing her face grim.

Recalling Quadran Pass and Dael, Tip looked 'round at the others and quietly said, [And perhaps a Dragon or two.]

Awed by the enormity of the task, they fell silent a moment, until Beau asked, [And after we've done them all in, then what?]

"Uh oh," whispered Tip, "I think he's got our scent."

Downslope, a horrid being stood among the crags: twelve feet tall, like a giant Rûck, it seemed, but massive and brutish and with a green-scaled skin. But no Rûck was this; instead it was an Ogru, and it snuffled the air, as if to catch the scent of a quarry. And now its glare seemed locked upon the heights above, where lay Tipperton and Beau.

"We've got to get out of here," hissed Tip.

"What about the Rûcks?" whispered Beau, pointing rightward, where was sited a maggot-folk sentry post on the ridge crest some two furlongs away.

Still the Troll snuffled the air drifting down from the heights.

"We can only hope they don't spot us," said Tip, glancing up at the February moon, full in the sky above.

The Ogru began climbing up among the crags.

"Let's go," breathed Tip, and down the back slope of the ridge they crept, down toward their ponies waiting in the shadows below.

And then a horn blatted.

"Oh lor', they've seen us," groaned Beau.

"Run!" barked Tip, and through the snow they fled, whiteness boiling in a wake behind.

Again the horn blatted, but its blare was chopped short in midcry.

"Tynvyr," grunted Beau, floundering downward, "or Picyn. Should we stop and help?"

"No," called Tip, scrambling. "Foxes can outrun an Ogru, but we afoot cannot."

And down they fled through cascading snow, to come to their ponies at last. Leaping astride—"Hai!"—away they flew, racing along the snow-laden valley and toward the Greatwood ahead. And as they dashed away, among the crags behind, the Ogru topped the ridge and bellowed in rage and frustration and raved at the winter sky.

March came and with it Springday, and lo! winter began to fade as it had always faded in years past. And folk faced into the warming winds and looked at the sky in wonder, for ever since the detonation of Karak and the destruction of Atala a chill grasp had fallen over all of the seasons . . . but now it seemed as if that grip had begun to loosen at last.

"Perhaps it's an omen," said Beau.

"Omen?" asked Linnet.

"That a tide has begun to turn somewhere," replied the buccan.

"Oh, I do hope so," replied Linnet, taking Beau's hand and raising it to her cheek.

"It is becoming too dangerous for us to watch from the Rimmen Spur," said Rynna. She looked 'round at the others there in the fog-laden glade as a damp April breeze wafted the mist past. "The Foul Folk patrols have doubled and redoubled again . . . as well as their sentry posts."

"To say nothing of the Ogrus," added Beau.

"Something is afoot," said Nix.

Farly frowned. "What can it be?"

"I dunno," said Nix, "but something . . . I can smell it."

Beau laughed, and when the others looked at him, said, "Perhaps it's just maggot-folk you're smelling."

Tip grinned, but then sobered. "Nix is right: something *is* afoot . . . else why all this activity? It's been months now that they've stepped up their patrols. They started 'round Winterday, and now spring has come. So what can it be that threatens Modru so?"

"Perhaps it's a way to keep us under control," said Rynna.

Linnet nodded and added, "Cooped in our woods, so to speak."

Tip slowly shook his head and said, "I dunno. Three years past, when we first heard of the Horde on the east of Darda Erynian, we thought it might be to keep the Hidden Ones hemmed in, a way to keep them from joining in the struggle against the Foul Folk. Yet I now believe that it was because Modru knew of the silver sword, and he didn't want Galarun to be able to get it."

Beau frowned in puzzlement. "But the sword was fetched in spite of the Horde, not to say that it isn't lost now. And so why would he keep Foul Folk on this border if it's not to keep the Hidden Ones from joining the High King when the time arrives?"

"Come again?" said Farly. "I got lost somewhere along the way."

Beau sighed. "If the Spawn were here to stop the sword from being fetched but utterly failed, then I ask you this: why are they yet still here?" Farly shrugged, but Beau continued: "The only reason I can think of is to keep the Hidden Ones bottled up."

Rynna slowly shook her head. "I don't think they could do that, Beau. That is, if the Hidden Ones ever decide to march—which I doubt—there just aren't enough maggot-folk to block all the borders of Darda Erynian or the Greatwood and keep them penned in."

"Regardless of why the Spawn are here," said Tipperton, "what are we going to do about the increased patrols and sentry posts?"

No one said aught for long moments, and finally Rynna cleared her throat. "We'll just have to be extra careful . . . and from now on, none of our patrols should go without Fox Riders scouting ahead. I'll speak to Tynvyr on it."

"I say, why don't we do something to cause them to pull some of their sentries down from the heights?" said Beau.

Rynna looked at Beau. "Such as . . . ?"

"Look, I'm tired of running and hiding and slipping aside, so how about we begin waylaying patrols? —Making them seem to vanish."

Nix frowned. "How would that help?"

Linnet's eyes lit with revelation, and she beamed at Beau.

"Oh, don't you see, Nix? By making patrols simply disappear, the others, they won't know what's happening. And they'll add more Spawn to each patrol in the hopes of thwarting whatever may come. And to do that, they'll have to take sentries and patrols away from the heights above."

"Aha!" said Nix, grinning at Beau. "A splendid deceit."

Farly nodded and then added, "I say, we could also send word to the Baeron watchers south and the Dylvana watchers north and have them join in making patrols, um, disappear. Perhaps it would clear out the Rimmen Spur all the faster."

All eyes turned to Rynna. "On the surface it seems a good plan," she said. "Let me think on it awhile . . . as well as see what Tynvyr has to say."

"Here they come," whispered Rynna. "Remember, if there are too many, let them pass. We want none to escape, for we would have all other Spawn remain in ignorance."

Rynna then turned to Picyn and repeated her words in Fey. Picyn nodded, then sprang to the back of his fox and gathered shadow about and slipped away in the night.

Past the shoulder of the hill tramped the maggot-folk.

"There's one with a bugle," said Rynna. "Tip."

Tipperton nodded. "I see him. I'll try to take him before he can sound his horn."

In that moment 'round the flank rode a Ghûl on Hèlsteed.

"Barn rats," spat Beau. "A Ghûl. We'll have to let them pass."

Rynna nodded, and in the chill April night the stealthy Warrows withdrew.

Two nights later, Tip led his pony toward the eaves of the forest, two slain Rûcks draped across the pony's back. Rynna, Beau, Linnet, Nix, and Farly followed, each of them leading ponies also burdened with dead maggot-folk. Into Blackwood they went, where down in the shadows Tynvyr hissed for them to stop. And they shoved the dead Spawn from the ponies and went back onto the wold to take up the remaining three Rûpt yet lying where they had been felled.

They reached the point of the ambush, and working swiftly, pulled their own arrows from the corpses—*thuck! thuck . . . !* —though, heeding Tynvyr's warning, they left the small lethal shafts of the Fox Riders untouched for fear of their fatal barbs.

As Tip and Beau lifted a dead Rûck up onto the back of a skittish pony now steadied by Rynna, Nix and Farly took up a second slain Rûck and did the same as Linnet soothed that wee mount. The four buccen then turned to the dead Hlôk and managed to heft the carcass over a third tremulous pony's back, while the dammen carefully scanned the ground—retrieving scimitars and cudgels and flails and helms and other such—and scuffed over soil stained with dark blood.

Again they returned to Blackwood, and again they shoved the corpses from the ponies to land with sodden thuds next to the others felled that night, Rynna and Linnet pitching down the Rûptish helms and weaponry as well.

They made one last trip back to the wold to see that all evidence of the ambush was gone, and when they returned to Blackwood, the arms and helms and bodies of the maggot-folk were no longer where they had been cast.

Over the next ten weeks, seven Rûcken patrols were made to vanish in this sector alone, the Warrows and Pysks waylaying them and haling their corpses into Blackwood, where the Spawn no longer came.

Yet there were also ambushes which they abandoned, for a Troll or Ghûl fared among the Spawn patrol, and these foe they shunned altogether—Ogrus being stone-hided, and Ghûls able to take dreadful wounds with little or no effect. And so to maintain the air of mystery—where maggot-folk simply disappeared with no cause evident—they let all such patrols pass unmolested.

Too, in the Greatwood to the south and Darda Erynian to the north, Baeron and Dylvana also waylaid patrols.

By mid-June as maggot-folk were pulled from the sentry posts to augment the vigilance along the eastern wold, Rûptish watchers became sparse along the Rimmen Spur, and Spaunen squads roved the ridges but sporadically, though Ogrus continued to wander along the high slopes and snuffle the air for spies. And so the patrols along the fringes of Darda Erynian and Darda Stor were strengthened, doubling and tripling in size, though the maggot-folk yielded even wider berth to these shadowy woods.

And although the Warrows and Pysks needed to exercise great caution when faring across the wold and in the heights above, still everything was going according to plan.

Summerday came—the summer solstice—and Fox Riders and Warrows alike celebrated together, unlike the ceremonies of the equinoxes, where the Pysks were guided by the moon rather than the sun.

For Pysks dedicated spring and fall to Elwydd, and they celebrated by Her light, holding their rites on the night of the full moon nearest each equinox.

But Summerday and Winterday were dedicated to Adon and the sun, and so the Pysks celebrated the solstices along with other Mithgarian folk . . .

. . . and now Summerday had come.

And it was on this day as well that the ground grumbled with a glad message sent from the aggregate of Eio Wa Suk nigh Bircehyll in the north: Crestan Pass had been freed at last, the Foul Folk driven away. Baeron and Dylvana were returning to Darda Erynian for a temporary rest, for war yet burned upon Mithgar, and their arms were needed elsewhere. Even so, even though they would yet be marching to war, still it was glad news indeed.

And so, in addition to a celebration of the turning of the seasons, and in addition to the Warrows celebrating the birthdays of everyone who'd had a birthday in the past year, Year's Long Day also became a victory celebration as well.

In the glade of the campsite, there was food and drink and singing and dancing, all to the lively melodies Tip and Rynna played—he on his lute, she on her pennywhistle—and the end of each tune was met with a resounding cheer. Song after song they played, throughout the afternoon. And as twilight fell Tipperton called wee Lark to him, the tot and Melli having come from the holding of the Springwater Warrows to celebrate Summerday. Lark was now two years old and a bit, and she stood seventeen inches tall. And as she sat at the feet of her da, Tip smiled down at her and began a haunting melody—Rynna softly accompanying him—and to the wonder and delight of all, Lark sang a wordless song in perfect accord, her voice now and again taking on the rustle of leaves in the wind.

It was as Tip played and sang the Elven song of the changing of the seasons, that Farly and Tynvyr and Picyn came riding through twilight and into the glade. And when the song was finished, Farly took Rynna and Tip aside and said, "Something is afoot in the Rimmens."

"Something afoot?" said Tip.

"What?" asked Rynna.

"I dunno," said Farly, "but there's a lot of movement."

"Movement?"

"Right. Foul Folk seen moving eastward."

"Eastward, eastward," muttered Tip. "What lies eastward?"

All gathered 'round in the candlelight as Tip laid out his maps on the small table. Once again Pysks stood about the edges, where they could see.

[This movement: where is it?] asked Tip.

[Up near the headwaters of the Rissanin,] said Farly, pointing into the Rimmen Ring. [Moving east within the crags.]

[Who brought this news?] asked Rynna, looking across at Tynvyr.

[Phero,] replied the Pysk. [She was scouting out the latest placement of Spaunen sentry posts when movement caught her eye. Great numbers of the Foul Folk move eastward, and they follow an old route where wagons can go, a supply train in their midst.]

[Where are they bound, I wonder?] asked Beau.

Tip shuffled his sketches about and then said, [Well, directly to the east lies Garia. It's mostly mountains—the Skarpals—where DelfLord Borl was killed. But why they would go there . . .]

[Oh, Tip, to the east also lies Bridgeton,] said Beau, stabbing a finger to the map. [Could that be their aim?]

Tip turned up his hands. [We won't know until we track them.]

[Track them?] Rynna looked at Tip, her eyes wide.

[Yes, love,] replied Tip. [Someone has to see what they are up to, and who better than us?]

"We are better at this than you," came a voice speaking Common.

Tip and the others turned. Aylissa stood in the doorway. Beside the wee Pysk were two others, two Pysks neither Tip nor Beau nor any of the Warrows had seen before.

"Lady Aylissa," exclaimed Tipperton.

Aylissa smiled. "Sir Tipperton, Lady Rynna, may I present my sire and dam: Mistress Jinnarin and Master Farrix, once of Darda Glain of Rwn, an isle that is no more."

"There they are," murmured Rynna.

Tip's gaze followed her outstretched arm. In the light of a last-quarter moon just now rising in the east, along an old trail through the stony mountains wended a column of Foul Folk.

"How many can there be?" asked Beau.

"Four, five hundred or so, I gauge," said Nix.

"No no, Nix. What I meant to ask was, how many have passed this point in the ten days since they were first spotted?"

"Oh," said Nix. "As to that, who can say?"

"Perhaps they are fleeing the fall of Crestan Pass," said Linnet.

Farrix shook his head. "Nay, Lady Linnet. They were on the move ere then. Marching south from the Grimwall, nigh where it joins the Gronfangs. We came to warn you."

"As you can see, we are not the ones who need warning," said Tipperton, "but someone east."

Rynna turned to Aylissa and Jinnarin and Farrix. "You must outpace them if possible and warn the folk at Bridgeton, should that seem to be their goal."

Aylissa nodded, but it was Farrix who replied. "Aye. We'll see where it is they are bound, but if it is somewhere past the Rimmens, we'll turn back after seeing that others carry the word beyond."

Beau frowned and said, "I say, by going to Bridgeton it seems you are not as shy about your presence as are the other Fox Riders we know."

Jinnarin laughed. "Not so, Sir Beau, although I must admit we may be bolder than most, for we have travelled around the world"—she reached out and took Farrix's hand—"Farrix and I, in Aravan's ship, the *Eroean*. Even so, it was necessity which drove us to such an uncommon act. And though we have sailed the world, still we let not just anyone see us, for our kind fear a repeat of foul deeds done to us long past. Yet, when necessity commands, there are those we turn to in trust: Elvenkind, Magekind, the Baeron . . . and now some Waerlinga. But even these we shun in ordinary times, lest our presence become commonplace.

"As to this mission, there are Baeron in the woods south of Bridgeton, and it is they whom we will ask to bear a warning unto the citizens of that town. Too, I deem they will carry on should we need give up the chase."

Beau smiled. "Oh, I see."

Rynna knelt. "You'll come back when you discern their goal."

Aylissa nodded. "Indeed, Adon willing, we shall return. Yet as to their goal, that we may never divine, for foul Modru drives them, and none knows his mind but his vile master Gyphon . . . and mayhap not even Him."

"Come," said Farrix. "We must hie." And he called his fox unto his side, Aylissa and Jinnarin doing likewise.

"Good fortune," said Linnet, as the Pysks mounted up, their tiny bows slung across their backs, wee lethal arrows in quivers at each of their hips, diminutive knapsacks slung across their shoulders and hanging at their sides.

"Good fortune to you as well," said Jinnarin.

And with cries of *"Hai, Rux!"* and *"Hai, Rhu!"* and *"Hai, Vex!"* the trio of riders darted away, the foxes scrambling down the back of the ridge through moonlight aslant and toward the foothills below.

*   *   *

A week passed, and then another, and then another still, and
yet no word came from Aylissa or her sire or dam.

And still Spawn moved through the Rimmens, heading east,
though their numbers diminished.

Toward the end of the seventh week there occurred a most
peculiar thing: the Foul Folk patrols and sentries vanished from
the eaves of Darda Erynian and the Greatwood: none were seen
north or south on the wold nor in the Rimmens above.

Over the following month or so, cautious scouts searched
along the wold and in the Rimmen Spur, yet no Spawn did they
see.

And still Aylissa and Jinnarin and Farrix had not returned.

"Where have they gone?" asked Linnet, as she and Beau carried a table out from the withy bower, a table which soon would
be laden with food for the Autumnday celebration. Beau
shrugged his shoulders but otherwise did not reply.

Rynna, carrying a tablecloth, gestured toward the risen sun of
the September morn as it burned away the lingering threads of
mist in the vale, though vaporous filaments yet tarried among
the trees. "Mayhap east through the Rimmens . . . following the
others."

Nix growled, "I said it before, and I'll say it again: something
foul is afoot."

"I agree, but what?" asked Farly.

Before Nix could answer, from the east there sounded a black-
oxen horn.

"Oh my," said Rynna, dropping the cloth and snatching up
her bow from where it leaned against the bower. "That's Tip's
horn."

She set an arrow to string, and her companions did likewise,
all but Beau who laded a stone in his sling. And as they spread
wide in a defensive stance, bursting out from the mist-entwined
trees came Tipperton riding at a gallop, Kell on a fox running at
his side. Tip set his horn to his lips once more and again belled
its resonant cry.

"The High King!" shouted Tipperton. "The High King has
called!"

33

*H*alting his pony before the withy bower, Tipperton sprang to the ground, while Kell and his fox darted on beyond, heading through the woods for Tynvyr's wee dwelling.

"The High King has called," declared Tipperton, puffing with excitement.

How—? Where—? When—? voices blurted.

Tip thrust forth his hands palms out to stop the babble. "We were passing the ford, Kell and I, when . . ."

[Rudd hears something,] said Kell, looking up at Tip on his pony.

The fox's ears were pricked and twitching, and he faced south across the shallow flow of the Rissanin, the animal sniffing the mist-laden air.

Tipperton dismounted and put his ear to the ground, and after a moment said, [I hear nothing.]

But still the fox faced southward, though now and again it looked over its shoulder at Kell, as if expecting a command.

[Let us to that stand of trees and watch,] said Kell.

Tipperton nodded and remounted, and to the grove they went, stopping just inside the edge.

Moments passed and moments more, and then above the swirl of water Tipperton faintly heard—[Hoofbeats!]

He took up his bow and set an arrow to string as did Kell, and from their covert they waited, as the thud of hoofbeats grew stronger.

[Sounds like several,] said Kell.

Tipperton nodded but remained silent.

[Mayhap it's Ghulka on Hèlsteeds returning,] said Kell.

[Mayhap,] replied Tip. [In which event, be ready to flee should they spot us.]

And they waited among the dripping foliage.

Kell spoke a word to Rudd, but what the command may have been, Tipperton did not know.

Louder still the hoofbeats came on, and now through the swirling vapor Tip and Kell could see cloaked riders: five of them altogether and running at a good clip, trailing two remounts apiece.

[Not Hèlsteeds,] hissed Tip, [but horses instead. Even so, stay well hidden, for it could be Hyrinians or Chabbains or other allies of Modru.]

[They ride in haste,] said Kell.

[Aye, and with little rest,] added Tip.

[How so?]

[The remounts,] replied Tip. [It means they cover long distances.]

Now the riders came to the ford, and they splashed to a gravel-bar in the center and halted, allowing the horses to drink.

And the riders themselves cast back their hoods and dismounted to take on water.

They were Elves—Lian.

Tip rode outward in the morning mist. "Hoy!"

Swords and long-knives appeared in hands as if they had been there all along.

"Hoy," again called Tipperton, slipping the arrow back into his quiver and urging his pony out from the trees and forward. "It's me, a Warrow—a Waerling, that is—Tipperton Thistledown." He turned and looked for Kell, but the tiny Pysk was nowhere to be seen, nor was Rudd, his fox.

"Tipperton?" called one. "Tipperton Thistledown?"

"Aye!" replied Tip, his pony now trotting onto the trace.

"Hál, and well met! I have heard of thee. I hight Falen."

Tip halted his steed at the water's edge and dismounted. "Heard of me?"

"Aye, from Dara Phais and Alor Loric. We fought side by side in Valon."

"Phais and Loric, you've seen them? Oh my. How are they? —It's been so very long."

"They fight at the right hand of Blaine."

"Then they found him, the High King, that is?" Tip smacked himself in the forehead. "Of course, you ninny, if they fight at his side then they had to have found him."

Falen broke out in laughter, as did the other four Elves.

Horses watered, the Lian led them out from the river, and Falen introduced the other riders as they shifted saddles to fresher mounts: Dara Lynna and Alori Landor, Kestian, and Ellidar.

At Tip's query, Falen said, "We ride to rallye allies to the High King's side."

"At last! Oh my, what an auspicious Autumnday this is. I will gather those who fight alongside me, and we will answer his call. Where is he?"

"In Pellar, fighting the Southerlings—Chabbains and Hyrinians and Kistanians—driving them eastward."

"In Pellar? How did he get there? I mean, last we heard, he was in the west, fighting Modru's Hordes."

Falen transferred his saddlebags to his new mount. "With a large army in a great fleet, he sailed 'round Vancha and broke the Kistanian blockade of the straits.

"Then he landed his force of Gelenders and Tholians and Jutlanders and Fjordlanders and Gothonians in Jugo and marched to Gûnarring Gap. In a coordinated attack, he from Valon, the Welleners and Trellians and Harthians and Rianians from Gûnar, together they broke the siege. A handful of Lian and Baeron were there as well, along with an army of Red Hills Drimma, and they swept the enemy away, the Foul Folk to hie into the Gûnarring, the Southerlings to flee east."

"And this took place at Gûnarring Gap?"

Falen nodded. "Aye."

"But a Gargon was there when last we knew."

"So we heard, but it was gone elsewhere when we came at the foe."

Tip frowned. "I wonder . . ."

Falen looked at him and cocked an eyebrow. "Thou dost wonder what, wee one?"

"The Gargon: I wonder if it was the same one that came here."

"A Draedan here?" Falen looked 'round, as if to see the monster standing nigh.

"A year and a half ago, it was," said Tip. "A Gargon warding this ford. It did terrible damage. In the end we killed it. —Or rather it was slain by one of the Eio Wa Suk."

"Hai!" crowed Lynna. "Dara Phais said thou wert a slayer of Mandraki, the one at Dendor thy first."

"Oh, it wasn't me," said Tip. "Imongar slew that one."

"Aye, but Imongar said that she would not have done it without thine aid."

"Imongar is with the King, too?"

"Aye," said Lynna. "Now she is, along with five other Magekind."

Kestian grinned at Tip. " 'Twould seem that Draedani are not safe 'round thee, Sir Tipperton."

Landor barked a laugh. "Mayhap 'tis the fate of each Mandrak to die at the hands of a Waerling. I will keep that in mind should Draedani come calling."

As the Lian laughed, Tip just shook his head and grinned but said nought in return.

Falen sobered and frowned and then looked at the buccan. "Didst thou say that Eio Wa Suk are nigh?"

Tipperton nodded. "No more than five leagues hence."

Falen nodded. "I have heard there is an aggregate nigh Bircehyll, where dwell the Dylvana."

"Yes," confirmed Tip, "there is."

"Ah, but would that we could send a message there, for—"

"But you can," interjected Tip. "The Pysks—"

"Thou dost know some Pysks?"

"Indeed. They are our allies." Tip looked about, but still he did not see Kell nor Rudd.

Falen glanced at the other Lian. " 'Twould save time," said Ellidar.

Falen nodded. "Sir Tipperton, wouldst thou send word unto the Dylvana court that the High King calls for all who can aid to come unto Pellar, unto Caer Pendwyr, and help beat back the foe?"

"Gladly," replied Tip. "Not only to the Dylvana, but I am told there is another aggregate well beyond Bircehyll, in the far north of Darda Erynian; we can call the north Greenhall Baeron as well. And since Crestan Pass is now freed, many will answer the call."

"Hai!" said Landor. "An auspicious Autumnday, indeed."

Falen turned to the others. "With the help of Sir Tipperton and the Pysks, and with the Eio Wa Suk sending word throughout Darda Erynian, it means we can now ride straight unto Mineholt North."

Tip grinned. "To summon Lord Bekki, aye?"

"Aye."

"What about Darda Galion and Arden Vale and Jord and—"

Falen pressed a palm out. "Other heralds ride to those realms, Sir Tipperton. We are to raise Darda Stor and Darda Erynian and Riamon and Mineholt North."

"Has the Greatwood yet been roused? If not, we can send messengers south."

Checking his cinch strap once again, Falen said, "No need, Sir Tipperton, for we came through The Clearing. Even now the Baeron who remained in Darda Stor are sending word unto their outposts to prepare for the long march."

"Well then, the Pysks and I will see that the message gets sent to Bircehyll and to the Baeron in the Great Greenhall beyond."

"Done and done, Sir Tipperton," said Falen as he swung into his saddle. "Tell them as well what I have told thee: the High King is hale; the siege at Gûnarring Gap is broken; the foe is on the run; and to Caer Pendwyr all who can aid are summoned."

"Wait," called Tip, as the others mounted as well.

Falen looked down at him.

"The Rûcks and such," said Tip, gesturing northerly, "the ones warding this wold, they disappeared a month or so back, yet they may be out there still: on the flats or in the Rimmens above. If you ride into trouble, hie for Darda Erynian, for Modru's lackeys are feared to come within."

Falen and the others grinned, and Dara Lynna said, "Ye have made it so, thou and the Fey?"

"And the Warrows and Dylvana and Baeron," added Tip.

"Hai!" called Lynna, and she flashed her sword on high.

Hai! called the others, likewise flourishing steel.

And then with cries of farewell and good fortune, the Elves galloped away, remounts trailing, morning mist swirling in their wake.

"Fair fortune to you as well," called Tipperton after, and then more quietly said, "fair fortune to us all."

"To Caer Pendwyr?" Rynna frowned at the map.

"Yes, love, to Caer Pendwyr," said Tip, sweeping his hand down across the chart, "some thousand miles away."

"A long journey," said Beau. "It will take much in the way of supplies."

"I've asked Kell to send a request for us to travel with the Dylvana," said Tip. "If so, we can lade our goods on their wagons."

"Regardless as to how we bear our goods, are we to leave Darda Erynian undefended?" asked Linnet.

"With the Hidden Ones staying fast, it will not be undefended," said Nix.

Linnet grudgingly nodded, but said, "Aye, 'tis true. But Nix, it's just that, well, what with the Springwater holding and all . . ."

"I don't like leaving them behind any more so than you," said Rynna, "but Nix is right. They'll be safe."

"Oh my. Are you going to leave Lark?" asked Farly.

"Not before I say good-bye," replied Rynna, and then she burst into tears

Instead of celebrating Autumnday, they rode back in but a single day to the Springwater holding to report the news. When they told of the summons, buccan and dammen alike clamored to go, each trying to outshout the other in order to be heard.

Notwithstanding the heated debate among the whole of the Springwater Warrows, of the seventy or so surviving Wee Folk only eight altogether would answer the High King's call: Tip, Rynna, Beau, Linnet, Nix, and Farly, along with two who had just come into their young-buccen years—Alver Bruk, brother of Winkton, who had been slain on the banks of the Argon, and Dinly Rill, whose entire family had been killed as they had fled from the Horde down the Rissanin. The remaining buccen and dammen were simply unsuited to take up the mantle of war: some were too young, others too old, some were ailing, others had injuries which got in the way, and some were needed to grow and harvest crops and gather firewood and bear water and forage for edibles and watch over the youngsters and oldsters and look after the few animals and other such responsibilities.

With the debate settled as to just who would stay and who would go, the next week in the holding was one of furious activity, and it was all aimed at supplying the eight who would be marching off to Pellar:

Hundreds of arrows were crafted—shafts were inspected for trueness and cut to length and fletched and nocked and fitted with kiln-fired glaze-hardened clay points, for there was no iron to spare. Too, the tiny kilns were used to fire and glaze clay bullets for slings. Blades were sharpened—daggers and long-knives, one of each for each of the eight—to act as a desperate last line of defense should any need them, for untrained Warrows were at great disadvantage blade on blade with a larger foe. Supplies were gathered: grain for ponies; food for Warrows; clothing, ropes, precious mirrors and carved wooden whistles for signalling, foraged medicks to add to Beau's supply, and other such necessary goods.

In this same week, the ground groaned with a message from the Eio Wa Suk, and a day later Picyn came riding to Rynna. [The Dylvana are pleased to include the Waerlinga within their ranks. They ask that you rendezvous with their force and the northern Baeron at Eryn Ford a fortnight hence.]

[That's just after the first-quarter moon,] said Linnet.

But Rynna said, [Fourteen days, only fourteen.] And she

glanced at Tip, then down at Lark, and tears brimmed in her eyes.

Tip took Rynna's hand and said in Twyll, [Love, you can always—]

[No, Tip. We've already settled this argument.] With her free hand Rynna brushed her cheeks. [No less than you, I too must answer the call of the High King. Lark will be safe with Melli and Prym.]

Tipperton nodded and turned to Picyn. [I would ask the Fey to keep special guard over this holding, for we answer the beck of the High King.]

Picyn nodded. [So shall it be, Sir Tipperton, for in serving the High King you and yours will act to protect Mithgar and all its kind, including the Fey.]

Tip grinned. [Well and good.]

They sat in silence for a moment, and then Farly asked, [What of the Foul Folk: are they back?]

[Neither in the Rimmens nor on the wold, the Spaunen, they've not returned,] said Picyn.

Tip shook his head in puzzlement. [Well, I don't know whether to be worried that they've disappeared . . . or glad that they've gone.]

[I choose glad,] said Dinly, laughing, the amber-eyed buccan sitting in council with the others.

[Still, it's a mystery,] said Alver, attending the council as well. [I mean, where could they have gone?]

[Perhaps we will find out when Aylissa and Jinnarin and Farrix return,] said Picyn.

[Only if the Spawn followed the others through the Rimmens,] said Farly.

[Oh my,] said Beau, [speaking of Aylissa and her sire and dam, they've been gone, what?]—he counted on his fingers—[five weeks now. I do hope that nothing untoward has happened to them.]

[Oh, Beau, don't say such things,] said Linnet. [We wouldn't want to call misfortune down on them.]

As Beau took Linnet's hand, Tipperton stood. [I'm going to go see to the ponies. It's time to water and feed.]

Nix and Alver and Dinly got up to follow.

One day before the first-quarter moon, they set out for the camp near Eryn Ford, Melli and Lark to accompany them as far as the campsite dell. The holding entire turned out to see them off—the eight who would ride to war—and many were the tears shed, not only among those staying behind but those riding away as well, and two weeping maidens moved alongside Alver and Dinly until the dammen were called back by their foster kin.

Into the sun-dappled autumn forest the Warrows rode, drawing pack ponies behind, while from the holding there came a rousing cheer, mingled with cries of good-bye.

Only Lark seemed unaffected, as she trilled to the few remaining birds flitting in the branches overhead among the turning leaves.

And off to one side within the trees, a vine-woven creature of leaves and twigs and tendrils kept pace.

"Lor' but it's hard leaving folks you've come to love," said Beau, as Tip caught up wee Lark running by, the tiny damman squealing in delight as her da turned her upside down and then righted her again.

"No harder than it is on them," said Linnet.

At Beau's puzzled look, Linnet added, "Back before I reached my young-damman years and was allowed to join in the fight, every time you rode away, Beau, I would weep for days."

Beau glanced at Melli, and she nodded and said, "At odd moments, that is."

Tip looked up from his giggling daughter and across the low fire pressing back the chill of the night. "Parting brings sorrow in its wake: tenderly sweet when lovers but separate until the morn, yet grievous in times of war."

Rynna looked at Tip and smiled and said, "How true, my love . . . as you and I know."

A rustle of leaves sounded from the darkness, though there was no breeze to stir them so.

"*Sshhhh, shhh . . .*" whispered Lark in return, and she struggled to get down. Tip set her afoot and she darted out toward the shadows.

"Oi, now," said Alver, reaching to grab her.

"Let her go," said Beau. "It's just Prym out there calling her babe."

Melli looked at Beau and smiled.

"What?" said Beau, looking back at her.

"You have changed, my lad," said Melli. "Yes, indeed, you have changed."

Tip laughed and took up his silver-stringed lute and struck an argent chord. "Shall I sing about the terrible Blackwood, with its ghosts and bogles and horrible *things* that seek the blood of those who would trespass this domain?"

Beau smiled grudgingly and said, "If you would sing of bogles

and seekers of blood, my snickering Tipperton, then Drearwood
should be your theme."

Tip drew in a deep breath and let it out, then said, "I'd rather
not, Beau, old friend; I prefer to forget that place altogether.
What say we have a merry tune instead?"

He glanced at Rynna and she took up her pennywhistle and
together they began "The Dish and the Spoon and the Big Yellow Moon."

And from the shadows at the edge of the firelight there came
Lark's laughter of glee.

They rode into the campsite in the noontide of the day of the
first-quarter moon, that half-orb just then rising in the east.
After unloading the supplies and caring for the ponies, they met
with Tynvyr. And still the wold and Rimmens were free of Foul
Folk for as far as the Pysk patrols ran and as far as watchers
could see. Even the Troll hole in Rimmen Spur was deserted, or
so Nia and Kell reported, having gone there three times now
and found it completely empty of all but Ogru stench.

And so with little to do, the Warrows settled down to wait.
The Dylvana and the Baeron would be here within but days, the
long trek to Pellar to follow.

And Rynna and Tipperton took Lark everywhere they went,
and sang to her and talked to her and told her many stories. They
embraced the wee tot often, showering her with their love.

On the second day after arriving in camp, three Pysks came
riding through the morning shadows and across the bowl of the
glade.

Rynna looked up from Lark to see them coming. "Quickly,
Tipperton," she called into the bower, "fetch Tynvyr and the
others; Farrix and Jinnarin and Aylissa are here."

[We followed them all the way to the Skarpals,] said Farrix.
He and Jinnarin and Aylissa stood about the map on the table
Tip and Beau had carried out from the bower so that all could
gather 'round. Tynvyr and Picyn stood on the table as well, and
crowding close were seven Warrows; the eighth, Farly, was not
among them, for he stood watch at the ford.

Melli was inside making tea, and Lark played under the
table.

Rynna frowned. [To the Skarpals?]

Aylissa nodded. [Aye.]

[No wonder you were gone so long,] said Tip, studying the
map. [That's all the way to Garia and back.]

Rynna looked at the map and frowned. [And the Foul Folk, they went into the mountains there?]

[Aye,] said Farrix, nodding.

[All of them?]

Again Farrix nodded. [All of them,] he affirmed.

[Wull, I hope DelfLord Borl's ghost finds a way of vengeance,] said Beau.

[Borl?] asked Dinly.

[Of Mineholt North,] said Beau. [He was killed by Rûck arrow in the Skarpal Mountains as he and others battled the retreating Spawn; the Foul Folk were fleeing the broken siege of Mineholt North, then Borl's delf, now Bekki's.]

[Say, just how did the Foul Folk cross the Ironwater River?] asked Tip, yet staring at the map.

[Oh no,] groaned Beau, [they didn't destroy Bridgeton, did they?]

Jinnarin shook her head. [Nay. Bridgeton is safe. When it became clear that Bridgeton was in the path, we raced ahead to alert the Baeron in the south woods, so that they could warn the city; even so, we were too late: the Spawn were already at Bridgeton. Nevertheless, they did not stop to attack the town. Instead, they crossed a deep ford to the north.]

[To the north?] said Tipperton, looking at his chart. [I see no ford there.]

[Nevertheless there is one,] said Farrix, striding across the map and placing his finger on the sketch of the Ironwater just north of Bridgeton. [Though quite deep—I would think not passable at all when the river is in spring flood—this is where they crossed.]

[Hmm.] Tipperton marked his map tentatively as he mused, [Perhaps this is what they did when marching the other direction to set siege on Mineholt North. They bypassed Bridgeton then as well.]

[They could have crossed on ice at that time,] said Beau, [for I think it was winter then. Regardless, this time they went 'round Bridgeton again, and it is safe.] He turned to Linnet. [They have some of the best mulled wine there.]

On the map, Tip wrote, *Deep Ford Here*, with an arrow to where Farrix pointed.

Farrix cocked his head 'round to read the words in Common and laughed. [Deep indeed. Even using the spanning ropes, the Rucha and Loka were just able to keep their noses above the water. The Trolls were the last to cross, and only under threat by the Ghûlka, though what a corpse-foe might do to a Troll, I have not even a hint.]

Dinly frowned. [Why would Ogrus be afraid of a river?]

[They sink like a rock in water,] said Jinnarin, grinning at Farrix, [completely unable to float or swim. Or so we discovered some long years back in a hidden cavern.]

[Bones like stones,] said Farrix.

[Ah,] said Dinly, enlightened.

Tipperton frowned. [It bothers me that they bypassed Bridgeton. —Oh, I'm certainly glad they did. It's just that it seems such a tempting target. What is the goal of a maggot-folk army if not to plunder cities?]

Beau held up a finger. [Hoy now, Tip, you said it yourself: the Rûcken army went 'round it on the way to Mineholt North.]

[Yes, but the Dwarvenholt was their goal, and so they had good reason to skirt it then, just as they disregarded Dael.]

Beau nodded, but added: [When the Mineholt siege was broken, they bypassed Bridgeton again as they fled.]

[They were running from an army of angry Dwarves, to say nothing of the Elves and Men.]

Beau laughed. [Angry Dwarves: nothing better to flee, eh?] As the others smiled, Beau sobered. [All I'm saying, Tip, is that every time the maggot-folk go past Bridgeton, they leave it alone.]

[Regardless as to their motives,] said Aylissa, [they marched to the Skarpals and within.]

[Retreating like the others, eh?] said Alver, looking at Beau.

Beau glanced at Tip and turned up his hands.

[Did you see any more maggot-folk?] asked Rynna. [The Spawn on the wold and those in the Rimmen Spur seem to have vanished.]

[Ah, so that's who they were,] said Farrix. [A belated group heading east as well.]

[They hie for the Skarpals, too,] said Aylissa, [or so we believe.]

[Fleeing to hide in the mountains,] said Dinly. [All of them run away.]

[Say, I wonder if this has to do with the High King breaking the siege at Gûnarring Gap?] said Beau. [Perhaps the reason they head for the Skarpals is that they think the war lost and they run for cover, just as Alver and Dinly say.]

Tip looked up from the map and shook his head. [Perhaps you are right, Beau, and the Skarpals is their final goal. But then again perhaps you are wrong and Modru has something else altogether in mi—]

"Hiyo! Hiyo!" came a shout.

They all glanced up from the table to see Farly come racing into camp.

"The Dylvana are here!" he cried as he galloped across the sward.

As Tip rolled his maps, Farly haled his pony up short and swung his leg across his saddle and leapt down. "The Dylvana are here and are setting up camp at Eryn Ford."

Rynna scooped up Lark and held onto her tightly, and Tipperton put his arms about both.

Dressed in their leathers and bearing their weaponry, eight Warrows came riding into the Elven camp, Rynna and Tipperton in the lead, Dinly and Alver coming last. And as Tipperton rode past, Dylvana hailed him . . . and hailed Beau following after.

Her blue eyes sparkling, Dara Vail came and walked alongside Tip as he rode toward the central tent, where Coron Ruar was said to be. "I was glad to hear thee yet lived, Tipperton, thou and Beau."

"Beau and I have come through some scrapes since I rode scout with you on the way to Mineholt North, Lady Vail," said Tip. "Scrapes: ah but what a gentle name for those dire dealings; nevertheless, they seemed to seek us out, as I imagine they did you."

"Aye. The Spaunen in Crestan Pass were stubborn, yet we prevailed in the end." Vail looked across at Rynna. "Is this—?"

"Oh, my pardon," blurted Tip. "Lady Vail, may I present Rynna Fenrush—er, that is, Rynna Fenrush Thistledown. Rynna, Lady Vail."

Vail's eyes widened, then she laughed merrily. "Oh but what splendid news."

Rynna smiled tentatively. "News?"

"That thou didst *not* die at the fall of Caer Lindor."

Rynna grinned widely. "Nay, lady, I did not." Then Rynna's smile vanished and she added, "Though many others did."

"Beau! Tipperton!" hailed a familiar voice.

Tip turned to see just as Beau exclaimed, "Melor!"

"Come sup with me this eve," called Melor, as he currycombed his horse, "and tell me what all has befallen."

"I will," replied Beau, then he gestured toward Linnet. "We will, and that's a promise."

Beau turned to Linnet. "A splendid healer. He taught me much."

Tip waved at Melor, turning to Vail as she said, "I wouldst that thou rejoin the scouts, Tipperton, for we need all to aid."

"Rynna is our leader," replied Tip. "But if she has no other plans for me, and if Lord Eilor requests, then so shall it be."

Vail's face fell. "Alor Eilor was slain in Crestan Pass. I am now chief scout."

"Oh my," said Tipperton . . .

. . . and they fared the rest of the way to Coron Ruar's tent in silence.

Two days later the Baeron came riding to Eryn Ford—huge men on huge horses, massive wagons drawn in their wake—and alongside their company was a band of Lian from Arden Vale, come down from Crestan Pass at the summons of High King Blaine. In addition among the Baeron also rode Dara Riatha's company, all of whom had been on the northern wold nigh Landover Ford at the time of the calling.

Everywhere Tip and Beau turned, it seemed, they found another friend; many were the reunions of the buccen with sundry of these warriors. Old acquaintances were renewed, and new acquaintances made, as Rynna and Linnet and the others were introduced to these comrades of old . . . though as Alver said, "Whoo, my head is spinning with names."

Among the Lian were the twins Gildor and Vanidor, along with Talar, Riatha, Ruar, Alaria, Arandar, and lovely, dark-haired Elissan—who smiled at Tip and winked, the buccan blushing furiously in remembrance of a particular exposed bath. And among the Baeron they found Wagonmaster Bwen and Braec and Durul, who now was chieftain, for Gara had been slain in the Grimwalls nigh Crestan Pass. And Bwen laughed hugely to see the buccen, and she called out, *"Thuas seasim mé agus síos cnag mé, Beau, Tip, hurá!"*

And so many of the reunions were bittersweet, for Tip and Beau learned of folk who had fallen in the war, folk they had come to cherish, folk they held in their hearts.

Yet there was little time to mourn and no time to celebrate, for on the morrow they would begin the march from Eryn Ford to Caer Pendwyr.

Dawn came to shadows slipping away after saying good-bye to the Warrows. Fires were quenched as Elven and Baeron and Waerlinga warriors broke camp. Horses and ponies were sad-dled, pack animals laden with goods, dray horses hitched to wagons, as all was made ready for the trek unto Pellar.

With tears running down her face, Rynna kissed Lark one last time and whispered, "I love you, my sweet one, I love you," then handed her over to Melli. Tipperton, his own cheeks wet, sat astride his pony, his good-byes already said.

Nix and Linnet and Beau all kissed Melli on the cheek, and

kissed little Lark as well, and then they turned to their ponies and mounted and fell in line after Rynna and Tip and rode forward two by two.

Vail spied the oncoming group of Waerlinga, and she summoned them to the fore, for all would be scouts but Beau, and he a healer in the vanguard.

Finally, at a signal from Coron Ruar, Dara Lyra raised a horn to her lips and blew a ringing call, and it echoed from limb and stone and hill on the cool October morn.

And slowly the column began to move forward, horses and ponies splashing into Eryn Ford and across, wagons rumbling after, all following the trail of the Elven scouts who were now some leagues ahead.

And as he rode into the water, Tipperton turned to take one long last look at his beloved Lark, and he raised his black-oxen horn and blew a ringing cry. And the hearts of all were lifted, wee Lark laughing in weeping Melli's arms. And away rode the Warrows, eight strong, eight warriors riding unto war midst a thousand Dylvana and twelve hundred Baeron and a hundred or so Lian, but Melli's tear-laden eyes saw only the precious eight.

34

*U*nder a high blue October sky, the army of Dylvana, Baeron, and Lian, along with eight Warrows, rode down the marge of the Greatwood. East-southeast they fared overland, the Rimmen Spur off to their left, Darda Stor to their right.

Tipperton, Beau, Alver, and Dinly rode together within the vanguard, while Rynna, Linnet, Nix, and Farly—being the most familiar with the territory—rode at the fore of the column to help lead the way.

On the morrow, all of the Warrows but two would ride scout, for the previous eve at the riverside camp, Vail had called them all together and had said . . .

"This will be the way of it: all but Sir Beau and Commander Rynna will ride scout—"

"What?" objected Rynna. "I am not to patrol? Look, I understand why Beau will not ride scout, for he is a healer and—"

"Hoy, now!" interjected Beau. "For a year and a half I have ridden scout along the marge of the Blackwood and up in the Rimmen Spur. Right?"

Linnet vigorously nodded. "Yes, and a better scout you could not—"

"Hold!" barked Vail. Then more softly, "Hold." She turned to Beau. "Healers are rarer than scouts, and Alor Melor has asked for thine aid. Is it not so?"

Beau sighed and reluctantly nodded, and Linnet put an arm about him and leaned her head against his shoulder.

"But what about me?" asked Rynna. "I am no healer."

Vail looked at the damman. "Nay, thou art not. Yet heed, thou art the commander of the Waerlinga, and as such thy place is with the other captains of this band and not out riding scout."

Rynna's jaw jutted out, and she glanced at Tip, fire glinting in her eye.

But Vail took in a deep breath and let it out and looked from Rynna to Beau. "I understand how ye both feel, for I, too, would rather be riding scout as in the days of yore"—she smiled at Tipperton, her partner of past—"yet as chief scout my place is with the vanguard, as is thy place, commander, just as it is with Beau."

Rynna glanced at Beau and looked at Tip and then turned to Vail and reluctantly agreed as well. But even as she did so a Dylvana runner came. "Commander Rynna, Chief Scout Vail, ye are requested to attend the council of captains in four candlemarks."

Vail nodded and said, "Even now it begins." She glanced at Rynna and, at the damman's nod, said to the runner, "We will be there."

Vail and the Warrows watched the runner go, and then Vail said to the six who would scout, "This will be the way of it: some days ye will ride patrol, other days ye will not. But most nights ye will camp with the column."

"Camp with the column?" asked Tipperton. "But does that give us time to get to and from station?"

Vail nodded. "Aye, for ye will ride on near-point and flank and rear, no more than league or two out from the column will ye range—"

"Two leagues? But what about the wide rangers and those on far-point?"

"Here alongside Darda Stor, a league or two is enough. 'Tis only after we reach the Plains of Pellar will any need range wide and far, and those tasks will be assigned to Dylvana, for they ride swift steeds, not ponies."

Vail looked at Tip, but he raised no more questions, and so she continued: "And speaking of swift steeds, each of ye will be paired with a Dylvana, for should there be a need to flee, the pony can be abandoned, and both scouts take flight on the horse. Thy added weight will not overslow them so."

"But in the woods a quick pony is just as fast as a horse," protested Nix. "I'd rather keep my steed, if you don't mind, than to cling to a Dylvana and flop along ragtag behind."

"Indeed," replied Vail. "Ponies are mayhap e'en swifter in the close woods than a horse. Yet in the open, a horse will outrun both pony and Hèlsteed."

"Hèlsteed?" asked Alver, looking at Dinly.

"Alver, if it's Hèlsteeds we're fleeing," said Dinly, "ragtag or not, I'll be most happy to flop along behind a Dylvana on a running Elven horse."

Smiling at Dinly's comment, Vail began assigning the posts they would ride . . .

These duties they would take up on the morrow, but for the nonce two dammen and two buccen rode at the fore of the vanguard, and four buccen rode within.

"How long will it take us to get there?" asked Beau.

Tipperton frowned. "If I remember correctly, Caer Pendwyr lies some nine hundred miles away as the raven flies, but by the route Vail indicated, we'll travel nigh a thousand altogether."

Beau groaned. "Why is it that we always seem to be crossing leagues and leagues of nothing but leagues and leagues merely to get where we're going. I mean, I felt like Tip and I had travelled half the world just to deliver a coin, and then another half the world from Dendor to Gron and from there to Blackwood. And here we go again, traipsing off to Caer Pendwyr, travelling half the world once more."

"Hoy now," said Nix, "that's three halves."

"Yar," agreed Dinly, chortling, "just how many halves does the world have?"

"A hundred and three," said Beau, glumly, "and we'll no doubt see them all."

In the lead, Coron Ruar glanced back at the Waerlinga and smiled and wondered why they were laughing.

As they rode a bit farther, Beau looked about and then said, "Well, Tip, at least we're among a lot of not-men."

Alver frowned. "Not-men?"

"Indeed," said Beau. "Elves and Warrows are not-men . . . and perhaps some of the Baeron."

"The Baeron aren't men?" asked Dinly, peering around at some of the huge riders on their huge horses.

Beau nodded. "Did you ever look at their eyes? Dark yellow, they are, like those of Wolves and Bears."

"But your eyes are amber, too," said Dinly, "just as are Linnet's and Rynna's and mine. And we're certainly not Wolves or Bears."

"Perhaps we're too small," snorted Alver. "More like ferrets or some such, eh, Beau?"

"You're one to talk, green-eyed Alver," shot back Beau, "I'd say you're more like to be a lizard."

Again the Warrows burst into laughter.

And once more Ruar looked back at them and marvelled at how they could be so merry while riding to deadly war.

East-southeast they fared for four days, the Warrows, all but Rynna and Beau, now riding scout. Tip was teamed with Dara Lyra, a scout he had ridden with once before: on the way to lift the siege from Mineholt North, together they had ambushed a Rûcken sentry as a vital part of a plan to deliver Braeton from a segment of Spawn. And now they were allied again to ride the land on the right flank of the column and a bit to the fore.

On the morning of the fifth day of setting out, the column turned southerly on a trace of a road and entered the Greatwood proper. It was an old trade route they followed, now grown over with disuse, yet it was mostly low scrub and small saplings which sought to impede the way, and so the wagons had little trouble following the brushy path, especially those which came last, as through the woodland they fared.

The forest was dressed in scarlet and gold, the leaves turning hue in the crisp fall air, though dashes of green lingered here and there. And down below the crimson and auric leaves, wherever shade fell so fell a chill, hinting of winter to come. Voles and limb-runners and other such small animals scurried thither and yon, collecting the last of provender to tide them over until the renewal of spring. Only a few birds were seen, and only now and again would one be heard to call, and that in the distance and brief, for most had already flown away to warmer climes abroad. The air itself seemed preternaturally still, all summer insects gone, but for a lone bee or two, searching out the last of what little nectar remained.

And down the overgrown two-track fared the column, hooves plodding, wagon wheels creaking and rumbling over uneven soil, all pressing down the rank weeds and brush and saplings into the humus beneath.

"One nice thing about this time of the year, Melor," said Beau, watching a limb-runner hie for its den, its cheeks stuffed with acorns or some such, "no midges, no gnats, no biting flies."

"Mayhap the very best time of all the seasons," said Melor, "with its pleasant days and cool nights."

"I'll agree to the days, Melor, but the nights are downright chill. In fact, the air is quite changeable."

As if to verify Beau's words, a sudden brisk breeze stirred across the forest above, the leaves whisking and rattling in response.

Beau drew his cloak about and looked up through the branches at the blue sky above. "What are the chances of a cloudburst, eh?"

"I would that it not rain, Beau, else the wagons are like to mire. Remember the trek across Riamon?"

"Yar, but it was September then and not October as now."

"Even so . . ."

Beau frowned and scanned the sky above, seeking clouds, finding none, as they plodded onward through the crisp woods on their southerly course to Pellar.

In the evening of the second day after entering the forest, they reached the edge of The Clearing, a place of significance to the Baeron, for here in normal times they came each mid-year, to sing of deeds done and to dance and to tell great tales and engage in contests, and to meet prospective mates, and to celebrate Summerday.

"I have been here before," said Tip, as he and Lyra moved across the yellowed grass of the great expanse the following morn.

"Oh?"

"Aye. Rynna and I rode to a Baeron village along the western brim. There we organized the watch on the eastern wold to guide travellers past the Spawn."

"Thou didst well, Tipperton."

"Oh, it was Aravan's idea to do so."

"Aravan?"

"Yes. By pure chance we came upon Galarun and Aravan and their company nigh Caer Lindor, and guided them past the Rûpt on the wold. This was when Galarun and the others were on their way to get the silver sword."

A look of sorrow crossed Lyra's face. "I see."

They rode in silence awhile longer, then Lyra said, "This woodland village: whence?"

Tip frowned. "Some twenty-five, thirty miles ahead. We should pass it on the way; it lies on the flank we ride."

The following morning they espied smoke rising in the sky.

"Oh my," said Tipperton. "That's near where lies the village."

Lyra nodded. "We go in caution, then. And should there be a need to flee, abandon thy pony for my horse."

Tipperton took a deep breath and patted his steed alongside the neck. "All right, but only at need."

Cautiously they rode forward, keeping to the tree line at the western fringe of The Clearing. Unconsciously and without taking his searching gaze from the broad lea ahead and the forest to their right, Tipperton loosened his bow in its saddle scabbard and made certain that his arrows were at hand.

Finally, Lyra said, "See the rising tendrils? I ween these are morning campfires, Tipperton."

"Not a burning village?"

"Nay. More like a gathering."

Tipperton nodded, but did not relax his vigilance.

Following one of the pickets, Tip and Lyra rode in among an encampment of Baeron—nearly four hundred all told—mustering for the march unto Caer Pendwyr in answer to the High King's call.

The two were escorted to meet with the newly elected chieftain of this group. As they came unto the central fire, a huge man looked up from a map. "If the morning light does not deceive, 'tis Tipperton Thistledown I see."

"Urel," cried Tip, dismounting. "I did not know if you escaped the fall of Caer Lindor."

"I did," rumbled the man, rubbing his chest as if soothing an old wound, "but it was touch-and-go. Had it not been for Silverleaf, I would not have survived. Yet had it not been for me bearing him out the west gate with Rutcha on my heels, then neither would have he." Urel laughed hugely, then said, "Come, sit with me and introduce me to your friend and have some tea. And after you tell me what you are doing in The Clearing, we'll trade war stories. I'll tell you of my adventures in Silverleaf's company, and you can tell me whether or no you delivered that coin, and what happened along the way."

The train of Dylvana and Baeron and Warrows arrived that evening at the camp in the lea, and after an evening meal, Ruar called a council.

"You've come at a good time," said Urel, "for our rendezvous here in The Clearing is set to be done on the day of the last-quarter moon."

"On the morrow," said Coron Ruar, Vail at his side canting her head in agreement.

"Aye," agreed Urel. "And if you will delay travel by one day, we will fare to Caer Pendwyr with you."

Ruar nodded and glanced at Chieftain Durul, who nodded likewise. And then the coron turned to Rynna. Somewhat surprised by his unspoken question, nevertheless Rynna said, "Indeed."

Ruar turned back to Urel. "You have how many, fifty or so beyond three hundred?"

"Aye, nearly four hundred," said Urel. "But not all Greatwood Baeron are gathering here; some will meet us at the southern bound, down along the Glave Hills in Pellar."

"How many of you then will there be?" asked Coron Ruar.

"Including those who are yet to arrive and those we will meet in the south, mayhap a thousand, all told."

"Ah, then will our combined forces number some three thousand three hundred altogether," said Ruar.

"Three thousand three hundred and eight," said Beau, and Ruar broke out laughing, and was joined by Bwen's guffaws.

"Three thousand three hundred and eight, indeed," the coron replied.

When Urel and others looked at Beau and Ruar and Bwen in puzzlement, Bwen said, "After the planning is done, I'll tell you the tale of Bekki and Brandt . . . a story of two thousand two hundred . . . and five."

"Yar," said Beau grinning, "only this time it's eight Warrows I'm adding to the total, and not two Warrows, two Elves, and a Dwarf."

They waited a day at the campsite as by ones and twos other Baeron arrived, but on the morning of the next day as planned, even as the last-quarter moon set in the west and the sun rose in the east, once again the column set forth, the ranks swelled by the four hundred Baeron from The Clearing.

South-southwest they fared all that day and the next, an occasional Baeron drifting in from the forest to join the column on the trek across the broad lea. And nigh the close of the second day, under lowering skies, they came to the trees of the Greatwood again, where they set camp that eve.

A drizzling rain fell through the night, to become blowing mist on the following morn, the vaporous air swirling chill, the moisture nought but damp cold sinking unto the bones. Beau clutched his cloak tightly 'round as he rode, and from the far rear he could hear Bwen cursing as another wagon became mired.

Beau looked up at Melor and said, "Hmph. The very best time of all the seasons, eh?"

Melor did not reply.

All that day and three more they went, the wains miring often on the narrow trace, yet it was the only lane through the crowded weald to the open land atop the long arc of the Great Escarpment ahead. At last on the evening of the fourth day they came to the fringe of the woods, the forest ending, the terrain before them open. Some twenty miles straight ahead the wold ended abruptly at the rim of the Great Escarpment, where stone plummeted down the sheer face, the land at the base to run another five or so miles unto the banks of the River Argon. Yet they would not travel to the brink and down, but would turn southeasterly instead and follow a route parallel to the steep precipice. For as the sheer bluff angled out from Bellon Falls some fifty leagues north and west, the mighty bluff curved southeasterly and away, two hundred and fifty miles or so in a long bend, the last hundred miles of which the cliff and the land atop slowly fell down a long, long slope to eventually descend to the level of the banks of the Argon flowing in the land below. And it was down this gradual decline the column would fare, heading toward Pellar.

And so the next day they turned leftward, faring down the gradual cant of the land, the river some twenty-five miles to their right but nigh a hundred miles straight ahead.

"Look," said Tipperton, haling his pony to a halt and leaping to the ground.

Lyra, too, dismounted to examine the track the buccan had found.

"Horses," said Tip, examining the spoor. "Heading south."

"Ponies, too," said Lyra.

"Oh?" Tipperton moved to where she knelt.

As Tipperton squatted to look at the trace of smaller hooves, Lyra stood and peered westerly. "There are more," she said. Tipperton got to his feet and looked to where she pointed, his gaze falling upon a wide southerly track beaten through the yellowing grass.

"Another column moving south," said Tipperton, "five or so miles rightward of ours and two or three days ahead. Many horses; many ponies."

Vail looked up from the map. "Come, let us speak to the council."

"With such a mix of steeds I would suggest it is Lian and Dwarves," said Urel. "When I fought in the Grimwalls in Silverleaf's company and alongside DelfLord Volki—as recent as three months past—his Dwarves rode ponies. Wouldn't abide horses except to pull wagons or a plow. It's them and their ponies, I would guess."

"From the Black Hole then, is that what you think?" asked Bwen.

"Aye, though they name it Kraggen-cor."

"Black Hole, Kraggen-cor, or Drimmen-deeve: by any name I think it is Drimma, marching to answer the High King's call," said Vail.

"Along with Lian from Darda Galion," said Riatha.

Tipperton frowned and looked at his map. "How did they cross the Argon? If it was by the ferry at Olorin Isle, given their number, they would have had to make many trips across and back. Too, then they would have had to cross the Rissanin thereafter, and there is no ferry there, though they could have come through Caer Lindor." Tip turned to Urel. "Did any of the border watch report such?"

Urel shook his head. "Nay. But you've got to recall, most of them were making their way to the rendezvous when this force would have come across the Argon to this side."

Eyes turned to Riatha. "I would say they mayhap added many ferries and first made the crossing at Olorin Isle, after which they moved the barges to the Rissanin where they were used to cross again."

Bwen glanced at the map and asked, "Why not cross but once . . . farther down the Argon?" Her finger stabbed to the map just below the Rissanin.

Melor smiled. "Even though Bellon Falls lies twenty leagues downstream, the closer to that mighty cataract, the more perilous is the Argon, for the Rissanin, the Rothro, the Quadrill, and the Cellener all add their flow to that of the Great River. Nay, I ween Dara Riatha is right, for 'tis better to make two crossings than to chance being swept over the brim of Bellon and into the Cauldron below."

"Regardless as to how one would cross," said Ruar, "we need to know who fares ahead." He turned to Vail. "Send scouts, but tell them to be wary until we know just who it is to the fore."

Vail nodded, but at Tip's hopeful look, she shook her head. "Nay, Tipperton, this is a deed which calls for fleet horses, not ponies."

Moments later, Cein and Arylin rode swiftly away from the camp, each Dylvana drawing two remounts behind. Tipperton watched them go, then he turned to Vail. "I do hope it's Lian and Dwarves they find and not some column of foe."

Vail nodded but did not reply.

Not quite a full day later, as camp was being set, Cein and Arylin came riding back. And soon the word was spread: the column ahead was indeed Lian from Darda Galion and Châkka from Kraggen-cor. And though DelfLord Volki was impatient to move onward, he and Coron Eiron and their combined forces would wait at their present camp by the River Argon for the Baeron and Dylvana to arrive.

"Good," said Beau by the fire that night. "More not-men."

Two more days they fared down the long slope to come to the river at last, where Coron Eiron's seven hundred Lian were encamped with Volki's twelve hundred Dwarves. And as Tipperton and the Warrows rode in among the waiting forces—

"Ho, Little Ryn!" called a voice.

Rynna was off her pony and running ere Tipperton saw who was calling. And as his dammia hurled herself into the Lian's arms to be swung 'round and 'round, "Silverleaf!" Tipperton cried.

But Vanidar did not hear him, so engaged was he with Rynna.

And as Tip dismounted, he saw Aravan standing nearby, the Alor's face yet cast with gloom.

"So you pledged to this rapscallion, eh?"

Rynna looked across the fire at Tipperton and grinned. "Oh, Silverleaf, he's no rapscallion, and I do love him so."

"So I remember from the days at Caer Lindor," said Silverleaf, "those hand-in-hand strolls on the wall." He glanced at Riatha and turned to Tipperton. "And as for being a rascal, nay, he is not, but the Hero of Dendor, or so I have heard."

"Don't forget Mineholt North," said Beau 'round a mouthful of crue.

Tipperton looked up from the silver strings of his lute and said, "You can't believe everything you hear. I was just one small cog in the millworks."

"But a cog without which the mill would not run," said Riatha, "or so do the legends say."

Tip's eyes widened. "Legends . . . ?"

Riatha nodded and gestured about the encampment. "Lady Bwen speaks of thee highly, as do others. And tales of thy feats at Dendor sing of heroic deeds."

Tip shook his head and said, "If you would cant legends of Warrows, then sing of Beau who found the cure for the plague. Sing of Rynna who saved me and Beau and led a Gargon to its death among the Groaning Stones. Sing of the Springwater Warrows who, though assailed by a Horde, delayed the advance until those who had survived the initial onslaught could reach the safety of Blackwood. Sing of those Warrows who died at the fall of Caer Lindor, the result of the Rivermen's treachery. Sing of Farly and Nix and Linnet and Alver and Dinly, heroes no less than any here."

As Tipperton fell silent, Riatha reached over her shoulder and drew the jade-handled sword from the green scabbard harnessed across her back and held it on high, its dark blade glinting as of starlight captured within. "Hál to the resolute Waerlinga, wherever they may be."

Silverleaf raised up his white-bone longbow, and Aravan hefted his crystal-bladed, black-hafted spear, and together with Riatha they cried, *Hál to the resolute Waerlinga, wherever they may be!*

While Alver and Dinly grinned, and Nix and Farly and Linnet looked at one another and shrugged, and Beau and Rynna and Tipperton sighed in resignation, elsewhere in the camp, Baeron and Dylvana and Lian and Dwarves turned at this call, and many nodded in agreement or raised a cup in salute.

Urged onward by Volki, the DelfLord impatient to get under way, by dawn the column was again moving southeasterly along the wold above the banks of the wide River Argon.

Nine days altogether they followed this route, the waterway to their right, the Greatwood to their left, the leaves turning russet and brown and cascading to the ground in these early days of November.

And on the eve of the ninth day they came to the northern reach of the Glave Hills, the northern reach of Pellar.

"How far is there left to go?" asked Dinly.

Tip looked at his map. "We've come nearly halfway, I'd judge: five hundred miles, altogether, with another five hundred to go."

Beau counted up on his fingers. "And we've been on the way for, let me see, twenty-eight days, I make it. So, that would put us in Caer Pendwyr, when? Ah, eight days into December?"

Linnet nodded, adding, "Two days after Elwydd's moon passes the next first quarter, then it is we should see the city."

"If nothing untoward happens ere then," said Rynna.

"What could happen?" asked Alver.

Rynna shrugged. "I've come to realize that Dame Fortune is quite fickle."

A silence fell among the Warrows.

Finally, Beau said, "I say, did you take note of Lady Riatha's sword, what with its dark blade and all, sparkling like stars trapped within."

"Perhaps it's one of those tokens of power," said Tipperton.

"Like Aravan's spear?" asked Rynna.

"That's a token of power?" asked Dinly. "I mean, I saw it had a crystal blade and a black haft, but I didn't think it, um, special."

"Oh, it's very special," said Rynna. "A dark crystal bound by argent silveron to an ebon staff. When I asked him about it, he would only say that it had a truename."

Dinly frowned. "Truename?"

"Aye. A word which invokes its power."

"Power?"

"It, um, *burns* when it touches flesh; I have seen it do such in battle . . . in the days before Caer Lindor fell."

Dinly sucked in a breath between his teeth and whispered, "Magic," as Tipperton said, "Oh my."

Beau's gaze fell upon the saddlebags where his red journal was stored. "Wizard's work, eh?"

Rynna turned up a hand. "He did not say."

Beau frowned, then said, "I wonder if Lady Riatha's sword or Silverleaf's white bow have truenames, and if so, what do you think they might do if and when invoked?"

Warrows looked at one another, yet none had an answer.

The next day as the column fared southerly, nearly six hundred Baeron emerged from the hills to join the march. They were those who had assembled in the south of the Greatwood and had waited to rendezvous with their brethren from the north. They fell in with Urel's group.

South went the column and south, the wagons and horses and ponies . . . and a thousand Dylvana, eight hundred Lian, twelve hundred Dwarves, twenty-two hundred Baeron, and eight Warrows, yielding altogether a total count of five thousand two hundred . . . and eight.

South-southwest they fared down the western reach of the Glaves, and on the evening of the fourth day of travel they came at last to the Plains of Pellar.

"Four hundred miles to go," said Tipperton, glancing up from his map and across the fire at Bwen. "From here the way should ease a bit."

Bwen wetted a finger and held it up in the wind and glanced up at the dark clouds scudding northeasterly across the full of the moon. She shook her head and said, "Not if the wind is bringing with it the November rains to come."

Braec grunted his agreement and then said, "Pray that it snows instead."

The rain began falling in the night, and by morning the ground was thoroughly soaked. Even so, Bwen spread the wagons wide in a long line such that none followed in the track of another. The vanguard was divided in twain: one to ride at the west end of the wagons, the other at the east. The main body of riders came behind the wagons, for as Bwen said, "I'll not have you out there in front churning up the good earth for my wheels to fall in."

Only the scouts were allowed to lead, and then only after Bwen lost the argument with Chieftain Durul.

Even so, the wains mired often, but the spare great horses of the Baeron swiftly pulled them free.

For two more days it rained off and on, the air damp with icy November chill, but the following morn dawned clear. Still the land was soft, and so, spread widely, south they went and south for days, the land drying as they fared, and on the fifth day Bwen declared that once more they could roll as a column, and on southward they went. And as they rode, Dinly said to Beau, "I see what you meant."

Frowning in puzzlement, Beau looked at Dinly.

"About travelling over half the world," clarified Dinly, gesturing at the wide featureless plain, nought but yellow grass and scrub and occasional stands of trees for as far as the eye could see. "I mean, could anything be duller than riding and camping and riding and camping and riding and camping and doing it for days on end? I mean, we hardly need to go out on near-scout; you can practically see everything there is to see without setting foot from here."

Beau looked out across the gently rolling land and nodded and said, "Still, Dinly, I'd rather have dull than war."

Linnet looked across at her buccaran and grinned. "With you, love, I think nothing will ever be dull. Peaceful, perhaps, but never dull."

Farther back in the column Rynna sighed, and Tipperton looked over at her. "Ryn?"

"Oh, I was just thinking: every step we take is but one more step farther away from Lark."

As Tipperton nodded, Rynna added, "Just one more reason Modru deserves to die . . . he and all of his ilk . . . Gyphon included."

A fortnight in all the march fared across the Plains of Pellar, striking for Caer Pendwyr, and in all that time though they covered mile after mile nothing seemed to change. Yet on the fifteenth day. . . .

"Look rightward, Tipperton."

On patrol, Tipperton and Lyra, as expected, had come upon Pendwyr Road.

Tipperton looked up from the tradeway and toward the north-west, where a league or so hence—"Riders," said Tip, "and not just a few."

"A column," said Lyra.

"Coming to answer the King's call?"

Lyra did not respond, but instead shaded her eyes and peered at the oncoming force.

Tip glanced back northeasterly, where out on the plains fared his own column. "Shall we ride back and warn—"

"Nay, Tipperton. Those coming along Pendwyr Road are Elves."

"Elves? But how can you—? Oh, right. Elven eagle eyes."

"They bear a banner: green on grey."

"Green on grey . . . Arden Vale! Let's go meet them."

Lyra shook her head. "They will be here soon enough."

"Well, if we're not going to meet them, then this." Tipperton raised his black-oxen horn to his lips and blew a ringing blast.

Long moments later and made faint by the distance, from the road northwest there returned a clarion cry.

That one to be followed by a third horn cry, this one from the plains to the northeast.

Lyra looked back toward their own column, then laughed.

"What?" said Tip.

"Thy call," said Lyra. "Weapons ready, the vanguard comes at haste."

Across the plains at a dead run came flying the Elven horses, with the ponies of the Dwarves and the great thundering mounts of the Baeron galloping after.

"Oops," said Tip, looking at his horn.

Ruar called out, "Hai, but it was good to run at last."

Both Urel and Durul patted the necks of their great horses and nodded in agreement, while DelfLord Volki growled.

Tipperton tried to look anywhere but at those staring down at him, including Rynna, giggling, along with laughing Beau.

Silverleaf grinned. "What say, Tipperton, that thou and I go to greet my cousins from Arden Vale?"

Tipperton looked up at Lyra, and she shrugged, then nodded.

The buccan leaped upon his pony and he and Vanidar spurred away, but ere they had gone more than a few loping strides, Tipperton looked over his shoulder at those behind and raised his black-oxen horn to his lips and blew another blast.

On the road aft the milling vanguard erupted in ringing cheers, while DelfLord Volki growled again, though his face broke into a smile.

*   *   *

Led by Alor Talarin, the force of Lian from Arden Vale numbered four hundred strong. And he merged his tally with the larger column, raising the whole of the combined legion to five thousand six hundred . . . and eight.

And though there were two chieftains and two corons and a Dwarven DelfLord among the host thus formed, and a Warrow commander as well, it was Silverleaf elected warleader.

Along Pendwyr Road they fared, heading for the distant city, Tip and Beau renewing acquaintances, among whom were Darai Alaria, Aris, and Jaith, and Alori Arandar, Inarion, Duron, and Flandrena.

When they camped that night, Aris and Jaith came unto the Warrow campfire. And Aris embraced Beau and said how wonderful it was for him to have found a cure for the plague, and they spoke of herbs and simples long into the night. And Jaith had brought a small harp, and she sat with Tipperton and they played and sang many tunes, Rynna and her pennywhistle joining in now and again.

And Linnet drew Rynna aside and whispered in her ear, and Rynna grinned and said for her to fear not, ". . . These are but old friends, my cousin, and though your mate and mine seem at times unaware of others about, 'tis you whom Beau will hold this night just as Tip will surely hold me."

Four days later, on the eve of the second of December, the column came unto the last of the empty plains below the city of Caer Pendwyr.

"Hmm," mused Rynna, frowning, "I would have expected more than just our legion to have answered the High King's call."

"Maybe we are the first," said Tip, though his heart was heavy with doubt.

Rynna nodded, but then added, "And maybe we are the last. We'll find out soon enough."

Even as she said so, emissaries came riding downslope from the headland above, and within two candlemarks, as the Warrows were rubbing down their ponies, a Dylvana rider came galloping, to stop at the Warrow campsite. "Warleader Vanidar requests thy presence, Commander Rynna."

"Silverleaf wants me now?"

"Aye," replied the rider, "and with thy pony." Without further word he spurred his horse and galloped onward.

Rynna looked at Tipperton as she cast a saddle blanket on the back of her steed and said, "Duty calls, love."

*   *   *

As the legion made camp on the plains, Silverleaf took with him six representatives—Corons Eiron and Ruar, Chieftains Urel and Durul, DelfLord Volki, and Commander Rynna—and up the slope and into the city they rode to confer with the steward there.

"We've come all this way just to find out he's not here?" asked Dinly.

"What good is a High King's call if he won't stay put?" growled Alver.

"I was afraid of this when I saw we were the only ones here," said Farly. "—Our legion, that is."

"Wull, if he's not here," asked Dinly, "just where *is* he?"

"Hush," said Nix, suppressing a yawn. "Let Rynna speak."

Overhead cold stars wheeled through the wee hours of the morning. Silverleaf and the others had returned late, and Rynna had awakened the Warrows to hear what had befallen.

And now as Rynna added another stick to the fire, she said, "The King's steward, Lord Voren, says Blaine is east of here, some seven hundred miles, along the Ironwater River."

"Oh no," groaned Dinly, looking at Beau. "Another half the world away. I don't, uh, I . . ."

Rynna glared Dinly to silence. "He pursued the Southerlings from Gûnarring Gap to there. They fled before the King and his host—those who broke the siege at the gap.

"East they ran, did the foe, the King close after: across Valon and over the Argon River they fled; across Pellar; and over the Ironwater, where they now stand.

"And the King holds on this side of the river, for the enemy wards the opposite shore, and to try to cross in the face of the foe is nought but begging for death."

"Oi, now wait a moment," said Farly. "They made no opposition at the Argon?"

Rynna shook her head. "The very same question I asked, Farly, but Lord Voren said no."

"Yet now they ward the Ironwater?" asked Farly. "Less wide, less formidable than the Argon?"

"Indeed," replied Rynna.

"Why there and not the Argon?" asked Tip.

"Voren thinks it's because Hèl's Crucible is at their backs, and it daunts them to think of fleeing across that wasteland dire."

Tip flipped through his maps and frowned. "Well, Lord Voren is right about that. —I mean, Hèl's Crucible is just beyond the Ironwater."

"Does the King have a plan?" asked Nix.

"Aye," replied Rynna. "Blaine believes the foe will soon have no choice but to abandon warding the opposite shore. Since they cannot live off that barren land, and with little in the way of supplies and nought but Hèl's Crucible at their backs, the King simply waits, rather like a siege, only this time 'tis the foe held at bay."

Beau sighed. "I suppose we've got a long ride ahead of us; as Dinly says, another half a world away."

Rynna grinned and shook her head. "No, Beau, not this time."

Linnet frowned at Rynna. "No? Are we just going to sit here?"

"That's what I'd like to know, too," chimed in Nix. "Are we to abandon the High King? Leave him deadlocked with the foe?"

"On the contrary," said Rynna. "You see, Silverleaf has a plan."

35

*T*he next morning the Warrows stood on the high northern bluffs of the headland and watched as a swift Fjordlander Dragonship set sail from the docks below. With spike-bearing, round wooden shields fixed at hand along its top wale and its square sail set by a beitass to catch at the wind, a crew of Human warriors with axes in their belts rowed the longship out of Hile Bay and toward the ocean beyond, soon to slip eastward through the indigo waters of the dark blue Avagon Sea. Amidships stood half a dozen horses separated one from the other by slender poles affixed thwartwise from wale to wale, and at the prow stood Vanidar, Aravan right behind, the warleader and his trusted advisor sailing away from the caer.

As they slid from sight 'round the shoulder of the headland, Rynna sighed and said, "Well, there they go, Silverleaf and Aravan, off to see King Blaine."

"Do you think his plan will really work?" asked Linnet. "—Using Dragonships for pontoons?"

"I don't see why not," said Nix. Then he pointed down at the long stone wharf. "Look, even now workers bear planks to the shipwrights below." On the jetty, men carted great loads of lumber toward the shipyard.

"Huah," grunted Beau. "Like a string of ants haling choice bits of fruit home to the hill."

"Well, as to the work these ants do, let us hope it bears sweet fruit as well," said Linnet.

"The fruit this will bear is more like to be bitter," said Rynna, "yet it is a crop we must harvest regardless."

Dinly yawned long and loud. "Oh my, but I don't think I got enough rest last night, and we rose ere the sun this day. And speaking of last night, Ryn, could you say again just how all this came about. I was rather sleepy, you know, and I think I may have missed something in the telling."

"Well, Dinly, speaking of getting up early, what say we have some breakfast, and Rynna can tell us then," said Beau. He looked at Linnet. "I could use a good wake-up cup of hot tea."

They stepped to their ponies and mounted and rode toward the camp, faring down the slope Silverleaf and his captains had ridden up the evening before. . . .

Bearing the flags of Darda Galion, Darda Erynian, Arden Vale, and Kraggen-cor, seven rode away from the camp of the legion and toward Caer Pendwyr above—Warleader Vanidar, Corons Eiron and Ruar, Chieftains Urel and Durul, DelfLord Volki, and Commander Rynna. Rynna felt somewhat out of place, having no flag of her own, but neither did the Baeron, and they seemed no less for the lack. Up the long slope they rode, to come at last to a steep embankment, the earthworks stretching out left and right, spanning the width of the headland. In three places along the rampart there stood heavy-timbered, wooden gates: center left, center right, and midmost. And above the gates stood warders, sentries in red-and-gold tabards. Vanidar had chosen to ride to the center gate, and now he and the others paused below.

"We have come in answer to the High King's call," said Silverleaf to the warders above, "and Lord Steward Voren has summoned us unto council. I am Warleader Vanidar, Lian Guardian"—he gestured to those behind—"and these are those whose armies I serve."

Rynna's eyes widened. *These are those whose* armies *he serves? Hmph! Eight Warrows. Some army.*

"Welcome, my Lord Vanidar," called down the gate captain, "we were told to expect you"—his gaze widened at the sight of Rynna—"though not the Elfchild you bring."

Before Vanidar could respond, Rynna said, "No Elfchild am I, but the commander of the force of Warrows."

Now the captain's eyes widened, and he breathed, "Waerlings." Recovering, he turned and spoke a command to unseen soldiers below, and Rynna could hear the rumble of a drawbar being pulled.

Through the gateway they rode, and beyond the earthen dike

were pitched row after row of tents, among which flew standards from poles, demarcating where soldiers from various lands were encamped.

Riding alongside Ruar, Rynna said, "I see most of the flags bear a golden griffin on a scarlet field."

" 'Tis Pellarion," replied the coron. "The High King's flag."

"Well, they greatly outnumber the others."

"As it should be," replied Ruar. "The remainder are but token forces, left here to show the unity of the Free Folk."

Riding at hand, Coron Eiron barked a laugh. At Rynna's inquiring look, he said, "I see that Lord Steward Voren has had the good sense to separate the Fjordlanders from the Jutlanders and from the Gelenders as well."

Rynna looked to where Eiron pointed: a blue-and-white streamer flew at one corner of the camp far to the right; while far to the left and diagonally across the whole of the ground flew a green, orange, and yellow banner; and entirely opposite at the third corner set a red, blue, and white flag.

Eiron shook his head. "Uneasy sits this truce, I would say."

"Truce?"

"Aye, for they are eld enemies but temporarily united against a common foe."

Ruar shook his head. "Humans."

Eiron cocked an eyebrow. "Forget not, Alor, we were once as mad as men."

Ruar reluctantly nodded, as across the encampment they rode.

They came to another wall, this one of stone and high, and once again were permitted entry through a warded gate, beyond which lay the city proper, with its cobblestone ways and buildings of stone and brick and tile, stucco and clay, most of which seemed to be joined to one another, though here and there were stand-alone structures. Narrow streets and alleyways twisted this way and that, the pave stones of variegated color. Shops occupied many first floors, with dwellings above. Glass windows displayed merchandise, the handiwork of crafters and artisans: milliners, coppersmiths, potters, jewelers, weavers, tanners, cobblers, coopers, clothiers, tailors, seamstresses, furniture makers, and the like.

Rynna's gaze widened at the sight of the many and varied shops, and more than one of each kind, for she had not dreamt that such could exist, so different from the village of Springwater. And onward they rode, Rynna's head turning this way and that, marvelling at the plentitude.

Footway traffic was light in the eve, and they saw only one

horse-drawn wain trundling through the streets, and this a water wagon. And Eiron said, "Pendwyr is a city without wells, and water is borne from shafts and springs down on the Plains of Pellar."

"Doesn't that make the city vulnerable to siege?" asked Rynna.

Eiron shook his head. "See the tile roofs? They are fitted with gutters and channels cunningly wrought to guide rainwater into cisterns for storing. The water from the plains merely augments the supply."

"It must rain often, then," observed Rynna.

"Aye," said Eiron. "Seldom does the city need rely wholly upon water from the plains."

"What about water needed to quench fires? Have they enough to do so?"

Eiron laughed. "Look about, wee one. This is a city of stone and brick and other such . . . things which do not burn."

Rynna gazed 'round, and the only wood her eye easily found was that of the brightly painted doors and shutters.

Eiron then said, "After the Chabbains destroyed Gleeds by fire—and were themselves destroyed—High King Rolun moved his court to the fort on this headland. And thinking upon the city just lost, 'Never again,' he declared, and he decreed that all buildings in Pendwyr must be made of stone, of brick, of that which would not burn."

"So it was then; so it is now," said Volki with an air of finality, and on through the city they fared.

Past shops and stores, past restaurants and cafés and tea shops, past inns and taverns, past large dwellings and small squares, past greengrocers and chirurgeons and herbalists they rode. And they crossed through several open-market squares, empty now that the day was done.

Finally they came to another gateway in a high stone wall running the width of the narrow peninsula. Again, Vanidar identified himself to the warders, and again they were permitted ingress. Beyond this wall the character of the buildings changed, for here were located a great courthouse, a tax hall, a large building housing the city guard with a jail above, a firehouse, a library, a census building, a hall of records, a cluster of university buildings, and other such—here was the face of government, the agencies and offices of the realm. Although impressed by the scale of the buildings within this quarter, it seemed cold and cheerless to Rynna and not nearly as marvelous as the city behind.

And as they rode forward, Caer Pendwyr loomed ahead, the

citadel tall with castellated walls all 'round and towers at each corner, all enclosing the castle of the High King. When she and the others drew near the caer, Rynna could see that it sat on a freestanding spire of stone towering up from the Avagon Sea below. The fortified pinnacle was connected to the headland by a pivot bridge, a span which could be swivelled aside by a crew in the castle to sever the fortress from the headland.

At the moment the bridge spanned the gulf, guards at either end.

They gave their names to a captain, and he summoned two pages, sending one to fetch Lord Voren to the north turret chamber and the other to guide them on their way.

They were led through corridors and up spiralling stairs to a room high within an outer turret, and although Rynna was thoroughly turned about, Volki declared that indeed they were in the north tower, the one overlooking Hile Bay.

No sooner had they arrived but the page who had been sent to fetch Lord Voren stepped to the door and breathlessly announced the steward's impending arrival. Moments later an elderly man came in—stooped in shoulder, but bright of eye— his head bald but for stray wisps of white hair all 'round.

"Come and sit about the table. No need to stand, eh? And do my old eyes deceive me? Or is it a Waerling in your midst?"

The old man smiled at Rynna, and he beckoned her to a chair at his side. "Come, come, wee one, I would have you at hand."

"But my lord, I am just a Warrow amid corons and chieftains and a DelfLord and a warleader, and I—"

"Nonsense," snapped the man. "I see Elves and Dwarves and even huge Baeron nearly every day—well, perhaps not every day, but certainly several times a year—but Waerlings, now, that's a different matter altogether. Besides, the page said you were a commander, and that's certainly good enough for me."

Silverleaf broke out in laughter. "Ah, little Ryn, resist not Lord Voren, for he has the right of it."

"Have you had aught to eat? No?" Voren turned to the page. "Boy, have food sent . . . and tea. On your way now, hop to."

As the page fled down the hallway, Voren turned to the others and said, "Now, about this army you bring . . ."

"How did the foe evade getting slaughtered as they came to the Argon?" asked Volki, the Dwarf stroking his black beard shot through with silver.

Voren pointed at the map at the point of the Argon Ferry. "Some were slain fighting a rearguard action, but most escaped. It seems they had floats waiting for them."

"Floats waiting?"

Lord Voren turned up a hand. "Perhaps they made them in anticipation of invading Pellar."

"They had not already done so? —Invaded Pellar, I mean?" asked Rynna.

Voren shook his head. "Oh, they sent token forces, but nothing of real threat." Voren gestured about. "It seems instead of capturing his city, they were more intent on capturing the King himself."

Rynna frowned. "Capturing?"

Voren nodded. "If the High King fell into the hands of Modru, 'twould be a terrible blow. But he outwitted them all and sent the foe fleeing across the Argon."

A scowl on his face, Volki nodded. "And how did the King cross in the teeth of their opposition?"

"They did not oppose him—"

"They made no opposition at the Argon?" interjected Rynna.

"—but fled instead," continued Lord Voren, "abandoning their floats and craft."

"Abandoning? They did not burn them?" Coron Eiron looked 'round at the others, all just as puzzled as he.

"Nay, they did not. King Blaine sent a company of Fjordlanders over and they fetched the floats and used them to ferry the host across. Even so, it took several days to get all to this side, to get all to the Pellarion shore. By then the foe had a good lead, and they fled across the land and over the Ironwater to Garia beyond."

"The King did not trap them against the near shore of that river either?" asked Durul.

Voren shook his head. "Nay. They were across when he arrived . . . and were arrayed to do battle on the opposite shore."

"Hmm," mused Ruar. "They did not oppose him at the Argon, a wider river to cross, yet they now do so at the Ironwater. This is a puzzle indeed."

"Aye," growled Volki. "The Ironwater is no Argon: a thousand feet across at most is the Ironwater, while the Argon alongside Pellar measures a mile or more."

"Forget not, Lord Ruar, DelfLord Volki, Hèl's Crucible is at their backs. King Blaine believes they are afraid to cross that wasteland. He holds them at siege."

"This Hèl's Crucible," said Rynna, "if they are afraid to cross it, just what is it like?"

"Oh, a terrible place, wee one," said Voren. "Look at the map, but heed me, for this is what it does and does not tell: surrounded by hills and separated from the Avagon Sea by a high shield wall, Hèl's Crucible is a hideous rift in the earth, ten leagues wide and forty long and some thousand feet deep here at the narrow seaward end but plunging down a mile or more here where it flares out wide, a vast chasm running all the way to the northwesterly end. In most places the sides are sheer or bear steeply down; in a few places, however, slopes lead down and in. Nothing grows in the depths therein, for the land is hot, baked, cracked as if raging fire burns 'neath. And down across that broad, yawning stretch of arid wasteland, there are leagues upon leagues of jagged black stone, broken, shattered, deep chasms and great heaps and long, jumbled runs, gaping crevices and holes disappearing into darkness within the mesh of stone. Were any to try to cross these parts of the shattered waste it would take them weeks to go but a few leagues, and even could they reach the opposite side, their clothing, their boots, their very skin would be in tatters. Beyond the black stone, there are places here and there where scalding water now and then shoots into the sky, and elsewhere are holes which vomit yellow melt onto wide flats of soft tawny stone. There are long, glittering ridges of clusters of crystal sharp as the sharpest of blades, as well as jagged fissures exhaling foul fumes and glowing with fire deep in their unplumbed abyssal depths. Across the 'scape, bubbling pools of boiling mud or thick, seeping black tar seek to trap the unwary, while smoldering crevices cleft in the barren earth spew out billowing smoke, black or yellow or grey. A hideous stench wafts over all. And some days the air is deadly down in the great rift, for the belch of foul smoke and tainted vapors fill low pockets within the basin—at times Hèl's Crucible entire—to thicken the air and kill all creatures therein, men included. For all these reasons and more, this is why Modru's armies fear to cross that land."

Volki cleared his throat and pointed to the place on the map where lay the city of Rhondor at the northwestern end of the rift. "Nevertheless, there are days when the wind blows the great cleft and its pockets sufficiently clear for the miners of Rhondor to quarry the worthy minerals within: white *foran*, yellow *siarka*, many-colored *sólas*—"

"They are not afraid of the deadly air?" asked Rynna.

Volki shook his head. "Just as we Châkka do in some of our mines, they too bear yellow-wings in cages to warn them of such. And the ores and rocks and crystals of Rhondor are of value dear."

Rynna looked across at the Dwarf. "Regardless as to the worth of what is mined therein, it sounds as if it is a hideous place to be, yellow-wings or no."

"Aye, little one, you have the right of it," said Voren, "and that's why the foe stands at siege."

"I take it the King has no floats at hand," said Urel.

"A few, chieftain, yet Blaine will not use them in that small number, for to throw his host a handful at a time against a waiting foe guarantees nought but defeat, and he will not do so. Hence, for the moment, he holds siege on this side, for there is no food where the enemy awaits, and their supplies are running low."

Silverleaf, who had been standing at the high window and looking down into the harbor below, turned about and said, "If he could win across with few losses, would King Blaine engage the foe?"

"Indeed, Lord Vanidar, he would."

Silverleaf smiled and said, "Well then, if thou wilt but lend me all thy shipwrights and all thy lumber and a few warriors from the host at camp before thy door, I have a plan."

". . . And so, that's how it came about," concluded Rynna. "Silverleaf explained his plan, and all the others embellished on it, and then I came and told you."

She looked about at the others and took a sip of tea.

"And a good plan it is," said Alver. "Right, Dinly?"

But that buccan—the one who had requested Rynna to retell the events of the meeting—that buccan, full of warm breakfast fare, had nodded off to sleep.

A sevenday passed and then another, yet Silverleaf and Aravan had not reappeared, and the army on the plains merely waited. The shipyards, however, were a hive of activity, the wrights working throughout the nights as well as the days: fifty of the Dragonships were measured and fitted thwartwise with wide, raftlike sections of heavy planks pinned to the underbracing, to span across from topwale to topwale and jut a yard beyond either side. Other raftlike sections of braced planking were made freestanding and later guided down atop those on the ships, where they were held in place by great wooden screws fitted through wide auger holes.

Too, sixteen of the huge Gothonian ships were made ready for sailing, the crews of the chosen vessels glad of something to do.

And even though not engaged in this work, the time fled swiftly for the Warrows, for on each of these days, by their commander's leave, they explored the city of Pendwyr, marvelling over the wonder of it all, Rynna herself in their midst. Never had they seen such a vast array of shops and dwellings, of inns and hostels, of places of goods and crafts. Even so, many of the businesses were but lightly staffed, and some were closed altogether. "What with the blockade and the burning of the ships in Arbalin," had explained Beth, a serving maid at the Red Moon, "it's the war and all. You should see it when peace is at hand and goods and people come in from all over the world. Now it's mostly soldiers and mariners, and a rowdy bunch at that, especially if Fjordlanders and Jutlanders happen to find one another in the same saloon."

"We have heard they do not get along," said Rynna.

"Not get along is putting it mildly, miss. If it weren't for the city watch, it'd come to murther, if you ask me. Though I am glad they are here, they need something to do beside stand ward at the city."

Rynna smiled to herself and looked at Tipperton, only to find him smiling, too. And then she said, "It's the war, all right, and I'd like to see the city in peacetime, when it is full to the brim. But tell me, Beth, what do you lack the most?"

"Oh, that's easy, miss: music. The playing of harps and flutes and lutes and drums. And the singing of songs. With war raging across the land, minstrels and bards are hard to come by, most having joined in the fight."

That night, the seventh after Silverleaf's army had arrived, and for the next nine nights as well, the Red Moon was filled with song, Tipperton and Rynna and Jaith and dark-haired Elissan playing and singing melodies—lute, pennywhistle, harp, and timbrel—ringing out the tunes.

And the inn was crowded with warriors, come to hear them play. And not a fight broke out on any of these nights, the soldiers at times singing along. Even Fjordlanders and Jutlanders caroled together, though from opposite sides of the room, Gelenders between joining in.

During one of the pauses for rest, as Tipperton and Beau quaffed an ale at the bar, Jaith and Rynna and Elissan huddled together at a table and now and again burst into laughter. And when Tipperton returned to the stage, and took up his lute, Rynna with her pennywhistle stepped to his side and said, "Keeping secrets, eh, of a certain bath in Arden vale?"

As Tip blushed furiously and glanced at Elissan, Rynna played the opening notes of "The Maiden and the Lad," and those in the tavern laughed and applauded at the familiar refrain. The buccan caught up with the song in the middle of the first chorus as the audience sang along.

Three days later a page came riding into the encampment, seeking Commander Rynna among others, and he handed her an invitation for the morrow night. Rynna called the Warrows together. "We are invited by Lord Steward Voren to a Winterday feast at the caer to celebrate Year's Long Night."

Dinly grinned. "Your entire Warrow army?"

Rynna laughed and nodded and said, "My entire Warrow army."

Linnet's face fell. "Oh, but I was hoping to join Beau and watch the Dwarves in their mid-of-night Winterday celebration to Elwydd. I mean, though I am not Châk-Sol as is Beau, when DelfLord Volki noted I was an adherent of Elwydd he granted me permission to do so. I would not care to miss it."

Tip frowned. "And I was hoping that you and I, Rynna, could step the turn of the seasons with the Dylvana and Lian at midnight as well."

"Wull, me now, I'd like to join the feast at the caer," said Nix, Dinly and Alver and Farly all nodding their agreement.

Rynna smiled and held up the invitation. "Fear not, for Lord Voren writes that the banquet will be over in good time for all folk to worship Year's Long Night in their very own special ways."

In the evening candlemarks of Winterday, as snow fell upon the land, and Warrows and Lian and Dylvana and Baeron and Dwarves made their way to the caer, muted singing could be heard drifting down from dwellings above the shops and from taverns and inns and hostels. It was Winterday, the First of Yule, and in spite of the war, folk would celebrate. Even so, some dwellings were quiet, though candles burned within, for those inside had lost kindred to battle, and this Yule was not happy for them.

Through the streets and past the second stone wall they rode, the looming facades of government staring coldly down as they fared by. Finally, across the swing-bridge they rode and into the courtyard beyond, where pages took charge of their mounts.

They were guided to a great banquet hall, a majordomo announcing the guests as they were ushered in. And as Rynna stepped forward, the majordomo called out, "Ladies and lords and honored guests, I present Commander Rynna Fenrush Thistledown and her entire army of Waerlings: Sir Tipperton Thistledown, Sir Beau Darby and Lady Linnet Fenrush Darby, Sir Nix Fenrush, Sir Farly Bourne, Sir Alver Bruk, and Sir Dinly Rill."

A murmur went 'round the chamber as Rynna and Tipperton, followed by the others, trod down three steps to the main floor, for though they were dressed in their very best leathers, still the Warrows seemed more like wee creatures of the woodlands than warriors of renown. With banquet tables ringed 'round the perimeter, the central space of the hall was open, and across the wide marble floor they fared toward the place reserved for them.

All eyes were upon the Warrows as they made their way past, for as Lord Voren had said, seldom did Waerlings come unto the High King's court. At the table they found their chairs sitting on blocks, raising the seats to a comfortable height for ones of their modest stature. Even so, like small children, they had to clamber up to take unto their places, much to the amusement of the other guests and to the embarrassment of the staff who had presumably thought of everything, though it was clear they had not. Still the Warrows seemed completely unfazed at having to climb up the chairs, happily chattering among themselves as they settled in.

The feast was well under way, when the great hall doors boomed open, conversation falling to nought, the majordomo rushing in to hammer the floor with his long staff and announce these late arrivals. But ere the words could leave the herald's lips, Rynna cried out, "Silverleaf, Aravan, you are back," as the two Lian strode across the wide vestibule and down the steps to the main floor.

"Lord Vanidar and Lord Aravan," announced the house steward, rapping his stave to the floor, but his words were lost in the babble of greetings.

Shaking snow from his cloak, Silverleaf strode to the central floor, and there he raised his hands. When silence fell, he said, "High King Blaine is well and sends his greetings and good wishes on this Winterday."

As this news was met with a resounding cheer, Rynna caught Aravan's eye.

[Our plan?] she mouthed silently.

He nodded.

Rynna turned to Tip and the others and grinned and said in Twyll, [Ready your slings and arrows, my entire Warrow army, for the King has agreed to the scheme.]

Across the sea in ships they sailed, an army of eight thousand six hundred and eight. And among the flotilla were fifty Dragonships, twenty-five of which were crewed by Fjordlanders, the remaining twenty-five by Jutes, three thousand warriors altogether, who would leave their ships upon the Ironwater and stand ward against the foe. All of the longboats bore the raftlike planking, more than enough altogether to carry out Silverleaf's plan.

As to the remaining five thousand six hundred and eight warriors, they were spread among the sixteen huge Gothonian ships, their horses and ponies as well, including the spare mounts and draft animals, and the wagons and wains, too.

The huge ships themselves were nearly two hundred feet long stem to stern, and some sixty feet across at the beam. Each had five decks altogether, the top deck and four below. And of these four lower decks, three were primarily for horses and ponies and feed and water, though some wains and supplies were kept there as well; the remaining deck housed warriors and sailors and wagons and wains and supplies. When the huge ships had been loaded, four at a time they had been maneuvered by sail and by rowers in towing dinghies to come alongside the long, stone dock, and wide doors in the *sides* of the ships had been opened and long gangways run out. Up these great ramps the horses and ponies had been led by the warriors and into the rows of narrow stalls, as many as four hundred steeds in all, their number spread over the three horse decks, the associated warriors to be clustered into but one. Wagons and wains had then been towed up, and the warriors brought their goods last of all.

It took three days altogether to simply lade all ships with their complement of horses and ponies and warriors and wagons and supplies, but they sailed on the very next tide, just after sunrise the following day. And when they reached the waters of the Avagon Sea, easterly they turned, the swift Dragonships surrounding the wallowing Gothonian vessels as would paladins protect dowager queens.

A sevenday or so it would take them to reach the Ironwater, given a favorable wind. And so they fared easterly and easterly some more, to finally swing to the north, the goal of the great ships the port of Adeo just this side of the Ironwater, while the goal of the Dragonships lay beyond.

Three days they sailed through the blue waters of the Avagon Sea, the wind brisk and following and the weather holding fair. In the distance larboard of the fleet lay the coast of Pellar, the land slowly slipping hindward as the great ships and their escort plowed on. Often the Warrows would gather in the bow of their huge weltering craft and watch the dolphins glide through the pellucid blue waters 'neath.

In the afternoon of the fourth day out, they were joined at the bowsprit rail by Volki and Gildor and Riatha. For long moments all watched as the dolphins swam before and under and 'round the prow, now and again falling back to come leaping across the low ripples and waves pushed outward by the bow.

"Would that we could play as do they," said Linnet, her voice wistful.

"They know nought of war," said Volki.

Riatha looked at Volki. "But they do, DelfLord. —Know of war, that is."

"They do?" said Tipperton, his eyes widening.

Riatha smiled. "Indeed, for at times they do battle with sharks and other predators, especially when protecting their young. Ask Aravan; he knows."

Volki growled. "But they do not wield weapons and great engines of siege and other such. It is not as if sharks come knocking at their door, as did the Foul Folk knock at ours."

Rynna frowned. "How so, DelfLord?"

"With a great ram, they came, and battered for entry to Kraggen-cor."

Gildor raised an eyebrow. "Great ram?"

"Aye. Ogru-driven and under a shield of brass and iron cladding, on wheels it came, its iron head shaped like a mighty fist, mounted on the end of a massive wooden beam," replied Volki, clenching his left hand and thrusting it forward to demonstrate.

"Ai," groaned Gildor. "An evil thing is that ram. Whelm they call it, though I name it Vile."

"You know of it?" asked Tipperton.

Gildor nodded, as did Riatha, and Gildor said, "Many a gate has it sundered and many a city has fallen before its hard knock. Dark was the day long past when it tore through the gates of Duellin."

"It was on Atala, neh?" asked Tip.

Riatha nodded.

Tip glanced at Gildor, then back to Riatha. "Were you there when the ram tore through the gates?"

Riatha shook her head. "Nay. Though Réin, my mother, was"—Riatha touched the hilt of her jade-handled sword—"and she bore Dunamís, the blade forged in Duellin by Dwynfor, the greatest swordsmith of all."

Volki grunted and nodded. "Even we Châkka hold Dwynfor to be the master of all bladesmiths."

"But what of Whelm and the gate?" asked Nix.

"And who attacked Duellin and why?" added Farly.

Riatha's silver-grey eyes darkened. "'Twas Modru, his lackeys that is."

"I knew it," gritted Volki.

"Argh," growled Dinly. "Modru again. Someday someone will kill Modru, and that will be that."

Gildor shook his head. "Be not so certain, my friend, for monsters are always aborning . . . or are being fashioned by monsters of their own."

"Monsters or not," said Farly, looking at Riatha, "again I ask: why would Modru attack Duellin? Just out of pure spite?"

Riatha made a small negating gesture. "Although spite may have been part of it, it is not all. This is what my mother has said:

"Nigh the beginning of the First Era, Modru came unto Duellin to purchase blades from Dwynfor—axes, swords, lances, pikes, and the like—but Dwynfor would not craft him any, for even then Modru was among the shunned. And so Modru turned to other smiths, Gilian not the least, yet she nor any within the city would aid the Black Mage.

"Enraged and swearing vengeance, Modru sailed away. And some centuries later, there came the invasion of the isle by Spaunen and Rovers and men from far-off Jûng. And among the engines they brought with them was Whelm.

"Boom! it knocked for entry, Boom! and Boom! and Boom! Driven by Trolls, at last the heavy gates of Duellin fell before the sinister fist.

"And the Rûpt and Rovers and Jûngarians poured through the breech.

"Hard-fought was the battle, every street, every building, every stride yielded in nought but furious struggle. Even so, the Spaunen and Kistanians and men of Jûng slowly gained sway, for they far outnumbered the defenders of Duellin.

"And they hammered their way toward the armories of Dwynfor and Gilian and other bladesmiths of renown.

"Three-quarters of the city was lost ere the Lian of Darda Immer arrived, and together with the defenders of Duellin they hurled the invaders back into the sea.

"And they sailed away defeated and took the mighty fist with them.

"So says Réin, Lian Guardian of that time; so says Réin my mother."

Silence fell upon the gathering, broken only by the creak of rope and timber and the *shssh* of water along the hull. Finally Beau said, "Tell me, DelfLord Volki, did Whelm hammer down the doors of Drimmen-deeve?"

Volki shook his head. "Nay. Though battered to their limit, the great gates of *daûn* yet stand."

"Ai," declared Gildor, "mighty are the workings of the Drimma to withstand such an evil token of power."

"Châkka cor," said Volki.

Rynna looked at Tipperton, her eyebrows raised. "Dwarven might," translated the buccan.

"Where is Whelm now?" asked Linnet. "Destroyed, I hope."

Volki shrugged. "I know not where lies Whelm, for the Squam took it away when they were routed. Yet when we caught up with them, Whelm was not at hand. I think it lies abandoned and lost among the crags of the Grimwalls."

Again they fell to silence, wind snapping the canvas above. But at last Gildor touched the hilts of his sword and long-knife and said, "Bale and Bane were forged in Duellin."

Riatha drew her jade-handled sword from its tooled green scabbard and said, "As was Dunamís." The shadowy blade glittered as if filled with stars.

Volki's eyes widened and he gasped, "Dark silveron! Your sword is made of dark silveron, Lady Riatha."

Beau looked at Tip in puzzlement and Tipperton shrugged, and Gildor, seeing the exchange, said, "Shadow starsilver is the rarest of all metals, my friends."

Volki nodded. "There are veins of starsilver in Kraggen-cor, and this is what Modru was after when he set siege on my realm."

"He wanted starsilver to forge his own blades?" asked Nix.

Volki turned up a hand. "After hearing the tale of his attempt at Duellin, it seems most likely, for no other metal yields such mighty weapons as does silveron, and silveron lies deep within my domain." Volki glanced with reverence at Riatha's blade, and added, "But only now and again do we find a nugget of the dark, and never any vein. Keep care of that weapon, my lady, for it is precious beyond all compare."

Riatha nodded and sheathed the blade.

Gildor sighed. "Alas, no more will Atalarian blades be forged in Duellin, for the isle is now gone into the sea."

After a moment Rynna asked, "Lady Riatha, was Talar the only one to escape?"

Riatha shook her head. "There were others, though precious few. Talar said he came across one in Gothan: Othran was his name, a Seer, a Mage. He was terribly damaged, yet refused aid, for he said he had a quest to fulfill and he was borne away east toward Rian. What was the quest, Othran did not say, and Talar did not know."

"My goodness," said Alver, "a quest, you say. I wonder how important it could have been to refuse aid and all."

Ere any could answer or speculate, orders were called out and sailors ran forth on the deck, unbelaying ropes and haling on them and swinging the yardarms around, all to a purpose—the changing of course—for they had finally rounded the Pellarion Cape and now swung north for the Ironwater.

The evening skies were dark with scudding clouds when the ships finally dropped anchor at the abandoned port of Adeo, its long stone pier crumbling in ruin, though it was sturdy enough for the task at hand. The Warrows stood adeck and watched as the first two great vessels were maneuvered to the dock, while a frigid wind blew steadily out of the north and east.

Standing nearby, Volki growled, "It is an ill wind which blows from Garia."

Beau took a deep breath. "You don't suppose it's Modru now, do you, raising a winter storm? They say he's master of the cold, you know."

Volki turned up his hands but otherwise did not reply.

And the Warrows all, they looked at the sky and shivered with a chill not born of the wind and drew their cloaks tightly 'round.

And still the raw wind blew, driving darkling clouds above.

It was Year's End Day, the last day of December, the last day of the two thousand one hundred ninety-eighth year of the Second Era of Mithgar. On the morrow their own ship would be haled to the dock, and their steeds and goods unladed . . . on the morrow, Year's Start Day, the first of January, two thousand one hundred ninety-nine, the very first day of the fifth deadly year of a great and terrible war.

36

*I*n all it took five more days to off-load the horses and ponies and warriors and wains and supplies from the ships. And all the time the chill wind blew from Garia, yet no snow flew on its wings, though the sky was laden with heavy clouds and a foul stench rode on the air, smelling of sulfer and slag and bearing an iron tang like that of fresh-spilled blood.

" 'Tis the smell of Hèl's Crucible, or so I am told," said Talar on the morn of the first day, the Elf standing at the ship's taffrail and watching the off-loading.

"No wonder the foe facing King Blaine refuse to retreat any farther," said Dinly, his nose wrinkled in disgust, "what with that reek awaiting them."

" 'Tis more than just a mere reek, wee one," said Riatha, leaning on the railing at her brother's side.

"More than a reek?"

"Aye. 'Tis the smell of death shouldst thou become ensnared within those foul vapors with no clean air to breathe."

"Oh my," said Dinly, turning to Rynna. As she nodded in agreement, Dinly added, "I must have fallen asleep when you told us of that."

"Come on, bucco," said Nix, gesturing at a nearby great coil of rope, "sit with me and I'll tell you again what Ryn said, but you must promise me you'll remain awake this time."

As the two buccen moved away, the others turned to watch

as another huge, weltering craft was maneuvered to the crumbling stone dock.

Finally all the ships were unladed, but even so each horse or pony had to wait a full day after reaching dry land to overcome the effects of the wallowing ships, for as Wagonleader Bwen amid her curses said, "There is something about boats which steeds do not like, and a day or so is needed for them to regain the touch of their hooves."

It was on the morn of this sixth day of the new year as the last of the off-loaded horses and ponies rested and regained their hooves that Aravan and an escort took up mounts unladed in the days before and rode away. Northwesterly up the Sea Road they went along the banks of the Ironwater and toward the High King's camp some thirty leagues hence. There they would tell King Blaine that all was ready for the plan to go forth.

And still the Fjordlander and Jutlander Dragonships rode at anchor, their platforms yet mounted thwartwise wale to wale. Yet on the morrow the swift craft would weigh anchor and sail a half mile north to the mouth of the river and turn northwesterly and in, heading upstream for the chosen place.

On the morrow as well, would Silverleaf's legion ride along the Sea Road to the rendezvous point.

But this night in the abandoned port city of Adeo would Silverleaf's legion wait.

In the middle of the night Beau startled awake, sitting up with a jolt. Beside him Linnet stirred and opened her eyes. "What is it, love?" she asked.

"I dunno," said Beau, looking about the encampment, with its low-banked fires and shadowy shapes scattered among the abandoned structures. "I thought I heard . . ."

Beau lay back down. "Hullo, there it is again."

"What?"

"Put your ear to the earth, love."

Linnet's eyes widened as she laid her head down and listened to the ground. From within there came a faint, deep knelling, rhythmic, patterned, as if someone were delving . . . or signalling.

Beau raised up on one elbow. "Do you know if there are any Groaning Stones about?"

Without taking her ear from the ground, Linnet said, "This is not a Stone talking. It sounds more like— Oh my, it's gone."

Beau pressed his own ear to the earth and listened a moment to the uneasy silence of the land, then said, "Well, it wasn't the drum of running hooves either, for I've heard them in the

ground, and they sound more like a thudding than this did."
Beau frowned and then cocked an eyebrow. "I say, you don't
suppose someone's digging a tunnel, do you?"

Linnet stood. "Let's get Rynna and go talk with DelfLord
Volki. He would know the sound of delving."

"It had a cadence, you say?"

"Yes, DelfLord," replied Linnet.

"And it was a deep knelling and not a tapping?"

Linnet nodded.

Volki turned to Bragga and Helki, two of his Châkka coun-
sellors and said, "Utruni," his word a statement, not a question.
They both nodded in agreement.

Linnet looked at Beau, her eyes wide. "Stone Giants?"

Volki grunted. "Aye, Stone Giants . . . for what you have
described is what we call Utruni signalling. It is much like
hammer-signalling through stone—"

"Hammer-signalling?" asked Rynna, Tip at her side.

"Aye. We Châkka often signal each other by hammer tapping
on stone, though in this case I deem it to be Stone Giants sending the messages. We at times hear the knells sounding within
the stone of our Châkkaholts."

"Can you read these signals of theirs?" asked Tipperton.

Regretfully, Volki shook his head.

"But why are they here?" asked Linnet.

"There is no guarantee they are nearby," said Bragga, running
a hand through his black hair. "Utruni signals can come from
afar, carried league upon league by the living stone below."

Volki nodded, his dark eyes casting back gleams in the firelight. "Some tell that the knells of Stone Giants can sound
across the whole of the world."

Tip sighed and looked at Beau. "I was hoping that they'd
come to help."

Helki stroked his grey beard. "Ah, would that it were, for it is
said that evil flees when the Earthmasters are nigh."

Beau frowned. "Earthmasters? Utruni? Stone Giants?"

Helki nodded.

"Let's hope that evil does flee, then," said Beau.

Helki shrugged. "It may be nought but an eld Châkias' tale."

Rynna frowned and glanced at Tip. "Old wives' tale," he supplied.

Rynna's eyes flashed with ire and she turned on Helki. "Eld
Châkias' tale, indeed. Hear the words of *this* old wife, Lord
Helki, and heed: many a tale has a basis in fact, told by old
wives or not."

Helki held up his hands in surrender as Volki broke out in

loud laughter. Finally, Volki mastered his humor and said to
Rynna, "Ah, commander, are you certain you are not a Châkian
in disguise?"

Of a sudden the storm left her eyes, and Rynna grinned.
"From what Tip tells me, I'm too short, though perhaps not by
much."

"Ah, but just as wonderfully beautiful," said Tip.

Volki started, as did Helki and Bragga, and a stern look came
over Volki's face and he said, "Châk-Sol Tipperton, we do not
speak of such."

Tipperton frowned in puzzlement and glanced at Rynna, but
nodded in assent.

A momentary uncomfortable silence followed, broken by
Beau, who yawned, then said, "Well, Stone Giants or not, for
me it's bed."

Volki nodded. "Indeed, we all need rest, for we ride on the
morrow at dawn."

"But what about the Utruni?" asked Linnet.

Volki turned up his hands. "What would you have us do, Lady
Linnet?"

Linnet looked at Beau and then Rynna and Tip. "Well . . .
uh . . . hmm. I suppose there is nothing we *can* do one way or
another."

Volki grinned. "Exactly so."

At last dawn came on this the seventh day of the new year,
and the Dragonships raised sails and set out for the mouth of
the Ironwater, and the column of warriors mounted up to ride,
Dwarves and Warrows on their ponies, Elves on fiery steeds,
and Baeron on their massive horses of war, Bwen and her wagons coming last of all.

Northwesterly they fared up the tradeway known as the Sea
Road, a route with one end anchored at the harbor of Adeo and
the other terminus at Dael in Riamon, with the city of Rhondor
at the far end of Hèl's Crucible nought but the first port of call.

Northwesterly they went and northwesterly, at a leisurely
gait, the fleet of Dragonships now riding upstream alongside,
keeping pace, Elven scouts on their fiery steeds riding far to the
flank and fore and rear. And although Commander Rynna had
objected, saying that her Warrow scouts should be out as well,
Silverleaf had pointed out that—unlike the hill country of the
opposite shore—the terrain on this side of the river was rela-
tively flat, where fleet horses would serve best. And so the Warrows rode their ponies among the Dwarven host.

All day they maintained the deliberate pace, and when

evening fell they had ridden some twenty-five miles altogether—halfway to their goal.

The Dragonships pulled into the southern shore and the
legion made camp for the night.

And still a chill wind blew out of Garia, pushing grey clouds
overhead.

Again at dawn they rode northwesterly, and when evening
fell they had reached the point on the Ironwater chosen by Silverleaf and Aravan weeks past, for here the riverbanks rose up
steeply some eight feet or so on either side, and the river itself
flowed gently a thousand or so feet wide.

By hooded lanterns and stealth in the night, the first of the
Dragonships—a Jutlander craft—drew parallel to the shore and
moored at the nearside upjutting bank, and the upper platform
was eased out to meet the land, the great wooden screws set to
hold it fast to the platform aboard the ship, while at the land-
ward end capped piles were driven through the holes and into
the earth to anchor all to the shore. Then a second Dragonship—a Fjordlander—was moored alongside the first, and its
upper platform slid out and fixed between, bridging from ship to
ship, the heavy wooden screws holding it fast. The third Dragonship—a Jutlander—drew alongside the second, and once
again the upper platform was fixed to span across. And so it
went into the night, Fjordlanders and Jutlanders alternating
craft and plying oars against the gentle flow of the current to
anchor a boat-length or so upstream and then pay out the moor-
ing line to ease back and set the ship in place, with Dragonship
after Dragonship positioning alongside one another and platform after platform bridging the gaps between.

Long did the Warrows watch, but then Rynna commanded that
they all get some rest. "Remember, sometime in darkness ere the
dawn, we will ride across, for there's twisting hill country beyond,
where once again we will scout, and I would have a rested 'army'
of worth rather than exhausted Warrows of burden."

And so, they took to their bedrolls, sleep coming quickly, and
none of the Warrows heard the faint knelling deep within the
earth, though Volki and his advisors did. They looked at one
another and nodded in agreement—it was Utruni signalling
indeed.

Just after mid of night the final ship—a Fjordlander craft—
was drawn into place, and an extra platform was brought forward and anchored to the land of the far bank by capped pilings
driven deeply.

In all it had taken thirty-six Dragonships and seventy-three platforms to span from shore to shore, eighteen of them Jutlander craft, eighteen Fjordlander. The remaining Dragonships rode at anchor, ready to fill in should there be a need. And in the dark of the night, Fjordlanders and Jutlanders stood on the far bank, gripping their axes and their sharp-spiked, round wooden shields, warding the foothold in enemy territory even as the legion rode by the light of hooded lanterns across the Dragonship pontoon bridge and to the opposite shore.

First crossed Dylvana and Lian, able to see in darkness better than Dwarves or Warrows or men, the Elves on their fiery steeds, swords unsheathed, spears abristle, bows nocked with arrows in hand, some Guardians in gleaming breastplate, but most in nought but leather.

Following the Elves came the Dwarves on their ponies, armed with crossbows and axes and war hammers at the ready, and armored in black-iron chain mail, with black-iron helms on their heads. They would set a perimeter ward inside that of the Elves. And across with them rode the Warrows.

Then came the Baeron on their massive horses, the huge men with their maces and morning stars and flails, and they began riding across to take up a perimeter ward with the others.

And by this time it was dawn, and Warrows and Elven scouts rode into the jagged hills beyond.

Yet just as the last of the Baeron started across, there sounded from the hills ahead a resonant horn cry, and over a craggy mound came Tipperton flying, his black-oxen horn sounding the alarm. From other points came ponies at a gallop, Warrows crouching low, Elves riding behind.

And in the hills aft there sounded flat horns blowing and thousands of voices yawling—*Rakka! Rakka!*—and over the crests and down came charging afoot a flood of sun-darkened men dressed in black on black—pantaloons and quilted vests and *branîs* overrobes and turbans with shawls flying out behind. Like a dark tide they ran down the slopes, howling and brandishing scimitars and *tabar* axes and short spears, *dhals* and *sipars* in hand, the small, round shields painted black, a clenched crimson fist centermost. Down they hurtled, some sounding the charge with trumps made of rams' horns while others waved red flags, each crimson banner marked with a clenched left fist of black. And howling *Rakka! Rakka! Rakka!* . . . they raised their weapons to strike as they rushed toward the defenders below.

In through the perimeter flew the Warrows, Elven scouts behind. The Baeron, yet mounted upon their massive horses, drew together at the ready and Urel and Durul called out to Silverleaf, yet what they said, Tipperton haling his pony to a halt did not hear.

And Dwarves and Lian and Dylvana, and Jutlanders and Fjordlanders braced for the onslaught.

Even as the Fists of Rakka charged down onto the flats, a sleet of arrows and crossbow bolts flew from the legion to hurtle into oncoming foe, sun-darkened men falling, pierced through, but undaunted the enemy came on. Another hail flew forth, and more of the foe fell, but still the men of Thyra and Sarain and Hurn shouted their war cries and plunged on. Silverleaf signalled to Larana and she blew her bugle, and the Baeron, now in formation, spurred their horses forward, the massive chargers flying in a wide wedge through the perimeter and toward the oncoming enemy, Elves and Dwarves and Fjordlanders and Jutes afoot running after the great galloping steeds.

And with clash and clang and shouts of *Adon!* and *Elwydd!* and *Garlon!* and *Fyrra!* and *Rakka!* the two armies collided, the great horses of the Baeron smashing into and through and over the ranks of the foe, though riders and horses were felled, brought down by spear and axe and blade.

Swords rived, axes hewed, spears pierced, mace and flail and hammer smashed and crushed. Blood and viscera and bone and brain flew wide, amid cries and shrieks and shouts of rage.

And from the rear flew arrows and sling bullets, sent winging by the Warrows now afoot. And everywhere they flew, enemies fell, yet there were only eight of the Wee Folk and myriad of the foe.

Though the Baeron on their horses had smashed through the enemy and beyond, still the Allies were outnumbered and were hurled back. Hindward they reeled, back toward the bridgehead, their perimeter growing ever shorter as they drew in toward the span. And the wee Warrows fell back and back, yet winging deadly slings and arrows. But then they had to cease: the perimeter became too crowded with allies for buccen and dammen to safely loose missiles past. Yet as the legion fell back, the tighter became the perimeter, the more difficult to break through, and the enemy's advance slowed and slowed, though the fierce struggle went on.

From the rear of the foe the Baeron again formed up and charged, and smashed into the enemy ranks, laying death about with their maces and flails and hammers, shattering skulls and arms, crushing necks, smashing ribs, and the horses flailed about with deadly hooves and trampled on any who fell.

Dwarven axes hewed, hammers bashed, and men fell screaming, and Fjordlander and Jutlander axes hewed as well, the spiked, round shields slamming into men to pierce the enemy through.

Elven spears stabbed over the heads of the Dwarves to take the enemy down, and gleaming Elven long-knives and swords—keen beyond reckoning, especially one of dark silveron—cut through sipar and dhal to hew flesh and blood and bone, arms and hands and heads flying wide, viscera spilling out.

Yet so, too, did the blades of the Fists of Rakka hew, tabars and scimitars and spears hacking and hewing and piercing. Dwarves fell, men, too, along with Elves cut down, and Tipperton and Beau and Rynna and Linnet wept to see such slaughter, as did Farly and Nix and Alver and Dinly, the Warrows ineffective now that they couldn't loose arrow or bullet at all.

And still the sun-darkened men drove inward, the Allies pressed back and back, some to come in among the gathered horses and ponies of Elf and Dwarf and Warrow. The steeds squealed and milled in fright, though some of the Elven horses lashed out with hoof and laid about with teeth, striking among the enemy, though now and again the one attacked was an ally instead.

"If we can get to ponies," shouted Tipperton, "we can lead steeds across the bridge and out of harm's way."

"You heard him," called Rynna. "Find a pony to ride." Warrows sprang forward and darted and dodged down among milling horses and horselings and fighting men and Dwarves and Elves, and they caught up ponies and leapt astride. But even as the Warrows did so, among the Allies came racing black-robed foe, a wedge of the enemy plunging for the bridge, lit oil lanterns in hand.

"They're going to burn the bridge!" shouted Tipperton, spurring forward, but only Beau and Alver heard him, those two buccen galloping after.

Even as he rode, Tipperton strung an arrow to bow, and he felled one of the Fists of Rakka, as a sling bullet took another in the back of the head, crashing into skull and brain, the black-robed man to tumble, his lantern smashing on the ground, flaming oil bursting outward.

Tipperton loosed a second arrow, and another man fell dead, even as Alver's shaft slammed into the back of yet one more. But, staggering, the arrow-struck man turned and triggered his heavy crossbow—"Alver, look out!" cried Tipperton—the bolt to crash into Alver's chest and knock him over the rear cantle to crash unto the ground, his pony to run on without him.

Tipperton screamed in rage and nocked an arrow, but it was

Beau's sling bullet that hammered into the man's eye and slew him.

Now the remaining men hurled their lanterns toward the bridge, some to smash onto wooden platforms, others to crash into Dragonships, still others missing altogether to plummet into the water below.

Though not burning with the intensity of Dwarven liquid fire, still oil was aflame on the span and in two of the boats below, and black-robed men stood athwart the path.

As Tipperton flew another arrow into the Fists of Rakka, from the far shore and westward there came a resonant horn cry, and the buccan turned to see—

—riders galloping, thousands of riders in the near distance, men and Elves racing along the Sea Road from the west, and in the lead rode Aravan and a redheaded warrior in scarlet-and-gold armor as well as a warrior with a white horsehair gaud flying out behind, and a host coming after.

"Aravan! Linde!" Tipperton cried, and he raised his own black-oxen horn to his lips and blew a ringing blast, and it was answered by Linde's pealing horn. And athwart the bridge the black-robed men quailed back to hear such a sound. And they turned to see the oncoming host, and fled back toward their own.

As Beau dismounted and ran to Alver, Tipperton pursued the fleeing burn squad and felled man after man, and now he was joined in the slaughter by Rynna and Linnet and Farly and Nix and Dinly, all winging arrows into the running men, and not a one survived.

Yet still the battle raged at the fore, Baeron and Fjordlanders and Jutlanders and Elves and Dwarves all crushing and slashing and hacking and piercing and felling black-robed men. But the Fists of Rakka gave as good as they got and slaughtered allies in turn.

But then from beyond the crest of the hills there sounded the cry of rams' horns, and at this signal the enemy struggled to break free, fighting to get clear of the melee. And Silverleaf signalled to Larana, and she blew the call to disengage, and men and Elves backed away in response, though Larana had to sound the call several times ere the Dwarves relinquished the fight.

And even as they disengaged, thundering across the bridge and through the flames came Aravan and Linde and the red-headed man in scarlet and gold, the host riding after.

And still the Fists of Rakka fled the field.

Again the legion flew arrows and bolts into the fleeing

enemy, the Warrows' shafts quite deadly, as were the arrows cast from Silverleaf's white-bone bow.

"My Lord High King," cried Silverleaf as Aravan and Linde and the redheaded man came riding nigh, "shall we pursue?"

Tipperton's mouth fell open. *So this is King Blaine, at last!*

He saw a slender man perhaps in his fifties, his hair flaming red, his eyes a grim steel-blue. He looked to be some six feet tall, though mounted on a horse as he was it was difficult to say. He was accoutered in scarlet-and-gold armor, and a golden griffin was embossed on his crimson shield, and gripped in his hand was a scarlet morning star.

"Nay, Vanidar, for the enemy pacing us on this side of the Ironwater is not far behind."

The enemy on this *side?* Tipperton looked at Rynna and mouthed [The Southerlings?]

She nodded in agreement.

And still the High King's host thundered across the bridge and through the fire, even as Fjordlanders and Jutes sought to extinguish the flames.

"Then, my lord, we should take up arms and make ready to meet them at last," said Silverleaf.

"Aye, Vanidar, do prepare. And while I deploy the host as it comes across this splendid bridge of yours, send scouts to see to the foe's whereabouts."

"We stand ready, my lord," said Rynna.

Turning to see who had spoken, "Waerlings!" called the King, his eyes widening, seeing the Wee Folk for the first time.

Linde and Aravan turned as well, and Linde said, "Ho, Sir Tipperton, I thought I recognized your horn."

The King's eyes widened again. "Sir Tipperton? The one who aided in the liberation of Mineholt North and delivered the coin to Agron?"

Tipperton nodded but added, "With Beau and Phais and Loric and Bekki, my lord, as well as with a host of others."

"And did you not aid Mage Imongar to slay the Gargon?"

" 'Twas her hand loosed the spear, my lord. I did but little to aid."

The High King smiled and said, " 'Tis not the way she tells it, Sir Tipperton, but regardless, well done." Then his eye took in the other Warrows, and he turned to Silverleaf. "These are your scouts, Lord Vanidar? I could not ask for better."

"Nay, thou couldst not," called a voice, and Tipperton looked up to see Phais and Loric riding nigh. The Dara and Alor leapt down and embraced the wee Warrow, and looked upon Rynna in wonder, for she had been said to be slain.

Yet war has little time for reunions, and ere other than mere greetings could be said—

"Aye, my lord," replied Silverleaf, "the Waerlinga are indeed worthy scouts, yet in this task I deem swift horses are needed rather than quick ponies."

Nix started to protest, but Rynna silenced him with a glance and said, "Nevertheless, Alor Vanidar, though Hyree and Kistan and Chabba come along the river, still someone needs keep track of the Fists of Rakka, and they fled into the twisting ways of the hills yon, and who better than we Warrows to keep pace with them therein?"

Silverleaf inclined his head. "So be it, Commander Rynna, send thy scouts after. Yet heed: as to thee, I would have thee remain in camp, for should we get the chance ere the foe arrives, a council of captains must needs be called."

Rynna's face fell, yet she nodded her agreement and turned to the other Warrows. "Tipperton, take Linnet with you. Nix, you ride with Dinly. Farly will take— I say, where is Alver?"

"He's dead," said Beau, just then coming in among the Warrows. "Slain by crossbow bolt."

Tipperton's heart plunged. *I had forgotten entirely. Oh, Alver, Alver.*

Tears welled in Rynna's eyes, and she angrily wiped them away.

"I can ride with Farly," said Beau.

Rynna shook her head. "No, Beau, you will need be here to help with the wounded. Farly will go with Nix and Dinly. Nix, ride west of Tipperton and—"

"But what about Alver?" asked Dinly. "Are we to just leave him lying while we ride off to—"

"I'll see that he's—" Beau began—

—but Rynna said, "This is war, Dinly. Remember Springwater, and know we cannot hope to escape unscathed. There have been and may yet be times when we can do nought but ride away from the dead . . . or even from the wounded. For you this is one of those times."

Dinly sighed and reluctantly nodded.

Rynna looked at the ground and then said, "Replenish your quivers and take that which is needed to scout. Dinly, you will ride back and report as soon as there is aught of significance to recount."

Tipperton stepped to Rynna and kissed her gently, then turned to Linnet as she embraced Beau. "Let's go."

Linnet kissed her own buccaran and hugged Rynna, then strode off with Tip toward the supply wagons on the far shore, Dinly, Nix, and Farly following.

And so, even as Elven scouts—Darai Vail and Arylin, Alori Flandrena and Elon—set forth along the shoreline upstream, Tipperton and Linnet and Farly and Dinly took to the craggy hills, while behind, Rynna and Beau stood and watched them ride over the crests and beyond.

And still the High King's host poured across the bridge, their numbers forty thousand in all. Even riding swiftly and in pairs, it would take until sundown and perhaps past for the full of the army to reach the eastern shore.

Last to cross would be a brigade of Red Hills Dwarves, their ponies having been outstripped in the race down the Ironwater to the Dragonboat bridge. Even so, even though no enemy was in sight, still DelfLord Okar and his fierce band stood ready to fight.

Even as the King's army crossed the span to take up positions to await the coming of the Lakh of Hyree and the Rovers of Kistan and the Askars of Chabba, the wounded members of Silverleaf's legion were borne to a place where Beau and other healers could tend the stricken. Later, after the King's host had all crossed the bridge, then the wounded would be carried to the far side of the Ironwater to be tended there, the worst of them to be carted down to the port of Adeo and laded aboard the ships.

A count of the wounded and dead was taken, and altogether the Fists of Rakka had slain over nine hundred warriors in Silverleaf's legion: two hundred fifty-six Baeron, one hundred forty-three Lian, one hundred twenty-eight Dylvana, one hundred forty-four Dwarves, one hundred ninety-seven Fjordlanders, one hundred eighty-two Jutes . . . and one Warrow. Another eighteen hundred or so allies had suffered grievous wounds and would no longer engage in battle in the near days to come.

As to the black-robed men, altogether twelve hundred had been slain outright, and another three thousand had been felled with deep wounds, and they lay afield and moaned in agony and called out in a strange tongue. These latter were questioned by the King's men, but even though suffering dreadful injury they yielded no useful information, for although hissing in distress, still they called upon Rakka to strike these infidels down and to grant themselves a glorious death in the service of Rakka, for by doing so they would win an eternal place beyond the sky in the paradise of *Jânní*.

And whelmed as they were by wounded allies, Beau and Melor and Aris and the other healers had time to tend only their own; the injured foe would have to wait.

* * *

"Why did they disengage?"

Vanidar looked 'round the hastily called captains' council—all captains having been summoned across the bridge to advise the King. Vanidar's gaze slid past DelfLord and coron and chieftain and skipskaptein and kapitän and field marshal and the like, and past Mage Farrin and High King Blaine himself to finally settle on Commander Rynna, for 'twas she who had asked. "A mystery that," said Silverleaf, "and I know not why they withdrew, for they had us outnumbered, and were driving us back and ever back." Silverleaf turned to King Blaine. "I deem they could have won the bridgehead and destroyed the way across ere you, my lord, arrived. Yet they withdrew, regardless."

"A tight fist is harder to crush than a loosely clasped one," growled DelfLord Volki. "And we were becoming a tight fist. Regardless, though, they would not have broken through the Châkka at the bridgehead itself."

Across the circle, DelfLord Okar clenched a fist in agreement.

"Perhaps thou art right, Lord Volki," replied Coron Ruar, "yet I, too, deem it a mystery they did not smash on through and tear down the bridge."

Volki snorted but otherwise did not reply.

"They did try to burn the bridge," said Rynna.

"It was but a small oil fire, neh?" asked Farrin, representing the Mages. At Rynna's nod, he added, "Not likely to have caused much damage unless it had been let burn."

Coron Eiron said, "I agree, but they withdrew ere then. Nay, I deem the Fists of Rakka made only a minor effort to take the bridge from us ere they ran unto the hills."

"Tell that to my slain warriors," gritted Chieftain Urel, the great Baeran scowling.

"That the Fists of Rakka were even in these hills came as a surprise," said King Blaine, "for I thought them in Alban still. Could they have marched across Garia and then Hèl's Crucible and by happenstance have been here?"

Those in council looked at one another, but none had an answer.

"That the Fists of Rakka were at this place—or even that they ran—is not the only mystery here," declared Field Marshal Burke, the leader of the men of Wellen, as he peered northwesterly through the glum day. "Where are the Hyrinians and Kistanians and Chabbains? Shouldn't they have come by now?"

All eyes turned to King Blaine. "We must needs wait on the scouts to report back."

"Even though the Fists of Rakka have withdrawn, and even though the Lakh and Rovers and the Askars are yet to arrive, still much of the day remains," said Chieftain Durul, "and so we must expect an attack. Too, in the night there is every chance they will try to take the bridge, either to use it themselves or to destroy it outright."

King Blaine nodded and gestured at the riders yet crossing the bridge. "Aye, but when my host is finally across, the foe will not find it easy to win through forty thousand men."

Silverleaf smiled at Okar's remark and added, "Thy numbers are grown beyond that, my lord, for the legion I command is at your hest as well."

Volki growled and said, "Forty thousand *men*? *Men*? You forget, King Blaine, in addition to *men*, Châkka and Dylvana and Lian and Baeron serve as well."

Rynna glared at Volki, and he quickly added, "Waerans, too."

DelfLord Okar said, "And the Châkka of the Red Hills, who have been with you since Gûnnaring Gap, several Lian from there also."

"And Magekind," said Farrin. "Our numbers are small, but you must add us in."

King Blaine laughed and threw up his hands. "I stand corrected by each and every one of you, for all Free Folk serve"—his eye singled out Rynna—"Waerlings not the least. Aye, the foe will not find it easy to win past us to the bridge."

"Perhaps not aland, my lord," said Skipskaptein Arnson, leader of the Fjordlanders, "but there is yet the water. I deem we should set craft upstream and down, for the enemy may try to swim the river and hole the hulls or send down floats afire."

"Ja," replied Kapitän Dolf. "The upstream side guard we will. The side downstream yours to guard it will be."

Arnson glared at the Jutlander, but nodded in agreement.

Blaine canted his head in assent. "That settled, the rest will be according to plan, lest someone has a new tactic to discuss."

Farrin cleared his throat. "This wind, my lord, I remind you: it has the taint of darkness."

Rynna's eyes widened. *Taint of darkness? Oh my.*

Silverleaf spoke: "Modru?"

Farrin shook his head. "I know not, for Modru and I have never crossed paths."

"Know you yet what it means?" asked the King.

Farrin shook his head. "If it is Modru, then mayhap a storm is brewing, but I cannot be certain."

Blaine frowned. "Then there's nought we can do until we face *whatever* the wind may bring."

"Clearly, my lord, we can prepare for a blizzard," said Phais, looking back along the Sea Road, where a thousand supply wagons and their escort now trundled into view. "In yon train are spare warm garments and blankets for those who need such." She gestured at the hills nearby. "And should a tempest come, yon crags will provide shelter of a sort."

"Agreed," said King Blaine. "My lords, make certain each warrior in your command is well prepared for a blizzard should one come riding on this tainted wind."

A murmur muttered about the council circle, but then Blaine held up his hand and asked, "Is there aught else we need discuss?"

Silence fell among the captains as the High King gazed to each and every one. When he looked at Volki, the DelfLord said, "We need deal with the dead; honor is due to each."

Silverleaf sighed. "Aye. Collect them on the far side of the river. But any honors due are to come after the fighting is done."

Volki nodded, as did they all, for in war the dead must wait for the living.

Even as the Dwarf agreed, a runner came to the circle. "Milord, a rider approaches!"

"Whereaway?" asked the King, standing.

"From the northwest along the river, this side."

"One of the scouts?"

"I know not, milord."

"Then we shall wait."

And still the King's army rode across the bridge.

Within moments Elon rode in among the host and was directed to the council. The Dylvana scout dismounted and said, "My lords, the Hyrinians, Kistanians, and Chabbains have turned northeasterly into the hills—"

Rynna's heart leapt to her throat. *The hills are where my Tipperton is, and Linnet and Nix and Farly and Dinly.*

"Toward Hèl's Crucible?" interjected Captain Donal of Gelen, a frown on his ruddy face.

"Aye," replied Elon.

Arth of the Wilderland, leader of the remnant of the Beacontor muster, grunted in surprise and brushed back a stray lock of red hair from his youthful brow, then asked, "Scouts yet follow them?"

"Darai Vail and Arylin and Alor Flandrena yet shadow, but there is more to report: glad tidings."

"Glad tidings?" asked Silverleaf.

"Aye, for no more than two leagues hence, allies come along this side of the Ironwater: King Loden of Riamon and DelfLord

Bekki of Mineholt North bring their forces to join with ours: nine hundred Drimma and some two thousand men."

"Hai!" called King Blaine. "Most welcome will they be."

"On this side of the river, you say?" asked Lugar of Trellinath.

Elon turned to the marshal, elderly yet hale. "They crossed at Rhondor to harass the foe and turn their attention away, hoping to give King Blaine's army a chance to cross over."

"Ha!" barked Kapitän Dolf. "Good it is that they did not, for as we have heard thirty thousand are the enemy, and fallen soon would have been the Riamoners and *der Zwergs.*"

DelfLord Volki snorted, then muttered to Rynna at his side, "Pah! Bekki's nine hundred Châkka alone could have held the foe at bay while the King and his men crossed at their ease."

Rynna smiled briefly, but, fretting, wondering, her thoughts were upon Tipperton and the others. . . .

"There they are," hissed Linnet, pointing.

Tipperton raised up to peer over the stony prominence. In the gorge below marched the Fists of Rakka, heading easterly.

Tip glanced at his sketch of the area, a sketch made long past at the map table of Coron Ruar, for when it was drawn, Tipperton did not know whence the war would take him, and so he had lightly traced all he could. Yet much detail was missing, and only the broadest outlines indicated what lay ahead.

"The only thing east is Hèl's Crucible," he murmured. "But given what we have heard of that place, surely they couldn't be heading there."

"Perhaps they have no choice, now that the High King is on this side of the river," replied Linnet.

"Perhaps not," said Tipperton, folding his sketches back into their waterproof wrapping. "Do you see any sign of Nix and Farly and Dinly? We will need send word back."

Linnet shook her head.

And so they watched and waited, and some candlemarks later, they slipped back downslope and retrieved their ponies and rode eastward after the marchers as the day waned.

In the night nigh the bridgehead the cries and moaning among the wounded Fists of Rakka dwindled and dwindled to finally cease altogether, and Dwarves came back into camp and cleaned their knives of blood.

And still a cold wind blew from Garia and across the legion and host.

Oh my," hissed Tipperton in the dawn. "Look ahead."

"Adon," breathed Linnet, "Hèl's Crucible."

They lay bellydown atop a ridge and peered easterly past the encamped Fists of Rakka below. Under the overcast sky they could see a vast rift in the earth, the near side nought but a jagged edge running out of the northwest and disappearing into the southeast, all obscured by a darkling haze. Even so, dim in the distance and steeply rising lay the far side, hills atop, with mountains looming vaguely beyond. From where the pair lay, they could not see the floor of the basin directly below the near-side brim, but two or so leagues outward and deeply down a thousand feet or so the bottom hove into view; leftward the floor plunged down and away, the bottom entirely beyond sight. Where they could see the floor of the rift, jumbles of jagged black stone ran in long, long stretches, and ragged fissures vomited dark smoke up and out, to be caught by the chill wind and spread wide in layers of grey, while elsewhere yellowish vapors belched forth to mingle with the dusky vapors and turn the westerly flow an ill-seeming, sickly brown . . . and the stench was nigh staggering. Under this cast of foul smoke, little else could be discerned, yet there was no question that this was indeed Hèl's Crucible.

"Lord, but what must it smell like in the bottom below when the wind doesn't blow down from those mountains afar," said Linnet, her face wrinkled in disgust.

"Bloody awful, if you ask me," said Tip. "Ryn says the vapors are deadly when the air in the basin is still."

"Oh my, but I would hate to have that reek in my nostrils if I were to die."

"Well then, let's take a pledge to remain out of Hèl's Crucible," said Tip, grinning.

They watched and waited for the Fists of Rakka to break camp, yet the black-robed men stayed put. And the day grew on toward the noontide, yet little below changed.

But then Linnet said, "I say, look there. Is that the King's host coming?"

Tipperton peered westerly where Linnet pointed. In the distance along the rim of the rift a mounted force stretched away for miles, with some men on foot trotting alongside the riders. Long did Tip look, his suspicions growing, and finally in the fore he could see—

"A flag, black and red," Tipperton gritted. "This is no host of the King."

"Then who?" asked Linnet.

"I think it may be the Southerlings—Hyrinians and Kistanians and Chabbains."

"How can you know?"

"I saw such in Valon, when Beau and Phais and Loric and I crossed that wide land. Too, I think the flag they bear is Modru's own."

Steadily the long column neared, and at last Tipperton could clearly see the standard they bore as it blew in the wind: it was a ring of fire on black.

"It *is* Modru's banner, Linnet. One of us is going to have to take this news back to—" began Tipperton—

—but Linnet hissed, "Movement behind and below."

Tipperton turned, and slipping uphill from rock to rock came—

"Nix!" sissed Linnet.

The buccan was clearly heading for their position. And now hoving into view behind Nix came Dinly . . . and then after him came Farly.

Nix flopped down next to Linnet and said, "You are going to have to take more care, sister of mine."

Linnet raised an eyebrow, and Nix added, "You were seen."

"Seen? By whom?"

"Well, not exactly you, Linnet, but your pony downslope instead. I believe it was Dara Vail who spotted it."

"Vail?" said Tipperton, looking about. "Where?"

Nix pointed westerly. "On the back side of yon hill, with Alor

Flandrena and Dara Arylin. Their own horses are among the crags below."

Tipperton looked long and at last saw the concealed horses.

"They have been tracking the army you see coming yon, and have asked us to bear the word back to King Blaine," said Nix.

"All of us?" asked Tipperton.

Nix shook his head. "I told her that we were trailing the Fists of Rakka, and that we would continue to do so. Besides, Ryn assigned Dinly to be the courier of news."

"Moreover," said Farly, "if the Fists hie in a direction elsewhere from the army the Elves are tracking, well then, someone needs to follow, and that is our task."

Tipperton nodded.

"Should I go now?" asked Dinly.

Tipperton shook his head. "Not yet, Dinly. Let's see what happens when these lackeys of Modru come together."

And so they waited as the multitude neared, closer and closer, until from below came the flat call of a ram's horn, to be answered by a horn from within the approaching ranks.

And still the long columns came on.

Moments passed and moments more, and of a sudden Tipperton groaned.

"What is it?" asked Linnet.

"See riding in the fore ranks?" said Tipperton.

"See what?" asked Nix.

"That man, the one on the dark horse."

"The one carrying a ragged bundle?" asked Farly.

"It is no bundle," said Tipperton, "but the corpse of his daughter instead."

Linnet gasped. "Corpse of—?"

"—His daughter," repeated Tipperton. "It is Mad Lord Tain, a Daelsman, a surrogate of Modru."

Tipperton turned to Dinly. "This news *must* reach King Blaine. For if Lord Tain is here, then so is the presence of Modru." As Dinly's eyes widened in understanding, an ephemeral thought flitted through Tipperton's mind, but ere he could capture it, it was gone. Nevertheless he said, "Something most foul is afoot, and I would have the King beware." Now Tipperton looked at Farly. "This news is too important for one alone to bear it."

Farly nodded and said, "I will also go."

Again they turned their attention to the army, and now it came in among the Fists of Rakka, the men of Hyree and Chabba and Kistan greeting those of Hurn and Sarain and Thyra.

And a score of men—Chabbains, Hyrinians, Kistanians, and

several Fists of Rakka—gathered around Lord Tain as he whispered unto the remains of his daughter, the corpse seeming no more than a bundle of twigs to the Warrows afar. Yet in moments Lord Tain turned unto those around him and clenched a fist and seemed to be hissing orders. After a while, again Lord Tain turned to the corpse he bore, yet just ere he did, he looked long at the hills above and seemed to laugh.

"So they have joined forces, have they?"

"Aye, my lord," said Farly, Dinly at his side nodding. "Right about here, or so Tipperton gauges." In the early-morning light, Farly pointed to a place on the map.

"And they marched off southeasterly along the rim of Hèl's Crucible," added Dinly.

King Blaine's eyes widened. "Southeasterly?"

"Aye, my lord. Southeasterly," said Dinly.

King Loden looked at the map and then at DelfLord Bekki. "You know more of this region, Lord Bekki. What could be their goal?"

Bekki shook his head. "They march toward the shield wall."

"They also march toward the sea," said Coron Eiron.

"Ships," replied Skipskaptein Arnson. "There may be ships awaiting them at the shores of the Avagon."

"We must not let them escape," growled DelfLord Volki.

King Blaine nodded and glanced at the others and finally at Linde. "Sound the horns. We will pursue."

"My lord," said Arth of the Wilderland, "forget not what these Waldans have said: the foe has a surrogate among them—"

"Coward Tain," gritted Bekki.

"—and where there is a surrogate, there also is Modru's eyes and ears and voice." The lad from Twoforks fell silent, awaiting his liege lord's response.

King Blaine nodded at Arth. "I know, Lord Arth, but remember, we defeated one of his Hordes at the battle of the downs, and a surrogate was with them there. Nay, I'll not forget that Modru's presence rides among them, yet I'll not let that stay my hand, for the fate of the Planes rides on that which we now do, and to do nought is to allow evil to reign."

"My lord," said Arnson, "seven of my ships are downstream of the bridge, and I can take those crews and set sail down the river and—"

"Do so," said King Blaine, ere the skipskaptein had finished, "and set fire to any enemy ships you find waiting."

Arnson smiled in triumph at his Jutlander counterpart and said, "I am sure Kapitän Dolf will be glad to hold ward at the bridge."

"Indeed," said King Blaine, even as Dolf glared at the Fjord-lander. "And now, Hrosmarshal Linde, sound the horn."

And so Linde sounded her black-oxen horn, and Larana her trump of silver, and host and legion mounted up, and in squads and companies and brigades they followed two Warrows wending into the hills.

And nigh Hèl's Crucible on a track through the crags, Arylin, Flandrena, and Vail, along with Tipperton, Linnet, and Nix, paralleled the march of the foe, turn by turn and from above the scouts keeping watch on the enemy.

The hideous stench of Hèl's Crucible wafted over all as the tainted vapors rode outward on the chill wind, but by this time all had become inured to the malodorous reek. In his and Linnet's turn to observe, now and again Tipperton's eye was drawn to the vast rift and the dimly seen foothills and mountains beyond, and each time he looked an elusive thought seemed to slip 'round the edges of his mind, yet the more he pursued it, the more it fled his grasp. Nevertheless, as he rode in the valleys behind the watch hills, he said to Vail, "I can't but help believe this is some viper's egg of a plan yet to be hatched by vile Modru."

"Why so, Tipperton? —Oh, not that I disbelieve thee, yet I would have thy thoughts."

"Well, although I cannot quite catch hold of a nagging suspicion on the edge of my mind, other things vex me as well, and I cannot read their riddle: look, the Fists of Rakka and the Lakh and Rovers and Askars make no effort to cover their tracks, nor do they go in stealth, taking advantage of the cover of these hills; they do not send sentries in among these ways to see if they are watched; 'tis almost as if they seek to be seen. Too, they veer not from this course, but the only thing ahead is the shield wall and beyond it a drop to the Avagon Sea."

"Perhaps 'tis there ships await them, or ships yet to come," said Flandrena, riding alongside.

"If not," said Linnet, "then when King Blaine and the host arrives he will have them trapped between Hèl's Crucible and the deep blue sea."

Vail nodded, then said, "As do thee, Tipperton, I, too, think something is afoot, for they move at a deliberate pace, slow and unhasty, as if"—Vail shook her head—"I know not."

Arylin signalled down from the hill above, and Vail said, "They continue their course."

Tipperton sighed, then said, "Come, Linnet, it's our turn to ride ahead and set watch. Let's do so from that hill yon."

Together they rode away, passing below the hill on which Arylin and Nix sat vigil.

"I am glad to see you survive, Lady Linde."

Linde sighed and looked down at the wee Waldan riding at hand. "There are but seventeen of us left, commander. Seventeen."

"So few?" Rynna glanced back at the meager number of Harlingar riding after.

Linde's face drew gaunt. "Aye. Of one thousand Jordians sent by King Ranor, only seventeen of the brigade yet live."

"Oh my," said Rynna.

They rode in silence for a while, and then Rynna asked, "Where is the Gargon's head you bore away when you left Darda Erynian."

"It is lost, Lady Rynna, lost, lying somewhere in the wrack of war. After the Battle of Gûnarring Gap it was gone."

"You fought there?"

"Aye. When word came that King Blaine had landed in Jugo, we set sail from Pendwyr and joined his force."

"And the battle . . . ?"

" 'Twas bloody, yet we won in the end."

Again they rode without speaking, wending among the crags and hills, but at last Rynna said almost to herself, "Like so many things."

An eyebrow raised, Linde looked at the Waldan.

Rynna sighed. "Many things lie somewhere, lost in the wreckage of war . . . innocence not the least of these."

Linnet and Tipperton watched as the column of foe marched along the rim of the rift below. Sheltered by the hills and out of view of the enemy, Vail and Flandrena made their way southeastward to take up the vigil atop the next craggy mound. Leftward, Nix and Arylin made their way down from the previous station. In the far distance rightward Tip and Linnet could see the shield wall and beyond it the indigo waters of the Avagon sea.

"How is the health of your father, Arth?"

Arth shook his head. "He is dead, Healer Darby, slain at the Battle of the Downs."

"Oh my, but I am sorry to hear of that," said Beau.

"It was just west of Stonehill," said Arth. "Da was a hero: saved the King's life."

"The mayor saved Blaine's life?"

"Aye. King Blaine was unhorsed. A Ghûl on Hèlsteed was riding him down. Da charged in between and engaged the foe and fought furiously. But Ghûls shrug off wounds that would slay any ordinary man, and in the end Da was speared through and fell."

"What of the King?"

"He caught up Da's horse and mounted and charged the Ghûl, but by this time I had won past and with my sword I took off the corpse-foe's head."

"Good," said Beau.

"The King then gave me command of the folk of the Beacontor muster, and we've been with him ever since, though nearly half altogether have been slain. I alone remain of the entire Company of Twoforks."

"You alone of all those men?" Sudden tears spilled down Beau's face.

Arth nodded, his own cheeks wet as well.

"They've stopped alongside the shield wall," said Nix, as Tipperton and Linnet came up the back of the hill to the crest in response to his signal.

Tipperton peered 'round the crag and down toward the enemy. As Nix had said, the foe stood on the broad flats along the rim of the rift, the shield wall stretching away eastward. Sheer and high was this barrier and some ten miles long, a perpendicular stone rampart spanning the width of the narrow neck between the ocean and the mighty rift below, the hundred-cubit-thick barricade keeping the two apart. Beyond the wall, beyond the foe, they could see the waters of the Avagon Sea and hear the roar of the ocean crashing against the hard stone.

"Have you seen any ships on the sea?" asked Linnet, taking a place beside Arylin.

"Nay," replied the Dara, "though they could be anchored beyond our sight at the base of the cliffs."

Linnet nodded and glanced at the rim, where the land dropped down steeply to an unseen shore below. "Vail and Flandrena rode ahead to look," said the damman.

"But if there are ships, then why are these forces waiting?" asked Nix. "Why aren't they climbing down the cliffs to board the craft?"

Ere any could answer—"Hist," said Arylin, "I ween they draw into formation."

"Be ready to cut and run," warned Nix, "for if indeed they are forming up, they may send sentries into these hills."

"Oh my," said Tipperton.

"What?" asked Linnet.

"They are facing back the way they came," replied Tipperton. "As if—"

"As if expecting someone," said Arylin.

"The High King," said Tipperton. "That's who they expect. I *knew* they were making no attempt to escape.

"A last stand?" asked Nix. "Are they making a last stand?"

Nix and Linnet turned to Tipperton, yet he looked to Dara Arylin. "Cornered foe oft make a final trial," she said, "and most dangerous are they then."

"But if they are expecting ships . . ." Linnet's words fell silent, but finally she added, "I think there are no ships there."

"We will soon know," said Tipperton, looking toward the ocean and seeking to see Vail and Flandrena but finding them not.

"Oh my, so this is Hèl's Crucible," said Rynna, as darkness descended on the land. "Now I know why Lord Steward Voren called it a terrible place."

Even as she said it, word came from the fore. They would spend the night encamped on the flats between the hills and the rift, and turn toward the enemy on the morrow, for scouts had seen their fires nigh the shield wall, no more than ten miles hence.

As Rynna prepared her bedroll, Beau and Farly and Dinly came to her side. And Rynna said, "Rest well this night, my dearest friends, for on the morrow we will fight. And although I would have this be the last battle of the war, I fear it is not."

"Not the last battle?" asked Dinly.

Beau looked up from spreading his bedroll. "No, Dinly. You see, these are but the Hyrinians and Chabbains and Rovers and the Fists of Rakka; Modru and the Foul Folk are yet on the loose. And it is Modru and his master Gyphon who drive all. Nay, until we can deal with them, the war will not be ended."

Glumly Dinly nodded, while Farly pulled biscuits of crue from his saddlebags to pass around. In spite of the fact that none had any appetite, they each took one.

"There are no ships directly below," said Vail, sitting down beside Tipperton and taking a wafer of mian from Arylin, "but sails approach from the southwest."

"Fjordlander sails," said Flandrena.

"Fjordlanders?" blurted Tipperton. "Have they thrown in with the foe?"

Vail shook her head. "I think not, Tipperton. Instead I ween King Blaine, acting on word borne by Farly and Dinly, has sent the Fjordlanders to stop any seaward escape by the enemy below."

"Ah," said Nix, taking another bite of mian. "Makes sense."

"How far down to the ocean?" asked Linnet. "—I mean, how high are the seaside cliffs?"

"Sixteen, seventeen fathoms, and sheer," replied Flandrena. "If enemy ships do come, 'tis not an easy climb up nor down."

"Thou canst bear such word back to King Blaine as well," said Arylin, looking from Tipperton to Linnet to Nix.

Vail raised an eyebrow.

"That the foe stands with their backs to a cliff with no ships waiting below," said Arylin, "but is instead arrayed to meet the host."

"I made a sketch of their deployment," said Tipperton, "though I still think that I should remain here while Linnet and Nix take it back."

Arylin shook her head. "Nay, for 'tis better that ye all three be with thy kind when the conflict comes. Vail, Flandrena and I will wait till the last to join with ours."

As Tipperton reluctantly agreed, Vail said, " 'Tis but some three or four leagues back to where Farly and Dinly parted to bear word back to the King, hence ye should await the host there if they have not already come."

Tipperton nodded and then stood and said to Nix and Linnet, "Let us be gone, and then."

Each of the Elves embraced the trio and kissed them, and then watched as down the hill and toward their ponies the Warrows went.

With a gentle kiss, Tipperton awakened his dammia. Together they quietly took up her blanket and slipped in among the nearby crags, even as Linnet and Beau did the same.

"There are no ships for the enemy," said Bekki, riding alongside Tipperton in the early-morning light. "And they fear to march through Hèl's Crucible. As you say, it seems they have readied themselves to make a last stand. Even so, it matters not, for we will soon make short shrift of them."

"I deem thou canst not be certain of that, Lord Bekki," said Loric, "for did we not hear the Fists of Rakka fought formidably at the Dragonboat bridge? And I can say the Battle at Gûnarring Gap was bloody indeed. Nay, I ween they will give good account of themselves, much to our regret."

"Pah!" snorted Bekki, but said no more.

"Tell us again, Tipperton," said Phais, "just how they are arrayed and the lay of the land nigh."

"In long rows, Phais: the Fists of Rakka out front; the Askars of Chabba next; then the mounted files of Hyrinians and Kistanians after them. Many of the Chabbains are armed with bows, but most wield short spears. The Fists of Rakka wield scimitars and axes and they bear small round shields, though some of the Fists are armed with crossbows. The Lakh of Hyree also bear small round shields but their swords are long and curved—like the sabers the Jordians wield—tulwars I think they are named. They also have bows at hand, strangely curved. The Rovers wield cutlasses and crossbows and spears."

Phais nodded, then said, "And the land?"

"They stand on the level ground between the brim of Hèl's Crucible to their right and the hills on their left, with their backs to the hundred-foot drop unto the Avagon Sea below."

"What lies in front?" asked Beau.

"A long flat like this," said Tipperton, gesturing at the broad expanse lying between the sheer fall into the rift to their left and the craggy hills in the near distance to their right and stretching out fore and aft of the moving host.

"They have their backs to the sun," growled Bekki.

"What sun?" asked Rynna, gesturing to the overcast above, yet sliding southwesterly overhead, driven by the chill wind.

"Should it come out," replied Bekki.

"And it is nought but a sheer fall to the foe's right?" asked Phais.

Tipperton shook his head. "Several hundred yards in front of the enemy's ranks, there seems to be a broad, broad slope down into Hèl's Crucible, the pitch itself mayhap a full mile wide. How gentle or steep, I cannot say, for we could not fully see it from our post."

"I say we drive them off the cliffs behind to fall into the sea," said Bekki.

"Or off the sheer drop to their right," added Nix.

"Or run them down the slope and into the foul air of Hèl's Crucible itself," said Linnet.

"The King says any one or all of these tactics will do," said Rynna, adding, "assuming they do not lay down their arms as the King will demand."

"Bah!" growled Bekki. "Were it mine to choose, I would not offer them surrender terms as King Blaine has said he will do."

"Better they surrender without a fight than to have them maim and kill our own," said Beau. "I'm sick of seeing so many warriors lying in their own leaking blood, weary of sewing and patching muscle and skin as if they were nought but shredded remnants of a torn garment, weary of dealing with broken bones, weary of pain and death and crippling harm . . . ah, me, but I am weary of war."

They rode awhile without speaking, but then Linde's horn sounded from the fore.

Loric looked at the others. " 'Tis the call to fall into formation as planned."

Bekki sighed and said, "May Elwydd shield ye all."

"May Her hand protect thou as well, Drimm Bekki, DelfLord of Mineholt North," replied Phais.

Bekki peered long at her, an unfathomable look in his eyes, but then he saluted with his war hammer and wheeled his pony rightward and to the fore, where the Châkka of Mineholt North rode in array.

"Take care, wee ones," said Phais, and then she and Loric also turned, and they cantered toward the Lian of Arden Vale.

"Remember," said Rynna, "if it comes to fighting, we are to circle to the far right, out where we will be free to cast arrows."

Farly shook his head. "I think the High King put us there just to get us out of the way."

"No, he did not," replied Rynna. "Silverleaf is the one who suggested it, and though we are but a handful and two, he knows how deadly we can be."

"Well, out of the way or not," said Tipperton, "I say we should get over there now, commander. I mean, I don't trust Modru to honor a grey flag."

Rynna nodded and spurred rightward, the others following, and among the ponies of the twenty-five hundred Dwarves and past the horses of six hundred Dylvana and eight hundred Lian and fourteen hundred Baeron and thirty-nine thousand men, the entire Wee Folk army of seven rode to their position wide to the right to cover the host's dextral flank.

In row after row came the King's host, each long row reaching across the wide flat between the hills to the right and the precipice to the left.

In the lead rode King Blaine and Silverleaf, with Larana to Silverleaf's right and Linde to the King's left. Couched in Larana's stirrup cup was a lance bearing a grey flag, and on Linde's lance flew the King's scarlet and gold.

In a row a short way behind the King were borne the many banners of the Allies, pennons of men and Elves and Dwarves, but no flags for the Warrows and the Baeron.

Directly after the standard bearers came the heavy horses with Baeron astride, maces and morning stars and war hammers in hand, for as Blaine had said, "I would have the foe tremble at the sight of such huge men and mounts; mayhap it will give the enemy pause should there be deceit in their hearts."

And following after the Baeron came row after row of men and Dwarves and Elves, armed and armored for war.

And two miles ahead and also arrayed in row after row stood the Lakh of Hyree and the Askars of Chabba and the Rovers of Kistan, along with the Fists of Rakka, all of them accoutered for war as well.

"Oh lordy," said Beau, "but what a throng. I swear, Tip, there's more foe here than ever was at Dendor."

Grimly, Tipperton nodded but otherwise did not reply as he and the Warrows pressed forward, riding along the right fore flank at the foot of the hills.

"Take note of the terrain," said Rynna, "for it may prove the difference between living and dying or between victory and defeat."

Even though Tip was thoroughly familiar with the lay of the land, for he had studied it well while making the sketch, a sketch he had shown to all, still he scanned the surround. To the right stood the craggy hills, a place of refuge at need. A broad flat stretched between these mounds and the precipice of Hèl's Crucible, a flat some thousand yards wide and running for miles along the rim of the rift. This flat between the hills and the brim would be the battleground if it came to combat. To the left yawned Hèl's Crucible itself, the bordering stone plummeting downward some thousand feet or so, the fall sheer alongside where the host now rode, but a quarter mile hence stood the long slope down into the vast basin, the slope Tip had observed from the hills above. Straight ahead were arrayed the foe, at their backs a hundred-foot fall to the deep Avagon Sea below. Stretching away to the enemy's right ran the shield wall, the steep stone plunging down into the basin, a sheer face between the rift and the ocean a hundred cubits beyond.

All was as Tip had last seen it; nothing seemed to have changed.

Tipperton looked up to the right. Somewhere in the hills above, Vail, Arylin, and Flandrena yet watched.

When the distance between the host and the foe came to a half mile or so, King Blaine signed to Linde, and she raised her black-oxen horn to her lips and blew a resonant call, and the host came to a stop.

Riding forward through the ranks came the emissaries who were to accompany King Blaine forward from this point. From the far right rode a wee Warrow on a pony. These emissaries arrayed themselves among the banners of the Allies, Rynna centermost and flanked by two Baeron, these three bereft of flags.

Now King Blaine looked behind and saw all was as planned, then he turned and nodded to Silverleaf and said, "Let us see if they are open to surrender."

"Beware treachery, my lord," gritted a voice from behind.

"I shall, Lord Bekki," replied the King without looking back.

Together, Blaine, Silverleaf, Larana, and Linde rode forward, the grey flag on the right, the scarlet and gold on the left. Directly behind rode the emissaries amid the many banners: Lian, Dylvana, Dwarves, Humans, Baeron, a Mage, and a single Warrow. Toward the foe they rode, coming at last to a point halfway between. There they stopped and waited.

The foe did not respond.

Long moments passed, a candlemark or so, yet neither ally nor foe stirred, and Rynna could hear the DelfLords growling among themselves, Bekki in particular.

And then Bekki cursed, "Kruk, Loden, look. There's Coward Tain."

Rynna stared at the enemy but a quarter mile away, where, centermost among them a man sat ahorse and seemed to be speaking to a bundle in his arms. Rynna shuddered, for although she had never seen Lord Tain before, she knew this bundle to be the corpse of his daughter Jolet.

Tipperton looked long at the enemy ranks, and he could make out Lord Tain astride a mount and whispering to the remains of his daughter, while gesticulating toward the host. Tip glanced at the cluster of emissaries: the King and Silverleaf and the others, notably Rynna, waiting at the midpoint.

Of a sudden, Lord Tain straightened and glared about—

—a shudder ran through Tipperton—

—the surrogate peered at the waiting King and his escort and laughed, then turned and spoke to someone at hand—

—and from the hills above there came a horn cry—

—Tipperton snapped his head around, and there on a crest stood Flandrena, sounding a signal of alarm and pointing northwesterly away from the foe, while thundering downslope toward the King's small assembly came Vail riding at speed—

—*Yaaaah . . . !* Shouted the enemy in a collective wordless howl, and forward charged the throng, mounted Hyrinians and Rovers hurtling toward the host, spears lowered, swords raised—

—*"Fly, Rynna, fly!"* cried Tipperton, stringing an arrow—
—Chabbains and the black-cloaked Fists of Rakka running forward afoot—
—Linde sounding her black-oxen horn, Larana her horn of silver . . .

Even as the heavy horses of the Baeron thundered forth and the ponies of Dwarves and the horses of men and Elves hammered after, the King shouted a command to his escort, and as one they readied weapons and shields and waited for the wave of allies to come.

All but Rynna, and she galloped her pony toward the right flank.

"Faster, Rynna!" cried Tipperton, afraid she would be run over by the oncoming Baeron, Linnet and Beau and Nix and Farly and Dinly shouting as well.

And even as she rode toward Tipperton and the other Warrows, Vail flashed past, galloping the opposite way, yelling in Sylva, but what she called out, none of the Warrows knew.

Yet Silverleaf shouted to Larana, and she blew a command on her silver horn, and within the charging ranks, Elves reined and turned opposite.

Tipperton's eyes flew wide. "What th—?" And he looked behind and saw riders coming, thousands upon thousands of riders, yellow flags flying, armored in dark scale and wide-flaring helms, long, curved swords in hand, great longbows drawn taut—
—and sleets of arrows both fore and aft flew from the oncoming foe's ranks, to strike down among the Allies, men and Elves and Dwarves to fall screaming even as a hail of arrows flew in return . . .

. . . and with a great clash of arms and armor and shrieks and shouts and battle cries, the armies collided, the Allies hammered fore and aft by foe even as Rynna flew free of the clash and galloped in among the Warrows.

"It was a trap!" shouted Tipperton, loosing arrow after arrow to fell the enemy.

"Dismount!" cried Rynna. "Take shelter among the crags. Make every shaft and sling bullet count."

"Who flies the yellow flag?" cried Dinly, as he drew his pony after and came in among the boulders.

Yet not a buccan nor damman knew the answer as they loosed arrows at the foe and Beau hurled sling bullets.

"Target the enemy archers," said Rynna, "for they are deadly."

Out on the flats amid the clash and clang and screams and cries of battle, taking terrible casualties the host drew together to face the two-pronged attack, all but the Baeron on their heavy horses, who had smashed entirely through the ranks of the seaward foe, but now were fighting their way back.

In the center 'round the King, rallied warriors dire: Dwarves with axes hewing; Elves with swords riving and spears piercing; men with maces and axes and swords bashing and hacking and hewing as well. Among those rallied was Aravan, his true-named Krystallopýr burning through flesh and bone. Riatha fought at his side, her glitter-dark blade keen beyond reckoning. Nigh her, Silverleaf's white bone bow was scabbarded in favor of his deadly long-knife. Magekind was there, too, but they withheld their <power> for the King had bade them to not spend it unless all was lost. Yet wholly outnumbered and assailed from both sides, the Allies were driven back and back as the foe swept in a semicircle to close ranks.

"They are too many," gritted Tipperton, even as he loosed an arrow to bring another enemy archer down.

"Oh lor'," cried Beau, "look, Tip! They are now driving the host toward Hèl's Crucible!"

With their backs to the great rift, King Blaine and the Allies were being hammered toward the brim, toward the long slope down and within.

Rynna wept as she loosed another shaft. "Oh, Tipperton, unless a miracle occurs, we are defeated." But still she fought on, as did the Warrows all, though bitter tears ran down.

Back and back were pressed the Allies, some now on the long slope, others to fall screaming to their doom over the brim and down.

Yet even facing annihilation, the host fought valiantly on, laying death about even as on them death fell.

Yet above the screams and shouts of Adon and Elwydd and Rakka and Gyphon, there came—

"Listen!" cried Tipperton, turning his head this way and that.

—a sound—

"Do you hear?"

—a deep horn cry—

"Do you hear, Rynna?"

—and another and another—

Tipperton raised his black-oxen horn to his lips and blew a ringing call—

A call which was answered by uncounted black-oxen horns blowing wildly, as the earth reverberated under the pounding of ten thousands of hooves.

"Oh, Rynna, my love, here comes your miracle!"

And thundering 'round the flanks of the hills and down the

flats, flags flying white horses on green, came riders and chariots with wheelblades spinning. And with lances lowered and sabers raised and bows drawn taut and spears in hand and horns calling out the charge—*Raw! Raw! Raw!*—and voices shouting *V'takku! V'takku!* in the war-tongue Valur, twenty thousand Harlingar charged. . . .

Jord had come at last.

And running full tilt they crashed into the yellow-flagged warriors and drove them aside, many to be hurled over the lip of the rift to fall shrieking to their deaths far below.

And even as DelfLord Valk and his pony-mounted army of Kachar arrived on the heels of the Jordians and fell upon the foe, there came a roaring blast of Mage-fire cleaving through the enemy. Following the path of the flame, High King Blaine and Silverleaf and the Allies drove up from the ramp and out to the hills, to split the foe in two. Hammering out wide, King Blaine turned his forces easterly, and along with King Ranor's Vanadurin on the west as well as the Dwarves of Kachar, they trapped the enemy against the rim. And even though yet outnumbered, they battered the foe back and back.

And fighting in rage and fury and aided at times by the Mages, together the men and Dwarves and Lian and Dylvana and Baeron—along with seven Warrows—drove the reeling enemy hindward and down the long ramp and down.

Seething and cursing and roaring battle cries, the Allies drove downward as well, hacking and slashing and piercing and bashing and driving the foe ever deeper. But at last the enemy turned and fled away, for they could not bring their greater numbers to bear. And with the foe in full flight—*Hahn, taa-roo! Hahn, taa-roo!*—rang the Jordian horns.

"Why do you sound the signal to withdraw?" shouted Tipperton to Linde riding nigh.

" 'Tis the King's command," she shouted back. "The enemy may be fleeing to lure us into a trap."

"Trap?"

"Aye. They yet outnumber us, and should we pursue them to the floor of the rift, they will have the advantage."

As Linde raised her own black-oxen horn to her lips, so too did Tipperton raise his, and they added their calls to the others—*Hahn, taa-roo! Hahn, taa-roo! Hahn, taa-roo taa-roo!*

And on a wide level roughly a mile down the ramp, the Allies disengaged, the Dwarves cursing at having to do so. And down and down fled the torn enemy into Hèl's Crucible below.

38

*T*hey are from Jûng," said Aravan, staring down the long, long ramp and into the dark basin below, night just now falling on the land. Behind them the slain were yet being collected, with the Dwarves casting the bodies of the foe over the rim to fall into the shadows below.

"Jûng?" asked Tipperton.

"A realm far to the east."

"Like Ryodo or Jinga?"

"Somewhat," replied Aravan. "Though Ryodo isolates itself from the rest of the world, calling all others uncouth foreigners, while Jinga trades with any and all who come unto her shores."

"And this Jûng . . . ?" asked Rynna.

"Filled with petty warlords and raiders," said Aravan, "unified under a mogul. It is his yellow flag they bear; the red star in the center is the mogul's mark. That they fall on the side of Gyphon surprises me not, though how they came to be here in Garia takes me somewhat aback."

"Why is that?" asked Linnet. "Is it far to Jûng?"

"Two thousand leagues, were you a bird," replied Aravan.

"Six thousand miles? Pah!" said Beau, standing at the edge of the circle and taking a quick meal ere returning to help with the wounded. "We alone have travelled that far, wouldn't you say so, Tip?"

"Ar, if I remember correctly, Beau, my friend," said Dinly,

grinning, "instead of a mere six thousand miles, it's three halfways around the world you claim altogether."

"Yar," chimed in Farly, laughing, "with a hundred more halves to go."

Beau pushed out his hands, a crue biscuit in one. "Wait, now, I am serious. Tip, you're the mapmaker here. Have we travelled altogether six thousand miles?"

"Perhaps if you add it all up," said Tipperton, "though it will have taken us four years to do so, come this February."

"Four years? Oh my," said Beau, sinking to his knees beside Linnet and reaching out to grasp her hand. "No wonder I'm tired of war."

The other Warrows sighed in agreement.

Aravan smiled sadly at the Wee Folk, the Guardian remembering the days when the Elves were yet mad. But he spoke not of the Elven Wars of Succession which lasted for ten millennia, nor of the hard times thereafter.

Overhead the clouds yet flowed in a blanket 'cross the night sky above, the glowing fires deep in the crevices of Hèl's Crucible casting dull red reflections here and there. Yet it was the night of the full moon, and as it rose, the running overcast shone from behind with a whiteness where the silvery light tried to break through. "Oh, perhaps it's an omen," said Linnet, looking at the paleness, "an omen of Elwydd's goodwill."

Beau peered at the flowing sky. "Let us hope," he said. "Indeed, let us hope." Beau then gave Linnet a quick kiss on the cheek and stood. "Ah, well, for me it's back to the wounded."

As Beau stepped away toward a cluster of distant lanterns, Tipperton sighed and gazed down the slope. Somewhere below, Rynna sat in the Kings' council with the captains and High King Blaine.

"We are yet outnumbered," growled Field Marshal Burke of Wellen.

"Aye, but we hold the high ground," replied Silverleaf, gesturing down the long ramp toward the enemy below, "an advantage we desperately need."

The slope itself was nearly two miles in length from the rim above to the floor of the basin beneath, with pitched runs of stony land separated by wide tracts of nigh level ground. It was on one of these level stretches nearly halfway down where the bulk of the host stood athwart the ramp, with the enemy all the way down in the rift, another mile farther on.

Above the host on a higher point of the slope the council sat with the King.

"My lord," said Rynna, "what do you plan to do? I mean, if the enemy stays where they are and we ride down to the base of the slope and meet them in combat in the rift, with their greater numbers they will have the upper hand."

By the light of the lantern the King fixed her with his steel-blue gaze. "Have you a suggestion, commander?"

Rynna nodded. "Offer them surrender terms again, and if they do not accept, then set a siege and wait them out until they have no choice but to accede."

"Bah," growled Volki. "I say we keep them trapped within, and when this cursed wind dies at last, we let the vapors take them."

Bekki sitting at Volki's side clenched a fist and nodded fiercely.

"They might march ere then," said Coron Eiron, "escape the rift altogether."

"Not on this side," said King Ranor, running a hand through his coppery hair, "for we will ride along the brim and stop them wherever they try to climb out."

"Aye," said Linde, "yet should they withdraw across the basin . . . ?"

"Then I fear they will escape," replied Ranor, "for not even the Harlingar, fleet as we are, can ride 'round to meet them ere they flee the rift below."

"What about riding along the top of the shield wall?" asked Arth of the Wilderland. "Can we not use it as a bridge to get from this side to that?"

Alor Talarin shook his head. "Nay, Lord Arth, it is too rough, too craggy. Flandrena says there are places atop the width of the wall where stone rises plumb for tens of feet. We could not win through."

King Ranor sighed and glanced toward the wall looming upward in the dark. "As I suspected."

"Then are you saying if they march away they may escape?" demanded DelfLord Okar.

"If they march for the far side, indeed," replied Ranor, regret in his dark grey eyes.

"Kruk!" spat Bekki, slamming a fist into palm.

Silence fell among the captains, and at last King Blaine said, "I deem Commander Rynna has the right of it: we will again offer terms of surrender. If they accept not, then we shall set siege. If the wind dies, Lord Volki, then we shall indeed let the vapors take them should they refuse to submit."

"And if they flee across the basin . . . ?" asked Okar.

"Then they will escape," replied Blaine.

A grumble went 'round the circle, and King Blaine raised his hands and when silence fell he asked, "Is there aught else of strategy to discuss?"

When no one spoke up, Blaine glanced at Farrin, and the Mage said, "My lords, have your warriors rest in shifts, for although we Mages will use our <powers> to see through the blackness and keep watch both below and above, still be ready, for we know not what the darkness may bring."

Again Blaine looked about, and when no one spoke, he said, "Then let us now speak of tactics: who will stand at the fore should there be an attack, and who will ward the flanks, and who will stand in reserve to thwart any breakthroughs. Does any have suggestions?"

Across the circle, Lord Arth raised his hand. . . .

"I say," said Beau late in the night, peering westerly along the rim through the dark, "but what is that stir among the host?"

Aravan turned about, then grinned back at the Waerling. "An ally comes."

"Just one?" asked Dinly, craning his neck to see.

"Nay," replied Aravan. "Seven allies in all."

"Just seven?" said Farly. "Seven thousand would be more welcome."

"If you ask Tip and Beau, I think they will agree these seven are worth seven thousand," said Aravan.

Now all the Warrows stood and looked.

Escorted by Loric and moving among the shadows cast by flickering firelight, there came the seven allies along the rim: one striding on two legs, the others padding on four.

"Dalavar!" cried Beau, running forward. "Shimmer!"

Alongside the Wolfmage came Greylight, Shimmer, Beam, Seeker, Trace, and Longshank.

"Longshank," breathed Tipperton, starting forward as well.

The other Warrows looked on in awe, for these great Silver Wolves, large as ponies, seemed appallingly fierce.

As Beau came running, Dalavar said a <word>, and all the Draega stopped.

Beau threw his arms about Shimmer's neck, and the Wolf suffered his touch. And Beau called back, "Linnet, come, there's someone I would have you meet."

Tipperton stepped before Longshank. "Hello, my friend."

Longshank's grin greeted the Warrow.

Now Tip looked up at Dalavar.

The Wolfmage smiled, his grin much like that of the 'Wolves. "I am glad to see you looking so well, Tipperton."

Passing his right hand over the Vulg scars on his left arm, Tipperton said, "And I am glad to see that you, too, are well, Mage Dalavar. When you left us in Jallorby, I feared you were heading for Gron."

"I say, Dalavar," called Beau, moving among the 'Wolves and stroking every one, even Greylight. "Just where *have* you and these rascals been?"

"In the Gwasp, destroying a Horde," said Dalavar darkly, as if remembering grim deeds.

"In the Gwasp!" blurted Beau.

"Adon," said Tipperton, "then you *did* return to Gron."

Dalavar inclined his head, but did not elaborate.

Timorously, Linnet arrived at Beau's side, and he took her by the hand. "Mage Dalavar, this is Linnet, my dammia. Linnet, Mage Dalavar."

"My lady," said Dalavar.

"I am glad we meet at last," said Linnet, "for Beau speaks often of you. But these Silver Wolves, now, even though Beau told me all about them—oh my—I did not think them so . . . so formidable."

Dalavar laughed. "Formidable indeed, though gentle with friends."

"Oh, but I do hope so," said Linnet, "for they look as if they could snap me all up in but a single bite."

As Dalavar laughed, Beau turned and drew Linnet after, stepping toward Shimmer.

Tipperton looked up at the Wolfmage and said, "I am glad you are here, for we can use all the help we can get. —You did come to help, neh?"

"I came to find King Blaine and offer him my aid, and perhaps he can use it well, for the ill wind blowing out of Garia and over this host bears the vile taint of foul Modru."

Tipperton's face fell. "Oh lor', just as we suspected."

After a restless night, chill dawn came, the sky yet covered by a dismal grey pall running westerly. Tipperton groaned awake to this gloomy cast, Rynna stirring as well. Tip glanced at the drifting murk above, then flopped over and buried his face in his blanket and, his voice muffled, said, "Oh but I would see the sun once more."

"Mmm?" murmured Rynna.

Tipperton rose up on his elbows. "The sun. I would see the sun."

Rynna opened her eyes to the grey sky, then closed them again.

"What's it been, love," asked Tipperton, "twelve, thirteen days under this dreary cast?"

Again Rynna opened her eyes. "Ever since we docked at Adeo."

Tip rolled over and sat up. "It's Modru's doing, or so says Dalavar."

"I saw him, you know," said Rynna, "and the Silver Wolves. I was coming up from council as they were going down."

Tip nodded. "He went to see Blaine."

Now Rynna sat up. "Does he know for certain that Modru is behind this weather? I mean, Farrin knew that the wind was not natural, but Mage-driven instead, yet he couldn't identify it as Modru's doings, for they had never crossed paths."

"I think so," replied Tipperton. "I mean, Beau says Dalavar tangled with Modru in the past. Too, he may have opposed Modru again in the Gwasp. And if that's what it takes, well then, Dalavar should know that foul taint."

A waft of sulfurous air blew across them. Rynna wrinkled her nose and said, "Perhaps Modru's taint smells somewhat like Hèl's Crucible."

Tipperton laughed and stood. "Speaking of Hèl's Crucible, what say after we break fast and take care of the ponies, we ride down the slope to the legion? I mean, I'd like to get a good look at what may become our next battleground. I've not yet been there, you know."

Rynna nodded, then grinned and said, "Let's ride with the entire Warrow army."

Down they rode and down, down the center of the mile-wide ramp, and as they descended they let the ponies find the way, for spread out before them was the basin of Hèl's Crucible, a stark vision, indeed:

Girdled by steep stone walls a thousand feet high or more, the great barren rift gaped wide. Three-quarters of a mile away to the right stood the shield wall, the stone dark and sheer and plunging into shadowed depths below. To the east at this end of the mighty cleft stood the far side, at this point but ten miles away. Leagues to the left the breech widened, spreading out to a breadth of thirty miles, more or less maintaining that width to the far end of the basin some forty leagues away; there where it widened the floor of the rift plunged down a mile or more, becoming deeper in places all the way to the end; but here nigh the shield wall it narrowed down from thirty miles to ten, its floor but a thousand feet deep. As Beau said, "Lor', it's somewhat like a bottle, and we are caught here in its neck."

Below and leftward, they could see but desolation, the land

hot, baked, cracked, with leagues of black stone heaped in shattered piles jagging across the floor in long, jumbled runs.
Beyond the black stone, whitish vapors, mayhap steam, surged
from holes in the ground, and far to the left yellow gas belched
upward from a great crack cleaving across tawny flats. Dark
smoke billowed from a conical ash pile nigh the opposite side,
and here and there on the ravaged earth pools of black bubbled
and oozed, as if the damaged ground itself were raddled with
open cankers seeping ebon pus.

"What a hideous place," said Dinly. "No wonder they call it
Hèl's Crucible."

Down they rode and down, coming at last unto the host
standing athwart the long, rough ramp, rubble and scree and
barren earth underfoot, the sides left and right pitching down
steeply. Continuing on, across the more or less level place they
fared among the ranks of the warriors, the Warrows at last
emerging beyond. There the slant pitched downward again, and
a mile or so downgrade and at the base of the broad, gritty slope
was arrayed the foe.

The Warrows reined to a stop and dismounted, and stepped
forward to see, and they found themselves next to Gildor and
Vanidor, the twin Lian brothers staring down at the ranks of
enemy. At hand stood Bekki, the Dwarf glaring down as well.

"Quite a number, eh, Tipperton?" said Vanidor.

"How many do you think there are?" asked Tip.

"Somewhat between sixty thousand and seventy," said
Vanidor, "or so we judge."

Gildor and Bekki nodded in agreement.

Rynna sighed. "Then we are yet outnumbered, for in council
last night a tally was taken: the count of those who are hale and
ready to fight totals to but fifty-seven thousand altogether."

"Bah," growled Bekki. "Outnumbered or not, we will defeat
them."

"Be not too certain, Lord Bekki," said Gildor, "for they are an
arduous foe."

A look of anguish crossed Beau's face, and he said, "Lord
Gildor is right, my friend, for our casualties were heavy: there
were nearly three thousand slain outright in the strife along the
rim, and seven thousand more who were wounded grievously,
seven thousand who will not soon see battle again." A tear
trickled down Beau's cheek, and Linnet reached out and took
his hand.

Bekki shook his head. "The cowardly enemy did not escape
unscathed, for the Châkka threw twelve or thirteen thousand of
the foe over the rim last night."

Rynna's face filled with distress. "You cast them over the brim?"

"Aye," replied Bekki, "by my orders as well as those of DelfLords Volki and Okar and Valk, they were thrown into the rift. Pah, unlike some we have battled in the past, these did not deserve the honor of fire or stone."

"But to cast them over the rim . . ."

"Fear not, lady, for most were dead by the time they were flung."

Rynna shook her head in fret but returned her gaze downslope.

"When will the King offer them surrender terms again?" asked Tip.

As Bekki snorted in disgust, Rynna said, "He proposes to do so at the noontide."

"Well then, that gives us some time to look over the terrain, just in case—"

Tipperton's words were interrupted by a horn call from below.

"Look!" cried Beau, pointing.

From the fore of the ranks of the enemy, a large party broke away from the main body and advanced onto the slope and up. In the lead strode a Chabbain bearing a grey flag, flanked left and right by more Chabbains, twenty-one warriors in all. In their wake rode some thirty or so horsemen—Kistanians, Hyrinians, Jûngarians—with a score of black-robed Fists of Rakka striding upslope behind. Midst them all rode Lord Tain bearing the corpse of his daughter Jolet.

A half mile up the slope they came, to one of the level flats. And there they stopped and planted the grey flag and blew the horn again.

The surrogate had come to parley.

"My Lord King, again I say beware treachery," said DelfLord Bekki, even as he slipped a throwing axe into his belt and took up his war hammer and shield. "There is no honor in their hearts."

"Nevertheless," said King Blaine, buckling on his sword, "we will go to meet them. I had planned on doing so in the noontide." As he slid a plain helm over his red hair, he added, "This merely advances our plans by several candlemarks." He mounted his grey horse and took his embossed shield from an attendant, then turned to the others. "Ready?"

Armed and armored and mounted all, the Corons and DelfLords and Marshals and Captains and Mages and Kings and

Chieftains and one Warrow Commander started down the slope, Vanidar Silverleaf at Blaine's right, Hrosmarshal Linde to his left and bearing the High King's scarlet-and-gold standard, Dara Arylin dextral of Vanidar and bearing the flag of truce.

Tipperton watched as Rynna rode down and away, his heart hammering in his chest. "I do not trust these foe to honor the grey flag."

At Tipperton's side, Mage Imongar said, "Neither do I, Sir Tipperton. Neither do I."

Now Tip looked across at the other Warrows. "Mount up," he gritted. "Mount up just in case."

Behind the Warrow army, Elves and Dwarves and Baeron and Mages and men mounted up as well.

Down they rode and down, coming ever nearer the foe, and Rynna shuddered, for now she could see Lord Tain, with his unclean white hair stringing down and his filthy white beard reaching to his waist; and he sat madly murmuring unto the long-dead burden he tenderly cradled in his own gaunt arms. Desiccated she was, her skin like leather drawn tight. Her teeth protruded in a gaping, rictus grin, her eyes nought but dark hollows. Rotted silken garments clung to her wasted frame, her left leg missing below the knee, the yellowed thighbone above showing through, a bit of tattered hose yet clinging. Her other leg and arms were wasted, drawn thin like jerky meat, the bones of her hands and remaining foot skeletal. Lord Tain held her close to his breast and kissed her and stroked what was left of her dark stringy hair and whispered of a glorious future ahead after her child was born.

Horror filled Rynna's heart at such a sight, yet a poignant sadness, too, and she turned her head away, tears streaming down.

Now the King and company reached the flat to come before the foe, and some ten yards from the surrogate, Blaine held up a hand and stopped. Behind him the emissaries stopped as well.

A black-cloaked Fist of Rakka stepped to Lord Tain's horse and led it forth from the ranks. Then he turned unto the surrogate and hissed, "*Gluktu!*"

Lord Tain's prattle and whispering ceased, and his deranged gaze was displaced, to be filled with a malevolent glare. No longer did a demented old man look through these eyes, but a vile being instead.

Slowly the surrogate's gaze slid across each and every one of the emissaries, and when his glare came unto Coron Eiron he laughed. "How is your son, my lord, yet fetching a silver blade? Oh, but dear me, I did forget: 'twas lost in the Dalgor Fens."

Again came the laughter, as Eiron's knuckles turned white on the hilt of his sheathed sword.

The surrogate's gaze slithered on down the line of emissaries, and when it came to Rynna, she shuddered under the malignant stare, and she knew 'twas Modru who glared out at her. Yet he looked upon Rynna in puzzlement, as if trying to determine just who or what she was, and where he might have seen her kind before.

His gaze finally left her and slid on down the line, passing over Dwarves and Baeron and Elves and men. But then he came unto Farrin and Dalavar, the Mages staring coldly back. "Bah! You bring neophytes with you, Dalavar? Novices above as well?"

Dalavar's Wolflike eyes bore into those of the surrogate, but neither he nor Farrin replied.

The surrogate glared at the Wolfmage and sneered, "That we are met for the third time bodes you ill, Dalavar, for two minor victories does not a war win. It is of no moment that you escaped me once at the Stones of Jalan and then again in the Gwasp, for this time I shall throw a collar about your mongrel scruff and bring you to heel. And think not to evade me by that bauble about your neck, for I am your master in concealment as you will see."

With a wave of hand the vile presence dismissed all the emissaries and turned its gaze upon High King Blaine.

Blaine stared back into the malevolent glare. "We did not come here to trade insults, Lord Modru, but to accept your surrender instead."

"Surrender? You fool. 'Tis you who should lay down your arms, for my victory here will be absolute. Did you not think it peculiar that when my forces left Gûnarring Gap they seemed prepared to come straightly here? Here where all your petty kings and corons and chieftains and DelfLords and other such rabble could gather? And did you not wonder why I did not destroy your paltry bridge but instead left it intact? Oh, it was a clever move to use Dragonships as pontoons, yet through my agents I watched them being fitted in the harbor of Pendwyr there in Hile Bay and realized your plan. But I let it proceed unmolested. Why you ask? Bah! Is it not obvious? Know this, Fool Blaine, I *drew* you here to Hèl's Crucible, you and your so-called Free Folk, for with but one blow at this place, I will eliminate all fools who oppose me, and when I have destroyed you entirely, Gyphon will rule, and *I* will be His regent."

Blaine looked grimly at the surrogate, but his words were for the one within. "You say such, Foul Modru, yet first you have to win, and at the moment, we hold the advantage."

"Advantage? Advantage? Imbecile Blaine!" The surrogate glanced at King Ranor in wrath, and then glared back at King Blaine. "That you hold the high ground is but an accident of these horse-lovers arriving unexpectedly, else you would be in the basin below, and *I* would hold the ground above. Even so, it is of no import, for you cannot prevail against that which I bring." Again the surrogate's face twisted in gloat. "What's that you ask? What is it I bring? Pah! Did you not know why the wind blows? Why *my* wind blows? It is to clear away the vapors in Hèl's Crucible for the march of my dread Swarm!" Now the surrogate glanced at Dalavar and laughed and gestured out into the rift and cried, "Behold!"

Of a sudden out on the floor of the basin, at a distance a rippling purled the air and where before there was nought but runs of shattered black stone and sulfurous rock and bubbling pustulant pools, a great Swarm stood revealed: thousands upon thousands upon thousands of Foul Folk, a hundred thousand or more—Rùcks, Hlôks, Ghûls on Hèlsteeds, dark Vulgs, hundreds of monstrous Trolls, and a dozen or more dreadful Gargons—all boiling forward in a seething, monstrous mass. And in the air high aloft flew a great, dark shape, mighty and massive and black, its vast leathery pinions churning: it was a Dragon dire.

And in that very same moment on the slope above, the elusive thought that had repeatedly escaped Tipperton now became crystal clear: those mountains afar were the *Skarpals*, the place where Jinnarin and Farrix and Aylissa had followed the Foul Folk when the Rûpt had fled. Nay! Not fled, but rather had assembled. *This* had been Modru's plan all along. He had drawn the Allies here to Hèl's Crucible; they had fallen into his trap.

And at Tipperton's side Mage Veran spoke a <word> then said to Imongar, "It is no illusion."

And Imongar gasped and her entire frame slumped in defeat. "Then we are lost, for we cannot prevail against so many Gargons, nor against the Dragon above."

And down where King Blaine and his emissaries stood, the surrogate turned and pointed at the oncoming Swarm. And the presence of Modru said, "Look well, Fool Blaine, for I myself ride in the fore of my might; I would see with my own eyes the victory I will win." At the head of the churning throng, a troika of Hèlsteeds drew a chariot rumbling across the floor below, driven by a figure in black, his features hidden behind a hideous iron mask. The surrogate turned back to King Blaine. "Surrender now or prepare for battle and think not to run, else I will loose Daagor from above, and he alone will shred and burn you all."

King Blaine, his features drawn grim, said, "Heed me, Foul Modru: we will not run nor will we surrender, Spawn, Gargons, renegade Dragon, or no."

Rage filled the surrogate's features, and Modru hissed, "*Now!*"

"Ware!" cried Bekki, flinging up his shield as, from under the concealment of black robes, the Fists of Rakka raised crossbows and stepped forward and aimed and loosed their bolts, some to strike flesh and bone, others to be deflected by iron.

And through the air tumbled a glitter as Bekki's axe flew in return to strike the surrogate full in the head, cleaving through flesh and bone and brain, blood and grey matter splashing wide as Lord Tain pitched over the rear cantle and to the ground, Jolet's corpse crashing down beside him to be smashed under the hooves of the Hyrinians and Kistanians charging forward, and the High King's counterattack.

"Rynna!" shouted Tipperton, spurring forward and racing downslope, Warrows galloping after, their surefooted ponies running full tilt. And behind them thundered the host, shouts of *Treachery!* and *Blaine!* and *Adon!* and *Elwydd!* and *Fyrra!* ringing through the air. And even as they did so, up from the basin below charged the combined army of the Chabbains and Hyrinians and Kistanians and Jûngarians and the Fists of Rakka.

Out on the floor of the basin, the vast Swarm of Foul Folk came on—Rûcks and Hlôks tramping forward, and Ghûls on Hèlsteeds riding, Trolls lumbering, Gargons stalking, a Dragon circling high above. Yet Modru did not let them race ahead but deliberately held them to their pace, for with his overpowering might, he knew certain victory was his. Even so, as a token of what was to come, he did loose his Vulgs to attack, for they would spread terror and poison among these *fools* who sought to oppose him.

Black and vicious, across the basin they sped, howling in savage glee. Yet down the slope came racing six silver shapes at the call of a seventh below.

Amid battle cries and shouts of rage and the clash of steel on steel, on the slope the two armies crashed together, swords and axes riving, spears piercing, maces smashing, morning stars and hammers crushing, tulwars and long, curved swords and scimitars and axes responding in kind, blades cleaving through flesh and bone and armor alike, with blunt-faced weapons crunching and pulping and breaking and pulverizing whatever it was they hammered.

"Rynna! Rynna!" shouted Tipperton, and in the melee he finally saw her just as her pony was slain, the animal to tumble down, its throat slashed, blood flying. Rynna fell hard to the ground beside it, landing on her left shoulder and losing her bow. A Fist of Rakka lunged toward her, his blade raised high, but in a flash Rynna was on her feet and running, the black-robed enemy in pursuit.

Ssss-thok! Tipperton's arrow took the foe in the throat, and he fell to his knees, clutching his neck, unable to breathe, his eyes wide and filled with death.

With Beau and Linnet and Farly and Nix and Dinly racing after, Tipperton shouted and spurred toward fleeing Rynna, the damman ducking and dodging among milling, bellowing men and Dwarves and Elves and Baeron.

Rynna spun to escape a Chabbain even as a Dwarf hewed the dusky man down from behind, but now she had turned toward the Warrows and looked up to see Tipperton galloping toward her even as he shouted her name.

Tipperton slowed and held out his arm and she grabbed it and, struggling, gasping in pain, her left arm useless, still she managed to swing up behind. "Ride to where bows will be effective," she cried, and Tipperton galloped toward the nearest edge of the slope.

"Dinly!" Tip heard Linnet shout, and looked back to see the buccan fall dead, pierced through by a spear. And cursing in grief, Tipperton and the others galloped on, Fists of Rakka in pursuit.

Down the steep side of the ramp they fled, their mounts barely able to keep their feet, and then Nix's pony tumbled tail over saddle, throwing Nix free to crash down the stony slant, the pony behind cartwheeling—*Crack!*—breaking its neck but still tumbling, slamming atop Nix and sliding on past to come to the bottom below, as the others reached the flat to gallop toward the towering shield wall.

Dazed, Nix managed to stagger to his feet, yet one foot seemed twisted at an angle. Even so, he started down the remainder of the steep pitch toward the bottom, but scrambling down after came the Fists of Rakka, and in the lead one of the black-robed men paused and aimed his crossbow and let fly the bolt. It struck Nix full in the back, and he tumbled down dead, sliding through rubble and scree to fetch up beside his pony.

"Nix!" screamed Linnet, wheeling about. "Nix!"

"Linnet, wait!" cried Beau, coming after.

Farly shouted in rage and galloped back toward the slope. And even as Linnet, sobbing, threw herself from her pony and took her brother Nix in her arms, Farly loosed an arrow to fly through the air and slay the crossbow bearer. The other black-robed men skidded to a halt and several began cocking crossbows. And still more Fists of Rakka came scrambling over the lip and down.

Beau slid his pony to a halt beside Linnet and cried, "Dammia, there are too many. We have to go." Even as he said it, he hurled a slingstone to fell one of the black-robed men, the foe to tumble down the slope and crash to the ground beside Linnet, a hole in his skull, his neck awry.

Yet sobbing, Linnet kissed Nix and closed his eyes and then sprang to her feet, just as a bolt slammed into the ground where she had been. She strung an arrow to bow and pierced the man through, and then leapt to her pony—"*Hai!*"—to race away, Fists of Rakka scrambling down after.

Tipperton and Rynna had turned as well, and when Linnet and Beau and Farly came galloping, Rynna called out, "We need make a stand in a place of defense. There are boulders on the talus at the base of the shield wall."

Pursued by twenty or more black-robed Fists of Rakka, toward the shield wall the Wee Folk galloped, passing by bubbling pools of steaming mud, the odor horrific. Past a long, glittering ridge of sharp crystal clusters they hammered, crystals sharp as the sharpest of blades. Past sulfurous vents they fled, yellow-brown smoke billowing out, and along a jagged fissure exhaling foul fumes from deep within its abyssal depths. But at last they came to the jumbled slope at the base of the shield wall, and dismounting and leading their ponies, up the rubble they went, with Fists of Rakka running in pursuit, and a battle between armies on the great slope aft, and Modru's vast Swarm churning across the basin behind.

"Look out, Farly!" But Linnet's call came too late, and the crossbow bolt punched through the buccan, and he fell dead at her feet.

Beau whirled his sling and loosed a bullet—*Crack!*—the man to scream and clutch at his head and fall backwards even as the others fled down and away.

Linnet scrambled on hands and knees to Farly, and she pressed her ear to the buccan's chest. Then with tears in her eyes she looked up at Beau and shook her head.

Tipperton glanced back at Rynna; she sat behind a boulder with her back to the shield wall, her arm in an improvised sling, for her left shoulder had been dislocated when she had slammed into the ground.

The remainder of the ponies had all been slain by the Fists of Rakka, the horselings unable to take adequate shelter behind fallen rock at the wall. And now Farly lay dead, and though Tipperton and Linnet and Beau yet had missiles, still the black-robed men were many, and the arrows few.

Again the Fists of Rakka came creeping upward, cautiously slipping from rock to rock, for the Warrows were more formidable than the black-robed men had ever imagined. Even so, to die in the service of Rakka won them eternal bliss, hence onward they came. Tipperton took careful aim just at the edge of a boulder, for that's where the one he targeted would appear.

Ssss . . . flew the arrow *thock!* to strike, the man to fall dead in the rubble and slide down a ways and stop.

The other Fists of Rakka again retreated.

Of a sudden, Rynna gasped.

"What is it?" hissed Tipperton.

She turned and pressed her ear against the shield wall. "The stone, Tipperton, there is a sound."

"A sound?"

"Yes, like—"

Yaaaaahhh . . . ! From below there came a collective yawl.

"Here they come again," said Beau, setting his sling atwirl.

Tipperton turned and peered past the boulder. Charging up the slope came the Fists of Rakka, running in the open and screaming in frenzy *Rakka! Rakka! Rakka!*

"Make every shot count!" yelled Tipperton. "Else we are doomed!"

But in the very moment he drew—

—from behind there came a *splitting* noise, as of cloven stone—

—and the Fists of Rakka cried out in fear and fled scrambling downward.

Rynna gasped and Linnet shrieked, and Tip and Beau spun about to see—

—a huge form emerging from the very stone itself and another form coming after.

And Tipperton looked up into great gemstone eyes staring outward and knew the Utruni had come.

Manlike they were but huge, taller than the tallest of Trolls—fifteen, sixteen, seventeen feet or perhaps more, the wee Warrows looking up at them could not say. There were seven of the Stone Giants and they wore no clothing nor did they carry any goods, and their skins bore hues of stone: grey, slate, tawny, rudden. Yet even though the Utruni were bare, whether or no they were male or female, neither Tipperton nor Beau nor Rynna nor Linnet could say. And as the Warrows scrambled backwards and out of the way, the giants stepped forth from the shield wall and sealed the stone behind, leaving no mark whatsoever. And they peered up into the sky, up where the Dragon flew, and then they looked down upon the floor of the basin, as if searching for, for . . .

. . . for what? None of the Wee Folk could say.

"Have you come to help?" called Tip.

Reacting in surprise, the Utruni turned toward Tipperton's voice, their gemstone stares searching for whoever had called out.

One of the Stone Giants spoke to the others, his voice deep, his words sounding somewhat like rock sliding upon rock, the others replying in the same tongue.

"Hiyo," called Tip, waving his arms. "I'm here."

With eyes like large diamonds, the greatest of the giants, pale buff in color, peered down toward the buccan, and in an eld form of Common said, "Ah, seest thee, ae naow do. Vapour ephemeral thou dost loken. Be ae riht: there be feower of ye?"

The grey Utrun shook its head. "Nae, Tholon. They be fif." The giant pointed down at Farly's body.

"Are you asking if we are four?" called Tip. "Asking if we are five?"

The one called Tholon cocked its head and then said, "Aye, though ye seemeth summat more solide than many who dwellen aboven, we be not want to stepe an ye."

"We must be difficult for them to see," said Rynna.

"Mage Farrin *did* say they can look right through solid stone," said Beau.

"Farrin?" said the grey Utrun. "Ye knowen Farrin?"

Beau nodded.

Again the giant asked. "Ye knowen Farrin?"

"Yes," called Tipperton, realizing that the Utrun could not see Beau's nod. "We do know Farrin. He is a friend and in dire straits, as are we all."

"Farrin didst techen we this dwer tunge," said the buff-hued giant, Tholon. Then he cocked his head and asked, "But who be ye?"

Tipperton stepped forward. "I am Tipperton Thistledown, and my companions are Rynna Thistledown and Beau and Linnet Darby"—Tipperton looked out at the rift, where Modru's seething Swarm boiled toward the ramp—"and we desperately need help."

The rudden giant pointed at Farly's body. "Thou hast nama feower, but ye be fif."

Tipperton's eyes teared, and he said, "The one lying there is slain. His name was Farly Bourne."

As one, the Stone Giants looked at Farly and made a clenching gesture with their right hands. And then the buff-colored Utrun turned to Tipperton and said, "Ae hight Tholon. Thæs be Orth, Flate, Umac, Chelk, Sidon, and Drit."

At the naming of each, without conscious thought Tipperton noted their gemstone eyes: sapphire, emerald, peridot, another emerald, ruby, and topaz, in addition to Tholon's diamond.

When Tholon fell silent, Tipperton, a plea in his voice, said, "Again I ask, did you come to help?"

"We be yet nae deciden Friend Tipperton," replied Orth.

"Oh, but you must help," implored Beau, gesturing out at the oncoming Swarm. "I mean, if you don't, then Gyphon will rule all, for Modru has come with his minions, and they are many and terrible and in numbers we cannot defeat: Rûcks, Hlôks, Vulgs, Ghûls on Hèlsteeds, Trolls, Gargons, and a Dragon."

"Se Drake?" asked Flate, pointing into the sky.

"It is Daagor," said Rynna.

Tipperton looked at her. "Daagor? The renegade? Daagor who vies with Black Kalgalath to be the greatest Dragon of all?"

Rynna nodded. "At the parley, Lord Tain—Modru—named him so."

"What does it matter?" said Beau, despairing. "Daagor, Skail, Sleeth, whoever, still it is a Dragon, a thing we cannot hope to defeat."

Tip, Beau, Rynna, Linnet: all turned to look upon the Drake high above . . . and then down at the rift below.

On the long slope the battle yet raged, Dwarves, Elves, Baeron, men, hewing and piercing and stabbing and bashing and crushing, shouting battle cries and calling out *Adon!* and *Elwydd!* and *Fyrra!* Calling out *Gyphon!* and *Rakka!* Calling out *Blaine!* and *Modru!* All while slaughtering one another.

"Oh my! Look there!" cried Linnet as the battle swirled. And in the midst of the clangor and chaos, great Bears raged, claws and teeth rending and tearing.

The Warrows looked at one another in wonderment, for how could such a thing be? And then Rynna said, "There is a legend 'round the Baeron . . ."

"Oh lor," said Beau, "that's right. Some Baeron are said to turn into Bears . . . that, or Wolves."

They turned and looked back, but the snarl of battle had

come in between and the huge Bears could no longer be seen. And as one, both Tip and Beau looked out on the basin below, and there they found Silver Wolves whirling in melee with Vulgs, slaughtered black creatures lying all 'round.

And then their gazes were drawn rightward, where across the floor of the rift came Modru in his iron mask, a troika of Hèl-steeds drawing his chariot, his vast Swarm churning after, Gargons and Trolls in their seething midst.

As the Warrows looked on at the overwhelming defeat at hand, behind them the great Stone Giants held rumbled converse in that sliding-rock tongue of theirs, and finally Tholon said, "Aye, we willa helpan. Yet ye seeth betera thanne we: hwær best to aiden?"

"Are you saying that you cannot see the great Swarm coming?" asked Tip.

"Aye. Se Trollth and Grægoni we seeth well; se Drake, too; 'twæs thæm we traked to this plæce hwil trieneth to deciden. Se rest be as vague as vapours."

"Oh, Tip," groaned Linnet, "there are too many Trolls for them to fight. Too many Gargons, too. And the Dragon, well, can even a Stone Giant tackle such a foe?"

"Argh!" said Beau. "Even though the Alliance holds the high ground, the Utruni have come too late, for the tide of battle is lost before the flood of Modru's forces." He turned and pounded his fist into the sheer stone, and said "We're nought but insignificant flies on this wall. There's no way—"

"That's it, Beau!" shouted Tipperton. "You've got it!"

"I what?" said Beau, wheeling 'round to look at Tipperton, but that buccan had turned to the giants.

In the midst of the melee arcane waves of fear washed over the combatants, for the Gargons were nearing and affecting all. Even so the battle raged on, for wrath and revenge and hatred and desperation powered the arms of ally and enemy alike.

And high on the slope King Blaine was tended by healers drawing a crossbow bolt from his forearm, the shaft having punched through shield and armor alike.

"Swift now," gritted the King, "for I must return to battle."

At his side stood Mage Farrin, and nearby pacing back and forth strode Linde, the Warrior Maiden anxious to rejoin the melee below.

"They can't hear me, can't hear me at all above the roar of battle," raged Tip, his black-oxen horn in hand, the buccan looking up at Tholon, the only Utrun left. "We cannot do it if they hear me not." Dejected, Tipperton turned to Rynna and said, "I might as well be whispering, for all the good it did."

Rynna peered out across the floor of the rift—Modru's Swarm now closing in on the ramp. Then she looked at the battle above, and groaning in defeat she spun toward the wall. Suddenly her eyes widened, and she whispered, "Sur Kolaré." Spinning toward Tipperton, she shouted, "I have it, Tip: Sur Kolaré! Whisper Hollow!"

Tipperton spread his hands. "But how can—?"

"Tholon will do it!" declared Rynna. She sighted a boulder at hand, then called to the Stone Giant and stepped to the barrier. "Can you shape the stone of the wall here before this boulder, hollow it out, cup it 'round concave, so its form would just embrace yon ramp were it to extend that far? A wide section I mean, fifty feet across and half as deep?"

Glancing at the ramp and then at the sheer barrier, Tholon stepped 'round the boulder and to the wall and with his great hands began shaping the stone, rock flowing under his touch. Remembering the contour of Sur Kolaré, Rynna watched closely and called out to the giant just how to curve the arc of the hollow being formed.

With hope in his eyes, Tipperton clambered up onto the boulder Rynna had selected.

And still on the slope below, the battle raged, a mighty clash and clangor, while above the King, now bandaged, prepared for combat.

Of a sudden nearby, "Hearken!" cried Linde, stopping in her tracks. " 'Tis a black-oxen horn calling."

"I hear," growled the King, drawing the cuff of his gauntlet over the dressing. "But why is it signalling withdraw? Is this a trick of Modru's?"

"I hear it as well, but whence does it blow?" said Mage Farrin, looking about, trying to find the source.

"There!" said Linde, pointing at the shield wall in the near distance.

Farrin looked where Linde pointed. "Utrun!" he proclaimed, now seeing the Stone Giant. "My Lord King Blaine, it is an Utrun."

"Utrun there is, yet 'tis a Waeran blowing the horn," said Linde. "And other Waerans to the side, waving desperately."

"Where?" asked Farrin.

"On yon rock he stands, facing the wall and blowing a Harlingar horn, the others leftward and waving," replied Linde. "It can only be Tipperton, and he sounds the signal to withdraw."

"Bah," growled King Blaine, "I yet think this is some fraud of Modru's."

Beside the King, Farrin said a <word> and narrowed his gaze and then said, "Nay, my Lord, 'tis no illusion but a true sight instead. 'Tis indeed a Waerling, and with an Utrun." Now Farrin turned to Blaine. "My lord, I suggest you do as he calls."

"But, Mage Farrin, we hold the high ground, 'tis the only advantage we have, and should we withdraw, we will find ourselves on the flats along the rim above, where the enemy will do us in."

"My lord," said Linde, gesturing at the oncoming Swarm, "we will lose regardless, for among the Foul Folk Modru brings Ogrus and Gargons and a Dragon, and we have no means to defeat them. Yet heed me:

"The Waldan blowing that horn conceived the plan which set Mineholt North free. He conceived the plan which freed Dendor, and he was one of the two who slew the Gargon outside that city's walls. And if I am not mistaken, one of the Waldana at his side is the very same one who conceived the plan which resulted in the destruction of another Gargon pursuing us through the Blackwood. And so this I say: if Tipperton Thistledown and Rynna Thistledown and an Utrun sound the signal to withdraw, then, my Lord High King Blaine, I say we must withdraw."

"But we know nothing of what he plans."

"Trust him, my lord. Trust them."

Blaine frowned and looked from Linde to the shield wall to Farrin, then out upon the Swarm boiling forward and finally back to the wall again. At last he said, "Well and good. We will withdraw. Sound the signal, Hrosmarshal Linde."

But the Allies weren't the only ones to hear Tip's horn, for Modru in his chariot heard it as well. And he turned his iron-veiled face toward the shield wall to see the Utrun and others standing there. And of a sudden behind his wrought mask his glaring eyes widened, and he howled in fury and gestured to Daagor above and said a <word> and then screamed directly into Daagor's ear, though the great Dragon was far, far aloft.

And the mighty Drake bellowed and folded his vast leathery wings and plunged roaring toward the distant wall.

"What's taking them so long?" shouted Beau, leaping and waving to attract attention, as Tipperton blew and blew, the sound of the black-oxen horn focused by the concave depression in the stone and hurled toward the ramp.

"Can they even hear the horn above the sounds of battle?" cried Linnet.

"Perhaps, perhaps," answered Rynna, "but we won't know unless and until—"

"Oh lor!" shouted Beau. "Look, above. Daagor comes."

Down plummeted the Dragon, down and down and down, hurtling toward the shield wall where Warrow and Utrun stood.

Linnet reached out for her buccaran's hand. "Oh, Beau, what will we do?"

And still the Swarm seethed toward the ramp; they had nearly reached the base.

"Listen!" shouted Rynna. "Listen! Oh, Tipperton, stop and listen!"

Tipperton turned and listened, and standing at the focal point of the shaped hollow, he clearly heard Harlingar horns blowing in the distance: *Hahn, taa-roo! Hahn, taa-roo! Hahn, taa-roo taa-roo!*

It was the command to withdraw.

Tipperton shouted—"Tholon, signal the others now!"—and leapt down from the rock.

Down plunged Daagor and down, and he drew in a great, deep breath.

Even as Tipperton leaped down, Tholon hammered on rock— once, twice, thrice—the entire wall ringing in response. The Utrun then split wide the stone, fissuring a passage inward.

Catching up Tipperton's lute and Beau's medical bag, retrieved from their crossbow-slain steeds, "Take Farly," said Linnet, and Beau stooped and lifted up the dead buccan, and the Warrows entered the cleft to find Chelk waiting, a phosphorescent glow in hand.

Daagor roared in fury, his flame blasting forth in a raging bolt, yet ere the blaze reached the crevice, the Utrun entered and sealed the stone after, the Dragonfire to strike and splash wide.

"I can't see a thing," said Tipperton, but then Chelk bent down and handed the buccan a double fistful of glowing lichen. Tipperton then remembered Bekki's tale of Durek and the Stone Giants in the depths of Kraggen-cor, and he knew he must be holding the stuff of Dwarven lanterns, the lichen brought here by Chelk specifically for the Warrows to use to illuminate their way. Tipperton gave over a handful to Rynna to spread the light out farther.

Whmp!

The wall juddered, as if something had struck it a great blow.

Tholon spoke in the sliding-rock tongue, and Chelk turned and began cleaving the stone, making a tunnel through.

Whmp!

Again the wall jolted.

Through an Utrun-made passage went the Warrows, following Chelk, Tholon coming after, sealing the stone behind.

Daagor roared and tore at the wall, flame blasting out in his fury. And he cast his senses forth; there were several Utruni in the rock—seven in all—as well as four of the Wee Folk.

His great claws rended stone in his anger, and the ground began to shudder, not only where he stood, but across the basin and up walls and along the rim as well.

On the ramp, the battle raged, the Allies fighting in withdrawal, the ground underfoot now wrenching.

The enemy disengaged, or attempted to, for here and there Châkka fought on, refusing to let the foe flee, though some Dwarves elsewhere had begun to withdraw under the insistent peal of horns.

And seven Silver Wolves came racing up the quaking ramp, six following Shifter, the Vulgs in the rift all slain.

And out on the juddering floor of the basin, black rock shattered and collapsed; fire burst forth from crevices deep, and geysers blasted boiling water skyward; mud exploded, black smoke billowed, and molten sulfur flowed yellow across the land. Crystalline ridges fractured, cracked, and shattered outward in shards, the air chiming and jingling in their wake.

And Modru screamed in fury, while his Swarm shrieked in dread, the land jolting underfoot. This could not be Daagor's doing, but that of cursed Utruni instead. Modru cast forth his own senses to locate the Stone Giants, and upon finding them, Modru's eyes flew wide and he shrilled in quavering terror.

And at the shield wall great wide cracks splintered upward, driven by the Utruni within, while off to one side within shuddering stone and stumbling their way up a long Utrun-made slope toward the westerly brim, wee Warrows followed a giant.

And down on the talus at the foot of the wall Daagor looked upward as a huge section of the great barrier from base to rim began to tilt inward, the immense slab leaning, leaning, leaning over, to fall with a thunderous crash, and in through the vast gape left behind roared the waters of the Avagon Sea.

And farther eastward another wide crack split upward through the stone, a second huge slab to break free and topple inward, and even more waters of the sea thundered in.

And following an Utrun-cloven tunnel, on westerly the War-rows went, Chelk leading, Tholon coming after, sealing the stone behind, Tipperton now carrying Farly's body over his shoulder, sharing the burden with Beau.

While under the raging waters, Daagor bellowed, flame blast-ing upward, the Dragon's bulk and great leathery wings pinned by unnumbered tons of mountainous stone lying atop him.

And a vast wave, hundreds of feet high, thundered in through the immense gap, hurling across the floor of the rift, the sea at last free to engulf the basin within, and it swept down upon the mighty Swarm, crashing over shrieking Rûcks and Hlôks and squealing Hèlsteeds and howling Ghûls. Trolls yawled in terror as they were swept under, their massive bones dragging them down. Gargons, too, plunged below the roaring billows, their own solidity dooming them.

And Modru's chariot was swept away, tumbling and lashing under the flood.

And another great slab crashed inward, more and more sea thundering after.

And the great waves crashed onto and over the ramp, sweep-ing Elves, Dwarves, Baeron, men, horses, ponies, and land away, the living and the dead, the wounded and the hale, ally and foe alike . . . though most of the Allies yet hale had withdrawn at the signal, had survived, some fleeing upward bearing wounded, all but barely ahead of the whelming deluge.

But lower down on the slope, none of the foe escaped.

And now the stone at the westerly end of the shield wall split open, and a giant emerged, Warrows following after. And when the Wee Folk had all come out, the Utrun went back into the crevice, sealing the stone behind.

Tipperton eased Farly's body to the ground and then stood with the others and watched the vast inundation.

And the air roared with the sound of water thundering in.

Even though he could not be heard by the others, his voice lost in the bellow, Beau stood on the rim and chanted:

> *"Seek the aid of those not men*
> *To quench the fires of war,*
> *Else Evil triumphant will ascend*
> *And rule forevermore."*

It was Rael's rede, at last its meaning clear, and Beau looked at Tipperton and received a grim nod in return, for now they both knew that somehow all was connected.

And then Beau turned to Linnet to find that she was weeping, and he took her in his arms to comfort her. And she leaned into Beau and said, "Oh, beloved, my Nix, our Nix, is lost forever beneath this flood." Though Beau did not hear her above the thunderous shout, he embraced her and stroked her hair.

At Tipperton's side Rynna's eyes widened, horrified, and Tipperton turned to see—

"No! No! I didn't mean for this to happen!" Tip's voice lost under the roar

—Fjordlander Dragonships come rushing through the gap, frantic crews yet aboard, the ships to roll and whip and thrash and finally plunge under the raging water, wooden shields, masts, sails, hull, men, all to vanish from sight in the thundering flow.

In the port of Adeo some twenty-five miles away, the huge Gothonian vessels swung about at anchor, some to drag their great drogue irons across the bottom ere catching to come to a halt.

And another great slab of shield wall toppled inward, and still more sea rushed in.

And down in the rift, hurling water smashed over all, pouring down into vast chasms and onto the burning lava below, the sea to flash into vapor and explode upward, great thunderous blasts jolting the air. And still geysers spewed steaming water up through the ice-cold, inrushing sea, while bubbling mud pits were swept into the torrent along with sulfurous melt, to turn the flow dark and sickly.

Shattered black stone and shards of crystal were swept up and borne northwesterly, along with the tumbling bodies of drowned Rûcks and Hlôks and Ghûls and Hèlsteeds and Trolls and Gargons, the water cascading them along the bottom, smashing, bludgeoning, rending the corpses as it thundered along to plunge down a mile-deep slope and into the wide depths below.

And beneath a great slab along the remnants of the shield wall, Daagor drowned, screaming in rage and fury and blasting flame even as he died.

And easterly, another slab fell into the basin, the shield wall now nearly all destroyed, the Avagon Sea roaring in triumph as it hurtled inward at last.

And still the water poured in, steam and detonations erupting upward from the bottom below.

And the High King looked on the rage and fury, Modru and his great Swarm gone, Daagor nowhere to be seen, the Hyrinians and Chabbains and Kistanians, the Fists of Rakka, the Throng of Jûng, all were drowned.

Drowned, too, were some of the Allies—Dwarves, men, Elves,

Baeron—those who had not been high enough up the slope when that first massive wave had struck, all casualties in this strife. King Blaine looked rightward where in the near distance four Wee Folk stood and one lay unmoving on the ground, and at this sight Blaine buried his face in his hands and sank to his knees and wept, bereavement sweeping over him, for so many friends, so many comrades, so many allies had died. Yet he wept in relief as well, for by unexpected stroke the battle was ended . . .

. . . And so too was ended the war.

39

*E*ight days later, when the host was finally ready to depart the environs of Hèl's Crucible, the waters of the Avagon Sea yet rushed in through the gap where the shield wall once had been, but its thunder had abated, diminishing throughout the days as the great rift had begun to fill. And here nigh the place where once had stood a wall, Tip and Beau, Rynna and Linnet, gazed down from above.

"Lor', but I never thought I'd ever look upon the making of a new sea," said Beau. "What do you think they'll call it?"

"Hèl's Ocean, I shouldn't wonder," replied Tipperton, pointing, where erupting upward came a blast of water, driven by an explosion far below.

"Farrin says the Utruni are going to calm the land," said Rynna, "working far below in the living stone to bring it all to rest. That's what they do, you know."

"There is fire down there, molten rock," came a gravelly voice from behind. It was Bekki. "The Stone Giants will be hard-pressed to work in a place little different from the bowels of a firemountain, a deadly dangerous place to be."

"Not anywhere I'd like to hang my hat," said Beau, hugging Linnet close.

"I came to say it is time to go," said Bekki.

Tip looked at Rynna and Linnet, then said, "We'll be right along."

Bekki nodded and turned and walked back toward the campsite.

Tip took a deep breath. "Well?"

Linnet nodded, then stepped to the rim and looked out on the forming sea. "Good-bye, Dinly. Good-bye, Nix." Linnet turned to look at the nearby cairn, but one among thousands. "Good-bye, Farly. May Elwydd hold you three in Her hand along with Alver, too."

Rynna, her shoulder healed by Mage Letha, stepped to the lip of what was once Hèl's Crucible, and she held Tipperton's bow, a red-shafted arrow fitted to string. Tipperton stepped up beside her, and he struck a lantern-striker to the woven red collar below the arrow head, and when it flared to life, Rynna drew the shaft to the full and let the arrow fly. Up it arced and up, loosed by an Elven bow, a phosphorescent streak running up through the clear dawn sky; far out above the waters it sailed, finally to arc over and down and down, to plunge at last into the dark flux of the inflowing sea.

"Good-bye, Alver and Dinly and Nix and Farly," she said, weeping. "We will hold you ever in our hearts."

Choking back tears, Tipperton and Beau stepped to their dammias, and taking them by the hand, slowly they trudged toward the host.

They fared back through the craggy hills and over the Dragonboat bridge. And when all the host had crossed over, the bridge was dismantled.

They rode to Caer Pendwyr in a fleet of Dragonships, did the wee Warrows, along with many of the captains and kings, along with DelfLords and corons and chieftains and other war-leaders.

Many more would come by the great Gothonian ships, while still others rode northerly and away, away toward Jord and Riamon and Mineholt North. Still even more fared westerly, striking for the Greatwood and Darda Erynian and Darda Galion and Kraggen-cor and Arden Vale beyond, or striking for Pellar and Valon and Jugo and Hoven. But many waited in the port of Adeo, waited for ships to come and take them to Tugal and Vancha and Basq, to Gelen and Gothon, some to sail to ports along the Ryngar Arm of the Weston Ocean, where they would disembark for Trellinath and Wellen, Dalara and Thol, or to ride through these lands to the Jillian Tors and Rian.

But Tip and Rynna and Beau and Linnet rode away in a Jutlander Dragonship, leaving Hèl's Crucible behind. Yet though they quitted the place itself, they could not escape its terrible memories; these they bore with them and away.

And down the Ironwater and into the deep blue of the Avagon Sea they rode, sailing south for three days to turn west. Four days later, seven in all after setting sail, they disembarked at the harbor of Pendwyr in Hile Bay, there below the High King's caer.

The city welcomed them with joy.

Uncomfortably, Tipperton turned about so that Rynna could see the fit of his new satin clothes, a deep sapphire blue to match his eyes, white ruffles and trimmings all 'round.

"Oh, but you look splendid, Tip," said Rynna, she herself clothed in a muted yellow gown, white ribbons crisscrossing her bodice.

Tipperton sighed.

"Come, now," said Linnet, "it can't be all that bad."

"It'll be right fun, if you ask me," said Beau, clothed in satin as well—brown with tan ruffles and trim. "We've done this before, you know, attended another ceremony that is, there in the city of Dendor."

His fists on his hips, Tip turned to Beau. "Right fun? Beau, if I remember correctly we were crawling about on the floor."

"Crawling about on the floor?" Linnet turned to Beau.

"Ah, well, hem, love, we couldn't see, you see, and we were trying to get to a place—"

"How undignified," said Linnet, the dammen gowned in brown, tan cording about her waist.

Tipperton laughed; Rynna, too. Beau looked at Linnet and grinned foolishly, and she broke into giggles.

Somewhere in the distance a gong sounded.

Tip drew in a deep breath and said, "Might as well get this over with."

Rynna slipped her arm through his, and likewise did Linnet take Beau's, and together they left their quarters in the High King's castle and stepped into the hall beyond.

On their way through the labyrinthine passages, they were joined by Bekki and Loric and Phais, and on they strode amicably, chatting of inconsequential things, Bekki growling that it all was a bother, Tipperton clearly agreeing. At last they came to the great throne chamber, and it was filled with hundreds of people, the conversation a babbling roar. Yet when the major-domo hammered his stave to the marble floor and announced

"Sir Tipperton Thistledown and Lady Rynna," and, "Sir Beau Darby and Lady Linnet," a hush came over the assembly. And when the Warrows stepped forward to come down into the hall, someone began to applaud, and then so did they all . . . and a cheering broke out, and the four wee ones were swept into the whirl of the crowd, lords and ladies pressing 'round, all talking at once.

Buccan and damman, they did their best to answer the questions put to them:

Yes, a village up along the Rissanin, a village now destroyed.

Silverroot and gwynthyme in equal proportions.

Yes, true gemstones. No no, their eyes, *not ours.*

Oh yes, it is *a splendid city.*

Mage Imongar at Dendor is the one who actually slew it.

From the Boskydells and the Wilderland.

One, a daughter. Her name is Lark.

A miller in Twoforks.

Yes, indeed, it was my Beau's words which reminded Tipperton of the tale of a giant and the fly on the wall, a wall broken by the giant, bringing ruin. And so Tipperton simply asked the Utruni to do the same.

Madam, I assure you, I am a full-grown Warrow and not an Elvenchild.

No, it was completely destroyed.

A Gjeenian penny: small and round with a hole in it.

It's nearly all filled with water now, a brand-new sea.

We met at Caer Lindor.

I don't see how he could have escaped; his body was never found. . . .

Buccan and dammen were greatly relieved when the major-domo hammered the floor and announced, "My lords and ladies, and honored guests, the Lord High King Blaine."

The crowd parted and pushed back to form a central aisle, and the Warrows found themselves off to one side and pressed all 'round by tall people.

"Barn rats," hissed Beau, "here we are again, Tip, unable to see a thing."

Linnet grabbed Beau's hand and said, "Well, you're not going to crawl about like a barn rat yourself just to get a peek."

As Blaine advanced down the aisle toward the distant throne, all men dropped to one knee as he passed, while the women curtseyed. Elves and Baeron bowed and Dwarves clenched right fists at their chests while canting their heads forward, and still the Warrows couldn't see.

And when the High King passed by their own general location, lords knelt and ladies curtseyed, and Beau and Tipperton dropped to one knee, while Rynna and Linnet curtseyed down.

Finally Blaine reached the dais and stepped up to his throne, and Lord Steward Voren, bearing scrolls, took station below and to the right.

King Blaine did not take his throne but stood at the edge of the dais instead, and he spoke unto the hushed crowd:

"We have come through a time of great darkness, a time when it seemed all was lost, yet in the end we did prevail, but not without great sacrifice. Many were those who died in this war, many sorely wounded as well, and we must honor those who gave so much, up to and including their all. And even though now is the time of celebration, for Adon has prevailed, still we must keep in mind the loved ones who will no longer stand beside us or answer to our call. Cherish those memories well, my friends, for, as I was told by a small trusted friend, as long as they are remembered they will live on in our hearts."

The King fell silent, and among the assembly there were muffled sobs, and down in the crowd Tipperton and Rynna and Linnet and Beau hugged one another and wept.

But then the King called out for a cheer, for the war was ended at last, and three huzzahs rose up in the chamber to ring the marble dome above.

Many were honored that evening—from the common born to nobility, from peasant to warrior to chieftain to king to DelfLord to coron—Humans, Dwarves, Baeron, Elves . . . and finally Warrows.

When Tipperton and Rynna and Beau and Linnet were finally called to come forth, at last the gathering parted and the Wee Folk stepped forward. When they finally stood on the dais before the King, he smiled at them and then said to the crowd, "These four were the key to the victory; without them all would have been lost, and Gyphon would now rule the Planes. Without them Mithgar would now be crushed under the heel of Modru. Yet Gyphon does not rule the Planes, nor does Modru rule this world, for these four conceived the plan which swept the foe away."

Now Blaine looked again at the four and said, "I have given away lands and titles and honors fitting the deeds done, yet I cannot conceive of anything in all of my power to bestow which would properly reward you for that which you did, for the whole of Mithgar, the whole of creation, owes you a debt none can ever repay. Yet this will I grant if it is within my power: name you your own reward, be it lands, titles, castles, riches, whatever it is you desire."

There was an indrawn gasp from all in the hall, for never had they heard of such a boon, and then a quietness descended, so utterly still that waves in the ocean far below could be heard through the very thick stone castle walls.

Beau shrugged and turned to Linnet, and she looked to Rynna. But Rynna stepped to Tipperton and whispered, "Name it, my love."

Tipperton looked out over the sea of faces, all folk waiting with bated breath, and finally he turned to High King Blaine and said, "There is but a single thing I would ask, my lord, and I ask it for all Warrowkind, and it is this: I would that we Warrows be excused from kneeling, for we are too short to see aught of pageantry when we are on our knees, especially when among or behind folk larger than ourselves. And if you would, a place up front would be nice, for when Big Folk stand before us, again we cannot see, kneeling, standing, or not."

Dead silence yet filled the hall, for had they heard rightly? The Warrow had requested virtually nought, the whole kingdom at his beck? And then the High King laughed, and called out, "Done and done." And as the King's laughter was echoed by all within, Tipperton embraced Rynna and winked at Beau.

Then Blaine raised his hands and when quietness fell, he said, "Let the word spread across the lands that I do here and now decree that for services rendered, never again shall *any* Warrow kneel in the presence of kings, queens, emperors, DelfLords, corons, chieftains, lords, ladies, dukes, earls, barons, or aught else of so-called royalty. Nought but a slight bow or curtsey will entirely suffice. Too, let the Wee Folk be given places of honor, where they may see and be seen."

Blaine glanced from lord to lady, coron to chieftain, king to queen, and when his eye swept across the Dwarves, Bekki stepped forward and proclaimed, "So you have said; so shall it be," and a shout of affirmation rose up from all.

Blaine then turned to Tipperton, and Lord Steward Voren stepped to the dais and handed the High King a small packet. And from it Blaine took a small pewter coin on a thong through a hole in its center. He signalled Tipperton to step forward, and he placed the dull token over Tipperton's head and about his neck and said, "Should there ever be a need, send this coin and I will come in all haste with all the force at my command."

With tears in his eyes, Tipperton looked up at Blaine and said, "My lord, should you ever have the need, send such a coin to us, and we will do the same."

Now there came a call for a speech, and Tipperton looked to

the other Warrows. Linnet smiled and Beau said, "They want to hear from you, bucco. Go on, tell 'em, Tip."

Tipperton looked at Rynna, and her eyes glistened as she nodded.

And he turned to the gathering, and a hush fell over them all. And then he said, "The King has told you of the terrible cost of the war—lost comrades, lost friends, lost brothers and cousins and fathers and mothers and daughters and sons." Tipperton held the pewter coin between finger and thumb and looked down at it on its thong, and then he looked up at the faces of the lords and ladies and honored guests waiting and said, "Know this, my friends: freedom is not free, for in times of darkness, in the fires of war, freedom is forged of iron, iron oft quenched by the blood of the innocent, a terrible price to pay. Yet to let evil rule is even more costly. No, my friends, freedom is not free, so cherish it and know its true value, for it is paid for by the highest coin of all."

Tipperton fell silent, and a hush filled the air. And then Bekki stepped forward and dropped to one knee and cried, *"Châkka amonu, Tipperton Thistledown, ko ka ska!"*

And the hall rang with cheers.

Two days later in the dawn, Tipperton and Rynna and Beau and Linnet rode out from Caer Pendwyr, a string of pack animals behind, Darda Erynian their goal. It was the sixth of February; four years ago on this very same day, Tip and Beau had set out from Twoforks bearing a coin toward an unknown end, and as Tipperton said to High King Blaine, "It just seems fitting that on this day we should start for home, our mission finally done." And so they rode away.

But they did not ride alone, for with them fared a cavalcade of others, heroes all, Phais and Loric and Bekki not the least of these. Men and Baeron and Dwarves and Lian and Dylvana all rode with the Warrows, each and every one heading for northerly homes: Kings Ranor and Loden; Chieftains Urel and Durul, DelfLord Volki, Corons Eiron and Ruar, and Prince Brandt and Hrosmarshal Linde, Vail and Arylin and Riatha and Talar, Talarin and Gildor and Vanidor and Vanidar and Aravan, and many others as well. And a crowd cheered as they rode through the streets of Caer Pendwyr and beyond, their loudest huzzahs for the Wee Folk riding in the midst. Out from the city they went, following Pendwyr Road, finally to depart that tradeway and strike out northerly.

And as they rode, King Loden laughed aloud, and when Beau

asked, Loden said, "Lord Bekki just now apologized for cheating me of my king's justice."

"Apologized?"

"Aye. For killing Lord Tain at Hèl's Crucible."

"Bekki slew the surrogate?"

"Split him with a thrown axe."

Rynna sighed and murmured to Tipperton, "I felt sorry for Lord Tain, mad as he was, for he knew nought of his role."

Tipperton nodded in agreement, but then shuddered, the memory of Jolet in his mind. He reached for his lute and said to Rynna, "What say we have a happy tune and drive these phantoms away."

A month and twelve days did they ride through snow and rain and sunny days warm and chill ere coming unto the wreck of Caer Lindor, sitting in ruins on its isle in the flow of the River Rissanin. And here came the parting of ways:

Coron Eiron, Vanidar Silverleaf, Riatha, Talar, Aravan, and other Lian turned west for Darda Galion. West as well rode DelfLord Volki and a cadre of Châkka, all heading for Kraggencor in the Grimwalls beyond.

Kings Ranor and Loden, Prince Brandt, and DelfLord Bekki and their retinues turned northeasterly to follow the river through the Greatwood and to the open wold, aiming for Jord and Riamon and Mineholt North. And with them fared Linde, the Warrior Maiden now acknowledged as King Ranor's only daughter, issue of an unsanctioned love. And she rode beside King Loden of Dael, a marriage-sealed alliance between Jord and Riamon perhaps in the offing, though the Warrior Maiden, free to choose, had neither said yea nor nay.

Turning back south to head for The Clearing went Chieftain Urel and a handful of Baeron, for they had guided all through the Greatwood to the Caer Lindor ruins.

Across the Rissanin and into Darda Erynian rode Chieftain Durul and Coron Ruar and Dara Vail and other Dylvana, along with Talarin of Arden Vale and Arylin, Aris, Gildor and Vanidor, Elissan, Jaith, and Loric and Phais. And with them rode Tipperton and Rynna and Beau and Linnet, all now heading for the holding of the Springwater Warrows.

But ere they went their own separate ways, DelfLord Bekki spoke softly unto Dara Phais, yet what he said was known only by them.

Crying out good-byes and farewells and wishing good fortunes to all, the small alliance parted, vowing one day to see one another again.

And away to the four winds they rode.

In midmorn of Springday, into the Springwater holding they came, Warrows calling out in gladness as among the withy-woven dwellings they fared.

With Lark in her arms Melli rushed out from her bower. "Oh, you're back, you're back," she joyfully cried. "Linnet, Rynna, Beau, Tipperton, Nix . . ." Melli frowned and looked among the Dylvana and Baeron and Lian and back down the trail, seeking her beloved son Nix. With dread in her eyes she looked up at Linnet, who broke out in tears, and so too did Melli weep, and Lark, wee Lark, yet in Melli's arms, began crying as well.

In the last week of April and accompanied by Fox Riders, Tipperton, Rynna, Lark, Melli, Beau, and Linnet set forth for Bircehyll, where Loric and Phais and Talar and a small contingent of Arden Vale Lian awaited them, for the Warrows would go onward to Twoforks, and Talar would see them safely there.

As to the Warrows of Springwater, those Wee Folk set out eastward on the very same day to return to their burnt hamlet nigh the headwaters of the Rissanin, vowing to rebuild their village come what may.

In early mid-June, the Warrows and their escort came to the western bound of Darda Erynian at the verge of the Landover Road. There they bade good-bye to Tynvyr and Picyn and Kell and Nia and Phero, the Pysks who had fared north with them. And accompanied by the Elves of Arden Vale, the Warrows rode on, crossing the River Argon at Landover Road Ford and onto the wold beyond.

To the eastern foot of Crestan Pass came Warrows and Lian, and to Beau's and Tipperton's delight, one of the Baeron toll keepers was Lady Bwen. And she heartily greeted the Warrows and fed all a whopping meal, and they talked long into the night of things shared, of hardships and joys and griefs.

They spent the next night at the peak of the pass, cold even though it was June. And the next day and the day after, down the western side they fared. But the following day, under the waterfall they rode and into Arden Vale, where they were greeted at the Lone Eld Tree by Dara Alaria, Captain of the South Ardenward.

It was Summerday when they reached the Elvenholt in Arden

Vale, and joy greeted them, and sadness, too, for many would never again celebrate the turn of the seasons.

Long did the Warrows spend in the Hidden Stand, Tip and Beau renewing old acquaintances, Rynna, Linnet, Melli, and Lark making acquaintances new. And Lark was fawned over incessantly, the tot grinning at the notice and babbling away in a polyglot of Sylva and Fey and Common and a tongue none knew but which sounded as a rustle of leaves.

And Tip and Beau spoke to Rael and told her the meaning of the rede she had uttered so long ago.

Yet at last in early autumn they once again set out for Twoforks. And with them rode an armed and armored cavalcade of Lian, for although Tip and Beau had once travelled alone across the breadth of Dhruousdarda, this time they would ride with a formidable escort, through that dangerous and dreadful wood.

Not even Lark took pleasure in the travel through Drearwood, for it was a tangled place of dark and dismal dread.

It was the dark of the moon when in late October they came unto Twoforks, where they found nought but ruin and old char, the entire village burned, weeds growing in the streets. No one came to greet them but the autumn wind.

"The Horde we saw that night long past, the Horde marching west through Drearwood," said Beau, "they did this. I wonder if any here had warning."

Tip shook his head, not knowing.

Loric came riding back among the wrack, Phais coming after, the other Elves yet searching. "We find no sign of survivors," said the Alor, "though there are scattered remains of those long dead."

"We will see they are given burial," added Phais.

Tip looked about, tears in his eyes. And then he said, "The eld dammen. I wonder . . ."

But when they came to the mill, it was burned as well. Only the great buhrstones yet remained, lying among ashes long dead.

Then Tipperton gazed northwesterly toward Beacontor and said, "Here it all began."

Beau shook his head. "No, Tip, for Linnet and Rynna it began in Springwater; for Bekki it began in Dael; for Phais and Loric, in the fringes of Drearwood; for others it began elsewhere. But it really began in a glade on Adonar, in a debate between Gyphon and Adon."

"Perhaps," said Tip, "it began before that, with the very creation itself, either that or with a sneeze in the Boskydells."

Beau laughed and said, "It *is* all connected, you know."

Rynna took a deep breath and let it out. "What will we do now?"

Tipperton shrugged, but Beau said, "We will go to my place in the Boskydells, that's what."

Tip looked from Beau to Rynna, Lark held in her arms, and he looked at Melli and Linnet, and seeing no objection from any he said, "Lead away, Beau. There's nothing for us here."

Over the next five days west they fared, to the Crossland Road and west. Past Beacontor they went, where the balefire had burned so very long ago. Along the southern flank of the Weiunwood they rode, Lark speaking to the trees now clothed in their autumn foliage, her voice a *shssh*ing call. Past Bogland Bottoms and on into Stonehill they went, where the citizens of that town were amazed to see a cavalcade of Elvenfolk escorting, it seemed, six insignificant Warrows.

They stayed that night and the next one as well in the White Unicorn, a large inn in the center of town. And on each of those nights Elves sang, but so, too, did Tipperton and Rynna, he playing his Elven lute, she her pennywhistle, and their songs were greeted with cheer, for the inn was filled to overflowing with folk who had come to listen.

The following morning the cavalcade rode out through the west gate of Stonehill, leaving behind puzzled citizenry wondering just what these Warrows might have done to deserve such a magnificent escort.

Southwesterly they turned, faring down the Crossland Road and along the southern flank of the Battle Downs, so named for the battle fought here where the High King and his host were victorious even though sorely outnumbered by the Horde of Foul Folk they faced. And they rode at a leisurely pace through the October days, the road now clasped within the Edgewood among leaves turned red and gold and russet in the crisp fall air.

In the early morning of the fourth day after leaving Stonehill, they saw ahead a great dark mass rearing up into the sky. It was the remarkable Spindlethorn Barrier, a formidable wall surrounding the Bosky entire. Befanged it was and dense, atangle with great spiked thorns, long and sharp and iron hard, living stilettoes, and even birds found it difficult to manage among its nigh impenetrable, interwoven branches. High it was, rearing up thirty, forty, and in some places fifty feet above the river valleys from which it sprang. Wide it was, reaching across broad river vales, no less than a mile anywhere, and in places greater than ten. And long it was, stretching completely around the Boskydells, from the Northwood down the River Spindle, and from the Updunes down the River Wenden, until the two rivers joined one another; but after their joining, no farther south did the 'Thorn grow. It was said that only the soil of the Bosky in these two river valleys would nourish the barrier, yet the War-rows had managed to cultivate a long stretch of it, reaching from the headwaters of the Spindle in the Northwood across to the headwaters of the Wenden in the Updunes, completing the Thornring entire. As to why it did not grow across the rest of the land and push all else aside remained a mystery; though the granddams said, *It's Adon's will*, while the granthers said, *It's the soil*, and neither knew the which of it for certain. There were only five ways through the barrier, passages like tunnels through the thorns: Spindle Ford in the northeast, The Bridge in the east, Tine Ford in the southeast, and Wenden Ford in the west, and the little-used northern tunnel through the ring there where the Northwood stood. In times of troubles these ways were stoppered with massive thorn barricades, plugging the pas-sages as would corks plug bottles. Only recently had word come that the war was ended, and the ways now stood open for any and all to pass through.

The cavalcade fared toward the eastern way.

But when they came to the barrier, the Elves stopped, Talarin saying, "We have brought ye safely to the land of the Waerlinga, yet we would not cause a stir by riding within. Hence we bid ye farewell here at the eastern gate."

And though the Warrows protested, Talarin would not be swayed, saying such a force of Elves entering would no doubt cause alarm, even if but temporarily. Even so, Talarin did promise that a time would come when by twos or threes Lian would visit.

And so, Phais and Loric embraced the Warrows and kissed them each good-bye, as did Aris and Elissan and Jaith. And when Phais came to Tip and Beau, tears running down their faces, tears in her eyes as well, she whispered, "Good-bye, my wee friends. Ye shall be in my thoughts forever." It was not until the Lian had ridden away that Tip realized just what she had said, ". . . in my thoughts forever," and she was an Elf.

Drawing pack ponies behind, into the thorn tunnel they rode, sunlight filtering down through the scarlet leaves overhead, Lark calling out, "*Ssshh, ssshh.*" Two miles they rode ere emerging from the wall, coming unto a wooden span set upon stone piers and bridging the River Spindle. They stopped and looked down at the water flowing below and the slash of sky overhead, and then they clattered on across and into the Spindlethorn tunnel beyond.

Three more miles they rode within, but at last they emerged into the sunlight at the far side. The countryside lying before them was one of rolling farmland, and the road they followed ran on to the west, cresting a rise to disappear only to be seen again topping the crest beyond.

"We've arrived," said Beau joyfully. Expansively he flourished his hand in a wide sweep and inhaled a great draught of air, reveling in the smell of the land: forest and field and clean-running streams and fertile soil above all. "This, my friends, is the Boskydells, the best place in all the world."

It was the last day of October, with a high blue sky overhead.

On they rode and in the evening they came to the village of Greenfields, and after an enquiry, they put up in the Happy Otter Inn, for the eld buccan they had asked said it brewed the best beer in all of Eastdell, which immediately started a quarrel with another eld buccan who favored the brew at the Green Frog, west aways in Tillok. Leaving the two eld buccen disputing one another, they rode to the western edge of town where the Happy Otter stood, Gorth Cotter, proprietor.

The beer was splendid.

The next morning on they continued west along the Crossland Road, reaching the town of Raffin and riding a bit beyond, to turn down a long dirt lane and come at last to Aunt Rose's farm, for although she was years passed away, Beau yet thought of this stead as the farm of his Aunt Rose.

The place was quite grown over in weeds and such, having been unlived in for several years now, and the house itself quite weathered; a small goat shed out back leaned precariously, all but ready to fall. Yet the apple trees were quite hale and burgeoning with crop, and the soil of the fields was fertile-dark.

Beau looked at the others and said, "With a bit of painting and yard and field work and other such, well, that should fix it right up."

On a chill day in November, Tip swung the scythe and sliced through another swath of dried weeds, while Beau raked the cuttings into a great pile. And as he raked, weed dust and dried pollen flew, and of a sudden Beau inhaled sharply and then loudly sneezed.

Tipperton paused and looked at the sky and so very soberly said, "Careful, Beau, you just might destroy the moon."

As Lark sat in the yard, her ear pressed to the trunk of an apple tree and her eyes wide as if hearing some twiggy secret, and as Melli rattled about in the kitchen, Linnet and Rynna sat on the porch, each sipping a good hot cup of tea. And they looked at one another and wondered why their buccarans, along the fence line, were laughing like a pair of loons.

EPILOGUE

Concerning Beau and Tip, they remained closemouthed about their wartime adventures, but everyone in the Bosky knew that they had been singular heroes of that war, for why else would Elves and Dwarves and even the High King come to see them. Why, it was even told that Stone Giants were seen emerging from the earth nigh the place where Tipperton and Rynna lived, but others pooh-poohed the notion, for who could believe such? Too, it was said that Silver Wolves were seen running across the fields of Eastdell, nigh Beau's place near Raffin—or so they did tell.

Some years after the Great War, a Wizard named Delgar came through the Boskydells specifically to see Beau Darby, mainly to congratulate him on finding the cure for the plague. It seems that Beau's red medical journal had been a gift from this Mage a number of years past, when Beau had been but a stripling. What else they might have said to one another remains unknown to this day.

Someone noted a peculiar thing about Tipperton and his wartime experiences: whenever anyone spoke of Dragonships and Fjordlanders, Tipperton would seem to withdraw, as if suffering from some hidden guilt concerning those men of the north, as if he were somehow responsible for the deaths of some in the war; ah, but who could put credence to such speculation? Besides, even if some Fjordlanders *did* die as a result of some act of Tipperton's, surely their deaths were inadvertent, wouldn't you say?

Tipperton never did take up the trade of a miller again, but instead became a bard, travelling with Rynna and Lark throughout the Seven Dells, and occasionally to other lands.

Too, it is said that Tipperton mastered the Elven rite celebrating the turning of the seasons—chant and song and steps—and passed the knowledge on to his descendants. Yet neither he nor those who followed knew the secret potency of the ritual; yet even had they known, still they knew not when or where on Mithgar they should sing and step and chant, knew neither the time nor place to loose the power hidden within. Perhaps one day Warrowkind would finally learn the arcane truth. . . .

Tipperton and Rynna and their subsequent brood took up residence outside of Eastpoint near the Spindlethorn, some tell that they did so on the insistence of Lark.

Speaking of Lark, she became even a more renowned bard than either her sire or dam, for no instrument defied her touch, the music to flow, her voice as sweet as her namesakes—the very larks themselves. Yet there was an air of mystery about this beautiful dammen, for it is said she spoke Twyll, Common, Fey, Sylva, and a strange language like the rustle of leaves in the wind. Too, it is said that she had a mysterious power over plants and trees, for her gardens were the wonder of all, and some even claim she could walk untouched through the Thornwall itself, but most discounted this wild rumor, for everyone knew that even birds and voles and other small creatures found it difficult to pass among the thickset thorns. Too, it is also said that a strange tall being, twigs and leaves and tendrils, would at times be seen in the night in Lark's company, but that was just wild rumor, too.

Both Tip and Beau, as well as Rynna and Linnet, lived long and useful lives, Tip and Rynna as bards bringing joy to the world, Beau and Linnet as healers bringing health to the sick.

As to others, this is known:

Bekki ruled Mineholt North for many a long year, and though he never married, other Châkka named their sons after him. Nearly four millennia following the time of this telling, one of these Châkka named Bekki, a Bekki of the Red Hills holt, sired a son named Brega . . . but that is another tale.

As to Linde, she and King Loden of Dael did marry, and she bore Loden a son, Garret, and when Garret was but nine, Loden was slain by raiders in Garia while on a trade mission. Linde led the campaign which destroyed the raiders, and a fiercer warrior the realm had never seen, and thereafter she was known as the Warrior Queen of Riamon. Until Garret came into his majority, Linde ruled the land; Garret was crowned king on his fifteenth birthday, but ever did the realm remember the beneficent rule of the fierce Warrior Queen Linde.

After the war, once more did Aravan return to the Dalgor Fens and long did he search for the Silver Sword. Yet he failed to find that token of power therein, and given the vision of Galarun's Death Rede, and Coron Eiron's description thereof, Aravan began a search for the yellow-eyed man who mayhap took the blade. For millennia upon millennia did he seek without success, but then an Impossible Child was born . . .

As far as anyone knows, Phais and Loric yet live.

Water poured into Hèl's Crucible for weeks; water flowed from the northern and eastern and southern seas into the Weston Ocean and through the Straits of Kistan into the Avagon Sea and thence into Hèl's Crucible, all oceans of Mithgar sinking a bit to do so, diminishing to fill the vast gullet of that deep rift. Long, too, did the land of Hèl's Crucible, though drowned, jolt and judder and quake, great gouts of steam exploding upward, and at times even fire, and it came to be known as Hèl's Ocean by some and as Hèl's Sea by others.

For years this ocean was restless, gas and vapors blowing upward from the depths and across the water, slaying ships' crews at times, at other times *thinning* the water as would a great cloud of bubbles thin the sea, and ships caught in these upsurges sank from sight never to be seen again; some said it was the ghost of a Dragon reaching up to drag ships down. The sailors themselves claimed it was the work of all the ghosts of the dead under the sea, for oft would witchfire come with these surges, or come with these terrible fogs, the poisonous vapors claiming the lives of any unlucky enough to be caught in the dreadful mists.

Too, the land about shivered and shook and sank; the craggy hills vanished downward; Hèl's Ocean spread wide. Rivers changed course—the Ironwater and the Storcha—to flow into the Hèl's Sea. Some said the quaking and upheaval was the work of the Utruni taming the land, taming the fires below, but others claimed it was but Hèl's Crucible itself remembering bygone days.

Long did Hèl's Ocean simmer and boil, steam gouting up, an occasional explosion, as if Hèl itself had drowned, but the Utruni working deep in the mantle managed to close magma vents and fissures, and finally the sea became somewhat tamed.

The city of Rhondor, its trade in minerals no more, did survive to become a major port city. And the citizenry of Rhondor renamed the ocean and called it the Inner Sea to make these waters seem more friendly, and so noted it on their maps, and it ultimately became known by this name. Even so, occasionally thereafter the waters would explode and spew, as a core of magma far below reached up from the gut of the world to come to the bed of the ocean, the molten fire to clash with water, elemental struggles anew. And sailors who knew of these violent quarrels would pray to the gods and the Stone Giants to see them safely through. Aye, the Inner Sea it is now called, a name not too untoward, yet those with long memories, Elves and others, name it Hèl's Crucible still.

As to the leaning Stone Tip and Rynna discovered among the destroyed aggregate in the Greatwood, it is said after it was set back upright by the Baeron, a Fox Rider ultimately communicated with it, and it was then used to relay messages. Even so, none discovered just how the aggregate had been shattered, for the ancient Stone only remembered that once it was among others of its kind and now it was not . . . and its grief was sorely heavy.

After the war, Kraggen-cor seemed somehow a more forbidding place, and deep within where starsilver lay there was an aura of fear. For some reason or other, when told of this ominous air, Tipperton Thistledown thought of the dread of Gargons, but then dismissed the idea altogether, for how could that be? For if a Gargon had come into Kraggen-cor, then surely the Dwarves would have fled. It would be many long centuries ere the answer to that enigma would come to light, and even then a mystery would remain. But that, too, is another tale.

Concerning Modru, some say he was slain at Hèl's Crucible, drowned under the waves, his body never recovered. Others claimed he fled far north to the Untended Lands, to the Barrens and beyond. It was said he dwelled in a black stone chamber deep under the ice and snow and away from the thundering wind. They said he was tended by Foul Folk as he plotted his dark revenge. Yet the answer to the question as to whether Modru lived or died would not be known for some four millennia altogether . . . the answer to come with a harbinger of doom, when the Dragonstar would score the sky.

Battered and beaten, a company of Humans returned from Neddra, crossing the in-between in the Gronfangs somewhere above Claw Spur. They had been fighting a strike-and-flee campaign against the Foul Folk, and had fought side by side with Elves who had crossed over with them. But given the small numbers of their combined force, it was a losing proposition at best, for they could be no more than a gadfly unto the vast count of Foul Folk therein. When the war ended, the Elves could but return along the bloodways to the High Plane, while the Humans could but come home to the Mid.

A year or so after the war ended, a Human, an ascetic Adonite warrior who had fought upon the High Plane, a man who would not give his name—for to do so was to abjure his sworn vows—crossed the in-between from Adonar unto Mithgar at the circle of stones. He came as a herald bearing witness, for he had beheld Gyphon's trial before the very gods Themselves; he travelled to Caer Pendwyr, where he was granted an audience with High King Blaine. And this is what the man said:

"My lord, Adon did visit these punishments upon Gyphon's creations:

"At the end of this year for a full sevenday a new star will burn in the heavens, and all folk who are not blood of this Plane but who aligned themselves with Gyphon, they will be banned from Adon's light: no longer will they be able to walk the world by day, but will wither swiftly to dust should the light of Mithgar's sun fall upon them, a ban which shall rule for as long as night follows day and day follows night.

"More, all Drakes who allied themselves with Gyphon's agent Modru will be reft of their fire to become Cold-drakes, and all of their male get and their get's male get down through the ages will be Cold-drakes as well.

"As to those folk of Mithgar who were deceived into following Gyphon, High Adon sets no sanctions, for He notes the flower of their manhood perished at the place you name Hèl's Crucible, and perhaps that is penalty enough.

"Regarding Gyphon Himself, He was cast into the Abyss to be imprisoned forever. Yet, heed, my lord, for ere He fell screaming into the nothingness below, He swore revenge, saying, 'Even now I have set into motion events You cannot stop. I shall return! I shall conquer! I shall rule!'

"Adon has sent me here to speak of these things, and to issue a warning for all to be ever vigilant, for who knows what Gyphon may achieve? He nearly ruled all creation.

"These things, my lord, Adon sent me to say. My message complete, I now go."

And with that, the man left the presence of the High King, even though Blaine bade him to stay. Yet when the palace guards stepped out before the stranger to stop him, it seems they could not lift a hand against the messenger of Adon.

Where he went is not known.

But on Year's Long Night and for seven nights in all, a new star—the Ban Star—blazed in the heavens, the nights so bright as to seem nearly day. And seven nights later it vanished forever, and Rûcks and Hlôks and Trolls and Ghûls and Hèlsteeds and all other Foul Folk as well as Black Mages could no longer withstand the sun but would crumble to dust were they caught in its light; nor did the renegade Dragons any longer breathe fire, but cast poisonous vapors and acid instead . . . and moreover suffered the Ban.

And the High King then declared 2E2000 the last year of the old Era, proclaiming Year's Start Day to be January 1, 3E1, hence beginning the new.

As to what Modru might have promised the renegade Drakes, those subsequently reft of their fire, there is only speculation. Mayhap he promised Daagor the Dragonstone or perhaps the death of Black Kalgalath; yet the Dragonstone itself at the time was indeed lost and Kalgalath hale and powerful. Some speculate that he promised Skail a mate, for some long years later that Drake was seen bearing a Kraken through the night skies above the Grimwall. And others believe perhaps he gave Sleeth information as to when the treasure-rich Dwarvenholt of Blackstone might be vulnerable, as future events would reveal. But all of these are different tales, different stories, some told, others not.

What is not recorded anywhere are the battles fought among Magekind, adherents of Gyphon and those of Adon fighting a mystical war on arcane battlefields, a tale which perhaps will never be told.

But this is not the time to speak of other stories, for herein are recorded the deeds of two unexpected heroes—Tipperton Thistledown and Beau Darby—and the heroes they met along the way. All other tales must await their turn, for it truly is all connected, you know.

Many things lie somewhere, lost in the wreckage of war . . . innocence not the least of these.

ABOUT THE AUTHOR

I was born April 4, 1932, in Moberly, Missouri, in the depths of the Great Depression. My dad and mom were factory workers, struggling to make ends meet. Yet my brother and sister and I didn't feel any neglect, for both of our parents loved to read and to read aloud, and both loved to play many games. And they included us in these pastimes.

When I was nine, my dad gave me a pulp magazine: it featured Captain Future, the quintessential science fiction pulp hero; I devoured the tale. This magazine more than anything else launched me into omnivorous reading: science fiction, fantasy, fairy tales, Oz books, and whatever else I could lay my hands on: westerns, mysteries, romances, the classics, and more: I read them all, and all was triggered by a magazine my dad gave me back when I was but nine.

Thank you, Mom; I really appreciate what you did. And thank you as well, Dad, wherever you are in that great beyond; that magazine you gave me when I was nine was a priceless gift. Thank you, Edmond Hamilton and Leigh Brackett, as well as a myriad others; you helped launch me into my engineering career, and the literary career which followed. Thank you, too, Captain Future . . . and Grag and Otho and the Brain, and Eek and Oog and all the others who helped that remarkable man. Without all of you and the Comet flying across vast reaches of space and doing in evil throughout the whole universe, perhaps this biography at the end of this book would never have been. . . . It *is* all connected, you know.